FU MANCHU

SAX ROHMER

ALSO AVAILABLE FROM PJM PUBLISHING

The 'Real' Wild West
The Lodger
The Evil Guest and Other Tales by J. Sheridan LeFanu
Collected Screenplays of Phillip J. Morledge
Deadeye - The True Story of 'Private Lives'

VIEW THE FULL CATALOGUE ONLINE AT
WWW.PJMORLEDGE.COM

FU MANCHU

SAX ROHMER

THREE COMPLETE NOVELS IN
ONE VOLUME

COLLECTED BY
PHILLIP J. MORLEDGE

WWW.PJMORLEDGE.COM

FU MANCHU
THIS EDITION
© Copyright Phillip J. Morledge 2008

ALL RIGHTS RESERVED

NO PART OF THIS BOOK MAY BE REPRODUCED IN ANY FORM,
BY PHOTOCOPYING OR BY ANY ELECTRONIC OR MECHANICAL MEANS,
INCLUDING INFORMATION STORAGE OR RETRIEVAL SYSTEMS,
WITHOUT PERMISSION IN WRITING FROM BOTH THE COPYRIGHT
OWNER AND THE PUBLISHER OF THIS BOOK.

COVER DESIGN BY PHILLIP J. MORLEDGE
ORIGINAL PHOTOGRAPH BY GAMERZERO

NEW EDITION PAPERBACK 2008

This Edition First Published August 2008
PJM Publishing Sheffield, England

ISBN 978-0-9559765-1-3

Printed in Great Britain for PJM Publishing

CONTENTS

THE INSIDIOUS DR FU MANCHU
1.

THE RETURN OF DR FU MANCHU
181.

THE HAND OF FU MANCHU
355.

THE INSIDIOUS DR FU MANCHU

by

SAX ROHMER

CHAPTER 1

"A GENTLEMAN to see you, Doctor."

From across the common a clock sounded the half-hour.

"Ten-thirty!" I said. "A late visitor. Show him up, if you please."

I pushed my writing aside and tilted the lamp-shade, as footsteps sounded on the landing. The next moment I had jumped to my feet, for a tall, lean man, with his square-cut, clean-shaven face sun-baked to the hue of coffee, entered and extended both hands, with a cry:

"Good old Petrie! Didn't expect me, I'll swear!"

It was Nayland Smith--whom I had thought to be in Burma!

"Smith," I said, and gripped his hands hard, "this is a delightful surprise! Whatever--however."

"Excuse me, Petrie!" he broke in. "Don't put it down to the sun!" And he put out the lamp, plunging the room into darkness.

I was too surprised to speak.

"No doubt you will think me mad," he continued, and, dimly, I could see him at the window, peering out into the road, "but before you are many hours older you will know that I have good reason to be cautious. Ah, nothing suspicious! Perhaps I am first this time." And, stepping back to the writing-table he relighted the lamp.

"Mysterious enough for you?" he laughed, and glanced at my unfinished MS. "A story, eh? From which I gather that the district is beastly healthy-- what, Petrie? Well, I can put some material in your way that, if sheer uncanny mystery is a marketable commodity, ought to make you independent of influenza and broken legs and shattered nerves and all the rest."

I surveyed him doubtfully, but there was nothing in his appearance to justify me in supposing him to suffer from delusions. His eyes were too bright, certainly, and a hardness now had crept over his face. I got out the whisky and siphon, saying:

"You have taken your leave early?"

"I am not on leave," he replied, and slowly filled his pipe. "I am on duty."

"On duty!" I exclaimed. "What, are you moved to London or something?"

"I have got a roving commission, Petrie, and it doesn't rest with me where I am to-day nor where I shall be to-morrow."

There was something ominous in the words, and, putting down my glass, its contents untasted, I faced round and looked him squarely in the eyes. "Out with it!" I said. "What is it all about?"

Smith suddenly stood up and stripped off his coat. Rolling back his left shirt-sleeve he revealed a wicked-looking wound in the fleshy part of the forearm. It was quite healed, but curiously striated for an inch or so around.

"Ever seen one like it?" he asked.

"Not exactly," I confessed. "It appears to have been deeply cauterized."

"Right! Very deeply!" he rapped. "A barb steeped in the venom of a hamadryad went in there!"

A shudder I could not repress ran coldly through me at mention of that most deadly of all the reptiles of the East.

"There's only one treatment," he continued, rolling his sleeve down again, "and that's with a sharp knife, a match, and a broken cartridge. I lay on my back, raving, for three days afterwards, in a forest that stank with malaria, but I should have been lying there now if I had hesitated. Here's the point. It was not an accident!"

"What do you mean?"

"I mean that it was a deliberate attempt on my life, and I am hard upon the tracks of the man who extracted that venom--patiently, drop by drop-- from the poison-glands of the snake, who prepared that arrow, and who caused it to be shot at me."

"What fiend is this?"

"A fiend who, unless my calculations are at fault is now in London, and who regularly wars with pleasant weapons of that kind. Petrie, I have traveled from Burma not in the interests of the British Government merely, but in the interests of the entire white race, and I honestly believe-- though I pray I may be wrong--that its survival depends largely upon the success of my mission."

To say that I was perplexed conveys no idea of the mental chaos created by these extraordinary statements, for into my humdrum suburban life Nayland Smith had brought fantasy of the wildest. I did not know what to think, what to believe.

"I am wasting precious time!" he rapped decisively, and, draining his glass, he stood up. "I came straight to you, because you are the only man I dare to trust. Except the big chief at headquarters, you are the only person in England, I hope, who knows that Nayland Smith has quitted Burma. I must have someone with me, Petrie, all the time--it's imperative! Can you put me up here, and spare a few days to the strangest business, I promise you, that ever was recorded in fact or fiction?"

I agreed readily enough, for, unfortunately, my professional duties were not onerous.

"Good man!" he cried, wringing my hand in his impetuous way. "We start now."

"What, to-night?"

"To-night! I had thought of turning in, I must admit. I have not dared to sleep for forty-eight hours, except in fifteen-minute stretches. But there is one move that must be made to-night and immediately. I must warn Sir Crichton Davey."

"Sir Crichton Davey--of the India--"

"Petrie, he is a doomed man! Unless he follows my instructions without question, without hesitation--before Heaven, nothing can save him! I do not know when the blow will fall, how it will fall, nor from whence, but I know that my first duty is to warn him. Let us walk down to the corner of the common and get a taxi."

How strangely does the adventurous intrude upon the humdrum; for, when it intrudes at all, more often than not its intrusion is sudden and unlooked for. To-day, we may seek for romance and fail to find it: unsought, it lies in wait for us at most prosaic corners of life's highway.

The drive that night, though it divided the drably commonplace from the wildly bizarre--though it was the bridge between the ordinary and the outre--has left no impression upon my mind. Into the heart of a weird mystery the cab bore me; and in reviewing my memories of those days I wonder that the busy thoroughfares through which we passed did not display before my eyes signs and portents--warnings.

It was not so. I recall nothing of the route and little of import that passed between us (we both were strangely silent, I think) until we were come to our journey's end. Then:

"What's this?" muttered my friend hoarsely.

Constables were moving on a little crowd of curious idlers who pressed about the steps of Sir Crichton Davey's house and sought to peer in at the open door. Without waiting for the cab to draw up to the curb, Nayland Smith recklessly leaped out and I followed close at his heels.

"What has happened?" he demanded breathlessly of a constable.

The latter glanced at him doubtfully, but something in his voice and bearing commanded respect.

"Sir Crichton Davey has been killed, sir."

Smith lurched back as though he had received a physical blow, and clutched my shoulder convulsively. Beneath the heavy tan his face had blanched, and his eyes were set in a stare of horror.

"My God!" he whispered. "I am too late!"

With clenched fists he turned and, pressing through the group of loungers, bounded up the steps. In the hall a man who unmistakably was a

Scotland Yard official stood talking to a footman. Other members of the household were moving about, more or less aimlessly, and the chilly hand of King Fear had touched one and all, for, as they came and went, they glanced ever over their shoulders, as if each shadow cloaked a menace, and listened, as it seemed, for some sound which they dreaded to hear. Smith strode up to the detective and showed him a card, upon glancing at which the Scotland Yard man said something in a low voice, and, nodding, touched his hat to Smith in a respectful manner.

A few brief questions and answers, and, in gloomy silence, we followed the detective up the heavily carpeted stair, along a corridor lined with pictures and busts, and into a large library. A group of people were in this room, and one, in whom I recognized Chalmers Cleeve, of Harley Street, was bending over a motionless form stretched upon a couch. Another door communicated with a small study, and through the opening I could see a man on all fours examining the carpet. The uncomfortable sense of hush, the group about the physician, the bizarre figure crawling, beetle-like, across the inner room, and the grim hub, around which all this ominous activity turned, made up a scene that etched itself indelibly on my mind.

As we entered Dr. Cleeve straightened himself, frowning thoughtfully.

"Frankly, I do not care to venture any opinion at present regarding the immediate cause of death," he said. "Sir Crichton was addicted to cocaine, but there are indications which are not in accordance with cocaine-poisoning. I fear that only a post-mortem can establish the facts--if," he added, "we ever arrive at them. A most mysterious case!"

Smith stepping forward and engaging the famous pathologist in conversation, I seized the opportunity to examine Sir Crichton's body.

The dead man was in evening dress, but wore an old smoking-jacket. He had been of spare but hardy build, with thin, aquiline features, which now were oddly puffy, as were his clenched hands. I pushed back his sleeve, and saw the marks of the hypodermic syringe upon his left arm. Quite mechanically I turned my attention to the right arm. It was unscarred, but on the back of the hand was a faint red mark, not unlike the imprint of painted lips. I examined it closely, and even tried to rub it off, but it evidently was caused by some morbid process of local inflammation, if it were not a birthmark.

Turning to a pale young man whom I had understood to be Sir Crichton's private secretary, I drew his attention to this mark, and inquired if it were constitutional. "It is not, sir," answered Dr. Cleeve, overhearing my question. "I have already made that inquiry. Does it suggest anything to your mind? I must confess that it affords me no assistance."

"Nothing," I replied. "It is most curious."

"Excuse me, Mr. Burboyne," said Smith, now turning to the secretary, "but Inspector Weymouth will tell you that I act with authority. I understand that Sir Crichton was--seized with illness in his study?"

"Yes--at half-past ten. I was working here in the library, and he inside, as was our custom."

"The communicating door was kept closed?"

"Yes, always. It was open for a minute or less about ten-twenty-five, when a message came for Sir Crichton. I took it in to him, and he then seemed in his usual health."

"What was the message?"

"I could not say. it was brought by a district messenger, and he placed it beside him on the table. It is there now, no doubt."

"And at half-past ten?"

"Sir Crichton suddenly burst open the door and threw himself, with a scream, into the library. I ran to him but he waved me back. His eyes were glaring horribly. I had just reached his side when he fell, writhing, upon the floor. He seemed past speech, but as I raised him and laid him upon the couch, he gasped something that sounded like 'The red hand!' Before I could get to bell or telephone he was dead!"

Mr. Burboyne's voice shook as he spoke the words, and Smith seemed to find this evidence confusing.

"You do not think he referred to the mark on his own hand?"

"I think not. From the direction of his last glance, I feel sure he referred to something in the study."

"What did you do? Having summoned the servants, I ran into the study. But there was absolutely nothing unusual to be seen. The windows were closed and fastened. He worked with closed windows in the hottest weather. There is no other door, for the study occupies the end of a narrow wing, so that no one could possibly have gained access to it, whilst I was in the library, unseen by me. Had someone concealed himself in the study earlier in the evening--and I am convinced that it offers no hiding-place-- he could only have come out again by passing through here."

Nayland Smith tugged at the lobe of his left ear, as was his habit when meditating.

"You had been at work here in this way for some time?"

"Yes. Sir Crichton was preparing an important book."

"Had anything unusual occurred prior to this evening?"

"Yes," said Mr. Burboyne, with evident perplexity; "though I attached no importance to it at the time. Three nights ago Sir Crichton came out to me, and appeared very nervous; but at times his nerves-- you know? Well, on this occasion he asked me to search the study. He had an idea that something was concealed there."

"Some THING or someone?"

"'Something' was the word he used. I searched, but fruitlessly, and he seemed quite satisfied, and returned to his work."

"Thank you, Mr. Burboyne. My friend and I would like a few minutes' private investigation in the study."

CHAPTER II

SIR CRICHTON DAVEY'S study was a small one, and a glance sufficed to show that, as the secretary had said, it offered no hiding-place. It was heavily carpeted, and over-full of Burmese and Chinese ornaments and curios, and upon the mantelpiece stood several framed photographs which showed this to be the sanctum of a wealthy bachelor who was no misogynist. A map of the Indian Empire occupied the larger part of one wall. The grate was empty, for the weather was extremely warm, and a green-shaded lamp on the littered writing-table afforded the only light. The air was stale, for both windows were closed and fastened.

Smith immediately pounced upon a large, square envelope that lay beside the blotting-pad. Sir Crichton had not even troubled to open it, but my friend did so. It contained a blank sheet of paper!

"Smell!" he directed, handing the letter to me. I raised it to my nostrils. It was scented with some pungent perfume.

"What is it?" I asked.

"It is a rather rare essential oil," was the reply, "which I have met with before, though never in Europe. I begin to understand, Petrie."

He tilted the lamp-shade and made a close examination of the scraps of paper, matches, and other debris that lay in the grate and on the hearth. I took up a copper vase from the mantelpiece, and was examining it curiously, when he turned, a strange expression upon his face.

"Put that back, old man," he said quietly.

Much surprised, I did as he directed.

"Don't touch anything in the room. It may he dangerous."

Something in the tone of his voice chilled me, and I hastily replaced the vase, and stood by the door of the study, watching him search, methodically, every inch of the room-- behind the books, in all the ornaments, in table drawers, in cupboards, on shelves.

"That will do," he said at last. "There is nothing here and I have no time to search farther."

We returned to the library.

"Inspector Weymouth," said my friend, "I have a particular reason for asking that Sir Crichton's body be removed from this room at once and the library locked. Let no one be admitted on any pretense whatever until you hear from me." It spoke volumes for the mysterious credentials borne by my friend that the man from Scotland Yard accepted his orders without demur, and, after a brief chat with Mr. Burboyne, Smith passed briskly downstairs. In the hall a man who looked like a groom out of livery was waiting.

"Are you Wills?" asked Smith.

"Yes, sir."

"It was you who heard a cry of some kind at the rear of the house about the time of Sir Crichton's death?"

"Yes, sir. I was locking the garage door, and, happening to look up at the window of Sir Crichton's study, I saw him jump out of his chair. Where he used to sit at his writing, sir, you could see his shadow on the blind. Next minute I heard a call out in the lane."

"What kind of call?"

The man, whom the uncanny happening clearly had frightened, seemed puzzled for a suitable description.

"A sort of wail, sir," he said at last. "I never heard anything like it before, and don't want to again."

"Like this?" inquired Smith, and he uttered a low, wailing cry, impossible to describe. Wills perceptibly shuddered; and, indeed, it was an eerie sound.

"The same, sir, I think," he said, "but much louder."

"That will do," said Smith, and I thought I detected a note of triumph in his voice. "But stay! Take us through to the back of the house."

The man bowed and led the way, so that shortly we found ourselves in a small, paved courtyard. It was a perfect summer's night, and the deep blue vault above was jeweled with myriads of starry points. How impossible it seemed to reconcile that vast, eternal calm with the hideous passions and fiendish agencies which that night had loosed a soul upon the infinite.

"Up yonder are the study windows, sir. Over that wall on your left is the back lane from which the cry came, and beyond is Regent's Park."

"Are the study windows visible from there?"

"Oh, yes, sir."

"Who occupies the adjoining house?"

"Major-General Platt-Houston, sir; but the family is out of town."

"Those iron stairs are a means of communication between the domestic offices and the servants' quarters, I take it?"

"Yes, sir."

"Then send someone to make my business known the Major-General's housekeeper; I want to examine those stairs."

Singular though my friend's proceedings appeared to me, I had ceased to wonder at anything. Since Nayland Smith's arrival at my rooms I seemed to have been moving through the fitful phases of a nightmare. My friend's account of how he came by the wound in his arm; the scene on our arrival at the house of Sir Crichton Davey; the secretary's story of the dying man's cry, "The red hand!"; the hidden perils of the study; the wail in the lane-- all were fitter incidents of delirium than of sane reality. So, when a white-faced butler made us known to a nervous old lady who proved to be the housekeeper of the next-door residence, I was not surprised at Smith's saying:

"Lounge up and down outside, Petrie. Everyone has cleared off now. It is getting late. Keep your eyes open and be on your guard. I thought I had the start, but he is here before me, and, what is worse, he probably knows by now that I am here, too."

With which he entered the house and left me out in the square, with leisure to think, to try to understand.

The crowd which usually haunts the scene of a sensational crime had been cleared away, and it had been circulated that Sir Crichton had died from natural causes. The intense heat having driven most of the residents out of town, practically I had the square to myself, and I gave myself up to a brief consideration of the mystery in which I so suddenly had found myself involved.

By what agency had Sir Crichton met his death? Did Nayland Smith know? I rather suspected that he did. What was the hidden significance of the perfumed envelope? Who was that mysterious personage whom Smith so evidently dreaded, who had attempted his life, who, presumably, had murdered Sir Crichton? Sir Crichton Davey, during the time that he had held office in India, and during his long term of service at home, had earned the good will of all, British and native alike. Who was his secret enemy?

Something touched me lightly on the shoulder.

I turned, with my heart fluttering like a child's. This night's work had imposed a severe strain even upon my callous nerves.

A girl wrapped in a hooded opera-cloak stood at my elbow, and, as she glanced up at me, I thought that I never had seen a face so seductively lovely nor of so unusual a type. With the skin of a perfect blonde, she had eyes and lashes as black as a Creole's, which, together with her full red lips, told me that this beautiful stranger, whose touch had so startled me, was not a child of our northern shores.

"Forgive me," she said, speaking with an odd, pretty accent, and laying a slim hand, with jeweled fingers, confidingly upon my arm, "if I startled you. But--is it true that Sir Crichton Davey has been--murdered?"

I looked into her big, questioning eyes, a harsh suspicion laboring in my mind, but could read nothing in their mysterious depths-- only I wondered anew at my questioner's beauty. The grotesque idea momentarily possessed me that, were the bloom of her red lips due to art and not to nature, their kiss would leave-- though not indelibly--just such a mark as I had seen upon the dead man's hand. But I dismissed the fantastic notion as bred of the night's horrors, and worthy only of a mediaeval legend. No doubt she was some friend or acquaintance of Sir Crichton who lived close by.

"I cannot say that he has been murdered," I replied, acting upon the latter supposition, and seeking to tell her what she asked as gently as possible.

"But he is--Dead?"

I nodded.

She closed her eyes and uttered a low, moaning sound, swaying dizzily. Thinking she was about to swoon, I threw my arm round her shoulder to support her, but she smiled sadly, and pushed me gently away.

"I am quite well, thank you," she said.

"You are certain? Let me walk with you until you feel quite sure of yourself."

She shook her head, flashed a rapid glance at me with her beautiful eyes, and looked away in a sort of sorrowful embarrassment, for which I was entirely at a loss to account. Suddenly she resumed:

"I cannot let my name be mentioned in this dreadful matter, but--I think I have some information--for the police. Will you give this to--whomever you think proper?"

She handed me a sealed envelope, again met my eyes with one of her dazzling glances, and hurried away. She had gone no more than ten or twelve yards, and I still was standing bewildered, watching her graceful, retreating figure, when she turned abruptly and came back.

Without looking directly at me, but alternately glancing towards a distant corner of the square and towards the house of Major-General Platt-Houston, she made the following extraordinary request:

"If you would do me a very great service, for which I always would be grateful,"--she glanced at me with passionate intentness--"when you have given my message to the proper person, leave him and do not go near him any more to-night!"

Before I could find words to reply she gathered up her cloak and ran. Before I could determine whether or not to follow her (for her words had aroused anew all my worst suspicions) she had disappeared! I heard the whir of a restarted motor at no great distance, and, in the instant that Nayland Smith came running down the steps, I knew that I had nodded at my post.

"Smith!" I cried as he joined me, "tell me what we must do!" And rapidly I acquainted him with the incident.

My friend looked very grave; then a grim smile crept round his lips.

"She was a big card to play," he said; "but he did not know that I held one to beat it."

"What! You know this girl! Who is she?"

"She is one of the finest weapons in the enemy's armory, Petrie. But a woman is a two-edged sword, and treacherous. To our great good fortune, she has formed a sudden predilection, characteristically Oriental, for yourself. Oh, you may scoff, but it is evident. She was employed to get this letter placed in my hands. Give it to me."

I did so.

"She has succeeded. Smell."

He held the envelope under my nose, and, with a sudden sense of nausea, I recognized the strange perfume.

"You know what this presaged in Sir Crichton's case? Can you doubt any longer? She did not want you to share my fate, Petrie."

"Smith," I said unsteadily, "I have followed your lead blindly in this horrible business and have not pressed for an explanation, but I must insist before I go one step farther upon knowing what it all means."

"Just a few steps farther," he rejoined; "as far as a cab. We are hardly safe here. Oh, you need not fear shots or knives. The man whose servants are watching us now scorns to employ such clumsy, tell-tale weapons."

Only three cabs were on the rank, and, as we entered the first, something hissed past my ear. missed both Smith and me by a miracle, and, passing over the roof of the taxi, presumably fell in the enclosed garden occupying the center of the square.

"What was that?" I cried.

"Get in--quickly!" Smith rapped back. "It was attempt number one! More than that I cannot say. Don't let the man hear. He has noticed nothing. Pull up the window on your side, Petrie, and look out behind. Good! We've started."

The cab moved off with a metallic jerk, and I turned and looked back through the little window in the rear.

"Someone has got into another cab. It is following ours, I think."

Nayland Smith lay back and laughed unmirthfully.

"Petrie," he said, "if I escape alive from this business I shall know that I bear a charmed life."

I made no reply, as he pulled out the dilapidated pouch and filled his pipe.

"You have asked me to explain matters," he continued, "and I will do so to the best of my ability. You no doubt wonder why a servant of the British Government, lately stationed in Burma, suddenly appears in London, in the character of a detective. I am here, Petrie--and I bear credentials from the very highest sources--because, quite by accident, I came upon a clew. Following it up, in the ordinary course of routine, I obtained evidence of the existence and malignant activity of a certain man. At the present stage of the case I should not be justified in terming him the emissary of an Eastern Power, but I may say that representations are shortly to be made to that Power's ambassador in London."

He paused and glanced back towards the pursuing cab.

"There is little to fear until we arrive home," he said calmly. "Afterwards there is much. To continue: This man, whether a fanatic or a duly appointed agent, is, unquestionably, the most malign and formidable personality existing in the known world today. He is a linguist who speaks with almost equal facility in any of the civilized languages, and in most of the barbaric. He is an adept in all the arts and sciences which a great university could teach him. He also is an adept in certain obscure arts and sciences which no university of to-day can teach. He has the brains of any three men of genius. Petrie, he is a mental giant."

"You amaze me!" I said.

"As to his mission among men. Why did M. Jules Furneaux fall dead in a Paris opera house? Because of heart failure? No! Because his last speech had shown that he held the key to the secret of Tongking. What became of the Grand Duke Stanislaus? Elopement? Suicide? Nothing of the kind. He alone was fully alive to Russia's growing peril. He alone knew the truth about Mongolia. Why was Sir Crichton Davey murdered? Because, had the work he was engaged upon ever seen the light it would have shown him to be the only living Englishman who understood the importance of the Tibetan frontiers. I say to you solemnly, Petrie, that these are but a few. Is there a man who would arouse the West to a sense of the awakening of the East, who would teach the deaf to hear, the blind to see, that the millions only await their leader? He will die. And this is only one phase of the devilish campaign. The others I can merely surmise."

"But, Smith, this is almost incredible! What perverted genius controls this awful secret movement?"

"Imagine a person, tall, lean and feline, high-shouldered, with a brow like Shakespeare and a face like Satan, a close-shaven skull, and long, magnetic eyes of the true cat-green. Invest him with all the cruel cunning of an entire Eastern race, accumulated in one giant intellect, with all the resources of science past and present, with all the resources, if you will, of a wealthy government-- which, however, already has denied all knowledge of his existence. Imagine that awful being, and you have a mental picture of Dr. Fu-Manchu, the yellow peril incarnate in one man."

CHAPTER III

I SANK into an arm-chair in my rooms and gulped down a strong peg of brandy.

"We have been followed here," I said. "Why did you make no attempt to throw the pursuers off the track, to have them intercepted?"

Smith laughed.

"Useless, in the first place. Wherever we went, HE would find us. And of what use to arrest his creatures? We could prove nothing against them. Further, it is evident that an attempt is to be made upon my life to-night-- and by the same means that proved so successful in the case of poor Sir Crichton."

His square jaw grew truculently prominent, and he leapt stormily to his feet, shaking his clenched fists towards the window.

"The villain!" he cried. "The fiendishly clever villain! I suspected that Sir Crichton was next, and I was right. But I came too late, Petrie! That hits me hard, old man. To think that I knew and yet failed to save him!"

He resumed his seat, smoking hard.

"Fu-Manchu has made the blunder common to all men of unusual genius," he said. "He has underrated his adversary. He has not given me credit for perceiving the meaning of the scented messages. He has thrown away one powerful weapon--to get such a message into my hands--and he thinks that once safe within doors, I shall sleep, unsuspecting, and die as Sir Crichton died. But without the indiscretion of your charming friend, I should have known what to expect when I receive her 'information'-- which by the way, consists of a blank sheet of paper."

"Smith," I broke in, "who is she?"

"She is either Fu-Manchu's daughter, his wife, or his slave. I am inclined to believe the last, for she has no will but his will, except"--with a quizzical glance--"in a certain instance."

"How can you jest with some awful thing--Heaven knows what-- hanging over your head? What is the meaning of these perfumed envelopes? How did Sir Crichton die?"

"He died of the Zayat Kiss. Ask me what that is and I reply 'I do not know.' The zayats are the Burmese caravanserais, or rest-houses. Along a certain route--upon which I set eyes, for the first and only time, upon Dr. Fu-Manchu--travelers who use them sometimes die as Sir Crichton died, with nothing to show the cause of death but a little mark upon the neck, face, or limb, which has earned, in those parts, the title of the 'Zayat Kiss.' The rest-houses along that route are shunned now. I have my theory and I hope to prove it to-night, if I live. It will be one more broken weapon in his fiendish armory, and it is thus, and thus only, that I can hope to crush him. This was my principal reason for not enlightening Dr. Cleeve. Even walls have ears where Fu-Manchu is concerned, so I feigned ignorance of the meaning of the mark, knowing that he would be almost certain to employ the same methods upon some other victim. I wanted an opportunity to study the Zayat Kiss in operation, and I shall have one."

"But the scented envelopes?"

"In the swampy forests of the district I have referred to a rare species of orchid, almost green, and with a peculiar scent, is sometimes met with. I recognized the heavy perfume at once. I take it that the thing which kills the traveler is attracted by this orchid. You will notice that the perfume clings to whatever it touches. I doubt if it can be washed off in the ordinary way. After at least one unsuccessful attempt to kill Sir Crichton-- you recall that he thought there was something concealed in his study on a previous occasion?--Fu-Manchu hit upon the perfumed envelopes. He may have a supply of these green orchids in his possession-- possibly to feed the creature."

"What creature? How could any kind of creature have got into Sir Crichton's room tonight?"

"You no doubt observed that I examined the grate of the study. I found a fair quantity of fallen soot. I at once assumed, since it appeared to be the only means of entrance, that something has been dropped down; and I took it for granted that the thing, whatever it was, must still be concealed either in the study or in the library. But when I had obtained the evidence of the groom, Wills, I perceived that the cry from the lane or from the park was a signal. I noted that the movements of anyone seated at the study table were visible, in shadow, on the blind, and that the study occupied the corner of a two-storied wing and, therefore, had a short chimney. What did the signal mean? That Sir Crichton had leaped up from his chair, and either had received the Zayat Kiss or had seen the thing which someone on the roof had lowered down the straight chimney. It was the signal to withdraw that deadly thing. By means of the iron stairway at the rear of Major-General Platt-Houston's, I quite easily, gained access to the roof above Sir Crichton's study-- and I found this."

Out from his pocket Nayland Smith drew a tangled piece of silk, mixed up with which were a brass ring and a number of unusually large-sized split-shot, nipped on in the manner usual on a fishing-line.

"My theory proven," he resumed. "Not anticipating a search on the roof, they had been careless. This was to weight the line and to prevent the creature clinging to the walls of the chimney. Directly it had dropped in the grate, however, by means of this ring I assume that the weighted line was withdrawn, and the thing was only held by one slender thread, which sufficed, though, to draw it back again when it had done its work. It might have got tangled, of course, but they reckoned on its making straight up the carved leg of the writing-table for the prepared envelope. From there to the hand of Sir Crichton--which, from having touched the envelope, would also be scented with the perfume--was a certain move."

"My God! How horrible!" I exclaimed, and glanced apprehensively into the dusky shadows of the room. "What is your theory respecting this creature-- what shape, what color--?"

"It is something that moves rapidly and silently. I will venture no more at present, but I think it works in the dark. The study was dark, remember, save for the bright patch beneath the reading-lamp. I have observed that the rear of this house is ivy-covered right up to and above your bedroom. Let us make ostentatious preparations to retire, and I think we may rely upon Fu-Manchu's servants to attempt my removal, at any rate--if not yours."

"But, my dear fellow, it is a climb of thirty-five feet at the very least."

"You remember the cry in the back lane? It suggested something to me, and I tested my idea--successfully. It was the cry of a dacoit. Oh, dacoity, though quiescent, is by no means extinct. Fu-Manchu has dacoits in his train, and probably it is one who operates the Zayat Kiss, since it was a dacoit who watched the window of the study this evening. To such a man an ivy-covered wall is a grand staircase."

The horrible events that followed are punctuated, in my mind, by the striking of a distant clock. It is singular how trivialities thus assert themselves in moments of high tension. I will proceed, then, by these punctuations, to the coming of the horror that it was written we should encounter.

The clock across the common struck two.

Having removed all traces of the scent of the orchid from our hands with a solution of ammonia Smith and I had followed the programme laid down. It was an easy matter to reach the rear of the house, by simply climbing a fence, and we did not doubt that seeing the light go out in the front, our unseen watcher would proceed to the back.

The room was a large one, and we had made up my camp-bed at one end, stuffing odds and ends under the clothes to lend the appearance of a sleeper, which device we also had adopted in the case of the larger bed. The perfumed envelope lay upon a little coffee table in the center of the floor, and Smith, with an electric pocket lamp, a revolver, and a brassey beside him, sat on cushions in the shadow of the wardrobe. I occupied a post between the windows.

No unusual sound, so far, had disturbed the stillness of the night. Save for the muffled throb of the rare all-night cars passing the front of the house, our vigil had been a silent one. The full moon had painted about the floor weird shadows of the clustering ivy, spreading the design gradually from the door, across the room, past the little table where the envelope lay, and finally to the foot of the bed.

The distant clock struck a quarter-past two.

A slight breeze stirred the ivy, and a new shadow added itself to the extreme edge of the moon's design.

Something rose, inch by inch, above the sill of the westerly window. I could see only its shadow, but a sharp, sibilant breath from Smith told me that he, from his post, could see the cause of the shadow.

Every nerve in my body seemed to be strung tensely. I was icy cold, expectant, and prepared for whatever horror was upon us.

The shadow became stationary. The dacoit was studying the interior of the room.

Then it suddenly lengthened, and, craning my head to the left, I saw a lithe, black-clad form, surmounted by a Yellow face, sketchy in the moonlight, pressed against the window-panes!

One thin, brown hand appeared over the edge of the lowered sash, which it grasped--and then another. The man made absolutely no sound whatever. The second hand disappeared--and reappeared. It held a small, square box. There was a very faint CLICK.

The dacoit swung himself below the window with the agility of an ape, as, with a dull, muffled thud, SOMETHING dropped upon the carpet!

"Stand still, for your life!" came Smith's voice, high-pitched.

A beam of white leaped out across the room and played full upon the coffee-table in the center.

Prepared as I was for something horrible, I know that I paled at sight of the thing that was running round the edge of the envelope.

It was an insect, full six inches long, and of a vivid, venomous, red color! It had something of the appearance of a great ant, with its long, quivering antennae and its febrile, horrible vitality; but it was proportionately longer of body and smaller of head, and had numberless rapidly moving legs. In short, it was a giant centipede, apparently of the scolopendra group, but of a form quite new to me.

These things I realized in one breathless instant; in the next-- Smith had dashed the thing's poisonous life out with one straight, true blow of the golf club!

I leaped to the window and threw it widely open, feeling a silk thread brush my hand as I did so. A black shape was dropping, with incredible agility from branch to branch of the ivy, and, without once offering a mark for a revolver-shot, it merged into the shadows beneath the trees of the garden. As I turned and switched on the light Nayland Smith dropped limply into a chair, leaning his head upon his hands. Even that grim courage had been tried sorely.

"Never mind the dacoit, Petrie," he said. "Nemesis will know where to find him. We know now what causes the mark of the Zayat Kiss. Therefore science is richer for our first brush with the enemy, and the enemy is poorer--unless he has any more unclassified centipedes. I understand now something that has been puzzling me since I heard of it-- Sir Crichton's stifled cry. When we remember that he was almost past speech, it is reasonable to suppose that his cry was not `The red hand!' but `The red ANT! Petrie, to think that I failed, by less than an hour, to save him from such an end!"

CHAPTER IV

"THE BODY OF A LASCAR, dressed in the manner usual on the P. & O. boats, was recovered from the Thames off Tilbury by the river police at six A.M. this morning. It is supposed that the man met with an accident in leaving his ship."

Nayland Smith passed me the evening paper and pointed to the above paragraph.

"For 'lascar' read 'dacoit,'" he said. "Our visitor, who came by way of the ivy, fortunately for us, failed to follow his instructions. Also, he lost the centipede and left a clew behind him. Dr. Fu-Manchu does not overlook such lapses."

It was a sidelight upon the character of the awful being with whom we had to deal. My very soul recoiled from bare consideration of the fate that would be ours if ever we fell into his hands.

The telephone bell rang. I went out and found that Inspector Weymouth of New Scotland Yard had called us up.

"Will Mr. Nayland Smith please come to the Wapping River Police Station at once," was the message.

Peaceful interludes were few enough throughout that wild pursuit.

"It is certainly something important," said my friend; "and, if Fu-Manchu is at the bottom of it--as we must presume him to be-- probably something ghastly."

A brief survey of the time-tables showed us that there were no trains to serve our haste. We accordingly chartered a cab and proceeded east.

Smith, throughout the journey, talked entertainingly about his work in Burma. Of intent, I think, he avoided any reference to the circumstances which first had brought him in contact with the sinister genius of the Yellow Movement. His talk was rather of the sunshine of the East than of its shadows.

But the drive concluded--and all too soon. In a silence which neither of us seemed disposed to break, we entered the police depot, and followed an officer who received us into the room where Weymouth waited.

The inspector greeted us briefly, nodding toward the table.

"Poor Cadby, the most promising lad at the Yard," he said; and his usually gruff voice had softened strangely.

Smith struck his right fist into the palm of his left hand and swore under his breath, striding up and down the neat little room. No one spoke for a moment, and in the silence I could hear the whispering of the Thames outside--of the Thames which had so many strange secrets to tell, and now was burdened with another.

The body lay prone upon the deal table--this latest of the river's dead-- dressed in rough sailor garb, and, to all outward seeming, a seaman of nondescript nationality--such as is no stranger in Wapping and Shadwell. His dark, curly hair clung clammily about the brown forehead; his skin was stained, they told me. He wore a gold ring in one ear, and three fingers of the left hand were missing.

"It was almost the same with Mason." The river police inspector was speaking. "A week ago, on a Wednesday, he went off in his own time on some funny business down St. George's way--and Thursday night the ten-o'clock boat got the grapnel on him off Hanover Hole. His first two fingers on the right hand were clean gone, and his left hand was mutilated frightfully."

He paused and glanced at Smith.

"That lascar, too," he continued, "that you came down to see, sir; you remember his hands?"

Smith nodded.

"He was not a lascar," he said shortly. "He was a dacoit."

Silence fell again.

I turned to the array of objects lying on the table--those which had been found in Cadby's clothing. None of them were noteworthy, except that which had been found thrust into the loose neck of his shirt. This last it was which had led the police to send for Nayland Smith, for it constituted the first clew which had come to light pointing to the authors of these mysterious tragedies.

It was a Chinese pigtail. That alone was sufficiently remarkable; but it was rendered more so by the fact that the plaited queue was a false one being attached to a most ingenious bald wig.

"You're sure it wasn't part of a Chinese make-up?" questioned Weymouth, his eye on the strange relic. "Cadby was clever at disguise."

Smith snatched the wig from my hands with a certain irritation, and tried to fit it on the dead detective.

"Too small by inches!" he jerked. "And look how it's padded in the crown. This thing was made for a most abnormal head."

He threw it down, and fell to pacing the room again.

"Where did you find him--exactly?" he asked.

"Limehouse Reach--under Commercial Dock Pier--exactly an hour ago."

"And you last saw him at eight o'clock last night?"--to Weymouth.

"Eight to a quarter past."

"You think he has been dead nearly twenty-four hours, Petrie?"

"Roughly, twenty-four hours," I replied.

"Then, we know that he was on the track of the Fu-Manchu group, that he followed up some clew which led him to the neighborhood of old Ratcliff Highway, and that he died the same night. You are sure that is where he was going?"

"Yes," said Weymouth; "He was jealous of giving anything away, poor chap; it meant a big lift for him if he pulled the case off. But he gave me to understand that he expected to spend last night in that district. He left the Yard about eight, as I've said, to go to his rooms, and dress for the job."

"Did he keep any record of his cases?"

"Of course! He was most particular. Cadby was a man with ambitions, sir! You'll want to see his book. Wait while I get his address; it's somewhere in Brixton."

He went to the telephone, and Inspector Ryman covered up the dead man's face.

Nayland Smith was palpably excited.

"He almost succeeded where we have failed, Petrie," he said. "There is no doubt in my mind that he was hot on the track of Fu-Manchu! Poor Mason had probably blundered on the scent, too, and he met with a similar fate. Without other evidence, the fact that they both died in the same way as the dacoit would be conclusive, for we know that Fu-Manchu killed the dacoit!"

"What is the meaning of the mutilated hands, Smith?"

"God knows! Cadby's death was from drowning, you say?"

"There are no other marks of violence."

"But he was a very strong swimmer, Doctor," interrupted Inspector Ryman. "Why, he pulled off the quarter-mile championship at the Crystal Palace last year! Cadby wasn't a man easy to drown. And as for Mason, he was an R.N.R., and like a fish in the water!"

Smith shrugged his shoulders helplessly.

"Let us hope that one day we shall know how they died," he said simply.

Weymouth returned from the telephone.

"The address is No.--Cold Harbor Lane," he reported. "I shall not be able to come along, but you can't miss it; it's close by the Brixton Police Station. There's no family, fortunately; he was quite alone in the world. His case-book isn't in the American desk, which you'll find in his sitting-room; it's in the cupboard in the corner--top shelf. Here are his keys, all intact. I think this is the cupboard key."

Smith nodded.

"Come on, Petrie," he said. "We haven't a second to waste."

Our cab was waiting, and in a few seconds we were speeding along Wapping High Street. We had gone no more than a few hundred yards, I think, when Smith suddenly slapped his open hand down on his knee.

"That pigtail!" he cried. "I have left it behind! We must have it, Petrie! Stop! Stop!"

The cab was pulled up, and Smith alighted.

"Don't wait for me," he directed hurriedly. "Here, take Weymouth's card. Remember where he said the book was? It's all we want. Come straight on to Scotland Yard and meet me there."

"But Smith," I protested, "a few minutes can make no difference!"

"Can't it!" he snapped. "Do you suppose Fu-Manchu is going to leave evidence like that lying about? It's a thousand to one he has it already, but there is just a bare chance."

It was a new aspect of the situation and one that afforded no room for comment; and so lost in thought did I become that the cab was outside the house for which I was bound ere I realized that we had quitted the purlieus of Wapping. Yet I had had leisure to review the whole troop of events which had crowded my life since the return of Nayland Smith from Burma. Mentally, I had looked again upon the dead Sir Crichton Davey, and with Smith had waited in the dark for the dreadful thing that had killed him. Now, with those remorseless memories jostling in my mind, I was entering the house of Fu-Manchu's last victim, and the shadow of that giant evil seemed to be upon it like a palpable cloud.

Cadby's old landlady greeted me with a queer mixture of fear and embarrassment in her manner.

"I am Dr. Petrie," I said, "and I regret that I bring bad news respecting Mr. Cadby."

"Oh, sir!" she cried. "Don't tell me that anything has happened to him!" And divining something of the mission on which I was come, for such sad duty often falls to the lot of the medical man: "Oh, the poor, brave lad!"

Indeed, I respected the dead man's memory more than ever from that hour, since the sorrow of the worthy old soul was quite pathetic, and spoke eloquently for the unhappy cause of it.

"There was a terrible wailing at the back of the house last night, Doctor, and I heard it again to-night, a second before you knocked. Poor lad! It was the same when his mother died."

At the moment I paid little attention to her words, for such beliefs are common, unfortunately; but when she was sufficiently composed I went on to explain what I thought necessary. And now the old lady's embarrassment took precedence of her sorrow, and presently the truth came out:

"There's a--young lady--in his rooms, sir."

I started. This might mean little or might mean much.

"She came and waited for him last night, Doctor--from ten until half-past-- and this morning again. She came the third time about an hour ago, and has been upstairs since."

"Do you know her, Mrs. Dolan?"

Mrs. Dolan grew embarrassed again.

"Well, Doctor," she said, wiping her eyes the while, "I DO. And God knows he was a good lad, and I like a mother to him; but she is not the girl I should have liked a son of mine to take up with."

At any other time, this would have been amusing; now, it might be serious. Mrs. Dolan's account of the wailing became suddenly significant, for perhaps it meant that one of Fu-Manchu's dacoit followers was watching the house, to give warning of any stranger's approach! Warning to whom? It was unlikely that I should forget the dark eyes of another of Fu-Manchu's servants. Was that lure of men even now in the house, completing her evil work?

"I should never have allowed her in his rooms--" began Mrs. Dolan again. Then there was an interruption.

A soft rustling retched my ears--intimately feminine. The girl was stealing down!

I leaped out into the hall, and she turned and fled blindly before me-- back up the stairs! Taking three steps at a time, I followed her, bounded into the room above almost at her heels, and stood with my back to the door.

She cowered against the desk by the window, a slim figure in a clinging silk gown, which alone explained Mrs. Dolan's distrust. The gaslight was turned very low, and her hat shadowed her face, but could not hide its startling, beauty, could not mar the brilliancy of the skin, nor dim the wonderful eyes of this modern Delilah. For it was she!

"So I came in time" I said grimly, and turned the key in the lock.

"Oh!" she panted at that, and stood facing me, leaning back with her jewel-laden hands clutching the desk edge.

"Give me whatever you have removed from here," I said sternly, "and then prepare to accompany me."

She took a step forward, her eyes wide with fear, her lips parted.

"I have taken nothing," she said. her breast was heaving tumultuously. "Oh, let me go! Please, let me go!" And impulsively she threw herself forward, pressing clasped hands against my shoulder and looking up into my face with passionate, pleading eyes.

It is with some shame that I confess how her charm enveloped me like a magic cloud. Unfamiliar with the complex Oriental temperament, I had laughed at Nayland Smith when he had spoken of this girl's infatuation. "Love in the East," he had said, "is like the conjurer's mango-tree; it is born, grows and flowers at the touch of a hand." Now, in those pleading eyes I read confirmation of his words. Her clothes or her hair exhaled a faint perfume. Like all Fu-Manchu's servants, she was perfectly chosen for her peculiar duties. Her beauty was wholly intoxicating.

But I thrust her away.

"You have no claim to mercy," I said. "Do not count upon any. What have you taken from here?"

She grasped the lapels of my coat.

"I will tell you all I can--all I dare," she panted eagerly, fearfully. "I should know how to deal with your friend, but with you I am lost! If you could only understand you would not be so cruel." Her slight accent added charm to the musical voice. "I am not free, as your English women are. What I do I must do, for it is the will of my master, and I am only a slave. Ah, you are not a man if you can give me to the police. You have no heart if you can forget that I tried to save you once."

I had feared that plea, for, in her own Oriental fashion, she certainly had tried to save me from a deadly peril once--at the expense of my friend. But I had feared the plea, for I did not know how to meet it. How could I give her up, perhaps to stand her trial for murder? And now I fell silent, and she saw why I was silent.

"I may deserve no mercy; I may be even as bad as you think; but what have YOU to do with the police? It is not your work to hound a woman to death. Could you ever look another woman in the eyes--one that you loved, and know that she trusted you--if you had done such a thing? Ah, I have no friend in all the world, or I should not be here. Do not be my enemy, my judge, and make me worse than I am; be my friend, and save me--from HIM." The tremulous lips were close to mine, her breath fanned my cheek. "Have mercy on me."

At that moment I honestly would have given half of my worldly possessions to have been spared the decision which I knew I must come to. After all, what proof had I that she was a willing accomplice of Dr. Fu-Manchu? Furthermore, she was an Oriental, and her code must necessarily be different from mine. Irreconcilable as the thing may be with Western ideas, Nayland Smith had really told me that he believed the girl to be a slave. Then there remained that other reason why I loathed the idea of becoming her captor. It was almost tantamount to betrayal! Must I soil my hands with such work?

Thus--I suppose--her seductive beauty argued against my sense of right. The jeweled fingers grasped my shoulders nervously, and her slim body quivered against mine as she watched me, with all her soul in her eyes, in an abandonment of pleading despair. Then I remembered the fate of the man in whose room we stood.

"You lured Cadby to his death," I said, and shook her off.

"No, no!" she cried wildly, clutching at me. "No, I swear by the holy name I did not! I did not! I watched him, spied upon him--yes! But, listen: it was because he would not be warned that he met his death. I could not save him! Ah, I am not so bad as that. I will tell you. I have taken his notebook and torn out the last pages and burnt them. Look! in the grate. The book was too big to steal away. I came twice and could not find it. There, will you let me go?"

"If you will tell me where and how to seize Dr. Fu-Manchu--yes."

Her hands dropped and she took a backward step. A new terror was to be read in her face.

"I dare not! I dare not!"

"Then you would--if you dared?"

She was watching me intently.

"Not if YOU would go to find him," she said.

And, with all that I thought her to be, the stern servant of justice that I would have had myself, I felt the hot blood leap to my cheek at all which the words implied. She grasped my arm.

Could you hide me from him if I came to you, and told you all I know?

"The authorities--"

"Ah!" Her expression changed. "They can put me on the rack if they choose, but never one word would I speak--never one little word."

She threw up her head scornfully. Then the proud glance softened again.

"But I will speak for you."

Closer she came, and closer, until she could whisper in my ear.

"Hide me from your police, from HIM, from everybody, and I will no longer be his slave."

My heart was beating with painful rapidity. I had not counted on this warring with a woman; moreover, it was harder than I could have dreamt of. For some time I had been aware that by the charm of her personality and the art of her pleading she bad brought me down from my judgment seat-- had made it all but impossible for me to give her up to justice. Now, I was disarmed--but in a quandary. What should I do? What COULD I do? I turned away from her and walked to the hearth, in which some paper ash lay and yet emitted a faint smell.

Not more than ten seconds elapsed, I am confident, from the time that I stepped across the room until I glanced back. But she had gone!

As I leapt to the door the key turned gently from the outside.

"Ma 'alesh!" came her soft whisper; "but I am afraid to trust you--yet. Be comforted, for there is one near who would have killed you had I wished it. Remember, I will come to you whenever you will take me and hide me."

Light footsteps pattered down the stairs. I heard a stifled cry from Mrs. Dolan as the mysterious visitor ran past her. The front door opened and closed.

CHAPTER V

"SHEN-YAN'S is a dope-shop in one of the burrows off the old Ratcliff Highway," said Inspector Weymouth.

"'Singapore Charlie's,' they call it. It's a center for some of the Chinese societies, I believe, but all sorts of opium-smokers use it. There have never been any complaints that I know of. I don't understand this."

We stood in his room at New Scotland Yard, bending over a sheet of foolscap upon which were arranged some burned fragments from poor Cadby's grate, for so hurriedly had the girl done her work that combustion had not been complete.

"What do we make of this?" said Smith. "`. . .Hunchback. . .lascar went up. . .unlike others. . .not return. . .till Shen-Yan' (there is no doubt about the name, I think) `turned me out. . . booming sound. . .lascar in. . .mortuary I could ident. . . not for days, or suspici. . .Tuesday night in a different make . . .snatch. . .pigtail. . .'"

"The pigtail again!" rapped Weymouth.

"She evidently burned the torn-out pages all together," continued Smith. "They lay flat, and this was in the middle. I see the hand of retributive justice in that, Inspector. Now we have a reference to a hunchback, and what follows amounts to this: A lascar (amongst several other persons) went up somewhere-- presumably upstairs--at Shen-Yan's, and did not come down again. Cadby, who was there disguised, noted a booming sound. Later, he identified the lascar in some mortuary. We have no means of fixing the date of this visit to Shen-Yan's, but I feel inclined to put down the `lascar' as the dacoit who was murdered by Fu-Manchu! It is sheer supposition, however. But that Cadby meant to pay another visit to the place in a different `make-up' or disguise, is evident, and that the Tuesday night proposed was last night is a reasonable deduction. The reference to a pigtail is principally interesting because of what was found on Cadby's body."

Inspector Weymouth nodded affirmatively, and Smith glanced at his watch.

"Exactly ten-twenty-three," he said. "I will trouble you, Inspector, for the freedom of your fancy wardrobe. There is time to spend an hour in the company of Shen-Yan's opium friends."

Weymouth raised his eyebrows.

"It might be risky. What about an official visit?"

Nayland Smith laughed.

"Worse than useless! By your own showing, the place is open to inspection. No; guile against guile! We are dealing with a Chinaman, with the incarnate essence of Eastern subtlety, with the most stupendous genius that the modern Orient has produced."

"I don't believe in disguises," said Weymouth, with a certain truculence. "It's mostly played out, that game, and generally leads to failure. Still, if you're determined, sir, there's an end of it. Foster will make your face up. What disguise do you propose to adopt?"

"A sort of Dago seaman, I think; something like poor Cadby. I can rely on my knowledge of the brutes, if I am sure of my disguise."

"You are forgetting me, Smith," I said.

He turned to me quickly.

"Petrie," he replied, "it is MY business, unfortunately, but it is no sort of hobby."

"You mean that you can no longer rely upon me?" I said angrily.

Smith grasped my hand, and met my rather frigid stare with a look of real concern on his gaunt, bronzed face.

"My dear old chap," he answered, "that was really unkind. You know that I meant something totally different."

"It's all right, Smith;" I said, immediately ashamed of my choler, and wrung his hand heartily. "I can pretend to smoke opium as well as another. I shall be going, too, Inspector."

As a result of this little passage of words, some twenty minutes later two dangerous-looking seafaring ruffians entered a waiting cab, accompanied by Inspector Weymouth, and were driven off into the wilderness of London's night. In this theatrical business there was, to my mind, something ridiculous--almost childish-- and I could have laughed heartily had it not been that grim tragedy lurked so near to farce.

The mere recollection that somewhere at our journey's end Fu-Manchu awaited us was sufficient to sober my reflections--Fu-Manchu, who, with all the powers represented by Nayland Smith pitted against him, pursued his dark schemes triumphantly, and lurked in hiding within this very area which was so sedulously patrolled--Fu-Manchu, whom I had never seen, but whose name stood for horrors indefinable! Perhaps I was destined to meet the terrible Chinese doctor to-night.

I ceased to pursue a train of thought which promised to lead to morbid depths, and directed my attention to what Smith was saying.

"We will drop down from Wapping and reconnoiter, as you say the place is close to the riverside. Then you can put us ashore somewhere below. Ryman can keep the launch close to the back of the premises, and your fellows will be hanging about near the front, near enough to hear the whistle."

"Yes," assented Weymouth; "I've arranged for that. If you are suspected, you shall give the alarm?"

"I don't know," said Smith thoughtfully. "Even in that event I might wait awhile."

"Don't wait too long," advised the Inspector. "We shouldn't be much wiser if your next appearance was on the end of a grapnel, somewhere down Greenwich Reach, with half your fingers missing."

The cab pulled up outside the river police depot, and Smith and I entered without delay, four shabby-looking fellows who had been seated in the office springing up to salute the Inspector, who followed us in.

"Guthrie and Lisle," he said briskly, "get along and find a dark corner which commands the door of Singapore Charlie's off the old Highway. You look the dirtiest of the troupe, Guthrie; you might drop asleep on the pavement, and Lisle can argue with you about getting home. Don't move till you hear the whistle inside or have my orders, and note everybody that goes in and comes out. You other two belong to this division?"

The C.I.D. men having departed, the remaining pair saluted again.

"Well, you're on special duty to-night. You've been prompt, but don't stick your chests out so much. Do you know of a back way to Shen-Yan's?"

The men looked at one another, and both shook their heads.

"There's an empty shop nearly opposite, sir," replied one of them. "I know a broken window at the back where we could climb in. Then we could get through to the front and watch from there."

"Good!" cried the Inspector. "See you are not spotted, though; and if you hear the whistle, don't mind doing a bit of damage, but be inside Shen-Yan's like lightning. Otherwise, wait for orders."

Inspector Ryman came in, glancing at the clock.

"Launch is waiting," he said.

"Right," replied Smith thoughtfully. "I am half afraid, though, that the recent alarms may have scared our quarry--your man, Mason, and then Cadby. Against which we have that, so far as he is likely to know, there has been no clew pointing to this opium den. Remember, he thinks Cadby's notes are destroyed."

"The whole business is an utter mystery to me," confessed Ryman. "I'm told that there's some dangerous Chinese devil hiding somewhere in London, and that you expect to find him at Shen-Yan's. Supposing he uses that place, which is possible, how do you know he's there to-night?"

"I don't," said Smith; "but it is the first clew we have had pointing to one of his haunts, and time means precious lives where Dr. Fu-Manchu is concerned."

"Who is he, sir, exactly, this Dr. Fu-Manchu?"

"I have only the vaguest idea, Inspector; but he is no ordinary criminal. He is the greatest genius which the powers of evil have put on earth for centuries. He has the backing of a political group whose wealth is enormous, and his mission in Europe is to PAVE THE WAY! Do you follow me? He is the advance-agent of a movement so epoch-making that not one Britisher, and not one American, in fifty thousand has ever dreamed of it."

Ryman stared, but made no reply, and we went out, passing down to the breakwater and boarding the waiting launch. With her crew of three, the party numbered seven that swung out into the Pool, and, clearing the pier, drew in again and hugged the murky shore.

The night had been clear enough hitherto, but now came scudding rainbanks to curtain the crescent moon, and anon to unveil her again and show the muddy swirls about us. The view was not extensive from the launch. Sometimes a deepening of the near shadows would tell of a moored barge, or lights high above our heads mark the deck of a large vessel. In the floods of moonlight gaunt shapes towered above; in the ensuing darkness only the oily glitter of the tide occupied the foreground of the night-piece.

The Surrey shore was a broken wall of blackness, patched with lights about which moved hazy suggestions of human activity. The bank we were following offered a prospect even more gloomy-- a dense, dark mass, amid which, sometimes, mysterious half-tones told of a dock gate, or sudden high lights leapt flaring to the eye.

Then, out of the mystery ahead, a green light grew and crept down upon us. A giant shape loomed up, and frowned crushingly upon the little craft. A blaze of light, the jangle of a bell, and it was past. We were dancing in the wash of one of the Scotch steamers, and the murk had fallen again.

Discords of remote activity rose above the more intimate throbbing of our screw, and we seemed a pigmy company floating past the workshops of Brobdingnagian toilers. The chill of the near water communicated itself to me, and I felt the protection of my shabby garments inadequate against it.

Far over on the Surrey shore a blue light--vaporous, mysterious-- flicked translucent tongues against the night's curtain. It was a weird, elusive flame, leaping, wavering, magically changing from blue to a yellowed violet, rising, falling.

"Only a gasworks," came Smith's voice, and I knew that he, too, had been watching those elfin fires. "But it always reminds me of a Mexican teocalli, and the altar of sacrifice."

The simile was apt, but gruesome. I thought of Dr. Fu-Manchu and the severed fingers, and could not repress a shudder.

"On your left, past the wooden pier! Not where the lamp is-- beyond that; next to the dark, square building--Shen-Yan's."

It was Inspector Ryman speaking.

"Drop us somewhere handy, then," replied Smith, "and lie close in, with your ears wide open. We may have to run for it, so don't go far away."

From the tone of his voice I knew that the night mystery of the Thames had claimed at least one other victim.

"Dead slow," came Ryman's order. "We'll put in to the Stone Stairs."

CHAPTER VI

A SEEMINGLY drunken voice was droning from a neighboring alleyway as Smith lurched in hulking fashion to the door of a little shop above which, crudely painted, were the words:

"SHEN-YAN, Barber."

I shuffled along behind him, and had time to note the box of studs, German shaving tackle and rolls of twist which lay untidily in the window ere Smith kicked the door open, clattered down three wooden steps, and pulled himself up with a jerk, seizing my arm for support.

We stood in a bare and very dirty room, which could only claim kinship with a civilized shaving-saloon by virtue of the grimy towel thrown across the back of the solitary chair. A Yiddish theatrical bill of some kind, illustrated, adorned one of the walls, and another bill, in what may have been Chinese, completed the decorations. From behind a curtain heavily brocaded with filth a little Chinaman appeared, dressed in a loose smock, black trousers and thick-soled slippers, and, advancing, shook his head vigorously.

"No shavee--no shavee," he chattered, simian fashion, squinting from one to the other of us with his twinkling eyes. "Too late! Shuttee shop!"

"Don't you come none of it wi' me!" roared Smith, in a voice of amazing gruffness, and shook an artificially dirtied fist under the Chinaman's nose. "Get inside and gimme an' my mate a couple o' pipes. Smokee pipe, you yellow scum--savvy?"

My friend bent forward and glared into the other's eyes with a vindictiveness that amazed me, unfamiliar as I was with this form of gentle persuasion.

"Kop 'old o' that," he said, and thrust a coin into the Chinaman's yellow paw. "Keep me waitin' an' I'll pull the dam' shop down, Charlie. You can lay to it."

"No hab got pipee--" began the other.

Smith raised his fist, and Yan capitulated.

"Allee lightee," he said. "Full up--no loom. You come see."

He dived behind the dirty curtain, Smith and I following, and ran up a dark stair. The next moment I found myself in an atmosphere which was literally poisonous. It was all but unbreathable, being loaded with opium fumes. Never before had I experienced anything like it. Every breath was an effort. A tin oil-lamp on a box in the middle of the floor dimly illuminated the horrible place, about the walls of which ten or twelve bunks were ranged and all of them occupied. Most of the occupants were lying motionless, but one or two were squatting in their bunks noisily sucking at the little metal pipes. These had not yet attained to the opium-smoker's Nirvana.

"No loom--samee tella you," said Shen-Yan, complacently testing Smith's shilling with his yellow, decayed teeth.

Smith walked to a corner and dropped cross-legged, on the floor, pulling me down with him.

"Two pipe quick," he said. "Plenty room. Two piecee pipe-- or plenty heap trouble."

A dreary voice from one of the bunks came:

"Give 'im a pipe, Charlie, curse yer! an' stop 'is palaver."

Yan performed a curious little shrug, rather of the back than of the shoulders, and shuffled to the box which bore the smoky lamp. Holding a needle in the flame, he dipped it, when red-hot, into an old cocoa tin, and withdrew it with a bead of opium adhering to the end. Slowly roasting this over the lamp, he dropped it into the bowl of the metal pipe which he held ready, where it burned with a spirituous blue flame.

"Pass it over," said Smith huskily, and rose on his knees with the assumed eagerness of a slave to the drug.

Yan handed him the pipe, which he promptly put to his lips, and prepared another for me.

"Whatever you do, don't inhale any," came Smith's whispered injunction.

It was with a sense of nausea greater even than that occasioned by the disgusting atmosphere of the den that I took the pipe and pretended to smoke. Taking my cue from my friend, I allowed my head gradually to sink lower and lower, until, within a few minutes, I sprawled sideways on the floor, Smith lying close beside me.

"The ship's sinkin'," droned a voice from one of the bunks. "Look at the rats."

Yan had noiselessly withdrawn, and I experienced a curious sense of isolation from my fellows--from the whole of the Western world. My throat was parched with the fumes, my head ached. The vicious atmosphere seemed contaminating. I was as one dropped--

Somewhere East of Suez, where the best is like the worst, And there ain't no Ten Commandments and a man can raise a thirst.

Smith began to whisper softly.

"We have carried it through successfully so far," he said. "I don't know if you have observed it, but there is a stair just behind you, half concealed by a ragged curtain. We are near that, and well in the dark. I have seen nothing suspicious so far--or nothing much. But if there was anything going forward it would no doubt be delayed until we new arrivals were well doped. S-SH!"

He pressed my arm to emphasize the warning. Through my half-closed eyes I perceived a shadowy form near the curtain to which he had referred. I lay like a log, but my muscles were tensed nervously.

The shadow materialized as the figure moved forward into the room with a curiously lithe movement.

The smoky lamp in the middle of the place afforded scant illumination, serving only to indicate sprawling shapes-- here an extended hand, brown or yellow, there a sketchy, corpse-like face; whilst from all about rose obscene sighings and murmurings in far-away voices--an uncanny, animal chorus. It was like a glimpse of the Inferno seen by some Chinese Dante. But so close to us stood the newcomer that I was able to make out a ghastly parchment face, with small, oblique eyes, and a misshapen head crowned with a coiled pigtail, surmounting a slight, hunched body. There was something unnatural, inhuman, about that mask like face, and something repulsive in the bent shape and the long, yellow hands clasped one upon the other.

Fu-Manchu, from Smith's account, in no way resembled this crouching apparition with the death's-head countenance and lithe movements; but an instinct of some kind told me that we were on the right scent-- that this was one of the doctor's servants. How I came to that conclusion, I cannot explain; but with no doubt in my mind that this was a member of the formidable murder group, I saw the yellow man creep nearer, nearer, silently, bent and peering.

He was watching us.

Of another circumstance I became aware, and a disquieting circumstance. There were fewer murmurings and sighings from the surrounding bunks. The presence of the crouching figure had created a sudden semi-silence in the den, which could only mean that some of the supposed opium-smokers had merely feigned coma and the approach of coma.

Nayland Smith lay like a dead man, and trusting to the darkness, I, too, lay prone and still, but watched the evil face bending lower and lower, until it came within a few inches of my own. I completely closed my eyes.

Delicate fingers touched my right eyelid. Divining what was coming, I rolled my eyes up, as the lid was adroitly lifted and lowered again. The man moved away.

I had saved the situation! And noting anew the hush about me-- a hush in which I fancied many pairs of ears listened--I was glad. For just a moment I realized fully how, with the place watched back and front, we yet were cut off, were in the hands of Far Easterns, to some extent in the power of members of that most inscrutably mysterious race, the Chinese.

"Good," whispered Smith at my side. "I don't think I could have done it. He took me on trust after that. My God! what an awful face. Petrie, it's the hunchback of Cadby's notes. Ah, I thought so. Do you see that?"

I turned my eyes round as far as was possible. A man had scrambled down from one of the bunks and was following the bent figure across the room.

They passed around us quietly, the little yellow man leading, with his curious, lithe gait, and the other, an impassive Chinaman, following. The curtain was raised, and I heard footsteps receding on the stairs.

"Don't stir," whispered Smith.

An intense excitement was clearly upon him, and he communicated it to me. Who was the occupant of the room above?

Footsteps on the stair, and the Chinaman reappeared, recrossed the floor, and went out. The little, bent man went over to another bunk, this time leading up the stair one who looked like a lascar.

"Did you see his right hand?" whispered Smith. "A dacoit! They come here to report and to take orders. Petrie, Dr. Fu-Manchu is up there."

"What shall we do?"--softly.

"Wait. Then we must try to rush the stairs. It would be futile to bring in the police first. He is sure to have some other exit. I will give the word while the little yellow devil is down here. You are nearer and will have to go first, but if the hunchback follows, I can then deal with him."

Our whispered colloquy was interrupted by the return of the dacoit, who recrossed the room as the Chinaman had done, and immediately took his departure. A third man, whom Smith identified as a Malay, ascended the mysterious stairs, descended, and went out; and a fourth, whose nationality it was impossible to determine, followed. Then, as the softly moving usher crossed to a bunk on the right of the outer door--

"Up you go, Petrie," cried Smith, for further delay was dangerous and further dissimulation useless.

I leaped to my feet. Snatching my revolver from the pocket of the rough jacket I wore, I bounded to the stair and went blundering up in complete darkness. A chorus of brutish cries clamored from behind, with a muffled scream rising above them all. But Nayland Smith was close behind as I raced along a covered gangway, in a purer air, and at my heels when I crashed open a door at the end and almost fell into the room beyond.

What I saw were merely a dirty table, with some odds and ends upon it of which I was too excited to take note, an oil-lamp swung by a brass chain above, and a man sitting behind the table. But from the moment that my gaze rested upon the one who sat there, I think if the place had been an Aladdin's palace I should have had no eyes for any of its wonders.

He wore a plain yellow robe, of a hue almost identical with that of his smooth, hairless countenance. His hands were large, long and bony, and he held them knuckles upward, and rested his pointed chin upon their thinness. He had a great, high brow, crowned with sparse, neutral-colored hair.

Of his face, as it looked out at me over the dirty table, I despair of writing convincingly. It was that of an archangel of evil, and it was wholly dominated by the most uncanny eyes that ever reflected a human soul, for they were narrow and long, very slightly oblique, and of a brilliant green. But their unique horror lay in a certain filminess (it made me think of the membrana nictitans in a bird) which, obscuring them as I threw wide the door, seemed to lift as I actually passed the threshold, revealing the eyes in all their brilliant iridescence.

I know that I stopped dead, one foot within the room, for the malignant force of the man was something surpassing my experience. He was surprised by this sudden intrusion--yes, but no trace of fear showed upon that wonderful face, only a sort of pitying contempt. And, as I paused, he rose slowly to his feet, never removing his gaze from mine.

"IT'S FU-MANCHU!" cried Smith over my shoulder, in a voice that was almost a scream. "IT'S FU-MANCHU! Cover him! Shoot him dead if--"

The conclusion of that sentence I never heard.

Dr. Fu-Manchu reached down beside the table, and the floor slipped from under me.

One last glimpse I had of the fixed green eyes, and with a scream I was unable to repress I dropped, dropped, dropped, and plunged into icy water, which closed over my head.

Vaguely I had seen a spurt of flame, had heard another cry following my own, a booming sound (the trap), the flat note of a police whistle. But when I rose to the surface impenetrable darkness enveloped me; I was spitting filthy, oily liquid from my mouth, and fighting down the black terror that had me by the throat--terror of the darkness about me, of the unknown depths beneath me, of the pit into which I was cast amid stifling stenches and the lapping of tidal water.

"Smith!" I cried. . . ."Help! Help!"

My voice seemed to beat back upon me, yet I was about to cry out again, when, mustering all my presence of mind and all my failing courage, I recognized that I had better employment of my energies, and began to swim straight ahead, desperately determined to face all the horrors of this place-- to die hard if die I must.

A drop of liquid fire fell through the darkness and hissed into the water beside me!

I felt that, despite my resolution, I was going mad.

Another fiery drop--and another!

I touched a rotting wooden post and slimy timbers. I had reached one bound of my watery prison. More fire fell from above, and the scream of hysteria quivered, unuttered, in my throat.

Keeping myself afloat with increasing difficulty in my heavy garments, I threw my head back and raised my eyes.

No more drops fell, and no more drops would fall; but it was merely a question of time for the floor to collapse. For it was beginning to emit a dull, red glow.

The room above me was in flames!

It was drops of burning oil from the lamp, finding passage through the cracks in the crazy flooring, which had fallen about me-- for the death trap had reclosed, I suppose, mechanically.

My saturated garments were dragging me down, and now I could hear the flames hungrily eating into the ancient rottenness overhead. Shortly that cauldron would be loosed upon my head. The glow of the flames grew brighter. . .and showed me the half-rotten piles upholding the building, showed me the tidal mark upon the slime-coated walls-- showed me that there was no escape!

By some subterranean duct the foul place was fed from the Thames. By that duct, with the outgoing tide, my body would pass, in the wake of Mason, Cadby, and many another victim!

Rusty iron rungs were affixed to one of the walls communicating with a trap-- but the bottom three were missing!

Brighter and brighter grew the awesome light the light of what should be my funeral pyre--reddening the oily water and adding a new dread to the whispering, clammy horror of the pit. But something it showed me. . .a projecting beam a few feet above the water. . .and directly below the iron ladder!

"Merciful Heaven!" I breathed. "Have I the strength?"

A desire for laughter claimed me with sudden, all but irresistible force. I knew what it portended and fought it down--grimly, sternly.

My garments weighed upon me like a suit of mail; with my chest aching dully, my veins throbbing to bursting, I forced tired muscles to work, and, every stroke an agony, approached the beam. Nearer I swam. . .nearer. Its shadow fell black upon the water, which now had all the seeming of a pool of blood. Confused sounds--a remote uproar--came to my ears. I was nearly spent. . .I was in the shadow of the beam! If I could throw up one arm. . .

A shrill scream sounded far above me!

"Petrie! Petrie!" (That voice must be Smith's!) "Don't touch the beam! For God's sake DON'T TOUCH THE BEAM! Keep afloat another few seconds and I can get to you!"

Another few seconds! Was that possible?

I managed to turn, to raise my throbbing head; and I saw the strangest sight which that night yet had offered.

Nayland Smith stood upon the lowest iron rung. . .supported by the hideous, crook-backed Chinaman, who stood upon the rung above!

"I can't reach him!"

It was as Smith hissed the words despairingly that I looked up-- and saw the Chinaman snatch at his coiled pigtail and pull it off! With it came the wig to which it was attached; and the ghastly yellow mask, deprived of its fastenings, fell from position! "Here! Here! Be quick! Oh! be quick! You can lower this to him! Be quick! Be quick!"

A cloud of hair came falling about the slim shoulders as the speaker bent to pass this strange lifeline to Smith; and I think it was my wonder at knowing her for the girl whom that day I had surprised in Cadby's rooms which saved my life.

For I not only kept afloat, but kept my gaze upturned to that beautiful, flushed face, and my eyes fixed upon hers--which were wild with fear . . .for me!

Smith, by some contortion, got the false queue into my grasp, and I, with the strength of desperation, by that means seized hold upon the lowest rung. With my friend's arm round me I realized that exhaustion was even nearer than I had supposed. My last distinct memory is of the bursting of the floor above and the big burning joist hissing into the pool beneath us. Its fiery passage, striated with light, disclosed two sword blades, riveted, edges up along the top of the beam which I had striven to reach.

"The severed fingers--" I said; and swooned.

How Smith got me through the trap I do not know--nor how we made our way through the smoke and flames of the narrow passage it opened upon. My next recollection is of sitting up, with my friend's arm supporting me and Inspector Ryman holding a glass to my lips.

A bright glare dazzled my eyes. A crowd surged about us, and a clangor and shouting drew momentarily nearer.

"It's the engines coming," explained Smith, seeing my bewilderment. "Shen-Yan's is in flames. It was your shot, as you fell through the trap, broke the oil-lamp."

"Is everybody out?"

"So far as we know."

"Fu-Manchu?"

Smith shrugged his shoulders.

"No one has seen him. There was some door at the back--"

"Do you think he may--"

"No," he said tensely. "Not until I see him lying dead before me shall I believe it."

Then memory resumed its sway. I struggled to my feet.

"Smith, where is she?" I cried. "Where is she?"

"I don't know," be answered.

"She's given us the slip, Doctor," said Inspector Weymouth, as a fire-engine came swinging round the corner of the narrow lane. "So has Mr. Singapore Charlie--and, I'm afraid, somebody else. We've got six or eight all-sorts, some awake and some asleep, but I suppose we shall have to let 'em go again. Mr. Smith tells me that the girl was disguised as a Chinaman. I expect that's why she managed to slip away."

I recalled how I had been dragged from the pit by the false queue, how the strange discovery which had brought death to poor Cadby had brought life to me, and I seemed to remember, too, that Smith had dropped it as he threw his arm about me on the ladder. Her mask the girl might have retained, but her wig, I felt certain, had been dropped into the water.

It was later that night, when the brigade still were playing, upon the blackened shell of what had been Shen-Yan's opium-shop, and Smith and I were speeding away in a cab from the scene of God knows how many crimes, that I had an idea.

"Smith," I said, "did you bring the pigtail with you that was found on Cadby?"

"Yes. I had hoped to meet the owner."

"Have you got it now?"

"No. I met the owner."

I thrust my hands deep into the pockets of the big pea-jacket lent to me by Inspector Ryman, leaning back in my corner.

"We shall never really excel at this business," continued Nayland Smith. "We are far too sentimental. I knew what it meant to us, Petrie, what it meant to the world, but I hadn't the heart. I owed her your life-- I had to square the account."

CHAPTER VII

NIGHT FELL on Redmoat. I glanced from the window at the nocturne in silver and green which lay beneath me. To the west of the shrubbery, with its broken canopy of elms and beyond the copper beech which marked the center of its mazes, a gap offered a glimpse of the Waverney where it swept into a broad. Faint bird-calls floated over the water. These, with the whisper of leaves, alone claimed the ear.

Ideal rural peace, and the music of an English summer evening; but to my eyes, every shadow holding fantastic terrors; to my ears, every sound a signal of dread. For the deathful hand of Fu-Manchu was stretched over Redmoat, at any hour to loose strange, Oriental horrors upon its inmates.

"Well," said Nayland Smith, joining me at the window, "we had dared to hope him dead, but we know now that he lives!"

The Rev. J. D. Eltham coughed nervously, and I turned, leaning my elbow upon the table, and studied the play of expression upon the refined, sensitive face of the clergyman.

"You think I acted rightly in sending for you, Mr. Smith?"

Nayland Smith smoked furiously.

"Mr. Eltham," he replied, "you see in me a man groping in the dark. I am to-day no nearer to the conclusion of my mission than upon the day when I left Mandalay. You offer me a clew; I am here. Your affair, I believe, stands thus: A series of attempted burglaries, or something of the kind, has alarmed your household. Yesterday, returning from London with your daughter, you were both drugged in some way and, occupying a compartment to yourselves, you both slept. Your daughter awoke, and saw someone else in the carriage-- a yellow-faced man who held a case of instruments in his hands."

"Yes; I was, of course, unable to enter into particulars over the telephone. The man was standing by one of the windows. Directly he observed that my daughter was awake, he stepped towards her."

"What did he do with the case in his hands?"

"She did not notice--or did not mention having noticed. In fact, as was natural, she was so frightened that she recalls nothing more, beyond the fact that she strove to arouse me, without succeeding, felt hands grasp her shoulders--and swooned."

"But someone used the emergency cord, and stopped the train."

"Greba has no recollection of having done so."

"Hm! Of course, no yellow-faced man was on the train. When did you awake?"

"I was aroused by the guard, but only when he had repeatedly shaken me."

"Upon reaching Great Yarmouth you immediately called up Scotland Yard? You acted very wisely, sir. How long were you in China?"

Mr. Eltham's start of surprise was almost comical.

"It is perhaps not strange that you should be aware of my residence in China, Mr. Smith," he said; "but my not having mentioned it may seem so. The fact is"--his sensitive face flushed in palpable embarrassment-- "I left China under what I may term an episcopal cloud. I have lived in retirement ever since. Unwittingly--I solemnly declare to you, Mr. Smith, unwittingly--I stirred up certain deep-seated prejudices in my endeavors to do my duty--my duty. I think you asked me how long I was in China? I was there from 1896 until 1900--four years."

"I recall the circumstances, Mr. Eltham," said Smith, with an odd note in his voice. "I have been endeavoring to think where I had come across the name, and a moment ago I remembered. I am happy to have met you, sir."

The clergyman blushed again like a girl, and slightly inclined his head, with its scanty fair hair.

"Has Redmoat, as its name implies, a moat round it? I was unable to see in the dusk." "It remains. Redmoat--a corruption of Round Moat-- was formerly a priory, disestablished by the eighth Henry in 1536." His pedantic manner was quaint at times. "But the moat is no longer flooded. In fact, we grow cabbages in part of it. If you refer to the strategic strength of the place"--he smiled, but his manner was embarrassed again--"it is considerable. I have barbed wire fencing, and--other arrangements. You see, it is a lonely spot," he added apologetically. "And now, if you will excuse me, we will resume these gruesome inquiries after the more pleasant affairs of dinner."

He left us.

"Who is our host?" I asked, as the door closed.

Smith smiled.

"You are wondering what caused the 'episcopal cloud?'" he suggested. "Well, the deep-seated prejudices which our reverend friend stirred up culminated in the Boxer Risings."

"Good heavens, Smith!" I said; for I could not reconcile the diffident personality of the clergyman with the memories which those words awakened.

"He evidently should be on our danger list," my friend continued quickly; "but he has so completely effaced himself of recent years that I think it probable that someone else has only just recalled his existence to mind. The Rev. J. D. Eltham, my dear Petrie, though he may be a poor hand at saving souls, at any rate, has saved a score of Christian women from death-- and worse."

"J. D. Eltham--" I began.

"Is `Parson Dan'!" rapped Smith, "the `Fighting Missionary,' the man who with a garrison of a dozen cripples and a German doctor held the hospital at Nan-Yang against two hundred Boxers. That's who the Rev. J. D. Eltham is! But what is he up to, now, I have yet to find out. He is keeping something back-- something which has made him an object of interest to Young China!"

During dinner the matters responsible for our presence there did not hold priority in the conversation. In fact, this, for the most part, consisted in light talk of books and theaters.

Greba Eltham, the clergyman's daughter, was a charming young hostess, and she, with Vernon Denby, Mr. Eltham's nephew, completed the party. No doubt the girl's presence, in part, at any rate, led us to refrain from the subject uppermost in our minds.

These little pools of calm dotted along the torrential course of the circumstances which were bearing my friend and me onward to unknown issues form pleasant, sunny spots in my dark recollections.

So I shall always remember, with pleasure, that dinner-party at Redmoat, in the old-world dining-room; it was so very peaceful, so almost grotesquely calm. For I, within my very bones, felt it to be the calm before the storm. When, later, we men passed to the library, we seemed to leave that atmosphere behind us.

"Redmoat," said the Rev. J. D. Eltham, "has latterly become the theater of strange doings."

He stood on the hearth-rug. A shaded lamp upon the big table and candles in ancient sconces upon the mantelpiece afforded dim illumination. Mr. Eltham's nephew, Vernon Denby, lolled smoking on the window-seat, and I sat near to him. Nayland Smith paced restlessly up and down the room.

"Some mouths ago, almost a year," continued the clergyman, "a burglarious attempt was made upon the house. There was an arrest, and the man confessed that he had been tempted by my collection." He waved his hand vaguely towards the several cabinets about the shadowed room.

"It was shortly afterwards that I allowed my hobby for-- playing at forts to run away with me." He smiled an apology. "I virtually fortified Redmoat--against trespassers of any kind, I mean. You have seen that the house stands upon a kind of large mound. This is artificial, being the buried ruins of a Roman outwork; a portion of the ancient castrum." Again he waved indicatively, this time toward the window.

"When it was a priory it was completely isolated and defended by its environing moat. Today it is completely surrounded by barbed-wire fencing. Below this fence, on the east, is a narrow stream, a tributary of the Waverney; on the north and west, the high road, but nearly twenty feet below, the banks being perpendicular. On the south is the remaining part of the moat--now my kitchen garden; but from there up to the level of the house is nearly twenty feet again, and the barbed wire must also be counted with.

"The entrance, as you know, is by the way of a kind of cutting. There is a gate at the foot of the steps (they are some of the original steps of the priory, Dr. Petrie), and another gate at the head."

He paused, and smiled around upon us boyishly.

"My secret defenses remain to be mentioned," he resumed; and, opening a cupboard, he pointed to a row of batteries, with a number of electric bells upon the wall behind. "The more vulnerable spots are connected at night with these bells," he said triumphantly. "Any attempt to scale the barbed wire or to force either gate would set two or more of these ringing. A stray cow raised one false alarm," he added, "and a careless rook threw us into a perfect panic on another occasion."

He was so boyish--so nervously brisk and acutely sensitive-- that it was difficult to see in him the hero of the Nan-Yang hospital. I could only suppose that he had treated the Boxers' raid in the same spirit wherein he met would-be trespassers within the precincts of Redmoat. It had been an escapade, of which he was afterwards ashamed, as, faintly, he was ashamed of his "fortifications." "But," rapped Smith, "it was not the visit of the burglar which prompted these elaborate precautions."

Mr. Eltham coughed nervously.

"I am aware," he said, "that having invoked official aid, I must be perfectly frank with you, Mr. Smith. It was the burglar who was responsible for my continuing the wire fence all round the grounds, but the electrical contrivance followed, later, as a result of several disturbed nights. My servants grew uneasy about someone who came, they said, after dusk. No one could describe this nocturnal visitor, but certainly we found traces. I must admit that.

"Then--I received what I may term a warning. My position is a peculiar one-- a peculiar one. My daughter, too, saw this prowling, person, over by the Roman castrum, and described him as a yellow man. It was the incident in the train following closely upon this other, which led me to speak to the police, little as I desired to--er--court publicity."

Nayland Smith walked to a window, and looked out across the sloping lawn to where the shadows of the shrubbery lay. A dog was howling dismally somewhere.

"Your defenses are not impregnable, after all, then?" he jerked. "On our way up this evening Mr. Denby was telling us about the death of his collie a few nights ago."

The clergyman's face clouded.

"That, certainly, was alarming," he confessed.

"I had been in London for a few days, and during my absence Vernon came down, bringing the dog with him. On the night of his arrival it ran, barking, into the shrubbery yonder, and did not come out. He went to look for it with a lantern, and found it lying among the bushes, quite dead. The poor creature had been dreadfully beaten about the head."

"The gates were locked," Denby interrupted, "and no one could have got out of the grounds without a ladder and someone to assist him. But there was so sign of a living thing about. Edwards and I searched every corner."

"How long has that other dog taken to howling?" inquired Smith.

"Only since Rex's death," said Denby quickly.

"It is my mastiff," explained the clergyman, "and he is confined in the yard. He is never allowed on this side of the house."

Nayland Smith wandered aimlessly about the library.

"I am sorry to have to press you, Mr. Eltham," he said, "but what was the nature of the warning to which you referred, and from whom did it come?"

Mr. Eltham hesitated for a long time.

"I have been so unfortunate," he said at last, "in my previous efforts, that I feel assured of your hostile criticism when I tell you that I am contemplating an immediate return to Ho-Nan!"

Smith jumped round upon him as though moved by a spring.

"Then you are going back to Nan-Yang?" he cried. "Now I understand! Why have you not told me before? That is the key for which I have vainly been seeking. Your troubles date from the time of your decision to return?"

"Yes, I must admit it," confessed the clergyman diffidently.

"And your warning came from China?"

"It did."

"From a Chinaman?"

"From the Mandarin, Yen-Sun-Yat."

"Yen-Sun-Yat! My good sir! He warned you to abandon your visit? And you reject his advice? Listen to me." Smith was intensely excited now, his eyes bright, his lean figure curiously strung up, alert. "The Mandarin Yen-Sun-Yat is one of the seven!"

"I do not follow you, Mr. Smith."

"No, sir. China to-day is not the China of '98. It is a huge secret machine, and Ho-Nan one of its most important wheels! But if, as I understand, this official is a friend of yours, believe me, he has saved your life! You would be a dead man now if it were not for your friend in China! My dear sir, you must accept his counsel."

Then, for the first time since I had made his acquaintance, "Parson Dan" showed through the surface of the Rev. J. D. Eltham.

"No, sir!" replied the clergyman--and the change in his voice was startling. "I am called to Nan-Yang. Only One may deter my going."

The admixture of deep spiritual reverence with intense truculence in his voice was dissimilar from anything I ever had heard.

"Then only One can protect you," cried Smith, "for, by Heaven, no

MAN will be able to do so! Your presence in Ho-Nan can do no possible good at present. It must do harm. Your experience in 1900 should be fresh in your memory."

"Hard words, Mr. Smith."

"The class of missionary work which you favor, sir, is injurious to international peace. At the present moment, Ho-Nan is a barrel of gunpowder; you would be the lighted match. I do not willingly stand between any man and what he chooses to consider his duty, but I insist that you abandon your visit to the interior of China!"

"You insist, Mr. Smith?"

"As your guest, I regret the necessity for reminding you that I hold authority to enforce it."

Denby fidgeted uneasily. The tone of the conversation was growing harsh and the atmosphere of the library portentous with brewing, storms.

There was a short, silent interval.

"This is what I had feared and expected," said the clergyman. "This was my reason for not seeking official protection."

"The phantom Yellow Peril," said Nayland Smith, "to-day materializes under the very eyes of the Western world."

"The `Yellow Peril'!"

"You scoff, sir, and so do others. We take the proffered right hand of friendship nor inquire if the hidden left holds a knife! The peace of the world is at stake, Mr. Eltham. Unknowingly, you tamper with tremendous issues."

Mr. Eltham drew a deep breath, thrusting both hands in his pockets.

"You are painfully frank, Mr. Smith," he said; "but I like you for it. I will reconsider my position and talk this matter over again with you to-morrow."

Thus, then, the storm blew over. Yet I had never experienced such an overwhelming sense of imminent peril-- of a sinister presence--as oppressed me at that moment. The very atmosphere of Redmoat was impregnated with Eastern devilry; it loaded the air like some evil perfume. And then, through the silence, cut a throbbing scream-- the scream of a woman in direst fear.

"My God, it's Greba!" whispered Mr. Eltham.

CHAPTER VIII

IN WHAT order we dashed down to the drawing-room I cannot recall. But none was before me when I leaped over the threshold and saw Miss Eltham prone by the French windows.

These were closed and bolted, and she lay with hands outstretched in the alcove which they formed. I bent over her. Nayland Smith was at my elbow.

"Get my bag" I said. "She has swooned. It is nothing serious."

Her father, pale and wide-eyed, hovered about me, muttering incoherently; but I managed to reassure him; and his gratitude when, I having administered a simple restorative, the girl sighed shudderingly and opened her eyes, was quite pathetic.

I would permit no questioning at that time, and on her father's arm she retired to her own rooms.

It was some fifteen minutes later that her message was brought to me. I followed the maid to a quaint little octagonal apartment, and Greba Eltham stood before me, the candlelight caressing the soft curves of her face and gleaming in the meshes of her rich brown hair.

When she had answered my first question she hesitated in pretty confusion.

"We are anxious to know what alarmed you, Miss Eltham."

She bit her lip and glanced with apprehension towards the window.

"I am almost afraid to tell father," she began rapidly. "He will think me imaginative, but you have been so kind. It was two green eyes! Oh! Dr. Petrie, they looked up at me from the steps leading to the lawn. And they shone like the eyes of a cat."

The words thrilled me strangely.

"Are you sure it was not a cat, Miss Eltham?"

"The eyes were too large, Dr. Petrie. There was something dreadful, most dreadful, in their appearance. I feel foolish and silly for having fainted, twice in two days! But the suspense is telling upon me, I suppose. Father thinks"--she was becoming charmingly confidential, as a woman often will with a tactful physician--"that shut up here we are safe from--whatever threatens us." I noted, with concern, a repetition of the nervous shudder. "But since our return someone else has been in Redmoat!"

"Whatever do you mean, Miss Eltham?"

"Oh! I don't quite know what I do mean, Dr. Petrie. What does it ALL mean? Vernon has been explaining to me that some awful Chinaman is seeking the life of Mr. Nayland Smith. But if the same man wants to kill my father, why has he not done so?"

"I am afraid you puzzle me."

"Of course, I must do so. But--the man in the train. He could have killed us both quite easily! And--last night someone was in father's room."

"In his room!"

"I could not sleep, and I heard something moving. My room is the next one. I knocked on the wall and woke father. There was nothing; so I said it was the howling of the dog that had frightened me."

"How, could anyone get into his room?"

"I cannot imagine. But I am not sure it was a man."

"Miss Eltham, you alarm me. What do you suspect?"

"You must think me hysterical and silly, but whilst father and I have been away from Redmoat perhaps the usual precautions have been neglected. Is there any creature, any large creature, which could climb up the wall to the window? Do you know of anything with a long, thin body?"

For a moment I offered no reply, studying the girl's pretty face, her eager, blue-gray eyes widely opened and fixed upon mine. She was not of the neurotic type, with her clear complexion and sun-kissed neck; her arms, healthily toned by exposure to the country airs, were rounded and firm, and she had the agile shape of a young Diana with none of the anaemic languor which breeds morbid dreams. She was frightened; yes, who would not have been? But the mere idea of this thing which she believed to be in Redmoat, without the apparition of the green eyes, must have prostrated a victim of "nerves."

"Have you seen such a creature, Miss Eltham?"

She hesitated again, glancing down and pressing her finger-tips together.

"As father awoke and called out to know why I knocked, I glanced from my window. The moonlight threw half the lawn into shadow, and just disappearing in this shadow was something-- something of a brown color, marked with sections!"

"What size and shape?"

"It moved so quickly I could form no idea of its shape; but I saw quite six feet of it flash across the grass!"

"Did you hear anything?"

"A swishing sound in the shrubbery, then nothing more."

She met my eyes expectantly. Her confidence in my powers of understanding and sympathy was gratifying, though I knew that I but occupied the position of a father-confessor.

"Have you any idea," I said, "how it came about that you awoke in the train yesterday whilst your father did not?"

"We had coffee at a refreshment-room; it must have been drugged in some way. I scarcely tasted mine, the flavor was so awful; but father is an old traveler and drank the whole of his cupful!"

Mr. Eltham's voice called from below.

"Dr. Petrie," said the girl quickly, "what do you think they want to do to him?"

"Ah!" I replied, "I wish I knew that."

"Will you think over what I have told you? For I do assure you there is something here in Redmoat--something that comes and goes in spite of father's `fortifications'? Caesar knows there is. Listen to him. He drags at his chain so that I wonder he does not break it."

As we passed downstairs the howling of the mastiff sounded eerily through the house, as did the clank-clank of the tightening chain as he threw the weight of his big body upon it.

I sat in Smith's room that night for some time, he pacing the floor smoking and talking.

"Eltham has influential Chinese friends," he said; "but they dare not have him in Nan-Yang at present. He knows the country as he knows Norfolk; he would see things!

"His precautions here have baffled the enemy, I think. The attempt in the train points to an anxiety to waste no opportunity. But whilst Eltham was absent (he was getting his outfit in London, by the way) they have been fixing some second string to their fiddle here. In case no opportunity offered before he returned, they provided for getting at him here!"

"But how, Smith?"

"That's the mystery. But the dead dog in the shrubbery is significant."

"Do you think some emissary of Fu-Manchu is actually inside the moat?"

"It's impossible, Petrie. You are thinking of secret passages, and so forth. There are none. Eltham has measured up every foot of the place. There isn't a rat hole left unaccounted for; and as for a tunnel under the moat, the house stands on a solid mass of Roman masonry, a former camp of Hadrian's time. I have seen a very old plan of the Round Moat Priory as it was called. There is no entrance and no exit save by the steps. So how was the dog killed?"

I knocked out my pipe on a bar of the grate.

"We are in the thick of it here," I said.

"We are always in the thick of it," replied Smith. "Our danger is no greater in Norfolk than in London. But what do they want to do? That man in the train with the case of instruments--WHAT instruments? Then the apparition of the green eyes to-night. Can they have been the eyes of Fu-

Manchu? Is some peculiarly unique outrage contemplated-- something calling for the presence of the master?"

"He may have to prevent Eltham's leaving England without killing him."

"Quite so. He probably has instructions to be merciful. But God help the victim of Chinese mercy!"

I went to my own room then. But I did not even undress, refilling my pipe and seating myself at the open window. Having looked upon the awful Chinese doctor, the memory of his face, with its filmed green eyes, could never leave me. The idea that he might be near at that moment was a poor narcotic.

The howling and baying of the mastiff was almost continuous.

When all else in Redmoat was still the dog's mournful note yet rose on the night with something menacing in it. I sat looking out across the sloping turf to where the shrubbery showed as a black island in a green sea. The moon swam in a cloudless sky, and the air was warm and fragrant with country scents.

It was in the shrubbery that Denby's collie had met his mysterious death-- that the thing seen by Miss Eltham had disappeared. What uncanny secret did it hold?

Caesar became silent.

As the stopping of a clock will sometimes awaken a sleeper, the abrupt cessation of that distant howling, to which I had grown accustomed, now recalled me from a world of gloomy imaginings.

I glanced at my watch in the moonlight. It was twelve minutes past midnight.

As I replaced it the dog suddenly burst out afresh, but now in a tone of sheer anger. He was alternately howling and snarling in a way that sounded new to me. The crashes, as he leapt to the end of his chain, shook the building in which he was confined. It was as I stood up to lean from the window and commanded a view of the corner of the house that he broke loose.

With a hoarse bay he took that decisive leap, and I heard his heavy body fall against the wooden wall. There followed a strange, guttural cry. . .and the growling of the dog died away at the rear of the house. He was out! But that guttural note had not come from the throat of a dog. Of what was he in pursuit?

At which point his mysterious quarry entered the shrubbery I do not know. I only know that I saw absolutely nothing, until Caesar's lithe shape was streaked across the lawn, and the great creature went crashing into the undergrowth.

Then a faint sound above and to my right told me that I was not the only spectator of the scene. I leaned farther from the window.

"Is that you, Miss Eltham?" I asked.

"Oh, Dr. Petrie!" she said. "I am so glad you are awake. Can we do nothing to help? Caesar will be killed."

"Did you see what he went after?"

"No," she called back, and drew her breath sharply.

For a strange figure went racing across the grass. It was that of a man in a blue dressing-gown, who held a lantern high before him, and a revolver in his right hand. Coincident with my recognition of Mr. Eltham he leaped, plunging into the shrubbery in the wake of the dog.

But the night held yet another surprise; for Nayland Smith's voice came:

"Come back! Come back, Eltham!"

I ran out into the passage and downstairs. The front door was open. A terrible conflict waged in the shrubbery, between the mastiff and something else. Passing round to the lawn, I met Smith fully dressed. He just had dropped from a first-floor window.

"The man is mad!" he snapped. "Heaven knows what lurks there! He should not have gone alone!"

Together we ran towards the dancing light of Eltham's lantern. The sounds of conflict ceased suddenly. Stumbling over stumps and lashed by low-sweeping branches, we struggled forward to where the clergyman knelt amongst the bushes. He glanced up with tears in his eyes, as was revealed by the dim light.

"Look!" he cried.

The body of the dog lay at his feet.

It was pitiable to think that the fearless brute should have met his death in such a fashion, and when I bent and examined him I was glad to find traces of life.

"Drag him out. He is not dead," I said.

"And hurry," rapped Smith, peering about him right and left.

So we three hurried from that haunted place, dragging the dog with us. We were not molested. No sound disturbed the now perfect stillness.

By the lawn edge we came upon Denby, half dressed; and almost immediately Edwards the gardener also appeared. The white faces of the house servants showed at one window, and Miss Eltham called to me from her room:

"Is he dead?"

"No," I replied; "only stunned."

We carried the dog round to the yard, and I examined his head. It had been struck by some heavy blunt instrument, but the skull was not broken. It is hard to kill a mastiff.

"Will you attend to him, Doctor?" asked Eltham. "We must see that the villain does not escape."

His face was grim and set. This was a different man from the diffident clergyman we knew: this was "Parson Dan" again.

I accepted the care of the canine patient, and Eltham with the others went off for more lights to search the shrubbery. As I was washing a bad wound between the mastiff's ears, Miss Eltham joined me. It was the sound of her voice, I think, rather than my more scientific ministration, which recalled Caesar to life. For, as she entered, his tail wagged feebly, and a moment later he struggled to his feet-- one of which was injured.

Having provided for his immediate needs, I left him in charge of his young mistress and joined the search party. They had entered the shrubbery from four points and drawn blank.

"There is absolutely nothing there, and no one can possibly have left the grounds," said Eltham amazedly.

We stood on the lawn looking at one another, Nayland Smith, angry but thoughtful, tugging at the lobe of his left ear, as was his habit in moments of perplexity.

CHAPTER IX

WITH THE first coming of light, Eltham, Smith and I tested the electrical contrivances from every point. They were in perfect order. It became more and more incomprehensible how anyone could have entered and quitted Redmoat during the night. The barbed-wire fencing was intact, and bore no signs of having been tampered with.

Smith and I undertook an exhaustive examination of the shrubbery.

At the spot where we had found the dog, some five paces to the west of the copper beech, the grass and weeds were trampled and the surrounding laurels and rhododendrons bore evidence of a struggle, but no human footprint could be found.

"The ground is dry," said Smith. "We cannot expect much."

"In my opinion," I said, "someone tried to get at Caesar; his presence is dangerous. And in his rage he broke loose."

"I think so, too," agreed Smith. "But why did this person make for here? And how, having mastered the dog, get out of Redmoat? I am open to admit the possibility of someone's getting in during the day whilst the gates are open, and hiding until dusk. But how in the name of all that's wonderful does he GET OUT? He must possess the attributes of a bird."

I thought of Greba Eltham's statements, reminding my friend of her description of the thing which she had seen passing into this strangely haunted shrubbery.

"That line of speculation soon takes us out of our depth, Petrie," he said. "Let us stick to what we can understand, and that may help us to a clearer idea of what, at present, is incomprehensible. My view of the case to date stands thus:

"(1) Eltham, having rashly decided to return to the interior of China, is warned by an official whose friendship he has won in some way to stay in England.

"(2) I know this official for one of the Yellow group represented in England by Dr. Fu-Manchu.

"(3) Several attempts, of which we know but little, to get at Eltham are frustrated, presumably by his curious `defenses.' An attempt in a train fails owing to Miss Eltham's distaste for refreshment-room coffee. An attempt here fails owing to her insomnia.

"(4) During Eltham's absence from Redmoat certain preparations are made for his return. These lead to:

"(a) The death of Denby's collie;

"(b) The things heard and seen by Miss Eltham;

"(c) The things heard and seen by us all last night."

"So that the clearing up of my fourth point--id est, the discovery of the nature of these preparations--becomes our immediate concern. The prime object of these preparations, Petrie, was to enable someone to gain access to Eltham's room. The other events are incidental. The dogs HAD to be got rid of, for instance; and there is no doubt that Miss Eltham's wakefulness saved her father a second time."

"But from what? For Heaven's sake, from what?"

Smith glanced about into the light-patched shadows.

"From a visit by someone--perhaps by Fu-Manchu himself," he said in a hushed voice. "The object of that visit I hope we may never learn; for that would mean that it had been achieved."

"Smith," I said, "I do not altogether understand you; but do you think he has some incredible creature hidden here somewhere? It would be like him."

"I begin to suspect the most formidable creature in the known world to be hidden here. I believe Fu-Manchu is somewhere inside Redmoat!"

Our conversation was interrupted at this point by Denby, who came to report that he had examined the moat, the roadside, and the bank of the stream, but found no footprints or clew of any kind.

"No one left the grounds of Redmoat last night, I think," he said. And his voice had awe in it.

That day dragged slowly on. A party of us scoured the neighborhood for traces of strangers, examining every foot of the Roman ruin hard by; but vainly.

"May not your presence here induce Fu-Manchu to abandon his plans?" I asked Smith.

"I think not," he replied. "You see, unless we can prevail upon him, Eltham sails in a fortnight. So the Doctor has no time to waste. Furthermore, I have an idea that his arrangements are of such a character that they MUST go forward. He might turn aside, of course, to assassinate me, if opportunity arose! But we know, from experience, that he permits nothing to interfere with his schemes."

There are few states, I suppose, which exact so severe a toll from one's nervous system as the ANTICIPATION of calamity.

All anticipation is keener, be it of joy or pain, than the reality whereof it is a mental forecast; but that inactive waiting at Redmoat, for the blow which we knew full well to be pending exceeded in its nerve taxation, anything, I hitherto had experienced.

I felt as one bound upon an Aztec altar, with the priest's obsidian knife raised above my breast!

Secret and malign forces throbbed about us; forces against which we had no armor. Dreadful as it was, I count it a mercy that the climax was reached so quickly. And it came suddenly enough; for there in that quiet Norfolk home we found ourselves at hand grips with one of the mysterious horrors which characterized the operations of Dr. Fu-Manchu. It was upon us before we realized it. There is no incidental music to the dramas of real life.

As we sat on the little terrace in the creeping twilight, I remember thinking how the peace of the scene gave the lie to my fears that we bordered upon tragic things. Then Caesar, who had been a docile patient all day, began howling again; and I saw Greba Eltham shudder.

I caught Smith's eye, and was about to propose our retirement indoors, when the party was broken up in more turbulent fashion. I suppose it was the presence of the girl which prompted Denby to the rash act, a desire personally to distinguish himself. But, as I recalled afterwards, his gaze had rarely left the shrubbery since dusk, save to seek her face, and now he leaped wildly to his feet, overturning his chair, and dashed across the grass to the trees.

"Did you see it?" he yelled. "Did you see it?"

He evidently carried a revolver. For from the edge of the shrubbery a shot sounded, and in the flash we saw Denby with the weapon raised.

"Greba, go in and fasten the windows," cried Eltham. "Mr. Smith, will you enter the bushes from the west. Dr. Petrie, east. Edwards, Edwards--" And he was off across the lawn with the nervous activity of a cat.

As I made off in an opposite direction I heard the gardener's voice from the lower gate, and I saw Eltham's plan. It was to surround the shrubbery.

Two more shots and two flashes from the dense heart of greenwood. Then a loud cry--I thought, from Denby--and a second, muffled one.

Following--silence, only broken by the howling of the mastiff.

I sprinted through the rose garden, leaped heedlessly over a bed of geranium and heliotrope, and plunged in among the bushes and under the elms. Away on the left I heard Edwards shouting, and Eltham's answering voice.

"Denby!" I cried, and yet louder: "Denby!"

But the silence fell again.

Dusk was upon Redmoat now, but from sitting in the twilight my eyes had grown accustomed to gloom, and I could see fairly well what lay before me. Not daring to think what might lurk above, below, around me, I pressed on into the midst of the thicket.

"Vernon!" came Eltham's voice from one side.

"Bear more to the right, Edwards," I heard Nayland Smith cry directly ahead of me.

With an eerie and indescribable sensation of impending disaster upon me, I thrust my way through to a gray patch which marked a break in the elmen roof. At the foot of the copper beech I almost fell over Eltham. Then Smith plunged into view. Lastly, Edwards the gardener rounded a big rhododendron and completed the party.

We stood quite still for a moment.

A faint breeze whispered through the beech leaves.

"Where is he?"

I cannot remember who put it into words; I was too dazed with amazement to notice. Then Eltham began shouting:

"Vernon! Vernon! VERNON!"

His voice pitched higher upon each repetition. There was something horrible about that vain calling, under the whispering beech, with shrubs banked about us cloaking God alone could know what.

From the back of the house came Caesar's faint reply.

"Quick! Lights!" rapped Smith. "Every lamp you have!"

Off we went, dodging laurels and privets, and poured out on to the lawn, a disordered company. Eltham's face was deathly pale, and his jaw set hard. He met my eye.

"God forgive me!" he said. "I could do murder to-night!"

He was a man composed of strange perplexities.

It seemed an age before the lights were found. But at last we returned to the bushes, really after a very brief delay; and ten minutes sufficed us to explore the entire shrubbery, for it was not extensive. We found his revolver, but there was no one there--nothing.

When we all stood again on the lawn, I thought that I had never seen Smith so haggard.

"What in Heaven's name can we do?" he muttered. "What does it mean?"

He expected no answer; for there was none to offer one.

"Search! Everywhere," said Eltham hoarsely.

He ran off into the rose garden, and began beating about among the flowers like a madman, muttering: "Vernon! Vernon!" For close upon an hour we all searched. We searched every square yard, I think, within the wire fencing, and found no trace. Miss Eltham slipped out in the confusion, and joined with the rest of us in that frantic hunt. Some of the servants assisted too.

It was a group terrified and awestricken which came together again on the terrace. One and then another would give up, until only Eltham and Smith were missing. Then they came back together from examining the steps to the lower gate.

Eltham dropped on to a rustic seat, and sank his head in his hands.

Nayland Smith paced up and down like a newly caged animal, snapping his teeth together and tugging at his ear.

Possessed by some sudden idea, or pressed to action by his tumultuous thoughts, he snatched up a lantern and strode silently off across the grass and to the shrubbery once more. I followed him. I think his idea was that he might surprise anyone who lurked there. He surprised himself, and all of us.

For right at the margin he tripped and fell flat. I ran to him.

He had fallen over the body of Denby, which lay there!

Denby had not been there a few moments before, and how he came to be there now we dared not conjecture. Mr. Eltham joined us, uttered one short, dry sob, and dropped upon his knees. Then we were carrying Denby back to the house, with the mastiff howling a marche funebre.

We laid him on the grass where it sloped down from the terrace. Nayland Smith's haggard face was terrible. But the stark horror of the thing inspired him to that, which conceived earlier, had saved Denby. Twisting suddenly to Eltham, he roared in a voice audible beyond the river:

"Heavens! we are fools! LOOSE THE DOG!"

"But the dog--" I began.

Smith clapped his hand over my mouth.

"I know he's crippled," he whispered. "But if anything human lurks there, the dog will lead us to it. If a MAN is there, he will fly! Why did we not think of it before. Fools, fools!" He raised his voice again. "Keep him on leash, Edwards. He will lead us."

The scheme succeeded.

Edwards barely had started on his errand when bells began ridging inside the house.

"Wait!" snapped Eltham, and rushed indoors.

A moment later he was out again, his eyes gleaming madly. "Above the moat," he panted. And we were off en masse round the edge of the trees.

It was dark above the moat; but not so dark as to prevent our seeing a narrow ladder of thin bamboo joints and silken cord hanging by two hooks from the top of the twelve-foot wire fence. There was no sound.

"He's out!" screamed Eltham. "Down the steps!"

We all ran our best and swiftest. But Eltham outran us. Like a fury he tore at bolts and bars, and like a fury sprang out into the road. Straight and white it showed to the acclivity by the Roman ruin. But no living thing moved upon it. The distant baying of the dog was borne to our ears.

"Curse it! he's crippled," hissed Smith. "Without him, as well pursue a shadow!"

A few hours later the shrubbery yielded up its secret, a simple one enough: A big cask sunk in a pit, with a laurel shrub cunningly affixed to its movable lid, which was further disguised with tufts of grass. A slender bamboo-jointed rod lay near the fence. It had a hook on the top, and was evidently used for attaching the ladder.

"It was the end of this ladder which Miss Eltham saw," said Smith, "as he trailed it behind him into the shrubbery when she interrupted him in her fathers room. He and whomever he had with him doubtless slipped in during the daytime--whilst Eltham was absent in London-- bringing the prepared cask and all necessary implements with them. They concealed themselves somewhere--probably in the shrubbery-- and during the night made the cache. The excavated earth would be disposed of on the flower-beds; the dummy bush they probably had ready. You see, the problem of getting IN was never a big one. But owing to the `defenses' it was impossible (whilst Eltham was in residence at any rate) to get OUT after dark. For Fu-Manchu's purposes, then, a working-base INSIDE Redmoat was essential. His servant--for he needed assistance-- must have been in hiding somewhere outside; Heaven knows where! During the day they could come or go by the gates, as we have already noted."

"You think it was the Doctor himself?"

"It seems possible. Whom else has eyes like the eyes Miss Eltham saw from the window last night?"

Then remains to tell the nature of the outrage whereby Fu-Manchu had planned to prevent Eltham's leaving England for China. This we learned from Denby. For Denby was not dead.

It was easy to divine that he had stumbled upon the fiendish visitor at the very entrance to his burrow; had been stunned (judging from the evidence, with a sand-bag), and dragged down into the cache--to which he must have lain in such dangerous proximity as to render detection of the dummy bush possible in removing him. The quickest expedient, then, had been to draw him beneath. When the search of the shrubbery was concluded, his body had been borne to the edge of the bushes and laid where we found it.

Why his life had been spared, I cannot conjecture, but provision had been made against his recovering consciousness and revealing the secret of the shrubbery. The ruse of releasing the mastiff alone had terminated the visit of the unbidden guest within Redmoat.

Denby made a very slow recovery; and, even when convalescent, consciously added not one fact to those we already had collated; his memory had completely deserted him!

This, in my opinion, as in those of the several specialists consulted, was due, not to the blow on the head, but to the presence, slightly below and to the right of the first cervical curve of the spine, of a minute puncture-- undoubtedly caused by a hypodermic syringe. Then, unconsciously, poor Denby furnished the last link in the chain; for undoubtedly, by means of this operation, Fu-Manchu had designed to efface from Eltham's mind his plans of return to Ho-Nan.

The nature of the fluid which could produce such mental symptoms was a mystery--a mystery which defied Western science: one of the many strange secrets of Dr. Fu-Manchu.

CHAPTER X

SINCE NAYLAND SMITH'S return from Burma I had rarely taken up a paper without coming upon evidences of that seething which had cast up Dr. Fu-Manchu. Whether, hitherto, such items had escaped my attention or had seemed to demand no particular notice, or whether they now became increasingly numerous, I was unable to determine.

One evening, some little time after our sojourn in Norfolk, in glancing through a number of papers which I had brought in with me, I chanced upon no fewer than four items of news bearing more or less directly upon the grim business which engaged my friend and I.

No white man, I honestly believe, appreciates the unemotional cruelty of the Chinese. Throughout the time that Dr. Fu-Manchu remained in England, the press preserved a uniform silence upon the subject of his existence. This was due to Nayland Smith. But, as a result, I feel assured that my account of the Chinaman's deeds will, in many quarters, meet with an incredulous reception.

I had been at work, earlier in the evening, upon the opening chapters of this chronicle, and I had realized how difficult it would be for my reader, amid secure and cozy surroundings, to credit any human being, with a callous villainy great enough to conceive and to put into execution such a death pest as that directed against Sir Crichton Davey.

One would expect God's worst man to shrink from employing--against however vile an enemy--such an instrument as the Zayat Kiss. So thinking, my eye was caught by the following:--

EXPRESS CORRESPONDENT

NEW YORK.

"Secret service men of the United States Government are searching the South Sea Islands for a certain Hawaiian from the island of Maui, who, it is believed, has been selling poisonous scorpions to Chinese in Honolulu anxious to get rid of their children.

"Infanticide, by scorpion and otherwise, among the Chinese, has increased so terribly that the authorities have started a searching inquiry, which has led to the hunt for the scorpion dealer of Maui.

"Practically all the babies that die mysteriously are unwanted girls, and in nearly every case the parents promptly ascribe the death to the bite of a scorpion, and are ready to produce some more or less poisonous insect in support of the statement.

"The authorities have no doubt that infanticide by scorpion bite is a growing practice, and orders have been given to hunt down the scorpion dealer at any cost."

Is it any matter for wonder that such a people had produced a Fu-Manchu? I pasted the cutting into a scrap-book, determined that, if I lived to publish my account of those days, I would quote it therein as casting a sidelight upon Chinese character.

A Reuter message to The Globe and a paragraph in The Star also furnished work for my scissors. Here were evidences of the deep-seated unrest, the secret turmoil, which manifested itself so far from its center as peaceful England in the person of the sinister Doctor.

"HONG KONG, Friday.

"Li Hon Hung, the Chinaman who fired at the Governor yesterday, was charged before the magistrate with shooting at him with intent to kill, which is equivalent to attempted murder. The prisoner, who was not defended, pleaded guilty. The Assistant Crown Solicitor, who prosecuted, asked for a remand until Monday, which was granted.

"Snapshots taken by the spectators of the outrage yesterday disclosed the presence of an accomplice, also armed with a revolver. It is reported that this man, who was arrested last night, was in possession of incriminating documentary evidence."

Later.

"Examination of the documents found on Li Hon Hung's accomplice has disclosed the fact that both men were well financed by the Canton Triad Society, the directors of which had enjoined the assassination of Sir F. M. or Mr. C. S., the Colonial Secretary. In a report prepared by the accomplice for dispatch to Canton, also found on his person, he expressed regret that the attempt had failed."--Reuter.

"It is officially reported in St. Petersburg that a force of Chinese soldiers and villagers surrounded the house of a Russian subject named Said Effendi, near Khotan, in Chinese Turkestan.

"They fired at the house and set it in flames. There were in the house about 100 Russians, many of whom were killed.

"The Russian Government has instructed its Minister at Peking to make the most vigorous representations on the subject."--Reuter.

Finally, in a Personal Column, I found the following:--

"HO-NAN. Have abandoned visit.--ELTHAM."

I had just pasted it into my book when Nayland Smith came in and threw himself into an arm-chair, facing me across the table. I showed him the cutting.

"I am glad, for Eltham's sake--and for the girl's," was his comment. "But it marks another victory for Fu-Manchu! Just Heaven! Why is retribution delayed!"

Smith's darkly tanned face had grown leaner than ever since he had begun his fight with the most uncanny opponent, I suppose, against whom a man ever had pitted himself. He stood up and began restlessly to pace the room, furiously stuffing tobacco into his briar.

"I have seen Sir Lionel Barton," he said abruptly; "and, to put the whole thing in a nutshell, he has laughed at me! During the months that I have been wondering where he had gone to he has been somewhere in Egypt. He certainly bears a charmed life, for on the evidence of his letter to The Times he has seen things in Tibet which Fu-Manchu would have the West blind to; in fact, I think he has found a new keyhole to the gate of the Indian Empire!"

Long ago we had placed the name of Sir Lionel Barton upon the list of those whose lives stood between Fu-Manchu and the attainment of his end. Orientalist and explorer, the fearless traveler who first had penetrated to Lhassa, who thrice, as a pilgrim, had entered forbidden Mecca, he now had turned his attention again to Tibet--thereby signing his own death-warrant.

"That he has reached England alive is a hopeful sign?" I suggested.

Smith shook his head, and lighted the blackened briar.

"England at present is the web," he replied. "The spider will be waiting. Petrie, I sometimes despair. Sir Lionel is an impossible man to shepherd. You ought to see his house at Finchley. A low, squat place completely hemmed in by trees. Damp as a swamp; smells like a jungle. Everything topsy-turvy. He only arrived to-day, and he is working and eating (and sleeping I expect), in a study that looks like an earthquake at Sotheby's auction-rooms. The rest of the house is half a menagerie and half a circus. He has a Bedouin groom, a Chinese body-servant, and Heaven only knows what other strange people!"

"Chinese!"

"Yes, I saw him; a squinting Cantonese he calls Kwee. I don't like him. Also, there is a secretary known as Strozza, who has an unpleasant face. He is a fine linguist, I understand, and is engaged upon the Spanish notes for Barton's forthcoming book on the Mayapan temples. By the way, all Sir Lionel's baggage disappeared from the landing-stage-- including his Tibetan notes."

"Significant!"

"Of course. But he argues that he has crossed Tibet from the Kuen-Lun to the Himalayas without being assassinated, and therefore that it is unlikely he will meet with that fate in London. I left him dictating the book from memory, at the rate of about two hundred words a minute."

"He is wasting no time."

"Wasting time! In addition to the Yucatan book and the work on Tibet, he has to read a paper at the Institute next week about some tomb he has unearthed in Egypt. As I came away, a van drove up from the docks and a couple of fellows delivered a sarcophagus as big as a boat. It is unique, according to Sir Lionel, and will go to the British Museum after he has examined it. The man crams six months' work into six weeks; then he is off again."

"What do you propose to do?"

"What CAN I do? I know that Fu-Manchu will make an attempt upon him. I cannot doubt it. Ugh! that house gave me the shudders. No sunlight, I'll swear, Petrie, can ever penetrate to the rooms, and when I arrived this afternoon clouds of gnats floated like motes wherever a stray beam filtered through the trees of the avenue. There's a steamy smell about the place that is almost malarious, and the whole of the west front is covered with a sort of monkey-creeper, which he has imported at some time or other. It has a close, exotic perfume that is quite in the picture. I tell you, the place was made for murder."

"Have you taken any precautions?"

"I called at Scotland Yard and sent a man down to watch the house, but--"

He shrugged his shoulders helplessly.

"What is Sir Lionel like?"

"A madman, Petrie. A tall, massive man, wearing a dirty dressing-gown of neutral color; a man with untidy gray hair and a bristling mustache, keen blue eyes, and a brown skin; who wears a short beard or rarely shaves-- I don't know which. I left him striding about among the thousand and one curiosities of that incredible room, picking his way through his antique furniture, works of reference, manuscripts, mummies, spears, pottery and what not--sometimes kicking a book from his course, or stumbling over a stuffed crocodile or a Mexican mask-- alternately dictating and conversing. Phew!"

For some time we were silent.

"Smith" I said, "we are making no headway in this business. With all the forces arrayed against him, Fu-Manchu still eludes us, still pursues his devilish, inscrutable way."

Nayland Smith nodded.

"And we don't know all," he said. "We mark such and such a man as one alive to the Yellow Peril, and we warn him--if we have time. Perhaps he escapes; perhaps he does not. But what do we know, Petrie, of those others who may die every week by his murderous agency? We cannot know EVERYONE who has read the riddle of China. I never see a report of someone found drowned, of an apparent suicide, of a sudden, though seemingly natural death, without wondering. I tell you, Fu-Manchu is omnipresent; his tentacles embrace everything. I said that Sir Lionel must bear a charmed life. The fact that WE are alive is a miracle."

He glanced at his watch.

"Nearly eleven," he said. "But sleep seems a waste of time-- apart from its dangers."

We heard a bell ring. A few moments later followed a knock at the room door.

"Come in!" I cried.

A girl entered with a telegram addressed to Smith. His jaw looked very square in the lamplight, and his eyes shone like steel as he took it from her and opened the envelope. He glanced at the form, stood up and passed it to me, reaching for his hat, which lay upon my writing-table.

"God help us, Petrie!" he said.

This was the message:

"Sir Lionel Barton murdered. Meet me at his house at once.--WEYMOUTH, INSPECTOR."

CHAPTER XI

ALTHOUGH WE avoided all unnecessary delay, it was close upon midnight when our cab swung round into a darkly shadowed avenue, at the farther end of which, as seen through a tunnel, the moonlight glittered upon the windows of Rowan House, Sir Lionel Barton's home.

Stepping out before the porch of the long, squat building, I saw that it was banked in, as Smith had said, by trees and shrubs. The facade showed mantled in the strange exotic creeper which he had mentioned, and the air was pungent with an odor of decaying vegetation, with which mingled the heavy perfume of the little nocturnal red flowers which bloomed luxuriantly upon the creeper.

The place looked a veritable wilderness, and when we were admitted to the hall by Inspector Weymouth I saw that the interior was in keeping with the exterior, for the hall was constructed from the model of some apartment in an Assyrian temple, and the squat columns, the low seats, the hangings, all were eloquent of neglect, being thickly dust-coated. The musty smell, too, was almost as pronounced here as outside, beneath the trees.

To a library, whose contents overflowed in many literary torrents upon the floor, the detective conducted us.

"Good heavens!" I cried, "what's that?"

Something leaped from the top of the bookcase, ambled silently across the littered carpet, and passed from the library like a golden streak. I stood looking after it with startled eyes. Inspector Weymouth laughed dryly.

"It's a young puma, or a civet-cat, or something, Doctor," he said. "This house is full of surprises--and mysteries."

His voice was not quite steady, I thought, and he carefully closed the door ere proceeding further.

"Where is he?" asked Nayland Smith harshly. "How was it done?"

Weymouth sat down and lighted a cigar which I offered him.

"I thought you would like to hear what led up to it--so far as we know-- before seeing him?"

Smith nodded.

"Well," continued the Inspector, "the man you arranged to send down from the Yard got here all right and took up a post in the road outside, where he could command a good view of the gates. He saw and heard nothing, until going on for half-past ten, when a young lady turned up and went in."

"A young lady?"

"Miss Edmonds, Sir Lionel's shorthand typist. She had found, after getting home, that her bag, with her purse in, was missing, and she came back to see if she had left it here. She gave the alarm. My man heard the row from the road and came in. Then he ran out and rang us up. I immediately wired for you."

"He heard the row, you say. What row?"

"Miss Edmonds went into violent hysterics!"

Smith was pacing the room now in tense excitement.

"Describe what he saw when he came in."

"He saw a negro footman--there isn't an Englishman in the house--trying to pacify the girl out in the hall yonder, and a Malay and another colored man beating their foreheads and howling. There was no sense to be got out of any of them, so he started to investigate for himself. He had taken the bearings of the place earlier in the evening, and from the light in a window on the ground floor had located the study; so he set out to look for the door. When he found it, it was locked from the inside."

"Well?"

"He went out and round to the window. There's no blind, and from the shrubbery you can see into the lumber-room known as the study. He looked in, as apparently Miss Edmonds had done before him. What he saw accounted for her hysterics."

Both Smith and I were hanging upon his words.

"All amongst the rubbish on the floor a big Egyptian mummy case was lying on its side, and face downwards, with his arms thrown across it, lay Sir Lionel Barton."

"My God! Yes. Go on."

"There was only a shaded reading-lamp alight, and it stood on a chair, shining right down on him; it made a patch of light on the floor, you understand." The Inspector indicated its extent with his bands. "Well, as the man smashed the glass and got the window open, and was just climbing in, he saw something else, so he says."

He paused.

"What did he see?" demanded Smith shortly.

"A sort of GREEN MIST, sir. He says it seemed to be alive. It moved over the floor, about a foot from the ground, going away from him and towards a curtain at the other end of the study."

Nayland Smith fixed his eyes upon the speaker.

"Where did he first see this green mist?"

"He says, Mr. Smith, that he thinks it came from the mummy case."

"Yes; go on."

"It is to his credit that he climbed into the room after seeing a thing like that. He did. He turned the body over, and Sir Lionel looked horrible. He was quite dead. Then Croxted--that's the man's name--went over to this curtain. There was a glass door--shut. He opened it, and it gave on a conservatory--a place stacked from the tiled floor to the glass roof with more rubbish. It was dark inside, but enough light came from the study--it's really a drawing-room, by the way-- as he'd turned all the lamps on, to give him another glimpse of this green, crawling mist. There are three steps to go down. On the steps lay a dead Chinaman."

"A dead Chinaman!"

"A dead CHINAMAN."

"Doctor seen them?" rapped Smith.

"Yes; a local man. He was out of his depth, I could see. Contradicted himself three times. But there's no need for another opinion--until we get the coroner's."

"And Croxted?"

"Croxted was taken ill, Mr. Smith, and had to be sent home in a cab."

"What ails him?"

Detective-Inspector Weymouth raised his eyebrows and carefully knocked the ash from his cigar.

"He held out until I came, gave me the story, and then fainted right away. He said that something in the conservatory seemed to get him by the throat."

"Did he mean that literally?"

"I couldn't say. We had to send the girl home, too, of course."

Nayland Smith was pulling thoughtfully at the lobe of his left ear.

"Got any theory?" he jerked.

Weymouth shrugged his shoulders.

"Not one that includes the green mist," he said. "Shall we go in now?"

We crossed the Assyrian hall, where the members of that strange household were gathered in a panic-stricken group. They numbered four. Two of them were negroes, and two Easterns of some kind. I missed the Chinaman, Kwee, of whom Smith had spoken, and the Italian secretary; and from the way in which my friend peered about the shadows of the hall I divined that he, too, wondered at their absence. We entered Sir Lionel's study--an apartment which I despair of describing.

Nayland Smith's words, "an earthquake at Sotheby's auction-rooms," leaped to my mind at once; for the place was simply stacked with curious litter--loot of Africa, Mexico and Persia. In a clearing by the hearth a gas stove stood upon a packing-case, and about it lay a number of utensils for camp cookery. The odor of rotting vegetation, mingled with the insistent perfume of the strange night-blooming flowers, was borne in through the open window.

In the center of the floor, beside an overturned sarcophagus, lay a figure in a neutral-colored dressing-gown, face downwards, and arms thrust forward and over the side of the ancient Egyptian mummy case.

My friend advanced and knelt beside the dead man.

"Good God!"

Smith sprang upright and turned with an extraordinary expression to Inspector Weymouth.

"You do not know Sir Lionel Barton by sight?" he rapped.

"No," began Weymouth, "but--"

"This is not Sir Lionel. This is Strozza, the secretary."

"What!" shouted Weymouth.

"Where is the other--the Chinaman--quick!" cried Smith.

"I have had him left where he was found--on the conservatory steps," said the Inspector.

Smith ran across the room to where, beyond the open door, a glimpse might be obtained of stacked-up curiosities. Holding back the curtain to allow more light to penetrate, he bent forward over a crumpled-up figure which lay upon the steps below.

"It is!" he cried aloud. "It is Sir Lionel's servant, Kwee."

Weymouth and I looked at one another across the body of the Italian; then our eyes turned together to where my friend, grim-faced, stood over the dead Chinaman. A breeze whispered through the leaves; a great wave of exotic perfume swept from the open window towards the curtained doorway.

It was a breath of the East--that stretched out a yellow hand to the West. It was symbolic of the subtle, intangible power manifested in Dr. Fu-Manchu, as Nayland Smith--lean, agile, bronzed with the suns of Burma, was symbolic of the clean British efficiency which sought to combat the insidious enemy.

"One thing is evident," said Smith: "no one in the house, Strozza excepted, knew that Sir Lionel was absent."

"How do you arrive at that?" asked Weymouth.

"The servants, in the hall, are bewailing him as dead. If they had seen him go out they would know that it must be someone else who lies here."

"What about the Chinaman?"

"Since there is no other means of entrance to the conservatory save through the study, Kwee must have hidden himself there at some time when his master was absent from the room."

"Croxted found the communicating door closed. What killed the Chinaman?"

"Both Miss Edmonds and Croxted found the study door locked from the inside. What killed Strozza?" retorted Smith.

"You will have noted," continued the Inspector, "that the secretary is wearing Sir Lionel's dressing-gown. It was seeing him in that, as she looked in at the window, which led Miss Edmonds to mistake him for her employer--and consequently to put us on the wrong scent."

"He wore it in order that anybody looking in at the window would be sure to make that mistake," rapped Smith.

"Why?" I asked.

"Because he came here for a felonious purpose. See." Smith stooped and took up several tools from the litter on the floor. "There lies the lid. He came to open the sarcophagus. It contained the mummy of some notable person who flourished under Meneptah II; and Sir Lionel told me that a number of valuable ornaments and jewels probably were secreted amongst the wrappings. He proposed to open the thing and to submit the entire contents to examination to-night. He evidently changed his mind--fortunately for himself."

I ran my fingers through my hair in perplexity.

"Then what has become of the mummy?"

Nayland Smith laughed dryly.

"It has vanished in the form of a green vapor apparently," he said. "Look at Strozza's face."

He turned the body over, and, used as I was to such spectacles, the contorted features of the Italian filled me with horror, so-- suggestive were they of a death more than ordinarily violent. I pulled aside the dressing-gown and searched the body for marks, but failed to find any. Nayland Smith crossed the room, and, assisted by the detective, carried Kwee, the Chinaman, into the study and laid him fully in the light. His puckered yellow face presented a sight even more awful than the other, and his blue lips were drawn back, exposing both upper and lower teeth. There were no marks of violence, but his limbs, like Strozza's, had been tortured during his mortal struggles into unnatural postures.

The breeze was growing higher, and pungent odor-waves from the damp shrubbery, bearing, too, the oppressive sweetness of the creeping, plant, swept constantly through the open window. Inspector Weymouth carefully relighted his cigar.

"I'm with you this far, Mr. Smith," he said. "Strozza, knowing Sir Lionel to be absent, locked himself in here to rifle the mummy case, for Croxted, entering by way of the window, found the key on the inside. Strozza didn't know that the Chinaman was hidden in the conservatory--"

"And Kwee did not dare to show himself, because he too was there for some mysterious reason of his own," interrupted Smith.

"Having got the lid off, something,--somebody--"

"Suppose we say the mummy?"

Weymouth laughed uneasily.

"Well, sir, something that vanished from a locked room without opening the door or the window killed Strozza."

"And something which, having killed Strozza, next killed the Chinaman, apparently without troubling to open the door behind which he lay concealed," Smith continued. "For once in a way, Inspector, Dr. Fu-Manchu has employed an ally which even his giant will was incapable entirely to subjugate. What blind force--what terrific agent of death--had he confined in that sarcophagus!"

"You think this is the work of Fu-Manchu?" I said. "If you are correct, his power indeed is more than human."

Something in my voice, I suppose, brought Smith right about. He surveyed me curiously.

"Can you doubt it? The presence of a concealed Chinaman surely is sufficient. Kwee, I feel assured, was one of the murder group, though probably he had only recently entered that mysterious service. He is unarmed, or I should feel disposed to think that his part was to assassinate Sir Lionel whilst, unsuspecting the presence of a hidden enemy, he was at work here. Strozza's opening the sarcophagus clearly spoiled the scheme."

"And led to the death--"

"Of a servant of Fu-Manchu. Yes. I am at a loss to account for that."

"Do you think that the sarcophagus entered into the scheme, Smith?"

My friend looked at me in evident perplexity.

"You mean that its arrival at the time when a creature of the Doctor--Kwee--was concealed here, may have been a coincidence?"

I nodded; and Smith bent over the sarcophagus, curiously examining the garish paintings with which it was decorated inside and out. It lay sideways upon the floor, and seizing it by its edge, he turned it over.

"Heavy," he muttered; "but Strozza must have capsized it as he fell. He would not have laid it on its side to remove the lid. Hallo!"

He bent farther forward, catching at a piece of twine, and out of the mummy case pulled a rubber stopper or "cork."

"This was stuck in a hole level with the floor of the thing," he said. "Ugh! it has a disgusting smell."

I took it from his hands, and was about to examine it, when a loud voice sounded outside in the hall. The door was thrown open, and a big man, who, despite the warmth of the weather, wore a fur-lined overcoat, rushed impetuously into the room.

"Sir Lionel!" cried Smith eagerly. "I warned you! And see, you have had a very narrow escape."

Sir Lionel Barton glanced at what lay upon the floor, then from Smith to myself, and from me to Inspector Weymouth. He dropped into one of the few chairs unstacked with books.

"Mr. Smith," he said, with emotion, "what does this mean? Tell me--quickly."

In brief terms Smith detailed the happenings of the night-- or so much as he knew of them. Sir Lionel Barton listened, sitting quite still the while--an unusual repose in a man of such evidently tremendous nervous activity.

"He came for the jewels," he said slowly, when Smith was finished; and his eyes turned to the body of the dead Italian. "I was wrong to submit him to the temptation. God knows what Kwee was doing in hiding. Perhaps he had come to murder me, as you surmise, Mr. Smith, though I find it hard to believe. But--I don't think this is the handiwork of your Chinese doctor." He fixed his gaze upon the sarcophagus.

Smith stared at him in surprise. "What do you mean, Sir Lionel?"

The famous traveler continued to look towards the sarcophagus with something in his blue eyes that might have been dread.

"I received a wire from Professor Rembold to-night," he continued. "You were correct in supposing that no one but Strozza knew of my absence. I dressed hurriedly and met the professor at the Traveler's. He knew that I was to read a paper next week upon"-- again he looked toward the mummy case--"the tomb of Mekara; and he knew that the sarcophagus had been brought, untouched, to England. He begged me not to open it."

Nayland Smith was studying the speaker's face.

"What reason did he give for so extraordinary a request?" he asked.

Sir Lionel Barton hesitated.

"One," he replied at last, "which amused me--at the time. I must inform you that Mekara--whose tomb my agent had discovered during my absence in Tibet, and to enter which I broke my return journey to Alexandria-- was a high priest and first prophet of Amen--under the Pharaoh of the Exodus; in short, one of the magicians who contested in magic arts with Moses. I thought the discovery unique, until Professor Rembold furnished me with some curious particulars respecting the death of M. Page le Roi, the French Egyptologist--particulars new to me."

We listened in growing surprise, scarcely knowing to what this tended.

"M. le Roi," continued Barton, "discovered, but kept secret, the tomb of Amenti--another of this particular brotherhood. It appears that he opened the mummy case on the spot-- these priests were of royal line, and are buried in the valley of Biban-le-Moluk. His Fellah and Arab servants deserted him for some reason--on seeing the mummy case--and he was found dead, apparently strangled, beside it. The matter was hushed up by the Egyptian Government. Rembold could not explain why. But he begged of me not to open the sarcophagus of Mekara."

A silence fell.

The strange facts regarding the sudden death of Page le Roi, which I now heard for the first time, had impressed me unpleasantly, coming from a man of Sir Lionel Barton's experience and reputation.

"How long had it lain in the docks?" jerked Smith.

"For two days, I believe. I am not a superstitious man, Mr. Smith, but neither is Professor Rembold, and now that I know the facts respecting Page le Roi, I can find it in my heart to thank God that I did not see. . .whatever came out of that sarcophagus."

Nayland Smith stared him hard in the face. "I am glad you did not, Sir Lionel," he said; "for whatever the priest Mekara has to do with the matter, by means of his sarcophagus, Dr. Fu-Manchu has made his first attempt upon your life. He has failed, but I hope you will accompany me from here to a hotel. He will not fail twice."

CHAPTER XII

IT WAS THE NIGHT following that of the double tragedy at Rowan House. Nayland Smith, with Inspector Weymouth, was engaged in some mysterious inquiry at the docks, and I had remained at home to resume my strange chronicle. And--why should I not confess it?--my memories had frightened me.

I was arranging my notes respecting the case of Sir Lionel Barton. They were hopelessly incomplete. For instance, I had jotted down the following queries:--(1) Did any true parallel exist between the death of M. Page le Roi and the death of Kwee, the Chinaman, and of Strozza? (2) What had become of the mummy of Mekara? (3) How had the murderer escaped from a locked room? (4) What was the purpose of the rubber stopper? (5) Why was Kwee hiding in the conservatory? (6) Was the green mist a mere subjective hallucination--a figment of Croxted's imagination-- or had he actually seen it?

Until these questions were satisfactorily answered, further progress was impossible. Nayland Smith frankly admitted that he was out of his depth. "It looks, on the face of it, more like a case for the Psychical Research people than for a plain Civil Servant, lately of Mandalay," he had said only that morning.

"Sir Lionel Barton really believes that supernatural agencies were brought into operation by the opening of the high priest's coffin. For my part, even if I believed the same, I should still maintain that Dr. Fu-Manchu controlled those manifestations. But reason it out for yourself and see if we arrive at any common center. Don't work so much upon the datum of the green mist, but keep to the FACTS which are established."

I commenced to knock out my pipe in the ash-tray; then paused, pipe in hand. The house was quite still, for my landlady and all the small household were out.

Above the noise of the passing tramcar I thought I had heard the hall door open. In the ensuing silence I sat and listened.

Not a sound. Stay! I slipped my hand into the table drawer, took out my revolver, and stood up.

There WAS a sound. Someone or something was creeping upstairs in the dark!

Familiar with the ghastly media employed by the Chinaman, I was seized with an impulse to leap to the door, shut and lock it. But the rustling sound proceeded, now, from immediately outside my partially opened door. I had not the time to close it; knowing somewhat of the horrors at the command of Fu-Manchu, I had not the courage to open it. My heart leaping wildly, and my eyes upon that bar of darkness with its gruesome potentialities, I waited--waited for whatever was to come. Perhaps twelve seconds passed in silence.

"Who's there?" I cried. "Answer, or I fire!"

"Ah! no," came a soft voice, thrillingly musical. "Put it down-- that pistol. Quick! I must speak to you."

The door was pushed open, and there entered a slim figure wrapped in a hooded cloak. My hand fell, and I stood, stricken to silence, looking into the beautiful dark eyes of Dr. Fu-Manchu's messenger-- if her own statement could be credited, slave. On two occasions this girl, whose association with the Doctor was one of the most profound mysteries of the case, had risked--I cannot say what; unnamable punishment, perhaps--to save me from death; in both cases from a terrible death. For what was she come now?

Her lips slightly parted, she stood, holding her cloak about her, and watching me with great passionate eyes.

"How--" I began.

But she shook her head impatiently.

"HE has a duplicate key of the house door," was her amazing statement. "I have never betrayed a secret of my master before, but you must arrange to replace the lock."

She came forward and rested her slim hands confidingly upon my shoulders. "I have come again to ask you to take me away from him," she said simply.

And she lifted her face to me.

Her words struck a chord in my heart which sang with strange music, with music so barbaric that, frankly, I blushed to find it harmony. Have I said that she was beautiful? It can convey no faint conception of her. With her pure, fair skin, eyes like the velvet darkness of the East, and red lips so tremulously near to mine, she was the most seductively lovely creature I ever had looked upon. In that electric moment my heart went out in sympathy to every man who had bartered honor, country, all for a woman's kiss.

"I will see that you are placed under proper protection," I said firmly, but my voice was not quite my own. "It is quite absurd to talk of slavery here in England. You are a free agent, or you could not be here now. Dr. Fu-Manchu cannot control your actions."

"Ah!" she cried, casting back her head scornfully, and releasing a cloud of hair, through whose softness gleamed a jeweled head-dress. "No? He cannot? Do you know what it means to have been a slave? Here, in your free England, do you know what it means--the razzia, the desert journey, the whips of the drivers, the house of the dealer, the shame. Bah!"

How beautiful she was in her indignation!

"Slavery is put down, you imagine, perhaps? You do not believe that to-day--TO-DAY--twenty-five English sovereigns will buy a Galla girl, who is brown, and"--whisper--"two hundred and fifty a Circassian, who is white. No, there is no slavery! So! Then what am I?"

She threw open her cloak, and it is a literal fact that I rubbed my eyes, half believing that I dreamed. For beneath, she was arrayed in gossamer silk which more than indicated the perfect lines of her slim shape; wore a jeweled girdle and barbaric ornaments; was a figure fit for the walled gardens of Stamboul--a figure amazing, incomprehensible, in the prosaic setting of my rooms.

"To-night I had no time to make myself an English miss," she said, wrapping her cloak quickly about her. "You see me as I am." Her garments exhaled a faint perfume, and it reminded me of another meeting I had had with her. I looked into the challenging eyes.

"Your request is but a pretense," I said. "Why do you keep the secrets of that man, when they mean death to so many?"

"Death! I have seen my own sister die of fever in the desert-- seen her thrown like carrion into a hole in the sand. I have seen men flogged until they prayed for death as a boon. I have known the lash myself. Death! What does it matter?"

She shocked me inexpressibly. Enveloped in her cloak again, and with only her slight accent to betray her, it was dreadful to hear such words from a girl who, save for her singular type of beauty, might have been a cultured European.

"Prove, then, that you really wish to leave this man's service. Tell me what killed Strozza and the Chinaman," I said.

She shrugged her shoulders.

"I do not know that. But if you will carry me off"--she clutched me nervously--"so that I am helpless, lock me up so that I cannot escape, beat me, if you like, I will tell you all I do know. While he is my master I will never betray him. Tear me from him--by force, do you understand, BY FORCE, and my lips will be sealed no longer. Ah! but you do not understand, with your `proper authorities'-- your police. Police! Ah, I have said enough."

A clock across the common began to strike. The girl started and laid her hands upon my shoulders again. There were tears glittering among the curved black lashes.

"You do not understand," she whispered. "Oh, will you never understand and release me from him! I must go. Already I have remained too long. Listen. Go out without delay. Remain out--at a hotel, where you will, but do not stay here."

"And Nayland Smith?"

"What is he to me, this Nayland Smith? Ah, why will you not unseal my lips? You are in danger--you hear me, in danger! Go away from here to-night."

She dropped her hands and ran from the room. In the open doorway she turned, stamping her foot passionately.

"You have hands and arms," she cried, "and yet you let me go. Be warned, then; fly from here--" She broke off with something that sounded like a sob.

I made no move to stay her--this beautiful accomplice of the arch-murderer, Fu-Manchu. I heard her light footsteps paltering down the stairs, I heard her open and close the door--the door of which Dr. Fu-Manchu held the key. Still I stood where she had parted from me, and was so standing when a key grated in the lock and Nayland Smith came running up.

"Did you see her?" I began.

But his face showed that he had not done so, and rapidly I told him of my strange visitor, of her words, of her warning.

"How can she have passed through London in that costume?" I cried in bewilderment. "Where can she have come from?"

Smith shrugged his shoulders and began to stuff broad-cut mixture into the familiar cracked briar.

"She might have traveled in a car or in a cab," he said; "and undoubtedly she came direct from the house of Dr. Fu-Manchu. You should have detained her, Petrie. It is the third time we have had that woman in our power, the third time we have let her go free."

"Smith," I replied, "I couldn't. She came of her own free will to give me a warning. She disarms me."

"Because you can see she is in love with you?" he suggested, and burst into one of his rare laughs when the angry flush rose to my cheek. "She is, Petrie why pretend to be blind to it? You don't know the Oriental mind as I do; but I quite understand the girl's position. She fears the English authorities, but would submit to capture by you! If you would only seize her by the hair, drag her to some cellar, hurl her down and stand over her with a whip, she would tell you everything she knows, and salve her strange Eastern conscience with the reflection that speech was forced from her. I am not joking; it is so, I assure you. And she would adore you for your savagery, deeming you forceful and strong!"

"Smith," I said, "be serious. You know what her warning meant before."

"I can guess what it means now," he rapped. "Hallo!"

Someone was furiously ringing the bell.

"No one at home?" said my friend. "I will go. I think I know what it is."

A few minutes later he returned, carrying a large square package.

"From Weymouth," he explained, "by district messenger. I left him behind at the docks, and he arranged to forward any evidence which subsequently he found. This will be fragments of the mummy."

"What! You think the mummy was abstracted?"

"Yes, at the docks. I am sure of it; and somebody else was in the sarcophagus when it reached Rowan House. A sarcophagus, I find, is practically airtight, so that the use of the rubber stopper becomes evident-- ventilation. How this person killed Strozza I have yet to learn."

"Also, how he escaped from a locked room. And what about the green mist?"

Nayland Smith spread his hands in a characteristic gesture.

"The green mist, Petrie, can be explained in several ways. Remember, we have only one man's word that it existed. It is at best a confusing datum to which we must not attach a fictitious importance."

He threw the wrappings on the floor and tugged at a twine loop in the lid of the square box, which now stood upon the table. Suddenly the lid came away, bringing with it a lead lining, such as is usual in tea-chests. This lining was partially attached to one side of the box, so that the action of removing the lid at once raised and tilted it.

Then happened a singular thing.

Out over the table billowed a sort of yellowish-green cloud-- an oily vapor--and an inspiration, it was nothing less, born of a memory and of some words of my beautiful visitor, came to me.

"RUN, SMITH!" I screamed. "The door! the door, for your life! Fu-Manchu sent that box!" I threw my arms round him. As he bent forward the moving vapor rose almost to his nostrils. I dragged him back and all but pitched him out on to the landing. We entered my bedroom, and there, as I turned on the light, I saw that Smith's tanned face was unusually drawn, and touched with pallor.

"It is a poisonous gas!" I said hoarsely; "in many respects identical with chlorine, but having unique properties which prove it to be something else--God and Fu-Manchu, alone know what! It is the fumes of chlorine that kill the men in the bleaching powder works. We have been blind--I particularly. Don't you see? There was no one in the sarcophagus, Smith, but there was enough of that fearful stuff to have suffocated a regiment!"

Smith clenched his fists convulsively.

"My God!" he said, "how can I hope to deal with the author of such a scheme? I see the whole plan. He did not reckon on the mummy case being overturned, and Kwee's part was to remove the plug with the aid of the string--after Sir Lionel had been suffocated. The gas, I take it, is heavier than air."

"Chlorine gas has a specific gravity of 2.470," I said; "two and a half times heavier than air. You can pour it from jar to jar like a liquid--if you are wearing a chemist's mask. In these respects this stuff appears to be similar; the points of difference would not interest you. The sarcophagus would have emptied through the vent, and the gas have dispersed, with no clew remaining--except the smell."

"I did smell it, Petrie, on the stopper, but, of course, was unfamiliar with it. You may remember that you were prevented from doing so by the arrival of Sir Lionel? The scent of those infernal flowers must partially have drowned it, too. Poor, misguided Strozza inhaled the stuff, capsized the case in his fall, and all the gas--"

"Went pouring under the conservatory door, and down the steps, where Kwee was crouching. Croxted's breaking the window created sufficient draught to disperse what little remained. It will have settled on the floor now. I will go and open both windows."

Nayland raised his haggard face.

"He evidently made more than was necessary to dispatch Sir Lionel Barton," he said; "and contemptuously--you note the attitude, Petrie?--contemptuously devoted the surplus to me. His contempt is justified. I am a child striving to cope with a mental giant. It is by no wit of mine that Dr. Fu-Manchu scores a double failure."

CHAPTER XIII

I WILL TELL YOU, now of a strange dream which I dreamed, and of the stranger things to which I awakened. Since, out of a blank--a void--this vision burst in upon my mind, I cannot do better than relate it, without preamble. It was thus:

I dreamed that I lay writhing on the floor in agony indescribable. My veins were filled with liquid fire, and but that stygian darkness was about me, I told myself that I must have seen the smoke arising from my burning body.

This, I thought, was death.

Then, a cooling shower descended upon me, soaked through skin and tissue to the tortured arteries and quenched the fire within. Panting, but free from pain, I lay--exhausted.

Strength gradually returning to me, I tried to rise; but the carpet felt so singularly soft that it offered me no foothold. I waded and plunged like a swimmer treading water; and all about me rose impenetrable walls of darkness, darkness all but palpable. I wondered why I could not see the windows. The horrible idea flashed to my mind that I was become blind!

Somehow I got upon my feet, and stood swaying dizzily. I became aware of a heavy perfume, and knew it for some kind of incense.

Then--a dim light was born, at an immeasurable distance away. It grew steadily in brilliance. It spread like a bluish-red stain-- like a liquid. It lapped up the darkness and spread throughout the room.

But this was not my room! Nor was it any room known to me.

It was an apartment of such size that its dimensions filled me with a kind of awe such as I never had known: the awe of walled vastness. Its immense extent produced a sensation of sound. Its hugeness had a distinct NOTE.

Tapestries covered the four walls. There was no door visible. These tapestries were magnificently figured with golden dragons; and as the serpentine bodies gleamed and shimmered in the increasing radiance, each dragon, I thought, intertwined its glittering coils more closely with those of another. The carpet was of such richness that I stood knee-deep in its pile. And this, too, was fashioned all over with golden dragons; and they seemed to glide about amid the shadows of the design--stealthily.

At the farther end of the hall--for hall it was--a huge table with dragons' legs stood solitary amid the luxuriance of the carpet. It bore scintillating globes, and tubes that held living organisms, and books of a size and in such bindings as I never had imagined, with instruments of a type unknown to Western science--a heterogeneous litter quite indescribable, which overflowed on to the floor, forming an amazing oasis in a dragon-haunted desert of carpet. A lamp hung above this table, suspended by golden chains from the ceiling-which was so lofty that, following the chains upward, my gaze lost itself in the purple shadows above.

In a chair piled high with dragon-covered cushions a man sat behind this table. The light from the swinging lamp fell fully upon one side of his face, as he leaned forward amid the jumble of weird objects, and left the other side in purplish shadow. From a plain brass bowl upon the corner of the huge table smoke writhed aloft and at times partially obscured that dreadful face.

From the instant that my eyes were drawn to the table and to the man who sat there, neither the incredible extent of the room, nor the nightmare fashion of its mural decorations, could reclaim my attention. I had eyes only for him.

For it was Dr. Fu-Manchu!

Something of the delirium which had seemed to fill my veins with fire, to people the walls with dragons, and to plunge me knee-deep in the carpet, left me. Those dreadful, filmed green eyes acted somewhat like a cold douche. I knew, without removing my gaze from the still face, that the walls no longer lived, but were merely draped in exquisite Chinese dragon tapestry. The rich carpet beneath my feet ceased to be as a jungle and became a normal carpet--extraordinarily rich, but merely a carpet. But the sense of vastness nevertheless remained, with the uncomfortable knowledge that the things upon the table and overflowing about it were all, or nearly all, of a fashion strange to me.

Then, and almost instantaneously, the comparative sanity which I had temporarily experienced began to slip from me again; for the smoke faintly penciled through the air--from the burning perfume on the table--grew in volume, thickened, and wafted towards me in a cloud of gray horror. It enveloped me, clammily. Dimly, through its oily wreaths, I saw the immobile yellow face of Fu-Manchu. And my stupefied brain acclaimed him a sorcerer, against whom unwittingly we had pitted our poor human wits. The green eyes showed filmy through the fog. An intense pain shot through my lower limbs, and, catching my breath, I looked down. As I did so, the points of the red slippers which I dreamed that I wore increased in length, curled sinuously upward, twined about my throat and choked the breath from my body!

Came an interval, and then a dawning like consciousness; but it was a false consciousness, since it brought with it the idea that my head lay softly pillowed and that a woman's hand caressed my throbbing forehead. Confusedly, as though in the remote past, I recalled a kiss--and the recollection thrilled me strangely. Dreamily content I lay, and a voice stole to my ears:

"They are killing him! they are killing him! Oh! do you not

understand?" In my dazed condition, I thought that it was I who had died, and that this musical girl-voice was communicating to me the fact of my own dissolution.

But I was conscious of no interest in the matter.

For hours and hours, I thought, that soothing hand caressed me. I never once raised my heavy lids, until there came a resounding crash that seemed to set my very bones vibrating--a metallic, jangling crash, as the fall of heavy chains. I thought that, then, I half opened my eyes, and that in the dimness I had a fleeting glimpse of a figure clad in gossamer silk, with arms covered with barbaric bangles and slim ankles surrounded by gold bands. The girl was gone, even as I told myself that she was an houri, and that I, though a Christian, had been consigned by some error to the paradise of Mohammed.

Then--a complete blank.

My head throbbed madly; my brain seemed to be clogged--inert; and though my first, feeble movement was followed by the rattle of a chain, some moments more elapsed ere I realized that the chain was fastened to a steel collar-- that the steel collar was clasped about my neck.

I moaned weakly.

"Smith!" I muttered, "Where are you? Smith!"

On to my knees I struggled, and the pain on the top of my skull grew all but insupportable. It was coming back to me now; how Nayland Smith and I had started for the hotel to warn Graham Guthrie; how, as we passed up the steps from the Embankment and into Essex Street, we saw the big motor standing before the door of one of the offices. I could recall coming up level with the car--a modern limousine; but my mind retained no impression of our having passed it-- only a vague memory of a rush of footsteps--a blow. Then, my vision of the hall of dragons, and now this real awakening to a worse reality.

Groping in the darkness, my hands touched a body that lay close beside me. My fingers sought and found the throat, sought and found the steel collar about it.

"Smith," I groaned; and I shook the still form. "Smith, old man-- speak to me! Smith!"

Could he be dead? Was this the end of his gallant fight with Dr. Fu-Manchu and the murder group? If so, what did the future hold for me-- what had I to face?

He stirred beneath my trembling hands.

"Thank God!" I muttered, and I cannot deny that my joy was tainted with selfishness. For, waking in that impenetrable darkness, and yet obsessed with the dream I had dreamed, I had known what fear meant, at the realization that alone, chained, I must face the dreadful Chinese doctor in the flesh. Smith began incoherent mutterings.

"Sand-bagged!. . .Look out, Petrie!. . .He has us at last!. . .Oh, Heavens!" . . .He struggled on to his knees, clutching at my hand.

"All right, old man," I said. "We are both alive! So let's be thankful."

A moment's silence, a groan, then:

"Petrie, I have dragged you into this. God forgive me--"

"Dry up, Smith," I said slowly. "I'm not a child. There is no question of being dragged into the matter. I'm here; and if I can be of any use, I'm glad I am here!"

He grasped my hand.

"There were two Chinese, in European clothes--lord, how my head throbs!-- in that office door. They sand-bagged us, Petrie--think of it!-- in broad daylight, within hail of the Strand! We were rushed into the car--and it was all over, before--" His voice grew faint. "God! they gave me an awful knock!"

"Why have we been spared, Smith? Do you think he is saving us for--"

"Don't, Petrie! If you had been in China, if you had seen what I have seen--"

Footsteps sounded on the flagged passage. A blade of light crept across the floor towards us. My brain was growing clearer. The place had a damp, earthen smell. It was slimy--some noisome cellar. A door was thrown open and a man entered, carrying a lantern. Its light showed my surmise to be accurate, showed the slime-coated walls of a dungeon some fifteen feet square-- shone upon the long yellow robe of the man who stood watching us, upon the malignant, intellectual countenance.

It was Dr. Fu-Manchu.

At last they were face to face--the head of the great Yellow Movement, and the man who fought on behalf of the entire white race. How can I paint the individual who now stood before us-- perhaps the greatest genius of modern times?

Of him it had been fitly said that he had a brow like Shakespeare and a face like Satan. Something serpentine, hypnotic, was in his very presence. Smith drew one sharp breath, and was silent. Together, chained to the wall, two mediaeval captives, living mockeries of our boasted modern security, we crouched before Dr. Fu-Manchu.

He came forward with an indescribable gait, cat-like yet awkward, carrying his high shoulders almost hunched. He placed the lantern in a niche in the wall, never turning away the reptilian gaze of those eyes which must haunt my dreams forever. They possessed a viridescence which hitherto I had supposed possible only in the eye of the cat--and the film intermittently clouded their brightness-- but I can speak of them no more.

I had never supposed, prior to meeting Dr. Fu-Manchu, that so intense a force of malignancy could radiate--from any human being. He spoke. His English was perfect, though at times his words were oddly chosen; his delivery alternately was guttural and sibilant.

"Mr. Smith and Dr. Petrie, your interference with my plans has gone too far. I have seriously turned my attention to you."

He displayed his teeth, small and evenly separated, but discolored in a way that was familiar to me. I studied his eyes with a new professional interest, which even the extremity of our danger could not wholly banish. Their greenness seemed to be of the iris; the pupil was oddly contracted--a pin-point.

Smith leaned his back against the wall with assumed indifference.

"You have presumed," continued Fu-Manchu, "to meddle with a world-change. Poor spiders--caught in the wheels of the inevitable! You have linked my name with the futility of the Young China Movement-- the name of Fu-Manchu! Mr. Smith, you are an incompetent meddler-- I despise you! Dr. Petrie, you are a fool--I am sorry for you!"

He rested one bony hand on his hip, narrowing the long eyes as he looked down on us. The purposeful cruelty of the man was inherent; it was entirely untheatrical. Still Smith remained silent.

"So I am determined to remove you from the scene of your blunders!" added Fu-Manchu.

"Opium will very shortly do the same for you!" I rapped at him savagely.

Without emotion he turned the narrowed eyes upon me.

"That is a matter of opinion, Doctor," he said. "You may have lacked the opportunities which have been mine for studying that subject-- and in any event I shall not be privileged to enjoy your advice in the future."

"You will not long outlive me," I replied. "And our deaths will not profit you, incidentally; because--" Smith's foot touched mine.

"Because?" inquired Fu-Manchu softly.

"Ah! Mr. Smith is so prudent! He is thinking that I have FILES!" He pronounced the word in a way that made me shudder. "Mr. Smith has seen a WIRE JACKET! Have you ever seen a wire jacket? As a surgeon its functions would interest you!"

I stifled a cry that rose to my lips; for, with a shrill whistling sound, a small shape came bounding into the dimly lit vault, then shot upward. A marmoset landed on the shoulder of Dr. Fu-Manchu and peered grotesquely into the dreadful yellow face. The Doctor raised his bony hand and fondled the little creature, crooning to it.

"One of my pets, Mr. Smith," he said, suddenly opening his eyes fully so that they blazed like green lamps. "I have others, equally useful. My scorpions--have you met my scorpions? No? My pythons and hamadryads? Then there are my fungi and my tiny allies, the bacilli. I have a collection in my laboratory quite unique. Have you ever visited Molokai, the leper island, Doctor? No? But Mr. Nayland Smith will be familiar with the asylum at Rangoon! And we must not forget my black spiders, with their diamond eyes-- my spiders, that sit in the dark and watch--then leap!"

He raised his lean hands, so that the sleeve of the robe fell back to the elbow, and the ape dropped, chattering, to the floor and ran from the cellar.

"O God of Cathay!" he cried, "by what death shall these die-- these miserable ones who would bind thine Empire, which is boundless!"

Like some priest of Tezcat he stood, his eyes upraised to the roof, his lean body quivering--a sight to shock the most unimpressionable mind.

"He is mad!" I whispered to Smith. "God help us, the man is a dangerous homicidal maniac!"

Nayland Smith's tanned face was very drawn, but he shook his head grimly.

"Dangerous, yes, I agree," he muttered; "his existence is a danger to the entire white race which, now, we are powerless to avert."

Dr. Fu-Manchu recovered himself, took up the lantern and, turning abruptly, walked to the door, with his awkward, yet feline gait. At the threshold be looked back.

"You would have warned Mr. Graham Guthrie?" he said, in a soft voice. "To-night, at half-past twelve, Mr. Graham Guthrie dies!"

Smith sat silent and motionless, his eyes fixed upon the speaker.

"You were in Rangoon in 1908?" continued Dr. Fu-Manchu-- "you remember the Call?"

From somewhere above us--I could not determine the exact direction-- came a low, wailing cry, an uncanny thing of falling cadences, which, in that dismal vault, with the sinister yellow-robed figure at the door, seemed to pour ice into my veins. Its effect upon Smith was truly extraordinary. His face showed grayly in the faint light, and I heard him draw a hissing breath through clenched teeth.

"It calls for you!" said Fu-Manchu. "At half-past twelve it calls for Graham Guthrie!"

The door closed and darkness mantled us again.

"Smith," I said, "what was that?" The horrors about us were playing havoc with my nerves.

"It was the Call of Siva!" replied Smith hoarsely.

"What is it? Who uttered it? What does it mean?"

"I don't know what it is, Petrie, nor who utters it. But it means death!"

CHAPTER XIV

THERE MAY BE SOME who could have lain, chained to that noisome cell, and felt no fear--no dread of what the blackness might hold. I confess that I am not one of these. I knew that Nayland Smith and I stood in the path of the most stupendous genius who in the world's history had devoted his intellect to crime. I knew that the enormous wealth of the political group backing Dr. Fu-Manchu rendered him a menace to Europe and to America greater than that of the plague. He was a scientist trained at a great university--an explorer of nature's secrets, who had gone farther into the unknown, I suppose, than any living man. His mission was to remove all obstacles--human obstacles-- from the path of that secret movement which was progressing in the Far East. Smith and I were two such obstacles; and of all the horrible devices at his command, I wondered, and my tortured brain refused to leave the subject, by which of them were we doomed to be dispatched?

Even at that very moment some venomous centipede might be wriggling towards me over the slime of the stones, some poisonous spider be preparing to drop from the roof! Fu-Manchu might have released a serpent in the cellar, or the air be alive with microbes of a loathsome disease!

"Smith," I said, scarcely recognizing my own voice, "I can't bear this suspense. He intends to kill us, that is certain, but--"

"Don't worry," came the reply; "he intends to learn our plans first."

"You mean--?"

"You heard him speak of his files and of his wire jacket?"

"Oh, my God!" I groaned; "can this be England?"

Smith laughed dryly, and I heard him fumbling with the steel collar about his neck.

"I have one great hope," he said, "since you share my captivity, but we must neglect no minor chance. Try with your pocket-knife if you can force the lock. I am trying to break this one."

Truth to tell, the idea had not entered my half-dazed mind, but I immediately acted upon my friend's suggestion, setting to work with the small blade of my knife. I was so engaged, and, having snapped one blade, was about to open another, when a sound arrested me. It came from beneath my feet.

"Smith," I whispered, "listen!"

The scraping and clicking which told of Smith's efforts ceased. Motionless, we sat in that humid darkness and listened.

Something was moving beneath the stones of the cellar. I held my breath; every nerve in my body was strung up.

A line of light showed a few feet from where we lay. It widened-- became an oblong. A trap was lifted, and within a yard of me, there rose a dimly seen head. Horror I had expected--and death, or worse. Instead, I saw a lovely face, crowned with a disordered mass of curling hair; I saw a white arm upholding the stone slab, a shapely arm clasped about the elbow by a broad gold bangle.

The girl climbed into the cellar and placed the lantern on the stone floor. In the dim light she was unreal--a figure from an opium vision, with her clinging silk draperies and garish jewelry, with her feet encased in little red slippers. In short, this was the houri of my vision, materialized. It was difficult to believe that we were in modern, up-to-date England; easy to dream that we were the captives of a caliph, in a dungeon in old Bagdad.

"My prayers are answered," said Smith softly. "She has come to save YOU."

"S-sh!" warned the girl, and her wonderful eyes opened widely, fearfully. "A sound and he will kill us all."

She bent over me; a key jarred in the lock which had broken my penknife-- and the collar was off. As I rose to my feet the girl turned and released Smith. She raised the lantern above the trap, and signed to us to descend the wooden steps which its light revealed.

"Your knife," she whispered to me. "Leave it on the floor. He will think you forced the locks. Down! Quickly!"

Nayland Smith, stepping gingerly, disappeared into the darkness. I rapidly followed. Last of all came our mysterious friend, a gold band about one of her ankles gleaming in the rays of the lantern which she carried. We stood in a low-arched passage.

"Tie your handkerchiefs over your eyes and do exactly as I tell you," she ordered.

Neither of us hesitated to obey her. Blind-folded, I allowed her to lead me, and Smith rested his hand upon my shoulder. In that order we proceeded, and came to stone steps, which we ascended.

"Keep to the wall on the left," came a whisper. "There is danger on the right."

With my free hand I felt for and found the wall, and we pressed forward. The atmosphere of the place through which we were passing was steamy, and loaded with an odor like that of exotic plant life. But a faint animal scent crept to my nostrils, too, and there was a subdued stir about me, infinitely suggestive--mysterious.

Now my feet sank in a soft carpet, and a curtain brushed my shoulder. A gong sounded. We stopped.

The din of distant drumming came to my ears.

"Where in Heaven's name are we?" hissed Smith in my ear; "that is a tom-tom!"

"S-sh! S-sh!"

The little hand grasping mine quivered nervously. We were near a door or a window, for a breath of perfume was wafted through the air; and it reminded me of my other meetings with the beautiful woman who was now leading us from the house of Fu-Manchu; who, with her own lips, had told me that she was his slave. Through the horrible phantasmagoria she flitted-- a seductive vision, her piquant loveliness standing out richly in its black setting of murder and devilry. Not once, but a thousand times, I had tried to reason out the nature of the tie which bound her to the sinister Doctor.

Silence fell.

"Quick! This way!"

Down a thickly carpeted stair we went. Our guide opened a door, and led us along a passage. Another door was opened; and we were in the open air. But the girl never tarried, pulling me along a graveled path, with a fresh breeze blowing in my face, and along until, unmistakably, I stood upon the river bank. Now, planking creaked to our tread; and looking downward beneath the handkerchief, I saw the gleam of water beneath my feet.

"Be careful!" I was warned, and found myself stepping into a narrow boat--a punt.

Nayland Smith followed, and the girl pushed the punt off and poled out into the stream.

"Don't speak!" she directed.

My brain was fevered; I scarce knew if I dreamed and was waking, or if the reality ended with my imprisonment in the clammy cellar and this silent escape, blindfolded, upon the river with a girl for our guide who might have stepped out of the pages of "The Arabian Nights" were fantasy--the mockery of sleep.

Indeed, I began seriously to doubt if this stream whereon we floated, whose waters plashed and tinkled about us, were the Thames, the Tigris, or the Styx.

The punt touched a bank.

"You will hear a clock strike in a few minutes," said the girl, with her soft, charming accent, "but I rely upon your honor not to remove the handkerchiefs until then. You owe me this."

"We do!" said Smith fervently.

I heard him scrambling to the bank, and a moment later a soft hand was placed in mine, and I, too, was guided on to terra firma. Arrived on the bank, I still held the girl's hand, drawing her towards me.

"You must not go back," I whispered. "We will take care of you. You must not return to that place."

"Let me go!" she said. "When, once, I asked you to take me from him, you spoke of police protection; that was your answer, police protection! You would let them lock me up--imprison me--and make me betray him! For what? For what?" She wrenched herself free. "How little you understand me. Never mind. Perhaps one day you will know! Until the clock strikes!"

She was gone. I heard the creak of the punt, the drip of the water from the pole. Fainter it grew, and fainter.

"What is her secret?" muttered Smith, beside me. "Why does she cling to that monster?"

The distant sound died away entirely. A clock began to strike; it struck the half-hour. In an instant my handkerchief was off, and so was Smith's. We stood upon a towing-path. Away to the left the moon shone upon the towers and battlements of an ancient fortress.

It was Windsor Castle.

"Half-past ten," cried Smith. "Two hours to save Graham Guthrie!"

We had exactly fourteen minutes in which to catch the last train to Waterloo; and we caught it. But I sank into a corner of the compartment in a state bordering upon collapse. Neither of us, I think, could have managed another twenty yards. With a lesser stake than a human life at issue, I doubt if we should have attempted that dash to Windsor station.

"Due at Waterloo at eleven-fifty-one," panted Smith. "That gives us thirty-nine minutes to get to the other side of the river and reach his hotel."

"Where in Heaven's name is that house situated? Did we come up or down stream?"

"I couldn't determine. But at any rate, it stands close to the riverside. It should be merely a question of time to identify it. I shall set Scotland Yard to work immediately; but I am hoping for nothing. Our escape will warn him."

I said no more for a time, sitting wiping the perspiration from my forehead and watching my friend load his cracked briar with the broadcut Latakia mixture.

"Smith," I said at last, "what was that horrible wailing we heard, and what did Fu-Manchu mean when he referred to Rangoon? I noticed how it affected you."

My friend nodded and lighted his pipe.

"There was a ghastly business there in 1908 or early in 1909," he replied: "an utterly mysterious epidemic. And this beastly wailing was associated with it."

"In what way? And what do you mean by an epidemic?"

"It began, I believe, at the Palace Mansions Hotel, in the cantonments. A young American, whose name I cannot recall, was staying there on business connected with some new iron buildings. One night he went to his room, locked the door, and jumped out of the window into the courtyard. Broke his neck, of course."

"Suicide?"

"Apparently. But there were singular features in the case. For instance, his revolver lay beside him, fully loaded!"

"In the courtyard?"

"In the courtyard!"

"Was it murder by any chance?"

Smith shrugged his shoulders.

"His door was found locked from the inside; had to be broken in."

"But the wailing business?"

"That began later, or was only noticed later. A French doctor, named Lafitte, died in exactly the same way."

"At the same place?"

"At the same hotel; but he occupied a different room. Here is the extraordinary part of the affair: a friend shared the room with him, and actually saw him go!"

"Saw him leap from the window?"

"Yes. The friend--an Englishman--was aroused by the uncanny wailing. I was in Rangoon at the time, so that I know more of the case of Lafitte than of that of the American. I spoke to the man about it personally. He was an electrical engineer, Edward Martin, and he told me that the cry seemed to come from above him."

"It seemed to come from above when we heard it at Fu-Manchu's house."

"Martin sat up in bed, it was a clear moonlight night-- the sort of moonlight you get in Burma. Lafitte, for some reason, had just gone to the window. His friend saw him look out. The next moment with a dreadful scream, he threw himself forward-- and crashed down into the courtyard!"

"What then?"

"Martin ran to the window and looked down. Lafitte's scream had aroused the place, of course. But there was absolutely nothing to account for the occurrence. There was no balcony, no ledge, by means of which anyone could reach the window."

"But how did you come to recognize the cry?"

"I stopped at the Palace Mansions for some time; and one night this uncanny howling aroused me. I heard it quite distinctly, and am never likely to forget it. It was followed by a hoarse yell. The man in the next room, an orchid hunter, had gone the same way as the others!"

"Did you change your quarters?"

"No. Fortunately for the reputation of the hotel--a first-class establishment-- several similar cases occurred elsewhere, both in Rangoon, in Prome and in Moulmein. A story got about the native quarter, and was fostered by some mad fakir, that the god Siva was reborn and that the cry was his call for victims; a ghastly story, which led to an outbreak of dacoity and gave the District Superintendent no end of trouble."

"Was there anything unusual about the bodies?"

"They all developed marks after death, as though they had been strangled! The marks were said all to possess a peculiar form, though it was not appreciable to my eye; and this, again, was declared to be the five heads of Siva."

"Were the deaths confined to Europeans?"

"Oh, no. Several Burmans and others died in the same way. At first there was a theory that the victims had contracted leprosy and committed suicide as a result; but the medical evidence disproved that. The Call of Siva became a perfect nightmare throughout Burma."

"Did you ever hear it again, before this evening?"

"Yes. I heard it on the Upper Irrawaddy one clear, moonlight night, and a Colassie--a deck-hand--leaped from the top deck of the steamer aboard which I was traveling! My God! to think that the fiend Fu-Manchu has brought That to England!"

"But brought what, Smith?" I cried, in perplexity. "What has he brought? An evil spirit? A mental disease? What is it? What CAN it be?"

"A new agent of death, Petrie! Something born in a plague-spot of Burma-- the home of much that is unclean and much that is inexplicable. Heaven grant that we be in time, and are able to save Guthrie."

CHAPTER XV

THE TRAIN WAS LATE, and as our cab turned out of Waterloo Station and began to ascend to the bridge, from a hundred steeples rang out the gongs of midnight, the bell of St. Paul's raised above them all to vie with the deep voice of Big Ben.

I looked out from the cab window across the river to where, towering above the Embankment, that place of a thousand tragedies, the light of some of London's greatest caravanserais formed a sort of minor constellation. From the subdued blaze that showed the public supper-rooms I looked up to the hundreds of starry points marking the private apartments of those giant inns.

I thought how each twinkling window denoted the presence of some bird of passage, some wanderer temporarily abiding in our midst. There, floor piled upon floor above the chattering throngs, were these less gregarious units, each something of a mystery to his fellow-guests, each in his separate cell; and each as remote from real human companionship as if that cell were fashioned, not in the bricks of London, but in the rocks of Hindustan!

In one of those rooms Graham Guthrie might at that moment be sleeping, all unaware that he would awake to the Call of Siva, to the summons of death. As we neared the Strand, Smith stopped the cab, discharging the man outside Sotheby's auction-rooms.

"One of the doctor's watch-dogs may be in the foyer," he said thoughtfully, "and it might spoil everything if we were seen to go to Guthrie's rooms. There must be a back entrance to the kitchens, and so on?"

"There is," I replied quickly. "I have seen the vans delivering there. But have we time?"

"Yes. Lead on."

We walked up the Strand and hurried westward. Into that narrow court, with its iron posts and descending steps, upon which opens a well-known wine-cellar, we turned. Then, going parallel with the Strand, but on the Embankment level, we ran round the back of the great hotel, and came to double doors which were open. An arc lamp illuminated the interior and a number of men were at work among the casks, crates and packages stacked about the place. We entered.

"Hallo!" cried a man in a white overall, "where d'you think you're going?"

Smith grasped him by the arm.

"I want to get to the public part of the hotel without being seen from the entrance hall," he said. "Will you please lead the way?"

"Here--" began the other, staring.

"Don't waste time!" snapped my friend, in that tone of authority which he knew so well how to assume. "It's a matter of life and death. Lead the way, I say!"

"Police, sir?" asked the man civilly.

"Yes," said Smith; "hurry!"

Off went our guide without further demur. Skirting sculleries, kitchens, laundries and engine-rooms, he led us through those mysterious labyrinths which have no existence for the guest above, but which contain the machinery that renders these modern khans the Aladdin's palaces they are. On a second-floor landing we met a man in a tweed suit, to whom our cicerone presented us.

"Glad I met you, sir. Two gentlemen from the police."

The man regarded us haughtily with a suspicious smile.

"Who are you?" he asked. "You're not from Scotland Yard, at any rate!"

Smith pulled out a card and thrust it into the speaker's hand.

"If you are the hotel detective," he said, "take us without delay to Mr. Graham Guthrie."

A marked change took place in the other's demeanor on glancing at the card in his hand.

"Excuse me, sir," he said deferentially, "but, of course, I didn't know who I was speaking to. We all have instructions to give you every assistance."

"Is Mr. Guthrie in his room?"

"He's been in his room for some time, sir. You will want to get there without being seen? This way. We can join the lift on the third floor."

Off we went again, with our new guide. In the lift:

"Have you noticed anything suspicious about the place to-night?" asked Smith.

"I have!" was the startling reply. "That accounts for your finding me where you did. My usual post is in the lobby. But about eleven o'clock, when the theater people began to come in I had a hazy sort of impression that someone or something slipped past in the crowd--something that had no business in the hotel."

We got out of the lift.

"I don't quite follow you," said Smith. "If you thought you saw something entering, you must have formed a more or less definite impression regarding it."

"That's the funny part of the business," answered the man doggedly. "I didn't! But as I stood at the top of the stairs I could have sworn that there was something crawling up behind a party-- two ladies and two gentlemen."

"A dog, for instance?"

"It didn't strike me as being a dog, sir. Anyway, when the party passed me, there was nothing there. Mind you, whatever it was, it hadn't come in by the front. I have made inquiries everywhere, but without result." He stopped abruptly. "No. 189--Mr. Guthrie's door, sir."

Smith knocked.

"Hallo!" came a muffled voice; "what do you want?"

"Open the door! Don't delay; it is important."

He turned to the hotel detective.

"Stay right there where you can watch the stairs and the lift," he instructed; "and note everyone and everything that passes this door. But whatever you see or hear, do nothing without my orders."

The man moved off, and the door was opened. Smith whispered in my ear:

"Some creature of Dr. Fu-Manchu is in the hotel!"

Mr. Graham Guthrie, British resident in North Bhutan, was a big, thick-set man--gray-haired and florid, with widely opened eyes of the true fighting blue, a bristling mustache and prominent shaggy brows. Nayland Smith introduced himself tersely, proffering his card and an open letter.

"Those are my credentials, Mr. Guthrie," he said; "so no doubt you will realize that the business which brings me and my friend, Dr. Petrie, here at such an hour is of the first importance."

He switched off the light.

"There is no time for ceremony," he explained. "It is now twenty-five minutes past twelve. At half-past an attempt will be made upon your life!"

"Mr. Smith," said the other, who, arrayed in his pajamas, was seated on the edge of the bed, "you alarm me very greatly. I may mention that I was advised of your presence in England this morning."

"Do you know anything respecting the person called Fu-Manchu--Dr. Fu-Manchu?"

"Only what I was told to-day--that he is the agent of an advanced political group."

"It is opposed to his interests that you should return to Bhutan. A more gullible agent would be preferable. Therefore, unless you implicitly obey my instructions, you will never leave England!"

Graham Guthrie breathed quickly. I was growing more used to the gloom, and I could dimly discern him, his face turned towards Nayland Smith, whilst with his hand he clutched the bed-rail. Such a visit as ours, I think, must have shaken the nerve of any man.

"But, Mr. Smith," he said, "surely I am safe enough here! The place is full of American visitors at present, and I have had to be content with a room right at the top; so that the only danger I apprehend is that of fire."

"There is another danger," replied Smith. "The fact that you are at the top of the building enhances that danger. Do you recall anything of the mysterious epidemic which broke out in Rangoon in 1908--the deaths due to the Call of Siva?"

"I read of it in the Indian papers," said Guthrie uneasily. "Suicides, were they not?" "No!" snapped Smith. "Murders!"

There was a brief silence.

"From what I recall of the cases," said Guthrie, "that seems impossible. In several instances the victims threw themselves from the windows of locked rooms--and the windows were quite inaccessible."

"Exactly," replied Smith; and in the dim light his revolver gleamed dully, as he placed it on the small table beside the bed. "Except that your door is unlocked, the conditions to-night are identical. Silence, please, I hear a clock striking."

It was Big Ben. It struck the half-hour, leaving the stillness complete. In that room, high above the activity which yet prevailed below, high above the supping crowds in the hotel, high above the starving crowds on the Embankment, a curious chill of isolation swept about me. Again I realized how, in the very heart of the great metropolis, a man may be as far from aid as in the heart of a desert. I was glad that I was not alone in that room-- marked with the death-mark of Fu-Manchu; and I am certain that Graham Guthrie welcomed his unexpected company.

I may have mentioned the fact before, but on this occasion it became so peculiarly evident to me that I am constrained to record it here-- I refer to the sense of impending danger which invariably preceded a visit from Fu-Manchu. Even had I not known that an attempt was to be made that night, I should have realized it, as, strung to high tension, I waited in the darkness. Some invisible herald went ahead of the dreadful Chinaman, proclaiming his coming to every nerve in one's body. It was like a breath of astral incense, announcing the presence of the priests of death.

A wail, low but singularly penetrating, falling in minor cadences to a new silence, came from somewhere close at hand.

"My God!" hissed Guthrie, "what was that?"

"The Call of Siva," whispered Smith.

"Don't stir, for your life!"

Guthrie was breathing hard.

I knew that we were three; that the hotel detective was within hail; that there was a telephone in the room; that the traffic of the Embankment moved almost beneath us; but I knew, and am not ashamed to confess, that King Fear had icy fingers about my heart. It was awful--that tense waiting--for--what?

Three taps sounded--very distinctly upon the window.

Graham Guthrie started so as to shake the bed.

"It's supernatural!" he muttered--all that was Celtic in his blood recoiling from the omen. "Nothing human can reach that window!" "S-sh!" from Smith. "Don't stir."

The tapping was repeated.

Smith softly crossed the room. My heart was beating painfully. He threw open the window. Further inaction was impossible. I joined him; and we looked out into the empty air.

"Don't come too near, Petrie!" he warned over his shoulder.

One on either side of the open window, we stood and looked down at the moving Embankment lights, at the glitter of the Thames, at the silhouetted buildings on the farther bank, with the Shot Tower starting above them all.

Three taps sounded on the panes above us.

In all my dealings with Dr. Fu-Manchu I had had to face nothing so uncanny as this. What Burmese ghoul had he loosed? Was it outside, in the air? Was it actually in the room?

"Don't let me go, Petrie!" whispered Smith suddenly. "Get a tight hold on me!"

That was the last straw; for I thought that some dreadful fascination was impelling my friend to hurl himself out! Wildly I threw my arms about him, and Guthrie leaped forward to help.

Smith leaned from the window and looked up.

One choking cry he gave--smothered, inarticulate--and I found him slipping from my grip--being drawn out of the window--drawn to his death!

"Hold him, Guthrie!" I gasped hoarsely. "My God, he's going! Hold him!"

My friend writhed in our grasp, and I saw him stretch his arm upward. The crack of his revolver came, and he collapsed on to the floor, carrying me with him.

But as I fell I heard a scream above. Smith's revolver went hurtling through the air, and, hard upon it, went a black shape-- flashing past the open window into the gulf of the night.

"The light! The light!" I cried.

Guthrie ran and turned on the light. Nayland Smith, his eyes starting from his head, his face swollen, lay plucking at a silken cord which showed tight about his throat.

"It was a Thug!" screamed Guthrie. "Get the rope off! He's choking!"

My hands a-twitch, I seized the strangling-cord.

"A knife! Quick!" I cried. "I have lost mine!"

Guthrie ran to the dressing-table and passed me an open penknife. I somehow forced the blade between the rope and Smith's swollen neck, and severed the deadly silken thing.

Smith made a choking noise, and fell back, swooning in my arms.

When, later, we stood looking down upon the mutilated thing which had been brought in from where it fell, Smith showed me a mark on the brow-- close beside the wound where his bullet had entered.

"The mark of Kali," he said. "The man was a phansigar-- a religious strangler. Since Fu-Manchu has dacoits in his service I might have expected that he would have Thugs. A group of these fiends would seem to have fled into Burma; so that the mysterious epidemic in Rangoon was really an outbreak of thuggee--on slightly improved lines! I had suspected something of the kind but, naturally, I had not looked for Thugs near Rangoon. My unexpected resistance led the strangler to bungle the rope. You have seen how it was fastened about my throat? That was unscientific. The true method, as practiced by the group operating in Burma, was to throw the line about the victim's neck and jerk him from the window. A man leaning from an open window is very nicely poised: it requires only a slight jerk to pitch him forward. No loop was used, but a running line, which, as the victim fell, remained in the hand of the murderer. No clew! Therefore we see at once what commended the system to Fu-Manchu."

Graham Guthrie, very pale, stood looking down at the dead strangler.

"I owe you my life, Mr. Smith," he said. "If you had come five minutes later--"

He grasped Smith's hand.

"You see," Guthrie continued, "no one thought of looking for a Thug in Burma! And no one thought of the ROOF! These fellows are as active as monkeys, and where an ordinary man would infallibly break his neck, they are entirely at home. I might have chosen my room especially for the business!"

"He slipped in late this evening," said Smith. "The hotel detective saw him, but these stranglers are as elusive as shadows, otherwise, despite their having changed the scene of their operations, not one could have survived."

"Didn't you mention a case of this kind on the Irrawaddy?" I asked.

"Yes," was the reply; "and I know of what you are thinking. The steamers of the Irrawaddy flotilla have a corrugated-iron roof over the top deck. The Thug must have been lying up there as the Colassie passed on the deck below."

"But, Smith, what is the motive of the Call?" I continued.

"Partly religious," he explained, "and partly to wake the victims! You are perhaps going to ask me how Dr. Fu-Manchu has obtained power over such people as phansigars? I can only reply that Dr. Fu-Manchu has secret knowledge of which, so far, we know absolutely nothing; but, despite all, at last I begin to score."

"You do," I agreed; "but your victory took you near to death."

"I owe my life to you, Petrie," he said. "Once to your strength of arm, and once to--"

"Don't speak of her, Smith," I interrupted. "Dr. Fu-Manchu may have discovered the part she played! In which event--"

"God help her!"

CHAPTER XVI

UPON THE FOLLOWING DAY we were afoot again, and shortly at handgrips with the enemy. In retrospect, that restless time offers a chaotic prospect, with no peaceful spot amid its turmoil's.

All that was reposeful in nature seemed to have become an irony and a mockery to us--who knew how an evil demigod had his sacrificial altars amid our sweetest groves. This idea ruled strongly in my mind upon that soft autumnal day.

"The net is closing in," said Nayland Smith.

"Let us hope upon a big catch," I replied, with a laugh.

Beyond where the Thames tided slumberously seaward showed the roofs of Royal Windsor, the castle towers showing through the autumn haze. The peace of beautiful Thames-side was about us.

This was one of the few tangible clews upon which thus far we had chanced; but at last it seemed indeed that we were narrowing the resources of that enemy of the white race who was writing his name over England in characters of blood. To capture Dr. Fu-Manchu we did not hope; but at least there was every promise of destroying one of the enemy's strongholds.

We had circled upon the map a tract of country cut by the Thames, with Windsor for its center. Within that circle was the house from which miraculously we had escaped--a house used by the most highly organized group in the history of criminology. So much we knew. Even if we found the house, and this was likely enough, to find it vacated by Fu-Manchu and his mysterious servants we were prepared. But it would be a base destroyed.

We were working upon a methodical plan, and although our cooperators were invisible, these numbered no fewer than twelve--all of them experienced men. Thus far we had drawn blank, but the place for which Smith and I were making now came clearly into view: an old mansion situated in extensive walled grounds. Leaving the river behind us, we turned sharply to the right along a lane flanked by a high wall. On an open patch of ground, as we passed, I noted a gypsy caravan. An old woman was seated on the steps, her wrinkled face bent, her chin resting in the palm of her hand.

I scarcely glanced at her, but pressed on, nor did I notice that my friend no longer was beside me. I was all anxiety to come to some point from whence I might obtain a view of the house; all anxiety to know if this was the abode of our mysterious enemy--the place where he worked amid his weird company, where he bred his deadly scorpions and his bacilli, reared his poisonous fungi, from whence he dispatched his murder ministers. Above all, perhaps, I wondered if this would prove to be the hiding-place of the beautiful slave girl who was such a potent factor in the Doctor's plans, but a two-edged sword which yet we hoped to turn upon Fu-Manchu. Even in the hands of a master, a woman's beauty is a dangerous weapon.

A cry rang out behind me. I turned quickly. And a singular sight met my gaze.

Nayland Smith was engaged in a furious struggle with the old gypsy woman! His long arms clasped about her, he was roughly dragging her out into the roadway, she fighting like a wild thing--silently, fiercely.

Smith often surprised me, but at that sight, frankly, I thought that he was become bereft of reason. I ran back; and I had almost reached the scene of this incredible contest, and Smith now was evidently hard put to it to hold his own when a man, swarthy, with big rings in his ears, leaped from the caravan.

One quick glance he threw in our direction, and made off towards the river.

Smith twisted round upon me, never releasing his hold of the woman.

"After him, Petrie!" he cried. "After him. Don't let him escape. It's a dacoit!"

My brain in a confused whirl; my mind yet disposed to a belief that my friend had lost his senses, the word "dacoit" was sufficient.

I started down the road after the fleetly running man. Never once did he glance behind him, so that he evidently had occasion to fear pursuit. The dusty road rang beneath my flying footsteps. That sense of fantasy, which claimed me often enough in those days of our struggle with the titanic genius whose victory meant the victory of the yellow races over the white, now had me fast in its grip again. I was an actor in one of those dream-scenes of the grim Fu-Manchu drama.

Out over the grass and down to the river's brink ran the gypsy who was no gypsy, but one of that far more sinister brotherhood, the dacoits. I was close upon his heels. But I was not prepared for him to leap in among the rushes at the margin of the stream; and seeing him do this I pulled up quickly. Straight into the water he plunged; and I saw that he held some object in his hand. He waded out; he dived; and as I gained the bank and looked to right and left he had vanished completely. Only ever--widening rings showed where he had been. I had him.

For directly he rose to the surface he would be visible from either bank, and with the police whistle which I carried I could, if necessary, summon one of the men in hiding across the stream. I waited. A wild-fowl floated serenely past, untroubled by this strange invasion of his precincts. A full minute I waited. From the lane behind me came Smith's voice:

"Don't let him escape, Petrie!"

Never lifting my eyes from the water, I waved my hand reassuringly. But still the dacoit did not rise. I searched the surface in all directions as far as my eyes could reach; but no swimmer showed above it. Then it was that I concluded he had dived too deeply, become entangled in the weeds and was drowned. With a final glance to right and left and some feeling of awe at this sudden tragedy-- this grim going out of a life at glorious noonday--I turned away. Smith had the woman securely; but I had not taken five steps towards him when a faint splash behind warned me. Instinctively I ducked. From whence that saving instinct arose I cannot surmise, but to it I owed my life. For as I rapidly lowered my head, something hummed past me, something that flew out over the grass bank, and fell with a jangle upon the dusty roadside. A knife!

I turned and bounded back to the river's brink. I heard a faint cry behind me, which could only have come from the gypsy woman. Nothing disturbed the calm surface of the water. The reach was lonely of rowers. Out by the farther bank a girl was poling a punt along, and her white-clad figure was the only living thing that moved upon the river within the range of the most expert knife-thrower.

To say that I was nonplused is to say less than the truth; I was amazed. That it was the dacoit who had shown me this murderous attention I could not doubt. But where in Heaven's name WAS he? He could not humanly have remained below water for so long; yet he certainly was not above, was not upon the surface, concealed amongst the reeds, nor hidden upon the bank.

There, in the bright sunshine, a consciousness of the eerie possessed me. It was with an uncomfortable feeling that my phantom foe might be aiming a second knife at my back that I turned away and hastened towards Smith. My fearful expectations were not realized, and I picked up the little weapon which had so narrowly missed me, and with it in my hand rejoined my friend.

He was standing with one arm closely clasped about the apparently exhausted woman, and her dark eyes were fixed upon him with an extraordinary expression.

"What does it mean, Smith?" I began.

But he interrupted me.

"Where is the dacoit?" he demanded rapidly.

"Since he seemingly possesses the attributes of a fish," I replied, "I cannot pretend to say."

The gypsy woman lifted her eyes to mine and laughed. Her laughter was musical, not that of such an old hag as Smith held captive; it was familiar, too.

I started and looked closely into the wizened face.

"He's tricked you," said Smith, an angry note in his voice. "What is that you have in your hand?"

I showed him the knife, and told him how it had come into my possession.

"I know," he rapped. "I saw it. He was in the water not three yards from where you stood. You must have seen him. Was there nothing visible?"

"Nothing."

The woman laughed again, and again I wondered.

"A wild-fowl," I added; "nothing else."

"A wild-fowl," snapped Smith. "If you will consult your recollections of the habits of wild-fowl you will see that this particular specimen was a RARA AVIS. It's an old trick, Petrie, but a good one, for it is used in decoying. A dacoit's head was concealed in that wild-fowl! It's useless. He has certainly made good his escape by now."

"Smith," I said, somewhat crestfallen, "why are you detaining this gypsy woman?"

"Gypsy woman!" he laughed, hugging her tightly as she made an impatient movement. "Use your eyes, old man."

He jerked the frowsy wig from her head, and beneath was a cloud of disordered hair that shimmered in the sunlight.

"A wet sponge will do the rest," he said.

Into my eyes, widely opened in wonder, looked the dark eyes of the captive; and beneath the disguise I picked out the charming features of the slave girl. There were tears on the whitened lashes, and she was submissive now.

"This time," said my friend hardly, "we have fairly captured her-- and we will hold her."

From somewhere up-stream came a faint call.

"The dacoit!"

Nayland Smith's lean body straightened; he stood alert, strung up.

Another call answered, and a third responded. Then followed the flatly shrill note of a police whistle, and I noted a column of black vapor rising beyond the wall, mounting straight to heaven as the smoke of a welcome offering.

The surrounded mansion was in flames!

"Curse it!" rapped Smith. "So this time we were right. But, of course, he has had ample opportunity to remove his effects. I knew that. The man's daring is incredible. He has given himself till the very last moment--and we blundered upon two of the outposts."

"I lost one."

"No matter. We have the other. I expect no further arrests, and the house will have been so well fired by the Doctor's servants that nothing can save it. I fear its ashes will afford us no clew, Petrie; but we have secured a lever which should serve to disturb Fu-Manchu's world."

He glanced at the queer figure which hung submissively in his arms. She looked up proudly.

"You need not hold me so tight," she said, in her soft voice. "I will come with you."

That I moved amid singular happenings, you, who have borne with me thus far, have learned, and that I witnessed many curious scenes; but of the many such scenes in that race--drama wherein Nayland Smith and Dr. Fu-Manchu played the leading parts, I remember none more bizarre than the one at my rooms that afternoon.

Without delay, and without taking the Scotland Yard men into our confidence, we had hurried our prisoner back to London, for my friend's authority was supreme. A strange trio we were, and one which excited no little comment; but the journey came to an end at last. Now we were in my unpretentious sitting-room-- the room wherein Smith first had unfolded to me the story of Dr. Fu-Manchu and of the great secret society which sought to upset the balance of the world--to place Europe and America beneath the scepter of Cathay.

I sat with my elbows upon the writing-table, my chin in my hands; Smith restlessly paced the floor, relighting his blackened briar a dozen times in as many minutes. In the big arm-chair the pseudo gypsy was curled up. A brief toilet had converted the wizened old woman's face into that of a fascinatingly pretty girl. Wildly picturesque she looked in her ragged Romany garb. She held a cigarette in her fingers and watched us through lowered lashes.

Seemingly, with true Oriental fatalism, she was quite reconciled to her fate, and ever and anon she would bestow upon me a glance from her beautiful eyes which few men, I say with confidence, could have sustained unmoved. Though I could not be blind to the emotions of that passionate Eastern soul, yet I strove not to think of them. Accomplice of an arch-murderer she might be; but she was dangerously lovely.

"That man who was with you," said Smith, suddenly turning upon her, "was in Burma up till quite recently. He murdered a fisherman thirty miles above Prome only a mouth before I left. The D.S.P. had placed a thousand rupees on his head. Am I right?"

The girl shrugged her shoulders.

"Suppose--What then?" she asked.

"Suppose I handed you over to the police?" suggested Smith. But he spoke without conviction, for in the recent past we both had owed our lives to this girl.

"As you please," she replied. "The police would learn nothing."

"You do not belong to the Far East," my friend said abruptly. "You may have Eastern blood in your veins, but you are no kin of Fu-Manchu."

"That is true," she admitted, and knocked the ash from her cigarette.

"Will you tell me where to find Fu-Manchu?"

She shrugged her shoulders again, glancing eloquently in my direction.

Smith walked to the door.

"I must make out my report, Petrie," he said. "Look after the prisoner."

And as the door closed softly behind him I knew what was expected of me; but, honestly, I shirked my responsibility. What attitude should I adopt? How should I go about my delicate task? In a quandary, I stood watching the girl whom singular circumstances saw captive in my rooms.

"You do not think we would harm you?" I began awkwardly. "No harm shall come to you. Why will you not trust us?"

She raised her brilliant eyes.

"Of what avail has your protection been to some of those others," she said; "those others whom HE has sought for?"

Alas! it had been of none, and I knew it well. I thought I grasped the drift of her words.

"You mean that if you speak, Fu-Manchu will find a way of killing you?"

"Of killing ME!" she flashed scornfully. "Do I seem one to fear for myself?"

"Then what do you fear?" I asked, in surprise.

She looked at me oddly.

"When I was seized and sold for a slave," she answered slowly, "my sister was taken, too, and my brother--a child." She spoke the word with a tender intonation, and her slight accent rendered it the more soft. "My sister died in the desert. My brother lived. Better, far better, that he had died, too."

Her words impressed me intensely.

"Of what are you speaking?" I questioned. "You speak of slave-raids, of the desert. Where did these things take place? Of what country are you?"

"Does it matter?" she questioned in turn. "Of what country am I? A slave has no country, no name."

"No name!" I cried.

"You may call me Karamaneh," she said. "As Karamaneh I was sold to Dr. Fu-Manchu, and my brother also he purchased. We were cheap at the price he paid." She laughed shortly, wildly.

"But he has spent a lot of money to educate me. My brother is all that is left to me in the world to love, and he is in the power of Dr. Fu-Manchu. You understand? It is upon him the blow will fall. You ask me to fight against Fu-Manchu. You talk of protection. Did your protection save Sir Crichton Davey?"

I shook my head sadly.

"You understand now why I cannot disobey my master's orders--why, if I would, I dare not betray him."

I walked to the window and looked out. How could I answer her arguments? What could I say? I heard the rustle of her ragged skirts, and she who called herself Karamaneh stood beside me. She laid her hand upon my arm.

"Let me go," she pleaded. "He will kill him! He will kill him!"

Her voice shook with emotion.

"He cannot revenge himself upon your brother when you are in no way to blame," I said angrily. "We arrested you; you are not here of your own free will."

She drew her breath sharply, clutching at my arm, and in her eyes I could read that she was forcing her mind to some arduous decision.

"Listen." She was speaking rapidly, nervously. "If I help you to take Dr. Fu-Manchu--tell you where he is to be found ALONE-- will you promise me, solemnly promise me, that you will immediately go to the place where I shall guide you and release my brother; that you will let us both go free?"

"I will," I said, without hesitation. "You may rest assured of it."

"But there is a condition," she added.

"What is it?"

"When I have told you where to capture him you must release me."

I hesitated. Smith often had accused me of weakness where this girl was concerned. What now was my plain duty? That she would utterly decline to speak under any circumstances unless it suited her to do so I felt assured. If she spoke the truth, in her proposed bargain there was no personal element; her conduct I now viewed in a new light. Humanity, I thought, dictated that I accept her proposal; policy also.

"I agree," I said, and looked into her eyes, which were aflame now with emotion, an excitement perhaps of anticipation, perhaps of fear.

She laid her hands upon my shoulders.

"You will be careful?" she said pleadingly.

"For your sake," I replied, "I shall."

"Not for my sake."

"Then for your brother's."

"No." Her voice had sunk to a whisper. "For your own."

CHAPTER XVII

A COOL breeze met us, blowing from the lower reaches of the Thames. Far behind us twinkled the dim lights of Low's Cottages, the last regular habitations abutting upon the marshes. Between us and the cottages stretched half-a-mile of lush land through which at this season there were, however, numerous dry paths. Before us the flats again, a dull, monotonous expanse beneath the moon, with the promise of the cool breeze that the river flowed round the bend ahead. It was very quiet. Only the sound of our footsteps, as Nayland Smith and I tramped steadily towards our goal, broke the stillness of that lonely place.

Not once but many times, within the last twenty minutes, I had thought that we were ill-advised to adventure alone upon the capture of the formidable Chinese doctor; but we were following out our compact with Karamaneh; and one of her stipulations had been that the police must not be acquainted with her share in the matter.

A light came into view far ahead of us.

"That's the light, Petrie," said Smith. "If we keep that straight before us, according to our information we shall strike the hulk."

I grasped the revolver in my pocket, and the presence of the little weapon was curiously reassuring. I have endeavored, perhaps in extenuation of my own fears, to explain how about Dr. Fu-Manchu there rested an atmosphere of horror, peculiar, unique. He was not as other men. The dread that he inspired in all with whom he came in contact, the terrors which he controlled and hurled at whomsoever cumbered his path, rendered him an object supremely sinister. I despair of conveying to those who may read this account any but the coldest conception of the man's evil power.

Smith stopped suddenly and grasped my arm. We stood listening. "What?" I asked.

"You heard nothing?"

I shook my head.

Smith was peering back over the marshes in his oddly alert way. He turned to me, and his tanned face wore a peculiar expression.

"You don't think it's a trap?" he jerked. "We are trusting her blindly."

Strange it may seem, but something within me rose in arms against the innuendo.

"I don't," I said shortly.

He nodded. We pressed on.

Ten minutes' steady tramping brought us within sight of the Thames. Smith and I both had noticed how Fu-Manchu's activities centered always about the London river. Undoubtedly it was his highway, his line of communication, along which he moved his mysterious forces. The opium den off Shadwell Highway, the mansion upstream, at that hour a smoldering shell; now the hulk lying off the marshes. Always he made his headquarters upon the river. It was significant; and even if to-night's expedition should fail, this was a clew for our future guidance.

"Bear to the right," directed Smith. "We must reconnoiter before making our attack."

We took a path that led directly to the river bank. Before us lay the gray expanse of water, and out upon it moved the busy shipping of the great mercantile city. But this life of the river seemed widely removed from us. The lonely spot where we stood had no kinship with human activity. Its dreariness illuminated by the brilliant moon, it looked indeed a fit setting for an act in such a drama as that wherein we played our parts. When I had lain in the East End opium den, when upon such another night as this I had looked out upon a peaceful Norfolk countryside, the same knowledge of aloofness, of utter detachment from the world of living men, had come to me.

Silently Smith stared out at the distant moving lights.

"Karamaneh merely means a slave," he said irrelevantly.

I made no comment.

"There's the hulk," he added.

The bank upon which we stood dipped in mud slopes to the level of the running tide. Seaward it rose higher, and by a narrow inlet-- for we perceived that we were upon a kind of promontory-- a rough pier showed. Beneath it was a shadowy shape in the patch of gloom which the moon threw far out upon the softly eddying water. Only one dim light was visible amid this darkness.

"That will be the cabin," said Smith.

Acting upon our prearranged plan, we turned and walked up on to the staging above the hulk. A wooden ladder led out and down to the deck below, and was loosely lashed to a ring on the pier. With every motion of the tidal waters the ladder rose and fell, its rings creaking harshly, against the crazy railing.

"How are we going to get down without being detected?" whispered Smith.

"We've got to risk it," I said grimly.

Without further words my friend climbed around on to the ladder and commenced to descend. I waited until his head disappeared below the level, and, clumsily enough, prepared to follow him.

The hulk at that moment giving an unusually heavy heave, I stumbled, and for one breathless moment looked down upon the glittering surface streaking the darkness beneath me. My foot had slipped, and but that I had a firm grip upon the top rung, that instant, most probably, had marked the end of my share in the fight with Fu-Manchu. As it was I had a narrow escape. I felt something slip from my hip pocket, but the weird creaking of the ladder, the groans of the laboring hulk, and the lapping of the waves about the staging drowned the sound of the splash as my revolver dropped into the river.

Rather, white-faced, I think, I joined Smith on the deck. He had witnessed my accident, but--

"We must risk it," he whispered in my ear. "We dare not turn back now."

He plunged into the semi-darkness, making for the cabin, I perforce following.

At the bottom of the ladder we came fully into the light streaming out from the singular apartments at the entrance to which we found ourselves. It was fitted up as a laboratory. A glimpse I had of shelves loaded with jars and bottles, of a table strewn with scientific paraphernalia, with retorts, with tubes of extraordinary shapes, holding living organisms, and with instruments--some of them of a form unknown to my experience. I saw too that books, papers and rolls of parchment littered the bare wooden floor. Then Smith's voice rose above the confused sounds about me, incisive, commanding:

"I have you covered, Dr. Fu-Manchu!"

For Fu-Manchu sat at the table.

The picture that he presented at that moment is one which persistently clings in my memory. In his long, yellow robe, his mask like, intellectual face bent forward amongst the riot of singular objects upon the table, his great, high brow gleaming in the light of the shaded lamp above him, and with the abnormal eyes, filmed and green, raised to us, he seemed a figure from the realms of delirium. But, most amazing circumstance of all, he and his surroundings tallied, almost identically, with the dream-picture which had come to me as I lay chained in the cell!

Some of the large jars about the place held anatomy specimens. A faint smell of opium hung in the air, and playing with the tassel of one of the cushions upon which, as upon a divan, Fu-Manchu was seated, leaped and chattered a little marmoset.

That was an electric moment. I was prepared for anything-- for anything except for what really happened.

The doctor's wonderful, evil face betrayed no hint of emotion. The lids flickered over the filmed eyes, and their greenness grew momentarily brighter, and filmed over again.

"Put up your hands!" rapped Smith, "and attempt no tricks." His voice quivered with excitement. "The game's up, Fu-Manchu. Find something to tie him up with, Petrie."

I moved forward to Smith's side, and was about to pass him in the narrow doorway. The hulk moved beneath our feet like a living thing groaning, creaking--and the water lapped about the rotten woodwork with a sound infinitely dreary.

"Put up your hands!" ordered Smith imperatively.

Fu-Manchu slowly raised his hands, and a smile dawned upon the impassive features--a smile that had no mirth in it, only menace, revealing as it did his even, discolored teeth, but leaving the filmed eyes inanimate, dull, inhuman.

He spoke softly, sibilantly.

"I would advise Dr. Petrie to glance behind him before he moves."

Smith's keen gray eyes never for a moment quitted the speaker. The gleaming barrel moved not a hair's-breadth. But I glanced quickly over my shoulder--and stifled a cry of pure horror.

A wicked, pock-marked face, with wolfish fangs bared, and jaundiced eyes squinting obliquely into mine, was within two inches of me. A lean, brown hand and arm, the great thews standing up like cords, held a crescent-shaped knife a fraction of an inch above my jugular vein. A slight movement must have dispatched me; a sweep of the fearful weapon, I doubt not, would have severed my head from my body.

"Smith!" I whispered hoarsely, "don't look around. For God's sake keep him covered. But a dacoit has his knife at my throat!"

Then, for the first time, Smith's hand trembled. But his glance never wavered from the malignant, emotionless countenance of Dr. Fu-Manchu. He clenched his teeth hard, so that the muscles stood out prominently upon his jaw.

I suppose that silence which followed my awful discovery prevailed but a few seconds. To me those seconds were each a lingering death.

There, below, in that groaning hulk, I knew more of icy terror than any of our meetings with the murder-group had brought to me before; and through my brain throbbed a thought: the girl had betrayed us!

"You supposed that I was alone?" suggested Fu-Manchu. "So I was."

Yet no trace of fear had broken through the impassive yellow mask when we had entered.

"But my faithful servant followed you," he added. "I thank him. The honors, Mr. Smith, are mine, I think?"

Smith made no reply. I divined that he was thinking furiously. Fu-Manchu moved his hand to caress the marmoset, which had leaped playfully upon his shoulder, and crouched there gibing at us in a whistling voice.

"Don't stir!" said Smith savagely. "I warn you!"

Fu-Manchu kept his hand raised.

"May I ask you how you discovered my retreat?" he asked.

"This hulk has been watched since dawn," lied Smith brazenly.

"So?" The Doctor's filmed eyes cleared for a moment. "And to-day you compelled me to burn a house, and you have captured one of my people, too.

I congratulate you. She would not betray me though lashed with scorpions."

The great gleaming knife was so near to my neck that a sheet of notepaper could scarcely have been slipped between blade and vein, I think; but my heart throbbed even more wildly when I heard those words.

"An impasse," said Fu-Manchu. "I have a proposal to make. I assume that you would not accept my word for anything?"

"I would not," replied Smith promptly.

"Therefore," pursued the Chinaman, and the occasional guttural alone marred his perfect English, "I must accept yours. Of your resources outside this cabin I know nothing. You, I take it, know as little of mine. My Burmese friend and Doctor Petrie will lead the way, then; you and I will follow. We will strike out across the marsh for, say, three hundred yards. You will then place your pistol on the ground, pledging me your word to leave it there. I shall further require your assurance that you will make no attempt upon me until I have retraced my steps. I and my good servant will withdraw, leaving you, at the expiration of the specified period, to act as you see fit. Is it agreed?"

Smith hesitated. Then:

"The dacoit must leave his knife also," he stipulated. Fu-Manchu smiled his evil smile again.

"Agreed. Shall I lead the way?"

"No!" rapped Smith. "Petrie and the dacoit first; then you; I last."

A guttural word of command from Fu-Manchu, and we left the cabin, with its evil odors, its mortuary specimens, and its strange instruments, and in the order arranged mounted to the deck.

"It will be awkward on the ladder," said Fu-Manchu. "Dr. Petrie, I will accept your word to adhere to the terms."

"I promise," I said, the words almost choking me.

We mounted the rising and dipping ladder, all reached the pier, and strode out across the flats, the Chinaman always under close cover of Smith's revolver. Round about our feet, now leaping ahead, now gamboling back, came and went the marmoset. The dacoit, dressed solely in a dark loincloth, walked beside me, carrying his huge knife, and sometimes glancing at me with his blood-lustful eyes. Never before, I venture to say, had an autumn moon lighted such a scene in that place.

"Here we part," said Fu-Manchu, and spoke another word to his follower.

The man threw his knife upon the ground.

"Search him, Petrie," directed Smith. "He may have a second concealed."

The Doctor consented; and I passed my hands over the man's scanty garments.

"Now search Fu-Manchu."

This also I did. And never have I experienced a similar sense of revulsion from any human being. I shuddered, as though I had touched a venomous reptile.

Smith drew down his revolver.

"I curse myself for an honorable fool," he said. "No one could dispute my right to shoot you dead where you stand."

Knowing him as I did, I could tell from the suppressed passion in Smith's voice that only by his unhesitating acceptance of my friend's word, and implicit faith in his keeping it, had Dr. Fu-Manchu escaped just retribution at that moment. Fiend though he was, I admired his courage; for all this he, too, must have known.

The Doctor turned, and with the dacoit walked back. Nayland Smith's next move filled me with surprise. For just as, silently, I was thanking God for my escape, my friend began shedding his coat, collar and waistcoat.

"Pocket your valuables, and do the same," he muttered hoarsely. "We have a poor chances but we are both fairly fit. To-night, Petrie, we literally have to run for our lives."

We live in a peaceful age, wherein it falls to the lot of few men to owe their survival to their fleetness of foot. At Smith's words I realized in a flash that such was to be our fate to-night.

I have said that the hulk lay off a sort of promontory. East and west, then, we had nothing to hope for. To the south was Fu-Manchu; and even as, stripped of our heavier garments, we started to run northward, the weird signal of a dacoit rose on the night and was answered--was answered again.

"Three, at least," hissed Smith; "three armed dacoits. Hopeless."

"Take the revolver," I cried. "Smith, it's--"

"No," he rapped, through clenched teeth. "A servant of the Crown in the East makes his motto: `Keep your word, though it break your neck!' I don't think we need fear it being used against us. Fu-Manchu avoids noisy methods."

So back we ran, over the course by which, earlier, we had come. It was, roughly, a mile to the first building--a deserted cottage-- and another quarter of a mile to any that was occupied.

Our chance of meeting a living soul, other than Fu-Manchu's dacoits, was practically nil.

At first we ran easily, for it was the second half-mile that would decide our fate. The professional murderers who pursued us ran like panthers, I knew; and I dare not allow my mind to dwell upon those yellow figures with the curved, gleaming, knives. For a long time neither of us looked back.

On we ran, and on--silently, doggedly.

Then a hissing breath from Smith warned me what to expect.

Should I, too, look back? Yes. It was impossible to resist the horrid fascination.

I threw a quick glance over my shoulder.

And never while I live shall I forget what I saw. Two of the pursuing dacoits had outdistanced their fellow (or fellows), and were actually within three hundred yards of us.

More like dreadful animals they looked than human beings, running bent forward, with their faces curiously up tilted. The brilliant moonlight gleamed upon bared teeth, as I could see, even at that distance, even in that quick, agonized glance, and it gleamed upon the crescent-shaped knives.

"As hard as you can go now," panted Smith. "We must make an attempt to break into the empty cottage. Only chance."

I had never in my younger days been a notable runner; for Smith I cannot speak. But I am confident that the next half-mile was done in time that would not have disgraced a crack man. Not once again did either of us look back. Yard upon yard we raced forward together. My heart seemed to be bursting. My leg muscles throbbed with pain. At last, with the empty cottage in sight, it came to that pass with me when another three yards looks as unattainable as three miles. Once I stumbled.

"My God!" came from Smith weakly.

But I recovered myself. Bare feet pattered close upon our heels, and panting breaths told how even Fu-Manchu's bloodhounds were hard put to it by the killing pace we had made.

"Smith," I whispered, "look in front. Someone!"

As through a red mist I had seen a dark shape detach itself from the shadows of the cottage, and merge into them again. It could only be another dacoit; but Smith, not heeding, or not hearing, my faintly whispered words, crashed open the gate and hurled himself blindly at the door.

It burst open before him with a resounding boom, and he pitched forward into the interior darkness. Flat upon the floor he lay, for as, with a last effort, I gained the threshold and dragged myself within, I almost fell over his recumbent body.

Madly I snatched at the door. His foot held it open. I kicked the foot away, and banged the door to. As I turned, the leading dacoit, his eyes starting from their sockets, his face the face of a demon leaped wildly through the gateway.

That Smith had burst the latch I felt assured, but by some divine accident my weak hands found the bolt. With the last ounce of strength spared to me I thrust it home in the rusty socket-- as a full six inches of shining steel split the middle panel and protruded above my head.

I dropped, sprawling, beside my friend.

A terrific blow shattered every pane of glass in the solitary window, and one of the grinning animal faces looked in.

"Sorry, old man," whispered Smith, and his voice was barely audible.

Weakly he grasped my hand. "My fault. I shouldn't have let, you come."

From the corner of the room where the black shadows lay flicked a long tongue of flame. Muffled, staccato, came the report. And the yellow face at the window was blotted out.

One wild cry, ending in a rattling gasp, told of a dacoit gone to his account.

A gray figure glided past me and was silhouetted against the broken window.

Again the pistol sent its message into the night, and again came the reply to tell how well and truly that message had been delivered. In the stillness, intense by sharp contrast, the sound of bare soles pattering upon the path outside stole to me. Two runners, I thought there were, so that four dacoits must have been upon our trail. The room was full of pungent smoke. I staggered to my feet as the gray figure with the revolver turned towards me. Something familiar there was in that long, gray garment, and now I perceived why I had thought so.

It was my gray rain-coat.

"Karamaneh," I whispered.

And Smith, with difficulty, supporting himself upright, and holding fast to the ledge beside the door, muttered something hoarsely, which sounded like "God bless her!"

The girl, trembling now, placed her hands upon my shoulders with that quaint, pathetic gesture peculiarly her own.

"I followed you," she said. "Did you not know I should follow you? But I had to hide because of another who was following also. I had but just reached this place when I saw you running towards me."

She broke off and turned to Smith.

"This is your pistol," she said naively. "I found it in your bag. Will you please take it!"

He took it without a word. Perhaps he could not trust himself to speak.

"Now go. Hurry!" she said. "You are not safe yet."

"But you?" I asked.

"You have failed," she replied. "I must go back to him. There is no other way."

Strangely sick at heart for a man who has just had a miraculous escape from death, I opened the door. Coatless, disheveled figures, my friend and I stepped out into the moonlight.

Hideous under the pale rays lay the two dead men, their glazed eyes up cast to the peace of the blue heavens. Karamaneh had shot to kill, for both had bullets in their brains. If God ever planned a more complex nature than hers--a nature more tumultuous with conflicting passions, I cannot conceive of it. Yet her beauty was of the sweetest; and in some respects she had the heart of a child--this girl who could shoot so straight.

"We must send the police to-night," said Smith. "Or the papers--"

"Hurry," came the girl's voice commandingly from the darkness of the cottage.

It was a singular situation. My very soul rebelled against it. But what could we do?

"Tell us where we can communicate," began Smith.

"Hurry. I shall be suspected. Do you want him to kill me!"

We moved away. All was very still now, and the lights glimmered faintly ahead. Not a wisp of cloud brushed the moon's disk.

"Good-night, Karamaneh," I whispered softly.

CHAPTER XVIII

TO PURSUE further the adventure on the marshes would be a task at once useless and thankless. In its actual and in its dramatic significance it concluded with our parting from Karamaneh. And in that parting I learned what Shakespeare meant by "Sweet Sorrow."

There was a world, I learned, upon the confines of which I stood, a world whose very existence hitherto had been unsuspected. Not the least of the mysteries which peeped from the darkness was the mystery of the heart of Karamaneh. I sought to forget her. I sought to remember her. Indeed, in the latter task I found one more congenial, yet, in the direction and extent of the ideas which it engendered, one that led me to a precipice.

East and West may not intermingle. As a student of world-policies, as a physician, I admitted, could not deny, that truth. Again, if Karamaneh were to be credited, she had come to Fu-Manchu a slave; had fallen into the hands of the raiders; had crossed the desert with the slave-drivers; had known the house of the slave-dealer. Could it be? With the fading of the crescent of Islam I had thought such things to have passed.

But if it were so?

At the mere thought of a girl so deliciously beautiful in the brutal power of slavers, I found myself grinding my teeth--closing my eyes in a futile attempt to blot out the pictures called up.

Then, at such times, I would find myself discrediting her story. Again, I would find myself wondering, vaguely, why such problems persistently haunted my mind. But, always, my heart had an answer. And I was a medical man, who sought to build up a family practice!-- who, in short, a very little time ago, had thought himself past the hot follies of youth and entered upon that staid phase of life wherein the daily problems of the medical profession hold absolute sway and such seductive follies as dark eyes and red lips find-- no place--are excluded!

But it is foreign from the purpose of this plain record to enlist sympathy for the recorder. The topic upon which, here, I have ventured to touch was one fascinating enough to me; I cannot hope that it holds equal charm for any other. Let us return to that which it is my duty to narrate and let us forget my brief digression.

It is a fact, singular, but true, that few Londoners know London. Under the guidance of my friend, Nayland Smith, I had learned, since his return from Burma, how there are haunts in the very heart of the metropolis whose existence is unsuspected by all but the few; places unknown even to the ubiquitous copy-hunting pressman.

Into a quiet thoroughfare not two minutes' walk from the pulsing life of Leicester Square, Smith led the way. Before a door sandwiched in between two dingy shop-fronts he paused and turned to me.

"Whatever you see or hear," he cautioned, "express no surprise."

A cab had dropped us at the corner. We both wore dark suits and fez caps with black silk tassels. My complexion had been artificially reduced to a shade resembling the deep tan of my friend's. He rang the bell beside the door.

Almost immediately it was opened by a negro woman--gross, hideously ugly.

Smith uttered something in voluble Arabic. As a linguist his attainments were a constant source of surprise. The jargons of the East, Far and Near, he spoke as his mother tongue. The woman immediately displayed the utmost servility, ushering us into an ill-lighted passage, with every evidence of profound respect. Following this passage, and passing an inner door, from beyond whence proceeded bursts of discordant music, we entered a little room bare of furniture, with coarse matting for mural decorations, and a pattern less red carpet on the floor. In a niche burned a common metal lamp.

The negress left us, and close upon her departure entered a very aged man with a long patriarchal beard, who greeted my friend with dignified courtesy. Following a brief conversation, the aged Arab--for such he appeared to be-- drew aside a strip of matting, revealing a dark recess. Placing his finger upon his lips, he silently invited us to enter.

We did so, and the mat was dropped behind us. The sounds of crude music were now much plainer, and as Smith slipped a little shutter aside I gave a start of surprise.

Beyond lay a fairly large apartment, having divans or low seats around three of its walls. These divans were occupied by a motley company of Turks, Egyptians, Greeks, and others; and I noted two Chinese. Most of them smoked cigarettes, and some were drinking. A girl was performing a sinuous dance upon the square carpet occupying the center of the floor, accompanied by a young negro woman upon a guitar and by several members of the assembly who clapped their hands to the music or hummed a low, monotonous melody.

Shortly after our entrance into the passage the dance terminated, and the dancer fled through a curtained door at the farther end of the room. A buzz of conversation arose.

"It is a sort of combined Wekaleh and place of entertainment for a certain class of Oriental residents in, or visiting, London," Smith whispered. "The old gentleman who has just left us is the proprietor or host. I have been here before on several occasions, but have always drawn blank."

He was peering out eagerly into the strange clubroom.

"Whom do you expect to find here?" I asked.

"It is a recognized meeting-place," said Smith in my ear. "It is almost a certainty that some of the Fu-Manchu group use it at times."

Curiously I surveyed all these faces which were visible from the spy-hole. My eyes rested particularly upon the two Chinamen.

"Do you recognize anyone?" I whispered.

"S-sh!"

Smith was craning his neck so as to command a sight of the doorway. He obstructed my view, and only by his tense attitude and some subtle wave of excitement which he communicated to me did I know that a new arrival was entering. The hum of conversation died away, and in the ensuing silence I heard the rustle of draperies. The newcomer was a woman, then. Fearful of making any noise I yet managed to get my eyes to the level of the shutter.

A woman in an elegant, flame-colored opera cloak was crossing the floor and coming in the direction of the spot where we were concealed. She wore a soft silk scarf about her head, a fold partly draped across her face. A momentary view I had of her--and wildly incongruous she looked in that place--and she had disappeared from sight, having approached someone invisible who sat upon the divan immediately beneath our point of vantage.

From the way in which the company gazed towards her, I divined that she was no habitué of the place, but that her presence there was as greatly surprising to those in the room as it was to me.

Whom could she be, this elegant lady who visited such a haunt--who, it would seem, was so anxious to disguise her identity, but who was dressed for a society function rather than for a midnight expedition of so unusual a character?

I began a whispered question, but Smith tugged at my arm to silence me. His excitement was intense. Had his keener powers enabled him to recognize the unknown?

A faint but most peculiar perfume stole to my nostrils, a perfume which seemed to contain the very soul of Eastern mystery. Only one woman known to me used that perfume--Karamaneh.

Then it was she!

At last my friend's vigilance had been rewarded. Eagerly I bent forward. Smith literally quivered in anticipation of a discovery. Again the strange perfume was wafted to our hiding-place; and, glancing neither to right nor left, I saw Karamaneh--for that it was she I no longer doubted--recross the room and disappear.

"The man she spoke to," hissed Smith. "We must see him! We must have him!"

He pulled the mat aside and stepped out into the anteroom. It was empty. Down the passage he led, and we were almost come to the door of the big room when it was thrown open and a man came rapidly out, opened the street door before Smith could reach him, and was gone, slamming it fast.

I can swear that we were not four seconds behind him, but when we gained the street it was empty. Our quarry had disappeared as if by magic. A big car was just turning the corner towards Leicester Square.

"That is the girl," rapped Smith; "but where in Heaven's name is the man to whom she brought the message? I would give a hundred pounds to know what business is afoot. To think that we have had such an opportunity and have thrown it away!"

Angry and nonplused he stood at the corner, looking in the direction of the crowded thoroughfare into which the car had been driven, tugging at the lobe of his ear, as was his habit in such moments of perplexity, and sharply clicking his teeth together. I, too, was very thoughtful. Clews were few enough in those days of our war with that giant antagonist. The mere thought that our trifling error of judgment tonight in tarrying a moment too long might mean the victory of Fu-Manchu, might mean the turning of the balance which a wise providence had adjusted between the white and yellow races, was appalling.

To Smith and me, who knew something of the secret influences at work to overthrow the Indian Empire, to place, it might be, the whole of Europe and America beneath an Eastern rule, it seemed that a great yellow hand was stretched out over London. Doctor Fu-Manchu was a menace to the civilized world. Yet his very existence remained unsuspected by the millions whose fate he sought to command.

"Into what dark scheme have we had a glimpse?" said Smith. "What State secret is to be filched? What faithful servant of the British Raj to be spirited away? Upon whom now has Fu-Manchu set his death seal?"

"Karamaneh on this occasion may not have been acting as an emissary of the Doctor's."

"I feel assured that she was, Petrie. Of the many whom this yellow cloud may at any moment envelop, to which one did her message refer? The man's instructions were urgent. Witness his hasty departure. Curse it!" He dashed his right clenched fist into the palm of his left hand. "I never had a glimpse of his face, first to last. To think of the hours I have spent in that place, in anticipation of just such a meeting--only to bungle the opportunity when it arose!" Scarce heeding what course we followed, we had come now to Piccadilly Circus, and had walked out into the heart of the night's traffic. I just dragged Smith aside in time to save him from the off-front wheel of a big Mercedes. Then the traffic was blocked, and we found ourselves dangerously penned in amidst the press of vehicles.

Somehow we extricated ourselves, jeered at by taxi-drivers, who naturally took us for two simple Oriental visitors, and just before that impassable barrier the arm of a London policeman was lowered and the stream moved on a faint breath of perfume became perceptible to me.

The cabs and cars about us were actually beginning to move again, and there was nothing for it but a hasty retreat to the curb. I could not pause to glance behind, but instinctively I knew that someone--someone who used that rare, fragrant essence-- was leaning from the window of the car.

"ANDAMAN--SECOND!" floated a soft whisper.

We gained the pavement as the pent-up traffic roared upon its way.

Smith had not noticed the perfume worn by the unseen occupant of the car, had not detected the whispered words. But I had no reason to doubt my senses, and I knew beyond question that Fu-Manchu's lovely slave, Karamaneh, had been within a yard of us, had recognized us, and had uttered those words for our guidance.

On regaining my rooms, we devoted a whole hour to considering what "ANDAMAN--SECOND" could possibly mean.

"Hang it all!" cried Smith, "it might mean anything-- the result of a race, for instance."

He burst into one of his rare laughs, and began to stuff broadcut mixture into his briar. I could see that he had no intention of turning in.

"I can think of no one--no one of note--in London at present upon whom it is likely that Fu-Manchu would make an attempt," he said, "except ourselves."

We began methodically to go through the long list of names which we had compiled and to review our elaborate notes. When, at last, I turned in, the night had given place to a new day. But sleep evaded me, and "ANDAMAN--SECOND" danced like a mocking phantom through my brain.

Then I heard the telephone bell. I heard Smith speaking.

A minute afterwards he was in my room, his face very grim.

"I knew as well as if I'd seen it with my own eyes that some black business was afoot last night," he said. "And it was. Within pistol-shot of us! Someone has got at Frank Norris West. Inspector Weymouth has just been on the 'phone."

"Norris West!" I cried, "the American aviator--and inventor--" "Of the West aero-torpedo--yes. He's been offering it to the English War Office, and they have delayed too long."

I got out of bed.

"What do you mean?"

"I mean that the potentialities have attracted the attention of Dr. Fu-Manchu!"

Those words operated electrically. I do not know how long I was in dressing, how long a time elapsed ere the cab for which Smith had 'phoned arrived, how many precious minutes were lost upon the journey; but, in a nervous whirl, these things slipped into the past, like the telegraph poles seen from the window of an express, and, still in that tense state, we came upon the scene of this newest outrage.

Mr. Norris West, whose lean, stoic face had latterly figured so often in the daily press, lay upon the floor in the little entrance hall of his chambers, flat upon his back, with the telephone receiver in his hand.

The outer door had been forced by the police. They had had to remove a piece of the paneling to get at the bolt. A medical man was leaning over the recumbent figure in the striped pajama suit, and Detective-Inspector

Weymouth stood watching him as Smith and I entered.

"He has been heavily drugged," said the Doctor, sniffing at West's lips, "but I cannot say what drug has been used. It isn't chloroform or anything of that nature. He can safely be left to sleep it off, I think."

I agreed, after a brief examination.

"It's most extraordinary," said Weymouth. "He rang up the Yard about an hour ago and said his chambers had been invaded by Chinamen. Then the man at the 'phone plainly heard him fall. When we got here his front door was bolted, as you've seen, and the windows are three floors up. Nothing is disturbed."

"The plans of the aero-torpedo?" rapped Smith.

"I take it they are in the safe in his bedroom," replied the detective, "and that is locked all right. I think he must have taken an overdose of something and had illusions. But in case there was anything in what he mumbled (you could hardly understand him) I thought it as well to send for you."

"Quite right," said Smith rapidly. His eyes shone like steel. "Lay him on the bed, Inspector."

It was done, and my friend walked into the bedroom.

Save that the bed was disordered, showing that West had been sleeping in it, there were no evidences of the extraordinary invasion mentioned by the drugged man. It was a small room-- the chambers were of that kind which are let furnished--and very neat. A safe with a combination lock stood in a corner. The window was open about a foot at the top. Smith tried the safe and found it fast. He stood for a moment clicking his teeth together, by which I knew him to be perplexed. He walked over to the window and threw it up. We both looked out.

"You see," came Weymouth's voice, "it is altogether too far from the court below for our cunning Chinese friends to have fixed a ladder with one of their bamboo rod arrangements. And, even if they could get up there, it's too far down from the roof--two more stories-- for them to have fixed it from there."

Smith nodded thoughtfully, at the same time trying the strength of an iron bar which ran from side to side of the window-sill. Suddenly he stooped, with a sharp exclamation. Bending over his shoulder I saw what it was that had attracted his attention.

Clearly imprinted upon the dust-coated gray stone of the sill was a confused series of marks--tracks call them what you will.

Smith straightened himself and turned a wondering look upon me.

"What is it, Petrie?" he said amazedly. "Some kind of bird has been here, and recently." Inspector Weymouth in turn examined the marks.

"I never saw bird tracks like these, Mr. Smith," he muttered.

Smith was tugging at the lobe of his ear.

"No," he returned reflectively; "come to think of it, neither did I."

He twisted around, looking at the man on the bed.

"Do you think it was all an illusion?" asked the detective.

"What about those marks on the window-sill?" jerked Smith.

He began restlessly pacing about the room, sometimes stopping before the locked safe and frequently glancing at Norris West.

Suddenly he walked out and briefly examined the other apartments, only to return again to the bedroom.

"Petrie," he said, "we are losing valuable time. West must be aroused."

Inspector Weymouth stared.

Smith turned to me impatiently. The doctor summoned by the police had gone. "Is there no means of arousing him, Petrie?" he said.

"Doubtless," I replied, "he could be revived if one but knew what drug he had taken."

My friend began his restless pacing again, and suddenly pounced upon a little phial of tabloids which had been hidden behind some books on a shelf near the bed. He uttered a triumphant exclamation.

"See what we have here, Petrie!" he directed, handing the phial to me. "It bears no label."

I crushed one of the tabloids in my palm and applied my tongue to the powder.

"Some preparation of chloral hydrate," I pronounced.

"A sleeping draught?" suggested Smith eagerly.

"We might try," I said, and scribbled a formula upon a leaf of my notebook. I asked Weymouth to send the man who accompanied him to call up the nearest chemist and procure the antidote.

During the man's absence Smith stood contemplating the unconscious inventor, a peculiar expression upon his bronzed face.

"ANDAMAN--SECOND," he muttered. "Shall we find the key to the riddle here, I wonder?"

Inspector Weymouth, who had concluded, I think, that the mysterious telephone call was due to mental aberration on the part of Norris West, was gnawing at his mustache impatiently when his assistant returned. I administered the powerful restorative, and although, as later transpired, chloral was not responsible for West's condition, the antidote operated successfully.

Norris West struggled into a sitting position, and looked about him with haggard eyes.

"The Chinamen! The Chinamen!" he muttered.

He sprang to his feet, glaring wildly at Smith and me, reeled, and almost fell.

"It is all right," I said, supporting him. "I'm a doctor. You have been unwell."

"Have the police come?" he burst out. "The safe--try the safe!"

"It's all right," said Inspector Weymouth. "The safe is locked-- unless someone else knows the combination, there's nothing to worry about."

"No one else knows it," said West, and staggered unsteadily to the safe. Clearly his mind was in a dazed condition, but, setting his jaw with a curious expression of grim determination, he collected his thoughts and opened the safe.

He bent down, looking in.

In some way the knowledge came to me that the curtain was about to rise on a new and surprising act in the Fu-Manchu drama.

"God!" he whispered--we could scarcely hear him--"the plans are gone!"

CHAPTER XIX

I HAVE NEVER seen a man quite so surprised as Inspector Weymouth.

"This is absolutely incredible!" he said. "There's only one door to your chambers. We found it bolted from the inside."

"Yes," groaned West, pressing his hand to his forehead. "I bolted it myself at eleven o'clock, when I came in."

"No human being could climb up or down to your windows. The plans of the aero-torpedo were inside a safe."

"I put them there myself," said West, "on returning from the War Office, and I had occasion to consult them after I had come in and bolted the door. I returned them to the safe and locked it. That it was still locked you saw for yourselves, and no one else in the world knows the combination."

"But the plans have gone," said Weymouth. "It's magic! How was it done? What happened last night, sir? What did you mean when you rang us up?"

Smith during this colloquy was pacing rapidly up and down the room. He turned abruptly to the aviator.

"Every fact you can remember, Mr. West, please," he said tersely; "and be as brief as you possibly can."

"I came in, as I said," explained West "about eleven o'clock and having made some notes relating to an interview arranged for this morning, I locked the plans in the safe and turned in."

"There was no one hidden anywhere in your chambers?" snapped Smith.

"There was not," replied West. "I looked. I invariably do. Almost immediately, I went to sleep."

"How many chloral tabloids did you take?" I interrupted.

Norris West turned to me with a slow smile.

"You're cute, Doctor," he said. "I took two. It's a bad habit, but I can't sleep without. They are specially made up for me by a firm in Philadelphia."

"How long sleep lasted, when it became filled with uncanny dreams, and when those dreams merged into reality, I do not know-- shall never know, I suppose. But out of the dreamless void a face came to me--closer--closer--and peered into mine.

"I was in that curious condition wherein one knows that one is dreaming and seeks to awaken--to escape. But a nightmare-like oppression held me. So I must lie and gaze into the seared yellow face that hung over me, for it would drop so close that I could trace the cicatrized scar running from the left ear to the corner of the mouth, and drawing up the lip like the lip of a snarling cur. I could look into the malignant, jaundiced eyes; I could hear the dim whispering of the distorted mouth-- whispering that seemed to counsel something--something evil. That whispering intimacy was indescribably repulsive. Then the wicked yellow face would be withdrawn, and would recede until it became as a pin's head in the darkness far above me-- almost like a glutinous, liquid thing.

"Somehow I got upon my feet, or dreamed I did--God knows where dreaming ended and reality began. Gentlemen maybe you'll conclude I went mad last night, but as I stood holding on to the bedrail I heard the blood throbbing through my arteries with a noise like a screw-propeller. I started laughing. The laughter issued from my lips with a shrill whistling sound that pierced me with physical pain and seemed to wake the echoes of the whole block. I thought myself I was going mad, and I tried to command my will-- to break the power of the chloral--for I concluded that I had accidentally taken an overdose.

"Then the walls of my bedroom started to recede, till at last I stood holding on to a bed which had shrunk to the size of a doll's cot, in the middle of a room like Trafalgar Square! That window yonder was such a long way off I could scarcely see it, but I could just detect a Chinaman--the owner of the evil yellow face--creeping through it. He was followed by another, who was enormously tall--so tall that, as they came towards me (and it seemed to take them something like half-an-hour to cross this incredible apartment in my dream), the second Chinaman seemed to tower over me like a cypress-tree.

"I looked up to his face--his wicked, hairless face. Mr. Smith, whatever age I live to, I'll never forget that face I saw last night--or did I see it? God knows! The pointed chin, the great dome of a forehead, and the eyes-- heavens above, the huge green eyes!"

He shook like a sick man, and I glanced at Smith significantly. Inspector Weymouth was stroking his mustache, and his mingled expression of incredulity and curiosity was singular to behold.

"The pumping of my blood," continued West, "seemed to be bursting my body; the room kept expanding and contracting. One time the ceiling would be pressing down on my head, and the Chinamen--sometimes I thought there were two of them, sometimes twenty--became dwarfs; the next instant it shot up like the roof of a cathedral.

"`Can I be awake,' I whispered, `or am I dreaming?'

"My whisper went sweeping in windy echoes about the walls, and was lost in the shadowy distances up under the invisible roof.

"`You are dreaming--yes.' It was the Chinaman with the green eyes who was addressing me, and the words that he uttered appeared to occupy an immeasurable time in the utterance. 'But at will I can render the subjective objective.' I don't think I can have dreamed those singular words, gentlemen. "And then he fixed the green eyes upon me--the blazing green eyes. I made no attempt to move. They seemed to be draining me of something vital--bleeding me of every drop of mental power. The whole nightmare room grew green, and I felt that I was being absorbed into its greenness.

"I can see what you think. And even in my delirium-- if it was delirium--I thought the same. Now comes the climax of my experience--my vision--I don't know what to call it. I SAW some WORDS issuing from my own mouth!"

Inspector Weymouth coughed discreetly. Smith whisked round upon him.

"This will be outside your experience, Inspector, I know," he said, "but Mr. Norris West's statement does not surprise me in the least. I know to what the experience was due."

Weymouth stared incredulously, but a dawning perception of the truth was come to me, too.

"How I SAW a SOUND I just won't attempt to explain; I simply tell you I saw it. Somehow I knew I had betrayed myself-- given something away."

"You gave away the secret of the lock combination!" rapped Smith.

"Eh!" grunted Weymouth.

But West went on hoarsely:

"Just before the blank came a name flashed before my eyes. It was 'Bayard Taylor.'"

At that I interrupted West.

"I understand!" I cried. "I understand! Another name has just occurred to me, Mr. West--that of the Frenchman, Moreau."

"You have solved the mystery," said Smith. "It was natural Mr. West should have thought of the American traveler, Bayard Taylor, though. Moreau's book is purely scientific. He has probably never read it."

"I fought with the stupor that was overcoming me," continued West, "striving to associate that vaguely familiar name with the fantastic things through which I moved. It seemed to me that the room was empty again. I made for the hall, for the telephone. I could scarcely drag my feet along. It seemed to take me half-an-hour to get there. I remember calling up Scotland Yard, and I remember no more."

There was a short, tense interval.

In some respects I was nonplused; but, frankly, I think Inspector Weymouth considered West insane. Smith, his hands locked behind his back, stared out of the window.

"ANDAMAN--SECOND" he said suddenly. "Weymouth, when is the first train to Tilbury?"

"Five twenty-two from Fenchurch Street," replied the Scotland Yard man promptly.

"Too late!" rapped my friend. "Jump in a taxi and pick up two good men to leave for China at once! Then go and charter a special to Tilbury to leave in twenty-five minutes. Order another cab to wait outside for me."

Weymouth was palpably amazed, but Smith's tone was imperative. The Inspector departed hastily.

I stared at Smith, not comprehending what prompted this singular course.

"Now that you can think clearly, Mr. West," he said, "of what does your experience remind you? The errors of perception regarding time; the idea of SEEING A SOUND; the illusion that the room alternately increased and diminished in size; your fit of laughter, and the recollection of the name Bayard Taylor. Since evidently you are familiar with that author's work-- 'The Land of the Saracen,' is it not?--these symptoms of the attack should be familiar, I think."

Norris West pressed his hands to his evidently aching head.

"Bayard Taylor's book," he said dully. "Yes!. . .I know of what my brain sought to remind me--Taylor's account of his experience under hashish. Mr. Smith, someone doped me with hashish!"

Smith nodded grimly.

"Cannabis indica," I said--"Indian hemp. That is what you were drugged with. I have no doubt that now you experience a feeling of nausea and intense thirst, with aching in the muscles, particularly the deltoid. I think you must have taken at least fifteen grains."

Smith stopped his perambulations immediately in front of West, looking into his dulled eyes.

"Someone visited your chambers last night," he said slowly, "and for your chloral tabloids substituted some containing hashish, or perhaps not pure hashish. Fu-Manchu is a profound chemist."

Norris West started.

"Someone substituted--" he began.

"Exactly," said Smith, looking at him keenly; "someone who was here yesterday. Have you any idea whom it could have been?"

West hesitated. "I had a visitor in the afternoon," he said, seemingly speaking the words unwillingly, "but--"

"A lady?" jerked Smith. "I suggest that it was a lady."

West nodded.

"You're quite right," he admitted. "I don't know how you arrived at the conclusion, but a lady whose acquaintance I made recently-- a foreign lady."

"Karamaneh!" snapped Smith.

"I don't know what you mean in the least, but she came here-- knowing this to be my present address--to ask me to protect her from a mysterious man who had followed her right from Charing Cross. She said he was down in the lobby, and naturally, I asked her to wait here whilst I went and sent him about his business."

He laughed shortly.

"I am over-old," he said, "to be guyed by a woman. You spoke just now of someone called Fu-Manchu. Is that the crook I'm indebted to for the loss of my plans? I've had attempts made by agents of two European governments, but a Chinaman is a novelty."

"This Chinaman," Smith assured him, "is the greatest novelty of his age. You recognize your symptoms now from Bayard Taylor's account?"

"Mr. West's statement," I said, "ran closely parallel with portions of Moreau's book on 'Hashish Hallucinations.' Only Fu-Manchu, I think, would have thought of employing Indian hemp. I doubt, though, if it was pure Cannabis indica. At any rate, it acted as an opiate--"

"And drugged Mr. West," interrupted Smith, "sufficiently to enable Fu-Manchu to enter unobserved."

"Whilst it produced symptoms which rendered him an easy subject for the Doctor's influence. It is difficult in this case to separate hallucination from reality, but I think, Mr. West, that Fu-Manchu must have exercised an hypnotic influence upon your drugged brain. We have evidence that he dragged from you the secret of the combination."

"God knows we have!" said West. "But who is this Fu-Manchu, and how-- how in the name of wonder did he get into my chambers?"

Smith pulled out his watch. "That," he said rapidly, "I cannot delay to explain if I'm to intercept the man who has the plans. Come along, Petrie; we must be at Tilbury within the hour. There is just a bare chance."

CHAPTER XX

IT WAS WITH my mind in a condition of unique perplexity that I hurried with Nayland Smith into the cab which waited and dashed off through the streets in which the busy life of London just stirred into being. I suppose I need not say that I could penetrate no farther into this, Fu-Manchu's latest plot, than the drugging of Norris West with hashish? Of his having been so drugged with Indian hemp--that is, converted temporarily into a maniac--would have been evident to any medical man who had heard his statement and noted the distressing after-effects which conclusively pointed to Indian hemp poisoning. Knowing something of the Chinese doctor's powers, I could understand that he might have extracted from West the secret of the combination by sheer force of will whilst the American was under the influence of the drug. But I could not understand how Fu-Manchu had gained access to locked chambers on the third story of a building.

"Smith," I said, "those bird tracks on the window-sill-- they furnish the key to a mystery which is puzzling me."

"They do," said Smith, glancing impatiently at his watch. "Consult your memories of Dr. Fu-Manchu's habits--especially your memories of his pets."

I reviewed in my mind the creatures gruesome and terrible which surrounded the Chinaman--the scorpions, the bacteria, the noxious things which were the weapons wherewith he visited death upon whomsoever opposed the establishment of a potential Yellow Empire. But no one of them could account for the imprints upon the dust of West's window-sill.

"You puzzle me, Smith," I confessed. "There is much in this extraordinary case that puzzles me. I can think of nothing to account for the marks."

"Have you thought of Fu-Manchu's marmoset?" asked Smith.

"The monkey!" I cried.

"They were the footprints of a small ape," my friend continued. "For a moment I was deceived as you were, and believed them to be the tracks of a large bird; but I have seen the footprints of apes before now, and a marmoset, though an American variety, I believe, is not unlike some of the apes of Burma."

"I am still in the dark," I said.

"It is pure hypothesis," continued Smith, "but here is the theory-- in lieu of a better one it covers the facts. The marmoset-- and it is contrary from the character of Fu-Manchu to keep any creature for mere amusement--is trained to perform certain duties.

"You observed the waterspout running up beside the window; you observed the iron bar intended to prevent a window-cleaner from falling out? For an ape the climb from the court below to the sill above was a simple one. He carried a cord, probably attached to his body. He climbed on to the sill, over the bar, and climbed down again. By means of this cord a rope was pulled up over the bar, by means of the rope one of those ladders of silk and bamboo. One of the Doctor's servants ascended--probably to ascertain if the hashish had acted successfully. That was the yellow dream-face which West saw bending over him. Then followed the Doctor, and to his giant will the drugged brain of West was a pliant instrument which he bent to his own ends. The court would be deserted at that hour of the night, and, in any event, directly after the ascent the ladder probably was pulled up, only to be lowered again when West had revealed the secret of his own safe and Fu-Manchu had secured the plans. The reclosing of the safe and the removing of the hashish tabloids, leaving no clew beyond the delirious ravings of a drug slave-- for so anyone unacquainted with the East must have construed West's story--is particularly characteristic. His own tabloids were returned, of course. The sparing of his life alone is a refinement of art which points to a past master."

"Karamaneh was the decoy again?" I said shortly.

"Certainly. Hers was the task to ascertain West's habits and to substitute the tabloids. She it was who waited in the luxurious car-- infinitely less likely to attract attention at that hour in that place than a modest taxi-- and received the stolen plans. She did her work well."

"Poor Karamaneh; she had no alternative! I said I would have given a hundred pounds for a sight of the messenger's face--the man to whom she handed them. I would give a thousand now!"

"ANDAMAN--SECOND," I said. "What did she mean?"

"Then it has not dawned upon you?" cried Smith excitedly, as the cab turned into the station. "The ANDAMAN, of the Oriental Navigation Company's line, leaves Tilbury with the next tide for China ports. Our man is a second-class passenger. I am wiring to delay her departure, and the special should get us to the docks inside of forty minutes."

Very vividly I can reconstruct in my mind that dash to the docks through the early autumn morning. My friend being invested with extraordinary powers from the highest authorities, by Inspector Weymouth's instructions the line had been cleared all the way.

Something of the tremendous importance of Nayland Smith's mission came home to me as we hurried on to the platform, escorted by the station-master, and the five of us--for Weymouth had two other C.I.D. men with him-- took our seats in the special.

Off we went on top speed, roaring through stations, where a glimpse might be had of wondering officials upon the platforms, for a special train was a novelty on the line. All ordinary traffic arrangements were held up until we had passed through, and we reached Tilbury in time which I doubt not constituted a record.

There at the docks was the great liner, delayed in her passage to the Far East by the will of my royally empowered companion. It was novel, and infinitely exciting.

"Mr. Commissioner Nayland Smith?" said the captain interrogatively, when we were shown into his room, and looked from one to another and back to the telegraph form which he held in his hand.

"The same, Captain," said my friend briskly. "I shall not detain you a moment. I am instructing the authorities at all ports east of Suez to apprehend one of your second-class passengers, should he leave the ship. He is in possession of plans which practically belong to the British Government!"
"Why not arrest him now?" asked the seaman bluntly.

"Because I don't know him. All second-class passengers' baggage will be searched as they land. I am hoping something from that, if all else fails. But I want you privately to instruct your stewards to watch any passenger of Oriental nationality, and to cooperate with the two Scotland Yard men who are joining you for the voyage. I look to you to recover these plans, Captain."

"I will do my best," the captain assured him.

Then, from amid the heterogeneous group on the dockside, we were watching the liner depart, and Nayland Smith's expression was a very singular one. Inspector Weymouth stood with us, a badly puzzled man. Then occurred the extraordinary incident which to this day remains inexplicable, for, clearly heard by all three of us, a guttural voice said:

"Another victory for China, Mr. Nayland Smith!"

I turned as though I had been stung. Smith turned also. My eyes passed from face to face of the group about us. None was familiar. No one apparently had moved away.

But the voice was the voice of DOCTOR FU-MANCHU.

As I write of it, now, I can appreciate the difference between that happening, as it appealed to us, and as it must appeal to you who merely read of it. It is beyond my powers to convey the sense of the uncanny which the episode created. Yet, even as I think of it, I feel again, though in lesser degree, the chill which seemed to creep through my veins that day.

From my brief history of the wonderful and evil man who once walked, by the way unsuspected, in the midst of the people of England-- near whom you, personally, may at some time unwittingly, have been-- I am aware that much must be omitted. I have no space for lengthy examinations of the many points but ill illuminated with which it is dotted. This incident at the docks is but one such point.

Another is the singular vision which appeared to me whilst I lay in the cellar of the house near Windsor. It has since struck me that it possessed peculiarities akin to those of a hashish hallucination. Can it be that we were drugged on that occasion with Indian hemp? Cannabis indica is a treacherous narcotic, as every medical man knows full well; but Fu-Manchu's knowledge of the drug was far in advance of our slow science. West's experience proved so much.

I may have neglected opportunities--later, you shall judge if I did so--opportunities to glean for the West some of the strange knowledge of the secret East. Perhaps, at a future time, I may rectify my errors. Perhaps that wisdom--the wisdom stored up by Fu-Manchu--is lost forever. There is, however, at least a bare possibility of its survival, in part; and I do not wholly despair of one day publishing a scientific sequel to this record of our dealings with the Chinese doctor.

CHAPTER XXI

TIME WORE ON and seemingly brought us no nearer, or very little nearer, to our goal. So carefully had my friend Nayland Smith excluded the matter from the press that, whilst public interest was much engaged with some of the events in the skein of mystery which he had come from Burma to unravel, outside the Secret Service and the special department of Scotland Yard few people recognized that the several murders, robberies and disappearances formed each a link in a chain; fewer still were aware that a baneful presence was in our midst, that a past master of the evil arts lay concealed somewhere in the metropolis; searched for by the keenest wits which the authorities could direct to the task, but eluding all-triumphant, contemptuous.

One link in that chain Smith himself for long failed to recognize. Yet it was a big and important link.

"Petrie," he said to me one morning, "listen to this:

"`. . .In sight of Shanghai--a clear, dark night. On board the deck of a junk passing close to seaward of the Andaman a blue flare started up. A minute later there was a cry of "Man overboard!"

"`Mr. Lewin, the chief officer, who was in charge, stopped the engines. A boat was put out. But no one was recovered. There are sharks in these waters. A fairly heavy sea was running.

"`Inquiry showed the missing man to be a James Edwards, second class, booked to Shanghai. I think the name was assumed. The man was some sort of Oriental, and we had had him under close observation. . . .'"

"That's the end of their report," exclaimed Smith.

He referred to the two C.I.D. men who had joined the Andaman at the moment of her departure from Tilbury.

He carefully lighted his pipe.

"IS it a victory for China, Petrie?" he said softly.

"Until the great war reveals her secret resources--and I pray that the day be not in my time--we shall never know," I replied.

Smith began striding up and down the room,

"Whose name," he jerked abruptly, "stands now at the head of our danger list?"

He referred to a list which we had compiled of the notable men intervening between the evil genius who secretly had invaded London and the triumph of his cause--the triumph of the yellow races.

I glanced at our notes. "Lord Southery," I replied.

Smith tossed the morning paper across to me.

"Look," he said shortly. "He's dead."

I read the account of the peer's death, and glanced at the long obituary notice; but no more than glanced at it. He had but recently returned from the East, and now, after a short illness, had died from some affection of the heart. There had been no intimation that his illness was of a serious nature, and even Smith, who watched over his flock-- the flock threatened by the wolf, Fu-Manchu--with jealous zeal, had not suspected that the end was so near.

"Do you think he died a natural death, Smith?" I asked.

My friend reached across the table and rested the tip of a long ringer upon one of the sub-headings to the account:

"SIR FRANK NARCOMBE SUMMONED TOO LATE."

"You see," said Smith, "Southery died during the night, but Sir Frank Narcombe, arriving a few minutes later, unhesitatingly pronounced death to be due to syncope, and seems to have noticed nothing suspicious."

I looked at him thoughtfully.

"Sir Frank is a great physician," I said slowly; "but we must remember he would be looking for nothing suspicious."

"We must remember," rapped Smith, "that, if Dr. Fu-Manchu is responsible for Southery's death, except to the eye of an expert there would be nothing suspicious to see. Fu-Manchu leaves no clews."

"Are you going around?" I asked.

Smith shrugged his shoulders.

"I think not," he replied. "Either a greater One than Fu-Manchu has taken Lord Southery, or the yellow doctor has done his work so well that no trace remains of his presence in the matter."

Leaving his breakfast untasted, he wandered aimlessly about the room, littering the hearth with matches as he constantly relighted his pipe, which went out every few minutes.

"It's no good, Petrie," he burst out suddenly; "it cannot be a coincidence. We must go around and see him."

An hour later we stood in the silent room, with its drawn blinds and its deathful atmosphere, looking down at the pale, intellectual face of Henry Stradwick, Lord Southery, the greatest engineer of his day. The mind that lay behind that splendid brow had planned the construction of the railway for which Russia had paid so great a price, had conceived the scheme for the canal which, in the near future, was to bring two great continents, a full week's journey nearer one to the other. But now it would plan no more.

"He had latterly developed symptoms of angina pectoris," explained the family physician; "but I had not anticipated a fatal termination so soon. I was called about two o'clock this morning, and found Lord Southery in a dangerously exhausted condition. I did all that was possible, and Sir Frank Narcombe was sent for. But shortly before his arrival the patient expired."

"I understand, Doctor, that you had been treating Lord Southery for angina pectoris?" I said.

"Yes," was the reply, "for some months."

"You regard the circumstances of his end as entirely consistent with a death from that cause?"

"Certainly. Do you observe anything unusual yourself? Sir Frank Narcombe quite agrees with me. There is surely no room for doubt?"

"No," said Smith, tugging reflectively at the lobe of his left ear. "We do not question the accuracy of your diagnosis in any way, sir."

The physician seemed puzzled.

"But am I not right in supposing that you are connected with the police?" asked the physician.

"Neither Dr. Petrie nor myself are in any way connected with the police," answered Smith. "But, nevertheless, I look to you to regard our recent questions as confidential."

As we were leaving the house, hushed awesomely in deference to the unseen visitor who had touched Lord Southery with gray, cold fingers, Smith paused, detaining a black-coated man who passed us on the stairs.

"You were Lord Southery's valet?"

The man bowed.

"Were you in the room at the moment of his fatal seizure?"

"I was, sir."

"Did you see or hear anything unusual--anything unaccountable?"

"Nothing, sir."

"No strange sounds outside the house, for instance?"

The man shook his head, and Smith, taking my arm, passed out into the street.

"Perhaps this business is making me imaginative," he said; "but there seems to be something tainting the air in yonder-- something peculiar to houses whose doors bear the invisible death-mark of Fu-Manchu."

"You are right, Smith!" I cried. "I hesitated to mention the matter, but I, too, have developed some other sense which warns me of the Doctor's presence. Although there is not a scrap of confirmatory evidence, I am as sure that he has brought about Lord Southery's death as if I had seen him strike the blow."

It was in that torturing frame of mind--chained, helpless, in our ignorance, or by reason of the Chinaman's supernormal genius--that we lived throughout the ensuing days. My friend began to look like a man consumed by a burning fever. Yet, we could not act.

In the growing dark of an evening shortly following I stood idly turning over some of the works exposed for sale outside a second-hand bookseller's in New Oxford Street. One dealing with the secret societies of China struck me as being likely to prove instructive, and I was about to call the shop man when I was startled to feel a hand clutch my arm.

I turned around rapidly--and was looking into the darkly beautiful eyes of Karamaneh! She--whom I had seen in so many guises-- was dressed in a perfectly fitting walking habit, and had much of her wonderful hair concealed beneath a fashionable hat.

She glanced about her apprehensively.

"Quick! Come round the corner. I must speak to you," she said, her musical voice thrilling with excitement.

I never was quite master of myself in her presence. He must have been a man of ice who could have been, I think for her beauty had all the bouquet of rarity; she was a mystery--and mystery adds charm to a woman. Probably she should have been under arrest, but I know I would have risked much to save her from it.

As we turned into a quiet thoroughfare she stopped and said:

"I am in distress. You have often asked me to enable you to capture Dr. Fu-Manchu. I am prepared to do so."

I could scarcely believe that I heard right.

"Your brother--" I began.

She seized my arm entreatingly, looking into my eyes.

"You are a doctor," she said. "I want you to come and see him now."

"What! Is he in London?"

"He is at the house of Dr. Fu-Manchu."

"And you would have me ---"

"Accompany me there, yes."

Nayland Smith, I doubted not, would have counseled me against trusting my life in the hands of this girl with the pleading eyes. Yet I did so, and with little hesitation; shortly we were traveling eastward in a closed cab. Karamaneh was very silent, but always when I turned to her I found her big eyes fixed upon me with an expression in which there was pleading, in which there was sorrow, in which there was something else--something indefinable, yet strangely disturbing. The cabman she had directed to drive to the lower end of the Commercial Road, the neighborhood of the new docks, and the scene of one of our early adventures with Dr. Fu-Manchu. The mantle of dusk had closed about the squalid activity of the East End streets as we neared our destination. Aliens of every shade of color were about us now, emerging from burrow-like alleys into the glare of the lamps upon the main road. In the short space of the drive we had passed from the bright world of the West into the dubious underworld of the East.

I do not know that Karamaneh moved; but in sympathy, as we neared the abode of the sinister Chinaman, she crept nearer to me, and when the cab was discharged, and together we walked down a narrow turning leading riverward, she clung to me fearfully, hesitated, and even seemed upon the point of turning back. But, overcoming her fear or repugnance, she led on, through a maze of alleyways and courts, wherein I hopelessly lost my bearings, so that it came home to me how wholly I was in the hands of this girl whose history was so full of shadows, whose real character was so inscrutable, whose beauty, whose charm truly might mask the cunning of a serpent.

I spoke to her.

"S-SH!" She laid her hand upon my arm, enjoining me to silence.

The high, drab brick wall of what looked like some part of a dock building loomed above us in the darkness, and the indescribable stenches of the lower Thames were borne to my nostrils through a gloomy, tunnel-like opening, beyond which whispered the river. The muffled clangor of waterside activity was about us. I heard a key grate in a lock, and Karamaneh drew me into the shadow of an open door, entered, and closed it behind her.

For the first time I perceived, in contrast to the odors of the court without, the fragrance of the peculiar perfume which now I had come to associate with her. Absolute darkness was about us, and by this perfume alone I knew that she, was near to me, until her hand touched mine, and I was led along an uncarpeted passage and up an uncarpeted stair. A second door was unlocked, and I found myself in an exquisitely furnished room, illuminated by the soft light of a shaded lamp which stood upon a low, inlaid table amidst a perfect ocean of silken cushions, strewn upon a Persian carpet, whose yellow richness was lost in the shadows beyond the circle of light.

Karamaneh raised a curtain draped before a doorway, and stood listening intently for a moment.

The silence was unbroken.

Then something stirred amid the wilderness of cushions, and two tiny bright eyes looked up at me. Peering closely, I succeeded in distinguishing, crouched in that soft luxuriance, a little ape. It was Dr. Fu-Manchu's marmoset. "This way," whispered Karamaneh.

Never, I thought, was a staid medical man committed to a more unwise enterprise, but so far I had gone, and no consideration of prudence could now be of avail.

The corridor beyond was thickly carpeted. Following the direction of a faint light which gleamed ahead, it proved to extend as a balcony across one end of a spacious apartment. Together we stood high up there in the shadows, and looked down upon such a scene as I never could have imagined to exist within many a mile of that district.

The place below was even more richly appointed than the room into which first we had come. Here, as there, piles of cushions formed splashes of gaudy color about the floor. Three lamps hung by chains from the ceiling, their light softened by rich silk shades. One wall was almost entirely occupied by glass cases containing chemical apparatus, tubes, retorts and other less orthodox indications of Dr. Fu-Manchu's pursuits, whilst close against another lay the most extraordinary object of a sufficiently extraordinary room-- a low couch, upon which was extended the motionless form of a boy. In the light of a lamp which hung directly above him, his olive face showed an almost startling resemblance to that of Karamaneh-- save that the girl's coloring was more delicate. He had black, curly hair, which stood out prominently against the white covering upon which he lay, his hands crossed upon his breast.

Transfixed with astonishment, I stood looking down upon him. The wonders of the "Arabian Nights" were wonders no longer, for here, in East-End London, was a true magician's palace, lacking not its beautiful slave lacking not its enchanted prince!

"It is Aziz, my brother," said Karamaneh.

We passed down a stairway on to the floor of the apartment. Karamaneh knelt and bent over the boy, stroking his hair and whispering to him lovingly. I, too, bent over him; and I shall never forget the anxiety in the girl's eyes as she watched me eagerly whilst I made a brief examination.

Brief, indeed, for even ere I had touched him I knew that the comely shell held no spark of life. But Karamaneh fondled the cold hands, and spoke softly in that Arabic tongue which long before I had divined must be her native language.

Then, as I remained silent, she turned and looked at me, read the truth in my eyes, and rose from her knees, stood rigidly upright, and clutched me tremblingly.

"He is not dead--he is NOT dead!" she whispered, and shook me as a child might, seeking to arouse me to a proper understanding. "Oh, tell me he is not ---"

"I cannot," I replied gently, "for indeed he is."

"No!" she said, wild-eyed, and raising her hands to her face as though half distraught. "You do not understand--yet you are a doctor. You do not understand ---"

She stopped, moaning to herself and looking from the handsome face of the boy to me. It was pitiful; it was uncanny. But sorrow for the girl predominated in my mind.

Then from somewhere I heard a sound which I had heard before in houses occupied by Dr. Fu-Manchu--that of a muffled gong.

"Quick!" Karamaneh had me by the arm. "Up! He has returned!"

She fled up the stairs to the balcony, I close at her heels. The shadows veiled us, the thick carpet deadened the sound of our tread, or certainly we must have been detected by the man who entered the room we had just quitted.

It was Dr. Fu-Manchu!

Yellow-robed, immobile, the inhuman green eyes glittering catlike even, it seemed, before the light struck them, he threaded his way through the archipelago of cushions and bent over the couch of Aziz.

Karamaneh dragged me down on to my knees.

"Watch!" she whispered. "Watch!"

Dr. Fu-Manchu felt for the pulse of the boy whom a moment since I had pronounced dead, and, stepping to the tall glass case, took out a long-necked flask of chased gold, and from it, into a graduated glass, he poured some drops of an amber liquid wholly unfamiliar to me. I watched him with all my eyes, and noted how high the liquid rose in the measure. He charged a needle-syringe, and, bending again over Aziz, made an injection.

Then all the wonders I had heard of this man became possible, and with an awe which any other physician who had examined Aziz must have felt, I admitted him a miracle-worker. For as I watched, all but breathless, the dead came to life! The glow of health crept upon the olive cheek--the boy moved-- he raised his hands above his head--he sat up, supported by the Chinese doctor!

Fu-Manchu touched some hidden bell. A hideous yellow man with a scarred face entered, carrying a tray upon which were a bowl containing some steaming fluid, apparently soup, what looked like oaten cakes, and a flask of red wine.

As the boy, exhibiting no more unusual symptoms than if he had just awakened from a normal sleep, commenced his repast, Karamaneh drew me gently along the passage into the room which we had first entered. My heart leaped wildly as the marmoset bounded past us to drop hand over hand to the lower apartment in search of its master.

"You see," said Karamaneh, her voice quivering, "he is not dead! But without Fu-Manchu he is dead to me. How can I leave him when he holds the life of Aziz in his hand?"

"You must get me that flask, or some of its contents," I directed. "But tell me, how does he produce the appearance of death?"

"I cannot tell you," she replied. "I do not know. It is something in the wine. In another hour Aziz will be again as you saw him. But see." And, opening a little ebony box, she produced a phial half filled with the amber liquid.

"Good!" I said, and slipped it into my pocket. "When will be the best time to seize Fu-Manchu and to restore your brother?"

"I will let you know," she whispered, and, opening the door, pushed me hurriedly from the room. "He is going away to-night to the north; but you must not come to-night. Quick! Quick! Along the passage. He may call me at any moment."

So, with the phial in my pocket containing a potent preparation unknown to Western science, and with a last long look into the eyes of Karamaneh, I passed out into the narrow alley, out from the fragrant perfumes of that mystery house into the place of Thames-side stenches.

CHAPTER XXII

"**WE MUST ARRANGE** for the house to be raided without delay," said Smith. "This time we are sure of our ally--"

"But we must keep our promise to her," I interrupted.

"You can look after that, Petrie," my friend said. "I will devote the whole of my attention to Dr. Fu-Manchu!" he added grimly.

Up and down the room he paced, gripping the blackened briar between his teeth, so that the muscles stood out squarely upon his lean jaws. The bronze which spoke of the Burmese sun enhanced the brightness of his gray eyes.

"What have I all along maintained?" he jerked, looking back at me across his shoulder--"that, although Karamaneh was one of the strongest weapons in the Doctor's armory, she was one which some day would be turned against him. That day has dawned."

"We must await word from her."

"Quite so."

He knocked out his pipe on the grate. Then:

"Have you any idea of the nature of the fluid in the phial?"

"Not the slightest. And I have none to spare for analytical purposes."

Nayland Smith began stuffing mixture into the hot pipe-bowl, and dropping an almost equal quantity on the floor.

"I cannot rest, Petrie," he said. "I am itching to get to work. Yet, a false move, and--" He lighted his pipe, and stood staring from the window.

"I shall, of course, take a needle-syringe with me," I explained.

Smith made no reply.

"If I but knew the composition of the drug which produced the semblance of death," I continued, "my fame would long survive my ashes."

My friend did not turn. But:

"She said it was something he put in the wine?" he jerked.

"In the wine, yes."

Silence fell. My thoughts reverted to Karamaneh, whom Dr. Fu-Manchu held in bonds stronger than any slave-chains. For, with Aziz, her brother, suspended between life and death, what could she do save obey the mandates of the cunning Chinaman? What perverted genius was his! If that treasury of obscure wisdom which he, perhaps alone of living men, had rifled, could but be thrown open to the sick and suffering, the name of Dr. Fu-Manchu would rank with the golden ones in the history of healing.

Nayland Smith suddenly turned, and the expression upon his face amazed me.

"Look up the next train to L--!" he rapped. "To L--? What--?"

"There's the Bradshaw. We haven't a minute to waste."

In his voice was the imperative note I knew so well; in his eyes was the light which told of an urgent need for action-- a portentous truth suddenly grasped.

"One in half-an-hour--the last."

"We must catch it."

No further word of explanation he vouchsafed, but darted off to dress; for he had spent the afternoon pacing the room in his dressing-gown and smoking without intermission.

Out and to the corner we hurried, and leaped into the first taxi upon the rank. Smith enjoined the man to hasten, and we were off-- all in that whirl of feverish activity which characterized my friend's movements in times of important action.

He sat glancing impatiently from the window and twitching at the lobe of his ear.

"I know you will forgive me, old man," he said, "but there is a little problem which I am trying to work out in my mind. Did you bring the things I mentioned?"

"Yes."

Conversation lapsed, until, just as the cab turned into the station, Smith said: "Should you consider Lord Southery to have been the first constructive engineer of his time, Petrie?"

"Undoubtedly," I replied.

"Greater than Von Homber, of Berlin?"

"Possibly not. But Von Homber has been dead for three years."

"Three years, is it?"

"Roughly."

"Ah!"

We reached the station in time to secure a non-corridor compartment to ourselves, and to allow Smith leisure carefully to inspect the occupants of all the others, from the engine to the guard's van. He was muffled up to the eyes, and he warned me to keep out of sight in the corner of the compartment. In fact, his behavior had me bursting with curiosity. The train having started:

"Don't imagine, Petrie," said Smith "that I am trying to lead you blindfolded in order later to dazzle you with my perspicacity. I am simply afraid that this may be a wild-goose chase. The idea upon which I am acting does not seem to have struck you. I wish it had. The fact would argue in favor of its being, sound."

"At present I am hopelessly mystified."

"Well, then, I will not bias you towards my view. But just study the situation, and see if you can arrive at the reason for this sudden journey. I shall be distinctly encouraged if you succeed."

But I did not succeed, and since Smith obviously was unwilling to enlighten me, I pressed him no more. The train stopped at Rugby, where he was engaged with the stationmaster in making some mysterious arrangements. At L--, however, their object became plain, for a high-power car was awaiting us, and into this we hurried and ere the greater number of passengers had reached the platform were being driven off at headlong speed along the moon-bathed roads.

Twenty minutes' rapid traveling, and a white mansion leaped into the line of sight, standing out vividly against its woody backing.

"Stradwick Hall," said Smith. "The home of Lord Southery. We are first--but Dr. Fu-Manchu was on the train."

Then the truth dawned upon the gloom of my perplexity.

CHAPTER XXIII

"YOUR EXTRAORDINARY proposal fills me with horror, Mr. Smith!"

The sleek little man in the dress suit, who looked like a head waiter (but was the trusted legal adviser of the house of Southery) puffed at his cigar indignantly. Nayland Smith, whose restless pacing had led him to the far end of the library, turned, a remote but virile figure, and looked back to where I stood by the open hearth with the solicitor.

"I am in your hands, Mr. Henderson," he said, and advanced upon the latter, his gray eyes ablaze. "Save for the heir, who is abroad on foreign service, you say there is no kin of Lord Southery to consider. The word rests with you. If I am wrong, and you agree to my proposal, there is none whose susceptibilities will suffer--"

"My own, sir!"

"If I am right, and you prevent me from acting, you become a murderer, Mr. Henderson."

The lawyer started, staring nervously up at Smith, who now towered over him menacingly.

"Lord Southery was a lonely man," continued my friend. "If I could have placed my proposition before one of his blood, I do not doubt what my answer had been. Why do you hesitate? Why do you experience this feeling of horror?"

Mr. Henderson stared down into the fire. His constitutionally ruddy face was pale.

"It is entirely irregular, Mr. Smith. We have not the necessary powers--"

Smith snapped his teeth together impatiently, snatching his watch from his pocket and glancing at it.

"I am vested with the necessary powers. I will give you a written order, sir."

"The proceeding savors of paganism. Such a course might be admissible in China, in Burma--"

"Do you weigh a life against such quibbles? Do you suppose that, granting MY irresponsibility, Dr. Petrie would countenance such a thing if be doubted the necessity?"

Mr. Henderson looked at me with pathetic hesitance.

"There are guests in the house--mourners who attended the ceremony to-day. They--"

"Will never know, if we are in error," interrupted Smith. "Good God! why do you delay?"

"You wish it to be kept secret?"

"You and I, Mr. Henderson, and Dr. Petrie will go now. We require no other witnesses. We are answerable only to our consciences."

The lawyer passed his hand across his damp brow.

"I have never in my life been called upon to come to so momentous a decision in so short a time," he confessed. But, aided by Smith's indomitable will, he made his decision. As its result, we three, looking and feeling like conspirators, hurried across the park beneath a moon whose placidity was a rebuke to the turbulent passions which reared their strangle-growth in the garden of England. Not a breath of wind stirred amid the leaves. The calm of perfect night soothed everything to slumber. Yet, if Smith were right (and I did not doubt him), the green eyes of Dr. Fu-Manchu had looked upon the scene; and I found myself marveling that its beauty had not wilted up. Even now the dread Chinaman must be near to us.

As Mr. Henderson unlocked the ancient iron gates he turned to Nayland Smith. His face twitched oddly.

"Witness that I do this unwillingly," he said--"most unwillingly."

"Mine be the responsibility," was the reply.

Smith's voice quivered, responsive to the nervous vitality pent up within that lean frame. He stood motionless, listening--and I knew for whom he listened. He peered about him to right and left-- and I knew whom he expected but dreaded to see.

Above us now the trees looked down with a solemnity different from the aspect of the monarchs of the park, and the nearer we came to our journey's end the more somber and lowering bent the verdant arch-- or so it seemed.

By that path, patched now with pools of moonlight, Lord Southery had passed upon his bier, with the sun to light his going; by that path several generations of Stradwicks had gone to their last resting-place.

To the doors of the vault the moon rays found free access. No branch, no leaf, intervened. Mr. Henderson's face looked ghastly. The keys which he carried rattled in his hand.

"Light the lantern," he said unsteadily.

Nayland Smith, who again had been peering suspiciously about into the shadows, struck a match and lighted the lantern which he carried. He turned to the solicitor.

"Be calm, Mr. Henderson," he said sternly. "It is your plain duty to your client."

"God be my witness that I doubt it," replied Henderson, and opened the door.

We descended the steps. The air beneath was damp and chill. It touched us as with clammy fingers; and the sensation was not wholly physical.

Before the narrow mansion which now sufficed Lord Southery, the great engineer whom kings had honored, Henderson reeled and clutched at me for support. Smith and I had looked to him for no aid in our uncanny task, and rightly.

With averted eyes he stood over by the steps of the tomb, whilst my friend and myself set to work. In the pursuit of my profession I had undertaken labors as unpleasant, but never amid an environment such as this. It seemed that generations of Stradwicks listened to each turn of every screw.

At last it was done, and the pallid face of Lord Southery questioned the intruding light. Nayland Smith's hand was as steady as a rigid bar when he raised the lantern. Later, I knew, there would be a sudden releasing of the tension of will--a reaction physical and mental-- but not until his work was finished.

That my own hand was steady I ascribed to one thing solely--professional zeal. For, under conditions which, in the event of failure and exposure, must have led to an unpleasant inquiry by the British Medical Association, I was about to attempt an experiment never before essayed by a physician of the white races.

Though I failed, though I succeeded, that it ever came before the B.M.A., or any other council, was improbable; in the former event, all but impossible. But the knowledge that I was about to practice charlatanry, or what any one of my fellow-practitioners must have designated as such, was with me. Yet so profound had my belief become in the extraordinary being whose existence was a danger to the world that I reveled in my immunity from official censure. I was glad that it had fallen to my lot to take at least one step-- though blindly--into the FUTURE of medical science.

So far as my skill bore me, Lord Southery was dead. Unhesitatingly, I would have given a death certificate, save for two considerations. The first, although his latest scheme ran contrary from the interests of Dr. Fu-Manchu, his genius, diverted into other channels, would serve the yellow group better than his death. The second, I had seen the boy Aziz raised from a state as like death as this.

From the phial of amber-hued liquid which I had with me, I charged the needle syringe. I made the injection, and waited.

"If he is really dead!" whispered Smith. "It seems incredible that he can have survived for three days without food. Yet I have known a fakir to go for a week."

Mr. Henderson groaned.

Watch in hand, I stood observing the gray face.

A second passed; another; a third. In the fourth the miracle began. Over the seemingly cold clay crept the hue of pulsing life. It came in waves--in waves which corresponded with the throbbing of the awakened heart; which swept fuller and stronger; which filled and quickened the chilled body.

As we rapidly freed the living man from the trappings of the dead one, Southery, uttering a stifled scream, sat up, looked about him with half-glazed eyes, and fell back. "My God!" cried Smith.

"It is all right," I said, and had time to note how my voice had assumed a professional tone. "A little brandy from my flask is all that is necessary now."

"You have two patients, Doctor," rapped my friend.

Mr. Henderson had fallen in a swoon to the floor of the vault.

"Quiet," whispered Smith; "HE is here."

He extinguished the light.

I supported Lord Southery. "What has happened?" he kept moaning. "Where am I? Oh, God! what has happened?"

I strove to reassure him in a whisper, and placed my traveling coat about him. The door at the top of the mausoleum steps we had reclosed but not relocked. Now, as I upheld the man whom literally we had rescued from the grave, I heard the door reopen. To aid Henderson I could make no move. Smith was breathing hard beside me. I dared not think what was about to happen, nor what its effects might be upon Lord Southery in his exhausted condition.

Through the Memphian dark of the tomb cut a spear of light, touching the last stone of the stairway.

A guttural voice spoke some words rapidly, and I knew that Dr. Fu-Manchu stood at the head of the stairs. Although I could not see my friend, I became aware that Nayland Smith had his revolver in his hand, and I reached into my pocket for mine.

At last the cunning Chinaman was about to fall into a trap. It would require all his genius, I thought, to save him to-night. Unless his suspicions were aroused by the unlocked door, his capture was imminent.

Someone was descending the steps.

In my right hand I held my revolver, and with my left arm about Lord Southery, I waited through ten such seconds of suspense as I have rarely known.

The spear of light plunged into the well of darkness again.

Lord Southery, Smith and myself were hidden by the angle of the wall; but full upon the purplish face of Mr. Henderson the beam shone. In some way it penetrated to the murk in his mind; and he awakened from his swoon with a hoarse cry, struggled to his feet, and stood looking up the stair in a sort of frozen horror.

Smith was past him at a bound. Something flashed towards him as the light was extinguished. I saw him duck, and heard the knife ring upon the floor.

I managed to move sufficiently to see at the top, as I fired up the stairs, the yellow face of Dr. Fu-Manchu, to see the gleaming, chatoyant eyes, greenly terrible, as they sought to pierce the gloom. A flying figure was racing up, three steps at a time (that of a brown man scantily clad). He stumbled and fell, by which I knew that he was hit; but went on again, Smith hard on his heels.

"Mr. Henderson!" I cried, "relight the lantern and take charge of Lord Southery. Here is my flask on the floor. I rely upon you."

Smith's revolver spoke again as I went bounding up the stair. Black against the square of moonlight I saw him stagger, I saw him fall. As he fell, for the third time, I heard the crack of his revolver.

Instantly I was at his side. Somewhere along the black aisle beneath the trees receding footsteps pattered.

"Are you hurt, Smith?" I cried anxiously.

He got upon his feet.

"He has a dacoit with him," he replied, and showed me the long curved knife which he held in his hand, a full inch of the blade bloodstained. "A near thing for me, Petrie."

I heard the whir of a restarted motor.

"We have lost him," said Smith.

"But we have saved Lord Southery," I said. "Fu-Manchu will credit us with a skill as great as his own."

"We must get to the car," Smith muttered, "and try to overtake them. Ugh! my left arm is useless."

"It would be mere waste of time to attempt to overtake them," I argued, "for we have no idea in which direction they will proceed."

"I have a very good idea," snapped Smith. "Stradwick Hall is less than ten miles from the coast. There is only one practicable means of conveying an unconscious man secretly from here to London."

"You think he meant to take him from here to London?"

"Prior to shipping him to China; I think so. His clearing-house is probably on the Thames."

"A boat?"

"A yacht, presumably, is lying off the coast in readiness. Fu-Manchu may even have designed to ship him direct to China."

Lord Southery, a bizarre figure, my traveling coat wrapped about him, and supported by his solicitor, who was almost as pale as himself, emerged from the vault into the moonlight.

"This is a triumph for you, Smith," I said.

The throb of Fu-Manchu's car died into faintness and was lost in the night's silence.

"Only half a triumph," he replied. "But we still have another chance-- the raid on his house. When will the word come from Karamaneh?"

Southery spoke in a weak voice.

"Gentlemen," he said, "it seems I am raised from the dead."

It was the weirdest moment of the night wherein we heard that newly buried man speak from the mold of his tomb.

"Yes," replied Smith slowly, "and spared from the fate of Heaven alone knows how many men of genius. The yellow society lacks a Southery, but that Dr. Fu-Manchu was in Germany three years ago I have reason to believe; so that, even without visiting the grave of your great Teutonic rival, who suddenly died at about that time, I venture to predict that they have a Von Homber. And the futurist group in China knows how to MAKE men work!"

CHAPTER XXIV

FROM THE RESCUE of Lord Southery my story bears me mercilessly on to other things. I may not tarry, as more leisurely penmen, to round my incidents; they were not of my choosing. I may not pause to make you better acquainted with the figure of my drama; its scheme is none of mine. Often enough, in those days, I found a fitness in the lines of Omar:

We are no other than a moving show Of Magic Shadow-shapes that come and go Round with the Sun-illumined Lantern held In Midnight by the Master of the Show.

But "the Master of the Show," in this case, was Dr. Fu-Manchu!

I have been asked many times since the days with which these records deal: Who WAS Dr. Fu-Manchu? Let me confess here that my final answer must be postponed. I can only indicate, at this place, the trend of my reasoning, and leave my reader to form whatever conclusion he pleases.

What group can we isolate and label as responsible for the overthrow of the Manchus? The casual student of modern Chinese history will reply: "Young China." This is unsatisfactory. What do we mean by Young China? In my own hearing Fu-Manchu had disclaimed, with scorn, association with the whole of that movement; and assuming that the name were not an assumed one, he clearly can have been no anti-Manchu, no Republican.

The Chinese Republican is of the mandarin class, but of a new generation which veneers its Confucianism with Western polish. These youthful and unbalanced reformers, in conjunction with older but no less ill-balanced provincial politicians, may be said to represent Young China. Amid such turmoils as this we invariably look for, and invariably find, a Third Party. In my opinion, Dr. Fu-Manchu was one of the leaders of such a party.

Another question often put to me was: Where did the Doctor hide during the time that he pursued his operations in London? This is more susceptible of explanation. For a time Nayland Smith supposed, as I did myself, that the opium den adjacent to the old Ratcliff Highway was the Chinaman's base of operations; later we came to believe that the mansion near Windsor was his hiding-place, and later still, the hulk lying off the downstream flats. But I think I can state with confidence that the spot which he had chosen for his home was neither of these, but the East End riverside building which I was the first to enter. Of this I am all but sure; for the reason that it not only was the home of Fu-Manchu, of Karamaneh, and of her brother, Aziz, but the home of something else-- of something which I shall speak of later.

The dreadful tragedy (or series of tragedies) which attended the raid upon the place will always mark in my memory the supreme horror of a horrible case. Let me endeavor to explain what occurred.

By the aid of Karamaneh, you have seen how we had located the whilom warehouse, which, from the exterior, was so drab and dreary, but which within was a place of wondrous luxury. At the moment selected by our beautiful accomplice, Inspector Weymouth and a body of detectives entirely surrounded it; a river police launch lay off the wharf which opened from it on the river-side; and this upon a singularly black night, than which a better could not have been chosen.

"You will fulfill your promise to me?" said Karamaneh, and looked up into my face.

She was enveloped in a big, loose cloak, and from the shadow of the hood her wonderful eyes gleamed out like stars.

"What do you wish us to do?" asked Nayland Smith.

"You--and Dr. Petrie," she replied swiftly, "must enter first, and bring out Aziz. Until he is safe--until he is out of that place-- you are to make no attempt upon--"

"Upon Dr. Fu-Manchu?" interrupted Weymouth; for Karamaneh hesitated to pronounce the dreaded name, as she always did. "But how can we be sure that there is no trap laid for us?"

The Scotland Yard man did not entirely share my confidence in the integrity of this Eastern girl whom he knew to have been a creature of the Chinaman's.

"Aziz lies in the private room," she explained eagerly, her old accent more noticeable than usual. "There is only one of the Burmese men in the house, and he--he dare not enter without orders!"

"But Fu-Manchu?"

"We have nothing to fear from him. He will be your prisoner within ten minutes from now! I have no time for words-- you must believe!" She stamped her foot impatiently. "And the dacoit?" snapped Smith.

"He also."

"I think perhaps I'd better come in, too," said Weymouth slowly.

Karamaneh shrugged her shoulders with quick impatience, and unlocked the door in the high brick wall which divided the gloomy, evil-smelling court from the luxurious apartments of Dr. Fu-Manchu.

"Make no noise," she warned. And Smith and myself followed her along the uncarpeted passage beyond.

Inspector Weymouth, with a final word of instruction to his second in command, brought up the rear. The door was reclosed; a few paces farther on a second was unlocked. Passing through a small room, unfurnished, a farther passage led us to a balcony. The transition was startling.

Darkness was about us now, and silence: a perfumed, slumberous darkness-- a silence full of mystery. For, beyond the walls of the apartment whereon we looked down waged the unceasing battle of sounds that is the hymn of the great industrial river. About the scented confines which bounded us now floated the smoke-laden vapors of the Lower Thames.

From the metallic but infinitely human clangor of dock-side life, from the unpleasant but homely odors which prevail where ships swallow in and belch out the concrete evidences of commercial prosperity, we had come into this incensed stillness, where one shaded lamp painted dim enlargements of its Chinese silk upon the nearer walls, and left the greater part of the room the darker for its contrast.

Nothing of the Thames-side activity--of the riveting and scraping--the bumping of bales--the bawling of orders--the hiss of steam-- penetrated to this perfumed place. In the pool of tinted light lay the deathlike figure of a dark-haired boy, Karamaneh's muffled form bending over him.

"At last I stand in the house of Dr. Fu-Manchu!" whispered Smith.

Despite the girl's assurance, we knew that proximity to the sinister Chinaman must be fraught with danger. We stood, not in the lion's den, but in the serpent's lair.

From the time when Nayland Smith had come from Burma in pursuit of this advance-guard of a cogent Yellow Peril, the face of Dr. Fu-Manchu rarely had been absent from my dreams day or night. The millions might sleep in peace--the millions in whose cause we labored!--but we who knew the reality of the danger knew that a veritable octopus had fastened upon England-- a yellow octopus whose head was that of Dr. Fu-Manchu, whose tentacles were dacoity, thuggee, modes of death, secret and swift, which in the darkness plucked men from life and left no clew behind.

"Karamaneh!" I called softly.

The muffled form beneath the lamp turned so that the soft light fell upon the lovely face of the slave girl. She who had been a pliant instrument in the hands of Fu-Manchu now was to be the means whereby society should be rid of him.

She raised her finger warningly; then beckoned me to approach.

My feet sinking in the rich pile of the carpet, I came through the gloom of the great apartment in to the patch of light, and, Karamaneh beside me, stood looking down upon the boy. It was Aziz, her brother; dead so far as Western lore had power to judge, but kept alive in that deathlike trance by the uncanny power of the Chinese doctor.

"Be quick," she said; "be quick! Awaken him! I am afraid."

From the case which I carried I took out a needle-syringe and a phial containing a small quantity of amber-hued liquid. It was a drug not to be found in the British Pharmacopoeia. Of its constitution I knew nothing. Although I had had the phial in my possession for some days I had not dared to devote any of its precious contents to analytical purposes. The amber drops spelled life for the boy Aziz, spelled success for the mission of Nayland Smith, spelled ruin for the fiendish Chinaman.

I raised the white coverlet. The boy, fully dressed, lay with his arms crossed upon his breast. I discerned the mark of previous injections as, charging the syringe from the phial, I made what I hoped would be the last of such experiments upon him. I would have given half of my small worldly possessions to have known the real nature of the drug which was now coursing through the veins of Aziz--which was tinting the grayed face with the olive tone of life; which, so far as my medical training bore me, was restoring the dead to life.

But such was not the purpose of my visit. I was come to remove from the house of Dr. Fu-Manchu the living chain which bound Karamaneh to him. The boy alive and free, the Doctor's hold upon the slave girl would be broken.

My lovely companion, her hands convulsively clasped, knelt and devoured with her eyes the face of the boy who was passing through the most amazing physiological change in the history of therapeutics. The peculiar perfume which she wore--which seemed to be a part of her-- which always I associated with her--was faintly perceptible. Karamaneh was breathing rapidly.

"You have nothing to fear," I whispered; "see, he is reviving. In a few moments all will be well with him."

The hanging lamp with its garishly colored shade swung gently above us, wafted, it seemed, by some draught which passed through the apartment. The boy's heavy lids began to quiver, and Karamaneh nervously clutched my arm, and held me so whilst we watched for the long-lashed eyes to open. The stillness of the place was positively unnatural; it seemed inconceivable that all about us was the discordant activity of the commercial East End. Indeed, this eerie silence was becoming oppressive; it began positively to appall me.

Inspector Weymouth's wondering face peeped over my shoulder.

"Where is Dr. Fu-Manchu?" I whispered, as Nayland Smith in turn appeared beside me. "I cannot understand the silence of the house--"

"Look about," replied Karamaneh, never taking her eyes from the face of Aziz.

I peered around the shadowy walls. Tall glass cases there were, shelves and niches: where once, from the gallery above, I had seen the tubes and retorts, the jars of unfamiliar organisms, the books of unfamiliar lore, the impedimenta of the occult student and man of science--the visible evidences of Fu-Manchu's presence. Shelves--cases--niches--were bare. Of the complicated appliances unknown to civilized laboratories, wherewith he pursued his strange experiments, of the tubes wherein he isolated the bacilli of unclassified diseases, of the yellow-bound volumes for a glimpse at which (had they known of their contents) the great men of Harley Street would have given a fortune--no trace remained. The silken cushions; the inlaid tables; all were gone.

The room was stripped, dismantled. Had Fu-Manchu fled? The silence assumed a new significance. His dacoits and kindred ministers of death all must have fled, too.

"You have let him escape us!" I said rapidly. "You promised to aid us to capture him--to send us a message-- and you have delayed until--"

"No," she said; "no!" and clutched at my arm again. "Oh! is he not reviving slowly? Are you sure you have made no mistake?"

Her thoughts were all for the boy; and her solicitude touched me. I again examined Aziz, the most remarkable patient of my busy professional career.

As I counted the strengthening pulse, he opened his dark eyes-- which were so like the eyes of Karamaneh--and, with the girl's eager arms tightly about him, sat up, looking wonderingly around.

Karamaneh pressed her cheek to his, whispering loving words in that softly spoken Arabic which had first betrayed her nationality to Nayland Smith. I handed her my flask, which I had filled with wine.

"My promise is fulfilled!" I said. "You are free! Now for Fu-Manchu! But first let us admit the police to this house; there is something uncanny in its stillness."

"No," she replied. "First let my brother be taken out and placed in safety. Will you carry him?"

She raised her face to that of Inspector Weymouth, upon which was written awe and wonder.

The burly detective lifted the boy as tenderly as a woman, passed through the shadows to the stairway, ascended, and was swallowed up in the gloom. Nayland Smith's eyes gleamed feverishly. He turned to Karamaneh.

"You are not playing with us?" he said harshly. "We have done our part; it remains for you to do yours."

"Do not speak so loudly," the girl begged. "HE is near us-- and, oh, God, I fear him so!"

"Where is he?" persisted my friend.

Karamaneh's eyes were glassy with fear now.

"You must not touch him until the police are here," she said-- but from the direction of her quick, agitated glances I knew that, her brother safe now, she feared for me, and for me alone. Those glances sent my blood dancing; for Karamaneh was an Eastern jewel which any man of flesh and blood must have coveted had he known it to lie within his reach. Her eyes were twin lakes of mystery which, more than once, I had known the desire to explore.

"Look--beyond that curtain"--her voice was barely audible--"but do not enter. Even as he is, I fear him."

Her voice, her palpable agitation, prepared us for something extraordinary. Tragedy and Fu-Manchu were never far apart. Though we were two, and help was so near, we were in the abode of the most cunning murderer who ever came out of the East.

It was with strangely mingled emotions that I crossed the thick carpet, Nayland Smith beside me, and drew aside the draperies concealing a door, to which Karamaneh had pointed. Then, upon looking into the dim place beyond, all else save what it held was forgotten.

We looked upon a small, square room, the walls draped with fantastic Chinese tapestry, the floor strewn with cushions; and reclining in a corner, where the faint, blue light from a lamp, placed upon a low table, painted grotesque shadows about the cavernous face-- was Dr. Fu-Manchu!

At sight of him my heart leaped--and seemed to suspend its functions, so intense was the horror which this man's presence inspired in me. My hand clutching the curtain, I stood watching him. The lids veiled the malignant green eyes, but the thin lips seemed to smile. Then Smith silently pointed to the hand which held a little pipe. A sickly perfume assailed my nostrils, and the explanation of the hushed silence, and the ease with which we had thus far executed our plan, came to me. The cunning mind was torpid-- lost in a brutish world of dreams.

Fu-Manchu was in an opium sleep!

The dim light traced out a network of tiny lines, which covered the yellow face from the pointed chin to the top of the great domed brow, and formed deep shadow pools in the hollows beneath his eyes. At last we had triumphed.

I could not determine the depth of his obscene trance; and mastering some of my repugnance, and forgetful of Karamaneh's warning, I was about to step forward into the room, loaded with its nauseating opium fumes, when a soft breath fanned my cheek.

"Do not go in!" came Karamaneh's warning voice--hushed--trembling.

Her little hand grasped my arm. She drew Smith and myself back from the door.

"There is danger there!" she whispered.

"Do not enter that room! The police must reach him in some way-- and drag him out! Do not enter that room!"

The girl's voice quivered hysterically; her eyes blazed into savage flame. The fierce resentment born of dreadful wrongs was consuming her now; but fear of Fu-Manchu held her yet. Inspector Weymouth came down the stairs and joined us.

"I have sent the boy to Ryman's room at the station," he said. "The divisional surgeon will look after him until you arrive, Dr. Petrie. All is ready now. The launch is just off the wharf and every side of the place under observation. Where's our man?"

He drew a pair of handcuffs from his pocket and raised his eyebrows interrogatively. The absence of sound-- of any demonstration from the uncanny Chinaman whom he was there to arrest--puzzled him.

Nayland Smith jerked his thumb toward the curtain.

At that, and before we could utter a word, Weymouth stepped to the draped door. He was a man who drove straight at his goal and saved reflections for subsequent leisure. I think, moreover, that the atmosphere of the place (stripped as it was it retained its heavy, voluptuous perfume) had begun to get a hold upon him. He was anxious to shake it off; to be up and doing.

He pulled the curtain aside and stepped into the room. Smith and I perforce followed him. Just within the door the three of us stood looking across at the limp thing which had spread terror throughout the Eastern and Western world. Helpless as Fu-Manchu was, he inspired terror now, though the giant intellect was inert--stupefied.

In the dimly lit apartment we had quitted I heard Karamaneh utter a stifled scream. But it came too late.

As though cast up by a volcano, the silken cushions, the inlaid table with its blue-shaded lamp, the garish walls, the sprawling figure with the ghastly light playing upon its features--quivered, and shot upward!

So it seemed to me; though, in the ensuing instant I remembered, too late, a previous experience of the floors of Fu-Manchu's private apartments; I knew what had indeed befallen us. A trap had been released beneath our feet.

I recall falling--but have no recollection of the end of my fall-- of the shock marking the drop. I only remember fighting for my life against a stifling something which had me by the throat. I knew that I was being suffocated, but my hands met only the deathly emptiness.

Into a poisonous well of darkness I sank. I could not cry out. I was helpless. Of the fate of my companions I knew nothing-- could surmise nothing. Then. . .all consciousness ended.

CHAPTER XXV

I WAS BEING carried along a dimly lighted, tunnel-like place, slung, sackwise, across the shoulder of a Burman. He was not a big man, but he supported my considerable weight with apparent ease. A deadly nausea held me, but the rough handling had served to restore me to consciousness. My hands and feet were closely lashed. I hung limply as a wet towel: I felt that this spark of tortured life which had flickered up in me must ere long finally become extinguished.

A fancy possessed me, in these the first moments of my restoration to the world of realities, that I had been smuggled into China; and as I swung head downward I told myself that the huge, puffy things which strewed the path were a species of giant toadstool, unfamiliar to me and possibly peculiar to whatever district of China I now was in.

The air was hot, steamy, and loaded with a smell as of rotting vegetation. I wondered why my bearer so scrupulously avoided touching any of the unwholesome-looking growths in passing through what seemed a succession of cellars, but steered a tortuous course among the bloated, unnatural shapes, lifting his bare brown feet with a catlike delicacy.

He passed under a low arch, dropped me roughly to the ground and ran back. Half stunned, I lay watching the agile brown body melt into the distances of the cellars. Their walls and roof seemed to emit a faint, phosphorescent light.

"Petrie!" came a weak voice from somewhere ahead. . . ."Is that you, Petrie?"

It was Nayland Smith!

"Smith!" I said, and strove to sit up. But the intense nausea overcame me, so that I all but swooned.

I heard his voice again, but could attach no meaning to the words which he uttered. A sound of terrific blows reached my ears, too. The Burman reappeared, bending under the heavy load which he bore. For, as he picked his way through the bloated things which grew upon the floors of the cellars, I realized that he was carrying the inert body of Inspector Weymouth. And I found time to compare the strength of the little brown man with that of a Nile beetle, which can raise many times its own weight. Then, behind him, appeared a second figure, which immediately claimed the whole of my errant attention.

"Fu-Manchu!" hissed my friend, from the darkness which concealed him.

It was indeed none other than Fu-Manchu--the Fu-Manchu whom we had thought to be helpless. The deeps of the Chinaman's cunning-- the fine quality of his courage, were forced upon me as amazing facts.

He had assumed the appearance of a drugged opium-smoker so well as to dupe me--a medical man; so well as to dupe Karamaneh-- whose experience of the noxious habit probably was greater than my own. And, with the gallows dangling before him, he had waited-- played the part of a lure-- whilst a body of police actually surrounded the place!

I have since thought that the room probably was one which he actually used for opium debauches, and the device of the trap was intended to protect him during the comatose period.

Now, holding a lantern above his head, the deviser of the trap where into we, mouse like, had blindly entered, came through the cellars, following the brown man who carried Weymouth. The faint rays of the lantern (it apparently contained a candle) revealed a veritable forest of the gigantic fungi--poisonously colored-- hideously swollen--climbing from the floor up the slimy walls-- climbing like horrid parasites to such part of the arched roof as was visible to me.

Fu-Manchu picked his way through the fungi ranks as daintily as though the distorted, tumid things had been viper-headed.

The resounding blows which I had noted before, and which had never ceased, culminated in a splintering crash. Dr. Fu-Manchu and his servant, who carried the apparently insensible detective, passed in under the arch, Fu-Manchu glancing back once along the passages. The lantern he extinguished, or concealed; and whilst I waited, my mind dully surveying, memories of all the threats which this uncanny being had uttered, a distant clamor came to my ears.

Then, abruptly, it ceased. Dr. Fu-Manchu had closed a heavy door; and to my surprise I perceived that the greater part of it was of glass. The will-o'-the-wisp glow which played around the fungi rendered the vista of the cellars faintly luminous, and visible to me from where I lay. Fu-Manchu spoke softly. His voice, its guttural note alternating with a sibilance on certain words, betrayed no traces of agitation. The man's unbroken calm had in it something inhuman. For he had just perpetrated an act of daring unparalleled in my experience, and, in the clamor now shut out by the glass door I tardily recognized the entrance of the police into some barricaded part of the house-- the coming of those who would save us--who would hold the Chinese doctor for the hangman!

"I have decided," he said deliberately, "that you are more worthy of my attention than I had formerly supposed. A man who can solve the secret of the Golden Elixir (I had not solved it; I had merely stolen some) should be a valuable acquisition to my Council. The extent of the plans of Mr. Commissioner Nayland Smith and of the English Scotland Yard it is incumbent upon me to learn. Therefore, gentlemen, you live--for the present!"

"And you'll swing," came Weymouth's hoarse voice, "in the near future! You and all your yellow gang!"

"I trust not," was the placid reply. "Most of my people are safe: some are shipped as lascars upon the liners; others have departed by different means. Ah!"

That last word was the only one indicative of excitement which had yet escaped him. A disk of light danced among the brilliant poison hues of the passages--but no sound reached us; by which I knew that the glass door must fit almost hermetically. It was much cooler here than in the place through which we had passed, and the nausea began to leave me, my brain to grow more clear. Had I known what was to follow I should have cursed the lucidity of mind which now came to me; I should have prayed for oblivion-- to be spared the sight of that which ensued.

"It's Logan!" cried Inspector Weymouth; and I could tell that he was struggling to free himself of his bonds. From his voice it was evident that he, too, was recovering from the effects of the narcotic which had been administered to us all.

"Logan!" he cried. "Logan! This way--HELP!"

But the cry beat back upon us in that enclosed space and seemed to carry no farther than the invisible walls of our prison.

"The door fits well," came Fu-Manchu's mocking voice. "It is fortunate for us all that it is so. This is my observation window, Dr. Petrie, and you are about to enjoy an unique opportunity of studying fungology. I have already drawn your attention to the anaesthetic properties of the lycoperdon, or common puff-ball. You may have recognized the fumes? The chamber into which you rashly precipitated yourselves was charged with them. By a process of my own I have greatly enhanced the value of the puff-ball in this respect. Your friend, Mr. Weymouth, proved the most obstinate subject; but he succumbed in fifteen seconds."

"Logan! Help! HELP! This way, man!"

Something very like fear sounded in Weymouth's voice now. Indeed, the situation was so uncanny that it almost seemed unreal. A group of men had entered the farthermost cellars, led by one who bore an electric pocket-lamp. The hard, white ray danced from bloated gray fungi to others of nightmare shape, of dazzling, venomous brilliance. The mocking, lecture-room voice continued:

"Note the snowy growth upon the roof, Doctor. Do not be deceived by its size. It is a giant variety of my own culture and is of the order empusa. You, in England, are familiar with the death of the common house-fly-- which is found attached to the window-pane by a coating of white mold. I have developed the spores of this mold and have produced a giant species. Observe the interesting effect of the strong light upon my orange and blue amanita fungus!"

Hard beside me I heard Nayland Smith groan, Weymouth had become suddenly silent. For my own part, I could have shrieked in pure horror. FOR I KNEW WHAT WAS COMING. I realized in one agonized instant the significance of the dim lantern, of the careful progress through the subterranean fungi grove, of the care with which Fu-Manchu and his servant had avoided touching any of the growths. I knew, now, that Dr. Fu-Manchu was the greatest fungologist the world had ever known; was a poisoner to whom the Borgias were as children--and I knew that the detectives blindly were walking into a valley of death.

Then it began--the unnatural scene--the saturnalia of murder.

Like so many bombs the brilliantly colored caps of the huge toadstool-like things alluded to by the Chinaman exploded, as the white ray sought them out in the darkness which alone preserved their existence. A brownish cloud--I could not determine whether liquid or powdery-- arose in the cellar.

I tried to close my eyes--or to turn them away from the reeling forms of the men who were trapped in that poison-hole. It was useless:

I must look.

The bearer of the lamp had dropped it, but the dim, eerily illuminated gloom endured scarce a second. A bright light sprang up-- doubtless at the touch of the fiendish being who now resumed speech:

"Observe the symptoms of delirium, Doctor!" Out there, beyond the glass door, the unhappy victims were laughing-- tearing their garments from their bodies--leaping--waving their arms-- were become MANIACS!

"We will now release the ripe spores of giant entpusa," continued the wicked voice. "The air of the second cellar being super-charged with oxygen, they immediately germinate. Ah! it is a triumph! That process is the scientific triumph of my life!"

Like powdered snow the white spores fell from the roof, frosting the writhing shapes of the already poisoned men. Before my horrified gaze, THE FUNGUS GREW; it spread from the head to the, feet of those it touched; it enveloped them as in glittering shrouds. . . .

"They die like flies!" screamed Fu-Manchu, with a sudden febrile excitement; and I felt assured of something I had long suspected: that that magnificent, perverted brain was the brain of a homicidal maniac--though Smith would never accept the theory.

"It is my fly-trap!" shrieked the Chinaman. "And I am the god of destruction!"

CHAPTER XXVI

THE CLAMMY TOUCH of the mist revived me. The culmination of the scene in the poison cellars, together with the effects of the fumes which I had inhaled again, had deprived me of consciousness. Now I knew that I was afloat on the river. I still was bound: furthermore, a cloth was wrapped tightly about my mouth, and I was secured to a ring in the deck.

By moving my aching head to the left I could look down into the oily water; by moving it to the right I could catch a glimpse of the empurpled face of Inspector Weymouth, who, similarly bound and gagged, lay beside me, but only of the feet and legs of Nayland Smith. For I could not turn my head sufficiently far to see more.

We were aboard an electric launch. I heard the hated guttural voice of Fu-Manchu, subdued now to its habitual calm, and my heart leaped to hear the voice that answered him. It was that of Karamaneh. His triumph was complete. Clearly his plans for departure were complete; his slaughter of the police in the underground passages had been a final reckless demonstration of which the Chinaman's subtle cunning would have been incapable had he not known his escape from the country to be assured.

What fate was in store for us? How would he avenge himself upon the girl who had betrayed him to his enemies? What portion awaited those enemies? He seemed to have formed the singular determination to smuggle me into China-- but what did he purpose in the case of Weymouth, and in the case of Nayland Smith?

All but silently we were feeling our way through the mist. Astern died the clangor of dock and wharf into a remote discord. Ahead hung the foggy curtain veiling the traffic of the great waterway; but through it broke the calling of sirens, the tinkling of bells.

The gentle movement of the screw ceased altogether. The launch lay heaving slightly upon the swells.

A distant throbbing grew louder--and something advanced upon us through the haze.

A bell rang and muffled by the fog a voice proclaimed itself-- a voice which I knew. I felt Weymouth writhing impotently beside me; heard him mumbling incoherently; and I knew that he, too, had recognized the voice.

It was that of Inspector Ryman of the river police and their launch was within biscuit-throw of that upon which we lay!

"'Hoy! 'Hoy!"

I trembled. A feverish excitement claimed me. They were hailing us.

We carried no lights; but now--and ignoring the pain which shot from my spine to my skull I craned my neck to the left--the port light of the police launch glowed angrily through the mist.

I was unable to utter any save mumbling sounds, and my companions were equally helpless. It was a desperate position. Had the police seen us or had they hailed at random? The light drew nearer.

"Launch, 'hoy!"

They had seen us! Fu-Manchu's guttural voice spoke shortly-- and our screw began to revolve again; we leaped ahead into the bank of darkness. Faint grew the light of the police launch--and was gone. But I heard Ryman's voice shouting.

"Full speed!" came faintly through the darkness. "Port! Port!"

Then the murk closed down, and with our friends far astern of us we were racing deeper into the fog banks--speeding seaward; though of this I was unable to judge at the time.

On we raced, and on, sweeping over growing swells. Once, a black, towering shape dropped down upon us. Far above, lights blazed, bells rang, vague cries pierced the fog. The launch pitched and rolled perilously, but weathered the wash of the liner which so nearly had concluded this episode. It was such a journey as I had taken once before, early in our pursuit of the genius of the Yellow Peril; but this was infinitely more terrible; for now we were utterly in Fu-Manchu's power.

A voice mumbled in my ear. I turned my bound-up face; and Inspector Weymouth raised his hands in the dimness and partly slipped the bandage from his mouth.

"I've been working at the cords since we left those filthy cellars," he whispered. "My wrists are all cut, but when I've got out a knife and freed my ankles--"

Smith had kicked him with his bound feet. The detective slipped the bandage back to position and placed his hands behind him again. Dr. Fu-Manchu, wearing a heavy overcoat but no hat, came aft. He was dragging Karamaneh by the wrists. He seated himself on the cushions near to us, pulling the girl down beside him. Now, I could see her face--and the expression in her beautiful eyes made me writhe.

Fu-Manchu was watching us, his discolored teeth faintly visible in the dim light, to which my eyes were becoming accustomed.

"Dr. Petrie," he said, "you shall be my honored guest at my home in China. You shall assist me to revolutionize chemistry. Mr. Smith, I fear you know more of my plans than I had deemed it possible for you to have learned, and I am anxious to know if you have a confidant. Where your memory fails you, and my files and wire jackets prove ineffectual, Inspector Weymouth's recollections may prove more accurate."

He turned to the cowering girl--who shrank away from him in pitiful, abject terror.

"In my hands, Doctor," he continued, "I hold a needle charged with a rare culture. It is the link between the bacilli and the fungi. You have seemed to display an undue interest in the peach and pearl which render my Karamaneh so delightful, In the supple grace of her movements and the sparkle of her eyes. You can never devote your whole mind to those studies which I have planned for you whilst such distractions exist. A touch of this keen point, and the laughing Karamaneh becomes the shrieking hag--the maniacal, mowing--"

Then, with an ox-like rush, Weymouth was upon him!

Karamaneh, wrought upon past endurance, with a sobbing cry, sank to the deck-- and lay still. I managed to writhe into a half-sitting posture, and Smith rolled aside as the detective and the Chinaman crashed down together.

Weymouth had one big hand at the Doctor's yellow throat; with his left he grasped the Chinaman's right. It held the needle.

Now, I could look along, the length of the little craft, and, so far as it was possible to make out in the fog, only one other was aboard-- the half-clad brown man who navigated her--and who had carried us through the cellars. The murk had grown denser and now shut us in like a box. The throb of the motor--the hissing breath of the two who fought-- with so much at issue--these sounds and the wash of the water alone broke the eerie stillness.

By slow degrees, and with a reptilian agility horrible to watch, Fu-Manchu was neutralizing the advantage gained by Weymouth. His clawish fingers were fast in the big man's throat; the right hand with its deadly needle was forcing down the left of his opponent. He had been underneath, but now he was gaining the upper place. His powers of physical endurance must have been truly marvelous. His breath was whistling through his nostrils significantly, but Weymouth was palpably tiring.

The latter suddenly changed his tactics. By a supreme effort, to which he was spurred, I think, by the growing proximity of the needle, he raised Fu-Manchu--by the throat and arm-- and pitched him sideways.

The Chinaman's grip did not relax, and the two wrestlers dropped, a writhing mass, upon the port cushions. The launch heeled over, and my cry of horror was crushed back into my throat by the bandage. For, as Fu-Manchu sought to extricate himself, he overbalanced-- fell back--and, bearing Weymouth with him--slid into the river!

The mist swallowed them up.

There are moments of which no man can recall his mental impressions, moments so acutely horrible that, mercifully, our memory retains nothing of the emotions they occasioned. This was one of them. A chaos ruled in my mind. I had a vague belief that the Burman, forward, glanced back. Then the course of the launch was changed. How long intervened between the tragic end of that Gargantuan struggle and the time when a black wall leaped suddenly up before us I cannot pretend to state.

With a sickening jerk we ran aground. A loud explosion ensued, and I clearly remember seeing the brown man leap out into the fog-- which was the last I saw of him.

Water began to wash aboard.

Fully alive to our imminent peril, I fought with the cords that bound me; but I lacked poor Weymouth's strength of wrist, and I began to accept as a horrible and imminent possibility, a death from drowning, within six feet of the bank.

Beside me, Nayland Smith was straining and twisting. I think his object was to touch Karamaneh, in the hope of arousing her. Where he failed in his project, the inflowing water succeeded. A silent prayer of thankfulness came from my very soul when I saw her stir--when I saw her raise her hands to her head-- and saw the big, horror-bright eyes gleam through the mist veil.

CHAPTER XXVII

WE QUITTED the wrecked launch but a few seconds before her stern settled down into the river. Where the mud-bank upon which we found ourselves was situated we had no idea. But at least it was terra firma and we were free from Dr. Fu-Manchu.

Smith stood looking out towards the river.

"My God!" he groaned. "My God!"

He was thinking, as I was, of Weymouth.

And when, an hour later, the police boat located us (on the mud-flats below Greenwich) and we heard that the toll of the poison cellars was eight men, we also heard news of our brave companion.

"Back there in the fog, sir," reported Inspector Ryman, who was in charge, and his voice was under poor command, "there was an uncanny howling, and peals of laughter that I'm going to dream about for weeks--"

Karamaneh, who nestled beside me like a frightened child, shivered; and I knew that the needle had done its work, despite Weymouth's giant strength.

Smith swallowed noisily.

"Pray God the river has that yellow Satan," he said. "I would sacrifice a year of my life to see his rat's body on the end of a grappling-iron!"

We were a sad party that steamed through the fog homeward that night. It seemed almost like deserting a staunch comrade to leave the spot-- so nearly as we could locate it--where Weymouth had put up that last gallant fight. Our helplessness was pathetic, and although, had the night been clear as crystal, I doubt if we could have acted otherwise, it came to me that this stinking murk was a new enemy which drove us back in coward retreat.

But so many were the calls upon our activity, and so numerous the stimulants to our initiative in those times, that soon we had matter to relieve our minds from this stress of sorrow.

There was Karamaneh to be considered--Karamaneh and her brother. A brief counsel was held, whereat it was decided that for the present they should be lodged at a hotel.

"I shall arrange," Smith whispered to me, for the girl was watching us, "to have the place patrolled night and day."

"You cannot suppose--"

"Petrie! I cannot and dare not suppose Fu-Manchu dead until with my own eyes I have seen him so!"

Accordingly we conveyed the beautiful Oriental girl and her brother away from that luxurious abode in its sordid setting. I will not dwell upon the final scene in the poison cellars lest I be accused of accumulating horror for horror's sake. Members of the fire brigade, helmed against contagion, brought out the bodies of the victims wrapped in their living shrouds. . . .

From Karamaneh we learned much of Fu-Manchu, little of herself.

"What am I? Does my poor history matter--to anyone?" was her answer to questions respecting herself.

And she would droop her lashes over her dark eyes.

The dacoits whom the Chinaman had brought to England originally numbered seven, we learned. As you, having followed me thus far, will be aware, we had thinned the ranks of the Burmans. Probably only one now remained in England. They had lived in a camp in the grounds of the house near Windsor (which, as we had learned at the time of its destruction, the Doctor had bought outright). The Thames had been his highway.

Other members of the group had occupied quarters in various parts of the East End, where sailormen of all nationalities congregate. Shen-Yan's had been the East End headquarters. He had employed the hulk from the time of his arrival, as a laboratory for a certain class of experiments undesirable in proximity to a place of residence.

Nayland Smith asked the girl on one occasion if the Chinaman had had a private sea-going vessel, and she replied in the affirmative. She had never been on board, however, had never even set eyes upon it, and could give us no information respecting its character. It had sailed for China.

"You are sure," asked Smith keenly, "that it has actually left?"

"I understood so, and that we were to follow by another route."

"It would have been difficult for Fu-Manchu to travel by a passenger boat?"

"I cannot say what were his plans."

In a state of singular uncertainty, then, readily to be understood, we passed the days following the tragedy which had deprived us of our fellow-worker.

Vividly I recall the scene at poor Weymouth's home, on the day that we visited it. I then made the acquaintance of the Inspector's brother. Nayland Smith gave him a detailed account of the last scene.

"Out there in the mist," he concluded wearily, "it all seemed very unreal."

"I wish to God it had been!"

"Amen to that, Mr. Weymouth. But your brother made a gallant finish. If ridding the world of Fu-Manchu were the only good deed to his credit, his life had been well spent."

James Weymouth smoked awhile in thoughtful silence. Though but four and a half miles S.S.E. of St. Paul's the quaint little cottage, with its rustic garden, shadowed by the tall trees which had so lined the village street before motor 'buses were, was a spot as peaceful and secluded as any in broad England. But another shadow lay upon it to-day--chilling, fearful. An incarnate evil had come out of the dim East and in its dying malevolence had touched this home.

"There are two things I don't understand about it, sir," continued Weymouth. "What was the meaning of the horrible laughter which the river police heard in the fog? And where are the bodies?"

Karamaneh, seated beside me, shuddered at the words. Smith, whose restless spirit granted him little repose, paused in his aimless wanderings about the room and looked at her.

In these latter days of his Augean labors to purge England of the unclean thing which had fastened upon her, my friend was more lean and nervous-looking than I had ever known him. His long residence in Burma had rendered him spare and had burned his naturally dark skin to a coppery hue; but now his gray eyes had grown feverishly bright and his face so lean as at times to appear positively emaciated. But I knew that he was as fit as ever.

"This lady may be able to answer your first question," he said. "She and her brother were for some time in the household of Dr. Fu-Manchu. In fact, Mr. Weymouth, Karamaneh, as her name implies, was a slave."

Weymouth glanced at the beautiful, troubled face with scarcely veiled distrust. "You don't look as though you had come from China, miss," he said, with a sort of unwilling admiration.

"I do not come from China," replied Karamaneh. "My father was a pure Bedawee. But my history does not matter." (At times there was something imperious in her manner; and to this her musical accent added force.) "When your brave brother, Inspector Weymouth, and Dr. Fu-Manchu, were swallowed up by the river, Fu-Manchu held a poisoned needle in his hand. The laughter meant that the needle had done its work. Your brother had become mad!"

Weymouth turned aside to hide his emotion. "What was on the needle?" he asked huskily.

"It was something which he prepared from the venom of a kind of swamp adder," she answered. "It produces madness, but not always death."

"He would have had a poor chance," said Smith, "even had he been in complete possession of his senses. At the time of the encounter we must have been some considerable distance from shore, and the fog was impenetrable."

"But how do you account for the fact that neither of the bodies have been recovered?"

"Ryman of the river police tells me that persons lost at that point are not always recovered--or not until a considerable time later."

There was a faint sound from the room above. The news of that tragic happening out in the mist upon the Thames had prostrated poor Mrs. Weymouth.

"She hasn't been told half the truth," said her brother-in-law. "She doesn't know about--the poisoned needle. What kind of fiend was this Dr. Fu-Manchu?" He burst out into a sudden blaze of furious resentment. "John never told me much, and you have let mighty little leak into the papers. What was he? Who was he?"

Half he addressed the words to Smith, half to Karamaneh.

"Dr. Fu-Manchu," replied the former, "was the ultimate expression of Chinese cunning; a phenomenon such as occurs but once in many generations. He was a superman of incredible genius, who, had he willed, could have revolutionized science. There is a superstition in some parts of China according to which, under certain peculiar conditions (one of which is proximity to a deserted burial-ground) an evil spirit of incredible age may enter unto the body of a new-born infant. All my efforts thus far have not availed me to trace the genealogy of the man called Dr. Fu-Manchu. Even Karamaneh cannot help me in this. But I have sometimes thought that he was a member of a certain very old Kiangsu family--and that the peculiar conditions I have mentioned prevailed at his birth!"

Smith, observing our looks of amazement, laughed shortly, and quite mirthlessly.

"Poor old Weymouth!" he jerked. "I suppose my labors are finished; but I am far from triumphant. Is there any improvement in Mrs. Weymouth's condition?"

"Very little," was the reply; "she has lain in a semi-conscious state since the news came. No one had any idea she would take it so. At one time we were afraid her brain was going. She seemed to have delusions."

Smith spun round upon Weymouth.

"Of what nature?" he asked rapidly.

The other pulled nervously at his mustache.

"My wife has been staying with her," he explained, "since--it happened; and for the last three nights poor John's widow has cried out at the same time--half-past two--that someone was knocking on the door."

"What door?"

"That door yonder--the street door."

All our eyes turned in the direction indicated.

"John often came home at half-past two from the Yard," continued Weymouth; "so we naturally thought poor Mary was wandering in her mind. But last night--and it's not to be wondered at--my wife couldn't sleep, and she was wide awake at half-past two."

"Well?"

Nayland Smith was standing before him, alert, bright-eyed.

"She heard it, too!"

The sun was streaming into the cozy little sitting-room; but I will confess that Weymouth's words chilled me uncannily. Karamaneh laid her hand upon mine, in a quaint, childish fashion peculiarly her own. Her hand was cold, but its touch thrilled me. For Karamaneh was not a child, but a rarely beautiful girl-- a pearl of the East such as many a monarch has fought for.

"What then?" asked Smith.

"She was afraid to move--afraid to look from the window!"

My friend turned and stared hard at me.

"A subjective hallucination, Petrie?"

"In all probability," I replied. "You should arrange that your wife be relieved in her trying duties, Mr. Weymouth. It is too great a strain for an inexperienced nurse."

CHAPTER XXVIII

OF ALL THAT WE had hoped for in our pursuit of Fu-Manchu how little had we accomplished. Excepting Karamaneh and her brother (who were victims and not creatures of the Chinese doctor's) not one of the formidable group had fallen alive into our hands. Dreadful crimes had marked Fu-Manchu's passage through the land. Not one-half of the truth (and nothing of the later developments) had been made public. Nayland Smith's authority was sufficient to control the press.

In the absence of such a veto a veritable panic must have seized upon the entire country; for a monster--a thing more than humanly evil--existed in our midst.

Always Fu-Manchu's secret activities had centered about the great waterway. There was much of poetic justice in his end; for the Thames had claimed him, who so long had used the stream as a highway for the passage to and fro for his secret forces. Gone now were the yellow men who had been the instruments of his evil will; gone was the giant intellect which had controlled the complex murder machine. Karamaneh, whose beauty he had used as a lure, at last was free, and no more with her smile would tempt men to death-- that her brother might live.

Many there are, I doubt not, who will regard the Eastern girl with horror. I ask their forgiveness in that I regarded her quite differently. No man having seen her could have condemned her unheard. Many, having looked into her lovely eyes, had they found there what I found, must have forgiven her almost any crime.

That she valued human life but little was no matter for wonder. Her nationality--her history--furnished adequate excuse for an attitude not condonable in a European equally cultured.

But indeed let me confess that hers was a nature incomprehensible to me in some respects. The soul of Karamaneh was a closed book to my short-sighted Western eyes. But the body of Karamaneh was exquisite; her beauty of a kind that was a key to the most extravagant rhapsodies of Eastern poets. Her eyes held a challenge wholly Oriental in its appeal; her lips, even in repose, were a taunt. And, herein, East is West and West is East.

Finally, despite her lurid history, despite the scornful self-possession of which I knew her capable, she was an unprotected girl-- in years, I believe, a mere child--whom Fate had cast in my way. At her request, we had booked passages for her brother and herself to Egypt. The boat sailed in three days. But Karamaneh's beautiful eyes were sad; often I detected tears on the black lashes. Shall I endeavor to describe my own tumultuous, conflicting emotions? It would be useless, since I know it to be impossible. For in those dark eyes burned a fire I might not see; those silken lashes veiled a message I dared not read.

Nayland Smith was not blind to the facts of the complicated situation. I can truthfully assert that he was the only man of my acquaintance who, having come in contact with Karamaneh, had kept his head.

We endeavored to divert her mind from the recent tragedies by a round of amusements, though with poor Weymouth's body still at the mercy of unknown waters Smith and I made but a poor show of gayety; and I took a gloomy pride in the admiration which our lovely companion everywhere excited. I learned, in those days, how rare a thing in nature is a really beautiful woman.

One afternoon we found ourselves at an exhibition of water colors in Bond Street. Karamaneh was intensely interested in the subjects of the drawings--which were entirely Egyptian. As usual, she furnished matter for comment amongst the other visitors, as did the boy, Aziz, her brother, anew upon the world from his living grave in the house of Dr. Fu-Manchu.

Suddenly Aziz clutched at his sister's arm, whispering rapidly in Arabic. I saw her peach like color fade; saw her become pale and wild-eyed--the haunted Karamaneh of the old days.

She turned to me.

"Dr. Petrie--he says that Fu-Manchu is here!"

"Where?"

Nayland Smith rapped out the question violently, turning in a flash from the picture which he was examining.

"In this room!" she whispered glancing furtively, affrightedly about her. "Something tells Aziz when HE is near--and I, too, feel strangely afraid. Oh, can it be that he is not dead!"

She held my arm tightly. Her brother was searching the room with big, velvet black eyes. I studied the faces of the several visitors; and Smith was staring about him with the old alert look, and tugging nervously at the lobe of his ear. The name of the giant foe of the white race instantaneously had strung him up to a pitch of supreme intensity.

Our united scrutinies discovered no figure which could have been that of the Chinese doctor. Who could mistake that long, gaunt shape, with the high, mummy-like shoulders, and the indescribable gait, which I can only liken to that of an awkward cat?

Then, over the heads of a group of people who stood by the doorway, I saw Smith peering at someone--at someone who passed across the outer room. Stepping aside, I, too, obtained a glimpse of this person.

As I saw him, he was a tall, old man, wearing a black Inverness coat and a rather shabby silk hat. He had long white hair and a patriarchal beard, wore smoked glasses and walked slowly, leaning upon a stick.

Smith's gaunt face paled. With a rapid glance at Karamaneh, he made off across the room.

Could it be Dr. Fu-Manchu?

Many days had passed since, already half-choked by Inspector Weymouth's iron grip, Fu-Manchu, before our own eyes, had been swallowed up by the Thames. Even now men were seeking his body, and that of his last victim. Nor had we left any stone unturned. Acting upon information furnished by Karamaneh, the police had searched every known haunt of the murder group. But everything pointed to the fact that the group was disbanded and dispersed; that the lord of strange deaths who had ruled it was no more.

Yet Smith was not satisfied. Neither, let me confess, was I. Every port was watched; and in suspected districts a kind of house-to-house patrol had been instituted. Unknown to the great public, in those days a secret war waged-- a war in which all the available forces of the authorities took the field against one man! But that one man was the evil of the East incarnate.

When we rejoined him, Nayland Smith was talking to the commissionaire at the door. He turned to me.

"That is Professor Jenner Monde," he said. "The sergeant, here, knows him well."

The name of the celebrated Orientalist of course was familiar to me, although I had never before set eyes upon him.

"The Professor was out East the last time I was there, sir," stated the commissionaire. "I often used to see him. But he's an eccentric old gentleman. Seems to live in a world of his own. He's recently back from China, I think."

Nayland Smith stood clicking his teeth together in irritable hesitation. I heard Karamaneh sigh, and, looking at her, I saw that her cheeks were regaining their natural color.

She smiled in pathetic apology.

"If he was here he is gone," she said. "I am not afraid now."

Smith thanked the commissionaire for his information and we quitted the gallery.

"Professor Jenner Monde," muttered my friend, "has lived so long in China as almost to be a Chinaman. I have never met him-- never seen him, before; but I wonder--"

"You wonder what, Smith?"

"I wonder if he could possibly be an ally, of the Doctor's!"

I stared at him in amazement.

"If we are to attach any importance to the incident at all," I said, "we must remember that the boy's impression--and Karamaneh's-- was that Fu-Manchu was present in person."

"I DO attach importance to the incident, Petrie; they are naturally sensitive to such impressions. But I doubt if even the abnormal organization of Aziz could distinguish between the hidden presence of a creature of the

Doctor's and that of the Doctor himself. I shall make a point of calling upon Professor Jenner Monde."

But Fate had ordained that much should happen ere Smith made his proposed call upon the Professor.

Karamaneh and her brother safely lodged in their hotel (which was watched night and day by four men under Smith's orders), we returned to my quiet suburban rooms.

"First," said Smith, "let us see what we can find out respecting Professor Monde."

He went to the telephone and called up New Scotland Yard. There followed some little delay before the requisite information was obtained. Finally, however, we learned that the Professor was something of a recluse, having few acquaintances, and fewer friends.

He lived alone in chambers in New Inn Court, Carey Street. A charwoman did such cleaning as was considered necessary by the Professor, who employed no regular domestic. When he was in London he might be seen fairly frequently at the British Museum, where his shabby figure was familiar to the officials. When he was not in London--that is, during the greater part of each year--no one knew where he went. He never left any address to which letters might be forwarded.

"How long has he been in London now?" asked Smith.

So far as could be ascertained from New Inn Court (replied Scotland Yard) roughly a week.

My friend left the telephone and began restlessly to pace the room. The charred briar was produced and stuffed with that broad cut Latakia mixture of which Nayland Smith consumed close upon a pound a week. He was one of those untidy smokers who leave tangled tufts hanging from the pipe-bowl and when they light up strew the floor with smoldering fragments.

A ringing came, and shortly afterwards a girl entered.

"Mr. James Weymouth to see you, sir."

"Hullo!" rapped Smith. "What's this?"

Weymouth entered, big and florid, and in some respects singularly like his brother, in others as singularly unlike. Now, in his black suit, he was a somber figure; and in the blue eyes I read a fear suppressed.

"Mr. Smith," he began, "there's something uncanny going on at Maple Cottage."

Smith wheeled the big arm-chair forward.

"Sit down, Mr. Weymouth," he said. "I am not entirely surprised. But you have my attention. What has occurred?"

Weymouth took a cigarette from the box which I proffered and poured out a peg of whisky. His hand was not quite steady.

"That knocking," he explained. "It came again the night after you were there, and Mrs. Weymouth--my wife, I mean-- felt that she couldn't spend another night there, alone" "Did she look out of the window?" I asked.

"No, Doctor; she was afraid. But I spent last night downstairs in the sitting-room--and *I* looked out!"

He took a gulp from his glass. Nayland Smith, seated on the edge of the table, his extinguished pipe in his hand, was watching him keenly.

"I'll admit I didn't look out at once," Weymouth resumed. "There was something so uncanny, gentlemen, in that knocking-- knocking--in the dead of the night. I thought"--his voice shook--"of poor Jack, lying somewhere amongst the slime of the river--and, oh, my God! it came to me that it was Jack who was knocking--and I dare not think what he--what it-- would look like!"

He leaned forward, his chin in his hand. For a few moments we were all silent.

"I know I funked," he continued huskily. "But when the wife came to the head of the stairs and whispered to me: 'There it is again. What in heaven's name can it be'--I started to unbolt the door. The knocking had stopped. Everything was very still. I heard Mary--HIS widow--sobbing, upstairs; that was all. I opened the door, a little bit at a time."

Pausing again, he cleared his throat, and went on:

"It was a bright night, and there was no one there--not a soul. But somewhere down the lane, as I looked out into the porch, I heard most awful groans! They got fainter and fainter. Then--I could have sworn I heard SOMEONE LAUGHING! My nerves cracked up at that; and I shut the door again."

The narration of his weird experience revived something of the natural fear which it had occasioned. He raised his glass, with unsteady hand, and drained it.

Smith struck a match and relighted his pipe. He began to pace the room again. His eyes were literally on fire.

"Would it be possible to get Mrs. Weymouth out of the house before to-night? Remove her to your place, for instance?" he asked abruptly.

Weymouth looked up in surprise.

"She seems to be in a very low state," he replied. He glanced at me. "Perhaps Dr. Petrie would give us an opinion?"

"I will come and see her," I said. "But what is your idea, Smith?"

"I want to hear that knocking!" he rapped. "But in what I may see fit to do I must not be handicapped by the presence of a sick woman."

"Her condition at any rate will admit of our administering an opiate," I suggested. "That would meet the situation?"

"Good!" cried Smith. He was intensely excited now. "I rely upon you to arrange something, Petrie. Mr. Weymouth"-- he turned to our visitor--"I shall be with you this evening not later than twelve o'clock."

Weymouth appeared to be greatly relieved. I asked him to wait whilst I prepared a drought for the patient. When he was gone:

"What do you think this knocking means, Smith?" I asked.

He tapped out his pipe on the side of the grate and began with nervous energy to refill it again from the dilapidated pouch.

"I dare not tell you what I hope, Petrie," he replied-- "nor what I fear."

CHAPTER XXIX

DUSK WAS FALLING when we made our way in the direction of Maple Cottage. Nayland Smith appeared to be keenly interested in the character of the district. A high and ancient wall bordered the road along which we walked for a considerable distance. Later it gave place to a rickety fence.

My friend peered through a gap in the latter.

"There is quite an extensive estate here," he said, "not yet cut up by the builder. It is well wooded on one side, and there appears to be a pool lower down."

The road was a quiet one, and we plainly heard the tread-- quite unmistakable--of an approaching policeman. Smith continued to peer through the hole in the fence, until the officer drew up level with us. Then:

"Does this piece of ground extend down to the village, constable?" he inquired.

Quite willing for a chat, the man stopped, and stood with his thumbs thrust in his belt.

"Yes, sir. They tell me three new roads will be made through it between here and the hill."

"It must be a happy hunting ground for tramps?"

"I've seen some suspicious-looking coves about at times. But after dusk an army might be inside there and nobody would ever be the wiser."

"Burglaries frequent in the houses backing on to it?"

"Oh, no. A favorite game in these parts is snatching loaves and bottles of milk from the doors, first thing, as they're delivered. There's been an extra lot of it lately. My mate who relieves me has got special instructions to keep his eye open in the mornings!" The man grinned. "It wouldn't be a very big case even if he caught anybody!" "No," said Smith absently; "perhaps not. Your business must be a dry one this warm weather. Good-night."

"Good-night, sir," replied the constable, richer by half-a-crown--"and thank you."

Smith stared after him for a moment, tugging reflectively at the lobe of his ear.

"I don't know that it wouldn't be a big case, after all," he murmured. "Come on, Petrie."

Not another word did he speak, until we stood at the gate of Maple Cottage. There a plain-clothes man was standing, evidently awaiting Smith.

He touched his hat.

"Have you found a suitable hiding-place?" asked my companion rapidly.

"Yes, sir," was the reply. "Kent--my mate--is there now. You'll notice that he can't be seen from here."

"No," agreed Smith, peering all about him. "He can't. Where is he?"

"Behind the broken wall," explained the man, pointing. "Through that ivy there's a clear view of the cottage door."

"Good. Keep your eyes open. If a messenger comes for me, he is to be intercepted, you understand. No one must be allowed to disturb us. You will recognize the messenger. He will be one of your fellows. Should he come-- hoot three times, as much like an owl as you can."

We walked up to the porch of the cottage. In response to Smith's ringing came James Weymouth, who seemed greatly relieved by our arrival.

"First," said my friend briskly, "you had better run up and see the patient."

Accordingly, I followed Weymouth upstairs and was admitted by his wife to a neat little bedroom where the grief-stricken woman lay, a wanly pathetic sight.

"Did you administer the draught, as directed?" I asked.

Mrs. James Weymouth nodded. She was a kindly looking woman, with the same dread haunting her hazel eyes as that which lurked in her husband's blue ones.

The patient was sleeping soundly. Some whispered instructions I gave to the faithful nurse and descended to the sitting-room. It was a warm night, and Weymouth sat by the open window, smoking. The dim light from the lamp on the table lent him an almost startling likeness to his brother; and for a moment I stood at the foot of the stairs scarce able to trust my reason. Then he turned his face fully towards me, and the illusion was lost.

"Do you think she is likely to wake, Doctor?" he asked.

"I think not," I replied.

Nayland Smith stood upon the rug before the hearth, swinging from one foot to the other, in his nervously restless way. The room was foggy with the fumes of tobacco, for he, too, was smoking.

At intervals of some five to ten minutes, his blackened briar (which I never knew him to clean or scrape) would go out. I think Smith used more matches than any other smoker I have ever met, and he invariably carried three boxes in various pockets of his garments.

The tobacco habit is infectious, and, seating myself in an arm-chair, I lighted a cigarette. For this dreary vigil I had come prepared with a bunch of rough notes, a writing-block, and a fountain pen. I settled down to work upon my record of the Fu-Manchu case.

Silence fell upon Maple Cottage. Save for the shuddering sigh which whispered through the over-hanging cedars and Smith's eternal match-striking, nothing was there to disturb me in my task. Yet I could make little progress. Between my mind and the chapter upon which I was at work a certain sentence persistently intruded itself. It was as though an unseen hand held the written page closely before my eyes. This was the sentence:

"Imagine a person, tall, lean, and feline, high-shouldered, with a brow like Shakespeare and a face like Satan, a close-shaven skull, and long, magnetic eyes of the true cat-green: invest him with all the cruel cunning of an entire Eastern race, accumulated in one giant intellect. . ."

Dr. Fu-Manchu! Fu-Manchu as Smith had described him to me on that night which now seemed so remotely distant--the night upon which I had learned of the existence of the wonderful and evil being born of that secret quickening which stirred in the womb of the yellow races.

As Smith, for the ninth or tenth time, knocked out his pipe on a bar of the grate, the cuckoo clock in the kitchen proclaimed the hour.

"Two," said James Weymouth.

I abandoned my task, replacing notes and writing-block in the bag that I had with me. Weymouth adjusted the lamp which had begun to smoke.

I tiptoed to the stairs and, stepping softly, ascended to the sick room. All was quiet, and Mrs. Weymouth whispered to me that the patient still slept soundly. I returned to find Nayland Smith pacing about the room in that state of suppressed excitement habitual with him in the approach of any crisis. At a quarter past two the breeze dropped entirely, and such a stillness reigned all about us as I could not have supposed possible so near to the ever-throbbing heart of the great metropolis. Plainly I could hear Weymouth's heavy breathing. He sat at the window and looked out into the black shadows under the cedars. Smith ceased his pacing and stood again on the rug very still. He was listening! I doubt not we were all listening.

Some faint sound broke the impressive stillness, coming from the direction of the village street. It was a vague, indefinite disturbance, brief, and upon it ensued a silence more marked than ever. Some minutes before, Smith had extinguished the lamp. In the darkness I heard his teeth snap sharply together.

The call of an owl sounded very clearly three times.

I knew that to mean that a messenger had come; but from whence or bearing what tidings I knew not. My friend's plans were incomprehensible to me, nor had I pressed him for any explanation of their nature, knowing him to be in that high-strung and somewhat irritable mood which claimed him at times of uncertainty--when he doubted the wisdom of his actions, the accuracy of his surmises. He gave no sign.

Very faintly I heard a clock strike the half-hour. A soft breeze stole again through the branches above. The wind I thought must be in a new quarter since I had not heard the clock before. In so lonely a spot it was difficult to believe that the bell was that of St. Paul's. Yet such was the fact.

And hard upon the ringing followed another sound--a sound we all had expected, had waited for; but at whose coming no one of us, I think, retained complete mastery of himself.

Breaking up the silence in a manner that set my heart wildly leaping it came-- an imperative knocking on the door!

"My God!" groaned Weymouth--but he did not move from his position at the window.

"Stand by, Petrie!" said Smith.

He strode to the door--and threw it widely open.

I know I was very pale. I think I cried out as I fell back-- retreated with clenched hands from before THAT which stood on the threshold.

It was a wild, unkempt figure, with straggling beard, hideously staring eyes. With its hands it clutched at its hair--at its chin; plucked at its mouth. No moonlight touched the features of this unearthly visitant, but scanty as was the illumination we could see the gleaming teeth-- and the wildly glaring eyes.

It began to laugh--peal after peal--hideous and shrill.

Nothing so terrifying had ever smote upon my ears. I was palsied by the horror of the sound.

Then Nayland Smith pressed the button of an electric torch which he carried. He directed the disk of white light fully upon the face in the doorway.

"Oh, God!" cried Weymouth. "It's John!"--and again and again: "Oh, God! Oh, God!"

Perhaps for the first time in my life I really believed (nay, I could not doubt) that a thing of another world stood before me. I am ashamed to confess the extent of the horror that came upon me. James Weymouth raised his hands, as if to thrust away from him that awful thing in the door. He was babbling--prayers, I think, but wholly incoherent.

"Hold him, Petrie!"

Smith's voice was low. (When we were past thought or intelligent action, he, dominant and cool, with that forced calm for which, a crisis over, he always paid so dearly, was thinking of the woman who slept above.)

He leaped forward; and in the instant that he grappled with the one who had knocked I knew the visitant for a man of flesh and blood--a man who shrieked and fought like a savage animal, foamed at the mouth and gnashed his teeth in horrid frenzy; knew him for a madman--knew him for the victim of Fu-Manchu-- not dead, but living--for Inspector Weymouth--a maniac!

In a flash I realized all this and sprang to Smith's assistance. There was a sound of racing footsteps and the men who had been watching outside came running into the porch. A third was with them; and the five of us (for Weymouth's brother had not yet grasped the fact that a man and not a spirit shrieked and howled in our midst) clung to the infuriated madman, yet barely held our own with him.

"The syringe, Petrie!" gasped Smith. "Quick! You must manage to make an injection!"

I extricated myself and raced into the cottage for my bag. A hypodermic syringe ready charged I had brought with me at Smith's request. Even in that thrilling moment I could find time to admire the wonderful foresight of my friend, who had divined what would befall--isolated the strange, pitiful truth from the chaotic circumstances which saw us at Maple Cottage that night.

Let me not enlarge upon the end of the awful struggle. At one time I despaired (we all despaired) of quieting the poor, demented creature. But at last it was done; and the gaunt, blood-stained savage whom we had known as Detective-Inspector Weymouth lay passive upon the couch in his own sitting-room. A great wonder possessed my mind for the genius of the uncanny being who with the scratch of a needle had made a brave and kindly man into this unclean, brutish thing.

Nayland Smith, gaunt and wild-eyed, and trembling yet with his tremendous exertions, turned to the man whom I knew to be the messenger from Scotland Yard.

"Well?" he rapped.

"He is arrested, sir," the detective reported. "They have kept him at his chambers as you ordered."

"Has she slept through it?" said Smith to me. (I had just returned from a visit to the room above.) I nodded.

"Is HE safe for an hour or two?"--indicating the figure on the couch. "For eight or ten," I replied grimly.

"Come, then. Our night's labors are not nearly complete."

CHAPTER XXX

LATER WAS FORTHCOMING evidence to show that poor Weymouth had lived a wild life, in hiding among the thick bushes of the tract of land which lay between the village and the suburb on the neighboring hill. Literally, he had returned to primitive savagery and some of his food had been that of the lower animals, though he had not scrupled to steal, as we learned when his lair was discovered.

He had hidden himself cunningly; but witnesses appeared who had seen him, in the dusk, and fled from him. They never learned that the object of their fear was Inspector John Weymouth. How, having escaped death in the Thames, he had crossed London unobserved, we never knew; but his trick of knocking upon his own door at half-past two each morning (a sort of dawning of sanity mysteriously linked with old custom) will be a familiar class of symptom to all students of alienation.

I revert to the night when Smith solved the mystery of the knocking.

In a car which he had in waiting at the end of the village we sped through the deserted streets to New Inn Court. I, who had followed Nayland Smith through the failures and successes of his mission, knew that to-night he had surpassed himself; had justified the confidence placed in him by the highest authorities.

We were admitted to an untidy room--that of a student, a traveler and a crank--by a plain-clothes officer. Amid picturesque and disordered fragments of a hundred ages, in a great carven chair placed before a towering statue of the Buddha, sat a hand-cuffed man. His white hair and beard were patriarchal; his pose had great dignity. But his expression was entirely masked by the smoked glasses which he wore.

Two other detectives were guarding the prisoner.

"We arrested Professor Jenner Monde as he came in, sir," reported the man who had opened the door. "He has made no statement. I hope there isn't a mistake."

"I hope not," rapped Smith.

He strode across the room. He was consumed by a fever of excitement. Almost savagely, he tore away the beard, tore off the snowy wig dashed the smoked glasses upon the floor.

A great, high brow was revealed, and green, malignant eyes, which fixed themselves upon him with an expression I never can forget.

IT WAS DR. FU-MANCHU!

One intense moment of silence ensued--of silence which seemed to throb. Then:

"What have you done with Professor Monde?" demanded Smith.

Dr. Fu-Manchu showed his even, yellow teeth in the singularly evil smile which I knew so well. A manacled prisoner he sat as unruffled as a judge upon the bench. In truth and in justice I am compelled to say that Fu-Manchu was absolutely fearless.

"He has been detained in China," he replied, in smooth, sibilant tones--"by affairs of great urgency. His well-known personality and ungregarious habits have served me well, here!"

Smith, I could see, was undetermined how to act; he stood tugging at his ear and glancing from the impassive Chinaman to the wondering detectives.

"What are we to do, sir?" one of them asked.

"Leave Dr. Petrie and myself alone with the prisoner, until I call you."

The three withdrew. I divined now what was coming.

"Can you restore Weymouth's sanity?" rapped Smith abruptly. "I cannot save you from the hangman, nor"--his fists clenched convulsively--"would I if I could; but--"

Fu-Manchu fixed his brilliant eyes upon him.

"Say no more, Mr. Smith," he interrupted; "you misunderstand me. I do not quarrel with that, but what I have done from conviction and what I have done of necessity are separated--are seas apart. The brave Inspector Weymouth I wounded with a poisoned needle, in self-defense; but I regret his condition as greatly as you do. I respect such a man. There is an antidote to the poison of the needle."

"Name it," said Smith.

Fu-Manchu smiled again.

"Useless," he replied. "I alone can prepare it. My secrets shall die with me. I will make a sane man of Inspector Weymouth, but no one else shall be in the house but he and I."

"It will be surrounded by police," interrupted Smith grimly.

"As you please," said Fu-Manchu. "Make your arrangements. In that ebony case upon the table are the instruments for the cure. Arrange for me to visit him where and when you will--"

"I distrust you utterly. It is some trick," jerked Smith.

Dr. Fu-Manchu rose slowly and drew himself up to his great height. His manacled hands could not rob him of the uncanny dignity which was his. He raised them above his head with a tragic gesture and fixed his piercing gaze upon Nayland Smith.

"The God of Cathay hear me," he said, with a deep, guttural note in his voice--"I swear--"

The most awful visitor who ever threatened the peace of England, the end of the visit of Fu-Manchu was characteristic--terrible--inexplicable.

Strange to relate, I did not doubt that this weird being had conceived some kind of admiration or respect for the man to whom he had wrought so terrible an injury. He was capable of such sentiments, for he entertained some similar one in regard to myself.

A cottage farther down the village street than Weymouth's was vacant, and in the early dawn of that morning became the scene of outre happenings. Poor Weymouth, still in a comatose condition, we removed there (Smith having secured the key from the astonished agent). I suppose so strange a specialist never visited a patient before--certainly not under such conditions.

For into the cottage, which had been entirely surrounded by a ring of police, Dr. Fu-Manchu was admitted from the closed car in which, his work of healing complete, he was to be borne to prison--to death!

Law and justice were suspended by my royally empowered friend that the enemy of the white race might heal one of those who had hunted him down!

No curious audience was present, for sunrise was not yet come; no concourse of excited students followed the hand of the Master; but within that surrounded cottage was performed one of those miracles of science which in other circumstances had made the fame of Dr. Fu-Manchu to live forever.

Inspector Weymouth, dazed, disheveled, clutching his head as a man who has passed through the Valley of the Shadow-- but sane--sane!--walked out into the porch!

He looked towards us--his eyes wild, but not with the fearsome wildness of insanity.

"Mr. Smith!" he cried--and staggered down the path--"Dr. Petrie! What--"

There came a deafening explosion. From EVERY visible window of the deserted cottage flames burst forth!

"QUICK!" Smith's voice rose almost to a scream--"into the house!"

He raced up the path, past Inspector Weymouth, who stood swaying there like a drunken man. I was close upon his heels. Behind me came the police.

The door was impassable! Already, it vomited a deathly heat, borne upon stifling fumes like those of the mouth of the Pit. We burst a window. The room within was a furnace!

"My God!" cried someone. "This is supernatural!"

"Listen!" cried another. "Listen!"

The crowd which a fire can conjure up at any hour of day or night, out of the void of nowhere, was gathering already. But upon all descended a pall of silence.

From the heat of the holocaust a voice proclaimed itself--a voice raised, not in anguish but in TRIUMPH! It chanted barbarically--and was still.

The abnormal flames rose higher--leaping forth from every window.

"The alarm!" said Smith hoarsely. "Call up the brigade!"

I come to the close of my chronicle, and feel that I betray a trust--the trust of my reader. For having limned in the colors at my command the fiendish Chinese doctor, I am unable to conclude my task as I should desire, unable, with any consciousness of finality, to write Finis to the end of my narrative.

It seems to me sometimes that my pen is but temporarily idle--that I have but dealt with a single phase of a movement having a hundred phases. One sequel I hope for, and against all the promptings of logic and Western bias. If my hope shall be realized I cannot, at this time, pretend to state.

The future, 'mid its many secrets, holds this precious one from me.

I ask you then, to absolve me from the charge of ill completing my work; for any curiosity with which this narrative may leave the reader burdened is shared by the writer.

With intent, I have rushed you from the chambers of Professor Jenner Monde to that closing episode at the deserted cottage; I have made the pace hot in order to impart to these last pages of my account something of the breathless scurry which characterized those happenings.

My canvas may seem sketchy: it is my impression of the reality. No hard details remain in my mind of the dealings of that night. Fu-Manchu arrested--Fu-Manchu, manacled, entering the cottage on his mission of healing; Weymouth, miraculously rendered sane, coming forth; the place in flames.

And then?

To a shell the cottage burned, with an incredible rapidity which pointed to some hidden agency; to a shell about ashes which held NO TRACE OF HUMAN BONES!

It has been asked of me: Was there no possibility of Fu-Manchu's having eluded us in the ensuing confusion? Was there no loophole of escape?

I reply, that so far as I was able to judge, a rat could scarce have quitted the building undetected. Yet that Fu-Manchu had, in some incomprehensible manner and by some mysterious agency, produced those abnormal flames, I cannot doubt. Did he voluntarily ignite his own funeral pyre?

As I write, there lies before me a soiled and creased sheet of vellum. It bears some lines traced in a cramped, peculiar, and all but illegible hand. This fragment was found by Inspector Weymouth (to this day a man mentally sound) in a pocket of his ragged garments.

When it was written I leave you to judge. How it came to be where Weymouth found it calls for no explanation:

"To Mr. Commissioner NAYLAND SMITH and Dr. PETRIE--

"Greeting! I am recalled home by One who may not be denied. In much that I came to do I have failed. Much that I have done I would undo; some little I have undone. Out of fire I came--the smoldering fire of a thing one day to be a consuming flame; in fire I go. Seek not my ashes. I am the lord of the fires! Farewell.

"FU-MANCHU."

Who has been with me in my several meetings with the man who penned that message I leave to adjudge if it be the letter of a madman bent upon self-destruction by strange means, or the gibe of a preternaturally clever scientist and the most elusive being ever born of the land of mystery--China.

For the present, I can aid you no more in the forming of your verdict. A day may come though I pray it do not--when I shall be able to throw new light upon much that is dark in this matter. That day, so far as I can judge, could only dawn in the event of the Chinaman's survival; therefore I pray that the veil be never lifted.

But, as I have said, there is another sequel to this story which I can contemplate with a different countenance. How, then, shall I conclude this very unsatisfactory account?

Shall I tell you, finally, of my parting with lovely, dark-eyed Karamaneh, on board the liner which was to bear her to Egypt?

No, let me, instead, conclude with the words of Nayland Smith:

"*I* sail for Burma in a fortnight, Petrie. I have leave to break my journey at the Ditch. How would a run up the Nile fit your programme? Bit early for the season, but you might find something to amuse you!

THE RETURN OF DR FU MANCHU

by

SAX ROHMER

CHAPTER 1

A MIDNIGHT SUMMONS

"**WHEN DID YOU** last hear from Nayland Smith?" asked my visitor.

I paused, my hand on the syphon, reflecting for a moment.

"Two months ago," I said; "he's a poor correspondent and rather soured, I fancy."

"What--a woman or something?"

"Some affair of that sort. He's such a reticent beggar, I really know very little about it."

I placed a whisky and soda before the Rev. J. D. Eltham, also sliding the tobacco jar nearer to his hand. The refined and sensitive face of the clergy-man offered no indication of the truculent character of the man. His scanty fair hair, already gray over the temples, was silken and soft-looking; in appearance he was indeed a typical English churchman; but in China he had been known as "the fighting missionary," and had fully deserved the title. In fact, this peaceful-looking gentleman had directly brought about the Boxer Risings!

"You know," he said, in his clerical voice, but meanwhile stuffing tobacco into an old pipe with fierce energy, "I have often wondered, Petrie--I have never left off wondering--"

"What?"

"That accursed Chinaman! Since the cellar place beneath the site of the burnt-out cottage in Dulwich Village--I have wondered more than ever."

He lighted his pipe and walked to the hearth to throw the match in the grate.

"You see," he continued, peering across at me in his oddly nervous way, "one never knows, does one? If I thought that Dr. Fu-Manchu lived; if I seriously suspected that that stupendous intellect, that wonderful genius, Petrie, er--" he hesitated characteristically--"survived, I should feel it my duty--"

"Well?" I said, leaning my elbows on the table and smiling slightly.

"If that Satanic genius were not indeed destroyed, then the peace of the world, may be threatened anew at any moment!"

He was becoming excited, shooting out his jaw in the truculent manner I knew, and snapping his fingers to emphasize his words; a man composed of the oddest complexities that ever dwelt beneath a clerical frock.

"He may have got back to China, Doctor!" he cried, and his eyes had the fighting glint in them. "Could you rest in peace if you thought that he lived? Should you not fear for your life every time that a night-call took you out alone? Why, man alive, it is only two years since he was here among us, since we were searching every shadow for those awful green eyes! What became of his band of assassins--his stranglers, his dacoits, his damnable poisons and insects and what-not --the army of creatures--"

He paused, taking a drink.

"You--" he hesitated diffidently--"searched in Egypt with Nayland Smith, did you not?"

I nodded.

"Contradict me if I am wrong," he continued; but my impression is that you were searching for the girl--the girl--Karamaneh, I think she was called?"

"Yes," I replied shortly; "but we could find no trace--no trace."

"You--er--were interested?"

"More than I knew," I replied, "until I realized that I had--lost her."

"I never met Karamaneh, but from your account, and from others, she was quite unusually--"

"She was very beautiful," I said, and stood up, for I was anxious to terminate that phase of the conversation.

Eltham regarded me sympathetically; he knew something of my search with Nayland Smith for the dark-eyed, Eastern girl who had brought romance into my drab life; he knew that I treasured my memories of her as I loathed and abhorred those of the fiendish, brilliant Chinese doctor who had been her master.

Eltham began to pace up and down the rug, his pipe bubbling furiously; and something in the way he carried his head reminded me momentarily of Nayland Smith. Certainly, between this pink-faced clergyman, with his deceptively mild appearance, and the gaunt, bronzed, and steely- eyed Burmese commissioner, there was externally little in common; but it was some little nervous trick in his carriage that conjured up through the smoky haze one distant summer evening when Smith had paced that very room as Eltham paced it now, when before my startled eyes he had rung up the curtain upon the savage drama in which, though I little suspected it then, Fate had cast me for a leading role.

I wondered if Eltham's thoughts ran parallel with mine. My own were centered upon the unforgettable figure of the murderous Chinaman. These words, exactly as Smith had used them, seemed once again to sound in my ears: "Imagine a person tall, lean, and feline, high shouldered, with a brow like Shakespeare and a face like Satan, a close-shaven skull, and long magnetic eyes of the true cat green. Invest him with all the cruel cunning of an entire Eastern race accumulated in one giant intellect, with all the resources of science, past and present, and you have a mental picture of Dr. Fu-Manchu, the 'Yellow Peril' incarnate in one man."

This visit of Eltham's no doubt was responsible for my mood; for this singular clergyman had played his part in the drama of two years ago.

"I should like to see Smith again," he said suddenly; "it seems a pity that a man like that should be buried in Burma. Burma makes a mess of the best of men, Doctor. You said he was not married?"

"No," I replied shortly, "and is never likely to be, now."

"Ah, you hinted at something of the kind."

"I know very little of it. Nayland Smith is not the kind of man to talk much."

"Quite so--quite so! And, you know, Doctor, neither am I; but"--he was growing painfully embarrassed--"it may be your due--I--er--I have a correspondent, in the interior of China--"

"Well?" I said, watching him in sudden eagerness.

"Well, I would not desire to raise--vain hopes--nor to occasion, shall I say, empty fears; but--er . . . no, Doctor!" He flushed like a girl--"It was wrong of me to open this conversation. Perhaps, when I know more--will you forget my words, for the time?"

The telephone bell rang.

"Hullo!" cried Eltham--"hard luck, Doctor!"--but I could see that he welcomed the interruption. "Why!" he added, "it is one o'clock!"

I went to the telephone.

"Is that Dr. Petrie?" inquired a woman's voice.

"Yes; who is speaking?"

"Mrs. Hewett has been taken more seriously ill. Could you come at once?"

"Certainly," I replied, for Mrs. Hewett was not only a profitable patient but an estimable lady--" I shall be with you in a quarter of an hour."

I hung up the receiver.

"Something urgent?" asked Eltham, emptying his pipe.

"Sounds like it. You had better turn in."

"I should much prefer to walk over with you, if it would not be intruding. Our conversation has ill prepared me for sleep."

"Right!" I said; for I welcomed his company; and three minutes later we were striding across the deserted common.

A sort of mist floated amongst the trees, seeming in the moonlight like a veil draped from trunk to trunk, as in silence we passed the Mound pond, and struck out for the north side of the common.

I suppose the presence of Eltham and the irritating recollection of his half-confidence were the responsible factors, but my mind persistently dwelt upon the subject of Fu-Manchu and the atrocities which he had committed during his sojourn in England. So actively was my imagination at work that I felt again the menace which so long had hung over me; I felt as though that murderous yellow cloud still cast its shadow upon England. And I found myself longing for the company of Nayland Smith. I cannot state what was the nature of Eltham's reflections, but I can guess; for he was as silent as I.

It was with a conscious effort that I shook myself out of this morbidly reflective mood, on finding that we had crossed the common and were come to the abode of my patient.

"I shall take a little walk," announced Eltham; for I gather that you don't expect to be detained long? I shall never be out of sight of the door, of course."

"Very well," I replied, and ran up the steps.

There were no lights to be seen in any of the windows, which circumstance rather surprised me, as my patient occupied, or had occupied when last I had visited her, a first-floor bedroom in the front of the house. My knocking and ringing produced no response for three or four minutes; then, as I persisted, a scantily clothed and half awake maid servant unbarred the door and stared at me stupidly in the moonlight.

"Mrs. Hewett requires me?" I asked abruptly.

The girl stared more stupidly than ever.

"No, sir," she said, "she don't, sir; she's fast asleep!"

"But some one 'phoned me!" I insisted, rather irritably, I fear.

"Not from here, sir," declared the now wide-eyed girl. "We haven't got a telephone, sir."

For a few moments I stood there, staring as foolishly as she; then abruptly I turned and descended the steps. At the gate I stood looking up and down the road. The houses were all in darkness. What could be the meaning of the mysterious summons? I had made no mistake respecting the name of my patient; it had been twice repeated over the telephone; yet that the call had not emanated from Mrs. Hewett's house was now palpably evident. Days had been when I should have regarded the episode as preluding some outrage, but to-night I felt more disposed to ascribe it to a silly practical joke.

Eltham walked up briskly.

"You're in demand to-night, Doctor," he said. "A young person called for you almost directly you had left your house, and, learning where you were gone, followed you."

"Indeed!" I said, a trifle incredulously. "There are plenty of other doctors if the case is an urgent one."

"She may have thought it would save time as you were actually up and dressed," explained Eltham; "and the house is quite near to here, I understand."

I looked at him a little blankly. Was this another effort of the unknown jester?

"I have been fooled once," I said. "That 'phone call was a hoax--"

"But I feel certain," declared Eltham, earnestly, "that this is genuine! The poor girl was dreadfully agitated; her master has broken his leg and is lying helpless: number 280, Rectory Grove."

"Where is the girl?" I asked, sharply.

"She ran back directly she had given me her message."

"Was she a servant?"

"I should imagine so: French, I think. But she was so wrapped up I had little more than a glimpse of her. I am sorry to hear that some one has played a silly joke on you, but believe me--" he was very earnest --"this is no jest. The poor girl could scarcely speak for sobs. She mistook me for you, of course."

"Oh!" said I grimly "well, I suppose I must go. Broken leg, you said? --and my surgical bag, splints and so forth, are at home!"

"My dear Petrie!" cried Eltham, in his enthusiastic way--"you no doubt can do something to alleviate the poor man's suffering immediately. I will run back to your rooms for the bag and rejoin you at 280, Rectory Grove."

"It's awfully good of you, Eltham--"

He held up his hand.

"The call of suffering humanity, Petrie, is one which I may no more refuse to hear than you."

I made no further protest after that, for his point of view was evident and his determination adamant, but told him where he would find the bag and once more set out across the moonbright common, he pursuing a westerly direction and I going east.

Some three hundred yards I had gone, I suppose, and my brain had been very active the while, when something occurred to me which placed a new complexion upon this second summons. I thought of the falsity of the first, of the improbability of even the most hardened practical joker practising his wiles at one o'clock in the morning. I thought of our recent conversation; above all I thought of the girl who had delivered the message to Eltham, the girl whom he had described as a French maid - whose personal charm had so completely enlisted his sympathies. Now, to this train of thought came a new one, and, adding it, my suspicion became almost a certainty.

I remembered (as, knowing the district, I should have remembered before) that there was no number 280 in Rectory Grove.

Pulling up sharply I stood looking about me. Not a living soul was in sight; not even a policeman. Where the lamps marked the main paths across the common nothing moved; in the shadows about me nothing stirred. But something stirred within me--a warning voice which for long had lain dormant.

What was afoot?

A breeze caressed the leaves overhead, breaking the silence with mysterious whisperings. Some portentous truth was seeking for admittance to my brain. I strove to reassure myself, but the sense of impending evil and of mystery became heavier. At last I could combat my strange fears no longer. I turned and began to run toward the south side of the common--toward my rooms--and after Eltham.

I had hoped to head him off, but came upon no sign of him. An all-night tramcar passed at the moment that I reached the high road, and as I ran around behind it I saw that my windows were lighted and that there was a light in the hall.

My key was yet in the lock when my housekeeper opened the door.

"There's a gentleman just come, Doctor," she began--

I thrust past her and raced up the stairs into my study.

Standing by the writing-table was a tall, thin man, his gaunt face brown as a coffee-berry and his steely gray eyes fixed upon me. My heart gave a great leap--and seemed to stand still.

It was Nayland Smith!

"Smith," I cried. "Smith, old man, by God, I'm glad to see you!"

He wrung my hand hard, looking at me with his searching eyes; but there was little enough of gladness in his face. He was altogether grayer than when last I had seen him--grayer and sterner.

"Where is Eltham?" I asked.

Smith started back as though I had struck him.

"Eltham!" he whispered--"Eltham! is Eltham here?"

"I left him ten minutes ago on the common--"

Smith dashed his right fist into the palm of his left hand and his eyes gleamed almost wildly.

"My God, Petrie!" he said, "am I fated always to come too late?"

My dreadful fears in that instant were confirmed. I seemed to feel my legs totter beneath me.

"Smith, you don't mean--"

"I do, Petrie!" His voice sounded very far away. "Fu-Manchu is here; and Eltham, God help him . . . is his first victim!"

CHAPTER 11

ELTHAM VANISHES

SMITH WENT RACING down the stairs like a man possessed. Heavy with such a foreboding of calamity as I had not known for two years, I followed him--along the hall and out into the road. The very peace and beauty of the night in some way increased my mental agitation. The sky was lighted almost tropically with such a blaze of stars as I could not recall to have seen since, my futile search concluded, I had left Egypt. The glory of the moonlight yellowed the lamps speckled across the expanse of the common. The night was as still as night can ever be in London. The dimming pulse of a cab or car alone disturbed the stillness.

With a quick glance to right and left, Smith ran across on to the common, and, leaving the door wide open behind me, I followed. The path which Eltham had pursued terminated almost opposite to my house. One's gaze might follow it, white and empty, for several hundred yards past the pond, and further, until it became overshadowed and was lost amid a clump of trees.

I came up with Smith, and side by side we ran on, whilst pantingly, I told my tale.

"It was a trick to get you away from him!" cried Smith. "They meant no doubt to make some attempt at your house, but as he came out with you, an alternative plan--"

Abreast of the pond, my companion slowed down, and finally stopped.

"Where did you last see Eltham?" he asked rapidly.

I took his arm, turning him slightly to the right, and pointed across the moonbathed common.

"You see that clump of bushes on the other side of the road?" I said. "There's a path to the left of it. I took that path and he took this. We parted at the point where they meet--"

Smith walked right down to the edge of the water and peered about over the surface.

What he hoped to find there I could not imagine. Whatever it had been he was disappointed, and he turned to me again, frowning perplexedly, and tugging at the lobe of his left ear, an old trick which reminded me of gruesome things we had lived through in the past.

"Come on," he jerked. "It may be amongst the trees."

From the tone of his voice I knew that he was tensed up nervously, and his mood but added to the apprehension of my own.

"What may be amongst the trees, Smith?" I asked.

He walked on.

"God knows, Petrie; but I fear--"

Behind us, along the highroad, a tramcar went rocking by, doubtless bearing a few belated workers homeward. The stark incongruity of the thing was appalling. How little those weary toilers, hemmed about with the commonplace, suspected that almost within sight from the car windows, in a place of prosy benches, iron railings, and unromantic, flickering lamps, two fellow men moved upon the border of a horror-land!

Beneath the trees a shadow carpet lay, its edges tropically sharp; and fully ten yards from the first of the group, we two, hatless both, and sharing a common dread, paused for a moment and listened.

The car had stopped at the further extremity of the common, and now with a moan that grew to a shriek was rolling on its way again. We stood and listened until silence reclaimed the night. Not a footstep could be heard. Then slowly we walked on. At the edge of the little coppice we stopped again abruptly.

Smith turned and thrust his pistol into my hand. A white ray of light pierced the shadows; my companion carried an electric torch. But no trace of Eltham was discoverable.

There had been a heavy shower of rain during the evening just before sunset, and although the open paths were dry again, under the trees the ground was still moist. Ten yards within the coppice we came upon tracks-- the tracks of one running, as the deep imprints of the toes indicated.

Abruptly the tracks terminated; others, softer, joined them, two sets converging from left and right. There was a confused patch, trailing off to the west; then this became indistinct, and was finally lost upon the hard ground outside the group.

For perhaps a minute, or more, we ran about from tree to tree, and from bush to bush, searching like hounds for a scent, and fearful of what we might find. We found nothing; and fully in the moonlight we stood facing one another. The night was profoundly still.

Nayland Smith stepped back into the shadows, and began slowly to turn his head from left to right, taking in the entire visible expanse of the common. Toward a point where the road bisected it he stared intently. Then, with a bound, he set off.

"Come on, Petrie!" he cried. " There they are!"

Vaulting a railing he went away over a field like a madman. Recovering from the shock of surprise, I followed him, but he was well ahead of me, and making for some vaguely seen object moving against the lights of the roadway.

Another railing was vaulted, and the corner of a second, triangular grass patch crossed at a hot sprint. We were twenty yards from the road when the sound of a starting motor broke the silence. We gained the graveled footpath only to see the taillight of the car dwindling to the north!

Smith leaned dizzily against a tree.

"Eltham is in that car!" he gasped. "Just God! are we to stand here and see him taken away to--"

He beat his fist upon the tree, in a sort of tragic despair. The nearest cab-rank was no great distance away, but, excluding the possibility of no cab being there, it might, for all practical purposes, as well have been a mile off.

The beat of the retreating motor was scarcely audible; the lights might but just be distinguished. Then, coming in an opposite direction, appeared the headlamp of another car, of a car that raced nearer and nearer to us, so that, within a few seconds of its first appearance, we found ourselves bathed in the beam of its headlights.

Smith bounded out into the road, and stood, a weird silhouette, with upraised arms, fully in its course!

The brakes were applied hurriedly. It was a big limousine, and its driver swerved perilously in avoiding Smith and nearly ran into me. But, the breathless moment past, the car was pulled up, head on to the railings; and a man in evening clothes was demanding excitedly what had happened. Smith, a hatless, disheveled figure, stepped up to the door.

"My name is Nayland Smith," he said rapidly--Burmese Commissioner." He snatched a letter from his pocket and thrust it into the hands of the bewildered man. "Read that. It is signed by another Commissioner--the Commissioner of Police."

With amazement written all over him, the other obeyed.

"You see," continued my friend, tersely--"it is carte blanche. I wish to commandeer your car, sir, on a matter of life and death!".

The other returned the letter.

"Allow me to offer it!" he said, descending. "My man will take your orders. I can finish my journey by cab. I am--"

But Smith did not wait to learn whom he might be.

"Quick!" he cried to the stupefied chauffeur--"You passed a car a minute ago--yonder. Can you overtake it?"

"I can try, sir, if I don't lose her track."

Smith leaped in, pulling me after him.

"Do it!" he snapped."There are no speed limits for me. Thanks! Goodnight, sir!"

We were off! The car swung around and the chase commenced.

One last glimpse I had of the man we had dispossessed, standing alone by the roadside, and at ever increasing speed, we leaped away in the track of Eltham's captors.

Smith was too highly excited for ordinary conversation, but he threw out short, staccato remarks.

"I have followed Fu-Manchu from Hongkong," he jerked. "Lost him at Suez. He got here a boat ahead of me. Eltham has been corresponding with some mandarin up-country. Knew that. Came straight to you. Only got in this evening. He--Fu-Manchu--has been sent here to get Eltham. My God! and he has him! He will question him! The interior of China--a seething pot, Petrie! They had to stop the leakage of information. He is here for that."

The car pulled up with a jerk that pitched me out of my seat, and the chauffeur leaped to the road and ran ahead. Smith was out in a trice, as the man, who had run up to a constable, came racing back.

"Jump in, sir--jump in!" he cried, his eyes bright with the lust of the chase; "they are making for Battersea!"

And we were off again.

Through the empty streets we roared on. A place of gasometers and desolate waste lots slipped behind and we were in a narrow way where gates of yards and a few lowly houses faced upon a prospect of high blank wall.

"Thames on our right," said Smith, peering ahead. "His rathole is by the river as usual. Hi!"-- he grabbed up the speaking-tube--"Stop! Stop!"

The limousine swung in to the narrow sidewalk, and pulled up close by a yard gate. I, too, had seen our quarry--a long, low bodied car, showing no inside lights. It had turned the next corner, where a street lamp shone greenly, not a hundred yards ahead.

Smith leaped out, and I followed him.

"That must be a cul de sac," he said, and turned to the eager-eyed chauffeur. "Run back to that last turning," he ordered, "and wait there, out of sight. Bring the car up when you hear a police-whistle."

The man looked disappointed, but did not question the order. As he began to back away, Smith grasped me by the arm and drew me forward.

"We must get to that corner," he said, "and see where the car stands, without showing ourselves."

CHAPTER III

THE WIRE JACKET

I SUPPOSE WE WERE not more than a dozen paces from the lamp when we heard the thudding of the motor. The car was backing out!

It was a desperate moment, for it seemed that we could not fail to be discovered. Nayland Smith began to look about him, feverishly, for a hiding-place, a quest in which I seconded with equal anxiety. And Fate was kind to us--doubly kind as after events revealed. A wooden gate broke the expanse of wall hard by upon the right, and, as the result of some recent accident, a ragged gap had been torn in the panels close to the top.

The chain of the padlock hung loosely; and in a second Smith was up, with his foot in this as in a stirrup. He threw his arm over the top and drew himself upright. A second later he was astride the broken gate.

"Up you come, Petrie!" he said, and reached down his hand to aid me.

I got my foot into the loop of chain, grasped at a projection in the gatepost and found myself up.

"There is a crossbar on this side to stand on," said Smith.

He climbed over and vanished in the darkness. I was still astride the broken gate when the car turned the corner, slowly, for there was scanty room; but I was standing upon the bar on the inside and had my head below the gap ere the driver could possibly have seen me.

"Stay where you are until he passes," hissed my companion, below. "There is a row of kegs under you."

The sound of the motor passing outside grew loud--louder--then began to die away. I felt about with my left foot; discerned the top of a keg, and dropped, panting, beside Smith.

"Phew!" I said--"that was a close thing! Smith--how do we know--"

"That we have followed the right car?" he interrupted. "Ask yourself the question: what would any ordinary man be doing motoring in a place like this at two o'clock in the morning?"

"You are right, Smith," I agreed. "Shall we get out again?"

"Not yet. I have an idea. Look yonder."

He grasped my arm, turning me in the desired direction.

Beyond a great expanse of unbroken darkness a ray of moonlight slanted into the place wherein we stood, spilling its cold radiance upon rows of kegs.

"That's another door," continued my friend—I now began dimly to perceive him beside me. "If my calculations are not entirely wrong, it opens on a wharf gate—"

A steam siren hooted dismally, apparently from quite close at hand.

"I'm right!" snapped Smith. "That turning leads down to the gate. Come on, Petrie!"

He directed the light of the electric torch upon a narrow path through the ranks of casks, and led the way to the further door. A good two feet of moonlight showed along the top. I heard Smith straining; then—

"These kegs are all loaded with grease!" he said, "and I want to reconnoiter over that door."

"I am leaning on a crate which seems easy to move," I reported. "Yes, it's empty. Lend a hand."

We grasped the empty crate, and between us, set it up on a solid pedestal of casks. Then Smith mounted to this observation platform and I scrambled up beside him, and looked down upon the lane outside.

It terminated as Smith had foreseen at a wharf gate some six feet to the right of our post. Piled up in the lane beneath us, against the warehouse door, was a stack of empty casks. Beyond, over the way, was a kind of ramshackle building that had possibly been a dwelling-house at some time. Bills were stuck in the ground-floor window indicating that the three floors were to let as offices; so much was discernible in that reflected moonlight.

I could hear the tide, lapping upon the wharf, could feel the chill from the river and hear the vague noises which, night nor day, never cease upon the great commercial waterway.

"Down!" whispered Smith. "Make no noise! I suspected it. They heard the car following!"

I obeyed, clutching at him for support; for I was suddenly dizzy, and my heart was leaping wildly—furiously.

"You saw her?" he whispered.

Saw her! yes, I had seen her! And my poor dream-world was toppling about me, its cities, ashes and its fairness, dust.

Peering from the window, her great eyes wondrous in the moonlight and her red lips parted, hair gleaming like burnished foam and her anxious gaze set upon the corner of the lane—was Karamaneh . . . Karamaneh whom once we had rescued from the house of this fiendish Chinese doctor; Karamaneh who had been our ally; in fruitless quest of whom,—when, too late, I realized how empty my life was become—I had wasted what little of the world's goods I possessed;—Karamaneh!

"Poor old Petrie," murmured Smith—"I knew, but I hadn't the heart—He has her again—God knows by what chains he holds her. But she's only a woman, old boy, and women are very much alike--very much alike from Charing Cross to Pagoda Road."

He rested his hand on my shoulder for a moment; I am ashamed to confess that I was trembling; then, clenching my teeth with that mechanical physical effort which often accompanies a mental one, I swallowed the bitter draught of Nayland Smith's philosophy. He was raising himself, to peer, cautiously, over the top of the door. I did likewise.

The window from which the girl had looked was nearly on a level with our eyes, and as I raised my head above the woodwork, I quite distinctly saw her go out of the room. The door, as she opened it, admitted a dull light, against which her figure showed silhouetted for a moment. Then the door was reclosed.

"We must risk the other windows," rapped Smith.

Before I had grasped the nature of his plan he was over and had dropped almost noiselessly upon the casks outside. Again I followed his lead.

"You are not going to attempt anything, singlehanded--against him?" I asked.

"Petrie--Eltham is in that house. He has been brought here to be put to the question, in the medieval, and Chinese, sense! Is there time to summon assistance?"

I shuddered. This had been in my mind, certainly, but so expressed it was definitely horrible--revolting, yet stimulating.

"You have the pistol," added Smith--"follow closely, and quietly."

He walked across the tops of the casks and leaped down, pointing to that nearest to the closed door of the house. I helped him place it under the open window. A second we set beside it, and, not without some noise, got a third on top.

Smith mounted.

His jaw muscles were very prominent and his eyes shone like steel; but he was as cool as though he were about to enter a theater and not the den of the most stupendous genius who ever worked for evil. I would forgive any man who, knowing Dr. Fu-Manchu, feared him; I feared him myself-- feared him as one fears a scorpion; but when Nayland Smith hauled himself up on the wooden ledge above the door and swung thence into the darkened room, I followed and was in close upon his heels. But I admired him, for he had every ampere of his self-possession in hand; my own case was different.

He spoke close to my ear.

"Is your hand steady? We may have to shoot."

I thought of Karamaneh, of lovely dark-eyed Karamaneh whom this wonderful, evil product of secret China had stolen from me--for so I now adjudged it.

"Rely upon me!" I said grimly. "I . . ."

The words ceased--frozen on my tongue.

There are things that one seeks to forget, but it is my lot often to remember the sound which at that moment literally struck me rigid with horror. Yet it was only a groan; but, merciful God! I pray that it may never be my lot to listen to such a groan again.

Smith drew a sibilant breath.

"It's Eltham!" he whispered hoarsely --"they're torturing--"

"No, no!" screamed a woman's voice--a voice that thrilled me anew, but with another emotion-

"Not that, not--"

I distinctly heard the sound of a blow. Followed a sort of vague scuffling. A door somewhere at the back of the house opened--and shut again. Some one was coming along the passage toward us!

"Stand back!" Smith's voice was low, but perfectly steady. "Leave it to me!"

Nearer came the footsteps and nearer. I could hear suppressed sobs. The door opened, admitting again the faint light--and Karamaneh came in. The place was quite unfurnished, offering no possibility of hiding; but to hide was unnecessary.

Her slim figure had not crossed the threshold ere Smith had his arm about the girl's waist and one hand clapped to her mouth. A stifled gasp she uttered, and he lifted her into the room.

I stepped forward and closed the door. A faint perfume stole to my nostrils--a vague, elusive breath of the East, reminiscent of strange days that, now, seemed to belong to a remote past. Karamaneh! that faint, indefinable perfume was part of her dainty personality; it may appear absurd--impossible--but many and many a time I had dreamt of it.

"In my breast pocket," rapped Smith; "the light."

I bent over the girl as he held her. She was quite still, but I could have wished that I had had more certain mastery of myself. I took the torch from Smith's pocket, and, mechanically, directed it upon the captive.

She was dressed very plainly, wearing a simple blue skirt, and white blouse. It was easy to divine that it was she whom Eltham had mistaken for a French maid. A brooch set with a ruby was pinned at the point where the blouse opened--gleaming fierily and harshly against the soft skin. Her face was pale and her eyes wide with fear.

"There is some cord in my right-hand pocket," said Smith; "I came provided. Tie her wrists."

I obeyed him, silently. The girl offered no resistance, but I think I never essayed a less congenial task than that of binding her white wrists. The jeweled fingers lay quite listlessly in my own.

"Make a good job of it!" rapped Smith, significantly.

A flush rose to my cheeks, for I knew well enough what he meant.

"She is fastened," I said, and I turned the ray of the torch upon her again.

Smith removed his hand from her mouth but did not relax his grip of her. She looked up at me with eyes in which I could have sworn there was no recognition. But a flush momentarily swept over her face, and left it pale again.

"We shall have to--gag her--"

"Smith, I can't do it!"

The girl's eyes filled with tears and she looked up at my companion pitifully.

"Please don't be cruel to me," she whispered, with that soft accent which always played havoc with my composure. "Every one--every one--is cruel to me. I will promise--indeed I will swear, to be quiet. Oh, believe me, if you can save him I will do nothing to hinder you." Her beautiful head drooped. "Have some pity for me as well."

"Karamaneh" I said. "We would have believed you once. We cannot, now."

She started violently.

"You know my name!" Her voice was barely audible. "Yet I have never seen you in my life--"

"See if the door locks," interrupted Smith harshly.

Dazed by the apparent sincerity in the voice of our lovely captive--vacant from wonder of it all--I opened the door, felt for, and found, a key.

We left Karamaneh crouching against the wall; her great eyes were turned towards me fascinatedly. Smith locked the door with much care. We began a tip-toed progress along the dimly lighted passage.

From beneath a door on the left, and near the end, a brighter light shone. Beyond that again was another door. A voice was speaking in the lighted room; yet I could have sworn that Karamaneh had come, not from there but from the room beyond--from the far end of the passage.

But the voice!--who, having once heard it, could ever mistake that singular voice, alternately guttural and sibilant!

Dr. Fu-Manchu was speaking!

"I have asked you," came with ever-increasing clearness (Smith had begun to turn the knob), "to reveal to me the name of your correspondent in Nan-Yang. I have suggested that he may be the Mandarin Yen-Sun-Yat, but you have declined to confirm me. Yet I know" (Smith had the door open a good three inches and was peering in) "that some official, some high official, is a traitor. Am I to resort again to the question to learn his name?"

Ice seemed to enter my veins at the unseen inquisitor's intonation of the words "the question." This was the Twentieth Century, yet there, in that damnable room . . .

Smith threw the door open.

Through a sort of haze, born mostly of horror, but not entirely, I saw Eltham, stripped to the waist and tied, with his arms upstretched, to a rafter in the ancient ceiling. A Chinaman who wore a slop-shop blue suit and who held an open knife in his hand, stood beside him. Eltham was ghastly white. The appearance of his chest puzzled me momentarily, then I realized that a sort of tourniquet of wire-netting was screwed so tightly about him that the flesh swelled out in knobs through the mesh. There was blood--

"God in heaven!" screamed Smith frenziedly--"they have the wire-jacket on him! Shoot down that damned Chinaman, Petrie! Shoot! Shoot!"

Lithely as a cat the man with the knife leaped around--but I raised the Browning, and deliberately--with a cool deliberation that came to me suddenly--shot him through the head. I saw his oblique eyes turn up to the whites; I saw the mark squarely between his brows; and with no word nor cry he sank to his knees and toppled forward with one yellow hand beneath him and one outstretched, Clutching--clutching-- convulsively. His pigtail came unfastened and began to uncoil, slowly, like a snake.

I handed the pistol to Smith; I was perfectly cool, now; and I leaped forward, took up the bloody knife from the floor and cut Eltham's lashings. He sank into my arms.

"Praise God," he murmured, weakly. "He is more merciful to me than perhaps I deserve. Unscrew . . . the jacket, Petrie . . . I think . . . I was very near to . . .. weakening. Praise the good God, Who . . . gave me . . . fortitude . . ."

I got the screw of the accursed thing loosened, but the act of removing the jacket was too agonizing for Eltham--man of iron though he was. I laid him swooning on the floor.

"Where is Fu-Manchu?"

Nayland Smith, from just within the door, threw out the query in a tone of stark amaze. I stood up--I could do nothing more for the poor victim at the moment--and looked about me. The room was innocent of furniture, save for heaps of rubbish on the floor, and a tin oil-lamp hung, on the wall. The dead Chinaman lay close beside Smith. There was no second door, the one window was barred, and from this room we had heard the voice, the unmistakable, unforgettable voice, of Dr. Fu-Manchu.

But Dr. Fu-Manchu was not there!

Neither of us could accept the fact for a moment; we stood there, looking from the dead man to the tortured man who only swooned, in a state of helpless incredulity.

Then the explanation flashed upon us both, simultaneously, and with a cry of baffled rage Smith leaped along the passage to the second door. It was wide open. I stood at his elbow when he swept its emptiness with the ray of his pocket-lamp.

There was a speaking-tube fixed between the two rooms!

Smith literally ground his teeth.

"Yet, Petrie," he said, "we have learnt something. Fu-Manchu had evidently promised Eltham his life if he would divulge the name of his correspondent. He meant to keep his word; it is a sidelight on his character."

"How so?"

"Eltham has never seen Dr. Fu-Manchu, but Eltham knows certain parts of China better than you know the Strand. Probably, if he saw Fu-Manchu, he would recognize him for whom he really is, and this, it seems, the Doctor is anxious to avoid."

We ran back to where we had left Karamaneh.

The room was empty!

"Defeated, Petrie!" said Smith, bitterly. "The Yellow Devil is loosed on London again!"

He leaned from the window and the skirl of a police whistle split the stillness of the night.

CHAPTER IV

THE CRY OF A NIGHTHAWK

SUCH WERE THE EPISODES that marked the coming of Dr. Fu-Manchu to London, that awakened fears long dormant and reopened old wounds--nay, poured poison into them. I strove desperately, by close attention to my professional duties, to banish the very memory of Karamaneh from my mind; desperately, but how vainly! Peace was for me no more, joy was gone from the world, and only mockery remained as my portion.

Poor Eltham we had placed in a nursing establishment, where his indescribable hurts could be properly tended: and his uncomplaining fortitude not infrequently made me thoroughly ashamed of myself. Needless to say, Smith had made such other arrangements as were necessary to safeguard the injured man, and these proved so successful that the malignant being whose plans they thwarted abandoned his designs upon the heroic clergyman and directed his attention elsewhere, as I must now proceed to relate.

Dusk always brought with it a cloud of apprehensions, for darkness must ever be the ally of crime; and it was one night, long after the clocks had struck the mystic hour "when churchyards yawn," that the hand of Dr. Fu-Manchu again stretched out to grasp a victim. I was dismissing a chance patient.

"Good night, Dr. Petrie," he said.

"Good night, Mr. Forsyth," I replied; and, having conducted my late visitor to the door, I closed and bolted it, switched off the light and went upstairs.

My patient was chief officer of one of the P. and O. boats. He had cut his hand rather badly on the homeward run, and signs of poisoning having developed, had called to have the wound treated, apologizing for troubling me at so late an hour, but explaining that he had only just come from the docks. The hall clock announced the hour of one as I ascended the stairs. I found myself wondering what there was in Mr. Forsyth's appearance which excited some vague and elusive memory. Coming to the top floor, I opened the door of a front bedroom and was surprised to find the interior in darkness.

"Smith!" I called.

"Come here and watch!" was the terse response. Nayland Smith was sitting in the dark at the open window and peering out across the common. Even as I saw him, a dim silhouette, I could detect that tensity in his attitude which told of high-strung nerves.

I joined him.

"What is it?" I said, curiously.

"I don't know. Watch that clump of elms."

His masterful voice had the dry tone in it betokening excitement. I leaned on the ledge beside him and looked out. The blaze of stars almost compensated for the absence of the moon and the night had a quality of stillness that made for awe. This was a tropical summer, and the common, with its dancing lights dotted irregularly about it, had an unfamiliar look tonight. The clump of nine elms showed as a dense and irregular mass, lacking detail.

Such moods as that which now claimed my friend are magnetic. I had no thought of the night's beauty, for it only served to remind me that somewhere amid London's millions was lurking an uncanny being, whose life was a mystery, whose very, existence was a scientific miracle.

"Where's your patient?" rapped Smith.

His abrupt query diverted my thoughts into a new channel. No footstep disturbed the silence of the highroad; where was my patient?

I craned from the window. Smith grabbed my arm.

"Don't lean out," he said.

I drew back, glancing at him surprisedly.

"For Heaven's sake, why not?"

"I'll tell you presently, Petrie. Did you see him?"

"I did, and I can't make out what he is doing. He seems to have remained standing at the gate for some reason."

"He has seen it!" snapped Smith. "Watch those elms."

His hand remained upon my arm, gripping it nervously. Shall I say that I was surprised? I can say it with truth. But I shall add that I was thrilled, eerily; for this subdued excitement and alert watching of Smith could only mean one thing:

Fu-Manchu!

And that was enough to set me watching as keenly as he; to set me listening; not only for sounds outside the house but for sounds within. Doubts, suspicions, dreads, heaped themselves up in my mind. Why was Forsyth standing there at the gate? I had never seen him before, to my knowledge, yet there was something oddly reminiscent about the man. Could it be that his visit formed part of a plot? Yet his wound had been genuine enough. Thus my mind worked, feverishly; such was the effect of an unspoken thought--Fu-Manchu.

Nayland Smith's grip tightened on my arm.

"There it is again, Petrie!" he whispered.

"Look, look!"

His words were wholly unnecessary. I, too, had seen it; a wonderful and uncanny sight. Out of the darkness under the elms, low down upon the ground, grew a vaporous blue light. It flared up, elfinish, then began to ascend. Like an igneous phantom, a witch flame, it rose, high--higher-- higher, to what I adjudged to be some twelve feet or more from the ground. Then, high in the air, it died away again as it had come!

"For God's sake, Smith, what was it?"

"Don't ask me, Petrie. I have seen it twice. We--"

He paused. Rapid footsteps sounded below. Over Smith's shoulder I saw Forsyth cross the road, climb the low rail, and set out across the common.

Smith sprang impetuously to his feet.

"We must stop him!" he said hoarsely; then, clapping a hand to my mouth as I was about to call out--"Not a sound, Petrie!"

He ran out of the room and went blundering downstairs in the dark, crying:

"Out through the garden--the side entrance!"

I overtook him as he threw wide the door of my dispensing room. Through it he ran and opened the door at the other end. I followed him out, closing it behind me. The smell from some tobacco plants in a neighboring flower-bed was faintly perceptible; no breeze stirred; and in the great silence I could hear Smith, in front of me, tugging at the bolt of the gate.

Then he had it open, and I stepped out, close on his heels, and left the door ajar.

"We must not appear to have come from your house," explained Smith rapidly. "I will go along the highroad and cross to the common a hundred yards up, where there is a pathway, as though homeward bound to the north side. Give me half a minute's start, then you proceed in an opposite direction and cross from the corner of the next road. Directly you are out of the light of the street lamps, get over the rails and run for the elms!"

He thrust a pistol into my hand and was off.

While he had been with me, speaking in that incisive, impetuous way of his, with his dark face close to mine, and his eyes gleaming like steel, I had been at one with him in his feverish mood, but now, when I stood alone, in that staid and respectable byway, holding a loaded pistol in my hand, the whole thing became utterly unreal.

It was in an odd frame of mind that I walked to the next corner, as directed; for I was thinking, not of Dr. Fu-Manchu, the great and evil man who dreamed of Europe and America under Chinese rule, not of Nayland Smith, who alone stood between the Chinaman and the realization of his monstrous schemes, not even of Karamaneh the slave girl, whose glorious beauty was a weapon of might in Fu-Manchu's hand, but of what impression I must have made upon a patient had I encountered one then.

Such were my ideas up to the moment that I crossed to the common and vaulted into the field on my right. As I began to run toward the elms I found myself wondering what it was all about, and for what we were come. Fifty yards west of the trees it occurred to me that if Smith had counted on cutting Forsyth off we were too late, for it appeared to me that he must already be in the coppice.

I was right. Twenty paces more I ran, and ahead of me, from the elms, came a sound. Clearly it came through the still air--the eerie hoot of a nighthawk. I could not recall ever to have heard the cry of that bird on the common before, but oddly enough I attached little significance to it until, in the ensuing instant, a most dreadful scream--a scream in which fear, and loathing, and anger were hideously blended--thrilled me with horror.

After that I have no recollection of anything until I found myself standing by the southernmost elm.

"Smith!" I cried breathlessly. "Smith! my God! where are you?"

As if in answer to my cry came an indescribable sound, a mingled sobbing and choking. Out from the shadows staggered a ghastly figure--that of a man whose face appeared to be streaked. His eyes glared at me madly and he mowed the air with his hands like one blind and insane with fear.

I started back; words died upon my tongue. The figure reeled and the man fell babbling and sobbing at my very feet.

Inert I stood, looking down at him. He writhed a moment--and was still. The silence again became perfect. Then, from somewhere beyond the elms, Nayland Smith appeared. I did not move. Even when he stood beside me, I merely stared at him fatuously.

"I let him walk to his death, Petrie," I heard dimly. "God forgive me -- God forgive me!"

The words aroused me.

"Smith"-- my voice came as a whisper--"for one awful moment I thought--"

"So did some one else," he rapped. "Our poor sailor has met the end designed for me, Petrie!"

At that I realized two things: I knew why Forsyth's face had struck me as being familiar in some puzzling way, and I knew why Forsyth now lay dead upon the grass. Save that he was a fair man and wore a slight mustache, he was, in features and build, the double of Nayland Smith!

CHAPTER V

THE NET

WE RAISED THE POOR VICTIM and turned him over on his back. I dropped upon my knees, and with unsteady fingers began to strike a match. A slight breeze was arising and sighing gently through the elms, but, screened by my hands, the flame of the match took life. It illuminated wanly the sun-baked face of Nayland Smith, his eyes gleaming with unnatural brightness. I bent forward, and the dying light of the match touched that other face.

"Oh, God!" whispered Smith.

A faint puff of wind extinguished the match.

In all my surgical experience I had never met with anything quite so horrible. Forsyth's livid face was streaked with tiny streams of blood, which proceeded from a series of irregular wounds. One group of these clustered upon his left temple, another beneath his right eye, and others extended from the chin down to the throat. They were black, almost like tattoo marks, and the entire injured surface was bloated indescribably. His fists were clenched; he was quite rigid.

Smith's piercing eyes were set upon me eloquently as I knelt on the path and made my examination--an examination which that first glimpse when Forsyth came staggering out from the trees had rendered useless-- a mere matter of form.

"He's quite dead, Smith," I said huskily. "It's--unnatural--it--"

Smith began beating his fist into his left palm and taking little, short, nervous strides up and down beside the dead man. I could hear a car humming along the highroad, but I remained there on my knees staring dully at the disfigured bloody face which but a matter of minutes since had been that of a clean looking British seaman. I found myself contrasting his neat, squarely trimmed mustache with the bloated face above it, and counting the little drops of blood which trembled upon its edge. There were footsteps approaching. I stood up. The footsteps quickened; and I turned as a constable ran up.

"What's this?" he demanded gruffly, and stood with his fists clenched, looking from Smith to me and down at that which lay between us. Then his hand flew to his breast; there was a silvern gleam and--

"Drop that whistle!" snapped Smith--and struck it from the man's hand. "Where's your lantern? Don't ask questions!"

The constable started back and was evidently debating upon his chances with the two of us, when my friend pulled a letter from his pocket and thrust it under the man's nose.

"Read that!" he directed harshly, "and then listen to my orders."

There was something in his voice which changed the officer's opinion of the situation. He directed the light of his lantern upon the open letter and seemed to be stricken with wonder.

"If you have any doubts," continued Smith--"you may not be familiar with the Commissioner's signature--you have only to ring up Scotland Yard from Dr. Petrie's house, to which we shall now return, to disperse them." He pointed to Forsyth. "Help us to carry him there. We must not be seen; this must be hushed up. You understand? It must not get into the press--"

The man saluted respectfully; and the three of us addressed ourselves to the mournful task. By slow stages we bore the dead man to the edge of the common, carried him across the road and into my house, without exciting attention even on the part of those vagrants who nightly slept out in the neighborhood.

We laid our burden upon the surgery table.

"You will want to make an examination, Petrie," said Smith in his decisive way, "and the officer here might 'phone for the ambulance. I have some investigations to make also. I must have the pocket lamp."

He raced upstairs to his room, and an instant later came running down again. The front door banged.

"The telephone is in the hall," I said to the constable.

"Thank you, sir."

He went out of the surgery as I switched on the lamp over the table and began to examine the marks upon Forsyth's skin. These, as I have said, were in groups and nearly all in the form of elongated punctures; a fairly deep incision with a pear-shaped and superficial scratch beneath it. One of the tiny wounds had penetrated the right eye.

The symptoms, or those which I had been enabled to observe as Forsyth had first staggered into view from among the elms, were most puzzling. Clearly enough, the muscles of articulation and the respiratory muscles had been affected; and now the livid face, dotted over with tiny wounds (they were also on the throat), set me mentally groping for a clue to the manner of his death.

No clue presented itself; and my detailed examination of the body availed me nothing. The gray herald of dawn was come when the police arrived with the ambulance and took Forsyth away.

I was just taking my cap from the rack when Nayland Smith returned.

"Smith!" I cried--"have you found anything?"

He stood there in the gray light of the hallway, tugging at the lobe of his left ear, an old trick of his.

The bronzed face looked very gaunt, I thought, and his eyes were bright with that febrile glitter which once I had disliked, but which I had learned from experience were due to tremendous nervous excitement. At such times he could act with icy coolness and his mental faculties seemed temporarily to acquire an abnormal keenness. He made no direct reply; but--

"Have you any milk?" he jerked abruptly.

So wholly unexpected was the question, that for a moment I failed to grasp it. Then--

"Milk!" I began.

"Exactly, Petrie! If you can find me some milk, I shall be obliged."

I turned to descend to the kitchen, when--

"The remains of the turbot from dinner, Petrie, would also be welcome, and I think I should like a trowel."

I stopped at the stairhead and faced him.

"I cannot suppose that you are joking, Smith," I said, "but--"

He laughed dryly.

"Forgive me, old man," he replied. "I was so preoccupied with my own train of thought that it never occurred to me how absurd my request must have sounded. I will explain my singular tastes later; at the moment, hustle is the watchword."

Evidently he was in earnest, and I ran downstairs accordingly, returning with a garden trowel, a plate of cold fish and a glass of milk.

"Thanks, Petrie," said Smith--"If you would put the milk in a jug--"

I was past wondering, so I simply went and fetched a jug, into which he poured the milk. Then, with the trowel in his pocket, the plate of cold turbot in one hand and the milk jug in the other, he made for the door. He had it open when another idea evidently occurred to him.

"I'll trouble you for the pistol, Petrie."

I handed him the pistol without a word.

"Don't assume that I want to mystify you," he added, "but the presence of any one else might jeopardize my plan. I don't expect to be long."

The cold light of dawn flooded the hallway momentarily; then the door closed again and I went upstairs to my study, watching Nayland Smith as he strode across the common in the early morning mist. He was making for the Nine Elms, but I lost sight of him before he reached them.

I sat there for some time, watching for the first glow of sunrise. A policeman tramped past the house, and, a while later, a belated reveler in evening clothes. That sense of unreality assailed me again. Out there in the gray mists a man who was vested with powers which rendered him a law unto himself, who had the British Government behind him in all that he might choose to do, who had been summoned from Rangoon to London on singular and dangerous business, was employing himself with a plate of cold turbot, a jug of milk, and a trowel!

Away to the right, and just barely visible, a traincar stopped by the common; then proceeded on its way, coming in a westerly direction. Its lights twinkled yellowly through the grayness, but I was less concerned with the approaching car than with the solitary traveler who had descended from it.

As the car went rocking by below me, I strained my eyes in an endeavor more clearly to discern the figure, which, leaving the highroad, had struck out across the common. It was that of a woman, who seemingly carried a bulky bag or parcel.

One must be a gross materialist to doubt that there are latent powers in man which man, in modern times, neglects, or knows not how to develop. I became suddenly conscious of a burning curiosity respecting this lonely traveler who traveled at an hour so strange. With no definite plan in mind, I went downstairs, took a cap from the rack, and walked briskly out of the house and across the common in a direction which I thought would enable me to head off the woman.

I had slightly miscalculated the distance, as Fate would have it, and with a patch of gorse effectually screening my approach, I came upon her, kneeling on the damp grass and unfastening the bundle which had attracted my attention. I stopped and watched her.

She was dressed in bedraggled fashion in rusty black, wore a common black straw hat and a thick veil; but it seemed to me that the dexterous hands at work untying the bundle were slim and white; and I perceived a pair of hideous cotton gloves lying on the turf beside her. As she threw open the wrappings and lifted out something that looked like a small shrimping net, I stepped around the bush, crossed silently the intervening patch of grass, and stood beside her.

A faint breath of perfume reached me--of a perfume which, like the secret incense of Ancient Egypt, seemed to assail my soul. The glamour of the Orient was in that subtle essence; and I only knew one woman who used it. I bent over the kneeling figure.

"Good morning," I said; "can I assist you in any way?"

She came to her feet like a startled deer, and flung away from me with the lithe movement of some Eastern dancing girl.

Now came the sun, and its heralding rays struck sparks from the jewels, upon the white fingers of this woman who wore the garments of a mendicant. My heart gave a great leap. It was with difficulty that I controlled my voice.

"There is no cause for alarm," I added.

She stood watching me; even through the coarse veil I could see how her eyes glittered. I stooped and picked up the net.

"Oh!" The whispered word was scarcely audible, but it was enough; I doubted no longer.

"This is a net for bird snaring," I said. "What strange bird are you seeking--Karamaneh?"

With a passionate gesture Karamaneh snatched off the veil, and with it the ugly black hat. The cloud of wonderful, intractable hair came rumpling about her face, and her glorious eyes blazed out upon me. How beautiful they were, with the dark beauty of an Egyptian night; how often had they looked into mine in dreams!

To labor against a ceaseless yearning for a woman whom one knows, upon evidence that none but a fool might reject, to be worthless--evil; is there any torture to which the soul of man is subject, more pitiless? Yet this was my lot, for what past sins assigned to me I was unable to conjecture; and this was the woman, this lovely slave of a monster, this creature of Dr. Fu-Manchu.

"I suppose you will declare that you do not know me!" I said harshly.

Her lips trembled, but she made no reply.

"It is very convenient to forget, sometimes," I ran on bitterly, then checked myself; for I knew that my words were prompted by a feckless desire to hear her defense, by a fool's hope that it might be an acceptable one.

I looked again at the net contrivance in my hand; it had a strong spring fitted to it and a line attached. Quite obviously it was intended for snaring.

"What were you about to do?" I demanded sharply--but in my heart, poor fool that I was, I found admiration for the exquisite arch of Karamaneh's lips, and reproach because they were so tremulous.

She spoke then.

"Dr. Petrie--"

"Well?"

"You seem to be--angry with me, not so much because of what I do, as because I do not remember you. Yet--"

"Kindly do not revert to the matter," I interrupted. "You have chosen, very conveniently, to forget that once we were friends. Please yourself. But answer my question."

She clasped her hands with a sort of wild abandon.

"Why do you treat me so!" she cried; she had the most fascinating accent imaginable. "Throw me into prison, kill me if you like, for what I have done!" She stamped her foot. "For what I have done! But do not torture me, try to drive me mad with your reproaches--that I forget you! I tell you--again I tell you--that until you came one night, last week, to rescue some one from--" There was the old trick of hesitating before the name of Fu-Manchu--" from him, I had never, never seen you!"

The dark eyes looked into mine, afire with a positive hunger for belief--or so I was sorely tempted to suppose. But the facts were against her.

"Such a declaration is worthless," I said, as coldly as I could. "You are a traitress; you betray those who are mad enough to trust you--"

"I am no traitress!" she blazed at me; her eyes were magnificent.

"This is mere nonsense. You think that it will pay you better to serve Fu-Manchu than to remain true to your friends. Your 'slavery'--for I take it you are posing as a slave again--is evidently not very harsh. You serve Fu-

Manchu, lure men to their destruction, and in return he loads you with jewels, lavishes gifts--"

"Ah! so!"

She sprang forward, raising flaming eyes to mine; her lips were slightly parted. With that wild abandon which betrayed the desert blood in her veins, she wrenched open the neck of her bodice and slipped a soft shoulder free of the garment. She twisted around, so that the white skin was but inches removed from me.

"These are some of the gifts that he lavishes upon me!"

I clenched my teeth. Insane thoughts flooded my mind. For that creamy skin was red with the marks of the lash!

She turned, quickly rearranging her dress, and watching me the while. I could not trust myself to speak for a moment, then:

"If I am a stranger to you, as you claim, why do you give me your confidence?" I asked.

"I have known you long enough to trust you!" she said simply, and turned her head aside.

"Then why do you serve this inhuman monster?"

She snapped her fingers oddly, and looked up at me from under her lashes. "Why do you question me if you think that everything I say is a lie?"

It was a lesson in logic--from a woman! I changed the subject.

"Tell me what you came here to do," I demanded.

She pointed to the net in my hands.

"To catch birds; you have said so yourself,"

"What bird?"

She shrugged her shoulders.

And now a memory was born within my brain; it was that of the cry of the nighthawk which had harbingered the death of Forsyth! The net was a large and strong one; could it be that some horrible fowl of the air--some creature unknown to Western naturalists--had been released upon the common last night? I thought of the marks upon Forsyth's face and throat; I thought of the profound knowledge of obscure and dreadful things possessed by the Chinaman

The wrapping, in which the net had been, lay at my feet. I stooped and took out from it a wicker basket. Karamaneh stood watching me and biting her lip, but she made no move to check me. I opened the basket. It contained a large phial, the contents of which possessed a pungent and peculiar smell.

I was utterly mystified.

"You will have to accompany me to my house," I said sternly.

Karamaneh upturned her great eyes to mine. They were wide with fear. She was on the point of speaking when I extended my hand to grasp her. At that, the look of fear was gone and one of rebellion held its place. Ere

I had time to realize her purpose, she flung back from me with that wild grace which I had met with in no other woman, turned and ran!

Fatuously, net and basket in hand, I stood looking after her. The idea of pursuit came to me certainly; but I doubted if I could have outrun her. For Karamaneh ran, not like a girl used to town or even country life, but with the lightness and swiftness of a gazelle; ran like the daughter of the desert that she was.

Some two hundred yards she went, stopped, and looked back. It would seem that the sheer joy of physical effort had aroused the devil in her, the devil that must lie latent in every woman with eyes like the eyes of Karamaneh.

In the ever brightening sunlight I could see the lithe figure swaying; no rags imaginable could mask its beauty. I could see the red lips and gleaming teeth. Then--and it was music good to hear, despite its taunt --she laughed defiantly, turned, and ran again!

I resigned myself to defeat; I blush to add, gladly! Some evidences of a world awakening were perceptible about me now. Feathered choirs hailed the new day joyously. Carrying the mysterious contrivance which I had captured from the enemy, I set out in the direction of my house, my mind very busy with conjectures respecting the link between this bird snare and the cry like that of a nighthawk which we had heard at the moment of Forsyth's death.

The path that I had chosen led me around the border of the Mound Pond --a small pool having an islet in the center. Lying at the margin of the pond I was amazed to see the plate and jug which Nayland Smith had borrowed recently!

Dropping my burden, I walked down to the edge of the water. I was filled with a sudden apprehension. Then, as I bent to pick up the now empty jug, came a hail:

"All right, Petrie! Shall join you in a moment!"

I started up, looked to right and left; but, although the voice had been that of Nayland Smith, no sign could I discern of his presence!

"Smith!" I cried--"Smith!"

"Coming!"

Seriously doubting my senses, I looked in the direction from which the voice had seemed to proceed--and there was Nayland Smith.

He stood on the islet in the center of the pond, and, as I perceived him, he walked down into the shallow water and waded across to me!

"Good heavens!" I began--

One of his rare laughs interrupted me.

"You must think me mad this morning, Petrie!" he said. "But I have made several discoveries. Do you know what that islet in the pond really is?"

"Merely an islet, I suppose--"

"Nothing of the kind; it is a burial mound, Petrie! It marks the site of one of the Plague Pits where victims were buried during the Great Plague of London. You will observe that, although you have seen it every morning for some years, it remains for a British Commissioner resident in Burma to acquaint you with its history! Hullo!"--the laughter was gone from his eyes, and they were steely hard again-- "what the blazes have we here!"

He picked up the net. "What! a bird trap!"

"Exactly!" I said.

Smith turned his searching gaze upon me. "Where did you find it, Petrie?"

"I did not exactly find it," I replied; and I related to him the circumstances of my meeting with Karamaneh.

He directed that cold stare upon me throughout the narrative, and when, with some embarrassment, I had told him of the girl's escape--

"Petrie," he said succinctly, "you are an imbecile!"

I flushed with anger, for not even from Nayland Smith, whom I esteemed above all other men, could I accept such words uttered as he had uttered them. We glared at one another.

"Karamaneh," he continued coldly, "is a beautiful toy, I grant you; but so is a cobra. Neither is suitable for playful purposes."

"Smith!" I cried hotly--"drop that! Adopt another tone or I cannot listen to you!"

"You must listen," he said, squaring his lean jaw truculently. "You are playing, not only with a pretty girl who is the favorite of a Chinese Nero, but with my life! And I object, Petrie, on purely personal grounds!"

I felt my anger oozing from me; for this was strictly just. I had nothing to say, and Smith continued:

"You know that she is utterly false, yet a glance or two from those dark eyes of hers can make a fool of you! A woman made a fool of me, once; but I learned my lesson; you have failed to learn yours. If you are determined to go to pieces on the rock that broke up Adam, do so! But don't involve me in the wreck, Petrie--for that might mean a yellow emperor of the world, and you know it!"

"Your words are unnecessarily brutal, Smith," I said, feeling very crestfallen, "but there--perhaps I fully deserve them all."

"You do!" he assured me, but he relaxed immediately. "A murderous attempt is made upon my life, resulting in the death of a perfectly innocent man in no way concerned. Along you come and let an accomplice, perhaps a participant, escape, merely, because she has a red mouth, or black lashes, or whatever it is that fascinates you so hopelessly!"

He opened the wicker basket, sniffing at the contents.

"Ah!" he snapped, "do you recognize this odor?"

"Certainly."

"Then you have some idea respecting Karamaneh's quarry?"

"Nothing of the kind!"

Smith shrugged his shoulders.

"Come along, Petrie," he said, linking his arm in mine.

We proceeded. Many questions there were that I wanted to put to him, but one above all.

"Smith," I said, "what, in Heaven's name, were you doing on the mound? Digging something up?"

"No," he replied, smiling dryly; "burying something!"

CHAPTER VI

UNDER THE ELMS

DUSK FOUND NAYLAND SMITH and me at the top bedroom window. We knew, now that poor Forsyth's body had been properly examined, that he had died from poisoning. Smith, declaring that I did not deserve his confidence, had refused to confide in me his theory of the origin of the peculiar marks upon the body.

"On the soft ground under the trees," he said, "I found his tracks right up to the point where something happened. There were no other fresh tracks for several yards around. He was attacked as he stood close to the trunk of one of the elms. Six or seven feet away I found some other tracks, very much like this."

He marked a series of dots upon the blotting pad at his elbow.

"Claws!" I cried. "That eerie call! like the call of a nighthawk--is it some unknown species of--flying thing?"

"We shall see, shortly; possibly to-night," was his reply. "Since, probably owing to the absence of any moon, a mistake was made," his jaw hardened at the thoughts of poor Forsyth--"another attempt along the same lines will almost certainly follow--you know Fu-Manchu's system?"

So in the darkness, expectant, we sat watching the group of nine elms. To-night the moon was come, raising her Aladdin's lamp up to the star world and summoning magic shadows into being. By midnight the highroad showed deserted, the common was a place of mystery; and save for the periodical passage of an electric car, in blazing modernity, this was a fit enough stage for an eerie drama.

No notice of the tragedy had appeared in print; Nayland Smith was vested with powers to silence the press. No detectives, no special constables, were posted. My friend was of opinion that the publicity which had been given to the deeds of Dr. Fu-Manchu in the past, together with the sometimes clumsy co-operation of the police, had contributed not a little to the Chinaman's success.

"There is only one thing to fear," he jerked suddenly; "he may not be ready for another attempt to-night."

"Why?"

"Since he has only been in England for a short time, his menagerie of venomous things may be a limited one at present."

Earlier in the evening there had been a brief but violent thunderstorm, with a tropical downpour of rain, and now clouds were scudding across the blue of the sky. Through a temporary rift in the veiling the crescent of the moon looked down upon us. It had a greenish tint, and it set me thinking of the filmed, green eyes of Fu-Manchu.

The cloud passed and a lake of silver spread out to the edge of the coppice, where it terminated at a shadow bank.

"There it is, Petrie!" hissed Nayland Smith.

A lambent light was born in the darkness; it rose slowly, unsteadily, to a great height, and died.

"It's under the trees, Smith!"

But he was already making for the door. Over his shoulder:

"Bring the pistol, Petrie!" he cried; "I have another. Give me at least twenty yards' start or no attempt may be made. But the instant I'm under the trees, join me."

Out of the house we ran, and over onto the common, which latterly had been a pageant ground for phantom warring. The light did not appear again; and as Smith plunged off toward the trees, I wondered if he knew what uncanny thing was hidden there. I more than suspected that he had solved the mystery.

His instructions to keep well in the rear I understood. Fu-Manchu, or the creature of Fu-Manchu, would attempt nothing in the presence of a witness. But we knew full well that the instrument of death which was hidden in the elm coppice could do its ghastly work and leave no clue, could slay and vanish. For had not Forsyth come to a dreadful end while Smith and I were within twenty yards of him?

Not a breeze stirred, as Smith, ahead of me—for I had slowed my pace—came up level with the first tree. The moon sailed clear of the straggling cloud wisps which alone told of the recent storm; and I noted that an irregular patch of light lay silvern on the moist ground under the elms where otherwise lay shadow.

He passed on, slowly. I began to run again. Black against the silvern patch, I saw him emerge—and look up.

"Be careful, Smith!" I cried—and I was racing under the trees to join him.

Uttering a loud cry, he leaped— away from the pool of light.

"Stand back, Petrie!" he screamed—"Back! further!"

He charged into me, shoulder lowered, and sent me reeling!

Mixed up with his excited cry I had heard a loud splintering and sweeping of branches overhead; and now as we staggered into the shadows it seemed that one of the elms was reaching down to touch us! So, at least, the phenomenon presented itself to my mind in that fleeting moment while Smith, uttering his warning cry, was hurling me back.

Then the truth became apparent.

With an appalling crash, a huge bough fell from above. One piercing, awful shriek there was, a crackling of broken branches, and a choking groan . . .

The crack of Smith's pistol close beside me completed my confusion of mind.

"Missed!" he yelled. "Shoot it, Petrie! On your left! For God's sake don't miss it!"

I turned. A lithe black shape was streaking past me. I fired--once--twice. Another frightful cry made yet more hideous the nocturne.

Nayland Smith was directing the ray of a pocket torch upon the fallen bough.

"Have you killed it, Petrie?" he cried.

"Yes, yes!"

I stood beside him, looking down. From the tangle of leaves and twigs an evil yellow face looked up at us. The features were contorted with agony, but the malignant eyes, wherein light was dying, regarded us with inflexible hatred. The man was pinned beneath the heavy bough; his back was broken; and as we watched, he expired, frothing slightly at the mouth, and quitted his tenement of clay, leaving those glassy eyes set hideously upon us.

"The pagan gods fight upon our side," said Smith strangely. "Elms have a dangerous habit of shedding boughs in still weather--particularly after a storm. Pan, god of the woods, with this one has performed Justice's work of retribution."

"I don't understand. Where was this man--"

"Up the tree, lying along the bough which fell, Petrie! That is why he left no footmarks. Last night no doubt he made his escape by swinging from bough to bough, ape fashion, and descending to the ground somewhere at the other side of the coppice."

He glanced at me.

"You are wondering, perhaps," he suggested, what caused the mysterious light? I could have told you this morning, but I fear I was in a bad temper, Petrie. It's very simple: a length of tape soaked in spirit or something of the kind, and sheltered from the view of any one watching from your windows, behind the trunk of the tree; then, the end ignited, lowered, still behind the tree, to the ground. The operator swinging it around, the flame ascended, of course. I found the unburned fragment of the tape last night, a few yards from here."

I was peering down at Fu-Manchu's servant, the hideous yellow man who lay dead in a bower of elm leaves.

"He has some kind of leather bag beside him," I began--

"Exactly!" rapped Smith. "In that he carried his dangerous instrument of death; from that he released it!"

"Released what?"

"What your fascinating friend came to recapture this morning."

"Don't taunt me, Smith!" I said bitterly. "Is it some species of bird?"

"You saw the marks on Forsyth's body, and I told you of those which I had traced upon the ground here. They were caused by claws, Petrie!"

"Claws! I thought so! But what claws?"

"The claws of a poisonous thing. I recaptured the one used last night, killed it--against my will--and buried it on the mound. I was afraid to throw it in the pond, lest some juvenile fisherman should pull it out and sustain a scratch. I don't know how long the claws would remain venomous."

"You are treating me like a child, Smith," I said slowly. "No doubt I am hopelessly obtuse, but perhaps you will tell me what this Chinaman carried in a leather bag and released upon Forsyth. It was something which you recaptured, apparently with the aid of a plate of cold turbot and a jug of milk! It was something, also, which Karamaneh had been sent to recapture with the aid--"

I stopped.

"Go on," said Nayland Smith, turning the ray to the left, "what did she have in the basket?"

"Valerian," I replied mechanically.

The ray rested upon the lithe creature that I had shot down.

It was a black cat!

"A cat will go through fire and water for valerian," said Smith; "but I got first innings this morning with fish and milk! I had recognized the imprints under the trees for those of a cat, and I knew, that if a cat had been released here it would still be hiding in the neighborhood, probably in the bushes. I finally located a cat, sure enough, and came for bait! I laid my trap, for the animal was too frightened to be approachable, and then shot it; I had to. That yellow fiend used the light as a decoy. The branch which killed him jutted out over the path at a spot where an opening in the foliage above allowed some moon rays to penetrate. Directly the victim stood beneath, the Chinaman uttered his bird cry; the one below looked up, and the cat, previously held silent and helpless in the leather sack, was dropped accurately upon his head!"

"But"--I was growing confused.

Smith stooped lower.

"The cat's claws are sheathed now," he said; "but if you could examine them you would find that they are coated with a shining black substance. Only Fu-Manchu knows what that substance is, Petrie, but you and I know what it can do!"

CHAPTER VII

ENTER MR. ABEL SLATTIN

"I DON'T BLAME YOU!" rapped Nayland Smith. "Suppose we say, then, a thousand pounds if you show us the present hiding-place of Fu-Manchu, the payment to be in no way subject to whether we profit by your information or not?"

Abel Slattin shrugged his shoulders, racially, and returned to the armchair which he had just quitted. He reseated himself, placing his hat and cane upon my writing-table.

"A little agreement in black and white?" he suggested smoothly.

Smith raised himself up out of the white cane chair, and, bending forward over a corner of the table, scribbled busily upon a sheet of notepaper with my fountain-pen.

The while he did so, I covertly studied our visitor. He lay back in the armchair, his heavy eyelids lowered deceptively. He was a thought overdressed--a big man, dark-haired and well groomed, who toyed with a monocle most unsuitable to his type. During the preceding conversation, I had been vaguely surprised to note Mr. Abel Slattin's marked American accent.

Sometimes, when Slattin moved, a big diamond which he wore upon the third finger of his right hand glittered magnificently. There was a sort of bluish tint underlying the dusky skin, noticeable even in his hands but proclaiming itself significantly in his puffy face and especially under the eyes. I diagnosed a laboring valve somewhere in the heart system.

Nayland Smith's pen scratched on. My glance strayed from our Semitic caller to his cane, lying upon the red leather before me. It was of most unusual workmanship, apparently Indian, being made of some kind of dark brown, mottled wood, bearing a marked resemblance to a snake's skin; and the top of the cane was carved in conformity, to represent the head of what I took to be a puff-adder, fragments of stone, or beads, being inserted to represent the eyes, and the whole thing being finished with an artistic realism almost startling.

When Smith had tossed the written page to Slattin, and he, having read it with an appearance of carelessness, had folded it neatly and placed it in his pocket, I said:

"You have a curio here?"

Our visitor, whose dark eyes revealed all the satisfaction which, by his manner, he sought to conceal, nodded and took up the cane in his hand.

"It comes from Australia, Doctor," he replied; "it's aboriginal work, and was given to me by a client. You thought it was Indian? Everybody does. It's my mascot."

"Really?"

"It is indeed. Its former owner ascribed magical powers to it! In fact, I believe he thought that it was one of those staffs mentioned in biblical history--"

"Aaron's rod?" suggested Smith, glancing at the cane.

"Something of the sort," said Slattin, standing up and again preparing to depart.

"You will 'phone us, then?" asked my friend.

"You will hear from me to-morrow," was the reply.

Smith returned to the cane armchair, and Slattin, bowing to both of us, made his way to the door as I rang for the girl to show him out.

"Considering the importance of his proposal," I began, as the door closed, "you hardly received our visitor with cordiality."

"I hate to have any relations with him," answered my friend; "but we must not be squeamish respecting our instruments in dealing with Dr. Fu-Manchu. Slattin has a rotten reputation--even for a private inquiry agent. He is little better than a blackmailer--"

"How do you know?"

"Because I called on our friend Weymouth at the Yard yesterday and looked up the man's record."

"Whatever for?"

"I knew that he was concerning himself, for some reason, in the case. Beyond doubt he has established some sort of communication with the Chinese group; I am only wondering--"

"You don't mean--"

"Yes--I do, Petrie! I tell you he is unscrupulous enough to stoop even to that."

No doubt, Slattin knew that this gaunt, eager-eyed Burmese commissioner was vested with ultimate authority in his quest of the mighty Chinaman who represented things unutterable, whose potentialities for evil were boundless as his genius, who personified a secret danger, the extent and nature of which none of us truly understood. And, learning of these things, with unerring Semitic instinct he had sought an opening in this glittering Rialto. But there were two bidders!

"You think he may have sunk so low as to become a creature of Fu-Manchu?" I asked, aghast.

"Exactly! If it paid him well I do not doubt that he would serve that master as readily as any other. His record is about as black as it well could be. Slattin is of course an assumed name; he was known as Lieutenant Pepley when he belonged to the New York Police, and he was kicked out of the service for complicity in an unsavory Chinatown case."

"Chinatown!"

"Yes, Petrie, it made me wonder, too; and we must not forget that he is undeniably a clever scoundrel."

"Shall you keep any appointment which he may suggest?"

"Undoubtedly. But I shall not wait until tomorrow."

"What!"

"I propose to pay a little informal visit to Mr. Abel Slattin, to-night."

"At his office?"

"No; at his private residence. If, as I more than suspect, his object is to draw us into some trap, he will probably report his favorable progress to his employer to-night!"

"Then we should have followed him!"

Nayland Smith stood up and divested himself of the old shooting-jacket.

"He has been followed, Petrie," he replied, with one of his rare smiles. "Two C.I.D. men have been watching the house all night!"

This was entirely characteristic of my friend's farseeing methods.

"By the way," I said, "you saw Eltham this morning. He will soon be convalescent. Where, in heaven's name, can he--"

"Don't be alarmed on his behalf, Petrie," interrupted Smith. "His life is no longer in danger."

I stared, stupidly.

"No longer in danger!"

"He received, some time yesterday, a letter, written in Chinese, upon Chinese paper, and enclosed in an ordinary business envelope, having a typewritten address and bearing a London postmark."

"Well?"

"As nearly as I can render the message in English, it reads: 'Although, because you are a brave man, you would not betray your correspondent in China, he has been discovered. He was a mandarin, and as I cannot write the name of a traitor, I may not name him. He was executed four days ago. I salute you and pray for your speedy recovery. Fu-Manchu.'"

"Fu-Manchu! But it is almost certainly a trap."

"On the contrary, Petrie--Fu-Manchu would not have written in Chinese unless he were sincere; and, to clear all doubt, I received a cable this morning reporting that the Mandarin Yen-Sun-Yat was assassinated in his own garden, in Nan-Yang, one day last week."

CHAPTER VIII

DR. FU-MANCHU STRIKES

TOGETHER WE MARCHED down the slope of the quiet, suburban avenue; to take pause before a small, detached house displaying the hatchet boards of the Estate Agent. Here we found unkempt laurel bushes and acacias run riot, from which arboreal tangle protruded the notice--"To be Let or Sold."

Smith, with an alert glance to right and left, pushed open the wooden gate and drew me in upon the gravel path. Darkness mantled all; for the nearest street lamp was fully twenty yards beyond.

From the miniature jungle bordering the path, a soft whistle sounded.

"Is that Carter?" called Smith, sharply.

A shadowy figure uprose, and vaguely I made it out for that of a man in the unobtrusive blue serge which is the undress uniform of the Force.

"Well?" rapped my companion.

"Mr. Slattin returned ten minutes ago, sir," reported the constable. "He came in a cab which he dismissed--"

"He has not left again?"

"A few minutes after his return," the man continued, "another cab came up, and a lady alighted."

"A lady!"

"The same, sir, that has called upon him before."

"Smith!" I whispered, plucking at his arm--"is it--"

He half turned, nodding his head; and my heart began to throb foolishly. For now the manner of Slattin's campaign suddenly was revealed to me. In our operations against the Chinese murder-group two years before, we had had an ally in the enemy's camp--Karamaneh the beautiful slave, whose presence in those happenings of the past had colored the sometimes sordid drama with the opulence of old Arabia; who had seemed a fitting figure for the romances of Bagdad during the Caliphate--Karamaneh, whom I had thought sincere, whose inscrutable Eastern soul I had presumed, fatuously, to have laid bare and analyzed.

Now, once again she was plying her old trade of go-between; professing to reveal the secrets of Dr. Fu-Manchu, and all the time--I could not doubt it--inveigling men into the net of this awful fisher.

Yesterday, I had been her dupe; yesterday, I had rejoiced in my captivity. To-day, I was not the favored one; to-day I had not been selected recipient of her confidences--confidences sweet, seductive, deadly: but Abel Slattin, a plausible rogue, who, in justice, should be immured in Sing Sing, was chosen out, was enslaved by those lovely mysterious eyes, was taking to his soul the lies which fell from those perfect lips, triumphant in a conquest that must end in his undoing; deeming, poor fool, that for love of him this pearl of the Orient was about to betray her master, to resign herself a prize to the victor!

Companioned by these bitter reflections, I had lost the remainder of the conversation between Nayland Smith and the police officer; now, casting off the succubus memory which threatened to obsess me, I put forth a giant mental effort to purge my mind of this uncleanness, and became again an active participant in the campaign against the Master --the director of all things noxious.

Our plans being evidently complete, Smith seized my arm, and I found myself again out upon the avenue. He led me across the road and into the gate of a house almost opposite. From the fact that two upper windows were illuminated, I adduced that the servants were retiring; the other windows were in darkness, except for one on the ground floor to the extreme left of the building, through the lowered venetian blinds whereof streaks of light shone out.

"Slattin's study!" whispered Smith. "He does not anticipate surveillance, and you will note that the window is wide open!"

With that my friend crossed the strip of lawn, and careless of the fact that his silhouette must have been visible to any one passing the gate, climbed carefully up the artificial rockery intervening, and crouched upon the window-ledge peering into the room.

A moment I hesitated, fearful that if I followed, I should stumble or dislodge some of the larva blocks of which the rockery was composed.

Then I heard that which summoned me to the attempt, whatever the cost.

Through the open window came the sound of a musical voice--a voice possessing a haunting accent, possessing a quality which struck upon my heart and set it quivering as though it were a gong hung in my bosom.

Karamaneh was speaking.

Upon hands and knees, heedless of damage to my garments, I crawled up beside Smith. One of the laths was slightly displaced and over this my friend was peering in. Crouching close beside him, I peered in also.

I saw the study of a business man, with its files, neatly arranged works of reference, roll-top desk, and Milner safe. Before the desk, in a revolving chair, sat Slattin. He sat half turned toward the window, leaning back and smiling; so that I could note the gold crown which preserved the lower left molar. In an armchair by the window, close, very close, and sitting with her back to me, was Karamaneh!

She, who, in my dreams, I always saw, was ever seeing, in an Eastern dress, with gold bands about her white ankles, with jewel-laden fingers, with jewels in her hair, wore now a fashionable costume and a hat that could only have been produced in Paris. Karamaneh was the one Oriental woman I had ever known who could wear European clothes; and as I watched that exquisite profile, I thought that Delilah must have been just such another as this, that, excepting the Empress Poppaea, history has record of no woman, who, looking so innocent, was yet so utterly vile.

"Yes, my dear," Slattin was saying, and through his monocle ogling his beautiful visitor, "I shall be ready for you to-morrow night."

I felt Smith start at the words.

"There will be a sufficient number of men?"

Karamaneh put the question in a strangely listless way.

"My dear little girl," replied Slattin, rising and standing looking down at her, with his gold tooth twinkling in the lamplight, "there will be a whole division, if a whole division is necessary."

He sought to take her white gloved hand, which rested upon the chair arm; but she evaded the attempt with seeming artlessness, and stood up. Slattin fixed his bold gaze upon her.

"So now, give me my orders," he said.

"I am not prepared to do so, yet," replied the girl, composedly; "but now that I know you are ready, I can make my plans."

She glided past him to the door, avoiding his outstretched arm with an artless art which made me writhe; for once I had been the willing victim of all these wiles.

"But--" began Slattin.

"I will ring you up in less than half an hour," said Karamaneh and without further ceremony, she opened the door.

I still had my eyes glued to the aperture in the blind, when Smith began tugging at my arm.

"Down! you fool!" he hissed harshly--"if she sees us, all is lost!"

Realizing this, and none too soon, I turned, and rather clumsily followed my friend. I dislodged a piece of granite in my descent; but, fortunately, Slattin had gone out into the hall and could not well have heard it.

We were crouching around an angle of the house, when a flood of light poured down the steps, and Karamaneh rapidly descended. I had a glimpse of a dark-faced man who evidently had opened the door for her, then all my thoughts were, centered upon that graceful figure receding from me in the direction of the avenue. She wore a loose cloak, and I saw this fluttering for a moment against the white gate posts; then she was gone.

Yet Smith did not move. Detaining me with his hand he crouched there against a quick-set hedge; until, from a spot lower down the hill, we heard the start of the cab which had been waiting. Twenty seconds elapsed, and from some other distant spot a second cab started.

"That's Weymouth!" snapped Smith. With decent luck, we should know Fu-Manchu's hiding-place before Slattin tells us!"

"But--"

"Oh! as it happens, he's apparently playing the game."--In the half-light, Smith stared at me significantly--"Which makes it all the more important," he concluded, "that we should not rely upon his aid!"

Those grim words were prophetic.

My companion made no attempt to communicate with the detective (or detectives) who shared our vigil; we took up a position close under the lighted study window and waited--waited.

Once, a taxi-cab labored hideously up the steep gradient of the avenue . . . It was gone. The lights at the upper windows above us became extinguished. A policeman tramped past the gateway, casually flashing his lamp in at the opening. One by one the illuminated windows in other houses visible to us became dull; then lived again as mirrors for the pallid moon. In the silence, words spoken within the study were clearly audible; and we heard someone--presumably the man who had opened the door--inquire if his services would be wanted again that night.

Smith inclined his head and hung over me in a tense attitude, in order to catch Slattin's reply.

"Yes, Burke," it came--"I want you to sit up until I return; I shall be going out shortly."

Evidently the man withdrew at that; for a complete silence followed which prevailed for fully half an hour. I sought cautiously to move my cramped limbs, unlike Smith, who seeming to have sinews of piano-wire, crouched beside me immovable, untiringly. Then loud upon the stillness, broke the strident note of the telephone bell.

I started, nervously, clutching at Smith's arm. It felt hard as iron to my grip.

"Hullo!" I heard Slattin call--"who is speaking? . . . Yes, yes! This is Mr. A. S. . . . I am to come at once ? . . . I know where--yes I . . . you will meet me there? . . . Good!--I shall be with you in half an hour . . . . Good-by!"

Distinctly I heard the creak of the revolving office-chair as Slattin rose; then Smith had me by the arm, and we were flying swiftly away from the door to take up our former post around the angle of the building. This gained:

"He's going to his death!" rapped Smith beside me; "but Carter has a cab from the Yard waiting in the nearest rank. We shall follow to see where he goes--for it is possible that Weymouth may have been thrown off the scent; then, when we are sure of his destination, we can take a hand in the game! We . . ."

The end of the sentence was lost to me--drowned in such a frightful wave of sound as I despair to describe. It began with a high, thin scream, which was choked off staccato fashion; upon it followed a loud and dreadful cry uttered with all the strength of Slattin's lungs--

"Oh, God!" he cried, and again--"Oh, God!"

This in turn merged into a sort of hysterical sobbing.

I was on my feet now, and automatically making for the door. I had a vague impression of Nayland Smith's face beside me, the eyes glassy with a fearful apprehension. Then the door was flung open, and, in the bright light of the hall-way, I saw Slattin standing--swaying and seemingly fighting with the empty air.

"What is it? For God's sake, what has happened!" reached my ears dimly --and the man Burke showed behind his master. White-faced I saw him to be; for now Smith and I were racing up the steps.

Ere we could reach him, Slattin, uttering another choking cry, pitched forward and lay half across the threshold.

We burst into the hall, where Burke stood with both his hands raised dazedly to his head. I could hear the sound of running feet upon the gravel, and knew that Carter was coming to join us.

Burke, a heavy man with a lowering, bull-dog type of face, collapsed onto his knees beside Slattin, and began softly to laugh in little rising peals.

"Drop that!" snapped Smith, and grasping him by the shoulders, he sent him spinning along the hallway, where he sank upon the bottom step of the stairs, to sit with his outstretched fingers extended before his face, and peering at us grotesquely through the crevices.

There were rustlings and subdued cries from the upper part of the house. Carter came in out of the darkness, carefully stepping over the recumbent figure; and the three of us stood there in the lighted hall looking down at Slattin.

"Help us to move him back," directed Smith, tensely; "far enough to close the door."

Between us we accomplished this, and Carter fastened the door. We were alone with the shadow of Fu-Manchu's vengeance; for as I knelt beside the body on the floor, a look and a touch sufficed to tell me that this was but clay from which the spirit had fled!

Smith met my glance as I raised my head, and his teeth came together with a loud snap; the jaw muscles stood out prominently beneath the dark skin; and his face was grimly set in that odd, half-despairful expression which I knew so well but which boded so ill for whomsoever occasioned it.

"Dead, Petrie!--already?"

"Lightning could have done the work no better. Can I turn him over?

Smith nodded.

Together we stooped and rolled the heavy body on its back. A flood of whispers came sibilantly from the stairway. Smith spun around rapidly, and glared upon the group of half-dressed servants.

"Return to your rooms!" he rapped, imperiously; "let no one come into the hall without my orders."

The masterful voice had its usual result; there was a hurried retreat to the upper landing. Burke, shaking like a man with an ague, sat on the lower step, pathetically drumming his palms upon his uplifted knees.

"I warned him, I warned him!" he mumbled monotonously, "I warned him, oh, I warned him!"

"Stand up!" shouted Smith--"stand up and come here!"

The man, with his frightened eyes turning to right and left, and seeming to search for something in the shadows about him, advanced obediently.

"Have you a flask?" demanded Smith of Carter.

The detective silently administered to Burke a stiff restorative.

"Now," continued Smith, "you, Petrie, will want to examine him, I suppose?" He pointed to the body. "And in the meantime I have some questions to put to you, my man."

He clapped his hand upon Burke's shoulder.

"My God!" Burke broke out, "I was ten yards from him when it happened!"

"No one is accusing you," said Smith, less harshly; but since you were the only witness, it is by your aid that we hope to clear the matter up."

Exerting a gigantic effort to regain control of himself, Burke nodded, watching my friend with a childlike eagerness. During the ensuing conversation, I examined Slattin for marks of violence; and of what I found, more anon.

"In the first place," said Smith, "you say that you warned him. When did you warn him and of what?"

"I warned him, sir, that it would come to this--"

"That what would come to this?"'

"His dealings with the Chinaman!"

"He had dealings with Chinamen?"

"He accidentally met a Chinaman at an East End gaming-house, a man he had known in Frisco--a man called Singapore Charlie--"

"What! Singapore Charlie!"

"Yes, sir, the same man that had a dope-shop, two years ago, down Ratcliffe way--"

"There was a fire--"

"But Singapore Charlie escaped, sir."

"And he is one of the gang?"

"He is one of what we used to call in New York, the Seven Group."

Smith began to tug at the lobe of his left ear, reflectively, as I saw out of the corner of my eye.

"The Seven Group!" he mused. "That is significant. I always suspected that Dr. Fu-Manchu and the notorious Seven Group were one and the same. Go on, Burke."

"Well, sir," the man continued, more calmly, "the lieutenant--"

"The lieutenant!" began Smith; then: "Oh! of course; Slattin used to be a police lieutenant!"

"Well, sir, he--Mr. Slattin--had a sort of hold on this Singapore Charlie, and two years ago, when he first met him, he thought that with his aid he was going to pull off the biggest thing of his life--"

"Forestall me, in fact?"

"Yes, sir; but you got in first, with the big raid and spoiled it."

Smith nodded grimly, glancing at the Scotland Yard man, who returned his nod with equal grimness.

"A couple of months ago," resumed Burke, "he met Charlie again down East, and the Chinaman introduced him to a girl--some sort of an Egyptian girl."

"Go on!" snapped Smith--"I know her."

"He saw her a good many times--and she came here once or twice. She made out that she and Singapore Charlie were prepared to give away the boss of the Yellow gang--"

"For a price, of course?"

"I suppose so," said Burke; "but I don't know. I only know that I warned him."

"H'm!" muttered Smith. "And now, what took place to-night?"

"He had an appointment here with the girl," began Burke

"I know all that," interrupted Smith. "I merely want to know, what took place after the telephone call?"

"Well, he told me to wait up, and I was dozing in the next room to the study--the dining-room--when the 'phone bell aroused me. I heard the lieutenant--Mr. Slattin, coming out, and I ran out too, but only in time to see him taking his hat from the rack--"

"But he wears no hat!"

"He never got it off the peg! Just as he reached up to take it, he gave a most frightful scream, and turned around like lightning as though some one had attacked him from behind!"

"There was no one else in the hall?"

"No one at all. I was standing down there outside the dining-room just by the stairs, but he didn't turn in my direction, he turned and looked right behind him--where there was no one--nothing. His cries were frightful."

Burke's voice broke, and he shuddered feverishly. "Then he made a rush for the front door. It seemed as though he had not seen me. He stood there screaming; but, before I could reach him, he fell. . . ."

Nayland Smith fixed a piercing gaze upon Burke.

"Is that all you know?" he demanded slowly.

"As God is my judge, sir, that's all I know, and all I saw. There was no living thing near him when he met his death."

"We shall see," muttered Smith. He turned to me--"What killed him?" he asked, shortly.

"Apparently, a minute wound on the left wrist," I replied, and, stooping, I raised the already cold hand in mine.

A tiny, inflamed wound showed on the wrist; and a certain puffiness was becoming observable in the injured hand and arm. Smith bent down and drew a quick, sibilant breath.

"You know what this is, Petrie?" he cried.

"Certainly. It was too late to employ a ligature and useless to inject ammonia. Death was practically instantaneous. His heart . . ."

There came a loud knocking and ringing.

"Carter!" cried Smith, turning to the detective, open that door to no one--no one. Explain who I am--"

"But if it is the inspector?--"

"I said, open the door to no one!" snapped Smith.

"Burke, stand exactly where you are! Carter, you can speak to whoever knocks, through the letter-box. Petrie, don't move for your life! It may be here, in the hallway!--"

CHAPTER IX

THE CLIMBER

OUR SEARCH OF THE HOUSE of Abel Slattin ceased only with the coming of the dawn, and yielded nothing but disappointment. Failure followed upon failure; for, in the gray light of the morning, our own quest concluded, Inspector Weymouth returned to report that the girl, Karamaneh, had thrown him off the scent.

Again he stood before me, the big, burly friend of old and dreadful days, a little grayer above the temples, which I set down for a record of former horrors, but deliberate, stoical, thorough, as ever. His blue eyes melted in the old generous way as he saw me, and he gripped my hand in greeting.

"Once again," he said, "your dark-eyed friend has been too clever for me, Doctor. But the track as far as I could follow, leads to the old spot. In fact,"--he turned to Smith, who, grim-faced and haggard, looked thoroughly ill in that gray light--"I believe Fu-Manchu's lair is somewhere near the former opium-den of Shen-Yan--'Singapore Charlie.'"

Smith nodded.

"We will turn our attention in that direction," he replied, "at a very early date."

Inspector Weymouth looked down at the body of Abel Slattin.

"How was it done?" he asked softly.

"Clumsily for Fu-Manchu," I replied. "A snake was introduced into the house by some means."

"By Karamaneh!" rapped Smith.

"Very possibly by Karamaneh," I continued firmly. "The thing has escaped us."

"My own idea," said Smith, "is that it was concealed about his clothing. When he fell by the open door it glided out of the house. We must have the garden searched thoroughly by daylight."

"He"--Weymouth glanced at that which lay upon the floor--"must be moved; but otherwise we can leave the place untouched, clear out the servants, and lock the house up."

"I have already given orders to that effect," answered Smith. He spoke wearily and with a note of conscious defeat in his voice. "Nothing has been disturbed;"--he swept his arm around comprehensively--"papers and so forth you can examine at leisure."

Presently we quitted that house upon which the fateful Chinaman had set his seal, as the suburb was awakening to a new day. The clank of milk-cans was my final impression of the avenue to which a dreadful minister of death had come at the bidding of the death lord. We left Inspector Weymouth in charge and returned to my rooms, scarcely exchanging a word upon the way.

Nayland Smith, ignoring my entreaties, composed himself for slumber in the white cane chair in my study. About noon he retired to the bathroom, and returning, made a pretense of breakfast; then resumed his seat in the cane armchair. Carter reported in the afternoon, but his report was merely formal. Returning from my round of professional visits at half past five, I found Nayland Smith in the same position; and so the day waned into evening, and dusk fell uneventfully.

In the corner of the big room by the empty fireplace, Nayland Smith lay, with his long, lean frame extended in the white cane chair. A tumbler, from which two straws protruded, stood by his right elbow, and a perfect continent of tobacco smoke lay between us, wafted toward the door by the draught from an open window. He had littered the hearth with matches and tobacco ash, being the most untidy smoker I have ever met; and save for his frequent rapping-out of his pipe bowl and perpetual striking of matches, he had shown no sign of activity for the past hour. Collarless and wearing an old tweed jacket, he had spent the evening, as he had spent the day, in the cane chair, only quitting it for some ten minutes, or less, to toy with dinner.

My several attempts at conversation had elicited nothing but growls; therefore, as dusk descended, having dismissed my few patients, I busied myself collating my notes upon the renewed activity of the Yellow Doctor, and was thus engaged when the 'phone bell disturbed me. It was Smith who was wanted, however; and he went out eagerly, leaving me to my task.

At the end of a lengthy conversation, he returned from the 'phone and began, restlessly, to pace the room. I made a pretense of continuing my labors, but covertly I was watching him. He was twitching at the lobe of his left ear, and his face was a study in perplexity. Abruptly he burst out:

"I shall throw the thing up, Petrie! Either I am growing too old to cope with such an adversary as Fu-Manchu, or else my intellect has become dull. I cannot seem to think clearly or consistently. For the Doctor, this crime, this removal of Slattin, is clumsy--unfinished. There are two explanations. Either he, too, is losing his old cunning or he has been interrupted!"

"Interrupted!"

"Take the facts, Petrie,"--Smith clapped his hands upon my table and bent down, peering into my eyes--"is it characteristic of Fu-Manchu to kill a man by the direct agency of a snake and to implicate one of his own damnable servants in this way?"

"But we have found no snake!"

"Karamaneh introduced one in some way. Do you doubt it?"

"Certainly Karamaneh visited him on the evening of his death, but you must be perfectly well aware that even if she had been arrested, no jury could convict her."

Smith resumed his restless pacings up and down.

"You are very useful to me, Petrie," he replied; as a counsel for the defense you constantly rectify my errors of prejudice. Yet I am convinced that our presence at Slattin's house last night prevented Fu-Manchu from finishing off this little matter as he had designed to do."

"What has given you this idea?"

"Weymouth is responsible. He has rung me up from the Yard. The constable on duty at the house where the murder was committed, reports that some one, less than an hour ago, attempted to break in."

"Break in!"

"Ah! you are interested? I thought the circumstance illuminating, also!"

"Did the officer see this person?"

"No; he only heard him. It was some one who endeavored to enter by the bathroom window, which, I am told, may be reached fairly easily by an agile climber."

"The attempt did not succeed?"

"No; the constable interrupted, but failed to make a capture or even to secure a glimpse of the man."

We were both silent for some moments; then:

"What do you propose to do?" I asked.

"We must not let Fu-Manchu's servants know," replied Smith, "but to-night I shall conceal myself in Slattin's house and remain there for a week or a day--it matters not how long--until that attempt is repeated. Quite obviously, Petrie, we have overlooked something which implicates the murderer with the murder! In short, either by accident, by reason of our superior vigilance, or by the clumsiness of his plans, Fu-Manchu for once in an otherwise blameless career, has left a clue!"

CHAPTER X

THE CLIMBER RETURNS

IN UTTER DARKNESS we groped our way through into the hallway of Slattin's house, having entered, stealthily, from the rear; for Smith had selected the study as a suitable base of operations. We reached it without mishap, and presently I found myself seated in the very chair which Karamaneh had occupied; my companion took up a post just within the widely opened door.

So we commenced our ghostly business in the house of the murdered man --a house from which, but a few hours since, his body had been removed. This was such a vigil as I had endured once before, when, with Nayland Smith and another, I had waited for the coming of one of Fu-Manchu's death agents.

Of all the sounds which, one by one, now began to detach themselves from the silence, there was a particular sound, homely enough at another time, which spoke to me more dreadfully than the rest. It was the ticking of the clock upon the mantelpiece; and I thought how this sound must have been familiar to Abel Slattin, how it must have formed part and parcel of his life, as it were, and how it went on now--tick- tick-tick-tick--whilst he, for whom it had ticked, lay unheeding-- would never heed it more.

As I grew more accustomed to the gloom, I found myself staring at his office chair; once I found myself expecting Abel Slattin to enter the room and occupy it. There was a little China Buddha upon the bureau in one corner, with a gilded cap upon its head, and as some reflection of the moonlight sought out this little cap, my thoughts grotesquely turned upon the murdered man's gold tooth.

Vague creakings from within the house, sounds as though of stealthy footsteps upon the stair, set my nerves tingling; but Nayland Smith gave no sign, and I knew that my imagination was magnifying these ordinary night sounds out of all proportion to their actual significance. Leaves rustled faintly outside the window at my back: I construed their sibilant whispers into the dreaded name--Fu-Manchu- Fu-Manchu--Fu-Manchu!

So wore on the night; and, when the ticking clock hollowly boomed the hour of one, I almost leaped out of my chair, so highly strung were my nerves, and so appallingly did the sudden clangor beat upon them. Smith, like a man of stone, showed no sign. He was capable of so subduing his constitutionally high-strung temperament, at times, that temporarily he became immune from human dreads. On such occasions he would be icily cool amid universal panic; but, his object accomplished, I have seen him in such a state of collapse, that utter nervous exhaustion is the only term by which I can describe it.

Tick-tick-tick-tick went the clock, and, with my heart still thumping noisily in my breast, I began to count the tickings; one, two, three, four, five, and so on to a hundred, and from one hundred to many hundreds.

Then, out from the confusion of minor noises, a new, arresting sound detached itself. I ceased my counting; no longer I noted the tick-tick of the clock, nor the vague creakings, rustlings and whispers. I saw Smith, shadowly, raise his hand in warning--in needless warning, for I was almost holding my breath in an effort of acute listening.

From high up in the house this new sound came from above the topmost room, it seemed, up under the roof; a regular squeaking, oddly familiar, yet elusive. Upon it followed a very soft and muffled thud; then a metallic sound as of a rusty hinge in motion; then a new silence, pregnant with a thousand possibilities more eerie than any clamor.

My mind was rapidly at work. Lighting the topmost landing of the house was a sort of glazed trap, evidently set in the floor of a loft-like place extending over the entire building. Somewhere in the red-tiled roof above, there presumably existed a corresponding skylight or lantern.

So I argued; and, ere I had come to any proper decision, another sound, more intimate, came to interrupt me.

This time I could be in no doubt; some one was lifting the trap above the stairhead--slowly, cautiously, and all but silently. Yet to my ears, attuned to trifling disturbances, the trap creaked and groaned noisily.

Nayland Smith waved to me to take a stand on the other side of the opened door--behind it, in fact, where I should be concealed from the view of any one descending the stair.

I stood up and crossed the floor to my new post.

A dull thud told of the trap fully raised and resting upon some supporting joist. A faint rustling (of discarded garments, I told myself) spoke to my newly awakened, acute perceptions, of the visitor preparing to lower himself to the landing. Followed a groan of woodwork submitted to sudden strain--and the unmistakable pad of bare feet upon the linoleum of the top corridor.

I knew now that one of Dr. Fu-Manchu's uncanny servants had gained the roof of the house by some means, had broken through the skylight and had descended by means of the trap beneath on to the landing.

In such a tensed-up state as I cannot describe, nor, at this hour mentally reconstruct, I waited for the creaking of the stairs which should tell of the creature's descent.

I was disappointed. Removed scarce a yard from me as he was, I could hear Nayland Smith's soft, staccato breathing; but my eyes were all for the darkened hallway, for the smudgy outline of the stair-rail with the faint patterning in the background which, alone, indicated the wall.

It was amid an utter silence, unheralded by even so slight a sound as those which I had acquired the power of detecting--that I saw the continuity of the smudgy line of stair-rail to be interrupted.

A dark patch showed upon it, just within my line of sight, invisible to Smith on the other side of the doorway, and some ten or twelve stairs up.

No sound reached me, but the dark patch vanished and reappeared three feet lower down.

Still I knew that this phantom approach must be unknown to my companion--and I knew that it was impossible for me to advise him of it unseen by the dreaded visitor.

A third time the dark patch--the hand of one who, ghostly, silent, was creeping down into the hallway--vanished and reappeared on a level with my eyes. Then a vague shape became visible; no more than a blur upon the dim design of the wall-paper . . . and Nayland Smith got his first sight of the stranger.

The clock on the mantelpiece boomed out the halfhour.

At that, such was my state (I blush to relate it) I uttered a faint cry!

It ended all secrecy--that hysterical weakness of mine. It might have frustrated our hopes; that it did not do so was in no measure due to me. But in a sort of passionate whirl, the ensuing events moved swiftly.

Smith hesitated not one instant. With a panther-like leap he hurled himself into the hall.

"The lights, Petrie!" he cried--"the lights! The switch is near the street-door!"

I clenched my fists in a swift effort to regain control of my treacherous nerves, and, bounding past Smith, and past the foot of the stair, I reached out my hand to the switch, the situation of which, fortunately, I knew.

Around I came, in response to a shrill cry from behind me--an inhuman cry, less a cry than the shriek of some enraged animal. . . .

With his left foot upon the first stair, Nayland Smith stood, his lean body bent perilously backward, his arms rigidly thrust out, and his sinewy fingers gripping the throat of an almost naked man--a man whose brown body glistened unctuously, whose shaven head was apish low, whose bloodshot eyes were the eyes of a mad dog! His teeth, upper and lower, were bared; they glistened, they gnashed, and a froth was on his lips. With both his hands, he clutched a heavy stick, and once-- twice, he brought it down upon Nayland Smith's head!

I leaped forward to my friend's aid; but as though the blows had been those of a feather, he stood like some figure of archaic statuary, nor for an instant relaxed the death grip which he had upon his adversary's throat.

Thrusting my way up the stairs, I wrenched the stick from the hand of the dacoit--for in this glistening brown man, I recognized one of that deadly brotherhood who hailed Dr. Fu-Manchu their Lord and Master.

I cannot dwell upon the end of that encounter; I cannot hope to make acceptable to my readers an account of how Nayland Smith, glassy-eyed, and with consciousness ebbing from him instant by instant, stood there, a realization of Leighton's "Athlete," his arms rigid as iron bars even after Fu-Manchu's servant hung limply in that frightful grip.

In his last moments of consciousness, with the blood from his wounded head trickling down into his eyes, he pointed to the stick which I had torn from the grip of the dacoit, and which I still held in my hand.

"Not Aaron's rod, Petrie!" he gasped hoarsely--"the rod of Moses!--Slattin's stick!"

Even in upon my anxiety for my friend, amazement intruded.

"But," I began--and turned to the rack in which Slattin's favorite cane at that moment reposed--had reposed at the time of his death.

Yes!-- there stood Slattin's cane; we had not moved it; we had disturbed nothing in that stricken house; there it stood, in company with an umbrella and a malacca.

I glanced at the cane in my hand. Surely there could not be two such in the world?

Smith collapsed on the floor at my feet.

"Examine the one in the rack, Petrie," he whispered, almost inaudibly, "but do not touch it. It may not be yet. . . ."

I propped him up against the foot of the stairs, and as the constable began knocking violently at the street door, crossed to the rack and lifted out the replica of the cane which I held in my hand.

A faint cry from Smith--and as if it had been a leprous thing, I dropped the cane instantly.

"Merciful God!" I groaned.

Although, in every other particular, it corresponded with that which I held--which I had taken from the dacoit--which he had come to substitute for the cane now lying upon the floor--in one dreadful particular it differed.

Up to the snake's head it was an accurate copy; but the head lived!

Either from pain, fear or starvation, the thing confined in the hollow tube of this awful duplicate was become torpid. Otherwise, no power on earth could have saved me from the fate of Abel Slattin; for the creature was an Australian death-adder.

CHAPTER XI

THE WHITE PEACOCK

NAYLAND SMITH wasted no time in pursuing the plan of campaign which he had mentioned to Inspector Weymouth. Less than forty-eight hours after quitting the house of the murdered Slattin, I found myself bound along Whitechapel Road upon strange enough business.

A very fine rain was falling, which rendered it difficult to see clearly from the windows; but the weather apparently had little effect upon the commercial activities of the district. The cab was threading a hazardous way through the cosmopolitan throng crowding the street. On either side of me extended a row of stalls, seemingly established in opposition to the more legitimate shops upon the inner side of the pavement.

Jewish hawkers, many of them in their shirt-sleeves, acclaimed the rarity of the bargains which they had to offer; and, allowing for the difference of costume, these tireless Israelites, heedless of climatic conditions, sweating at their mongery, might well have stood, not in a squalid London thoroughfare, but in an equally squalid market-street of the Orient.

They offered linen and fine raiment; from footgear to hair-oil their wares ranged. They enlivened their auctioneering with conjuring tricks and witty stories, selling watches by the aid of legerdemain, and fancy vests by grace of a seasonable anecdote.

Poles, Russians, Serbs, Roumanians, Jews of Hungary, and Italians of Whitechapel mingled in the throng. Near East and Far East rubbed shoulders. Pidgin English contested with Yiddish for the ownership of some tawdry article offered by an auctioneer whose nationality defied conjecture, save that always some branch of his ancestry had drawn nourishment from the soil of Eternal Judea.

Some wearing mens' caps, some with shawls thrown over their oily locks, and some, more true to primitive instincts, defying, bare-headed, the unkindly elements, bedraggled women--more often than not burdened with muffled infants--crowded the pavements and the roadway, thronged about the stalls like white ants about some choicer carrion.

And the fine drizzling rain fell upon all alike, pattering upon the hood of the taxi-cab, trickling down the front windows; glistening upon the unctuous hair of those in the street who were hatless; dewing the bare arms of the auctioneers, and dripping, melancholy, from the tarpaulin coverings of the stalls. Heedless of the rain above and of the mud beneath, North, South, East, and West mingled their cries, their bids, their blandishments, their raillery, mingled their persons in that joyless throng.

Sometimes a yellow face showed close to one of the streaming windows; sometimes a black-eyed, pallid face, but never a face wholly sane and healthy. This was an underworld where squalor and vice went hand in hand through the beautiless streets, a melting-pot of the world's outcasts; this was the shadowland, which last night had swallowed up Nayland Smith.

Ceaselessly I peered to right and left, searching amid that rain-soaked company for any face known to me. Whom I expected to find there, I know not, but I should have counted it no matter for surprise had I detected amid that ungracious ugliness the beautiful face of Karamaneh the Eastern slave-girl, the leering yellow face of a Burmese dacoit, the gaunt, bronzed features of Nayland Smith; a hundred times I almost believed that I had seen the ruddy countenance of Inspector Weymouth, and once (at which instant my heart seemed to stand still) I suffered from the singular delusion that the oblique green eyes of Dr. Fu-Manchu peered out from the shadows between two stalls.

It was mere phantasy, of course, the sick imaginings of a mind overwrought. I had not slept and had scarcely tasted food for more than thirty hours; for, following up a faint clue supplied by Burke, Slattin's man, and, like his master, an ex-officer of New York Police, my friend, Nayland Smith, on the previous evening had set out in quest of some obscene den where the man called Shen-Yan--former keeper of an opium-shop--was now said to be in hiding.

Shen-Yan we knew to be a creature of the Chinese doctor, and only a most urgent call had prevented me from joining Smith upon this promising, though hazardous expedition.

At any rate, Fate willing it so, he had gone without me; and now--although Inspector Weymouth, assisted by a number of C. I. D. men, was sweeping the district about me--to the time of my departure nothing whatever had been heard of Smith. The ordeal of waiting finally had proved too great to be borne. With no definite idea of what I proposed to do, I had thrown myself into the search, filled with such dreadful apprehensions as I hope never again to experience.

I did not know the exact situation of the place to which Smith was gone, for owing to the urgent case which I have mentioned, I had been absent at the time of his departure; nor could Scotland Yard enlighten me upon this point. Weymouth was in charge of the case--under Smith's direction--and since the inspector had left the Yard, early that morning, he had disappeared as completely as Smith, no report having been received from him.

As my driver turned into the black mouth of a narrow, ill-lighted street, and the glare and clamor of the greater thoroughfare died behind me, I sank into the corner of the cab burdened with such a sense of desolation as mercifully comes but rarely.

We were heading now for that strange settlement off the West India Dock Road, which, bounded by Limehouse Causeway and Pennyfields, and narrowly confined within four streets, composes an unique Chinatown, a miniature of that at Liverpool, and of the greater one in San Francisco. Inspired with an idea which promised hopefully, I raised the speaking tube.

"Take me first to the River Police Station," I directed; "along Ratcliffe Highway."

The man turned and nodded comprehendingly, as I could see through the wet pane.

Presently we swerved to the right and into an even narrower street. This inclined in an easterly direction, and proved to communicate with a wide thoroughfare along which passed brilliantly lighted electric trams. I had lost all sense of direction, and when, swinging to the left and to the right again, I looked through the window and perceived that we were before the door of the Police Station, I was dully surprised.

In quite mechanical fashion I entered the depot. Inspector Ryman, our associate in one of the darkest episodes of the campaign with the Yellow Doctor two years before, received me in his office.

By a negative shake of the head, he answered my unspoken question.

"The ten o'clock boat is lying off the Stone Stairs, Doctor," he said, "and co-operating with some of the Scotland Yard men who are dragging that district--"

I shuddered at the word "dragging"; Ryman had not used it literally, but nevertheless it had conjured up a dread possibility--a possibility in accordance with the methods of Dr. Fu-Manchu. All within space of an instant I saw the tide of Limehouse Reach, the Thames lapping about the green-coated timbers of a dock pier; and rising--falling-- sometimes disclosing to the pallid light a rigid hand, sometimes a horribly bloated face--I saw the body of Nayland Smith at the mercy of those oily waters. Ryman continued:

"There is a launch out, too, patrolling the riverside from here to Tilbury. Another lies at the breakwater"--he jerked his thumb over his shoulder. "Should you care to take a run down and see for yourself?"

"No, thanks," I replied, shaking my head. "You are doing all that can be done. Can you give me the address of the place to which Mr. Smith went last night?"

"Certainly," said Ryman; "I thought you knew it. You remember Shen-Yan's place--by Limehouse Basin? Well, further east--east of the Causeway, between Gill Street and Three Colt Street--is a block of wooden buildings. You recall them?"

"Yes," I replied. "Is the man established there again, then?"

"It appears so, but, although you have evidently not been informed of the fact, Weymouth raided the establishment in the early hours of this morning!"

"Well?" I cried.

"Unfortunately with no result," continued the inspector. "The notorious Shen-Yan was missing, and although there is no real doubt that the place is used as a gaming-house, not a particle of evidence to that effect could be obtained. Also--there was no sign of Mr. Nayland Smith, and no sign of the American, Burke, who had led him to the place."

"Is it certain that they went there?"

"Two C. I. D. men who were shadowing, actually saw the pair of them enter. A signal had been arranged, but it was never given; and at about half past four, the place was raided."

"Surely some arrests were made?"

"But there was no evidence!" cried Ryman. "Every inch of the rat-burrow was searched. The Chinese gentleman who posed as the proprietor of what he claimed to be a respectable lodging-house offered every facility to the police. What could we do?"

"I take it that the place is being watched?"

"Certainly," said Ryman. "Both from the river and from the shore. Oh! they are not there! God knows where they are, but they are not there!"

I stood for a moment in silence, endeavoring to determine my course; then, telling Ryman that I hoped to see him later, I walked out slowly into the rain and mist, and nodding to the taxi-driver to proceed to our original destination, I re-entered the cab.

As we moved off, the lights of the River Police depot were swallowed up in the humid murk, and again I found myself being carried through the darkness of those narrow streets, which, like a maze, hold secret within their labyrinth mysteries as great, and at least as foul, as that of Pasiphae.

The marketing centers I had left far behind me; to my right stretched the broken range of riverside buildings, and beyond them flowed the Thames, a stream more heavily burdened with secrets than ever was Tiber or Tigris. On my left, occasional flickering lights broke through the mist, for the most part the lights of taverns; and saving these rents in the veil, the darkness was punctuated with nothing but the faint and yellow luminance of the street lamps.

Ahead was a black mouth, which promised to swallow me up as it had swallowed up my friend.

In short, what with my lowered condition and consequent frame of mind, and what with the traditions, for me inseparable from that gloomy quarter of London, I was in the grip of a shadowy menace which at any moment might become tangible--I perceived, in the most commonplace objects, the yellow hand of Dr. Fu-Manchu.

When the cab stopped in a place of utter darkness, I aroused myself with an effort, opened the door, and stepped out into the mud of a narrow lane. A high brick wall frowned upon me from one side, and, dimly perceptible, there towered a smoke stack, beyond. On my right uprose the side of a wharf building, shadowly, and some distance ahead, almost obscured by the drizzling rain, a solitary lamp flickered, I turned up the collar of my raincoat, shivering, as much at the prospect as from physical chill.

"You will wait here," I said to the man; and, feeling in my breast-pocket, I added: "If you hear the note of a whistle, drive on and rejoin me."

He listened attentively and with a certain eagerness. I had selected him that night for the reason that he had driven Smith and myself on previous occasions and had proved himself a man of intelligence.

Transferring a Browning pistol from my hip-pocket to that of my raincoat, I trudged on into the mist.

The headlights of the taxi were swallowed up behind me, and just abreast of the street lamp I stood listening.

Save for the dismal sound of rain, and the trickling of water along the gutters, all about me was silent. Sometimes this silence would be broken by the distant, muffled note of a steam siren; and always, forming a sort of background to the near stillness, was the remote din of riverside activity.

I walked on to the corner just beyond the lamp. This was the street in which the wooden buildings were situated. I had expected to detect some evidences of surveillances, but if any were indeed being observed, the fact was effectively masked. Not a living creature was visible, peer as I could.

Plans, I had none, and perceiving that the street was empty, and that no lights showed in any of the windows, I passed on, only to find that I had entered a cul-de-sac.

A rickety gate gave access to a descending flight of stone steps, the bottom invisible in the denser shadows of an archway, beyond which, I doubted not, lay the river.

Still uninspired by any definite design, I tried the gate and found that it was unlocked. Like some wandering soul, as it has since seemed to me, I descended. There was a lamp over the archway, but the glass was broken, and the rain apparently had extinguished the light; as I passed under it, I could hear the gas whistling from the burner.

Continuing my way, I found myself upon a narrow wharf with the Thames flowing gloomily beneath me. A sort of fog hung over the river, shutting me in. Then came an incident.

Suddenly, quite near, there arose a weird and mournful cry--a cry indescribable, and inexpressibly uncanny!

I started back so violently that how I escaped falling into the river I do not know to this day. That cry, so eerie and so wholly unexpected, had unnerved me; and realizing the nature of my surroundings, and the folly of my presence alone in such a place, I began to edge back toward the foot of the steps, away from the thing that cried; when--a great white shape uprose like a phantom before me! . . .

There are few men, I suppose, whose lives have been crowded with so many eerie happenings as mine, but this phantom thing which grew out of the darkness, which seemed about to envelope me, takes rank in my memory amongst the most fearsome apparitions which I have witnessed.

I knew that I was frozen with a sort of supernatural terror. I stood there with hands clenched, staring--staring at that white shape, which seemed to float.

As I stared, every nerve in my body thrilling, I distinguished the outline of the phantom. With a subdued cry, I stepped forward. A new sensation claimed me. In that one stride I passed from the horrible to the bizarre.

I found myself confronted with something tangible, certainly, but something whose presence in that place was utterly extravagant--could only be reconcilable in the dreams of an opium slave.

Was I awake, was I sane? Awake and sane beyond doubt, but surely moving, not in the purlieus of Limehouse, but in the fantastic realms of fairyland.

Swooping, with open arms, I rounded up in an angle against the building and gathered in this screaming thing which had inspired in me so keen a terror.

The great, ghostly fan was closed as I did so, and I stumbled back toward the stair with my struggling captive tucked under my arm; I mounted into one of London's darkest slums, carrying a beautiful white peacock!

CHAPTER XII

DARK EYES LOOKED INTO MINE

MY ADVENTURE HAD DONE nothing to relieve the feeling of unreality which held me enthralled. Grasping the struggling bird firmly by the body, and having the long white tail fluttering a yard or so behind me, I returned to where the taxi waited.

"Open the door!" I said to the man--who greeted me with such a stare of amazement that I laughed outright, though my mirth was but hollow.

He jumped into the road and did as I directed. Making sure that both windows were closed, I thrust the peacock into the cab and shut the door upon it.

"For God's sake, sir!" began the driver--

"It has probably escaped from some collector's place on the riverside," I explained, "but one never knows. See that it does not escape again, and if at the end of an hour, as arranged, you do not hear from me, take it back with you to the River Police Station."

"Right you are, sir," said the man, remounting his seat. "It's the first time I ever saw a peacock in Limehouse!"

It was the first time I had seen one, and the incident struck me as being more than odd; it gave me an idea, and a new, faint hope. I returned to the head of the steps, at the foot of which I had met with this singular experience, and gazed up at the dark building beneath which they led. Three windows were visible, but they were broken and neglected. One, immediately above the arch, had been pasted up with brown paper, and this was now peeling off in the rain, a little stream of which trickled down from the detached corner to drop, drearily, upon the stone stairs beneath.

Where were the detectives? I could only assume that they had directed their attention elsewhere, for had the place not been utterly deserted, surely I had been challenged.

In pursuit of my new idea, I again descended the steps. The persuasion (shortly to be verified) that I was close upon the secret hold of the Chinaman, grew stronger, unaccountably. I had descended some eight steps, and was at the darkest part of the archway or tunnel, when confirmation of my theories came to me.

A noose settled accurately upon my shoulders, was snatched tightly about my throat, and with a feeling of insupportable agony at the base of my skull, and a sudden supreme knowledge that I was being strangled--hanged--I lost consciousness!

How long I remained unconscious, I was unable to determine at the time, but I learned later, that it was for no more than half an hour; at any rate, recovery was slow.

The first sensation to return to me was a sort of repetition of the asphyxia. The blood seemed to be forcing itself into my eyes--I choked --I felt that my end was come. And, raising my hands to my throat, I found it to be swollen and inflamed. Then the floor upon which I lay seemed to be rocking like the deck of a ship, and I glided back again into a place of darkness and forgetfulness.

My second awakening was heralded by a returning sense of smell; for I became conscious of a faint, exquisite perfume.

It brought me to my senses as nothing else could have done, and I sat upright with a hoarse cry. I could have distinguished that perfume amid a thousand others, could have marked it apart from the rest in a scent bazaar. For me it had one meaning, and one meaning only-- Karamaneh.

She was near to me, or had been near to me!

And in the first moments of my awakening, I groped about in the darkness blindly seeking her.

Then my swollen throat and throbbing head, together with my utter inability to move my neck even slightly, reminded me of the facts as they were. I knew in that bitter moment that Karamaneh was no longer my friend; but, for all her beauty and charm, was the most heartless, the most fiendish creature in the service of Dr. Fu-Manchu. I groaned aloud in my despair and misery.

Something stirred, near to me in the room, and set my nerves creeping with a new apprehension. I became fully alive to the possibilities of the darkness.

To my certain knowledge, Dr. Fu-Manchu at this time had been in England for fully three months, which meant that by now he must be equipped with all the instruments of destruction, animate and inanimate, which dread experience had taught me to associate with him.

Now, as I crouched there in that dark apartment listening for a repetition of the sound, I scarcely dared to conjecture what might have occasioned it, but my imagination peopled the place with reptiles which writhed upon the floor, with tarantulas and other deadly insects which crept upon the walls, which might drop upon me from the ceiling at any moment.

Then, since nothing stirred about me, I ventured to move, turning my shoulders, for I was unable to move my aching head; and I looked in the direction from which a faint, very faint, light proceeded.

A regular tapping sound now began to attract my attention, and, having turned about, I perceived that behind me was a broken window, in places patched with brown paper; the corner of one sheet of paper was detached, and the rain trickled down upon it with a rhythmical sound.

In a flash I realized that I lay in the room immediately above the archway; and listening intently, I perceived above the other faint sounds of the night, or thought that I perceived, the hissing of the gas from the extinguished lamp-burner.

Unsteadily I rose to my feet, but found myself swaying like a drunken man. I reached out for support, stumbling in the direction of the wall. My foot came in contact with something that lay there, and I pitched forward and fell. . . .

I anticipated a crash which would put an end to my hopes of escape, but my fall was comparatively noiseless--for I fell upon the body of a man who lay bound up with rope close against the wall!

A moment I stayed as I fell, the chest of my fellow captive rising and falling beneath me as he breathed. Knowing that my life depended upon retaining a firm hold upon myself, I succeeded in overcoming the dizziness and nausea which threatened to drown my senses, and, moving back so that I knelt upon the floor, I fumbled in my pocket for the electric lamp which I had placed there. My raincoat had been removed whilst I was unconscious, and with it my pistol, but the lamp was untouched.

I took it out, pressed the button, and directed the ray upon the face of the man beside me.

It was Nayland Smith!

Trussed up and fastened to a ring in the wall he lay, having a cork gag strapped so tightly between his teeth that I wondered how he had escaped suffocation.

But, although a grayish pallor showed through the tan of his skin, his eyes were feverishly bright, and there, as I knelt beside him, I thanked heaven, silently but fervently.

Then, in furious haste, I set to work to remove the gag. It was most ingeniously secured by means of leather straps buckled at the back of his head, but I unfastened these without much difficulty, and he spat out the gag, uttering an exclamation of disgust.

"Thank God, old man!" he said, huskily. "Thank God that you are alive! I saw them drag you in, and I thought . . ."

"I have been thinking the same about you for more than twenty-four hours," I said, reproachfully. "Why did you start without--"

"I did not want you to come, Petrie," he replied. "I had a sort of premonition. You see it was realized; and instead of being as helpless as I, Fate has made you the instrument of my release. Quick! You have a knife? Good!" The old, feverish energy was by no means extinguished in him. "Cut the ropes about my wrists and ankles, but don't otherwise disturb them--"

I set to work eagerly.

"Now," Smith continued, "put that filthy gag in place again--but you need not strap it so tightly! Directly they find that you are alive, they will treat you the same--you understand? She has been here three times--"

"Karamaneh?" . . .

"Ssh!"

I heard a sound like the opening of a distant door.

"Quick! the straps of the gag!" whispered Smith, "and pretend to recover consciousness just as they enter--"

Clumsily I followed his directions, for my fingers were none too steady, replaced the lamp in my pocket, and threw myself upon the floor.

Through half-shut eyes, I saw the door open and obtained a glimpse of a desolate, empty passage beyond. On the threshold stood Karamaneh. She held in her hand a common tin oil lamp which smoked and flickered with every movement, filling the already none too cleanly air with an odor of burning paraffin. She personified the outre; nothing so incongruous as her presence in that place could well be imagined. She was dressed as I remembered once to have seen her two years before, in the gauzy silks of the harem. There were pearls glittering like great tears amid the cloud of her wonderful hair. She wore broad gold bangles upon her bare arms, and her fingers were laden with jewelry. A heavy girdle swung from her hips, defining the lines of her slim shape, and about one white ankle was a gold band.

As she appeared in the doorway I almost entirely closed my eyes, but my gaze rested fascinatedly upon the little red slippers which she wore.

Again I detected the exquisite, elusive perfume, which, like a breath of musk, spoke of the Orient; and, as always, it played havoc with my reason, seeming to intoxicate me as though it were the very essence of her loveliness.

But I had a part to play, and throwing out one clenched hand so that my fist struck upon the floor, I uttered a loud groan, and made as if to rise upon my knees.

One quick glimpse I had of her wonderful eyes, widely opened and turned upon me with such an enigmatical expression as set my heart leaping wildly--then, stepping back, Karamaneh placed the lamp upon the boards of the passage and clapped her hands.

As I sank upon the floor in assumed exhaustion, a Chinaman with a perfectly impassive face, and a Burman, whose pock-marked, evil countenance was set in an apparently habitual leer, came running into the room past the girl.

With a hand which trembled violently, she held the lamp whilst the two yellow ruffians tied me. I groaned and struggled feebly, fixing my gaze upon the lamp-bearer in a silent reproach which was by no means without its effect.

She lowered her eyes, and I could see her biting her lip, whilst the color gradually faded from her cheeks. Then, glancing up again quickly, and still meeting that reproachful stare, she turned her head aside altogether, and rested one hand upon the wall, swaying slightly as she did so.

It was a singular ordeal for more than one of that incongruous group; but in order that I may not be charged with hypocrisy or with seeking to hide my own folly, I confess, here, that when again I found myself in darkness, my heart was leaping not because of the success of my strategy, but because of the success of that reproachful glance which I had directed toward the lovely, dark-eyed Karamaneh, toward the faithless, evil Karamaneh! So much for myself.

The door had not been closed ten seconds, ere Smith again was spitting out the gag, swearing under his breath, and stretching his cramped limbs free from their binding. Within a minute from the time of my trussing, I was a free man again; save that look where I would--to right, to left, or inward, to my own conscience--two dark eyes met mine, enigmatically.

"What now?" I whispered.

"Let me think," replied Smith. A false move would destroy us."

"How long have you been here?"

"Since last night."

"Is Fu-Manchu--"

"Fu-Manchu is here!" replied Smith, grimly--and not only Fu-Manchu, but--another."

"Another!"

"A higher than Fu-Manchu, apparently. I have an idea of the identity of this person, but no more than an idea. Something unusual is going on, Petrie; otherwise I should have been a dead man twenty-four hours ago. Something even more important than my death engages Fu-Manchu's attention--and this can only be the presence of the mysterious visitor. Your seductive friend, Karamaneh, is arrayed in her very becoming national costume in his honor, I presume." He stopped abruptly; then added: "I would give five hundred pounds for a glimpse of that visitor's face!"

"Is Burke--"

"God knows what has become of Burke, Petrie! We were both caught napping in the establishment of the amiable Shen-Yan, where, amid a very mixed company of poker players, we were losing our money like gentlemen."

"But Weymouth--"

"Burke and I had both been neatly sand-bagged, my dear Petrie, and removed elsewhere, some hours before Weymouth raided the gaming-house. Oh! I don't know how they smuggled us away with the police watching the place; but my presence here is sufficient evidence of the fact. Are you armed?"

"No; my pistol was in my raincoat, which is missing."

In the dim light from the broken window, I could see Smith tugging reflectively at the lobe of his left ear.

"I am without arms, too," he mused. "We might escape from the window--"

"It's a long drop!"

"Ah! I imagined so. If only I had a pistol, or a revolver--"

"What should you do?"

"I should present myself before the important meeting, which, I am assured, is being held somewhere in this building; and to-night would see the end of my struggle with the Fu-Manchu group--the end of the whole Yellow menace! For not only is Fu-Manchu here, Petrie, with all his gang of assassins, but he whom I believe to be the real head of the group--a certain mandarin--is here also!"

CHAPTER XIII

THE SACRED ORDER

SMITH STEPPED QUIETLY across the room and tried the door. It proved to be unlocked, and an instant later, we were both outside in the passage. Coincident with our arrival there, arose a sudden outcry from some place at the westward end. A high-pitched, grating voice, in which guttural notes alternated with a serpent-like hissing, was raised in anger.

"Dr. Fu-Manchu!" whispered Smith, grasping my arm.

Indeed, it was the unmistakable voice of the Chinaman, raised hysterically in one of those outbursts which in the past I had diagnosed as symptomatic of dangerous mania.

The voice rose to a scream, the scream of some angry animal rather than anything human. Then, chokingly, it ceased. Another short sharp cry followed--but not in the voice of Fu-Manchu--a dull groan, and the sound of a fall.

With Smith still grasping my wrist, I shrank back into the doorway, as something that looked in the darkness like a great ball of fluff came rapidly along the passage toward me. Just at my feet the thing stopped and I made it out for a small animal. The tiny, gleaming eyes looked up at me, and, chattering wickedly, the creature bounded past and was lost from view.

It was Dr. Fu-Manchu's marmoset.

Smith dragged me back into the room which we had just left. As he partly reclosed the door, I heard the clapping of hands. In a condition of most dreadful suspense, we waited; until a new, ominous sound proclaimed itself. Some heavy body was being dragged into the passage. I heard the opening of a trap. Exclamations in guttural voices told of a heavy task in progress; there was a great straining and creaking--whereupon the trap was softly reclosed.

Smith bent to my ear.

"Fu-Manchu has chastised one of his servants," he whispered. "There will be food for the grappling-irons to-night!"

I shuddered violently, for, without Smith's words, I knew that a bloody deed had been done in that house within a few yards of where we stood.

In the new silence, I could hear the drip, drip, drip of the rain outside the window; then a steam siren hooted dismally upon the river, and I thought how the screw of that very vessel, even as we listened, might be tearing the body of Fu-Manchu's servant!

"Have you some one waiting?" whispered Smith, eagerly.

"How long was I insensible?"

"About half an hour."

"Then the cabman will be waiting."

"Have you a whistle with you?"

I felt in my coat pocket.

"Yes," I reported.

"Good! Then we will take a chance."

Again we slipped out into the passage and began a stealthy progress to the west. Ten paces amid absolute darkness, and we found ourselves abreast of a branch corridor. At the further end, through a kind of little window, a dim light shone.

"See if you can find the trap," whispered Smith; "light your lamp."

I directed the ray of the pocket-lamp upon the floor, and there at my feet was a square wooden trap. As I stooped to examine it, I glanced back, painfully, over my shoulder--and saw Nayland Smith tiptoeing away from me along the passage toward the light!

Inwardly I cursed his folly, but the temptation to peep in at that little window proved too strong for me, as it had proved too strong for him.

Fearful that some board would creak beneath my tread, I followed; and side by side we two crouched, looking into a small rectangular room. It was a bare and cheerless apartment with unpapered walls and carpetless floor. A table and a chair constituted the sole furniture.

Seated in the chair, with his back toward us, was a portly Chinaman who wore a yellow, silken robe. His face, it was impossible to see; but he was beating his fist upon the table, and pouring out a torrent of words in a thin, piping voice. So much I perceived at a glance; then, into view at the distant end of the room, paced a tall, high-shouldered figure--a figure unforgettable, at once imposing and dreadful, stately and sinister.

With the long, bony hands behind him, fingers twining and intertwining serpentinely about the handle of a little fan, and with the pointed chin resting on the breast of the yellow robe, so that the light from the lamp swinging in the center of the ceiling gleamed upon the great, dome-like brow, this tall man paced somberly from left to right.

He cast a sidelong, venomous glance at the voluble speaker out of half-shut eyes; in the act they seemed to light up as with an internal luminance; momentarily they sparkled like emeralds; then their brilliance was filmed over as in the eyes of a bird when the membrane is lowered.

My blood seemed to chill, and my heart to double its pulsations; beside me Smith was breathing more rapidly than usual. I knew now the explanation of the feeling which had claimed me when first I had descended the stone stairs. I knew what it was that hung like a miasma over that house. It was the aura, the glamour, which radiated from this wonderful and evil man as light radiates from radium. It was the vril, the force, of Dr. Fu-Manchu.

I began to move away from the window. But Smith held my wrist as in a vise. He was listening raptly to the torrential speech of the Chinaman who sat in the chair; and I perceived in his eyes the light of a sudden comprehension.

As the tall figure of the Chinese doctor came pacing into view again, Smith, his head below the level of the window, pushed me gently along the passage.

Regaining the site of the trap, he whispered to me: "We owe our lives, Petrie, to the national childishness of the Chinese! A race of ancestor worshipers is capable of anything, and Dr. Fu-Manchu, the dreadful being who has rained terror upon Europe stands in imminent peril of disgrace for having lost a decoration."

"What do you mean, Smith?"

"I mean that this is no time for delay, Petrie! Here, unless I am greatly mistaken, lies the rope by means of which you made your entrance. It shall be the means of your exit. Open the trap!"

Handling the lamp to Smith, I stooped and carefully raised the trap-door. At which moment, a singular and dramatic thing happened.

A softly musical voice--the voice of my dreams!--spoke.

"Not that way! O God, not that way!"

In my surprise and confusion I all but let the trap fall, but I retained sufficient presence of mind to replace it gently. Standing upright, I turned . . . and there, with her little jeweled hand resting upon Smith's arm, stood Karamaneh!

In all my experience of him, I had never seen Nayland Smith so utterly perplexed. Between anger, distrust and dismay, he wavered; and each passing emotion was written legibly upon the lean bronzed features. Rigid with surprise, he stared at the beautiful face of the girl. She, although her hand still rested upon Smith's arm, had her dark eyes turned upon me with that same enigmatical expression. Her lips were slightly parted, and her breast heaved tumultuously.

This ten seconds of silence in which we three stood looking at one another encompassed the whole gamut of human emotion. The silence was broken by Karamaneh.

"They will be coming back that way!" she whispered, bending eagerly toward me. (How, in the most desperate moments, I loved to listen to that odd, musical accent!) "Please, if you would save your life, and spare mine, trust me!"--She suddenly clasped her hands together and looked up into my face, passionately-- "Trust me--just for once--and I will show you the way!"

Nayland Smith never removed his gaze from her for a moment, nor did he stir.

"Oh!" she whispered, tremulously, and stamped one little red slipper upon the floor. "Won't you heed me? Come, or it will be too late!"

I glanced anxiously at my friend; the voice of Dr. Fu-Manchu, now raised in anger, was audible above the piping tones of the other Chinaman.

And as I caught Smith's eye, in silent query--the trap at my feet began slowly to lift!

Karamaneh stifled a little sobbing cry; but the warning came too late. A hideous yellow face with oblique squinting eyes, appeared in the aperture.

I found myself inert, useless; I could neither think nor act. Nayland Smith, however, as if instinctively, delivered a pitiless kick at the head protruding above the trap.

A sickening crushing sound, with a sort of muffled snap, spoke of a broken jaw-bone; and with no word or cry, the Chinaman fell. As the trap descended with a bang, I heard the thud of his body on the stone stairs beneath.

But we were lost. Karamaneh fled along one of the passages lightly as a bird, and disappeared as Dr. Fu-Manchu, his top lip drawn up above his teeth in the manner of an angry jackal, appeared from the other.

"This way!" cried Smith, in a voice that rose almost to a shriek-- "this way!"--and he led toward the room overhanging the steps.

Off we dashed with panic swiftness, only to find that this retreat also was cut off. Dimly visible in the darkness was a group of yellow men, and despite the gloom, the curved blades of the knives which they carried glittered menacingly. The passage was full of dacoits!

Smith and I turned, together, The trap was raised again, and the Burman, who had helped to tie me, was just scrambling up beside Dr. Fu-Manchu, who stood there watching us, a shadowy, sinister figure.

"The game's up, Petrie!" muttered Smith. "It has been a long fight, but Fu-Manchu wins!"

"Not entirely!" I cried. I whipped the police whistle from my pocket, and raised it to my lips; but brief as the interval had been, the dacoits were upon me.

A sinewy brown arm shot over my shoulder and the whistle was dashed from my grasp. Then came a whirl of maelstrom fighting with Smith and myself ever sinking lower amid a whirlpool, as it seemed, of blood-lustful eyes, yellow fangs, and gleaming blades.

I had some vague idea that the rasping voice of Fu-Manchu broke once through the turmoil, and when, with my wrists tied behind me, I emerged from the strife to find myself lying beside Smith in the passage, I could only assume that the Chinaman had ordered his bloody servants to take us alive; for saving numerous bruises and a few superficial cuts, I was unwounded.

The place was utterly deserted again, and we two panting captives found ourselves alone with Dr. Fu-Manchu. The scene was unforgettable; that dimly lighted passage, its extremities masked in shadow, and the tall, yellow-robed figure of the Satanic Chinaman towering over us where we lay.

He had recovered his habitual calm, and as I peered at him through the gloom I was impressed anew with the tremendous intellectual force of the man. He had the brow of a genius, the features of a born ruler; and even in that moment I could find time to search my memory, and to discover that the face, saving the indescribable evil of its expression, was identical with that of Seti, the mighty Pharaoh who lies in the Cairo Museum.

Down the passage came leaping and gamboling the doctor's marmoset. Uttering its shrill, whistling cry, it leaped onto his shoulder, clutched with its tiny fingers at the scanty, neutral-colored hair upon his crown, and bent forward, peering grotesquely into that still, dreadful face.

Dr. Fu-Manchu stroked the little creature; and crooned to it, as a mother to her infant. Only this crooning, and the labored breathing of Smith and myself, broke that impressive stillness.

Suddenly the guttural voice began:

"You come at an opportune time, Mr. Commissioner Nayland Smith, and Dr. Petrie; at a time when the greatest man in China flatters me with a visit. In my absence from home, a tremendous honor has been conferred upon me, and, in the hour of this supreme honor, dishonor and calamity have befallen! For my services to China--the New China, the China of the future--I have been admitted by the Sublime Prince to the Sacred Order of the White Peacock."

Warming to his discourse, he threw wide his arms, hurling the chattering marmoset fully five yards along the corridor.

"O god of Cathay!" he cried, sibilantly, "in what have I sinned that this catastrophe has been visited upon my head! Learn, my two dear friends, that the sacred white peacock brought to these misty shores for my undying glory, has been lost to me! Death is the penalty of such a sacrilege; death shall be my lot, since death I deserve."

Covertly Smith nudged me with his elbow. I knew what the nudge was designed to convey; he would remind me of his words--anent the childish trifles which sway the life of intellectual China.

Personally, I was amazed. That Fu-Manchu's anger, grief, sorrow and resignation were real, no one watching him, and hearing his voice, could doubt.

He continued:

"By one deed, and one deed alone, may I win a lighter punishment. By one deed, and the resignation of all my titles, all my lands, and all my honors, may I merit to be spared to my work--which has only begun."

I knew now that we were lost, indeed; these were confidences which our graves should hold inviolate! He suddenly opened fully those blazing green eyes and directed their baneful glare upon Nayland Smith.

"The Director of the Universe," he continued, softly, "has relented toward me. To-night, you die! To-night, the arch-enemy of our caste shall be no more. This is my offering--the price of redemption . . ."

My mind was working again, and actively. I managed to grasp the stupendous truth--and the stupendous possibility.

Dr. Fu-Manchu was in the act of clapping his hands, when I spoke.

"Stop!" I cried.

He paused, and the weird film, which sometimes became visible in his eyes, now obscured their greenness, and lent him the appearance of a blind man.

"Dr. Petrie," he said, softly, "I shall always listen to you with respect."

"I have an offer to make," I continued, seeking to steady my voice. "Give us our freedom, and I will restore your shattered honor--I will restore the sacred peacock!"

Dr. Fu-Manchu bent forward until his face was so close to mine that I could see the innumerable lines which, an intricate network, covered his yellow skin.

"Speak!" he hissed. "You lift up my heart from a dark pit!"

"I can restore your white peacock," I said; "I and I alone, know where it is!"--and I strove not to shrink from the face so close to mine.

Upright shot the tall figure; high above his head Fu-Manchu threw his arms--and a light of exaltation gleamed in the now widely opened, catlike eyes.

"O god!" he screamed, frenziedly--"O god of the Golden Age! like a phoenix I arise from the ashes of myself!" He turned to me. "Quick! Quick! make your bargain! End my suspense!"

Smith stared at me like a man dazed; but, ignoring him, I went on:

"You will release me, now, immediately. In another ten minutes it will be too late; my friend will remain. One of your--servants--can accompany me, and give the signal when I return with the peacock. Mr. Nayland Smith and yourself, or another, will join me at the corner of the street where the raid took place last night. We shall then give you ten minutes grace, after which we shall take whatever steps we choose."

"Agreed!" cried Fu-Manchu. "I ask but one thing from an Englishman; your word of honor?"

"I give it."

"I, also," said Smith, hoarsely.

Ten minutes later, Nayland Smith and I, standing beside the cab, whose lights gleamed yellowly through the mist, exchanged a struggling, frightened bird for our lives--capitulated with the enemy of the white race.

With characteristic audacity--and characteristic trust in the British sense of honor--Dr. Fu-Manchu came in person with Nayland Smith, in response to the wailing signal of the dacoit who had accompanied me. No word was spoken, save that the cabman suppressed a curse of amazement; and the Chinaman, his sinister servant at his elbow, bowed low--and left us, surely to the mocking laughter of the gods!

CHAPTER XIV

THE COUGHING HORROR

I LEAPED UP in bed with a great start.

My sleep was troubled often enough in these days, which immediately followed our almost miraculous escape, from the den of Fu-Manchu; and now as I crouched there, nerves aquiver--listening--listening--I could not be sure if this dank panic which possessed me had its origin in nightmare or in something else.

Surely a scream, a choking cry for help, had reached my ears; but now, almost holding my breath in that sort of nervous tensity peculiar to one aroused thus, I listened, and the silence seemed complete. Perhaps I had been dreaming . . .

"Help! Petrie! Help! . . ."

It was Nayland Smith in the room above me!

My doubts were dissolved; this was no trick of an imagination disordered. Some dreadful menace threatened my friend. Not delaying even to snatch my dressing-gown, I rushed out on to the landing, up the stairs, bare-footed as I was, threw open the door of Smith's room and literally hurled myself in.

Those cries had been the cries of one assailed, had been uttered, I judged, in the brief interval of a life and death struggle; had been choked off . . .

A certain amount of moonlight found access to the room, without spreading so far as the bed in which my friend lay. But at the moment of my headlong entrance, and before I had switched on the light, my gaze automatically was directed to the pale moonbeam streaming through the window and down on to one corner of the sheep-skin rug beside the bed.

There came a sound of faint and muffled coughing.

What with my recent awakening and the panic at my heart, I could not claim that my vision was true; but across this moonbeam passed a sort of gray streak, for all the world as though some long thin shape had been withdrawn, snakelike, from the room, through the open window . . . From somewhere outside the house, and below, I heard the cough again, followed by a sharp cracking sound like the lashing of a whip.

I depressed the switch, flooding the room with light, and as I leaped forward to the bed a word picture of what I had seen formed in my mind; and I found that I was thinking of a gray feather boa.

"Smith!" I cried (my voice seemed to pitch itself, unwilled, in a very high key), "Smith, old man!"

He made no reply, and a sudden, sorrowful fear clutched at my heart-strings. He was lying half out of bed flat upon his back, his head at a dreadful angle with his body. As I bent over him and seized him by the shoulders, I could see the whites of his eyes. His arms hung limply, and his fingers touched the carpet.

"My God!" I whispered--"what has happened?"

I heaved him back onto the pillow, and looked anxiously into his face. Habitually gaunt, the flesh so refined away by the consuming nervous energy of the man as to reveal the cheekbones in sharp prominence, he now looked truly ghastly. His skin was so sunbaked as to have changed constitutionally; nothing could ever eradicate that tan. But to-night a fearful grayness was mingled with the brown, his lips were purple . . . and there were marks of strangulation upon the lean throat--ever darkening weals made by clutching fingers.

He began to breathe stentoriously and convulsively, inhalation being accompanied by a significant gurgling in the throat. But now my calm was restored in face of a situation which called for professional attention.

I aided my friend's labored respirations by the usual means, setting to work vigorously; so that presently he began to clutch at his inflamed throat which that murderous pressure had threatened to close.

I could hear sounds of movement about the house, showing that not I alone had been awakened by those hoarse screams.

"It's all right, old man," I said, bending over him; "brace up!"

He opened his eyes--they looked bleared and bloodshot--and gave me a quick glance of recognition.

"It's all right, Smith!" I said--"no! don't sit up; lie there for a moment."

I ran across to the dressing-table, whereon I perceived his flask to lie, and mixed him a weak stimulant with which I returned to the bed.

As I bent over him again, my housekeeper appeared in the doorway, pale and wide-eyed.

"There is no occasion for alarm," I said over my shoulder; "Mr. Smith's nerves are overwrought and he was awakened by some disturbing dream. You can return to bed, Mrs. Newsome."

Nayland Smith seemed to experience much difficulty in swallowing the contents of the tumbler which I held to his lips; and, from the way in which he fingered the swollen glands, I could see that his throat, which I had vigorously massaged, was occasioning him great pain. But the danger was past, and already that glassy look was disappearing from his eyes, nor did they protrude so unnaturally.

"God, Petrie!" he whispered, "that was a near shave! I haven't the strength of a kitten!"

"The weakness will pass off," I replied; "there will be no collapse, now. A little more fresh air..."

I stood up, glancing at the windows, then back at Smith, who forced a wry smile in answer to my look.

"Couldn't be done, Petrie," he said, huskily.

His words referred to the state of the windows. Although the night was oppressively hot, these were only opened some four inches at top and bottom. Further opening was impossible because of iron brackets screwed firmly into the casements which prevented the windows being raised or lowered further.

It was a precaution adopted after long experience of the servants of Dr. Fu-Manchu.

Now, as I stood looking from the half-strangled man upon the bed to those screwed-up windows, the fact came home to my mind that this precaution had proved futile. I thought of the thing which I had likened to a feather boa; and I looked at the swollen weals made by clutching fingers upon the throat of Nayland Smith.

The bed stood fully four feet from the nearest window.

I suppose the question was written in my face; for, as I turned again to Smith, who, having struggled upright, was still fingering his injured throat ruefully:

"God only knows, Petrie! he said; "no human arm could have reached me . . ."

For us, the night was ended so far as sleep was concerned. Arrayed in his dressing-gown, Smith sat in the white cane chair in my study with a glass of brandy-and-water beside him, and (despite my official prohibition) with the cracked briar which had sent up its incense in many strange and dark places of the East and which yet survived to perfume these prosy rooms in suburban London, steaming between his teeth. I stood with my elbow resting upon the mantelpiece looking down at him where he sat.

"By God! Petrie," he said, yet again, with his fingers straying gently over the surface of his throat, "that was a narrow shave--a damned narrow shave!"

"Narrower than perhaps you appreciate, old man," I replied. "You were a most unusual shade of blue when I found you . . ."

"I managed," said Smith evenly, "to tear those clutching fingers away for a moment and to give a cry for help. It was only for a moment, though. Petrie! they were fingers of steel--of steel!"

"The bed," I began . . .

"I know that," rapped Smith. "I shouldn't have been sleeping in it, had it been within reach of the window; but, knowing that the doctor avoids noisy methods, I had thought myself fairly safe so long as I made it impossible for any one actually to enter the room . . ."

"I have always insisted, Smith," I cried, "that there was danger! What of poisoned darts? What of the damnable reptiles and insects which form part of the armory of Fu-Manchu?"

"Familiarity breeds contempt, I suppose," he replied. "But as it happened none of those agents was employed. The very menace that I sought to avoid reached me somehow. It would almost seem that Dr. Fu-Manchu deliberately accepted the challenge of those screwed-up windows! Hang it all, Petrie! one cannot sleep in a room hermetically sealed, in weather like this! It's positively Burmese; and although I can stand tropical heat, curiously enough the heat of London gets me down almost immediately."

"The humidity; that's easily understood. But you'll have to put up with it in the future. After nightfall our windows must be closed entirely, Smith."

Nayland Smith knocked out his pipe upon the side of the fireplace. The bowl sizzled furiously, but without delay he stuffed broad-cut mixture into the hot pipe, dropping a liberal quantity upon the carpet during the process. He raised his eyes to me, and his face was very grim.

"Petrie," he said, striking a match on the heel of his slipper, "the resources of Dr. Fu-Manchu are by no means exhausted. Before we quit this room it is up to us to come to a decision upon a certain point." He got his pipe well alight. "What kind of thing, what unnatural, distorted creature, laid hands upon my throat to-night? I owe my life, primarily, to you, old man, but, secondarily, to the fact that I was awakened, just before the attack--by the creature's coughing--by its vile, high-pitched coughing . . ."

I glanced around at the books upon my shelves. Often enough, following some outrage by the brilliant Chinese doctor whose genius was directed to the discovery of new and unique death agents, we had obtained a clue in those works of a scientific nature which bulk largely in the library of a medical man. There are creatures, there are drugs, which, ordinarily innocuous, may be so employed as to become inimical to human life; and in the distorting of nature, in the disturbing of balances and the diverting of beneficent forces into strange and dangerous channels, Dr. Fu-Manchu excelled. I had known him to enlarge, by artificial culture, a minute species of fungus so as to render it a powerful agent capable of attacking man; his knowledge of venomous insects has probably never been paralleled in the history of the world; whilst, in the sphere of pure toxicology, he had, and has, no rival; the Borgias were children by comparison. But, look where I would, think how I might, no adequate explanation of this latest outrage seemed possible along normal lines.

"There's the clue," said Nayland Smith, pointing to a little ash-tray upon the table near by. "Follow it if you can."

But I could not.

"As I have explained," continued my friend, "I was awakened by a sound of coughing; then came a death grip on my throat, and instinctively my hands shot out in search of my attacker. I could not reach him; my hands came in contact with nothing palpable. Therefore I clutched at the fingers which were dug into my windpipe, and found them to be small--as the marks show--and hairy. I managed to give that first cry for help, then with all my strength I tried to unfasten the grip that was throttling the life out of me. At last I contrived to move one of the hands, and I called out again, though not so loudly. Then both the hands were back again; I was weakening; but I clawed like a madman at the thin, hairy arms of the strangling thing, and with a blood-red mist dancing before my eyes, I seemed to be whirling madly round and round until all became a blank. Evidently I used my nails pretty freely--and there's the trophy."

For the twentieth time, I should think, I carried the ash-tray in my hand and laid it immediately under the table-lamp in order to examine its contents. In the little brass bowl lay a blood-stained fragment of grayish hair attached to a tatter of skin. This fragment of epidermis had an odd bluish tinge, and the attached hair was much darker at the roots than elsewhere. Saving its singular color, it might have been torn from the forearm of a very hirsute human; but although my thoughts wandered unfettered, north, south, east and west; although, knowing the resources of Fu-Manchu, I considered all the recognized Mongolian types, and, in quest of hirsute mankind, even roamed far north among the blubbering Esquimo; although I glanced at Australasia, at Central Africa, and passed in mental review the dark places of the Congo, nowhere in the known world, nowhere in the history of the human species, could I come upon a type of man answering to the description suggested by our strange clue.

Nayland Smith was watching me curiously as I bent over the little brass ash-tray.

"You are puzzled," he rapped in his short way.

So am I--utterly puzzled. Fu-Manchu's gallery of monstrosities clearly has become reinforced; for even if we identified the type, we should not be in sight of our explanation."

"You mean," I began . . .

"Fully four feet from the window, Petrie, and that window but a few inches open! Look"--he bent forward, resting his chest against the table, and stretched out his hand toward me. "You have a rule there; just measure."

Setting down the ash-tray, I opened out the rule and measured the distance from the further edge of the table to the tips of Smith's fingers.

"Twenty-eight inches--and I have a long reach!" snapped Smith, withdrawing his arm and striking a match to relight his pipe." There's one thing, Petrie, often proposed before, which now we must do without delay. The ivy must be stripped from the walls at the back. It's a pity, but we can not afford to sacrifice our lives to our sense of the aesthetic. What do you make of the sound like the cracking of a whip?"

"I make nothing of it, Smith," I replied, wearily. "It might have been a thick branch of ivy breaking beneath the weight of a climber."

"Did it sound like it?"

"I must confess that the explanation does not convince me, but I have no better one."

Smith, permitting his pipe to go out, sat staring straight before him, and tugging at the lobe of his left ear.

"The old bewilderment is seizing me," I continued. "At first, when I realized that Dr. Fu-Manchu was back in England, when I realized that an elaborate murder-machine was set up somewhere in London, it seemed unreal, fantastical. Then I met--Karamaneh! She, whom we thought to be his victim, showed herself again to be his slave. Now, with Weymouth and Scotland Yard at work, the old secret evil is established again in our midst, unaccountably--our lives are menaced--sleep is a danger-- every shadow threatens death . . . oh! it is awful."

Smith remained silent; he did not seem to have heard my words. I knew these moods and had learnt that it was useless to seek to interrupt them. With his brows drawn down, and his deep-set eyes staring into space, he sat there gripping his cold pipe so tightly that my own jaw muscles ached sympathetically. No man was better equipped than this gaunt British Commissioner to stand between society and the menace of the Yellow Doctor; I respected his meditations, for, unlike my own, they were informed by an intimate knowledge of the dark and secret things of the East, of that mysterious East out of which Fu-Manchu came, of that jungle of noxious things whose miasma had been wafted Westward with the implacable Chinaman.

I walked quietly from the room, occupied with my own bitter reflections.

CHAPTER XV

BEWITCHMENT

"YOU SAY YOU HAVE two items of news for me?" said Nayland Smith, looking across the breakfast table to where Inspector Weymouth sat sipping coffee.

"There are two points--yes," replied the Scotland Yard man, whilst Smith paused, egg-spoon in hand, and fixed his keen eyes upon the speaker. "The first is this: the headquarters of the Yellow group is no longer in the East End."

"How can you be sure of that?"

"For two reasons. In the first place, that district must now be too hot to hold Dr. Fu-Manchu; in the second place, we have just completed a house-to-house inquiry which has scarcely overlooked a rathole or a rat. That place where you say Fu-Manchu was visited by some Chinese mandarin; where you, Mr. Smith," and--glancing in my direction--"you, Doctor, were confined for a time--"

"Yes?" snapped Smith, attacking his egg.

"Well," continued the inspector, "it is all deserted, now. There is not the slightest doubt that the Chinaman has fled to some other abode. I am certain of it. My second piece of news will interest you very much, I am sure. You were taken to the establishment of the Chinaman, Shen-Yan, by a certain ex-officer of New York Police-- Burke . . ."

"Good God!" cried Smith, looking up with a start; "I thought they had him!"

"So did I," replied Weymouth grimly; "but they haven't! He got away in the confusion following the raid, and has been hiding ever since with a cousin, a nurseryman out Upminster way . . ."

"Hiding?" snapped Smith.

"Exactly--hiding. He has been afraid to stir ever since, and has scarcely shown his nose outside the door. He says he is watched night and day."

"Then how . . ."

"He realized that something must be done," continued the inspector, "and made a break this morning. He is so convinced of this constant surveillance that he came away secretly, hidden under the boxes of a market-wagon. He landed at Covent Garden in the early hours of this morning and came straight away to the Yard."

"What is he afraid of exactly?"

Inspector Weymouth put down his coffee cup and bent forward slightly.

"He knows something," he said in a low voice, "and they are aware that he knows it!"

"And what is this he knows?"

Nayland Smith stared eagerly at the detective.

"Every man has his price," replied Weymouth with a smile, "and Burke seems to think that you are a more likely market than the police authorities."

"I see," snapped Smith. "He wants to see me?"

"He wants you to go and see him," was the reply. "I think he anticipates that you may make a capture of the person or persons spying upon him."

"Did he give you any particulars?"

"Several. He spoke of a sort of gipsy girl with whom he had a short conversation one day, over the fence which divides his cousin's flower plantations from the lane adjoining."

"Gipsy girl!" I whispered, glancing rapidly at Smith.

"I think you are right, Doctor," said Weymouth with his slow smile; "it was Karamaneh. She asked him the way to somewhere or other and got him to write it upon a loose page of his notebook, so that she should not forget it."

"You hear that, Petrie?" rapped Smith.

"I hear it," I replied, "but I don't see any special significance in the fact."

"I do!" rapped Smith; "I didn't sit up the greater part of last night thrashing my weary brains for nothing! But I am going to the British Museum to-day, to confirm a certain suspicion." He turned to Weymouth. "Did Burke go back?" he demanded abruptly.

"He returned hidden under the empty boxes," was the reply. "Oh! you never saw a man in such a funk in all your life!"

"He may have good reasons," I said.

"He has good reasons!" replied Nayland Smith grimly; "if that man really possesses information inimical to the safety of Fu-Manchu, he can only escape doom by means of a miracle similar to that which has hitherto protected you and me."

"Burke insists," said Weymouth at this point, that something comes almost every night after dusk, slinking about the house--it's an old farmhouse, I understand; and on two or three occasions he has been awakened (fortunately for him he is a light sleeper) by sounds of coughing immediately outside his window. He is a man who sleeps with a pistol under his pillow, and more than once, on running to the window, he has had a vague glimpse of some creature leaping down from the tiles of the roof, which slopes up to his room, into the flower beds below . . ."

"Creature!" said Smith, his gray eyes ablaze now--"you said creature!"

"I used the word deliberately," replied Weymouth, "because Burke seems to have the idea that it goes on all fours."

There was a short and rather strained silence. Then:

"In descending a sloping roof," I suggested, "a human being would probably employ his hands as well as his feet."

"Quite so," agreed the inspector. "I am merely reporting the impression of Burke."

"Has he heard no other sound?" rapped Smith; "one like the cracking of dry branches, for instance?"

"He made no mention of it," replied Weymouth, staring.

"And what is the plan?"

"One of his cousin's vans," said Weymouth, with his slight smile, "has remained behind at Covent Garden and will return late this afternoon. I propose that you and I, Mr. Smith, imitate Burke and ride down to Upminster under the empty boxes!"

Nayland Smith stood up, leaving his breakfast half finished, and began to wander up and down the room, reflectively tugging at his ear. Then he began to fumble in the pockets of his dressing-gown and finally produced the inevitable pipe, dilapidated pouch, and box of safety matches. He began to load the much-charred agent of reflection.

"Do I understand that Burke is actually too afraid to go out openly even in daylight?" he asked suddenly.

"He has not hitherto left his cousin's plantations at all," replied Weymouth. "He seems to think that openly to communicate with the authorities, or with you, would be to seal his death warrant."

"He's right," snapped Smith.

"Therefore he came and returned secretly," continued the inspector; "and if we are to do any good, obviously we must adopt similar precautions. The market wagon, loaded in such a way as to leave ample space in the interior for us, will be drawn up outside the office of Messrs. Pike and Pike, in Covent Garden, until about five o'clock this afternoon. At, say, half past four, I propose that we meet there and embark upon the journey."

The speaker glanced in my direction interrogatively.

"Include me in the program," I said. "Will there be room in the wagon?"

"Certainly," was the reply; "it is most commodious, but I cannot guarantee its comfort."

Nayland Smith promenaded the room, unceasingly, and presently he walked out altogether, only to return ere the inspector and I had had time to exchange more than a glance of surprise, carrying a brass ash-tray. He placed this on a corner of the breakfast table before Weymouth.

"Ever seen anything like that?" he inquired.

The inspector examined the gruesome relic with obvious curiosity, turning it over with the tip of his little finger and manifesting considerable repugnance--in touching it at all. Smith and I watched him in silence, and, finally, placing the tray again upon the table, he looked up in a puzzled way.

"It's something like the skin of a water rat," he said.

Nayland Smith stared at him fixedly.

"A water rat? Now that you come to mention it, I perceive a certain resemblance--yes. But"--he had been wearing a silk scarf about his throat and now he unwrapped it--"did you ever see a water rat that could make marks like these?"

Weymouth started to his feet with some muttered exclamation.

"What is this?" he cried. "When did it happen, and how?"

In his own terse fashion, Nayland Smith related the happenings of the night. At the conclusion of the story:

"By heaven!" whispered Weymouth, "the thing on the roof--the coughing thing that goes on all fours, seen by Burke..."

"My own idea exactly!" cried Smith . . .

"Fu-Manchu," I said excitedly, "has brought some new, some dreadful creature, from Burma..."

"No, Petrie," snapped Smith, turning upon me suddenly. "Not from Burma--from Abyssinia."

That day was destined to be an eventful one; a day never to be forgotten by any of us concerned in those happenings which I have to record. Early in the morning Nayland Smith set off for the British Museum to pursue his mysterious investigations, and having performed my brief professional round (for, as Nayland Smith had remarked on one occasion, this was a beastly healthy district), I found, having made the necessary arrangements, that, with over three hours to spare, I had nothing to occupy my time until the appointment in Covent Garden Market. My lonely lunch completed, a restless fit seized me, and I felt unable to remain longer in the house. Inspired by this restlessness, I attired myself for the adventure of the evening, not neglecting to place a pistol in my pocket, and, walking to the neighboring Tube station, I booked to Charing Cross, and presently found myself rambling aimlessly along the crowded streets. Led on by what link of memory I know not, I presently drifted into New Oxford Street, and looked up with a start--to learn that I stood before the shop of a second-hand bookseller where once two years before I had met Karamaneh.

The thoughts conjured up at that moment were almost too bitter to be borne, and without so much as glancing at the books displayed for sale, I crossed the roadway, entered Museum Street, and, rather in order to distract my mind than because I contemplated any purchase, began to examine the Oriental Pottery, Egyptian statuettes, Indian armor, and other curios, displayed in the window of an antique dealer.

But, strive as I would to concentrate my mind upon the objects in the window, my memories persistently haunted me, and haunted me to the exclusion even of the actualities. The crowds thronging the Pavement, the traffic in New Oxford Street, swept past unheeded; my eyes saw nothing of pot nor statuette, but only met, in a misty imaginative world, the glance of two other eyes--the dark and beautiful eyes of Karamaneh. In the exquisite tinting of a Chinese vase dimly perceptible in the background of the shop, I perceived only the blushing cheeks of Karamaneh; her face rose up, a taunting phantom, from out of the darkness between a hideous, gilded idol and an Indian sandalwood screen.

I strove to dispel this obsessing thought, resolutely fixing my attention upon a tall Etruscan vase in the corner of the window, near to the shop door. Was I losing my senses indeed? A doubt of my own sanity momentarily possessed me. For, struggle as I would to dispel the illusion--there, looking out at me over that ancient piece of pottery, was the bewitching face of the slave-girl!

Probably I was glaring madly, and possibly I attracted the notice of the passers-by; but of this I cannot be certain, for all my attention was centered upon that phantasmal face, with the cloudy hair, slightly parted red lips, and the brilliant dark eyes which looked into mine out of the shadows of the shop.

It was bewildering--it was uncanny; for, delusion or verity, the glamour prevailed. I exerted a great mental effort, stepped to the door, turned the handle, and entered the shop with as great a show of composure as I could muster.

A curtain draped in a little door at the back of one counter swayed slightly, with no greater violence than may have been occasioned by the draught. But I fixed my eyes upon this swaying curtain almost fiercely . . . as an impassive half-caste of some kind who appeared to be a strange cross between a Graeco-Hebrew and a Japanese, entered and quite unemotionally faced me, with a slight bow.

So wholly unexpected was this apparition that I started back.

"Can I show you anything, sir?" inquired the new arrival, with a second slight inclination of the head.

I looked at him for a moment in silence. Then:

"I thought I saw a lady of my acquaintance here a moment ago," I said. "Was I mistaken?"

"Quite mistaken, sir," replied the shopman, raising his black eyebrows ever so slightly; "a mistake possibly due to a reflection in the window. Will you take a look around now that you are here?"

"Thank you," I replied, staring him hard in the face; "at some other time."

I turned and quitted the shop abruptly. Either I was mad, or Karamaneh was concealed somewhere therein.

However, realizing my helplessness in the matter, I contented myself with making a mental note of the name which appeared above the establishment--J. Salaman--and walked on, my mind in a chaotic condition and my heart beating with unusual rapidity.

CHAPTER XVI

THE QUESTING HANDS

WITHIN MY VIEW, from the corner of the room where I sat in deepest shadow, through the partly opened window (it was screwed, like our own) were rows of glass-houses gleaming in the moonlight, and, beyond them, orderly ranks of flower-beds extending into a blue haze of distance. By reason of the moon's position, no light entered the room, but my eyes, from long watching, were grown familiar with the darkness, and I could see Burke quite clearly as he lay in the bed between my post and the window. I seemed to be back again in those days of the troubled past when first Nayland Smith and I had come to grips with the servants of Dr. Fu-Manchu. A more peaceful scene than this flower-planted corner of Essex it would be difficult to imagine; but, either because of my knowledge that its peace was chimerical, or because of that outflung consciousness of danger which, actually, or in my imagination, preceded the coming of the Chinaman's agents, to my seeming the silence throbbed electrically and the night was laden with stilly omens.

Already cramped by my journey in the market-cart, I found it difficult to remain very long in any one position. What information had Burke to sell? He had refused, for some reason, to discuss the matter that evening, and now, enacting the part allotted him by Nayland Smith, he feigned sleep consistently, although at intervals he would whisper to me his doubts and fears.

All the chances were in our favor to-night; for whilst I could not doubt that Dr. Fu-Manchu was set upon the removal of the ex-officer of New York police, neither could I doubt that our presence in the farm was unknown to the agents of the Chinaman. According to Burke, constant attempts had been made to achieve Fu-Manchu's purpose, and had only been frustrated by his (Burke's) wakefulness.

There was every probability that another attempt would be made to-night.

Any one who has been forced by circumstance to undertake such a vigil as this will be familiar with the marked changes (corresponding with phases of the earth's movement) which take place in the atmosphere, at midnight, at two o'clock, and again at four o'clock. During those fours hours falls a period wherein all life is at its lowest ebb, and every Physician is aware that there is a greater likelihood of a patient's passing between midnight and four A. M., than at any other period during the cycle of the hours.

To-night I became specially aware of this lowering of vitality, and now, with the night at that darkest phase which precedes the dawn, an indescribable dread, such as I had known before in my dealings with the Chinaman, assailed me, when I was least prepared to combat it. The stillness was intense. Then:

"Here it is!" whispered Burke from the bed.

The chill at the very center of my being, which but corresponded with the chill of all surrounding nature at that hour, became intensified, keener, at the whispered words.

I rose stealthily out of my chair, and from my nest of shadows watched --watched intently, the bright oblong of the window . . .

Without the slightest heralding sound--a black silhouette crept up against the pane . . . the silhouette of a small, malformed head, a dog-like head, deep-set in square shoulders. Malignant eyes peered intently in. Higher it arose--that wicked head--against the window, then crouched down on the sill and became less sharply defined as the creature stooped to the opening below. There was a faint sound of sniffing.

Judging from the stark horror which I experienced, myself, I doubted, now, if Burke could sustain the role allotted him. In beneath the slightly raised window came a hand, perceptible to me despite the darkness of the room. It seemed to project from the black silhouette outside the pane, to be thrust forward--and forward--and forward . . . that small hand with the outstretched fingers.

The unknown possesses unique terrors; and since I was unable to conceive what manner of thing this could be, which, extending its incredibly long arms, now sought the throat of the man upon the bed, I tasted of that sort of terror which ordinarily one knows only in dreams.

"Quick, sir--quick!" screamed Burke, starting up from the pillow.

The questing hands had reached his throat!

Choking down an urgent dread that I had of touching the thing which reached through the window to kill the sleeper, I sprang across the room and grasped the rigid, hairy forearms.

Heavens! Never have I felt such muscles, such tendons, as those beneath the hirsute skin! They seemed to be of steel wire, and with a sudden frightful sense of impotence, I realized that I was as powerless as a child to relax that strangle-hold. Burke was making the most frightful sounds and quite obviously was being asphyxiated before my eyes!

"Smith!" I cried, "Smith! Help! help! for God's sake!"

Despite the confusion of my mind I became aware of sounds outside and below me. Twice the thing at the window coughed; there was an incessant, lash-like cracking, then some shouted words which I was unable to make out; and finally the staccato report of a pistol.

Snarling like that of a wild beast came from the creature with the hairy arms, together with renewed coughing. But the steel grip relaxed not one iota.

I realized two things: the first, that in my terror at the suddenness of the attack I had omitted to act as pre-arranged: the second, that I had discredited the strength of the visitant, whilst Smith had foreseen it.

Desisting in my vain endeavor to pit my strength against that of the nameless thing, I sprang back across the room and took up the weapon which had been left in my charge earlier in the night, but which I had been unable to believe it would be necessary to employ. This was a sharp and heavy axe, which Nayland Smith, when I had met him in Covent Garden, had brought with him, to the great amazement of Weymouth and myself.

As I leaped back to the window and uplifted this primitive weapon, a second shot sounded from below, and more fierce snarling, coughing, and guttural mutterings assailed my ears from beyond the pane.

Lifting the heavy blade, I brought it down with all my strength upon the nearer of those hairy arms where it crossed the window-ledge, severing muscle, tendon and bone as easily as a knife might cut cheese. . . .

A shriek--a shriek neither human nor animal, but gruesomely compounded of both--followed . . . and merged into a choking cough. Like a flash the other shaggy arm was withdrawn, and some vaguely-seen body went rolling down the sloping red tiles and crashed on to the ground beneath.

With a second piercing shriek, louder than that recently uttered by Burke, wailing through the night from somewhere below, I turned desperately to the man on the bed, who now was become significantly silent. A candle, with matches, stood upon a table hard by, and, my fingers far from steady, I set about obtaining a light. This accomplished, I stood the candle upon the little chest-of-drawers and returned to Burke's side.

"Merciful God!" I cried.

Of all the pictures which remain in my memory, some of them dark enough, I can find none more horrible than that which now confronted me in the dim candle-light. Burke lay crosswise on the bed, his head thrown back and sagging; one rigid hand he held in the air, and with the other grasped the hairy forearm which I had severed with the ax; for, in a death-grip, the dead fingers were still fastened, vise-like, at his throat.

His face was nearly black, and his eyes projected from their sockets horribly. Mastering my repugnance, I seized the hideous piece of bleeding anatomy and strove to release it. It defied all my efforts; in death it was as implacable as in life. I took a knife from my pocket, and, tendon by tendon, cut away that uncanny grip from Burke's throat . . .

But my labor was in vain. Burke was dead!

I think I failed to realize this for some time. My clothes were sticking clammily to my body; I was bathed in perspiration, and, shaking furiously, I clutched at the edge of the window, avoiding the bloody patch upon the ledge, and looked out over the roofs to where, in the more distant plantations, I could hear excited voices. What had been the meaning of that scream which I had heard but to which in my frantic state of mind I had paid comparatively little attention?

There was a great stirring all about me.

"Smith!" I cried from the window; "Smith, for mercy's sake where are you?"

Footsteps came racing up the stairs. Behind me the door burst open and Nayland Smith stumbled into the room.

"God!" he said, and started back in the doorway.

"Have you got it, Smith?" I demanded hoarsely. "In sanity's name what is it--what is it?"

"Come downstairs," replied Smith quietly, "and see for yourself." He turned his head aside from the bed.

Very unsteadily I followed him down the stairs and through the rambling old house out into the stone-paved courtyard. There were figures moving at the end of a long alleyway between the glass houses, and one, carrying a lantern, stooped over something which lay upon the ground.

"That's Burke's cousin with the lantern," whispered Smith in my ear; "don't tell him yet."

I nodded, and we hurried up to join the group. I found myself looking down at one of those thick-set Burmans whom I always associated with Fu-Manchu's activities. He lay quite flat, face downward; but the back of his head was a shapeless blood-dotted mass, and a heavy stock-whip, the butt end ghastly because of the blood and hair which clung to it, lay beside him. I started back appalled as Smith caught my arm.

"It turned on its keeper!" he hissed in my ear. "I wounded it twice from below, and you severed one arm; in its insensate fury, its unreasoning malignity, it returned--and there lies its second victim..."

"Then..."

"It's gone, Petrie! It has the strength of four men even now. Look!"

He stooped, and from the clenched left hand of the dead Burman, extracted a piece of paper and opened it.

"Hold the lantern a moment," he said.

In the yellow light he glanced at the scrap of paper.

"As I expected--a leaf of Burke's notebook; it worked by scent." He turned to me with an odd expression in his gray eyes. "I wonder what piece of my personal property Fu-Manchu has pilfered," he said, "in order to enable it to sleuth me?"

He met the gaze of the man holding the lantern.

"Perhaps you had better return to the house," he said, looking him squarely in the eyes.

The other's face blanched.

"You don't mean, sir--you don't mean . . ."

"Brace up!" said Smith, laying his hand upon his shoulder. "Remember-- he chose to play with fire!"

One wild look the man cast from Smith to me, then went off, staggering, toward the farm.

"Smith," I began . . .

He turned to me with an impatient gesture.

"Weymouth has driven into Upminster," he snapped; "and the whole district will be scoured before morning. They probably motored here, but the sounds of the shots will have enabled whoever was with the car to make good his escape. And exhausted from loss of blood, its capture is only a matter of time, Petrie."

CHAPTER XVII

ONE DAY IN RANGOON

NAYLAND SMITH returned from the telephone. Nearly twenty-four hours had elapsed since the awful death of Burke.

"No news, Petrie," he said, shortly. "It must have crept into some inaccessible hole to die."

I glanced up from my notes. Smith settled into the white cane armchair, and began to surround himself with clouds of aromatic smoke. I took up a half-sheet of foolscap covered with penciled writing in my friend's cramped characters, and transcribed the following, in order to complete my account of the latest Fu-Manchu outrage:

"The Amharun, a Semitic tribe allied to the Falashas, who have been settled for many generations in the southern province of Shoa (Abyssinia) have been regarded as unclean and outcast, apparently since the days of Menelek--son of Suleyman and the Queen of Sheba--from whom they claim descent. Apart from their custom of eating meat cut from living beasts, they are accursed because of their alleged association with the Cynocephalus hamadryas (Sacred Baboon). I, myself, was taken to a hut on the banks of the Hawash and shown a creature . . . whose predominant trait was an unreasoning malignity toward . . . and a ferocious tenderness for the society of its furry brethren. Its powers of scent were fully equal to those of a bloodhound, whilst its abnormally long forearms possessed incredible strength . . . a Cynocephalyte such as this, contracts phthisis even in the more northern provinces of Abyssinia . . ."

"You have not explained to me, Smith," I said, having completed this note, "how you got in touch with Fu-Manchu; how you learnt that he was not dead, as we had supposed, but living--active."

Nayland Smith stood up and fixed his steely eyes upon me with an indefinable expression in them. Then:

"No," he replied; "I haven't. Do you wish to know?"

"Certainly," I said with surprise; "is there any reason why I should not?"

"There is no real reason," said Smith; "or"--staring at me very hard--"I hope there is no real reason."

"What do you mean?"

"Well"--he grabbed up his pipe from the table and began furiously to load it--"I blundered upon the truth one day in Rangoon. I was walking out of a house which I occupied there for a time, and as I swung around the corner into the main street, I ran into--literally ran into . . ."

Again he hesitated oddly; then closed up his pouch and tossed it into the cane chair. He struck a match.

"I ran into Karamaneh," he continued abruptly, and began to puff away at his pipe, filling the air with clouds of tobacco smoke.

I caught my breath. This was the reason why he had kept me so long in ignorance of the story. He knew of my hopeless, uncrushable sentiments toward the gloriously beautiful but utterly hypocritical and evil Eastern girl who was perhaps the most dangerous of all Dr. Fu-Manchu's servants; for the power of her loveliness was magical, as I knew to my cost.

"What did you do?" I asked quietly, my fingers drumming upon the table.

"Naturally enough," continued Smith, "with a cry of recognition I held out both my hands to her, gladly. I welcomed her as a dear friend regained; I thought of the joy with which you would learn that I had found the missing one; I thought how you would be in Rangoon just as quickly as the fastest steamer could get you there . . ."

"Well?"

"Karamaneh started back and treated me to a glance of absolute animosity. No recognition was there, and no friendliness--only a sort of scornful anger."

He shrugged his shoulders and began to walk up and down the room.

"I do not know what you would have done in the circumstances, Petrie, but I--"

"Yes?"

"I dealt with the situation rather promptly, I think. I simply picked her up without another word, right there in the public street, and raced back into the house, with her kicking and fighting like a little demon! She did not shriek or do anything of that kind, but fought silently like a vicious wild animal. Oh! I had some scars, I assure you; but I carried her up into my office, which fortunately was empty at the time, plumped her down in a chair, and stood looking at her."

"Go on," I said rather hollowly; "what next?"

"She glared at me with those wonderful eyes, an expression of implacable hatred in them! Remembering all that we had done for her; remembering our former friendship; above all, remembering you--this look of hers almost made me shiver. She was dressed very smartly in European fashion, and the whole thing had been so sudden that as I stood looking at her I half expected to wake up presently and find it all a day-dream. But it was real--as real as her enmity. I felt the need for reflection, and having vainly endeavored to draw her into conversation, and elicited no other answer than this glare of hatred--I left her there, going out and locking the door behind me."

"Very high-handed?"

"A commissioner has certain privileges, Petrie, and any action I might choose to take was not likely to be questioned. There was only one window to the office, and it was fully twenty feet above the level; it overlooked a narrow street off the main thoroughfare (I think I have explained that the house stood on a corner) so I did not fear her escaping. I had an important engagement which I had been on my way to fulfil when the encounter took place, and now, with a word to my native servant--who chanced to be downstairs--I hurried off."

Smith's pipe had gone out as usual, and he proceeded to relight it, whilst, with my eyes lowered, I continued to drum upon the table.

"This boy took her some tea later in the afternoon," he continued, "and apparently found her in a more placid frame of mind. I returned immediately after dusk, and he reported that when last he had looked in, about half an hour earlier, she had been seated in an armchair reading a newspaper (I may mention that everything of value in the office was securely locked up!) I was determined upon a certain course by this time, and I went slowly upstairs, unlocked the door, and walked into the darkened office. I turned up the light . . . the place was empty!"

"Empty!"

"The window was open, and the bird flown! Oh! it was not so simple a flight--as you would realize if you knew the place. The street, which the window overlooked, was bounded by a blank wall, on the opposite side, for thirty or forty yards along; and as we had been having heavy rains, it was full of glutinous mud. Furthermore, the boy whom I had left in charge had been sitting in the doorway immediately below the office window watching for my return ever since his last visit to the room above . . ."

"She must have bribed him," I said bitterly--"or corrupted him with her infernal blandishments."

"I'll swear she did not," rapped Smith decisively. "I know my man, and I'll swear she did not. There were no marks in the mud of the road to show that a ladder had been placed there; moreover, nothing of the kind could have been attempted whilst the boy was sitting in the doorway; that was evident. In short, she did not descend into the roadway and did not come out by the door . . ."

"Was there a gallery outside the window?"

"No; it was impossible to climb to right or left of the window or up on to the roof. I convinced myself of that."

"But, my dear man!" I cried, "you are eliminating every natural mode of egress! Nothing remains but flight."

"I am aware, Petrie, that nothing remains but flight; in other words I have never to this day understood how she quitted the room. I only know that she did."

"And then?"

"I saw in this incredible escape the cunning hand of Dr. Fu-Manchu--saw it at once. Peace was ended; and I set to work along certain channels without delay. In this manner I got on the track at last, and learned, beyond the possibility of doubt, that the Chinese doctor lived--nay! was actually on his way to Europe again!"

There followed a short silence. Then:

"I suppose it's a mystery that will be cleared up some day," concluded Smith; "but to date the riddle remains intact." He glanced at the clock. "I have an appointment with Weymouth; therefore, leaving you to the task of solving this problem which thus far has defied my own efforts, I will get along."

He read a query in my glance.

"Oh! I shall not be late," he added; "I think I may venture out alone on this occasion without personal danger."

Nayland Smith went upstairs to dress, leaving me seated at my writing table, deep in thought. My notes upon the renewed activity of Dr. Fu-Manchu were stacked at my left hand, and, opening a new writing block, I commenced to add to them particulars of this surprising event in Rangoon which properly marked the opening of the Chinaman's second campaign. Smith looked in at the door on his way out, but seeing me thus engaged, did not disturb me.

I think I have made it sufficiently evident in these records that my practice was not an extensive one, and my hour for receiving patients arrived and passed with only two professional interruptions.

My task concluded, I glanced at the clock, and determined to devote the remainder of the evening to a little private investigation of my own. From Nayland Smith I had preserved the matter a secret, largely because I feared his ridicule; but I had by no means forgotten that I had seen, or had strongly imagined that I had seen, Karamaneh--that beautiful anomaly, who (in modern London) asserted herself to be a slave--in the shop of an antique dealer not a hundred yards from the British Museum!

A theory was forming in my brain, which I was burningly anxious to put to the test. I remembered how, two years before, I had met Karamaneh near to this same spot; and I had heard Inspector Weymouth assert positively that Fu-Manchu's headquarters were no longer in the East End, as of yore. There seemed to me to be a distinct probability that a suitable center had been established for his reception in this place, so much less likely to be suspected by the authorities. Perhaps I attached too great a value to what may have been a delusion; perhaps my theory rested upon no more solid foundation than the belief that I had seen Karamaneh in the shop of the curio dealer. If her appearance there should prove to have been phantasmal, the structure of my theory would be shattered at its base. To-night I should test my premises, and upon the result of my investigations determine my future action.

CHAPTER XVIII

THE SILVER BUDDHA

MUSEUM STREET certainly did not seem a likely spot for Dr. Fu-Manchu to establish himself, yet, unless my imagination had strangely deceived me, from the window of the antique dealer who traded under the name of J. Salaman, those wonderful eyes of Karamaneh like the velvet midnight of the Orient, had looked out at me.

As I paced slowly along the pavement toward that lighted window, my heart was beating far from normally, and I cursed the folly which, in spite of all, refused to die, but lingered on, poisoning my life. Comparative quiet reigned in Museum Street, at no time a busy thoroughfare, and, excepting another shop at the Museum end, commercial activities had ceased there. The door of a block of residential chambers almost immediately opposite to the shop which was my objective, threw out a beam of light across the pavement, but not more than two or three people were visible upon either side of the street.

I turned the knob of the door and entered the shop.

The same dark and immobile individual whom I had seen before, and whose nationality defied conjecture, came out from the curtained doorway at the back to greet me.

"Good evening, sir," he said monotonously, with a slight inclination of the head; "is there anything which you desire to inspect?"

"I merely wish to take a look around," I replied. "I have no particular item in view."

The shop man inclined his head again, swept a yellow hand comprehensively about, as if to include the entire stock, and seated himself on a chair behind the counter.

I lighted a cigarette with such an air of nonchalance as I could summon to the operation, and began casually to inspect the varied objects of interest loading the shelves and tables about me. I am bound to confess that I retain no one definite impression of this tour. Vases I handled, statuettes, Egyptian scarabs, bead necklaces, illuminated missals, portfolios of old prints, jade ornaments, bronzes, fragments of rare lace, early printed books, Assyrian tablets, daggers, Roman rings, and a hundred other curiosities, leisurely, and I trust with apparent interest, yet without forming the slightest impression respecting any one of them.

Probably I employed myself in this way for half an hour or more, and whilst my hands busied themselves among the stock of J. Salaman, my mind was occupied entirely elsewhere. Furtively I was studying the shopman himself, a human presentment of a Chinese idol; I was listening and watching; especially I was watching the curtained doorway at the back of the shop.

"We close at about this time, sir," the man interrupted me, speaking in the emotionless, monotonous voice which I had noted before.

I replaced upon the glass counter a little Sekhet boat, carved in wood and highly colored, and glanced up with a start. Truly my methods were amateurish; I had learnt nothing; I was unlikely to learn anything. I wondered how Nayland Smith would have conducted such an inquiry, and I racked my brains for some means of penetrating into the recesses of the establishment. Indeed, I had been seeking such a plan for the past half an hour, but my mind had proved incapable of suggesting one.

Why I did not admit failure I cannot imagine, but, instead, I began to tax my brains anew for some means of gaining further time; and, as I looked about the place, the shopman very patiently awaiting my departure, I observed an open case at the back of the counter. The three lower shelves were empty, but upon the fourth shelf squatted a silver Buddha.

"I should like to examine the silver image yonder," I said; "what price are you asking for it?"

"It is not for sale, sir," replied the man, with a greater show of animation than he had yet exhibited.

"Not for sale!" I said, my eyes ever seeking the curtained doorway; "how's that?"

"It is sold."

"Well, even so, there can be no objection to my examining it?"

"It is not for sale, sir."

Such a rebuff from a tradesman would have been more than sufficient to call for a sharp retort at any other time, but now it excited the strangest suspicions. The street outside looked comparatively deserted, and prompted, primarily, by an emotion which I did not pause to analyze, I adopted a singular measure; without doubt I relied upon the unusual powers vested in Nayland Smith to absolve me in the event of error. I made as if to go out into the street, then turned, leaped past the shopman, ran behind the counter, and grasped at the silver Buddha!

That I was likely to be arrested for attempted larceny I cared not; the idea that Karamaneh was concealed somewhere in the building ruled absolutely, and a theory respecting this silver image had taken possession of my mind. Exactly what I expected to happen at that moment I cannot say, but what actually happened was far more startling than anything I could have imagined.

At the instant that I grasped the figure I realized that it was attached to the woodwork; in the next I knew that it was a handle . . . as I tried to pull it toward me I became aware that this handle was the handle of a door. For that door swung open before me, and I found myself at the foot of a flight of heavily carpeted stairs.

Anxious as I had been to proceed a moment before, I was now trebly anxious to retire, and for this reason: on the bottom step of the stair, facing me, stood Dr. Fu-Manchu!

CHAPTER XIX

DR. FU-MANCHU'S LABORATORY

I CANNOT CONCEIVE that any ordinary mortal ever attained to anything like an intimacy with Dr. Fu-Manchu; I cannot believe that any man could ever grow used to his presence, could ever cease to fear him. I suppose I had set eyes upon Fu-Manchu some five or six times prior to this occasion, and now he was dressed in the manner which I always associated with him, probably because it was thus I first saw him. He wore a plain yellow robe, and, with his pointed chin resting upon his bosom, he looked down at me, revealing a great expanse of the marvelous brow with its sparse, neutral-colored hair.

Never in my experience have I known such force to dwell in the glance of any human eye as dwelt in that of this uncanny being. His singular affliction (if affliction it were), the film or slight membrane which sometimes obscured the oblique eyes, was particularly evident at the moment that I crossed the threshold, but now, as I looked up at Dr. Fu-Manchu, it lifted-- revealing the eyes in all their emerald greenness.

The idea of physical attack upon this incredible being seemed childish --inadequate. But, following that first instant of stupefaction, I forced myself to advance upon him.

A dull, crushing blow descended on the top of my skull, and I became oblivious of all things.

My return to consciousness was accompanied by tremendous pains in my head, whereby, from previous experience, I knew that a sandbag had been used against me by some one in the shop, presumably by the immobile shopman. This awakening was accompanied by none of those hazy doubts respecting previous events and present surroundings which are the usual symptoms of revival from sudden unconsciousness; even before I opened my eyes, before I had more than a partial command of my senses, I knew that, with my wrists handcuffed behind me, I lay in a room which was also occupied by Dr. Fu-Manchu. This absolute certainty of the Chinaman's presence was evidenced, not by my senses, but only by an inner consciousness, and the same that always awoke into life at the approach not only of Fu-Manchu in person but of certain of his uncanny servants.

A faint perfume hung in the air about me; I do not mean that of any essence or of any incense, but rather the smell which is suffused by Oriental furniture, by Oriental draperies; the indefinable but unmistakable perfume of the East.

Thus, London has a distinct smell of its own, and so has Paris, whilst the difference between Marseilles and Suez, for instance, is even more marked.

Now, the atmosphere surrounding me was Eastern, but not of the East that I knew; rather it was Far Eastern. Perhaps I do not make myself very clear, but to me there was a mysterious significance in that perfumed atmosphere. I opened my eyes.

I lay upon a long low settee, in a fairly large room which was furnished as I had anticipated in an absolutely Oriental fashion. The two windows were so screened as to have lost, from the interior point of view, all resemblance to European windows, and the whole structure of the room had been altered in conformity, bearing out my idea that the place had been prepared for Fu-Manchu's reception some time before his actual return. I doubt if, East or West, a duplicate of that singular apartment could be found.

The end in which I lay, was, as I have said, typical of an Eastern house, and a large, ornate lantern hung from the ceiling almost directly above me. The further end of the room was occupied by tall cases, some of them containing books, but the majority filled with scientific paraphernalia; rows of flasks and jars, frames of test- tubes, retorts, scales, and other objects of the laboratory. At a large and very finely carved table sat Dr. Fu-Manchu, a yellow and faded volume open before him, and some dark red fluid, almost like blood, bubbling in a test-tube which he held over the flame of a Bunsen-burner.

The enormously long nail of his right index finger rested upon the opened page of the book to which he seemed constantly to refer, dividing his attention between the volume, the contents of the test- tube, and the progress of a second experiment, or possibly a part of the same, which was taking place upon another corner of the littered table.

A huge glass retort (the bulb was fully two feet in diameter), fitted with a Liebig's Condenser, rested in a metal frame, and within the bulb, floating in an oily substance, was a fungus some six inches high, shaped like a toadstool, but of a brilliant and venomous orange color. Three flat tubes of light were so arranged as to cast violet rays upward into the retort, and the receiver, wherein condensed the product of this strange experiment, contained some drops of a red fluid which may have been identical with that boiling in the test- tube.

These things I perceived at a glance: then the filmy eyes of Dr. Fu-Manchu were raised from the book, turned in my direction, and all else was forgotten.

"I regret," came the sibilant voice, "that unpleasant measures were necessary, but hesitation would have been fatal. I trust, Dr. Petrie, that you suffer no inconvenience?"

To this speech no reply was possible, and I attempted none.

"You have long been aware of my esteem for your acquirements," continued the Chinaman, his voice occasionally touching deep guttural notes, "and you will appreciate the pleasure which this visit affords me. I kneel at the feet of my silver Buddha. I look to you, when you shall have overcome your prejudices--due to ignorance of my true motives--to assist me in establishing that intellectual control which is destined to be the new World Force. I bear you no malice for your ancient enmity, and even now"--he waved one yellow hand toward the retort--"I am conducting an experiment designed to convert you from your misunderstanding, and to adjust your perspective."

Quite unemotionally he spoke, then turned again to his book, his test- tube and retort, in the most matter-of-fact way imaginable. I do not think the most frenzied outburst on his part, the most fiendish threats, could have produced such effect upon me as those cold and carefully calculated words, spoken in that unique voice which rang about the room sibilantly. In its tones, in the glance of the green eyes, in the very pose of the gaunt, high-shouldered body, there was power--force.

I counted myself lost, and in view of the doctor's words, studied the progress of the experiment with frightful interest. But a few moments sufficed in which to realize that, for all my training, I knew as little of chemistry--of chemistry as understood by this man's genius-- as a junior student in surgery knows of trephining. The process in operation was a complete mystery to me; the means and the end alike incomprehensible.

Thus, in the heavy silence of that room, a silence only broken by the regular bubbling from the test tube, I found my attention straying from the table to the other objects surrounding it; and at one of them my gaze stopped and remained chained with horror.

It was a glass jar, some five feet in height and filled with viscous fluid of a light amber color. Out from this peered a hideous, dog-like face, low browed, with pointed ears and a nose almost hoggishly flat. By the death-grin of the face the gleaming fangs were revealed; and the body, the long yellow-gray body, rested, or seemed to rest, upon short, malformed legs, whilst one long limp arm, the right, hung down straightly in the preservative. The left arm had been severed above the elbow.

Fu-Manchu, finding his experiment to be proceeding favorably, lifted his eyes to me again.

"You are interested in my poor Cynocephalyte?" he said; and his eyes were filmed like the eyes of one afflicted with cataract. "He was a devoted servant, Dr. Petrie, but the lower influences in his genealogy, sometimes conquered. Then he got out of hand; and at last he was so ungrateful toward those who had educated him, that, in one of those paroxysms of his, he attacked and killed a most faithful Burman, one of my oldest followers."

Fu-Manchu returned to his experiment.

Not the slightest emotion had he exhibited thus far, but had chatted with me as any other scientist might chat with a friend who casually visits his laboratory. The horror of the thing was playing havoc with my own composure, however. There I lay, fettered, in the same room with this man whose existence was a menace to the entire white race, whilst placidly he pursued an experiment designed, if his own words were believable, to cut me off from my kind--to wreak some change, psychological or physiological I knew not; to place me, it might be, upon a level with such brute-things as that which now hung, half floating, in the glass jar!

Something I knew of the history of that ghastly specimen, that thing neither man nor ape; for within my own knowledge had it not attempted the life of Nayland Smith, and was it not I who, with an ax, had maimed it in the instant of one of its last slayings?

Of these things Dr. Fu-Manchu was well aware, so that his placid speech was doubly, trebly horrible to my ears. I sought, furtively, to move my arms, only to realize that, as I had anticipated, the handcuffs were chained to a ring in the wall behind me. The establishments of Dr. Fu-Manchu were always well provided with such contrivances as these.

I uttered a short, harsh laugh. Fu-Manchu stood up slowly from the table, and, placing the test-tube in a rack, stood the latter carefully upon a shelf at his side.

"I am happy to find you in such good humor," he said softly. "Other affairs call me; and, in my absence, that profound knowledge of chemistry, of which I have had evidence in the past, will enable you to follow with intelligent interest the action of these violet rays upon this exceptionally fine specimen of Siberian amanita muscaria. At some future time, possibly when you are my guest in China--which country I am now making arrangements for you to visit--I shall discuss with you some lesser-known properties of this species; and I may say that one of your first tasks when you commence your duties as assistant in my laboratory in Kiang-su, will be to conduct a series of twelve experiments, which I have outlined, into other potentialities of this unique fungus."

He walked quietly to a curtained doorway, with his cat-like yet awkward gait, lifted the drapery, and, with a slight nod in my direction, went out of the room.

CHAPTER XX

THE CROSS BAR

HOW LONG I LAY THERE alone I had no means of computing. My mind was busy with many matters, but principally concerned with my fate in the immediate future. That Dr. Fu-Manchu entertained for me a singular kind of regard, I had had evidence before. He had formed the erroneous opinion that I was an advanced scientist who could be of use to him in his experiments and I was aware that he cherished a project of transporting me to some place in China where his principal laboratory was situated. Respecting the means which he proposed to employ, I was unlikely to forget that this man, who had penetrated further along certain byways of science than seemed humanly possible, undoubtedly was master of a process for producing artificial catalepsy. It was my lot, then, to be packed in a chest (to all intents and purposes a dead man for the time being) and despatched to the interior of China!

What a fool I had been. To think that I had learned nothing from my long and dreadful experience of the methods of Dr. Fu-Manchu; to think that I had come alone in quest of him; that, leaving no trace behind me, I had deliberately penetrated to his secret abode!

I have said that my wrists were manacled behind me, the manacles being attached to a chain fastened in the wall. I now contrived, with extreme difficulty, to reverse the position of my hands; that is to say, I climbed backward through the loop formed by my fettered arms, so that instead of their being locked behind me, they now were locked in front.

Then I began to examine the fetters, learning, as I had anticipated, that they fastened with a lock. I sat gazing at the steel bracelets in the light of the lamp which swung over my head, and it became apparent to me that I had gained little by my contortion.

A slight noise disturbed these unpleasant reveries. It was nothing less than the rattling of keys!

For a moment I wondered if I had heard aright, or if the sound portended the coming of some servant of the doctor, who was locking up the establishment for the night. The jangling sound was repeated, and in such a way that I could not suppose it to be accidental. Some one was deliberately rattling a small bunch of keys in an adjoining room.

And now my heart leaped wildly--then seemed to stand still.

With a low whistling cry a little gray shape shot through the doorway by which Fu-Manchu had retired, and rolled, like a ball of fluff blown by the wind, completely under the table which bore the weird scientific appliances of the Chinaman; the advent of the gray object was accompanied by a further rattling of keys.

My fear left me, and a mighty anxiety took its place. This creature which now crouched chattering at me from beneath the big table was Fu-Manchu's marmoset, and in the intervals of its chattering and grimacing, it nibbled, speculatively, at the keys upon the ring which it clutched in its tiny hands. Key after key it sampled in this manner, evincing a growing dissatisfaction with the uncrackable nature of its find.

One of those keys might be that of the handcuffs!

I could not believe that the tortures of Tantulus were greater than were mine at this moment. In all my hopes of rescue or release, I had included nothing so strange, so improbable as this. A sort of awe possessed me; for if by this means the key which should release me should come into my possession, how, ever again, could I doubt a beneficent Providence?

But they were not yet in my possession; moreover, the key of the handcuffs might not be amongst the bunch.

Were there no means whereby I could induce the marmoset to approach me?

Whilst I racked my brains for some scheme, the little animal took the matter out of my hands. Tossing the ring with its jangling contents a yard or so across the carpet in my direction, it leaped in pursuit, picked up the ring, whirled it over its head, and then threw a complete somersault around it. Now it snatched up the keys again, and holding them close to its ear, rattled them furiously. Finally, with an incredible spring, it leaped onto the chain supporting the lamp above my head, and with the garish shade swinging and spinning wildly, clung there looking down at me like an acrobat on a trapeze. The tiny, bluish face, completely framed in grotesque whiskers, enhanced the illusion of an acrobatic comedian. Never for a moment did it release its hold upon the key-ring.

My suspense now was intolerable. I feared to move, lest, alarming the marmoset, it should run off again, taking the keys with it. So as I lay there, looking up at the little creature swinging above me, the second wonder of the night came to pass.

A voice that I could never forget, strive how I would, a voice that haunted my dreams by night, and for which by day I was ever listening, cried out from some adjoining room.

"Ta'ala hina!" it called. "Ta'ala hina, Peko!"

It was Karamaneh!

The effect upon the marmoset was instantaneous. Down came the bunch of keys upon one side of the shade, almost falling on my head, and down leaped the ape upon the other. In two leaps it had traversed the room and had vanished through the curtained doorway.

If ever I had need of coolness it was now; the slightest mistake would be fatal. The keys had slipped from the mattress of the divan, and now lay just beyond reach of my fingers. Rapidly I changed my position, and sought, without undue noise, to move the keys with my foot.

I had actually succeeded in sliding them back on to the mattress, when, unheralded by any audible footstep, Karamaneh came through the doorway, holding the marmoset in her arms. She wore a dress of fragile muslin material, and out from its folds protruded one silk-stockinged foot, resting in a highheeled red shoe. . . .

For a moment she stood watching me, with a sort of enforced composure; then her glance strayed to the keys lying upon the floor. Slowly, and with her eyes fixed again upon my face, she crossed the room, stooped, and took up the key-ring.

It was one of the poignant moments of my life; for by that simple act all my hopes had been shattered!

Any poor lingering doubt that I may have had, left me now. Had the slightest spark of friendship animated the bosom of Karamaneh most certainly she would have overlooked the presence of the keys--of the keys which represented my one hope of escape from the clutches of the fiendish Chinaman.

There is a silence more eloquent than words. For half a minute or more, Karamaneh stood watching me--forcing herself to watch me--and I looked up at her with a concentrated gaze in which rage and reproach must have been strangely mingled. What eyes she had!--of that blackly lustrous sort nearly always associated with unusually dark complexions; but Karamaneh's complexion was peachlike, or rather of an exquisite and delicate fairness which reminded me of the petal of a rose. By some I had been accused of raving about this girl's beauty, but only by those who had not met her; for indeed she was astonishingly lovely.

At last her eyes fell, the long lashes drooped upon her cheeks. She turned and walked slowly to the chair in which Fu-Manchu had sat. Placing the keys upon the table amid the scientific litter, she rested one dimpled elbow upon the yellow page of the book, and with her chin in her palm, again directed upon me that enigmatical gaze.

I dared not think of the past, of the past in which this beautiful, treacherous girl had played a part; yet, watching her, I could not believe, even now, that she was false! My state was truly a pitiable one; I could have cried out in sheer anguish. With her long lashes partly lowered, she watched me awhile, then spoke; and her voice was music which seemed to mock me; every inflection of that elusive accent reopened, lancet-like, the ancient wound.

"Why do you look at me so?" she said, almost in a whisper. "By what right do you reproach me?--Have you ever offered me friendship, that I should repay you with friendship? When first you came to the house where I was, by the river--came to save some one from" (there was the familiar hesitation which always preceded the name of Fu-Manchu) "from--him, you treated me as your enemy, although--I would have been your friend . . ."

There was appeal in the soft voice, but I laughed mockingly, and threw myself back upon the divan.

Karamaneh stretched out her hands toward me, and I shall never forget the expression which flashed into those glorious eyes; but, seeing me intolerant of her appeal, she drew back and quickly turned her head aside. Even in this hour of extremity, of impotent wrath, I could find no contempt in my heart for her feeble hypocrisy; with all the old wonder I watched that exquisite profile, and Karamaneh's very deceitfulness was a salve--for had she not cared she would not have attempted it!

Suddenly she stood up, taking the keys in her hands, and approached me.

"Not by word, nor by look," she said, quietly, "have you asked for my friendship, but because I cannot bear you to think of me as you do, I will prove that I am not the hypocrite and the liar you think me. You will not trust me, but I will trust you."

I looked up into her eyes, and knew a pagan joy when they faltered before my searching gaze. She threw herself upon her knees beside me, and the faint exquisite perfume inseparable from my memories of her, became perceptible, and seemed as of old to intoxicate me. The lock clicked . . . and I was free.

Karamaneh rose swiftly to her feet as I stood upright and outstretched my cramped arms. For one delirious moment her bewitching face was close to mine, and the dictates of madness almost ruled; but I clenched my teeth and turned sharply aside. I could not trust myself to speak.

With Fu-Manchu's marmoset again gamboling before us, she walked through the curtained doorway into the room beyond. It was in darkness, but I could see the slave-girl in front of me, a slim silhouette, as she walked to a screened window, and, opening the screen in the manner of a folding door, also threw up the window.

"Look!" she whispered.

I crept forward and stood beside her. I found myself looking down into Museum Street from a first-floor window! Belated traffic still passed along New Oxford Street on the left, but not a solitary figure was visible to the right, as far as I could see, and that was nearly to the railings of the Museum. Immediately opposite, in one of the flats which I had noticed earlier in the evening, another window was opened. I turned, and in the reflected light saw that Karamaneh held a cord in her hand. Our eyes met in the semi-darkness.

She began to haul the cord into the window, and, looking upward, I perceived that is was looped in some way over the telegraph cables which crossed the street at that point. It was a slender cord, and it appeared to be passed across a joint in the cables almost immediately above the center of the roadway. As it was hauled in, a second and stronger line attached to it was pulled, in turn, over the cables, and thence in by the window. Karamaneh twisted a length of it around a metal bracket fastened in the wall, and placed a light wooden crossbar in my hand.

"Make sure that there is no one in the street," she said, craning out and looking to right and left, "then swing across. The length of the rope is just sufficient to enable you to swing through the open window opposite, and there is a mattress inside to drop upon. But release the bar immediately, or you may be dragged back. The door of the room in which you will find yourself is unlocked, and you have only to walk down the stairs and out into the street."

I peered at the crossbar in my hand, then looked hard at the girl beside me. I missed something of the old fire of her nature; she was very subdued, tonight.

"Thank you, Karamaneh," I said, softly.

She suppressed a little cry as I spoke her name, and drew back into the shadows.

"I believe you are my friend," I said, "but I cannot understand. Won't you help me to understand?"

I took her unresisting hand, and drew her toward me. My very soul seemed to thrill at the contact of her lithe body . . .

She was trembling wildly and seemed to be trying to speak, but although her lips framed the words no sound followed. Suddenly comprehension came to me. I looked down into the street, hitherto deserted . . . and into the upturned face of Fu-Manchu.

Wearing a heavy fur-collared coat, and with his yellow, malignant countenance grotesquely horrible beneath the shade of a large tweed motor cap, he stood motionless, looking up at me. That he had seen me, I could not doubt; but had he seen my companion?

In a choking whisper Karamaneh answered my unspoken question.

"He has not seen me! I have done much for you; do in return a small thing for me. Save my life!"

She dragged me back from the window and fled across the room to the weird laboratory where I had lain captive. Throwing herself upon the divan, she held out her white wrists and glanced significantly at the manacles.

"Lock them upon me!" she said, rapidly. "Quick! quick!"

Great as was my mental disturbance, I managed to grasp the purpose of this device. The very extremity of my danger found me cool. I fastened the manacles, which so recently had confined my own wrists, upon the slim wrists of Karamaneh. A faint and muffled disturbance, doubly ominous because there was nothing to proclaim its nature, reached me from some place below, on the ground floor.

"Tie something around my mouth!" directed Karamaneh with nervous rapidity. As I began to look about me:--"Tear a strip from my dress, "she said; "do not hesitate--be quick! be quick!"

I seized the flimsy muslin and tore off half a yard or so from the hem of the skirt. The voice of Dr Fu-Manchu became audible. He was speaking rapidly, sibilantly, and evidently was approaching--would be upon me in a matter of moments. I fastened the strip of fabric over the girl's mouth and tied it behind, experiencing a pang half pleasurable and half fearful as I found my hands in contact with the foamy luxuriance of her hair.

Dr. Fu-Manchu was entering the room immediately beyond.

Snatching up the bunch of keys, I turned and ran, for in another instant my retreat would be cut off. As I burst once more into the darkened room I became aware that a door on the further side of it was open; and framed in the opening was the tall, high-shouldered figure of the Chinaman, still enveloped in his fur coat and wearing the grotesque cap. As I saw him, so he perceived me; and as I sprang to the window, he advanced.

I turned desperately and hurled the bunch of keys with all my force into the dimly-seen face...

Either because they possessed a chatoyant quality of their own (as I had often suspected), or by reason of the light reflected through the open window, the green eyes gleamed upon me vividly like those of a giant cat. One short guttural exclamation paid tribute to the accuracy of my aim; then I had the crossbar in my hand. I threw one leg across the sill, and dire as was my extremity, hesitated for an instant ere trusting myself to the flight . . .

A vise-like grip fastened upon my left ankle.

Hazily I became aware that the dark room was flooded with figures. The whole yellow gang were upon me--the entire murder-group composed of units recruited from the darkest place of the East!

I have never counted myself a man of resource, and have always envied Nayland Smith his possession of that quality, in him extraordinarily developed; but on this occasion the gods were kind to me, and I resorted to the only device, perhaps, which could have saved me. Without releasing my hold upon the crossbar, I clutched at the ledge with the fingers of both hands and swung back into the room my right leg, which was already across the sill. With all my strength I kicked out. My heel came in contact, in sickening contact, with a human head; beyond doubt that I had split the skull of the man who held me.

The grip upon my ankle was released automatically; and now consigning all my weight to the rope I slipped forward, as a diver, across the broad ledge and found myself sweeping through the night like a winged thing . . .

The line, as Karamaneh had assured me, was of well-judged length. Down I swept to within six or seven feet of the street level, then up, at ever decreasing speed, toward the vague oblong of the open window beyond.

I hope I have been successful, in some measure, in portraying the varied emotions which it was my lot to experience that night, and it may well seem that nothing more exquisite could remain for me. Yet it was written otherwise; for as I swept up to my goal, describing the inevitable arc which I had no power to check, I saw that one awaited me.

Crouching forward half out of the open window was a Burmese dacoit, a cross-eyed, leering being whom I well remembered to have encountered two years before in my dealings with Dr. Fu-Manchu. One bare, sinewy arm held rigidly at right angles before his breast, he clutched a long curved knife and waited--waited--for the critical moment when my throat should be at his mercy!

I have said that a strange coolness had come to my aid; even now it did not fail me, and so incalculably rapid are the workings of the human mind that I remember complimenting myself upon an achievement which Smith himself could not have bettered, and this in the immeasurable interval which intervened between the commencement of my upward swing and my arrival on a level with the window.

I threw my body back and thrust my feet forward. As my legs went through the opening, an acute pain in one calf told me that I was not to escape scatheless from the night's melee. But the dacoit went rolling over in the darkness of the room, as helpless in face of that ramrod stroke as the veriest infant . . .

Back I swept upon my trapeze, a sight to have induced any passing citizen to question his sanity. With might and main I sought to check the swing of the pendulum, for if I should come within reach of the window behind I doubted not that other knives awaited me. It was no difficult feat, and I succeeded in checking my flight. Swinging there above Museum Street I could even appreciate, so lucid was my mind, the ludicrous element of the situation.

I dropped. My wounded leg almost failed me; and greatly shaken, but with no other serious damage, I picked myself up from the dust of the roadway. It was a mockery of Fate that the problem which Nayland Smith had set me to solve, should have been solved thus; for I could not doubt that by means of the branch of a tall tree or some other suitable object situated opposite to Smith's house in Rangoon, Karamaneh had made her escape as tonight I had made mine.

Apart from the acute pain in my calf I knew that the dacoit's knife had bitten deeply, by reason of the fact that a warm liquid was trickling down into my boot. Like any drunkard I stood there in the middle of the road looking up at the vacant window where the dacoit had been, and up at the window above the shop of J. Salaman where I knew Fu-Manchu to be. But for some reason the latter window had been closed or almost closed, and as I stood there this reason became apparent to me.

The sound of running footsteps came from the direction of New Oxford Street. I turned--to see two policemen bearing down upon me!

This was a time for quick decisions and prompt action. I weighed all the circumstances in the balance, and made the last vital choice of the night; I turned and ran toward the British Museum as though the worst of Fu-Manchu's creatures, and not my allies the police, were at my heels!

No one else was in sight, but, as I whirled into the Square, the red lamp of a slowly retreating taxi became visible some hundred yards to the left. My leg was paining me greatly, but the nature of the wound did not interfere with my progress; therefore I continued my headlong career, and ere the police had reached the end of Museum Street I had my hand upon the door handle of the cab--for, the Fates being persistently kind to me, the vehicle was for hire.

"Dr. Cleeve's, Harley Street!" I shouted at the man. "Drive like hell!

It's an urgent case."

I leaped into the cab.

Within five seconds from the time that I slammed the door and dropped back panting upon the cushions, we were speeding westward toward the house of the famous pathologist, thereby throwing the police hopelessly off the track.

Faintly to my ears came the purr of a police whistle. The taxi-man evidently did not hear the significant sound. Merciful Providence had rung down the curtain; for to-night my role in the yellow drama was finished.

CHAPTER XXI

CRAGMIRE TOWER

LESS THAN TWO HOURS LATER, Inspector Weymouth and a party of men from Scotland Yard raided the house in Museum Street. They found the stock of J. Salaman practically intact, and, in the strangely appointed rooms above, every evidence of a hasty outgoing. But of the instruments, drugs and other laboratory paraphernalia not one item remained. I would gladly have given my income for a year, to have gained possession of the books, alone; for, beyond all shadow of doubt, I knew them to contain formula calculated to revolutionize the science of medicine.

Exhausted, physically and mentally, and with my mind a whispering- gallery of conjectures (it were needless for me to mention whom respecting) I turned in, gratefully, having patched up the slight wound in my calf.

I seemed scarcely to have closed my eyes, when Nayland Smith was shaking me into wakefulness.

"You are probably tired out," he said; "but your crazy expedition of last night entitles you to no sympathy. Read this; there is a train in an hour. We will reserve a compartment and you can resume your interrupted slumbers in a corner seat."

As I struggled upright in bed, rubbing my eyes sleepily, Smith handed me the Daily Telegraph, pointing to the following paragraph upon the literary page:

Messrs. M---- announce that they will publish shortly the long delayed work of Kegan Van Roon, the celebrated American traveler, Orientalist and psychic investigator, dealing with his recent inquiries in China. It will be remembered that Mr. Van Roon undertook to motor from Canton to Siberia last winter, but met with unforeseen difficulties in the province of Ho-Nan. He fell into the hands of a body of fanatics and was fortunate to escape with his life. His book will deal in particular with his experiences in Ho-Nan, and some sensational revelations regarding the awakening of that most mysterious race, the Chinese, are promised. For reasons of his own he has decided to remain in England until the completion of his book (which will be published simultaneously in New York and London) and has leased Cragmire Tower, Somersetshire, in which romantic and historical residence he will collate his notes and prepare for the world a work ear-marked as a classic even before it is published.

I glanced up from the paper, to find Smith's eyes fixed upon me, inquiringly.

"From what I have been able to learn," he said, evenly, "we should reach Saul, with decent luck, just before dusk."

As he turned, and quitted the room without another word, I realized, in a flash, the purport of our mission; I understood my friend's ominous calm, betokening suppressed excitement.

The Fates were with us (or so it seemed); and whereas we had not hoped to gain Saul before sunset, as a matter of fact, the autumn afternoon was in its most glorious phase as we left the little village with its oldtime hostelry behind us and set out in an easterly direction, with the Bristol Channel far away on our left and a gently sloping upland on our right.

The crooked high-street practically constituted the entire hamlet of Saul, and the inn, "The Wagoners," was the last house in the street. Now, as we followed the ribbon of moor-path to the top of the rise, we could stand and look back upon the way we had come; and although we had covered fully a mile of ground, it was possible to detect the sunlight gleaming now and then upon the gilt lettering of the inn sign as it swayed in the breeze. The day had been unpleasantly warm, but was relieved by this same sea breeze, which, although but slight, had in it the tang of the broad Atlantic. Behind us, then, the foot-path sloped down to Saul, unpeopled by any living thing; east and northeast swelled the monotony of the moor right out to the hazy distance where the sky began and the sea remotely lay hidden; west fell the gentle gradient from the top of the slope which we had mounted, and here, as far as the eye could reach, the country had an appearance suggestive of a huge and dried-up lake. This idea was borne out by an odd blotchiness, for sometimes there would be half a mile or more of seeming moorland, then a sharply defined change (or it seemed sharply defined from that bird's-eye point of view). A vivid greenness marked these changes, which merged into a dun-colored smudge and again into the brilliant green; then the moor would begin once more.

"That will be the Tor of Glastonbury, I suppose," said Smith, suddenly peering through his field-glasses in an easterly direction; "and yonder, unless I am greatly mistaken, is Cragmire Tower."

Shading my eyes with my hand, I also looked ahead, and saw the place for which we were bound; one of those round towers, more common in Ireland, which some authorities have declared to be of Phoenician origin. Ramshackle buildings clustered untidily about its base, and to it a sort of tongue of that oddly venomous green which patched the lowlands, shot out and seemed almost to reach the towerbase. The land for miles around was as flat as the palm of my hand, saving certain hummocks, lesser tors, and irregular piles of boulders which dotted its expanse. Hills and uplands there were in the hazy distance, forming a sort of mighty inland bay which I doubted not in some past age had been covered by the sea. Even in the brilliant sunlight the place had something of a mournful aspect, looking like a great dried- up pool into which the children of giants had carelessly cast stones.

We met no living soul upon the moor. With Cragmire Tower but a quarter of a mile off, Smith paused again, and raising his powerful glasses swept the visible landscape.

"Not a sign. Petrie," he said, softly; "yet . . ."

Dropping the glasses back into their case, my companion began to tug at his left ear.

"Have we been over-confident?" he said, narrowing his eyes in speculative fashion. "No less than three times I have had the idea that something, or some one, has just dropped out of sight, behind me, as I focused . . ."

"What do you mean, Smith?"

"Are we"--he glanced about him as though the vastness were peopled with listening Chinamen--"followed?"

Silently we looked into one another's eyes, each seeking for the dread which neither had named. Then:

"Come on Petrie!" said Smith, grasping my arm; and at quick march we were off again.

Cragmire Tower stood upon a very slight eminence, and what had looked like a green tongue, from the moorland slopes above, was in fact a creek, flanked by lush land, which here found its way to the sea. The house which we were come to visit consisted in a low, two-story building, joining the ancient tower on the east with two smaller outbuildings. There was a miniature kitchen-garden, and a few stunted fruit trees in the northwest corner; the whole being surrounded by a gray stone wall.

The shadow of the tower fell sharply across the path, which ran up almost alongside of it. We were both extremely warm by reason of our long and rapid walk on that hot day, and this shade should have been grateful to us, In short, I find it difficult to account for the unwelcome chill which I experienced at the moment that I found myself at the foot of the time-worn monument. I know that we both pulled up sharply and looked at one another as though acted upon by some mutual disturbance.

But not a sound broke the stillness save a remote murmuring, until a solitary sea gull rose in the air and circled directly over the tower, uttering its mournful and unmusical cry. Automatically to my mind sprang the lines of the poem:

Far from all brother-men, in the weird of the fen, With God's creatures I bide, 'mid the birds that I ken; Where the winds ever dree, where the hymn of the sea Brings a message of peace from the ocean to me.

Not a soul was visible about the premises; there was no sound of human activity and no dog barked. Nayland Smith drew a long breath, glanced back along the way we had come, then went on, following the wall, I beside him, until we came to the gate. It was unfastened, and we walked up the stone path through a wilderness of weeds. Four windows of the house were visible, two on the ground floor and two above. Those on the ground floor were heavily boarded up, those above, though glazed, boasted neither blinds nor curtains. Cragmire Tower showed not the slightest evidence of tenancy.

We mounted three steps and stood before a tremendously massive oaken door. An iron bell-pull, ancient and rusty, hung on the right of the door, and Smith, giving me an odd glance, seized the ring and tugged it.

From somewhere within the building answered a mournful clangor, a cracked and toneless jangle, which, seeming to echo through empty apartments, sought and found an exit apparently by way of one of the openings in the round tower; for it was from above our heads that the noise came to us.

It died away, that eerie ringing--that clanging so dismal that it could chill my heart even then with the bright sunlight streaming down out of the blue; it awoke no other response than the mournful cry of the sea gull circling over our heads. Silence fell. We looked at one another, and we were both about to express a mutual doubt when, unheralded by any unfastening of bolts or bars, the oaken door was opened, and a huge mulatto, dressed in white, stood there regarding us.

I started nervously, for the apparition was so unexpected, but Nayland Smith, without evidence of surprise, thrust a card into the man's hand.

"Take my card to Mr. Van Roon, and say that I wish to see him on important business," he directed, authoritatively.

The mulatto bowed and retired. His white figure seemed to be swallowed up by the darkness within, for beyond the patch of uncarpeted floor revealed by the peeping sunlight, was a barn-like place of densest shadow. I was about to speak, but Smith laid his hand upon my arm warningly, as, out from the shadows the mulatto returned. He stood on the right of the door and bowed again.

"Be pleased to enter," he said, in his harsh, negro voice. "Mr. Van Roon will see you."

The gladness of the sun could no longer stir me; a chill and sense of foreboding bore me company, as beside Nayland Smith I entered Cragmire Tower.

CHAPTER XXII

THE MULATTO

THE ROOM IN WHICH Van Roon received us was roughly of the shape of an old-fashioned keyhole; one end of it occupied the base of the tower, upon which the remainder had evidently been built. In many respects it was a singular room, but the feature which caused me the greatest amazement was this:--it had no windows!

In the deep alcove formed by the tower sat Van Roon at a littered table, upon which stood an oil reading-lamp, green shaded, of the "Victoria" pattern, to furnish the entire illumination of the apartment. That bookshelves lined the rectangular portion of this strange study I divined, although that end of the place was dark as a catacomb. The walls were wood-paneled, and the ceiling was oaken beamed. A small bookshelf and tumble-down cabinet stood upon either side of the table, and the celebrated American author and traveler lay propped up in a long split-cane chair. He wore smoked glasses, and had a clean-shaven, olive face, with a profusion of jet black hair. He was garbed in a dirty red dressing-gown, and a perfect fog of cigar smoke hung in the room. He did not rise to greet us, but merely extended his right hand, between two fingers whereof he held Smith's card.

"You will excuse the seeming discourtesy of an invalid, gentlemen?" he said; "but I am suffering from undue temerity in the interior of China!"

He waved his hand vaguely, and I saw that two rough deal chairs stood near the table. Smith and I seated ourselves, and my friend, leaning his elbow upon the table, looked fixedly at the face of the man whom we had come from London to visit. Although comparatively unfamiliar to the British public, the name of Van Roon was well-known in American literary circles; for he enjoyed in the United States a reputation somewhat similar to that which had rendered the name of our mutual friend, Sir Lionel Barton, a household word in England. It was Van Roon who, following in the footsteps of Madame Blavatsky, had sought out the haunts of the fabled mahatmas in the Himalayas, and Van Roon who had essayed to explore the fever swamps of Yucatan in quest of the secret of lost Atlantis; lastly, it was Van Roon, who, with an overland car specially built for him by a celebrated American firm, had undertaken the journey across China.

I studied the olive face with curiosity. Its natural impassivity was so greatly increased by the presence of the colored spectacles that my study was as profitless as if I had scrutinized the face of a carven Buddha. The mulatto had withdrawn, and in an atmosphere of gloom and tobacco smoke, Smith and I sat staring, perhaps rather rudely, at the object of our visit to the West Country.

"Mr. Van Roon," began my friend abruptly, "you will no doubt have seen this paragraph. It appeared in this morning's Daily Telegraph."

He stood up, and taking out the cutting from his notebook, placed it on the table.

"I have seen this--yes," said Van Roon, revealing a row of even, white teeth in a rapid smile. "Is it to this paragraph that I owe the pleasure of seeing you here?"

"The paragraph appeared in this morning's issue," replied Smith. "An hour from the time of seeing it, my friend, Dr. Petrie, and I were entrained for Bridgewater."

"Your visit delights me, gentlemen, and I should be ungrateful to question its cause; but frankly I am at a loss to understand why you should have honored me thus. I am a poor host, God knows; for what with my tortured limb, a legacy from the Chinese devils whose secrets I surprised, and my semi-blindness, due to the same cause, I am but sorry company."

Nayland Smith held up his right hand deprecatingly. Van Roon tendered a box of cigars and clapped his hands, whereupon the mulatto entered.

"I see that you have a story to tell me, Mr. Smith," he said; "therefore I suggest whisky-and-soda--or you might prefer tea, as it is nearly tea time?"

Smith and I chose the former refreshment, and the soft-footed half-breed having departed upon his errand, my companion, leaning forward earnestly across the littered table, outlined for Van Roon the story of Dr. Fu-Manchu, the great and malign being whose mission in England at that moment was none other than the stoppage of just such information as our host was preparing to give to the world.

"There is a giant conspiracy, Mr. Van Roon," he said, "which had its birth in this very province of Ho-Nan, from which you were so fortunate to escape alive; whatever its scope or limitations, a great secret society is established among the yellow races. It means that China, which has slumbered for so many generations, now stirs in that age-long sleep. I need not tell you how much more it means, this seething in the pot . . ."

"In a word," interrupted Van Roon, pushing Smith's glass across the table "you would say?--"

"That your life is not worth that!" replied Smith, snapping his fingers before the other's face.

A very impressive silence fell. I watched Van Roon curiously as he sat propped up among his cushions, his smooth face ghastly in the green light from the lamp-shade. He held the stump of a cigar between his teeth, but, apparently unnoticed by him, it had long since gone out. Smith, out of the shadows, was watching him, too. Then:

"Your information is very disturbing," said the American. "I am the more disposed to credit your statement because I am all too painfully aware of the existence of such a group as you mention, in China, but that they had an agent here in England is something I had never conjectured. In seeking out this solitary residence I have unwittingly done much to assist their designs . . . But--my dear Mr. Smith, I am very remiss! Of course you will remain tonight, and I trust for some days to come?"

Smith glanced rapidly across at me, then turned again to our host.

"It seems like forcing our company upon you," he said, "but in your own interests I think it will be best to do as you are good enough to suggest. I hope and believe that our arrival here has not been noticed by the enemy; therefore it will be well if we remain concealed as much as possible for the present, until we have settled upon some plan."

"Hagar shall go to the station for your baggage," said the American rapidly, and clapped his hands, his usual signal to the mulatto.

Whilst the latter was receiving his orders I noticed Nayland Smith watching him closely; and when he had departed:

"How long has that man been in your service?" snapped my friend.

Van Roon peered blindly through his smoked glasses.

"For some years," he replied; "he was with me in India--and in China."

"Where did you engage him?"

"Actually, in St. Kitts."

"H'm," muttered Smith, and automatically he took out and began to fill his pipe.

"I can offer you no company but my own, gentlemen," continued Van Roon, "but unless it interferes with your plans, you may find the surrounding district of interest and worthy of inspection, between now and dinner time. By the way, I think I can promise you quite a satisfactory meal, for Hagar is a model chef."

"A walk would be enjoyable," said Smith, "but dangerous."

"Ah! perhaps you are right. Evidently you apprehend some attempt upon me?"

"At any moment!"

"To one in my crippled condition, an alarming outlook! However, I place myself unreservedly in your hands. But really, you must not leave this interesting district before you have made the acquaintance of some of its historical spots. To me, steeped as I am in what I may term the lore of the odd, it is a veritable wonderland, almost as interesting, in its way, as the caves and jungles of Hindustan depicted by Madame Blavatsky."

His high-pitched voice, with a certain labored intonation, not quite so characteristically American as was his accent, rose even higher; he spoke with the fire of the enthusiast.

"When I learned that Cragmire Tower was vacant," he continued, "I leaped at the chance (excuse the metaphor, from a lame man!). This is a ghost hunter's paradise. The tower itself is of unknown origin, though probably Phoenician, and the house traditionally sheltered Dr. Macleod, the necromancer, after his flight from the persecution of James of Scotland. Then, to add to its interest, it borders on Sedgemoor, the scene of the bloody battle during the Monmouth rising, whereat a thousand were slain on the field. It is a local legend that the unhappy Duke and his staff may be seen, on stormy nights, crossing the path which skirts the mire, after which this building is named, with flaming torches held aloft."

"Merely marsh-lights, I take it?" interjected Smith, gripping his pipe hard between his teeth.

"Your practical mind naturally seeks a practical explanation," smiled Van Roon, "but I myself have other theories. Then in addition to the charms of Sedgemoor--haunted Sedgemoor--on a fine day it is quite possible to see the ruins of Glastonbury Abbey from here; and Glastonbury Abbey, as you may know, is closely bound up with the history of alchemy. It was in the ruins of Glastonbury Abbey that the adept Kelly, companion of Dr. Dee, discovered, in the reign of Elizabeth, the famous caskets of St. Dunstan, containing the two tinctures . . ."

So he ran on, enumerating the odd charms of his residence, charms which for my part I did not find appealing. Finally:

"We cannot presume further upon your kindness," said Nayland Smith, standing up. "No doubt we can amuse ourselves in the neighborhood of the house until the return of your servant."

"Look upon Cragmire Tower as your own, gentlemen!" cried Van Roon. "Most of the rooms are unfurnished, and the garden is a wilderness, but the structure of the brickwork in the tower may interest you archaeologically, and the view across the moor is at least as fine as any in the neighborhood."

So, with his brilliant smile and a gesture of one thin yellow hand, the crippled traveler made us free of his odd dwelling. As I passed out from the room close at Smith's heels, I glanced back, I cannot say why. Van Roon already was bending over his papers, in his green shadowed sanctuary, and the light shining down upon his smoked glasses created the odd illusion that he was looking over the tops of the lenses and not down at the table as his attitude suggested. However, it was probably ascribable to the weird chiaroscuro of the scene, although it gave the seated figure an oddly malignant appearance, and I passed out through the utter darkness of the outer room to the front door. Smith opening it, I was conscious of surprise to find dusk come--to meet darkness where I had looked for sunlight.

The silver wisps which had raced along the horizon, as we came to Cragmire Tower, had been harbingers of other and heavier banks. A stormy sunset smeared crimson streaks across the skyline, where a great range of clouds, like the oily smoke of a city burning, was banked, mountain topping mountain, and lighted from below by this angry red. As we came down the steps and out by the gate, I turned and looked across the moor behind us. A sort of reflection from this distant blaze encrimsoned the whole landscape. The inland bay glowed sullenly, as if internal fires and not reflected light were at work; a scene both wild and majestic.

Nayland Smith was staring up at the cone-like top of the ancient tower in a curious, speculative fashion. Under the influence of our host's conversation I had forgotten the reasonless dread which had touched me at the moment of our arrival, but now, with the red light blazing over Sedgemoor, as if in memory of the blood which had been shed there, and with the tower of unknown origin looming above me, I became very uncomfortable again, nor did I envy Van Roon his eerie residence. The proximity of a tower of any kind, at night, makes in some inexplicable way for awe, and to-night there were other agents, too.

"What's that?" snapped Smith suddenly, grasping my arm.

He was peering southward, toward the distant hamlet, and, starting violently at his words and the sudden grasp of his hand, I, too, stared in that direction.

"We were followed, Petrie," he almost whispered. "I never got a sight of our follower, but I'll swear we were followed. Look! there's something moving over yonder!"

Together we stood staring into the dusk; then Smith burst abruptly into one of his rare laughs, and clapped me upon the shoulder.

"It's Hagar, the mulatto!" he cried--"and our grips. That extraordinary American with his tales of witch-lights and haunted abbeys has been playing the devil with our nerves."

Together we waited by the gate until the half-caste appeared on the bend of the path with a grip in either hand. He was a great, muscular fellow with a stoic face, and, for the purpose of visiting Saul, presumably, he had doffed his white raiment and now wore a sort of livery, with a peaked cap.

Smith watched him enter the house. Then:

"I wonder where Van Roon obtains his provisions and so forth," he muttered. "It's odd they knew nothing about the new tenant of Cragmire Tower at 'The Wagoners.'"

There came a sort of sudden expectancy into his manner for which I found myself at a loss to account. He turned his gaze inland and stood there tugging at his left ear and clicking his teeth together. He stared at me, and his eyes looked very bright in the dusk, for a sort of red glow from the sunset touched them; but he spoke no word, merely taking my arm and leading me off on a rambling walk around and about the house. Neither of us spoke a word until we stood at the gate of Cragmire Tower again; then:

"I'll swear, now, that we were followed here today!" muttered Smith.

The lofty place immediately within the doorway proved, in the light of a lamp now fixed in an iron bracket, to be a square entrance hall meagerly furnished. The closed study door faced the entrance, and on the left of it ascended an open staircase up which the mulatto led the way. We found ourselves on the floor above, in a corridor traversing the house from back to front. An apartment on the immediate left was indicated by the mulatto as that allotted to Smith. It was a room of fair size, furnished quite simply but boasting a wardrobe cupboard, and Smith's grip stood beside the white enameled bed. I glanced around, and then prepared to follow the man, who had awaited me in the doorway.

He still wore his dark livery, and as I followed the lithe, broad-shouldered figure along the corridor, I found myself considering critically his breadth of shoulder and the extraordinary thickness of his neck.

I have repeatedly spoken of a sort of foreboding, an elusive stirring in the depths of my being of which I became conscious at certain times in my dealings with Dr. Fu-Manchu and his murderous servants. This sensation, or something akin to it, claimed me now, unaccountably, as I stood looking into the neat bedroom, on the same side of the corridor but at the extreme end, wherein I was to sleep.

A voiceless warning urged me to return; a kind of childish panic came fluttering about my heart, a dread of entering the room, of allowing the mulatto to come behind me.

Doubtless this was no more than a sub-conscious product of my observations respecting his abnormal breadth of shoulder. But whatever the origin of the impulse, I found myself unable to disobey it. Therefore, I merely nodded, turned on my heel and went back to Smith's room.

I closed the door, then turned to face Smith, who stood regarding me.

"Smith," I said, "that man sends cold water trickling down my spine!"

Still regarding me fixedly, my friend nodded his head.

"You are curiously sensitive to this sort of thing," he replied slowly; "I have noticed it before as a useful capacity. I don't like the look of the man myself. The fact that he has been in Van Roon's employ for some years goes for nothing. We are neither of us likely to forget Kwee, the Chinese servant of Sir Lionel Barton, and it is quite possible that Fu-Manchu has corrupted this man as he corrupted the other. It is quite possible . . ."

His voice trailed off into silence, and he stood looking across the room with unseeing eyes, meditating deeply. It was quite dark now outside, as I could see through the uncurtained window, which opened upon the dreary expanse stretching out to haunted Sedgemoor. Two candles were burning upon the dressing table; they were but recently lighted, and so intense was the stillness that I could distinctly hear the spluttering of one of the wicks, which was damp. Without giving the slightest warning of his intention, Smith suddenly made two strides forward, stretched out his long arms, and snuffed the pair of candles in a twinkling.

The room became plunged in impenetrable darkness.

"Not a word, Petrie!" whispered my companion.

I moved cautiously to join him, but as I did so, perceived that he was moving too. Vaguely, against the window I perceived him silhouetted. He was looking out across the moor, and:

"See! see!" he hissed.

With my heart thumping furiously in my breast, I bent over him; and for the second time since our coming to Cragmire Tower, my thoughts flew to "The Fenman."

There are shades in the fen; ghosts of women and men Who have sinned and have died, but are living again. O'er the waters they tread, with their lanterns of dread, And they peer in the pools--in the pools of the dead...

A light was dancing out upon the moor, a witchlight that came and went unaccountably, up and down, in and out, now clearly visible, now masked in the darkness!

"Lock the door!" snapped my companion--"if there's a key."

I crept across the room and fumbled for a moment; then:

"There is no key," I reported.

"Then wedge the chair under the knob and let no one enter until I return!" he said, amazingly.

With that he opened the window to its fullest extent, threw his leg over the sill, and went creeping along a wide concrete ledge, in which ran a leaded gutter, in the direction of the tower on the right!

Not pausing to follow his instructions respecting the chair, I craned out of the window, watching his progress, and wondering with what sudden madness he was bitten. Indeed, I could not credit my senses, could not believe that I heard and saw aright. Yet there out in the darkness on the moor moved the will-o'-the-wisp, and ten yards along the gutter crept my friend, like a great gaunt cat. Unknown to me he must have prospected the route by daylight, for now I saw his design. The ledge terminated only where it met the ancient wall of the tower, and it was possible for an agile climber to step from it to the edge of the unglazed window some four feet below, and to scramble from that point to the stone fence and thence on to the path by which we had come from Saul.

This difficult operation Nayland Smith successfully performed, and, to my unbounded amazement, went racing into the darkness toward the dancing light, headlong, like a madman! The night swallowed him up, and between my wonder and my fear my hands trembled so violently that I could scarce support myself where I rested, with my full weight upon the sill.

I seemed now to be moving through the fevered phases of a nightmare. Around and below me Cragmire Tower was profoundly silent, but a faint odor of cookery was now perceptible. Outside, from the night, came a faint whispering as of the distant sea, but no moon and no stars relieved the impenetrable blackness. Only out over the moor the mysterious light still danced and moved.

One--two--three--four--five minutes passed. The light vanished and did not appear again. Five more age-long minutes elapsed in absolute silence, whilst I peered into the darkness of the night and listened, every nerve in my body tense, for the return of Nayland Smith. Yet two more minutes, which embraced an agony of suspense, passed in the same fashion; then a shadowy form grew, phantomesque, out of the gloom; a moment more, and I distinctly heard the heavy breathing of a man nearly spent, and saw my friend scrambling up toward the black embrasure in the tower. His voice came huskily, pantingly:

"Creep along and lend me a hand, Petrie! I am nearly winded."

I crept through the window, steadied my quivering nerves by an effort of the will, and reached the end of the ledge in time to take Smith's extended hand and to draw him up beside me against the wall of the tower. He was shaking with his exertions, and must have fallen, I think, without my assistance. Inside the room again:

"Quick! light the candles!" he breathed hoarsely.

"Did any one come?"

"No one--nothing."

Having expended several matches in vain, for my fingers twitched nervously, I ultimately succeeded in relighting the candles.

"Get along to your room!" directed Smith. "Your apprehensions are unfounded at the moment, but you may as well leave both doors wide open!"

I looked into his face--it was very drawn and grim, and his brow was wet with perspiration, but his eyes had the fighting glint, and I knew that we were upon the eve of strange happenings.

CHAPTER XXIII

A CRY ON THE MOOR

OF THE EVENTS intervening between this moment and that when death called to us out of the night, I have the haziest recollections. An excellent dinner was served in the bleak and gloomy dining-room by the mulatto, and the crippled author was carried to the head of the table by this same Herculean attendant, as lightly as though he had but the weight of a child.

Van Roon talked continuously, revealing a deep knowledge of all sorts of obscure matters; and in the brief intervals, Nayland Smith talked also, with almost feverish rapidity. Plans for the future were discussed. I can recall no one of them.

I could not stifle my queer sentiments in regard to the mulatto, and every time I found him behind my chair I was hard put to repress an shudder. In this fashion the strange evening passed; and to the accompaniment of distant, muttering thunder, we two guests retired to our chambers in Cragmire Tower. Smith had contrived to give me my instructions in a whisper, and five minutes after entering my own room, I had snuffed the candles, slipped a wedge, which he had given me, under the door, crept out through the window onto the guttered ledge, and joined Smith in his room. He, too, had extinguished his candles, and the place was in darkness. As I climbed in, he grasped my wrist to silence me, and turned me forcibly toward the window.

"Listen!" he said.

I turned and looked out upon a prospect which had been a fit setting for the witch scene in Macbeth. Thunder clouds hung low over the moor, but through them ran a sort of chasm, or rift, allowing a bar of lurid light to stretch across the drear, from east to west--a sort of lane walled by darkness. There came a remote murmuring, as of a troubled sea--a hushed and distant chorus; and sometimes in upon it broke the drums of heaven. In the west lightning flickered, though but faintly, intermittently.

Then came the call.

Out of the blackness of the moor it came, wild and distant--"Help! help!"

"Smith!" I whispered--"what is it? What. . ."

"Mr. Smith!" came the agonized cry . . . "Nayland Smith, help! for God's sake. . . ."

"Quick, Smith!" I cried, "quick, man! It's Van Roon--he's been dragged out . . . they are murdering him . . ."

Nayland Smith held me in a vise-like grip, silent, unmoved!

Louder and more agonized came the cry for aid, and I became more than ever certain that it was poor Van Roon who uttered it.

"Mr. Smith! Dr. Petrie! for God's sake come . . . or . . . it will be . . . too . . . late . . ."

"Smith!" I said, turning furiously upon my friend, "if you are going to remain here whilst murder is done, I am not!"

My blood boiled now with hot resentment. It was incredible, inhuman, that we should remain there inert whilst a fellow man, and our host to boot, was being done to death out there in the darkness. I exerted all my strength to break away; but although my efforts told upon him, as his loud breathing revealed, Nayland Smith clung to me tenaciously. Had my hands been free, in my fury, I could have struck him, for the pitiable cries, growing fainter, now, told their own tale. Then Smith spoke shortly and angrily--breathing hard between the words.

"Be quiet, you fool!" he snapped; "it's little less than an insult, Petrie, to think me capable of refusing help where help is needed!"

Like a cold douche his words acted; in that instant I knew myself a fool.

"You remember the Call of Siva?" he said, thrusting me away irritably, "--two years ago, and what it meant to those who obeyed it?"

"You might have told me . . ."

"Told you! You would have been through the window before I had uttered two words!"

I realized the truth of his assertion, and the justness of his anger.

"Forgive me, old man," I said, very crestfallen, "but my impulse was a natural one, you'll admit. You must remember that I have been trained never to refuse aid when aid is asked."

"Shut up, Petrie!" he growled; "forget it."

The cries had ceased now, entirely, and a peal of thunder, louder than any yet, echoed over distant Sedgemoor. The chasm of light splitting the heavens closed in, leaving the night wholly black.

"Don't talk!" rapped Smith; "act! You wedged your door?"

"Yes."

"Good. Get into that cupboard, have your Browning ready, and keep the door very slightly ajar."

He was in that mood of repressed fever which I knew and which always communicated itself to me. I spoke no further word, but stepped into the wardrobe indicated and drew the door nearly shut. The recess just accommodated me, and through the aperture I could see the bed, vaguely, the open window, and part of the opposite wall. I saw Smith cross the floor, as a mighty clap of thunder boomed over the house.

A gleam of lightning flickered through the gloom.

I saw the bed for a moment, distinctly, and it appeared to me that Smith lay therein, with the sheets pulled up over his head. The light was gone, and I could hear big drops of rain pattering upon the leaden gutter below the open window.

My mood was strange, detached, and characterized by vagueness. That Van Roon lay dead upon the moor I was convinced; and--although I recognized that it must be a sufficient one--I could not even dimly divine the reason why we had refrained from lending him aid. To have failed to save him, knowing his peril, would have been bad enough; to have refused, I thought was shameful. Better to have shared his fate--yet . . .

The downpour was increasing, and beating now a regular tattoo upon the gutterway. Then, splitting the oblong of greater blackness which marked the casement, quivered dazzlingly another flash of lightning in which I saw the bed again, with that impression of Smith curled up in it. The blinding light died out; came the crash of thunder, harsh and fearsome, more imminently above the tower than ever. The building seemed to shake.

Coming as they did, horror and the wrath of heaven together, suddenly, crashingly, black and angry after the fairness of the day, these happenings and their setting must have terrorized the stoutest heart; but somehow I seemed detached, as I have said, and set apart from the whirl of events; a spectator. Even when a vague yellow light crept across the room from the direction of the door, and flickered unsteadily on the bed, I remained unmoved to a certain degree, although passively alive to the significance of the incident. I realized that the ultimate issue was at hand, but either because I was emotionally exhausted, or from some other cause, the pending climax failed to disturb me.

Going on tiptoe, in stockinged feet, across my field of vision, passed Kegan Van Roon! He was in his shirt-sleeves and held a lighted candle in one hand whilst with the other he shaded it against the draught from the window. He was a cripple no longer, and the smoked glasses were discarded; most of the light, at the moment when first I saw him, shone upon his thin, olive face, and at sight of his eyes much of the mystery of Cragmire Tower was resolved. For they were oblique, very slightly, but nevertheless unmistakably oblique. Though highly educated, and possibly an American citizen, Van Roon was a Chinaman!

Upon the picture of his face as I saw it then, I do not care to dwell. It lacked the unique horror of Dr. Fu-Manchu's unforgettable countenance, but possessed a sort of animal malignancy which the latter lacked . . . He approached within three or four feet of the bed, peering--peering. Then, with a timidity which spoke well for Nayland Smith's reputation, paused and beckoned to some one who evidently stood in the doorway behind him. As he did so I noted that the legs of his trousers were caked with greenish brown mud nearly up to the knees.

The huge mulatto, silent-footed, crossed to the bed in three strides. He was stripped to the waist, and, excepting some few professional athletes, I had never seen a torso to compare with that which, brown and glistening, now bent over Nayland Smith. The muscular development was simply enormous; the man had a neck like a column, and the thews around his back and shoulders were like ivy tentacles wreathing some gnarled oak.

Whilst Van Roon, his evil gaze upon the bed, held the candle aloft, the mulatto, with a curious preparatory writhing movement of the mighty shoulders, lowered his outstretched fingers to the disordered bed linen . . .

I pushed open the cupboard door and thrust out the Browning. As I did so a dramatic thing happened. A tall, gaunt figure shot suddenly upright from beyond the bed. It was Nayland Smith!

Upraised in his hand he held a heavy walking cane. I knew the handle to be leaded, and I could judge of the force with which he wielded it by the fact that it cut the air with a keen swishing sound. It descended upon the back of the mulatto's skull with a sickening thud, and the great brown body dropped inert upon the padded bed--in which not Smith, but his grip, reposed. There was no word, no cry. Then:

"Shoot, Petrie! Shoot the fiend! Shoot . . ."

Van Roon, dropping the candle, in the falling gleam of which I saw the whites of the oblique eyes turned and leaped from the room with the agility of a wild cat. The ensuing darkness was split by a streak of lightning . . . and there was Nayland Smith scrambling around the foot of the bed and making for the door in hot pursuit.

We gained it almost together. Smith had dropped the cane, and now held his pistol in his hand. Together we fired into the chasm of the corridor, and in the flash, saw Van Roon hurling himself down the stairs. He went silently in his stockinged feet, and our own clatter was drowned by the awful booming of the thunder which now burst over us again.

Crack!--crack!--crack! Three times our pistols spat venomously after the flying figure . . . then we had crossed the hall below and were in the wilderness of the night with the rain descending upon us in sheets. Vaguely I saw the white shirt-sleeves of the fugitive near the corner of the stone fence. A moment he hesitated, then darted away inland, not toward Saul, but toward the moor and the cup of the inland bay.

"Steady, Petrie! steady!" cried Nayland Smith. He ran, panting, beside me. "It is the path to the mire." He breathed sibilantly between every few words. It was out there . . . that he hoped to lure us . . . with the cry for help."

A great blaze of lightning illuminated the landscape as far as the eye could see. Ahead of us a flying shape, hair lank and glistening in the downpour, followed a faint path skirting that green tongue of morass which we had noted from the upland. It was Kegan Van Roon. He glanced over his shoulder, showing a yellow, terror-stricken face. We were gaining upon him. Darkness fell, and the thunder cracked and boomed as though the very moor were splitting about us.

"Another fifty yards, Petrie," breathed Nayland Smith, "and after that it's unchartered ground."

On we went through the rain and the darkness; then:

"Slow up! slow up!" cried Smith. "It feels soft!"

Indeed, already I had made one false step--and the hungry mire had fastened upon my foot, almost tripping me.

"Lost the path!"

We stopped dead. The falling rain walled us in. I dared not move, for I knew that the mire, the devouring mire, stretched, eager, close about my feet. We were both waiting for the next flash of lightning, I think, but, before it came, out of the darkness ahead of us rose a cry that sometimes rings in my ears to this hour. Yet it was no more than a repetition of that which had called to us, deathfully, awhile before.

"Help! help! for God's sake help! Quick! I am sinking . . ."

Nayland Smith grasped my arm furiously.

"We dare not move, Petrie--we dare not move!" he breathed. "It's God's justice--visible for once."

Then came the lightning; and--ignoring a splitting crash behind us--we both looked ahead, over the mire.

Just on the edge of the venomous green path, not thirty yards away, I saw the head and shoulders and upstretched, appealing arms of Van Roon. Even as the lightning flickered and we saw him, he was gone; with one last, long, drawn-out cry, horribly like the mournful wail of a sea gull, he was gone!

That eerie light died, and in the instant before the sound of the thunder came shatteringly, we turned about . . . in time to see Cragmire Tower, a blacker silhouette against the night, topple and fall! A red glow began to be perceptible above the building. The thunder came booming through the caverns of space. Nayland Smith lowered his wet face close to mine and shouted in my ear:

"Kegan Van Roon never returned from China. It was a trap. Those were two creatures of Dr. Fu-Manchu . . ."

The thunder died away, hollowly, echoing over the distant sea . . .

"That light on the moor to-night?"

"You have not learned the Morse Code, Petrie. It was a signal, and it read:--S M I T H . . . SOS."

"Well?"

"I took the chance, as you know. And it was Karamaneh! She knew of the plot to bury us in the mire. She had followed from London, but could do nothing until dusk. God forgive me if I've misjudged her--for we owe her our lives to-night."

Flames were bursting up from the building beside the ruin of the ancient tower which had faced the storms of countless ages only to succumb at last. The lightning literally had cloven it in twain.

"The mulatto? . . ."

Again the lightning flashed, and we saw the path and began to retrace our steps. Nayland Smith turned to me; his face was very grim in that unearthly light, and his eyes shone like steel.

"I killed him, Petrie . . . as I meant to do."

From out over Sedgemoor it came, cracking and rolling and booming toward us, swelling in volume to a stupendous climax, that awful laughter of Jove the destroyer of Cragmire Tower.

CHAPTER XXIV

STORY OF THE GABLES

IN LOOKING OVER my notes dealing with the second phase of Dr. Fu-Manchu's activities in England, I find that one of the worst hours of my life was associated with the singular and seemingly inconsequent adventure of the fiery hand. I shall deal with it in this place, begging you to bear with me if I seem to digress.

Inspector Weymouth called one morning, shortly after the Van Roon episode, and entered upon a surprising account of a visit to a house at Hampstead which enjoyed the sinister reputation of being uninhabitable.

"But in what way does the case enter into your province?" inquired Nayland Smith, idly tapping out his pipe on a bar of the grate.

We had not long finished breakfast, but from an early hour Smith had been at his eternal smoking, which only the advent of the meal had interrupted.

"Well," replied the inspector, who occupied a big armchair near the window, "I was sent to look into it, I suppose, because I had nothing better to do at the moment."

"Ah!" jerked Smith, glancing over his shoulder.

The ejaculation had a veiled significance; for our quest of Dr. Fu-Manchu had come to an abrupt termination by reason of the fact that all trace of that malignant genius, and of the group surrounding him, had vanished with the destruction of Cragmire Tower.

"The house is called the Gables," continued the Scotland Yard man, "and I knew I was on a wild goose chase from the first--"

"Why?" snapped Smith.

"Because I was there before, six months ago or so--just before your present return to England--and I knew what to expect."

Smith looked up with some faint dawning of interest perceptible in his manner.

"I was unaware," he said with a slight smile, "that the cleaning-up of haunted houses came within the jurisdiction of Scotland Yard. I am learning something."

"In the ordinary way," replied the big man good-humoredly, "it doesn't. But a sudden death always excites suspicion, and--"

"A sudden death?" I said, glancing up; "you didn't explain that the ghost had killed any one!"

"I'm afraid I'm a poor hand at yarn-spinning, Doctor," said Weymouth, turning his blue, twinkling eyes in my direction. "Two people have died at the Gables within the last six months."

"You begin to interest me," declared Smith, and there came something of the old, eager look into his gaunt face, as, having lighted his pipe, he tossed the match-end into the hearth.

"I had hoped for some little excitement, myself," confessed the inspector. "This dead-end, with not a ghost of a clue to the whereabouts of the yellow fiend, has been getting on my nerves--"

Nayland Smith grunted sympathetically.

"Although Dr. Fu-Manchu has been in England for some months, now," continued Weymouth, "I have never set eyes upon him; the house we raided in Museum Street proved to be empty; in a word, I am wasting my time. So that I volunteered to run up to Hampstead and look into the matter of the Gables, principally as a distraction. It's a queer business, but more in the Psychical Research Society's line than mine, I'm afraid. Still, if there were no Dr. Fu-Manchu it might be of interest to you--and to you, Dr. Petrie, because it illustrates the fact, that, given the right sort of subject, death can be brought about without any elaborate mechanism--such as our Chinese friends employ."

"You interest me more and more," declared Smith, stretching himself in the long, white cane rest-chair.

"Two men, both fairly sound, except that the first one had an asthmatic heart, have died at the Gable without any one laying a little finger upon them. Oh! there was no jugglery! They weren't poisoned, or bitten by venomous insects, or suffocated, or anything like that. They just died of fear--stark fear."

With my elbows resting upon the table cover, and my chin in my hands, I was listening attentively, now, and Nayland Smith, a big cushion behind his head, was watching the speaker with a keen and speculative look in those steely eyes of his.

"You imply that Dr. Fu-Manchu has something to learn from the Gables?" he jerked.

Weymouth nodded stolidly.

"I can't work up anything like amazement in these days," continued the latter; "every other case seems stale and hackneyed alongside the case. But I must confess that when the Gables came on the books of the Yard the second time, I began to wonder. I thought there might be some tangible clue, some link connecting the two victims; perhaps some evidence of robbery or of revenge--of some sort of motive. In short, I hoped to find evidence of human agency at work, but, as before, I was disappointed."

"It's a legitimate case of a haunted house, then?" said Smith.

"Yes; we find them occasionally, these uninhabitable places, where there is something, something malignant and harmful to human life, but something that you cannot arrest, that you cannot hope to bring into court."

"Ah," replied Smith slowly; "I suppose you are right. There are historic instances, of course: Glamys Castle and Spedlins Tower in Scotland, Peel Castle, Isle of Man, with its Maudhe Dhug, the gray lady of Rainham Hall, the headless horses of Caistor, the Wesley ghost of Epworth Rectory, and others. But I have never come in personal contact with such a case, and if I did I should feel very humiliated to have to confess that there was any agency which could produce a physical result--death--but which was immune from physical retaliation."

Weymouth nodded his head again.

"I might feel a bit sour about it, too," he replied, "if it were not that I haven't much pride left in these days, considering the show of physical retaliation I have made against Dr. Fu-Manchu."

"A home thrust, Weymouth!" snapped Nayland Smith, with one of those rare, boyish laughs of his. "We're children to that Chinese doctor, Inspector, to that weird product of a weird people who are as old in evil as the pyramids are old in mystery. But about the Gables?"

"Well, it's an uncanny place. You mentioned Glamys Castle a moment ago, and it's possible to understand an old stronghold like that being haunted, but the Gables was only built about 1870; it's quite a modern house. It was built for a wealthy Quaker family, and they occupied it, uninterruptedly and apparently without anything unusual occurring, for over forty years. Then it was sold to a Mr. Maddison--and Mr. Maddison died there six months ago."

"Maddison?" said Smith sharply, staring across at Weymouth. "What was he? Where did he come from?"

"He was a retired tea-planter from Colombo," replied the inspector.

"Colombo?"

"There was a link with the East, certainly, if that's what you are thinking; and it was this fact which interested me at the time, and which led me to waste precious days and nights on the case. But there was no mortal connection between this liverish individual and the schemes of Dr. Fu-Manchu. I'm certain of that."

"And how did he die?" I asked, interestedly.

"He just died in his chair one evening, in the room which he used as a library. It was his custom to sit there every night, when there were no visitors, reading, until twelve o'clock--or later. He was a bachelor, and his household consisted of a cook, a housemaid, and a man who had been with him for thirty years, I believe. At the time of Mr. Maddison's death, his household had recently been deprived of two of its members. The cook and housemaid both resigned one morning, giving as their reason the fact that the place was haunted."

"In what way?"

"I interviewed the precious pair at the time, and they told me absurd and various tales about dark figures wandering along the corridors and bending over them in bed at night, whispering; but their chief trouble was a continuous ringing of bells about the house."

"Bells?"

"They said that it became unbearable. Night and day there were bells ringing all over the house. At any rate, they went, and for three or four days the Gables was occupied only by Mr. Maddison and his man, whose name was Stevens. I interviewed the latter also, and he was an altogether more reliable witness; a decent, steady sort of man whose story impressed me very much at the time."

"Did he confirm the ringing?"

"He swore to it--a sort of jangle, sometimes up in the air, near the ceilings, and sometimes under the floor, like the shaking of silver bells."

Nayland Smith stood up abruptly and began to pace the room, leaving great trails of blue-gray smoke behind him.

"Your story is sufficiently interesting, Inspector," he declared, "even to divert my mind from the eternal contemplation of the Fu-Manchu problem. This would appear to be distinctly a case of an 'astral bell' such as we sometimes hear of in India."

"It was Stevens," continued Weymouth, "who found Mr. Maddison. He (Stevens) had been out on business connected with the household arrangements, and at about eleven o'clock he returned, letting himself in with a key. There was a light in the library, and getting no response to his knocking, Stevens entered. He found his master sitting bolt upright in a chair, clutching the arms with rigid fingers and staring straight before him with a look of such frightful horror on his face, that Stevens positively ran from the room and out of the house. Mr. Maddison was stone dead. When a doctor, who lives at no great distance away, came and examined him, he could find no trace of violence whatever; he had apparently died of fright, to judge from the expression on his face."

"Anything else?"

"Only this: I learnt, indirectly, that the last member of the Quaker family to occupy the house had apparently witnessed the apparition, which had led to his vacating the place. I got the story from the wife of a man who had been employed as gardener there at that time. The apparition--which he witnessed in the hallway, if I remember rightly-- took the form of a sort of luminous hand clutching a long, curved knife."

"Oh, Heavens!" cried Smith, and laughed shortly; "that's quite in order!"

"This gentleman told no one of the occurrence until after he had left the house, no doubt in order that the place should not acquire an evil reputation. Most of the original furniture remained, and Mr. Maddison took the house furnished. I don't think there can be any doubt that what killed him was fear at seeing a repetition--"

"Of the fiery hand?" concluded Smith.

"Quite so. Well, I examined the Gables pretty closely, and, with another Scotland Yard man, spent a night in the empty house. We saw nothing; but once, very faintly, we heard the ringing of bells."

Smith spun around upon him rapidly.

"You can swear to that?" he snapped.

"I can swear to it," declared Weymouth stolidly. "It seemed to be over our heads. We were sitting in the dining-room. Then it was gone, and we heard nothing more whatever of an unusual nature. Following the death of Mr. Maddison, the Gables remained empty until a while ago, when a French gentleman, name Lejay, leased it--"

"Furnished?"

"Yes; nothing was removed--"

"Who kept the place in order?"

"A married couple living in the neighborhood undertook to do so. The man attended to the lawn and so forth, and the woman came once a week, I believe, to clean up the house."

"And Lejay?"

"He came in only last week, having leased the house for six months. His family were to have joined him in a day or two, and he, with the aid of the pair I have just mentioned, and assisted by a French servant he brought over with him, was putting the place in order. At about twelve o'clock on Friday night this servant ran into a neighboring house screaming 'the fiery hand!' and when at last a constable arrived and a frightened group went up the avenue of the Gables, they found M. Lejay, dead in the avenue, near the steps just outside the hall door! He had the same face of horror . . ."

"What a tale for the press!" snapped Smith.

The owner has managed to keep it quiet so far, but this time I think it will leak into the press--yes."

There was a short silence; then:

"And you have been down to the Gables again?"

"I was there on Saturday, but there's not a scrap of evidence. The man undoubtedly died of fright in the same way as Maddison. The place ought to be pulled down; it's unholy."

"Unholy is the word," I said. "I never heard anything like it. This M. Lejay had no enemies?--there could be no possible motive?"

"None whatever. He was a business man from Marseilles, and his affairs necessitated his remaining in or near London for some considerable time; therefore, he decided to make his headquarters here, temporarily, and leased the Gables with that intention."

Nayland Smith was pacing the floor with increasing rapidity; he was tugging at the lobe of his left ear and his pipe had long since gone out.

CHAPTER XXV

THE BELLS

I STARTED TO MY FEET as a tall, bearded man swung open the door and hurled himself impetuously into the room. He wore a silk hat, which fitted him very ill, and a black frock coat which did not fit him at all.

"It's all right, Petrie!" cried the apparition; "I've leased the Gables!"

It was Nayland Smith! I stared at him in amazement

"The first time I have employed a disguise," continued my friend rapidly, "since the memorable episode of the false pigtail." He threw a small brown leather grip upon the floor. "In case you should care to visit the house, Petrie, I have brought these things. My tenancy commences to-night!"

Two days had elapsed, and I had entirely forgotten the strange story of the Gables which Inspector Weymouth had related to us; evidently it was otherwise with my friend, and utterly at a loss for an explanation of his singular behavior, I stooped mechanically and opened the grip. It contained an odd assortment of garments, and amongst other things several gray wigs and a pair of gold-rimmed spectacles.

Kneeling there with this strange litter about me, I looked up amazedly. Nayland Smith, with the unsuitable silk hat set right upon the back of his head, was pacing the room excitedly, his fuming pipe protruding from the tangle of factitious beard.

"You see, Petrie," he began again, rapidly, "I did not entirely trust the agent. I've leased the house in the name of Professor Maxton . . ."

"But, Smith," I cried, "what possible reason can there be for disguise?"

"There's every reason," he snapped.

"Why should you interest yourself in the Gables?"

"Does no explanation occur to you?"

"None whatever; to me the whole thing smacks of stark lunacy."

"Then you won't come?"

"I've never stuck at anything, Smith," I replied, "however undignified, when it has seemed that my presence could be of the slightest use."

As I rose to my feet, Smith stepped in front of me, and the steely gray eyes shone out strangely from the altered face. He clapped his hands upon my shoulders.

"If I assure you that your presence is necessary to my safety," he said--"that if you fail me I must seek another companion--will you come?"

Intuitively, I knew that he was keeping something back, and I was conscious of some resentment, but nevertheless my reply was a foregone conclusion, and--with the borrowed appearance of an extremely untidy old man--I crept guiltily out of my house that evening and into the cab which Smith had waiting.

The Gables was a roomy and rambling place lying back a considerable distance from the road. A semicircular drive gave access to the door, and so densely wooded was the ground, that for the most part the drive was practically a tunnel--a verdant tunnel. A high brick wall concealed the building from the point of view of any one on the roadway, but either horn of the crescent drive terminated at a heavy, wrought-iron gateway.

Smith discharged the cab at the corner of the narrow and winding road upon which the Gables fronted. It was walled in on both sides; on the left the wall being broken by tradesmen's entrances to the houses fronting upon another street, and on the right following, uninterruptedly, the grounds of the Gables. As we came to the gate:

"Nothing now," said Smith, pointing into the darkness of the road before us, "except a couple of studios, until one comes to the Heath."

He inserted the key in the lock of the gate and swung it creakingly open. I looked into the black arch of the avenue, thought of the haunted residence that lay hidden somewhere beyond, of those who had died in it--especially of the one who had died there under the trees-- and found myself out of love with the business of the night.

"Come on!" said Nayland Smith briskly, holding the gate open; "there should be a fire in the library and refreshments, if the charwoman has followed instructions."

I heard the great gate clang to behind us. Even had there been any moon (and there was none) I doubted if more than a patch or two of light could have penetrated there. The darkness was extraordinary. Nothing broke it, and I think Smith must have found his way by the aid of some sixth sense. At any rate, I saw nothing of the house until I stood some five paces from the steps leading up to the porch. A light was burning in the hallway, but dimly and inhospitably; of the facade of the building I could perceive little.

When we entered the hall and the door was closed behind us, I began wondering anew what purpose my friend hoped to serve by a vigil in this haunted place. There was a light in the library, the door of which was ajar, and on the large table were decanters, a siphon, and some biscuits and sandwiches. A large grip stood upon the floor, also. For some reason which was a mystery to me, Smith had decided that we must assume false names whilst under the roof of the Gables; and:

"Now, Pearce," he said, "a whisky-and-soda before we look around?"

The proposal was welcome enough, for I felt strangely dispirited, and, to tell the truth, in my strange disguise, not a little ridiculous.

All my nerves, no doubt, were highly strung, and my sense of hearing unusually acute, for I went in momentary expectation of some uncanny happening. I had not long to wait. As I raised the glass to my lips and glanced across the table at my friend, I heard the first faint sound heralding the coming of the bells.

It did not seem to proceed from anywhere within the library, but from some distant room, far away overhead. A musical sound it was, but breaking in upon the silence of that ill-omened house, its music was the music of terror. In a faint and very sweet cascade it rippled; a ringing as of tiny silver bells.

I set down my glass upon the table, and rising slowly from the chair in which I had been seated, stared fixedly at my companion, who was staring with equal fixity at me. I could see that I had not been deluded; Nayland Smith had heard the ringing, too.

"The ghosts waste no time!" he said softly. "This is not new to me; I spent an hour here last night and heard the same sound . . ."

I glanced hastily around the room. It was furnished as a library, and contained a considerable collection of works, principally novels. I was unable to judge of the outlook, for the two lofty windows were draped with heavy purple curtains which were drawn close. A silk shaded lamp swung from the center of the ceiling, and immediately over the table by which I stood. There was much shadow about the room; and now I glanced apprehensively about me, but especially toward the open door.

In that breathless suspense of listening we stood awhile; then:

"There it is again!" whispered Smith, tensely.

The ringing of bells was repeated, and seemingly much nearer to us; in fact it appeared to come from somewhere above, up near the ceiling of the room in which we stood. Simultaneously, we looked up, then Smith laughed, shortly.

"Instinctive, I suppose," he snapped; "but what do we expect to see in the air?"

The musical sound now grew in volume; the first tiny peal seemed to be reinforced by others and by others again, until the air around about us was filled with the pealings of these invisible bell-ringers.

Although, as I have said, the sound was rather musical than horrible, it was, on the other hand, so utterly unaccountable as to touch the supreme heights of the uncanny. I could not doubt that our presence had attracted these unseen ringers to the room in which we stood, and I knew quite well that I was growing pale. This was the room in which at least one unhappy occupant of the Gables had died of fear. I recognized the fact that if this mere overture were going to affect my nerves to such an extent, I could not hope to survive the ordeal of the night; a great effort was called for. I emptied my glass at a gulp, and stared across the table at Nayland Smith with a sort of defiance. He was standing very upright and motionless, but his eyes were turning right and left, searching every visible corner of the big room.

"Good!" he said in a very low voice. "The terrorizing power of the Unknown is boundless, but we must not get in the grip of panic, or we could not hope to remain in this house ten minutes."

I nodded without speaking. Then Smith, to my amazement, suddenly began to speak in a loud voice, a marked contrast to that, almost a whisper, in which he had spoken formerly.

"My dear Pearce," he cried, "do you hear the ringing of bells?"

Clearly the latter words were spoken for the benefit of the unseen intelligence controlling these manifestations; and although I regarded such finesse as somewhat wasted, I followed my friend's lead and replied in a voice as loud as his own:

"Distinctly, Professor!"

Silence followed my words, a silence in which both stood watchful and listening. Then, very faintly, I seemed to detect the silvern ringing receding away through distant rooms. Finally it became inaudible, and in the stillness of the Gables I could distinctly hear my companion breathing. For fully ten minutes we two remained thus, each momentarily expecting a repetition of the ringing, or the coming of some new and more sinister manifestation. But we heard nothing and saw nothing.

"Hand me that grip, and don't stir until I come back!" hissed Smith in my ear.

He turned and walked out of the library, his boots creaking very loudly in that awe-inspiring silence.

Standing beside the table, I watched the open door for his return, crushing down a dread that another form than his might suddenly appear there.

I could hear him moving from room to room, and presently, as I waited in hushed, tense watchfulness, he came in, depositing the grip upon the table. His eyes were gleaming feverishly.

"The house is haunted, Pearce!" he cried. "But no ghost ever frightened me! Come, I will show you your room."

CHAPTER XXVI

THE FIERY HAND

SMITH WALKED AHEAD of me upstairs; he had snapped up the light in the hallway, and now he turned and cried back loudly:

"I fear we should never get servants to stay here."

Again I detected the appeal to a hidden Audience; and there was something very uncanny in the idea. The house now was deathly still; the ringing had entirely subsided. In the upper corridor my companion, who seemed to be well acquainted with the position of the switches, again turned up all the lights, and in pursuit of the strange comedy which he saw fit to enact, addressed me continuously in the loud and unnatural voice which he had adopted as part of his disguise.

We looked into a number of rooms all well and comfortably furnished, but although my imagination may have been responsible for the idea, they all seemed to possess a chilly and repellent atmosphere. I felt that to essay sleep in any one of them would be the merest farce, that the place to all intents and purposes was uninhabitable, that something incalculably evil presided over the house.

And through it all, so obtuse was I, that no glimmer of the truth entered my mind. Outside again in the long, brightly lighted corridor, we stood for a moment as if a mutual anticipation of some new event pending had come to us. It was curious that sudden pulling up and silent questioning of one another; because, although we acted thus, no sound had reached us. A few seconds later our anticipation was realized. From the direction of the stairs it came--a low wailing in a woman's voice; and the sweetness of the tones added to the terror of the sound. I clutched at Smith's arm convulsively whilst that uncanny cry rose and fell--rose and fell--and died away.

Neither of us moved immediately. My mind was working with feverish rapidity and seeking to run down a memory which the sound had stirred into faint quickness. My heart was still leaping wildly when the wailing began again, rising and falling in regular cadence. At that instant I identified it.

During the time Smith and I had spent together in Egypt, two years before, searching for Karamaneh, I had found myself on one occasion in the neighborhood of a native cemetery near to Bedrasheen. Now, the scene which I had witnessed there rose up again vividly before me, and I seemed to see a little group of black-robed women clustered together about a native grave; for the wailing which now was dying away again in the Gables was the same, or almost the same, as the wailing of those Egyptian mourners.

The house was very silent again, now. My forehead was damp with perspiration, and I became more and more convinced that the uncanny ordeal must prove too much for my nerves. Hitherto, I had accorded little credence to tales of the supernatural, but face to face with such manifestations as these, I realized that I would have faced rather a group of armed dacoits, nay! Dr. Fu-Manchu himself, than have remained another hour in that ill-omened house.

My companion must have read as much in my face. But he kept up the strange, and to me, purposeless comedy, when presently he spoke.

"I feel it to be incumbent upon me to suggest," he said, "that we spend the night at a hotel after all."

He walked rapidly downstairs and into the library and began to strap up the grip.

"After all," he said, "there may be a natural explanation of what we've heard; for it is noteworthy that we have actually seen nothing. It might even be possible to get used to the ringing and the wailing after a time. Frankly, I am loath to go back on my bargain!"

Whilst I stared at him in amazement, he stood there indeterminate as it seemed, Then:

"Come, Pearce!" he cried loudly, "I can see that you do not share my views; but for my own part I shall return to-morrow and devote further attention to the phenomena."

Extinguishing the light, he walked out into the hallway, carrying the grip in his hand. I was not far behind him. We walked toward the door together, and:

"Turn the light out, Pearce," directed Smith; the switch is at your elbow. We can see our way to the door well enough, now."

In order to carry out these instructions, it became necessary for me to remain a few paces in the rear of my companion, and I think I have never experienced such a pang of nameless terror as pierced me at the moment of extinguishing the light; for Smith had not yet opened the door, and the utter darkness of the Gables was horrible beyond expression. Surely darkness is the most potent weapon of the Unknown. I know that at the moment my hand left the switch, I made for the door as though the hosts of hell pursued me. I collided violently with Smith. He was evidently facing toward me in the darkness, for at the moment of our collision, he grasped my shoulder as in a vise.

"My God, Petrie! look behind you!" he whispered.

I was enabled to judge of the extent and reality of his fear by the fact that the strange subterfuge of addressing me always as Pearce was forgotten. I turned, in a flash. . . .

Never can I forget what I saw. Many strange and terrible memories are mine, memories stranger and more terrible than those of the average man; but this thing which now moved slowly down upon us through the impenetrable gloom of that haunted place, was (if the term be understood) almost absurdly horrible. It was a medieval legend come to life in modern

London; it was as though some horrible chimera of the black and ignorant past was become create and potent in the present.

A luminous hand--a hand in the veins of which fire seemed to run so that the texture of the skin and the shape of the bones within were perceptible--in short a hand of glowing, fiery flesh clutching a short knife or dagger which also glowed with the same hellish, internal luminance, was advancing upon us where we stood--was not three paces removed!

What I did or how I came to do it, I can never recall. In all my years I have experienced nothing to equal the stark panic which seized upon me then. I know that I uttered a loud and frenzied cry; I know that I tore myself like a madman from Smith's restraining grip . . .

"Don't touch it! Keep away, for your life!" I heard . . .

But, dimly I recollect that, finding the thing approaching yet nearer, I lashed out with my fists--madly, blindly--and struck something palpable . . .

What was the result, I cannot say. At that point my recollections merge into confusion. Something or some one (Smith, as I afterwards discovered) was hauling me by main force through the darkness; I fell a considerable distance onto gravel which lacerated my hands and gashed my knees. Then, with the cool night air fanning my brow, I was running, running--my breath coming in hysterical sobs. Beside me fled another figure. . . . And my definite recollections commence again at that point. For this companion of my flight from the Gables threw himself roughly against me to alter my course.

"Not that way! not that way!" came pantingly.

"Not on to the Heath . . . we must keep to the roads . . ."

It was Nayland Smith. That healing realization came to me, bringing such a gladness as no words of mine can express nor convey. Still we ran on.

"There's a policeman's lantern," panted my companion. "They'll attempt nothing, now!"

I gulped down the stiff brandy-and-soda, then glanced across to where Nayland Smith lay extended in the long, cane chair.

"Perhaps you will explain," I said, "for what purpose you submitted me to that ordeal. If you proposed to correct my skepticism concerning supernatural manifestations, you have succeeded."

"Yes," said my companion, musingly, "they are devilishly clever; but we knew that already."

I stared at him, fatuously.

"Have you ever known me to waste my time when there was important work to do?" he continued. "Do you seriously believe that my ghost-hunting was undertaken for amusement? Really, Petrie, although you are very fond of assuring me that I need a holiday, I think the shoe is on the other foot!"

From the pocket of his dressing-gown, he took out a piece of silk fringe which had apparently been torn from a scarf, and rolling it into a ball, tossed it across to me.

"Smell!" he snapped.

I did as he directed--and gave a great start. The silk exhaled a faint perfume, but its effect upon me was as though some one had cried aloud:--

"Karamaneh!"

Beyond doubt the silken fragment had belonged to the beautiful servant of Dr. Fu-Manchu, to the dark-eyed, seductive Karamaneh. Nayland Smith was watching me keenly.

"You recognize it--yes?"

I placed the piece of silk upon the table, slightly shrugging my shoulders.

"It was sufficient evidence in itself," continued my friend, "but I thought it better to seek confirmation, and the obvious way was to pose as a new lessee of the Gables . . ."

"But, Smith," I began . . .

"Let me explain, Petrie. The history of the Gables seemed to be susceptible of only one explanation; in short it was fairly evident to me that the object of the manifestations was to insure the place being kept empty. This idea suggested another, and with them both in mind, I set out to make my inquiries, first taking the precaution to disguise my identity, to which end Weymouth gave me the freedom of Scotland Yard's fancy wardrobe. I did not take the agent into my confidence, but posed as a stranger who had heard that the house was to let furnished and thought it might suit his purpose. My inquiries were directed to a particular end, but I failed to achieve it at the time. I had theories, as I have said, and when, having paid the deposit and secured possession of the keys, I was enabled to visit the place alone, I was fortunate enough to obtain evidence to show that my imagination had not misled me.

"You were very curious the other morning, I recall, respecting my object in borrowing a large brace and bit. My object, Petrie, was to bore a series of holes in the wainscoting of various rooms at the Gables--in inconspicuous positions, of course . . ."

"But, my dear Smith!" I cried, "you are merely adding to my mystification."

He stood up and began to pace the room in his restless fashion.

"I had cross-examined Weymouth closely regarding the phenomenon of the bell-ringing, and an exhaustive search of the premises led to the discovery that the house was in such excellent condition that, from ground-floor to attic, there was not a solitary crevice large enough to admit of the passage of a mouse."

I suppose I must have been staring very foolishly indeed, for Nayland Smith burst into one of his sudden laughs.

"A mouse, I said, Petrie!" he cried. "With the brace-and-bit I rectified that matter. I made the holes I have mentioned, and before each set a trap baited with a piece of succulent, toasted cheese. Just open that grip!"

The light at last was dawning upon my mental darkness, and I pounced upon the grip, which stood upon a chair near the window, and opened it. A sickly smell of cooked cheese assailed my nostrils.

"Mind your fingers!" cried Smith; "some of them are still set, possibly."

Out from the grip I began to take mouse-traps! Two or three of them were still set but in the case of the greater number the catches had slipped. Nine I took out and placed upon the table, and all were empty. In the tenth there crouched, panting, its soft furry body dank with perspiration, a little white mouse!

"Only one capture!" cried my companion, "showing how well-fed the creatures were. Examine his tail!"

But already I had perceived that to which Smith would draw my attention, and the mystery of the "astral bells" was a mystery no longer. Bound to the little creature's tail, close to the root, with fine soft wire such as is used for making up bouquets, were three tiny silver bells. I looked across at my companion in speechless surprise.

"Almost childish, is it not?" he said; "yet by means of this simple device the Gables has been emptied of occupant after occupant. There was small chance of the trick being detected, for, as I have said, there was absolutely no aperture from roof to basement by means of which one of them could have escaped into the building."

"Then . . ."

"They were admitted into the wall cavities and the rafters, from some cellar underneath, Petrie, to which, after a brief scamper under the floors and over the ceilings, they instinctively returned for the food they were accustomed to receive, and for which, even had it been possible (which it was not) they had no occasion to forage."

I, too, stood up; for excitement was growing within me. I took up the piece of silk from the table.

"Where did you find this?" I asked, my eyes upon Smith's keen face.

"In a sort of wine cellar, Petrie," he replied, "under the stair. There is no cellar proper to the Gables--at least no such cellar appears in the plans."

"But . . ."

"But there is one beyond doubt--yes! It must be part of some older building which occupied the site before the Gables was built. One can only surmise that it exists, although such a surmise is a fairly safe one, and the entrance to the subterranean portion of the building is situated beyond doubt in the wine cellar. Of this we have at least two evidences:--the finding of the fragment of silk there, and the fact that in one case at least--as I learned--the light was extinguished in the library unaccountably. This could only have been done in one way: by manipulating the main switch, which is also in the wine cellar."

"But Smith!" I cried, "do you mean that Fu-Manchu . . ."

Nayland Smith turned in his promenade of the floor, and stared into my eyes.

"I mean that Dr. Fu-Manchu has had a hiding-place under the Gables for an indefinite period!" he replied. "I always suspected that a man of his genius would have a second retreat prepared for him, anticipating the event of the first being discovered. Oh! I don't doubt it! The place probably is extensive, and I am almost certain--though the point has to be confirmed--that there is another entrance from the studio further along the road. We know, now, why our recent searchings in the East End have proved futile; why the house in Museum Street was deserted; he has been lying low in this burrow at Hampstead!"

"But the hand, Smith, the luminous hand . . ."

Nayland Smith laughed shortly.

"Your superstitious fears overcame you to such an extent, Petrie--and I don't wonder at it; the sight was a ghastly one--that probably you don't remember what occurred when you struck out at that same ghostly hand?"

"I seemed to hit something."

"That was why we ran. But I think our retreat had all the appearance of a rout, as I intended that it should. Pardon my playing upon your very natural fears, old man, but you could not have simulated panic half so naturally! And if they had suspected that the device was discovered, we might never have quitted the Gables alive. It was touch-and-go for a moment."

"But . . ."

"Turn out the light!" snapped my companion.

Wondering greatly, I did as he desired. I turned out the light . . . and in the darkness of my own study I saw a fiery fist being shaken at me threateningly! . . . The bones were distinctly visible, and the luminosity of the flesh was truly ghastly.

"Turn on the light, again!" cried Smith.

Deeply mystified, I did so . . . and my friend tossed a little electric pocket-lamp on to the writing-table.

"They used merely a small electric lamp fitted into the handle of a glass dagger," he said with a sort of contempt. "It was very effective, but the luminous hand is a phenomenon producible by any one who possesses an electric torch."

"The Gables--will be watched?"

"At last, Petrie, I think we have Fu-Manchu--in his own trap!"

CHAPTER XXVII

THE NIGHT OF THE RAID

"**DASH IT ALL, PETRIE!**" cried Smith, "this is most annoying!"

The bell was ringing furiously, although midnight was long past. Whom could my late visitor be? Almost certainly this ringing portended an urgent case. In other words, I was not fated to take part in what I anticipated would prove to be the closing scene of the Fu-Manchu drama.

"Every one is in bed," I said, ruefully; "and how can I possibly see a patient--in this costume?"

Smith and I were both arrayed in rough tweeds, and anticipating the labors before us, had dispensed with collars and wore soft mufflers. It was hard to be called upon to face a professional interview dressed thus, and having a big tweed cap pulled down over my eyes.

Across the writing-table we confronted one another in dismayed silence, whilst, below, the bell sent up its ceaseless clangor.

"It has to be done, Smith," I said, regretfully. "Almost certainly it means a journey and probably an absence of some hours."

I threw my cap upon the table, turned up my coat to hide the absence of collar, and started for the door. My last sight of Smith showed him standing looking after me, tugging at the lobe of his ear and clicking his teeth together with suppressed irritability. I stumbled down the dark stairs, along the hall, and opened the front door. Vaguely visible in the light of a street lamp which stood at no great distance away, I saw a slender man of medium height confronting me. From the shadowed face two large and luminous eyes looked out into mine. My visitor, who, despite the warmth of the evening, wore a heavy greatcoat, was an Oriental!

I drew back, apprehensively; then:

"Ah! Dr. Petrie!" he said in a softly musical voice which made me start again, "to God be all praise that I have found you!"

Some emotion, which at present I could not define, was stirring within me. Where had I seen this graceful Eastern youth before? Where had I heard that soft voice?

"Do you wish to see me professionally?" I asked--yet even as I put the question, I seemed to know it unnecessary.

"So you know me no more?" said the stranger--and his teeth gleamed in a slight smile.

Heavens! I knew now what had struck that vibrant chord within me! The voice, though infinitely deeper, yet had an unmistakable resemblance to the dulcet tones of Karamaneh--of Karamaneh whose eyes haunted my dreams, whose beauty had done much to embitter my years.

The Oriental youth stepped forward, with outstretched hand.

"So you know me no more?" he repeated; "but I know you, and give praise to Allah that I have found you!"

I stepped back, pressed the electric switch, and turned, with leaping heart, to look into the face of my visitor. It was a face of the purest Greek beauty, a face that might have served as a model for Praxiteles; the skin had a golden pallor, which, with the crisp black hair and magnetic yet velvety eyes, suggested to my fancy that this was the young Antinious risen from the Nile, whose wraith now appeared to me out of the night. I stifled a cry of surprise, not unmingled with gladness.

It was Aziz - the brother of Karamaneh!

Never could the entrance of a figure upon the stage of a drama have been more dramatic than the coming of Aziz upon this night of all nights. I seized the outstretched hand and drew him forward, then reclosed the door and stood before him a moment in doubt.

A vaguely troubled look momentarily crossed the handsome face; with the Oriental's unerring instinct, he had detected the reserve of my greeting. Yet, when I thought of the treachery of Karamaneh, when I remember how she, whom we had befriended, whom we had rescued from the house of Fu-Manchu, now had turned like the beautiful viper that she was to strike at the hand that caressed her; when I thought how to-night we were set upon raiding the place where the evil Chinese doctor lurked in hiding, were set upon the arrest of that malignant genius and of all his creatures, Karamaneh amongst them, is it strange that I hesitated? Yet, again, when I thought of my last meeting with her, and of how, twice, she had risked her life to save me . . .

So, avoiding the gaze of the lad, I took his arm, and in silence we two ascended the stairs and entered my study . . . where Nayland Smith stood bolt upright beside the table, his steely eyes fixed upon the face of the new arrival.

No look of recognition crossed the bronzed features, and Aziz who had started forward with outstretched hands, fell back a step and looked pathetically from me to Nayland Smith, and from the grim commissioner back again to me. The appeal in the velvet eyes was more than I could tolerate, unmoved.

"Smith," I said shortly, "you remember Aziz?"

Not a muscle visibly moved in Smith's face, as he snapped back:

"I remember him perfectly."

"He has come, I think, to seek our assistance."

"Yes, yes!" cried Aziz laying his hand upon my arm with a gesture painfully reminiscent of Karamaneh--"I came only to-night to London. Oh, my gentlemen! I have searched, and searched, and searched, until I am weary. Often I have wished to die. And then at last I come to Rangoon . . ."

"To Rangoon!" snapped Smith, still with the gray eyes fixed almost fiercely upon the lad's face.

"To Rangoon--yes; and there I heard news at last. I hear that you have seen her--have seen Karamaneh--that you are back in London." He was not entirely at home with his English. "I know then that she must be here, too. I ask them everywhere, and they answer 'yes.' Oh, Smith Pasha!"--he stepped forward and impulsively seized both Smith's hands --"You know where she is--take me to her!"

Smith's face was a study in perplexity, now. In the past we had befriended the young Aziz, and it was hard to look upon him in the light of an enemy. Yet had we not equally befriended his sister?--and she . . .

At last Smith glanced across at me where I stood just within the doorway.

"What do you make of it, Petrie?" he said harshly. "Personally I take it to mean that our plans have leaked out." He sprang suddenly back from Aziz and I saw his glance traveling rapidly over the slight figure as if in quest of concealed arms. "I take it to be a trap!"

A moment he stood so, regarding him, and despite my well-grounded distrust of the Oriental character, I could have sworn that the expression of pained surprise upon the youth's face was not simulated but real. Even Smith, I think, began to share my view; for suddenly he threw himself into the white cane rest-chair, and, still fixedly regarding Aziz:

"Perhaps I have wronged you," he said. "If I have, you shall know the reason presently. Tell your own story!"

There was a pathetic humidity in the velvet eyes of Aziz--eyes so like those others that were ever looking into mine in dreams--as glancing from Smith to me he began, hands outstretched, characteristically, palms upward and fingers curling, to tell in broken English the story of his search for Karamaneh . . .

"It was Fu-Manchu, my kind gentlemen - it was the hakim who is really not a man at all, but an efreet. He found us again less than four days after you had left us, Smith Pasha! . . . He found us in Cairo, and to Karamaneh he made the forgetting of all things--even of me--even of me . . ."

Nayland Smith snapped his teeth together sharply; then:

"What do you mean by that?" he demanded.

For my own part I understood well enough, remembering how the brilliant Chinese doctor once had performed such an operation as this upon poor Inspector Weymouth; how, by means of an injection of some serum prepared (as Karamaneh afterwards told us) from the venom of a swamp adder or similar reptile, he had induced amnesia, or complete loss of memory. I felt every drop of blood recede from my cheeks.

"Smith!" I began . . .

"Let him speak for himself," interrupted my friend sharply.

"They tried to take us both," continued Aziz still speaking in that soft, melodious manner, but with deep seriousness. "I escaped, I, who am swift of foot, hoping to bring help."--He shook his head sadly-- "But, except the All Powerful, who is so powerful as the Hakim Fu-Manchu? I hid, my gentlemen, and watched and waited, one--two-- three weeks. At last I saw her again, my sister, Karamaneh; but ah! she did not know me, did not know me, Aziz her brother! She was in an arabeeyeh, and passed me quickly along the Sharia en-Nahhasin. I ran, and ran, and ran, crying her name, but although she looked back, she did not know me--she did not know me! I felt that I was dying, and presently I fell--upon the steps of the Mosque of Abu."

He dropped the expressive hands wearily to his sides and sank his chin upon his breast.

"And then?" I said, huskily--for my heart was fluttering like a captive bird.

"Alas! from that day to this I see her no more, my gentlemen. I travel, not only in Egypt, but near and far, and still I see her no more until in Rangoon I hear that which brings me to England again"--he extended his palms naively--"and here I am--Smith Pasha."

Smith sprang upright again and turned to me.

"Either I am growing over-credulous," he said, or Aziz speaks the truth. But"--he held up his hand--"you can tell me all that at some other time, Petrie! We must take no chances. Sergeant Carter is downstairs with the cab; you might ask him to step up. He and Aziz can remain here until our return."

CHAPTER XXVIII

THE SAMURAI'S SWORD

THE MUFFLED DRUMMING of sleepless London seemed very remote from us, as side by side we crept up the narrow path to the studio. This was a starry but moonless night, and the little dingy white building with a solitary tree peeping, in silhouette, above the glazed roof, bore an odd resemblance to one of those tombs which form a city of the dead so near to the city of feverish life on the slopes of the Mokattam Hills. This line of reflection proved unpleasant, and I dismissed it sternly from my mind.

The shriek of a train-whistle reached me, a sound which breaks the stillness of the most silent London night, telling of the ceaseless, febrile life of the great world-capital whose activity ceases not with the coming of darkness. Around and about us a very great stillness reigned, however, and the velvet dusk which, with the star-jeweled sky, was strongly suggestive of an Eastern night--gave up no sign to show that it masked the presence of more than twenty men. Some distance away on our right was the Gables, that sinister and deserted mansion which we assumed, and with good reason, to be nothing less than the gateway to the subterranean abode of Dr. Fu-Manchu; before us was the studio, which, if Nayland Smith's deductions were accurate, concealed a second entrance to the same mysterious dwelling.

As my friend, glancing cautiously all about him, inserted the key in the lock, an owl hooted dismally almost immediately above our heads. I caught my breath sharply, for it might be a signal; but, looking upward, I saw a great black shape float slantingly from the tree beyond the studio into the coppice on the right which hemmed in the Gables. Silently the owl winged its uncanny flight into the greater darkness of the trees, and was gone. Smith opened the door and we stepped into the studio. Our plans had been well considered, and in accordance with these, I now moved up beside my friend, who was dimly perceptible to me in the starlight which found access through the glass roof, and pressed the catch of my electric pocket-lamp . . .

I suppose that by virtue of my self-imposed duty as chronicler of the deeds of Dr. Fu-Manchu--the greatest and most evil genius whom the later centuries have produced, the man who dreamt of an universal Yellow Empire--I should have acquired a certain facility in describing bizarre happenings. But I confess that it fails me now as I attempt in cold English to portray my emotions when the white beam from the little lamp cut through the darkness of the studio, and shone fully upon the beautiful face of Karamaneh!

Less than six feet away from me she stood, arrayed in the gauzy dress of the harem, her fingers and slim white arms laden with barbaric jewelry! The light wavered in my suddenly nerveless hand, gleaming momentarily upon bare ankles and golden anklets, upon little red leather shoes.

I spoke no word, and Smith was as silent as I; both of us, I think, were speechless rather from amazement than in obedience to the evident wishes of Fu-Manchu's slave-girl. Yet I have only to close my eyes at this moment to see her as she stood, one finger raised to her lips, enjoining us to silence. She looked ghastly pale in the light of the lamp, but so lovely that my rebellious heart threatened already, to make a fool of me.

So we stood in that untidy studio, with canvases and easels heaped against the wall and with all sorts of litter about us, a trio strangely met, and one to have amused the high gods watching through the windows of the stars.

"Go back!" came in a whisper from Karamaneh.

I saw the red lips moving and read a dreadful horror in the widely opened eyes, in those eyes like pools of mystery to taunt the thirsty soul. The world of realities was slipping past me; I seemed to be losing my hold on things actual; I had built up an Eastern palace about myself and Karamaneh wherein, the world shut out, I might pass the hours in reading the mystery of those dark eyes. Nayland Smith brought me sharply to my senses.

"Steady with the light, Petrie!" he hissed in my, ear. "My skepticism has been shaken, to-night, but I am taking no chances."

He moved from my side and forward toward that lovely, unreal figure which stood immediately before the model's throne and its background of plush curtains. Karamaneh started forward to meet him, suppressing a little cry, whose real anguish could not have been simulated.

"Go back! go back!" she whispered urgently, and thrust out her hands against Smith's breast. "For God's sake, go back! I have risked my life to come here to-night. He knows, and is ready!". . .

The words were spoken with passionate intensity, and Nayland Smith hesitated. To my nostrils was wafted that faint, delightful perfume which, since one night, two years ago, it had come to disturb my senses, had taunted me many times as the mirage taunts the parched Sahara traveler. I took a step forward.

"Don't move!" snapped Smith.

Karamaneh clutched frenziedly at the lapels of his coat.

"Listen to me!" she said, beseechingly and stamped one little foot upon the floor--"listen to me! You are a clever man, but you know nothing of a woman's heart--nothing--nothing--if seeing me, hearing me, knowing, as you do know, I risk, you can doubt that I speak the truth. And I tell you that it is death to go behind those curtains-- that he . . ."

"That's what I wanted to know!" snapped Smith. His voice quivered with excitement.

Suddenly grasping Karamaneh by the waist, he lifted her and set her aside; then in three bounds he was on to the model's throne and had torn the Plush curtains bodily from their fastenings.

How it occurred I cannot hope to make dear, for here my recollections merge into a chaos. I know that Smith seemed to topple forward amid the purple billows of velvet, and his muffled cry came to me:

"Petrie! My God, Petrie!" . . .

The pale face of Karamaneh looked up into mine and her hands were clutching me, but the glamour of her personality had lost its hold, for I knew--heavens, how poignantly it struck home to me!--that Nayland Smith was gone to his death. What I hoped to achieve, I know not, but hurling the trembling girl aside, I snatched the Browning pistol from my coat pocket, and with the ray of the lamp directed upon the purple mound of velvet, I leaped forward.

I think I realized that the curtains had masked a collapsible trap, a sheer pit of blackness, an instant before I was precipitated into it, but certainly the knowlege came too late. With the sound of a soft, shuddering cry in my ears, I fell, dropping lamp and pistol, and clutching at the fallen hangings. But they offered me no support. My head seemed to be bursting; I could utter only a hoarse groan, as I fell--fell--fell . . .

When my mind began to work again, in returning consciousness, I found it to be laden with reproach. How often in the past had we blindly hurled ourselves into just such a trap as this? Should we never learn that where Fu-Manchu was, impetuosity must prove fatal? On two distinct occasions in the past we had been made the victims of this device, yet even although we had had practically conclusive evidence that this studio was used by Dr. Fu-Manchu, we had relied upon its floor being as secure as that of any other studio, we had failed to sound every foot of it ere trusting our weight to its support. . . .

"There is such a divine simplicity in the English mind that one may lay one's plans with mathematical precision, and rely upon the Nayland Smiths and Dr. Petries to play their allotted parts. Excepting two faithful followers, my friends are long since departed. But here, in these vaults which time has overlooked and which are as secret and as serviceable to-day as they were two hundred years ago, I wait patiently, with my trap set, like the spider for the fly! . . ."

To the sound of that taunting voice, I opened my eyes. As I did so I strove to spring upright--only to realize that I was tied fast to a heavy ebony chair inlaid with ivory, and attached by means of two iron brackets to the floor.

"Even children learn from experience," continued the unforgettable voice, alternately guttural and sibilant, but always as deliberate as though the speaker were choosing with care words which should perfectly clothe his thoughts. "For 'a burnt child fears the fire,' says your English adage. But Mr. Commissioner Nayland Smith, who enjoys the confidence of the India Office, and who is empowered to control the movements of the Criminal Investigation Department, learns nothing from experience. He is less than a child, since he has twice rashly precipitated himself into a chamber charged with an anesthetic prepared, by a process of my own, from the lycoperdon or Common Puff-ball."

I became fully master of my senses, and I became fully alive to a stupendous fact. At last it was ended; we were utterly in the power of Dr. Fu-Manchu; our race was run.

I sat in a low vaulted room. The roof was of ancient brickwork, but the walls were draped with exquisite Chinese fabric having a green ground whereon was a design representing a grotesque procession of white peacocks. A green carpet covered the floor, and the whole of the furniture was of the same material as the chair to which I was strapped, viz:--ebony inlaid with ivory. This furniture was scanty. There was a heavy table in one corner of the dungeonesque place, on which were a number of books and papers. Before this table was a high-backed, heavily carven chair. A smaller table stood upon the right of the only visible opening, a low door partially draped with bead work curtains, above which hung a silver lamp. On this smaller table, a stick of incense, in a silver holder, sent up a pencil of vapor into the air, and the chamber was loaded with the sickly sweet fumes. A faint haze from the incense-stick hovered up under the roof.

In the high-backed chair sat Dr. Fu-Manchu, wearing a green robe upon which was embroidered a design, the subject of which at first glance was not perceptible, but which presently I made out to be a huge white peacock. He wore a little cap perched upon the dome of his amazing skull, and with one clawish hand resting upon the ebony of the table, be sat slightly turned toward me, his emotionless face a mask of incredible evil. In spite of, or because of, the high intellect written upon it, the face of Dr. Fu-Manchu was more utterly repellent than any I have ever known, and the green eyes, eyes green as those of a cat in the darkness, which sometimes burned like witch lamps, and sometimes were horribly filmed like nothing human or imaginable, might have mirrored not a soul, but an emanation of hell, incarnate in this gaunt, high-shouldered body.

Stretched flat upon the floor lay Nayland Smith, partially stripped, his arms thrown back over his head and his wrists chained to a stout iron staple attached to the wall; he was fully conscious and staring intently at the Chinese doctor. His bare ankles also were manacled, and fixed to a second chain, which quivered tautly across the green carpet and passed out through the doorway, being attached to something beyond the curtain, and invisible to me from where I sat.

Fu-Manchu was now silent. I could hear Smith's heavy breathing and hear my watch ticking in my pocket. I suddenly realized that although my body was lashed to the ebony chair, my hands and arms were free. Next, looking dazedly about me, my attention was drawn to a heavy sword which stood hilt upward against the wall within reach of my hand. It was a magnificent piece, of Japanese workmanship; a long, curved Damascened blade having a double-handed hilt of steel, inlaid with gold, and resembling fine Kuft work. A host of possibilities swept through my mind. Then I perceived that the sword was attached to the wall by a thin steel chain some five feet in length.

"Even if you had the dexterity of a Mexican knife-thrower," came the guttural voice of Fu-Manchu, "you would be unable to reach me, dear Dr. Petrie."

The Chinaman had read my thoughts.

Smith turned his eyes upon me momentarily, only to look away again in the direction of Fu-Manchu. My friend's face was slightly pale beneath the tan, and his jaw muscles stood out with unusual prominence. By this fact alone did he reveal his knowledge that he lay at the mercy of this enemy of the white race, of this inhuman being who himself knew no mercy, of this man whose very genius was inspired by the cool, calculated cruelty of his race, of that race which to this day disposes of hundreds, nay! thousands, of its unwanted girl-children by the simple measure of throwing them down a well specially dedicated to the purpose.

"The weapon near your hand," continued the Chinaman, imperturbably, "is a product of the civilization of our near neighbors, the Japanese, a race to whose courage I prostrate myself in meekness. It is the sword of a samurai, Dr. Petrie. It is of very great age, and was, until an unfortunate misunderstanding with myself led to the extinction of the family, a treasured possession of a noble Japanese house . . ."

The soft voice, into which an occasional sibilance crept, but which never rose above a cool monotone, gradually was lashing me into fury, and I could see the muscles moving in Smith's jaws as he convulsively clenched his teeth; whereby I knew that, impotent, he burned with a rage at least as great as mine. But I did not speak, and did not move.

"The ancient tradition of seppuku," continued the Chinaman, "or hara-kiri, still rules, as you know, in the great families of Japan. There is a sacred ritual, and the samurai who dedicates himself to this honorable end, must follow strictly the ritual. As a physician, the exact nature of the ceremony might possibly interest you, Dr. Petrie, but a technical account of the two incisions which the sacrificant employs in his self-dismissal, might, on the other hand, bore Mr. Nayland Smith. Therefore I will merely enlighten you upon one little point, a minor one, but interesting to the student of human nature. In short, even a samurai--and no braver race has ever honored the world--sometimes hesitates to complete the operation. The weapon near to your hand, my dear Dr. Petrie, is known as the Friend's Sword. On such occasions as we are discussing, a trusty friend is given the post--an honored one of standing behind the brave man who offers himself to his gods, and should the latter's courage momentarily fail him, the friend with the trusty blade (to which now I especially direct your attention) diverts the hierophant's mind from his digression, and rectifies his temporary breach of etiquette by severing the cervical vertebrae of the spinal column with the friendly blade--which you can reach quite easily, Dr. Petrie, if you care to extend your hand."

Some dim perceptions of the truth was beginning to creep into my mind. When I say a perception of the truth, I mean rather of some part of the purpose of Dr. Fu-Manchu; of the whole horrible truth, of the scheme which had been conceived by that mighty, evil man, I had no glimmering, but I foresaw that a frightful ordeal was before us both.

"That I hold you in high esteem," continued Fu-Manchu, "is a fact which must be apparent to you by this time, but in regard to your companion, I entertain very different sentiments. . . ."

Always underlying the deliberate calm of the speaker, sometimes showing itself in an unusually deep guttural, sometimes in an unusually serpentine sibilance, lurked the frenzy of hatred which in the past had revealed itself occasionally in wild outbursts. Momentarily I expected such an outburst now, but it did not come.

"One quality possessed by Mr. Nayland Smith," resumed the Chinaman, "I admire; I refer to his courage. I would wish that so courageous a man should seek his own end, should voluntarily efface himself from the path of that world-movement which he is powerless to check. In short, I would have him show himself a samurai. Always his friend, you shall remain so to the end, Dr. Petrie. I have arranged for this."

He struck lightly a little silver gong, dependent from the corner of the table, whereupon, from the curtained doorway, there entered a short, thickly built Burman whom I recognized for a dacoit. He wore a shoddy blue suit, which had been made for a much larger man; but these things claimed little of my attention, which automatically was directed to the load beneath which the Burman labored.

Upon his back he carried a sort of wire box rather less than six feet long, some two feet high, and about two feet wide. In short, it was a stout framework covered with fine wire-netting on the top, sides and ends, but being open at the bottom. It seemed to be made in five sections or to contain four sliding partitions which could be raised or lowered at will. These were of wood, and in the bottom of each was cut a little arch. The arches in the four partitions varied in size, so that whereas the first was not more than five inches high, the fourth opened almost to the wire roof of the box or cage; and a fifth, which was but little higher than the first, was cut in the actual end of the contrivance.

So intent was I upon this device, the purpose of which I was wholly unable to divine, that I directed the whole of my attention upon it. Then, as the Burman paused in the doorway, resting a corner of the cage upon the brilliant carpet, I glanced toward Fu-Manchu, He was watching Nayland Smith, and revealing his irregular yellow teeth--the teeth of an opium smoker--in the awful mirthless smile which I knew.

"God!" whispered Smith--"the Six Gates!"

"The knowledge of my beautiful country serves you well," replied Fu-Manchu gently.

Instantly I looked to my friend . . . and every drop of blood seemed to recede from my heart, leaving it cold in my breast. If I did not know the purpose of the cage, obviously Smith knew it all too well. His pallor had grown more marked, and although his gray eyes stared defiantly at the Chinaman, I, who knew him, could read a deathly horror in their depths.

The dacoit, in obedience to a guttural order from Dr. Fu-Manchu, placed the cage upon the carpet, completely covering Smith's body, but leaving his neck and head exposed. The seared and pock-marked face set in a sort of placid leer, the dacoit adjusted the sliding partitions to Smith's recumbent form, and I saw the purpose of the graduated arches. They were intended to divide a human body in just such fashion, and, as I realized, were most cunningly shaped to that end. The whole of Smith's body lay now in the wire cage, each of the five compartments whereof was shut off from its neighbor.

The Burman stepped back and stood waiting in the doorway. Dr. Fu-Manchu, removing his gaze from the face of my friend, directed it now upon me.

"Mr. Commissioner Nayland Smith shall have the honor of acting as hierophant, admitting himself to the Mysteries," said Fu-Manchu softly, "and you, Dr. Petrie, shall be the Friend."

CHAPTER XXIX

THE SIX GATES

HE GLANCED TOWARD the Burman, who retired immediately, to re-enter a moment later carrying a curious leather sack, in shape not unlike that of a sakka or Arab water-carrier. Opening a little trap in the top of the first compartment of the cage (that is, the compartment which covered Smith's bare feet and ankles) he inserted the neck of the sack, then suddenly seized it by the bottom and shook it vigorously. Before my horrified gaze four huge rats came tumbling out from the bag into the cage! The dacoit snatched away the sack and snapped the shutter fast. A moving mist obscured my sight, a mist through which I saw the green eyes of Dr. Fu-Manchu fixed upon me, and through which, as from a great distance, his voice, sunk to a snake-like hiss, came to my ears.

"Cantonese rats, Dr. Petrie, the most ravenous in the world . . . they have eaten nothing for nearly a week!"

Then all became blurred as though a painter with a brush steeped in red had smudged out the details of the picture. For an indefinite period, which seemed like many minutes yet probably was only a few seconds, I saw nothing and heard nothing; my sensory nerves were dulled entirely. From this state I was awakened and brought back to the realities by a sound which ever afterward I was doomed to associate with that ghastly scene.

This was the squealing of the rats.

The red mist seemed to disperse at that, and with frightfully intense interest, I began to study the awful torture to which Nayland Smith was being subjected. The dacoit had disappeared, and Fu-Manchu placidly was watching the four lean and hideous animals in the cage. As I also turned my eyes in that direction, the rats overcame their temporary fear, and began . . .

"You have been good enough to notice," said the Chinaman, his voice still sunk in that sibilant whisper, "my partiality for dumb allies. You have met my scorpions, my death-adders, my baboon-man. The uses of such a playful little animal as a marmoset have never been fully appreciated before, I think, but to an indiscretion of this last-named pet of mine, I seem to remember that you owed something in the past, Dr. Petrie . . ."

Nayland Smith stifled a deep groan. One rapid glance I ventured at his face. It was a grayish hue, now, and dank with perspiration. His gaze met mine.

The rats had almost ceased squealing.

"Much depends upon yourself, Doctor," continued Fu-Manchu, slightly raising his voice. "I credit Mr. Commissioner Nayland Smith with courage high enough to sustain the raising of all the gates; but I estimate the strength of your friendship highly, also, and predict that you will use the sword of the samurai certainly not later than the time when I shall raise the third gate. . . ."

A low shuddering sound, which I cannot hope to describe, but alas I can never forget, broke from the lips of the tortured man.

"In China," resumed Fu-Manchu, "we call this quaint fancy the Six Gates of joyful Wisdom. The first gate, by which the rats are admitted, is called the Gate of joyous Hope; the second, the Gate of Mirthful Doubt. The third gate is poetically named, the Gate of True Rapture, and the fourth, the Gate of Gentle Sorrow. I once was honored in the friendship of an exalted mandarin who sustained the course of joyful Wisdom to the raising of the Fifth Gate (called the Gate of Sweet Desires) and the admission of the twentieth rat. I esteem him almost equally with my ancestors. The Sixth, or Gate Celestial-- whereby a man enters into the joy of Complete Understanding--I have dispensed with, here, substituting a Japanese fancy of an antiquity nearly as great and honorable. The introduction of this element of speculation, I count a happy thought, and accordingly take pride to myself."

"The sword, Petrie!" whispered Smith. I should not have recognized his voice, but he spoke quite evenly and steadily. "I rely upon you, old man, to spare me the humiliation of asking mercy from that yellow fiend!"

My mind throughout this time had been gaining a sort of dreadful clarity. I had avoided looking at the sword of hara-kiri, but my thoughts had been leading me mercilessly up to the point at which we were now arrived. No vestige of anger, of condemnation of the inhuman being seated in the ebony chair, remained; that was past. Of all that had gone before, and of what was to come in the future, I thought nothing, knew nothing. Our long fight against the yellow group, our encounters with the numberless creatures of Fu-Manchu, the dacoits-- even Karamaneh--were forgotten, blotted out. I saw nothing of the strange appointments of that subterranean chamber; but face to face with the supreme moment of a lifetime, I was alone with my poor friend --and God.

The rats began squealing again. They were fighting . . .

"Quick, Petrie! Quick, man! I am weakening . . . ."

I turned and took up the samurai sword. My hands were very hot and dry, but perfectly steady, and I tested the edge of the heavy weapon upon my left thumb-nail as quietly as one might test a razor blade. It was as keen, this blade of ghastly history, as any razor ever wrought in Sheffield. I seized the graven hilt, bent forward in my chair, and raised the Friend's Sword high above my head. With the heavy weapon poised there, I looked into my friend's eyes. They were feverishly bright, but never in all my days, nor upon the many beds of suffering which it had been my lot to visit, had I seen an expression like that within them.

"The raising of the First Gate is always a crucial moment," came the guttural voice of the Chinaman. Although I did not see him, and barely heard his words, I was aware that he had stood up and was bending forward over the lower end of the cage.

"Now, Petrie! now! God bless you . . . and good-by . . ."

From somewhere--somewhere remote--I heard a hoarse and animal-like cry, followed by the sound of a heavy fall. I can scarcely bear to write of that moment, for I had actually begun the downward sweep of the great sword when that sound came--a faint Hope, speaking of aid where I had thought no aid possible.

How I contrived to divert the blade, I do not know to this day; but I do know that its mighty sweep sheared a lock from Smith's head and laid bare the scalp. With the hilt in my quivering hands I saw the blade bite deeply through the carpet and floor above Nayland Smith's skull. There, buried fully two inches in the woodwork, it stuck, and still clutching the hilt, I looked to the right and across the room--I looked to the curtained doorway.

Fu-Manchu, with one long, claw-like hand upon the top of the First Gate, was bending over the trap, but his brilliant green eyes were turned in the same direction as my own--upon the curtained doorway.

Upright within it, her beautiful face as pale as death, but her great eyes blazing with a sort of splendid madness, stood Karamaneh!

She looked, not at the tortured man, not at me, but fully at Dr. Fu-Manchu. One hand clutched the trembling draperies; now she suddenly raised the other, so that the jewels on her white arm glittered in the light of the lamp above the door. She held my Browning pistol! Fu-Manchu sprang upright, inhaling sibilantly, as Karamaneh pointed the pistol point blank at his high skull and fired. . . .

I saw a little red streak appear, up by the neutral colored hair, under the black cap. I became as a detached intelligence, unlinked with the corporeal, looking down upon a thing which for some reason I had never thought to witness.

Fu-Manchu threw up both arms, so that the sleeves of the green robe fell back to the elbows. He clutched at his head, and the black cap fell behind him. He began to utter short, guttural cries; he swayed backward--to the right--to the left then lurched forward right across the cage. There he lay, writhing, for a moment, his baneful eyes turned up, revealing the whites; and the great gray rats, released, began leaping about the room. Two shot like gray streaks past the slim figure in the doorway, one darted behind the chair to which I was lashed, and the fourth ran all around against the wall . . . Fu-Manchu, prostrate across the overturned cage, lay still, his massive head sagging downward.

I experienced a mental repetition of my adventure in the earlier evening--I was dropping, dropping, dropping into some bottomless pit . . . warm arms were about my neck; and burning kisses upon my lips.

CHAPTER XXX

THE CALL OF THE EAST

I SEEMED TO HAUL myself back out of the pit of unconsciousness by the aid of two little hands which clasped my own. I uttered a sigh that was almost a sob, and opened my eyes.

I was sitting in the big red-leathern armchair in my own study . . . and a lovely but truly bizarre figure, in a harem dress, was kneeling on the carpet at my feet; so that my first sight of the world was the sweetest sight that the world had to offer me, the dark eyes of Karamaneh, with tears trembling like jewels upon her lashes!

I looked no further than that, heeded not if there were others in the room beside we two, but, gripping the jewel-laden fingers in what must have been a cruel clasp, I searched the depths of the glorious eyes in ever growing wonder. What change had taken place in those limpid, mysterious pools? Why was a wild madness growing up within me like a flame? Why was the old longing returned, ten-thousandfold, to snatch that pliant, exquisite shape to my breast?

No word was spoken, but the spoken words of a thousand ages could not have expressed one tithe of what was held in that silent communion. A hand was laid hesitatingly on my shoulder. I tore my gaze away from the lovely face so near to mine, and glanced up.

Aziz stood at the back of my chair.

"God is all merciful," he said. "My sister is restored to us" (I loved him for the plural); "and she remembers."

Those few words were enough; I understood now that this lovely girl, who half knelt, half lay, at my feet, was not the evil, perverted creature of Fu-Manchu whom we had gone out to arrest with the other vile servants of the Chinese doctor, but was the old, beloved companion of two years ago, the Karamaneh for whom I had sought long and wearily in Egypt, who had been swallowed up and lost to me in that land of mystery.

The loss of memory which Fu-Manchu had artificially induced was subject to the same inexplicable laws which ordinarily rule in cases of amnesia. The shock of her brave action that night had begun to effect a cure; the sight of Aziz had completed it.

Inspector Weymouth was standing by the writing-table. My mind cleared rapidly now, and standing up, but without releasing the girl's hands, so that I drew her up beside me, I said:

"Weymouth--where is--?"

"He's waiting to see you, Doctor," replied the inspector.

A pang, almost physical, struck at my heart.

"Poor, dear old Smith!" I cried, with a break in my voice.

Dr. Gray, a neighboring practitioner, appeared in the doorway at the moment that I spoke the words.

"It's all right, Petrie," he said, reassuringly; "I think we took it in time. I have thoroughly cauterized the wounds, and granted that no complication sets in, he'll be on his feet again in a week or two."

I suppose I was in a condition closely bordering upon the hysterical. At any rate, my behavior was extraordinary. I raised both my hands above my head.

"Thank God!" I cried at the top of my voice, "thank God!--thank God!"

"Thank Him, indeed," responded the musical voice of Aziz. He spoke with all the passionate devoutness of the true Moslem.

Everything, even Karamaneh was forgotten, and I started for the door as though my life depended upon my speed. With one foot upon the landing, I turned, looked back, and met the glance of Inspector Weymouth.

"What have you done with--the body?" I asked.

"We haven't been able to get to it. That end of the vault collapsed two minutes after we hauled you out!"

As I write, now, of those strange days, already they seem remote and unreal. But, where other and more dreadful memories already are grown misty, the memory of that evening in my rooms remains clear-cut and intimate. It marked a crisis in my life.

During the days that immediately followed, whilst Smith was slowly recovering from his hurts, I made my plans deliberately; I prepared to cut myself off from old associations--prepared to exile myself, gladly; how gladly I cannot hope to express in mere cold words.

That my friend approved of my projects, I cannot truthfully state, but his disapproval at least was not openly expressed. To Karamaneh I said nothing of my plans, but her complete reliance in my powers to protect her, now, from all harm, was at once pathetic and exquisite.

Since, always, I have sought in these chronicles to confine myself to the facts directly relating to the malignant activity of Dr. Fu-Manchu, I shall abstain from burdening you with details of my private affairs. As an instrument of the Chinese doctor, it has sometimes been my duty to write of the beautiful Eastern girl; I cannot suppose that my readers have any further curiosity respecting her from the moment that Fate freed her from that awful servitude. Therefore, when I shall have dealt with the episodes which marked our voyage to Egypt--I had opened negotiations in regard to a practice in Cairo--I may honorably lay down my pen.

These episodes opened, dramatically, upon the second night of the voyage from Marseilles.

CHAPTER XXXI

"MY SHADOW LIES UPON YOU"

I SUPPOSE I DID NOT awake very readily. Following the nervous vigilance of the past six months, my tired nerves, in the enjoyment of this relaxation, were rapidly recuperating. I no longer feared to awake to find a knife at my throat, no longer dreaded the darkness as a foe.

So that the voice may have been calling (indeed, had been calling) for some time, and of this I had been hazily conscious before finally I awoke. Then, ere the new sense of security came to reassure me, the old sense of impending harm set my heart leaping nervously. There is always a certain physical panic attendant upon such awakening in the still of night, especially in novel surroundings. Now, I sat up abruptly, clutching at the rail of my berth and listening.

There was a soft thudding on my cabin door, and a voice, low and urgent, was crying my name.

Through the open porthole the moonlight streamed into my room, and save for a remote and soothing throb, inseparable from the progress of a great steamship, nothing else disturbed the stillness; I might have floated lonely upon the bosom of the Mediterranean. But there was the drumming on the door again, and the urgent appeal:

"Dr. Petrie! Dr. Petrie!"

I threw off the bedclothes and stepped on to the floor of the cabin, fumbling hastily for my slippers. A fear that something was amiss, that some aftermath, some wraith of the dread Chinaman, was yet to come to disturb our premature peace, began to haunt me. I threw open the door.

Upon the gleaming deck, blackly outlined against a wondrous sky, stood a man who wore a blue greatcoat over his pyjamas, and whose unstockinged feet were thrust into red slippers. It was Platts, the Marconi operator.

"I'm awfully sorry to disturb you, Dr. Petrie," he said, "and I was even less anxious to arouse your neighbor; but somebody seems to be trying to get a message, presumably urgent, through to you."

"To me!" I cried.

"I cannot make it out," admitted Platts, running his fingers through disheveled hair, "but I thought it better to arouse you. Will you come up?"

I turned without a word, slipped into my dressing-gown, and with Platts passed aft along the deserted deck. The sea was as calm as a great lake. Ahead, on the port bow, an angry flambeau burned redly beneath the peaceful vault of the heavens. Platts nodded absently in the direction of the weird flames.

"Stromboli," he said; "we shall be nearly through the Straits by breakfast-time."

We mounted the narrow stair to the Marconi deck. At the table sat Platts' assistant with the Marconi attachment upon his head--an apparatus which always set me thinking of the electric chair.

"Have you got it?" demanded my companion as we entered the room.

"It's still coming through," replied the other without moving, "but in the same jerky fashion. Every time I get it, it seems to have gone back to the beginning--just Dr. Petrie--Dr. Petrie."

He began to listen again for the elusive message. I turned to Platts.

"Where is it being sent from?" I asked.

Platts shook his head.

"That's the mystery," he declared. "Look!"--and he pointed to the table; "according to the Marconi chart, there's a Messagerie boat due west between us and Marseilles, and the homeward-bound P. & O. which we passed this morning must be getting on that way also, by now. The Isis is somewhere ahead, but I've spoken to all these, and the message comes from none of them."

"Then it may come from Messina."

"It doesn't come from Messina," replied the man at the table, beginning to write rapidly.

Platts stepped forward and bent over the message which the other was writing.

"Here it is!" he cried, excitedly; "we're getting it."

Stepping in turn to the table, I leaned over between the two and read these words as the operator wrote them down:

Dr. Petrie--my shadow . . .

I drew a quick breath and gripped Platts' shoulder harshly. His assistant began fingering the instrument with irritation.

"Lost it again!" he muttered.

"This message," I began . . .

But again the pencil was traveling over the paper:

--lies upon you all . . . end of message.

The operator stood up and unclasped the receivers from his ears. There, high above the sleeping ship's company, with the carpet of the blue Mediterranean stretched indefinitely about us, we three stood looking at one another. By virtue of a miracle of modern science, some one, divided from me by mile upon mile of boundless ocean, had spoken --and had been heard.

"Is there no means of learning," I said, "from whence this message emanated?"

Platts shook his head, perplexedly.

"They gave no code word," he said. "God knows who they were. It's a strange business and a strange message. Have you any sort of idea, Dr. Petrie, respecting the identity of the sender?"

I stared him hard in the face; an idea had mechanically entered my mind, but one of which I did not choose to speak, since it was opposed to human possibility.

But, had I not seen with my own eyes the bloody streak across his forehead as the shot fired by Karamaneh entered his high skull, had I not known, so certainly as it is given to man to know, that the giant intellect was no more, the mighty will impotent, I should have replied:

"The message is from Dr. Fu-Manchu!"

My reflections were rudely terminated and my sinister thoughts given new stimulus, by a loud though muffled cry which reached me from somewhere in the ship, below. Both my companions started as violently as I, whereby I knew that the mystery of the wireless message had not been without its effect upon their minds also. But whereas they paused in doubt, I leaped from the room and almost threw myself down the ladder.

It was Karamaneh who had uttered that cry of fear and horror!

Although I could perceive no connection betwixt the strange message and the cry in the night, intuitively I linked them, intuitively I knew that my fears had been well-grounded; that the shadow of Fu-Manchu still lay upon us.

Karamaneh occupied a large stateroom aft on the main deck; so that I had to descend from the upper deck on which my own room was situated to the promenade deck, again to the main deck and thence proceed nearly the whole length of the alleyway.

Karamaneh and her brother, Aziz, who occupied a neighboring room, met me, near the library. Karamaneh's eyes were wide with fear; her peerless coloring had fled, and she was white to the lips. Aziz, who wore a dressing-gown thrown hastily over his night attire, had his arm protectively about the girl's shoulders.

"The mummy!" she whispered tremulously--the mummy!"

There came a sound of opening doors, and several passengers, whom Karamaneh cries had alarmed, appeared in various stages of undress. A stewardess came running from the far end of the alleyway, and I found time to wonder at my own speed; for, starting from the distant Marconi deck, yet I had been the first to arrive upon the scene.

Stacey, the ship's doctor, was quartered at no great distance from the spot, and he now joined the group. Anticipating the question which trembled upon the lips of several of those about me:

"Come to Dr. Stacey's room," I said, taking Karamaneh arm; "we will give you something to enable you to sleep." I turned to the group. "My patient has had severe nerve trouble," I explained, "and has developed somnambulistic tendencies."

I declined the stewardess' offer of assistance, with a slight shake of the head, and shortly the four of us entered the doctor's cabin, on the deck above. Stacey carefully closed the door. He was an old fellow student of mine, and already he knew much of the history of the beautiful Eastern girl and her brother Aziz.

"I fear there's mischief afoot, Petrie," he said.

"Thanks to your presence of mind, the ship's gossips need know nothing of it."

I glanced at Karamaneh who, since the moment of my arrival had never once removed her gaze from me; she remained in that state of passive fear in which I had found her, the lovely face pallid; and she stared at me fixedly in a childish, expressionless way which made me fear that the shock to which she had been subjected, whatever its nature, had caused a relapse into that strange condition of forgetfulness from which a previous shock had aroused her. I could see that Stacey shared my view, for:

"Something has frightened you," he said gently, seating himself on the arm of Karamaneh chair and patting her hand as if to reassure her. "Tell us all about it."

For the first time since our meeting that night, the girl turned her eyes from me and glanced up at Stacey, a sudden warm blush stealing over her face and throat and as quickly departing, to leave her even more pale than before. She grasped Stacey's hand in both her own--and looked again at me.

"Send for Mr. Nayland Smith without delay!" she said, and her sweet voice was slightly tremulous. "He must be put on his guard!"

I started up.

"Why?" I said. "For God's sake tell us what has happened!"

Aziz who evidently was as anxious as myself for information, and who now knelt at his sister's feet looking at her with that strange love, which was almost adoration, in his eyes, glanced back at me and nodded his head rapidly.

"Something"--Karamaneh paused, shuddering violently--"some dreadful thing, like a mummy escaped from its tomb, came into my room to-night through the porthole . . ."

"Through the porthole?" echoed Stacey, amazedly.

"Yes, yes, through the porthole! A creature tall and very, very thin. He wore wrappings--yellow wrappings--swathed about his head, so that only his eyes, his evil gleaming eyes, were visible. . . . From waist to knees he was covered, also, but his body, his feet, and his legs were bare . . ."

"Was he--?" I began . . .

"He was a brown man, yes"--Karamaneh divining my question, nodded, and the shimmering cloud of her wonderful hair, hastily confined, burst free and rippled about her shoulders. "A gaunt, fleshless brown man, who bent, and writhed bony fingers--so!"

"A thug!" I cried.

"He--it--the mummy thing--would have strangled me if I had slept, for he crouched over the berth--seeking--seeking . . ."

I clenched my teeth convulsively.

"But I was sitting up--"

"With the light on?" interrupted Stacey in surprise.

"No," added Karamaneh; "the light was out." She turned her eyes toward me, as the wonderful blush overspread her face once more. "I was sitting thinking. It all happened within a few seconds, and quite silently. As the mummy crouched over the berth, I unlocked the door and leaped out into the passage. I think I screamed; I did not mean to. Oh, Dr. Stacey, there is not a moment to spare! Mr. Nayland Smith must be warned immediately. Some horrible servant of Dr. Fu-Manchu is on the ship!"

CHAPTER XXXII

THE TRAGEDY

NAYLAND SMITH leaned against the edge of the dressing-table, attired in pyjamas. The little stateroom was hazy with smoke, and my friend gripped the charred briar between his teeth and watched the blue-gray clouds arising from the bowl, in an abstracted way. I knew that he was thinking hard, and from the fact that he had exhibited no surprise when I had related to him the particular's of the attack upon Karamaneh I judged that he had half anticipated something of the kind. Suddenly he stood up, staring at me fixedly.

"Your tact has saved the situation, Petrie," he snapped. "It failed you momentarily, though, when you proposed to me just now that we should muster the lascars for inspection. Our game is to pretend that we know nothing--that we believe Karamaneh to have had a bad dream."

"But, Smith," I began--

"It would be useless, Petrie," he interrupted me. "You cannot suppose that I overlooked the possibility of some creature of the doctor's being among the lascars. I can assure you that not one of them answers to the description of the midnight assailant. From the girl's account we have to look (discarding the idea of a revivified mummy) for a man of unusual height--and there's no lascar of unusual height on board; and from the visible evidence, that he entered the stateroom through the porthole, we have to look for a man more than normally thin. In a word, the servant of Dr. Fu-Manchu who attempted the life of Karamaneh is either in hiding on the ship, or, if visible, is disguised."

With his usual clarity of vision, Nayland Smith had visualized the facts of the case; I passed in mental survey each one of the passengers, and those of the crew whose appearances were familiar to me, with the result that I had to admit the justice of my friend's conclusions. Smith began to pace the narrow strip of carpet between the dressing-table and the door. Suddenly he began again. "From our knowledge of Fu-Manchu and of the group surrounding him (and, don't forget, surviving him)--we may further assume that the wireless message was no gratuitous piece of melodrama, but that it was directed to a definite end. Let us endeavor to link up the chain a little. You occupy an upper deck berth; so do I. Experience of the Chinaman has formed a habit in both of us; that of sleeping with closed windows. Your port was fastened and so was my own. Karamaneh is quartered on the main deck, and her brother's stateroom opens into the same alleyway. Since the ship is in the Straits of Messina, and the glass set fair, the stewards have not closed the portholes nightly at present. We know that that of Karamaneh's stateroom was open. Therefore, in any attempt upon our quartet, Karamaneh would automatically be selected for the victim, since failing you or myself she may be regarded as being the most obnoxious to Dr. Fu-Manchu.

I nodded comprehendingly. Smith's capacity for throwing the white light of reason into the darkest places often amazed me.

"You may have noticed," he continued, "that Karamaneh's room is directly below your own. In the event of any outcry, you would be sooner upon the scene than I should, for instance, because I sleep on the opposite side of the ship. This circumstance I take to be the explanation of the wireless message, which, because of its hesitancy (a piece of ingenuity very characteristic of the group), led to your being awakened and invited up to the Marconi deck; in short, it gave the would-be assassin a better chance of escaping before your arrival."

I watched my friend in growing wonder. The strange events, seemingly having no link, took their places in the drama, and became well-ordered episodes in a plot that only a criminal genius could have devised. As I studied the keen, bronzed face, I realized to the full the stupendous mental power of Dr. Fu-Manchu, measuring it by the criterion of Nayland Smith's. For the cunning Chinaman, in a sense, had foiled this brilliant man before me, whereby, if by nought else, I might know him a master of his evil art.

"I regard the episode," continued Smith, "as a posthumous attempt of the doctor's; a legacy of hate which may prove more disastrous than any attempt made upon us by Fu-Manchu in life. Some fiendish member of the murder group is on board the ship. We must, as always, meet guile with guile. There must be no appeal to the captain, no public examination of passengers and crew. One attempt has failed; I do not doubt that others will be made. At present, you will enact the role of physician-in-attendance upon Karamaneh, and will put it about for whom it may interest that a slight return of her nervous trouble is causing her to pass uneasy nights. I can safely leave this part of the case to you, I think?"

I nodded rapidly.

"I haven't troubled to make inquiries," added Smith, "but I think it probable that the regulation respecting closed ports will come into operation immediately we have passed the Straits, or at any rate immediately there is any likelihood of bad weather."

"You mean--"

"I mean that no alteration should be made in our habits. A second attempt along similar lines is to be apprehended--to-night. After that we may begin to look out for a new danger."

"I pray we may avoid it," I said fervently.

As I entered the saloon for breakfast in the morning, I was subjected to solicitous inquiries from Mrs. Prior, the gossip of the ship. Her room adjoined Karamaneh's and she had been one of the passengers aroused by the girl's cries in the night. Strictly adhering to my role, I explained that my patient was threatened with a second nervous breakdown, and was subject to vivid and disturbing dreams. One or two other inquiries I met in the same way, ere escaping to the corner table reserved to us.

That iron-bound code of conduct which rules the Anglo-Indian, in the first days of the voyage had threatened to ostracize Karamaneh and Aziz, by reason of the Eastern blood to which their brilliant but peculiar type of beauty bore witness. Smith's attitude, however--and, in a Burmese commissioner, it constituted something of a law--had done much to break down the barriers; the extraordinary beauty of the girl had done the rest. So that now, far from finding themselves shunned, the society of Karamaneh and her romantic-looking brother was universally courted. The last inquiry that morning, respecting my interesting patient, came from the bishop of Damascus, a benevolent old gentleman whose ancestry was not wholly innocent of Oriental strains, and who sat at a table immediately behind me. As I settled down to my porridge, he turned his chair slightly and bent to my ear.

"Mrs. Prior tells me that your charming friend was disturbed last night," he whispered. "She seems rather pale this morning; I sincerely trust that she is suffering no ill-effect."

I swung around, with a smile. Owing to my carelessness, there was a slight collision, and the poor bishop, who had been invalided to England after typhoid, in order to undergo special treatment, suppressed an exclamation of pain, although his fine dark eyes gleamed kindly upon me through the pebbles of his gold-rimmed pince-nez.

Indeed, despite his Eastern blood, he might have posed for a Sadler picture, his small and refined features seeming out of place above the bulky body.

"Can you forgive my clumsiness," I began--

But the bishop raised his small, slim fingered hand of old ivory hue, deprecatingly.

His system was supercharged with typhoid bacilli, and, as sometimes occurs, the superfluous "bugs" had sought exit. He could only walk with the aid of two stout sticks, and bent very much at that. His left leg had been surgically scraped to the bone, and I appreciated the exquisite torture to which my awkwardness had subjected him. But he would entertain no apologies, pressing his inquiry respecting Karamaneh in the kindly manner which had made him so deservedly popular on board.

"Many thanks for your solicitude," I said; "I have promised her sound repose to-night, and since my professional reputation is at stake, I shall see that she secures it."

In short, we were in pleasant company, and the day passed happily enough and without notable event. Smith spent some considerable time with the chief officer, wandering about unfrequented parts of the ship. I learned later that he had explored the lascars' quarters, the forecastle, the engine-room, and had even descended to the stokehold; but this was done so unostentatiously that it occasioned no comment.

With the approach of evening, in place of that physical contentment which usually heralds the dinner-hour, at sea, I experienced a fit of the seemingly causeless apprehension which too often in the past had harbingered the coming of grim events; which I had learnt to associate with the nearing presence of one of Fu-Manchu's death-agents. In view of the facts, as I afterwards knew them to be, I cannot account for this.

Yet, in an unexpected manner, my forebodings were realized. That night I was destined to meet a sorrow surpassing any which my troubled life had known. Even now I experience great difficulty in relating the matters which befell, in speaking of the sense of irrevocable loss which came to me. Briefly, then, at about ten minutes before the dining hour, whilst all the passengers, myself included, were below, dressing, a faint cry arose from somewhere aft on the upper deck--a cry which was swiftly taken up by other voices, so that presently a deck steward echoed it immediately outside my own stateroom:

"Man overboard! Man overboard!"

All my premonitions rallying in that one sickening moment, I sprang out on the deck, half dressed as I was, and leaping past the boat which swung nearly opposite my door, craned over the rail, looking astern.

For a long time I could detect nothing unusual. The engine-room telegraph was ringing--and the motion of the screws momentarily ceased; then, in response to further ringing, recommenced, but so as to jar the whole structure of the vessel; whereby I knew that the engines were reversed. Peering intently into the wake of the ship, I was but dimly aware of the ever growing turmoil around me, of the swift mustering of a boat's crew, of the shouted orders of the third-officer. Suddenly I saw it--the sight which was to haunt me for succeeding days and nights.

Half in the streak of the wake and half out of it, I perceived the sleeve of a white jacket, and, near to it, a soft felt hat. The sleeve rose up once into clear view, seemed to describe a half-circle in the air then sink back again into the glassy swell of the water. Only the hat remained floating upon the surface.

By the evidence of the white sleeve alone I might have remained unconvinced, although upon the voyage I had become familiar enough with the drill shooting-jacket, but the presence of the gray felt hat was almost conclusive.

The man overboard was Nayland Smith!

I cannot hope, writing now, to convey in any words at my command, a sense, even remote, of the utter loneliness which in that dreadful moment closed coldly down upon me.

To spring overboard to the rescue was a natural impulse, but to have obeyed it would have been worse than quixotic. In the first place, the drowning man was close upon half a mile astern; in the second place, others had seen the hat and the white coat as clearly as I; among them the third-officer, standing upright in the stern of the boat--which, with commendable promptitude had already been swung into the water. The steamer was being put about, describing a wide arc around the little boat dancing on the deep blue rollers. . . .

Of the next hour, I cannot bear to write at all. Long as I had known him, I was ignorant of my friend's powers as a swimmer, but I judged that he must have been a poor one from the fact that he had sunk so rapidly in a calm sea. Except the hat, no trace of Nayland Smith remained when the boat got to the spot.

CHAPTER XXXIII

THE MUMMY

DINNER WAS OUT of the question that night for all of us. Karamaneh who had spoken no word, but, grasping my hands, had looked into my eyes--her own glassy with unshed tears--and then stolen away to her cabin, had not since reappeared. Seated upon my berth, I stared unseeingly before me, upon a changed ship, a changed sea and sky upon another world. The poor old bishop, my neighbor, had glanced in several times, as he hobbled by, and his spectacles were unmistakably humid; but even he had vouchsafed no word, realizing that my sorrow was too deep for such consolation.

When at last I became capable of connected thought, I found myself faced by a big problem. Should I place the facts of the matter, as I knew them to be, before the captain? or could I hope to apprehend Fu-Manchu's servant by the methods suggested by my poor friend? That Smith's death was an accident, I did not believe for a moment; it was impossible not to link it with the attempt upon Karamaneh. In my misery and doubt, I determined to take counsel with Dr. Stacey. I stood up, and passed out on to the deck.

Those passengers whom I met on my way to his room regarded me in respectful silence. By contrast, Stacey's attitude surprised and even annoyed me.

"I'd be prepared to stake all I possess--although it's not much," he said, "that this was not the work of your hidden enemy."

He blankly refused to give me his reasons for the statement and strongly advised me to watch and wait but to make no communication to the captain.

At this hour I can look back and savor again something of the profound dejection of that time. I could not face the passengers; I even avoided Karamaneh and Aziz. I shut myself in my cabin and sat staring aimlessly into the growing darkness. The steward knocked, once, inquiring if I needed anything, but I dismissed him abruptly. So I passed the evening and the greater part of the night.

Those groups of promenaders who passed my door, invariably were discussing my poor friend's tragic end; but as the night wore on, the deck grew empty, and I sat amid a silence that in my miserable state I welcomed more than the presence of any friend, saving only the one whom I should never welcome again.

Since I had not counted the bells, to this day I have only the vaguest idea respecting the time whereat the next incident occurred which it is my duty to chronicle. Perhaps I was on the verge of falling asleep, seated there as I was; at any rate, I could scarcely believe myself awake, when, unheralded by any footsteps to indicate his coming, some one who seemed to be crouching outside my stateroom, slightly raised himself and peered in through the porthole--which I had not troubled to close.

He must have been a fairly tall man to have looked in at all, and although his features were indistinguishable in the darkness, his outline, which was clearly perceptible against the white boat beyond, was unfamiliar to me. He seemed to have a small, and oddly swathed head, and what I could make out of the gaunt neck and square shoulders in some way suggested an unnatural thinness; in short, the smudgy silhouette in the porthole was weirdly like that of a mummy!

For some moments I stared at the apparition; then, rousing myself from the apathy into which I had sunk, I stood up very quickly and stepped across the room. As I did so the figure vanished, and when I threw open the door and looked out upon the deck . . . the deck was wholly untenanted!

I realized at once that it would be useless, even had I chosen the course, to seek confirmation of what I had seen from the officer on the bridge: my own berth, together with the one adjoining--that of the bishop--was not visible from the bridge.

For some time I stood in my doorway, wondering in a disinterested fashion which now I cannot explain, if the hidden enemy had revealed himself to me, or if disordered imagination had played me a trick. Later, I was destined to know the truth of the matter, but when at last I fell into a troubled sleep, that night, I was still in some doubt upon the point.

My state of mind when I awakened on the following day was indescribable; I found it difficult to doubt that Nayland Smith would meet me on the way to the bathroom as usual, with the cracked briar fuming between his teeth. I felt myself almost compelled to pass around to his stateroom in order to convince myself that he was not really there. The catastrophe was still unreal to me, and the world a dream-world. Indeed I retain scarcely any recollections of the traffic of that day, or of the days that followed it until we reached Port Said.

Two things only made any striking appeal to my dulled intelligence at that time. These were: the aloof attitude of Dr. Stacey, who seemed carefully to avoid me; and a curious circumstance which the second officer mentioned in conversation one evening as we strolled up and down the main deck together.

"Either I was fast asleep at my post, Dr. Petrie," he said, "or last night, in the middle watch, some one or something came over the side of the ship just aft the bridge, slipped across the deck, and disappeared."

I stared at him wonderingly.

"Do you mean something that came up out of the sea?" I said.

"Nothing could very well have come up out of the sea," he replied, smiling slightly, "so that it must have come up from the deck below."

"Was it a man?"

"It looked like a man, and a fairly tall one, but be came and was gone like a flash, and I saw no more of him up to the time I was relieved. To tell you the truth, I did not report it because I thought I must have been dozing; it's a dead slow watch, and the navigation on this part of the run is child's play."

I was on the point of telling him what I had seen myself, two evenings before, but for some reason I refrained from doing so, although I think had I confided in him he would have abandoned the idea that what he had seen was phantasmal; for the pair of us could not very well have been dreaming. Some malignant presence haunted the ship; I could not doubt this; yet I remained passive, sunk in a lethargy of sorrow.

We were scheduled to reach Port Said at about eight o'clock in the evening, but by reason of the delay occasioned so tragically, I learned that in all probability we should not arrive earlier than midnight, whilst passengers would not go ashore until the following morning. Karamaneh who had been staring ahead all day, seeking a first glimpse of her native land, was determined to remain up until the hour of our arrival, but after dinner a notice was posted up that we should not be in before two A.M. Even those passengers who were the most enthusiastic thereupon determined to postpone, for a few hours, their first glimpse of the land of the Pharaohs and even to forego the sight--one of the strangest and most interesting in the world--of Port Said by night.

For my own part, I confess that all the interest and hope with which I had looked forward to our arrival, had left me, and often I detected tears in the eyes of Karamaneh whereby I knew that the coldness in my heart had manifested itself even to her. I had sustained the greatest blow of my life, and not even the presence of so lovely a companion could entirely recompense me for the loss of my dearest friend.

The lights on the Egyptian shore were faintly visible when the last group of stragglers on deck broke up. I had long since prevailed upon Karamaneh to retire, and now, utterly sick at heart, I sought my own stateroom, mechanically undressed, and turned in.

It may, or may not be singular that I had neglected all precautions since the night of the tragedy; I was not even conscious of a desire to visit retribution upon our hidden enemy; in some strange fashion I took it for granted that there would be no further attempts upon Karamaneh, Aziz, or myself. I had not troubled to confirm Smith's surmise respecting the closing of the portholes; but I know now for a fact that, whereas they had been closed from the time of our leaving the Straits of Messina, to-night, in sight of the Egyptian coast, the regulation was relaxed again. I cannot say if this is usual, but that it occurred on this ship is a fact to which I can testify--a fact to which my attention was to be drawn dramatically.

The night was steamingly hot, and because I welcomed the circumstance that my own port was widely opened, I reflected that those on the lower decks might be open also. A faint sense of danger stirred within me; indeed, I sat upright and was about to spring out of my berth when that occurred which induced me to change my mind.

All passengers had long since retired, and a midnight silence descended upon the ship, for we were not yet close enough to port for any unusual activities to have commenced.

Clearly outlined in the open porthole there suddenly arose that same grotesque silhouette which I had seen once before.

Prompted by I know not what, I lay still and simulated heavy breathing; for it was evident to me that I must be partly visible to the watcher, so bright was the night. For ten--twenty--thirty seconds he studied me in absolute silence, that gaunt thing so like a mummy; and, with my eyes partly closed, I watched him, breathing heavily all the time. Then, making no more noise than a cat, he moved away across the deck, and I could judge of his height by the fact that his small, swathed head remained visible almost to the time that he passed to the end of the white boat which swung opposite my stateroom.

In a moment I slipped quietly to the floor, crossed, and peered out of the porthole; so that at last I had a clear view of the sinister mummy-man. He was crouching under the bow of the boat, and attaching to the white rails, below, a contrivance of a kind with which I was not entirely unfamiliar. This was a thin ladder of silken rope, having bamboo rungs, with two metal hooks for attaching it to any suitable object.

The one thus engaged was, as Karamaneh had declared, almost superhumanly thin. His loins were swathed in a sort of linen garment, and his head so bound about, turban fashion, that only his gleaming eyes remained visible. The bare limbs and body were of a dusky yellow color, and, at sight of him, I experienced a sudden nausea.

My pistol was in my cabin-trunk, and to have found it in the dark, without making a good deal of noise, would have been impossible. Doubting how I should act, I stood watching the man with the swathed head whilst he threw the end of the ladder over the side, crept past the bow of the boat, and swung his gaunt body over the rail, exhibiting the agility of an ape. One quick glance fore and aft he gave, then began to swarm down the ladder: in which instant I knew his mission.

With a choking cry, which forced itself unwilled from my lips, I tore at the door, threw it open, and sprang across the deck. Plans, I had none, and since I carried no instrument wherewith to sever the ladder, the murderer might indeed have carried out his design for all that I could have done to prevent him, were it not that another took a hand in the game. . . .

At the moment that the mummy-man--his head now on a level with the deck--perceived me, he stopped dead. Coincident with his stopping, the crack of a pistol shot sounded--from immediately beyond the boat.

Uttering a sort of sobbing sound, the creature fell--then clutched, with straining yellow fingers, at the rails, and, seemingly by dint of a great effort, swarmed along aft some twenty feet, with incredible swiftness and agility, and clambered onto the deck.

A second shot cracked sharply; and a voice (God! was I mad!) cried: "Hold him, Petrie!"

Rigid with fearful astonishment I stood, as out from the boat above me leaped a figure attired solely in shirt and trousers. The newcomer leaped away in the wake of the mummy-man--who had vanished around the corner by the smoke-room. Over his shoulder he cried back at me:

"The bishop's stateroom! See that no one enters!"

I clutched at my head--which seemed to be fiery hot; I realized in my own person the sensation of one who knows himself mad.

For the man who pursued the mummy was Nayland Smith!

I stood in the bishop's state-room, Nayland Smith, his gaunt face wet with perspiration, beside me, handling certain odd looking objects which littered the place, and lay about amid the discarded garments of the absent cleric.

"Pneumatic pads!" he snapped. "The man was a walking air-cushion!" He gingerly fingered two strange rubber appliances. "For distending the cheeks," he muttered, dropping them disgustedly on the floor. "His hands and wrists betrayed him, Petrie. He wore his cuff unusually long but he could not entirely hide his bony wrists. To have watched him, whilst remaining myself unseen, was next to impossible; hence my device of tossing a dummy overboard, calculated to float for less than ten minutes! It actually floated nearly fifteen, as a matter of fact, and I had some horrible moments!"

"Smith!" I said--"how could you submit me . . ."

He clapped his hands on my shoulders.

"My dear old chap--there was no other way, believe me. From that boat I could see right into his stateroom, but, once in, I dare not leave it--except late at night, stealthily! The second spotted me one night and I thought the game was up, but evidently he didn't report it."

"But you might have confided . . ."

"Impossible! I'll admit I nearly fell to the temptation that first night; for I could see into your room as well as into his!" He slapped me boisterously on the back, but his gray eyes were suspiciously moist. "Dear old Petrie! Thank God for our friends! But you'd be the first to admit, old man, that you're a dead rotten actor! Your portrayal of grief for the loss of a valued chum would not have convinced a soul on board!

"Therefore I made use of Stacey, whose callous attitude was less remarkable. Gad, Petrie! I nearly bagged our man the first night! The elaborate plan--Marconi message to get you out of the way, and so forth--had miscarried, and he knew the porthole trick would be useless once we got into the open sea. He took a big chance. He discarded his clerical guise and peeped into your room--you remember?--but you were awake, and I made no move when he slipped back to his own cabin; I wanted to take him red-handed."

"Have you any idea . . ."

"Who he is? No more than where he is! Probably some creature of Dr. Fu-Manchu specially chosen for the purpose; obviously a man of culture, and probably of thug ancestry. I hit him--in the shoulder; but even then he ran like a hare. We've searched the ship, without result. He may have gone overboard and chanced the swim to shore . . ."

We stepped out onto the deck. Around us was that unforgettable scene--Port Said by night. The ship was barely moving through the glassy water, now. Smith took my arm and we walked forward. Above us was the mighty peace of Egypt's sky ablaze with splendor; around and about us moved the unique turmoil of the clearing-house of the Near East.

"I would give much to know the real identity of the bishop of Damascus," muttered Smith.

He stopped abruptly, snapping his teeth together and grasping my arm as in a vise. Hard upon his words had followed the rattling clangor as the great anchor was let go; but horribly intermingled with the metallic roar there came to us such a fearful, inarticulate shrieking as to chill one's heart.

The anchor plunged into the water of the harbor; the shrieking ceased. Smith turned to me, and his face was tragic in the light of the arc lamp swung hard by.

"We shall never know," he whispered. "God forgive him--he must be in bloody tatters now. Petrie, the poor fool was hiding in the chainlocker!"

A little hand stole into mine. I turned quickly. Karamaneh stood beside me. I placed my arm about her shoulders, drawing her close; and I blush to relate that all else was forgotten.

For a moment, heedless of the fearful turmoil forward, Nayland Smith stood looking at us. Then he turned, with his rare smile, and walked aft.

"Perhaps you're right, Petrie!" he said.

THE HAND OF FU MANCHU

by

SAX ROHMER

CHAPTER 1

THE TRAVELER FROM TIBET

"WHO'S THERE?" I called sharply.

I turned and looked across the room. The window had been widely opened when I entered, and a faint fog haze hung in the apartment, seeming to veil the light of the shaded lamp. I watched the closed door intently, expecting every moment to see the knob turn. But nothing happened.

"Who's there?" I cried again, and, crossing the room, I threw open the door.

The long corridor without, lighted only by one inhospitable lamp at a remote end, showed choked and yellowed with this same fog so characteristic of London in November. But nothing moved to right nor left of me. The New Louvre Hotel was in some respects yet incomplete, and the long passage in which I stood, despite its marble facings, had no air of comfort or good cheer; palatial it was, but inhospitable.

I returned to the room, reclosing the door behind me, then for some five minutes or more I stood listening for a repetition of that mysterious sound, as of something that both dragged and tapped, which already had arrested my attention. My vigilance went unrewarded. I had closed the window to exclude the yellow mist, but subconsciously I was aware of its encircling presence, walling me in, and now I found myself in such a silence as I had known in deserts but could scarce have deemed possible in fog-bound London, in the heart of the world's metropolis, with the traffic of the Strand below me upon one side and the restless life of the river upon the other.

It was easy to conclude that I had been mistaken, that my nervous system was somewhat overwrought as a result of my hurried return from Cairo--from Cairo where I had left behind me many a fondly cherished hope. I addressed myself again to the task of unpacking my steamer-trunk and was so engaged when again a sound in the corridor outside brought me upright with a jerk.

A quick footstep approached the door, and there came a muffled rapping upon the panel.

This time I asked no question, but leapt across the room and threw the door open. Nayland Smith stood before me, muffled up in a heavy traveling coat, and with his hat pulled down over his brows.

"At last!" I cried, as my friend stepped in and quickly reclosed the door.

Smith threw his hat upon the settee, stripped off the great-coat, and pulling out his pipe began to load it in feverish haste.

"Well," I said, standing amid the litter cast out from the trunk, and watching him eagerly, "what's afoot?"

Nayland Smith lighted his pipe, carelessly dropping the match-end upon the floor at his feet.

"God knows what *is* afoot this time, Petrie!" he replied. "You and I have lived no commonplace lives; Dr. Fu-Manchu has seen to that; but if I am to believe what the Chief has told me to-day, even stranger things are ahead of us!"

I stared at him wonder-stricken.

"That is almost incredible," I said; "terror can have no darker meaning than that which Dr. Fu-Manchu gave to it. Fu-Manchu is dead, so what have we to fear?"

"We have to fear," replied Smith, throwing himself into a corner of the settee, "the Si-Fan!"

I continued to stare, uncomprehendingly.

"The Si-Fan----"

"I always knew and you always knew," interrupted Smith in his short, decisive manner, "that Fu-Manchu, genius that he was, remained nevertheless the servant of another or others. He was not the head of that organization which dealt in wholesale murder, which aimed at upsetting the balance of the world. I even knew the name of one, a certain mandarin, and member of the Sublime Order of the White Peacock, who was his immediate superior. I had never dared to guess at the identity of what I may term the Head Center."

He ceased speaking, and sat gripping his pipe grimly between his teeth, whilst I stood staring at him almost fatuously. Then--

"Evidently you have much to tell me," I said, with forced calm.

I drew up a chair beside the settee and was about to sit down.

"Suppose you bolt the door," jerked my friend.

I nodded, entirely comprehending, crossed the room and shot the little nickel bolt into its socket.

"Now," said Smith as I took my seat, "the story is a fragmentary one in which there are many gaps. Let us see what we know. It seems that the despatch which led to my sudden recall (and incidentally yours) from Egypt to London and which only reached me as I was on the point of embarking at Suez for Rangoon, was prompted by the arrival here of Sir Gregory Hale, whilom attaché at the British Embassy, Peking. So much, you will remember, was conveyed in my instructions."

"Quite so."

"Furthermore, I was instructed, you'll remember, to put up at the New Louvre Hotel; therefore you came here and engaged this suite whilst I reported to the chief. A stranger business is before us, Petrie, I verily believe, than any we have known hitherto. In the first place, Sir Gregory Hale is here."

"Here?"

"In the New Louvre Hotel. I ascertained on the way up, but not by direct inquiry, that he occupies a suite similar to this, and incidentally on the same floor."

"His report to the India Office, whatever its nature, must have been a sensational one."

"He has made no report to the India Office."

"What! made no report?"

"He has not entered any office whatever, nor will he receive any representative. He's been playing at Robinson Crusoe in a private suite here for close upon a fortnight--*id est* since the time of his arrival in London!"

I suppose my growing perplexity was plainly visible, for Smith suddenly burst out with his short, boyish laugh.

"Oh! I told you it was a strange business," he cried.

"Is he mad?"

Nayland Smith's gaiety left him; he became suddenly stern and grim.

"Either mad, Petrie, stark raving mad, or the savior of the Indian Empire--perhaps of all Western civilization. Listen. Sir Gregory Hale, whom I know slightly and who honors me, apparently, with a belief that I am the only man in Europe worthy of his confidence, resigned his appointment at Peking some time ago, and set out upon a private expedition to the Mongolian frontier with the avowed intention of visiting some place in the Gobi Desert. From the time that he actually crossed the frontier he disappeared for nearly six months, to reappear again suddenly and dramatically in London. He buried himself in this hotel, refusing all visitors and only advising the authorities of his return by telephone. He demanded that *I* should be sent to see him; and--despite his eccentric methods--so great is the Chief's faith in Sir Gregory's knowledge of matters Far Eastern, that behold, here I am."

He broke off abruptly and sat in an attitude of tense listening. Then--

"Do you hear anything, Petrie?" he rapped.

"A sort of tapping?" I inquired, listening intently myself the while.

Smith nodded his head rapidly.

We both listened for some time, Smith with his head bent slightly forward and his pipe held in his hands; I with my gaze upon the bolted door. A faint mist still hung in the room, and once I thought I detected a slight sound from the bedroom beyond, which was in darkness. Smith noted me turn my head, and for a moment the pair of us stared into the gap of the doorway. But the silence was complete.

"You have told me neither much nor little, Smith," I said, resuming for some reason, in a hushed voice. "Who or what is this Si-Fan at whose existence you hint?"

Nayland Smith smiled grimly.

"Possibly the real and hitherto unsolved riddle of Tibet, Petrie," he replied--"a mystery concealed from the world behind the veil of Lamaism." He stood up abruptly, glancing at a scrap of paper which he took from his pocket--"Suite Number 14a," he said. "Come along! We have not a moment to waste. Let us make our presence known to Sir Gregory-- the man who has dared to raise that veil."

CHAPTER 11

THE MAN WITH THE LIMP

"LOCK THE DOOR" said Smith significantly, as we stepped into the corridor.

I did so and had turned to join my friend when, to the accompaniment of a sort of hysterical muttering, a door further along, and on the opposite side of the corridor, was suddenly thrown open, and a man whose face showed ghastly white in the light of the solitary lamp beyond, literally hurled himself out. He perceived Smith and myself immediately. Throwing one glance back over his shoulder he came tottering forward to meet us.

"My God! I can't stand it any longer!" he babbled, and threw himself upon Smith, who was foremost, clutching pitifully at him for support. "Come and see him, sir--for Heaven's sake come in! I think he's dying; and he's going mad. I never disobeyed an order in my life before, but I can't help myself--I can't help myself!"

"Brace up!" I cried, seizing him by the shoulders as, still clutching at Nayland Smith, he turned his ghastly face to me. "Who are you, and what's your trouble?"

"I'm Beeton, Sir Gregory Hale's man."

Smith started visibly, and his gaunt, tanned face seemed to me to have grown perceptively paler.

"Come on, Petrie!" he snapped. "There's some devilry here."

Thrusting Beeton aside he rushed in at the open door--upon which, as I followed him, I had time to note the number, 14a. It communicated with a suite of rooms almost identical with our own. The sitting-room was empty and in the utmost disorder, but from the direction of the principal bedroom came a most horrible mumbling and gurgling sound--a sound utterly indescribable. For one instant we hesitated at the threshold--hesitated to face the horror beyond; then almost side by side we came into the bedroom....

Only one of the two lamps was alight--that above the bed; and on the bed a man lay writhing. He was incredibly gaunt, so that the suit of tropical twill which he wore hung upon him in folds, showing if such evidence were necessary, how terribly he was fallen away from his constitutional habit. He wore a beard of at least ten days' growth, which served to accentuate the cavitous hollowness of his face. His eyes seemed starting from their sockets as he lay upon his back uttering inarticulate sounds and plucking with skinny fingers at his lips.

Smith bent forward peering into the wasted face; and then started back with a suppressed cry.

"Merciful God! can it be Hale?" he muttered. "What does it mean? what does it mean?"

I ran to the opposite side of the bed, and placing my arms under the writhing man, raised him and propped a pillow at his back. He continued to babble, rolling his eyes from side to side hideously; then by degrees they seemed to become less glazed, and a light of returning sanity entered them. They became fixed; and they were fixed upon Nayland Smith, who bending over the bed, was watching Sir Gregory (for Sir Gregory I concluded this pitiable wreck to be) with an expression upon his face compound of many emotions.

"A glass of water," I said, catching the glance of the man Beeton, who stood trembling at the open doorway.

Spilling a liberal quantity upon the carpet, Beeton ultimately succeeded in conveying the glass to me. Hale, never taking his gaze from Smith, gulped a little of the water and then thrust my hand away. As I turned to place the tumbler upon a small table the resumed the wordless babbling, and now, with his index finger, pointed to his mouth.

"He has lost the power of speech!" whispered Smith.

"He was stricken dumb, gentlemen, ten minutes ago," said Beeton in a trembling voice. "He dropped off to sleep out there on the floor, and I brought him in here and laid him on the bed. When he woke up he was like that!"

The man on the bed ceased his inchoate babbling and now, gulping noisily, began to make quick nervous movements with his hands.

"He wants to write something," said Smith in a low voice. "Quick! hold him up!" He thrust his notebook, open at a blank page, before the man whose movement were numbered, and placed a pencil in the shaking right hand.

Faintly and unevenly Sir Gregory commenced to write--whilst I supported him. Across the bent shoulders Smith silently questioned me, and my reply was a negative shake of the head.

The lamp above the bed was swaying as if in a heavy draught; I remembered that it had been swaying as we entered. There was no fog in the room, but already from the bleak corridor outside it was entering; murky, yellow clouds steaming in at the open door. Save for the gulping of the dying man, and the sobbing breaths of Beeton, there was no sound. Six irregular lines Sir Gregory Hale scrawled upon the page; then suddenly his body became a dead weight in my arms. Gently I laid him back upon the pillows, gently his finger from the notebook, and, my head almost touching Smith's as we both craned forward over the page, read, with great difficulty, the following:--

"Guard my diary.... Tibetan frontier ... Key of India. Beware man ... with the limp. Yellow ... rising. Watch Tibet ... the *Si-Fan*...."

From somewhere outside the room, whether above or below I could not be sure, came a faint, dragging sound, accompanied by a *tap--tap--tap*....

CHAPTER III

"SAKYA MUNI"

THE FAINT DISTURBANCE faded into silence again. Across the dead man's body I met Smith's gaze. Faint wreaths of fog floated in from the outer room. Beeton clutched the foot of the bed, and the structure shook in sympathy with his wild trembling. That was the only sound now; there was absolutely nothing physical so far as my memory serves to signalize the coming of the brown man.

Yet, stealthy as his approach had been, something must have warned us. For suddenly, with one accord, we three turned upon the bed, and stared out into the room from which the fog wreaths floated in.

Beeton stood nearest to the door, but, although he turned, he did not go out, but with a smothered cry crouched back against the bed. Smith it was who moved first, then I followed, and close upon his heels burst into the disordered sitting-room. The outer door had been closed but not bolted, and what with the tinted light, diffused through the silken Japanese shade, and the presence of fog in the room, I was almost tempted to believe myself the victim of a delusion. What I saw or thought I saw was this:--

A tall screen stood immediately inside the door, and around its end, like some materialization of the choking mist, glided a lithe, yellow figure, a slim, crouching figure, wearing a sort of loose robe. An impression I had of jet-black hair, protruding from beneath a little cap, of finely chiseled features and great, luminous eyes, then, with no sound to tell of a door opened or shut, the apparition was gone.

"You saw him, Petrie!--you saw him!" cried Smith.

In three bounds he was across the room, had tossed the screen aside and thrown open the door. Out he sprang into the yellow haze of the corridor, tripped, and, uttering a cry of pain, fell sprawling upon the marble floor. Hot with apprehension I joined him, but he looked up with a wry smile and began furiously rubbing his left shin.

"A queer trick, Petrie," he said, rising to his feet; "but nevertheless effective."

He pointed to the object which had occasioned his fall. It was a small metal chest, evidently of very considerable weight, and it stood immediately outside the door of Number 14a.

"That was what he came for, sir! That was what he came for! You were too quick for him!"

Beeton stood behind us, his horror-bright eyes fixed upon the box.

"Eh?" rapped Smith, turning upon him.

"That's what Sir Gregory brought to England," the man ran on almost hysterically; "that's what he's been guarding this past two weeks, night and day, crouching over it with a loaded pistol. That's what cost him his life, sir. He's had no peace, day or night, since he got it...."

We were inside the room again now, Smith bearing the coffer in his arms, and still the man ran on:

"He's never slept for more than an hour at a time, that I know of, for weeks past. Since the day we came here he hasn't spoken to another living soul, and he's lain there on the floor at night with his head on that brass box, and sat watching over it all day."

"'Beeton!' he'd cry out, perhaps in the middle of the night--'Beeton-- do you hear that damned woman!' But although I'd begun to think I could hear something, I believe it was the constant strain working on my nerves and nothing else at all.

"Then he was always listening out for some one he called 'the man with the limp.' Five and six times a night he'd have me up to listen with him. 'There he goes, Beeton!' he'd whisper, crouching with his ear pressed flat to the door. 'Do you hear him dragging himself along?'

"God knows how I've stood it as I have; for I've known no peace since we left China. Once we got here I thought it would be better, but it's been worse.

"Gentlemen have come (from the India Office, I believe), but he would not see them. Said he would see no one but Mr. Nayland Smith. He had never lain in his bed until to-night, but what with taking no proper food nor sleep, and some secret trouble that was killing him by inches, he collapsed altogether a while ago, and I carried him in and laid him on the bed as I told you. Now he's dead--now he's dead."

Beeton leant up against the mantelpiece and buried his face in his hands, whilst his shoulders shook convulsively. He had evidently been greatly attached to his master, and I found something very pathetic in this breakdown of a physically strong man. Smith laid his hands upon his shoulders.

"You have passed through a very trying ordeal," he said, "and no man could have done his duty better; but forces beyond your control have proved too strong for you. I am Nayland Smith."

The man spun around with a surprising expression of relief upon his pale face.

"So that whatever can be done," continued my friend, "to carry out your master's wishes, will be done now. Rely upon it. Go into your room and lie down until we call you."

"Thank you, sir, and thank God you are here," said Beeton dazedly, and with one hand raised to his head he went, obediently, to the smaller bedroom and disappeared within.

"Now, Petrie," rapped Smith, glancing around the littered floor, "since

I am empowered to deal with this matter as I see fit, and since you are a medical man, we can devote the next half-hour, at any rate, to a strictly confidential inquiry into this most perplexing case. I propose that you examine the body for any evidences that may assist you determining the cause of death, whilst I make a few inquiries here."

I nodded, without speaking, and went into the bedroom. It contained not one solitary item of the dead man's belongings, and in every way bore out Beeton's statement that Sir Gregory had never inhabited it. I bent over Hale, as he lay fully dressed upon the bed.

Saving the singularity of the symptom which had immediately preceded death--viz., the paralysis of the muscles of articulation--I should have felt disposed to ascribe his end to sheer inanition; and a cursory examination brought to light nothing contradictory to that view. Not being prepared to proceed further in the matter at the moment I was about to rejoin Smith, whom I could hear rummaging about amongst the litter of the outer room, when I made a curious discovery.

Lying in a fold of the disordered bed linen were a few petals of some kind of blossom, three of them still attached to a fragment of slender stalk.

I collected the tiny petals, mechanically, and held them in the palm of my hand studying them for some moments before the mystery of their presence there became fully appreciable to me. Then I began to wonder. The petals (which I was disposed to class as belonging to some species of *Curcas* or Physic Nut), though bruised, were fresh, and therefore could not have been in the room for many hours. How had they been introduced, and by whom? Above all, what could their presence there at that time portend?

"Smith," I called, and walked towards the door carrying the mysterious fragments in my palm. "Look what I have found upon the bed."

Nayland Smith, who was bending over an open despatch case which he had placed upon a chair, turned--and his glance fell upon the petals and tiny piece of stem.

I think I have never seen so sudden a change of expression take place in the face of any man. Even in that imperfect light I saw him blanch. I saw a hard glitter come into his eyes. He spoke, evenly, but hoarsely:

"Put those things down----there, on the table; anywhere."

I obeyed him without demur; for something in his manner had chilled me with foreboding.

"You did not break that stalk?"

"No. I found it as you see it."

"Have you smelled the petals?"

I shook my head. Thereupon, having his eyes fixed upon me with the strangest expression in their gray depths, Nayland Smith said a singular thing.

"Pronounce, slowly, the words *Sâkya Mûni*,'" he directed.

I stared at him, scarce crediting my senses; but----

"I mean it!" he rapped. "Do as I tell you."

"Sâkya Mûni," I said, in ever increasing wonder.

Smith laughed unmirthfully.

"Go into the bathroom and thoroughly wash your hands," was his next order. "Renew the water at least three times." As I turned to fulfill his instructions, for I doubted no longer his deadly earnestness: "Beeton!" he called.

Beeton, very white-faced and shaky, came out from the bedroom as I entered the bathroom, and whist I proceeded carefully to cleanse my hands I heard Smith interrogating him.

"Have any flowers been brought into the room today, Beeton?"

"Flowers, sir? Certainly not. Nothing has ever been brought in here but what I have brought myself."

"You are certain of that?"

"Positive."

"Who brought up the meals, then?"

"If you'll look into my room here, sir, you'll see that I have enough tinned and bottled stuff to last us for weeks. Sir Gregory sent me out to buy it on the day we arrived. No one else had left or entered these rooms until you came to-night."

I returned to find Nayland Smith standing tugging at the lobe of his left ear in evident perplexity. He turned to me.

"I find my hands over full," he said. "Will you oblige me by telephoning for Inspector Weymouth? Also, I should be glad if you would ask M. Samarkan, the manager, to see me here immediately."

As I was about to quit the room--

"Not a word of our suspicions to M. Samarkan," he added; "not a word about the brass box."

I was far along the corridor ere I remembered that which, remembered earlier, had saved me the journey. There was a telephone in every suite. However, I was not indisposed to avail myself of an opportunity for a few moments' undisturbed reflection, and, avoiding the lift, I descended by the broad, marble staircase.

To what strange adventure were we committed? What did the brass coffer contain which Sir Gregory had guarded night and day? Something associated in some way with Tibet, something which he believed to be "the key of India" and which had brought in its train, presumably, the sinister "man with a limp."

Who was the "man with the limp"? What was the Si-Fan? Lastly, by what conceivable means could the flower, which my friend evidently regarded with extreme horror, have been introduced into Hale's room, and why had I been required to pronounce the words "Sâkya Mûni"?

So ran my reflections--at random and to no clear end; and, as is often the case in such circumstances, my steps bore them company; so that all at once I became aware that instead of having gained the lobby of the hotel, I had taken some wrong turning and was in a part of the building entirely unfamiliar to me.

A long corridor of the inevitable white marble extended far behind me. I had evidently traversed it. Before me was a heavily curtained archway. Irritably, I pulled the curtain aside, learnt that it masked a glass-paneled door, opened this door--and found myself in a small court, dimly lighted and redolent of some pungent, incense-like perfume.

One step forward I took, then pulled up abruptly. A sound had come to my ears. From a second curtained doorway, close to my right hand, it came--a sound of muffled *tapping*, together with that of something which dragged upon the floor.

Within my brain the words seemed audibly to form: "The man with the limp!"

I sprang to the door; I had my hand upon the drapery ... when a woman stepped out, barring the way!

No impression, not even a vague one, did I form of her costume, save that she wore a green silk shawl, embroidered with raised white figures of birds, thrown over her head and shoulders and draped in such fashion that part of her face was concealed. I was transfixed by the vindictive glare of her eyes, of her huge dark eyes.

They were ablaze with anger--but it was not this expression within them which struck me so forcibly as the fact that they were in some way familiar.

Motionless, we faced one another. Then--

"You go away," said the woman--at the same time extending her arms across the doorway as barriers to my progress.

Her voice had a husky intonation; her hands and arms, which were bare and of old ivory hue, were laden with barbaric jewelry, much of it tawdry silverware of the bazaars. Clearly she was a half-caste of some kind, probably a Eurasian.

I hesitated. The sounds of dragging and tapping had ceased. But the presence of this grotesque Oriental figure only increased my anxiety to pass the doorway. I looked steadily into the black eyes; they looked into mine unflinchingly.

"You go away, please," repeated the woman, raising her right hand and pointing to the door whereby I had entered. "These private rooms. What you doing here?"

Her words, despite her broken English, served to recall to me the fact that I was, beyond doubt, a trespasser! By what right did I presume to force my way into other people's apartments?

"There is some one in there whom I must see," I said, realizing, however, that my chance of doing so was poor.

"You see nobody," she snapped back uncompromisingly. "You go away!"

She took a step towards me, continuing to point to the door. Where had I previously encountered the glance of those splendid, savage eyes?

So engaged was I with this taunting, partial memory, and so sure, if the woman would but uncover her face, of instantly recognizing her, that still I hesitated. Whereupon, glancing rapidly over her shoulder into whatever place lay beyond the curtained doorway, she suddenly stepped back and vanished, drawing the curtains to with an angry jerk.

I heard her retiring footsteps; then came a loud bang. If her object in intercepting me had been to cover the slow retreat of some one she had succeeded.

Recognizing that I had cut a truly sorry figure in the encounter, I retraced my steps.

By what route I ultimately regained the main staircase I have no idea; for my mind was busy with that taunting memory of the two dark eyes looking out from the folds of the green embroidered shawl. Where, and when, had I met their glance before?

To that problem I sought an answer in vain.

The message despatched to New Scotland Yard, I found M. Samarkan, long famous as a *maître d' hôtel* in Cairo, and now host of London's newest and most palatial *khan*. Portly, and wearing a gray imperial, M. Samarkan had the manners of a courtier, and the smile of a true Greek.

I told him what was necessary, and no more, desiring him to go to suite 14a without delay and also without arousing unnecessary attention. I dropped no hint of foul play, but M. Samarkan expressed profound (and professional) regret that so distinguished, though unprofitable, a patron should have selected the New Louvre, thus early in its history, as the terminus of his career.

"By the way," I said, "have you Oriental guests with you, at the moment?"

"No, monsieur," he assured me.

"Not a certain Oriental lady?" I persisted.

M. Samarkan slowly shook his head.

"Possibly monsieur has seen one of the *ayahs?* There are several Anglo-Indian families resident in the New Louvre at present."

An *ayah?* It was just possible, of course. Yet ...

CHAPTER IV

THE FLOWER OF SILENCE

"WE ARE DEALING NOW," said Nayland Smith, pacing restlessly up and down our sitting-room, "not, as of old, with Dr. Fu-Manchu, but with an entirely unknown quantity--the Si-Fan."

"For Heaven's sake!" I cried, "what is the Si-Fan?"

"The greatest mystery of the mysterious East, Petrie. Think. You know, as I know, that a malignant being, Dr. Fu-Manchu, was for some time in England, engaged in 'paving the way' (I believe those words were my own) for nothing less than a giant Yellow Empire. That dream is what millions of Europeans and Americans term 'the Yellow Peril! Very good. Such an empire needs must have----"

"An emperor!"

Nayland Smith stopped his restless pacing immediately in front of me.

"Why not an *empress*, Petrie!" he rapped.

His words were something of a verbal thunderbolt; I found myself at loss for any suitable reply.

"You will perhaps remind me," he continued rapidly, "of the lowly place held by women in the East. I can cite notable exceptions, ancient and modern. In fact, a moment's consideration by a hypothetical body of Eastern dynast-makers not of an emperor but of an empress. Finally, there is a persistent tradition throughout the Far East that such a woman will one day rule over the known peoples. I was assured some years ago, by a very learned pundit, that a princess of incalculably ancient lineage, residing in some secret monastery in Tartary or Tibet, was to be the future empress of the world. I believe this tradition, or the extensive group who seek to keep it alive and potent, to be what is called the Si-Fan!"

I was past greater amazement; but--

"This lady can be no longer young, then?" I asked.

"On the contrary, Petrie, she remains always young and beautiful by means of a continuous series of reincarnations; also she thus conserves the collated wisdom of many ages. In short, she is the archetype of Lamaism. The real secret of Lama celibacy is the existence of this immaculate ruler, of whom the Grand Lama is merely a high priest. She has, as attendants, maidens of good family, selected for their personal charms, and rendered dumb in order that they may never report what they see and hear."

"Smith!" I cried, "this is utterly incredible!"

"Her body slaves are not only mute, but blind; for it is death to look upon her beauty unveiled."

I stood up impatiently.

"You are amusing yourself," I said.

Nayland Smith clapped his hands upon my shoulders, in his own impulsive fashion, and looked earnestly into my eyes.

"Forgive me, old man," he said, "if I have related all these fantastic particulars as though I gave them credence. Much of this is legendary, I know, some of it mere superstition, but--I am serious now, Petrie-- *part of it is true.*"

I stared at the square-cut, sun-tanned face; and no trace of a smile lurked about that grim mouth. "Such a woman may actually exist, Petrie, only in legend; but, nevertheless, she forms the head center of that giant conspiracy in which the activities of Dr. Fu-Manchu were merely a part. Hale blundered on to this stupendous business; and from what I have gathered from Beeton and what I have seen for myself, it is evident that in yonder coffer"--he pointed to the brass chest standing hard by--"Hale got hold of something indispensable to the success of this vast Yellow conspiracy. That he was followed here, to the very hotel, by agents of this mystic Unknown is evident. But," he added grimly, "they have failed in their object!"

A thousand outrageous possibilities fought for precedence in my mind.

"Smith!" I cried, "the half-caste woman whom I saw in the hotel ..."

Nayland Smith shrugged his shoulders.

"Probably, as M. Samarkan suggests, an *ayah!*" he said; but there was an odd note in his voice and an odd look in his eyes.

"Then again, I am almost certain that Hale's warning concerning 'the man with the limp' was no empty one. Shall you open the brass chest?"

"At present, decidedly *no*. Hale's fate renders his warning one that I dare not neglect. For I was with him when he died; and they cannot know how much *I* know. How did he die? How did he die? How was the Flower of Silence introduced into his closely guarded room?"

"The Flower of Silence?"

Smith laughed shortly and unmirthfully.

"I was once sent for," he said, "during the time that I was stationed in Upper Burma, to see a stranger--a sort of itinerant Buddhist priest, so I understood, who had desired to communicate some message to me personally. He was dying--in a dirty hut on the outskirts of Manipur, up in the hills. When I arrived I say at a glance that the man was a Tibetan monk. He must have crossed the river and come down through Assam; but the nature of his message I never knew. He had lost the power of speech! He was gurgling, inarticulate, just like poor Hale. A few moments after my arrival he breathed his last. The fellow who had guided me to the place bent over him--I shall always remember the scene--then fell back as though he had stepped upon an adder.

"'He holds the Flower Silence in his hand!' he cried--'the Si-Fan! the Si-Fan!'--and bolted from the hut."

"When I went to examine the dead man, sure enough he held in one hand a little crumpled spray of flowers. I did not touch it with my fingers naturally, but I managed to loop a piece of twine around the stem, and by that means I gingerly removed the flowers and carried them to an orchid-hunter of my acquaintance who chanced to be visiting Manipur.

"Grahame--that was my orchid man's name--pronounced the specimen to be an unclassified species of *jatropha;* belonging to the *Curcas* family. He discovered a sort of hollow thorn, almost like a fang, amongst the blooms, but was unable to surmise the nature of its functions. He extracted enough of a certain fixed oil from the flowers, however, to have poisoned the pair of us!"

"Probably the breaking of a bloom ..."

"Ejects some of this acrid oil through the thorn? Practically the uncanny thing stings when it is hurt? That is my own idea, Petrie. And I can understand how these Eastern fanatics accept their sentence-- silence and death--when they have deserved it, at the hands of their mysterious organization, and commit this novel form of *hara-kiri.* But I shall not sleep soundly with that brass coffer in my possession until I know by what means Sir Gregory was induced to touch a Flower of Silence, and by what means it was placed in his room!"

"But, Smith, why did you direct me to-night to repeat the words, 'Sâkya Mûni'?"

Smith smiled in a very grim fashion.

"It was after the episode I have just related that I made the acquaintance of that pundit, some of whose statements I have already quoted for your enlightenment. He admitted that the Flower of Silence was an instrument frequently employed by a certain group, adding that, according to some authorities, one who had touched the flower might escape death by immediately pronouncing the sacred name of Buddha. He was no fanatic himself, however, and, marking my incredulity, he explained that the truth was this;--

"No one whose powers of speech were imperfect could possibly pronounce correctly the words 'Sâkya Mûni.' Therefore, since the first effects of this damnable thing is instantly to tie the tongue, the uttering of the sacred name of Buddha becomes practically a test whereby the victim my learn whether the venom has entered his system or not!"

I repressed a shudder. An atmosphere of horror seemed to be enveloping us, foglike.

"Smith," I said slowly, "we must be on our guard," for at last I had run to earth that elusive memory. "Unless I am strangely mistaken, the 'man' who so mysteriously entered Hale's room and the supposed *ayah* whom I met downstairs are one and the same. Two, at least, of the Yellow group are actually here in the New Louvre!"

The light of the shaded lamp shone down upon the brass coffer on the table beside me. The fog seemed to have cleared from the room somewhat, but since in the midnight stillness I could detect the muffled sounds of sirens from the river and the reports of fog signals from the railways, I concluded that the night was not yet wholly clear of the choking mist. In accordance with a pre-arranged scheme we had decided to guard "the key of India" (whatever it might be) turn and turn about through the night. In a word--we feared to sleep unguarded. Now my watch informed me that four o'clock approached, at which hour I was to arouse Smith and retire to sleep to my own bedroom.

Nothing had disturbed my vigil--that is, nothing definite. True once, about half an hour earlier, I had thought I heard the dragging and tapping sound from somewhere up above me; but since the corridor overhead was unfinished and none of the rooms opening upon it yet habitable, I concluded that I had been mistaken. The stairway at the end of our corridor, which communicated with that above, was still blocked with bags of cement and slabs of marble, in fact.

Faintly to my ears came the booming of London's clocks, beating out the hour of four. But still I sat beside the mysterious coffer, indisposed to awaken my friend any sooner than was necessary, particularly since I felt in no way sleepy myself.

I was to learn a lesson that night: the lesson of strict adherence to a compact. I had arranged to awaken Nayland Smith at four; and because I dallied, determined to finish my pipe ere entering his bedroom, almost it happened that Fate placed it beyond my power ever to awaken him again.

At ten minutes past four, amid a stillness so intense that the creaking of my slippers seemed a loud disturbance, I crossed the room and pushed open the door of Smith's bedroom. It was in darkness, but as I entered I depressed the switch immediately inside the door, lighting the lamp which swung form the center of the ceiling.

Glancing towards the bed, I immediately perceived that there was something different in its aspect, but at first I found this difference difficult to define. I stood for a moment in doubt. Then I realized the nature of the change which had taken place.

A lamp hung above the bed, attached to a movable fitting, which enabled it to be raised or lowered at the pleasure of the occupant. When Smith had retired he was in no reading mood, and he had not even lighted the reading-lamp, but had left it pushed high up against the ceiling.

It was the position of this lamp which had changed. For now it swung so low over the pillow that the silken fringe of the shade almost touched my friend's face as he lay soundly asleep with one lean brown hand outstretched upon the coverlet.

I stood in the doorway staring, mystified, at this phenomenon; I might have stood there without intervening, until intervention had been too late, were it not that, glancing upward toward the wooden block from which ordinarily the pendant hung, I perceived that no block was visible, but only a round, black cavity from which the white flex supporting the lamp swung out.

Then, uttering a horse cry which rose unbidden to my lips, I sprang wildly across the room ... for now I had seen something else!

Attached to one of the four silken tassels which ornamented the lamp-shade, so as almost to rest upon the cheek of the sleeping man, was a little corymb of bloom ... the *Flower of Silence!*

Grasping the shade with my left hand I seized the flex with my right, and as Smith sprang upright in bed, eyes wildly glaring, I wrenched with all my might. Upward my gaze was set; and I glimpsed a yellow hand, with long, pointed finger nails. There came a loud resounding snap; an electric spark spat venomously from the circular opening above the bed; and, with the cord and lamp still fast in my grip, I went rolling across the carpet--as the other lamp became instantly extinguished.

Dimly I perceived Smith, arrayed in pyjamas, jumping out upon the opposite side of the bed.

"Petrie, Petrie!" he cried, "where are you? what has happened?"

A laugh, little short of hysterical, escaped me. I gathered myself up and made for the lighted sitting-room.

"Quick, Smith!" I said--but I did not recognize my own voice. "Quick--come out of that room."

I crossed to the settee, and shaking in every limb, sank down upon it. Nayland Smith, still wild-eyed, and his face a mask of bewilderment, came out of the bedroom and stood watching me.

"For God's sake what has happened, Petrie?" he demanded, and began clutching at the lobe of his left ear and looking all about the room dazedly.

"The Flower of Silence!" I said; "some one has been at work in the top corridor.... Heaven knows when, for since we engaged these rooms we have not been much away from them ... the same device as in the case of poor Hale.... You would have tried to brush the thing away ..."

A light of understanding began to dawn in my friend's eyes. He drew himself stiffly upright, and in a loud, harsh voice uttered the words: "Sâkya Mûni"--and again: "Sâkya Mûni."

"Thank God!" I said shakily. "I was not too late."

Nayland Smith, with much rattling of glass, poured out two stiff pegs from the decanter. Then--

"*Ssh!*what's that?" he whispered.

He stood, tense, listening, his head cast slightly to one side.

A very faint sound of shuffling and tapping was perceptible, coming, as I thought, from the incomplete stairway communicating with the upper corridor.

"The man with the limp!" whispered Smith.

He bounded to the door and actually had one hand upon the bolt, when he turned, and fixed his gaze upon the brass box.

"No!" he snapped; "there are occasions when prudence should rule. Neither of us must leave these rooms to-night!"

CHAPTER V
JOHN KI'S

"WHAT IS THE MEANING OF SI-FAN?" asked Detective-sergeant Fletcher.

He stood looking from the window at the prospect below; at the trees bordering the winding embankment; at the ancient monolith which for unnumbered ages had looked across desert sands to the Nile, and now looked down upon another river of many mysteries. The view seemed to absorb his attention. He spoke without turning his head.

Nayland Smith laughed shortly.

"The Si-Fan are the natives of Eastern Tibet," he replied.

"But the term has some other significance, sir?" said the detective; his words were more of an assertion than a query.

"It has," replied my friend grimly. "I believe it to be the name, or perhaps the sigil, of an extensive secret society with branches stretching out into every corner of the Orient."

We were silent for awhile. Inspector Weymouth, who sat in a chair near the window, glanced appreciatively at the back of his subordinate, who still stood looking out. Detective-sergeant Fletcher was one of Scotland Yard's coming men. He had information of the first importance to communicate, and Nayland Smith had delayed his departure upon an urgent errand in order to meet him.

"Your case to date, Mr. Smith," continued Fletcher, remaining with hands locked behind him, staring from the window, "reads something like this, I believe: A brass box, locked, contents unknown, has come into your possession. It stands now upon the table there. It was brought from Tibet by a man who evidently thought that it had something to do with the Si-Fan. He is dead, possibly by the agency of members of this group. No arrests have been made. You know that there are people here in London who are anxious to regain the box. You have theories respecting the identity of some of them, but there are practically no facts."

Nayland Smith nodded his head.

"Exactly!" he snapped.

"Inspector Weymouth, here," continued Fletcher, "has put me in possession of such facts as are known to him, and I believe that I have had the good fortune to chance upon a valuable one."

"You interest me, Sergeant Fletcher," said Smith. "What is the nature of this clue?"

"I will tell you," replied the other, and turned briskly upon his heel to face us.

He had a dark, clean-shaven face, rather sallow complexion, and deep-set, searching eyes. There was decision in the square, cleft chin and strong character in the cleanly chiseled features. His manner was alert.

"I have specialized in Chinese crime," he said; "much of my time is spent amongst our Asiatic visitors. I am fairly familiar with the Easterns who use the port of London, and I have a number of useful acquaintances among them."

Nayland Smith nodded. Beyond doubt Detective-sergeant Fletcher knew his business.

"To my lasting regret," Fletcher continued, "I never met the late Dr. Fu-Manchu. I understand, sir, that you believe him to have been a high official of this dangerous society? However, I think we may get in touch with some other notabilities; for instance, I'm told that one of the people you're looking for has been described as 'the man with the limp'?"

Smith, who had been about to relight his pipe, dropped the match on the carpet and set his foot upon it. His eyes shone like steel.

"'The man with the limp,'" he said, and slowly rose to his feet--"what do you know of the man with the limp?"

Fletcher's face flushed slightly; his words had proved more dramatic than he had anticipated.

"There's a place down Shadwell way," he replied, "of which, no doubt, you will have heard; it has no official title, but it is known to habitués as the Joy-Shop...."

Inspector Weymouth stood up, his burly figure towering over that of his slighter confrère.

"I don't think you know John Ki's, Mr. Smith," he said. "We keep all those places pretty well patrolled, and until this present business cropped up, John's establishment had never given us any trouble."

"What is this Joy-Shop?" I asked.

"A resort of shady characters, mostly Asiatics," replied Weymouth. "It's a gambling-house, an unlicensed drinking-shop, and even worse-- but it's more use to us open than it would be shut."

"It is one of my regular jobs to keep an eye on the visitors to the Joy-Shop," continued Fletcher. "I have many acquaintances who use the place. Needless to add, they don't know my real business! Well, lately several of them have asked me if I know who the man is that hobbles about the place with two sticks. Everybody seems to have heard him, but no one has seen him."

Nayland Smith began to pace the floor restlessly.

"I have heard him myself," added Fletcher, "but never managed to get so much as a glimpse of him. When I learnt about this Si-Fan mystery, I realized that he might very possibly be the man for whom you're looking--and a golden opportunity has cropped up for you to visit the Joy-Shop, and, if our luck remains in, to get a peep behind the scenes."

"I am all attention," snapped Smith.

"A woman called Zarmi has recently put in an appearance at the Joy-Shop. Roughly speaking, she turned up at about the same time as the unseen man with the limp...."

Nayland Smith's eyes were blazing with suppressed excitement; he was pacing quickly up and down the floor, tugging at the lobe of his left ear.

"She is--different in some way from any other woman I have ever seen in the place. She's a Eurasian and good-looking, after a tigerish fashion. I have done my best"--he smiled slightly--"to get in her good books, and up to a point I've succeeded. I was there last night, and Zarmi asked me if I knew what she called a 'strong feller.'

"'These,' she informed me, contemptuously referring to the rest of the company, 'are poor weak Johnnies!'

"I had nothing definite in view at the time, for I had not then heard about your return to London, but I thought it might lead to something anyway, so I promised to bring a friend along to-night. I don't know what we're wanted to do, but ..."

"Count on me!" snapped Smith. "I will leave all details to you and to Weymouth, and I will be at New Scotland Yard this evening in time to adopt a suitable disguise. Petrie"--he turned impetuously to me--"I fear I shall have to go without you; but I shall be in safe company, as you see, and doubtless Weymouth can find you a part in his portion of the evening's program."

He glanced at his watch.

"Ah! I must be off. If you will oblige me, Petrie, by putting the brass box into my smaller portmanteau, whilst I slip my coat on, perhaps Weymouth, on his way out, will be good enough to order a taxi. I shall venture to breathe again once our unpleasant charge is safely deposited in the bank vaults!"

CHAPTER VI

THE SI-FAN MOVE

A SLIGHT DRIZZLING rain was falling as Smith entered the cab which the hall-porter had summoned. The brown bag in his hand contained the brass box which actually was responsible for our presence in London. The last glimpse I had of him through the glass of the closed window showed him striking a match to light his pipe--which he rarely allowed to grow cool.

Oppressed with an unaccountable weariness of spirit, I stood within the lobby looking out upon the grayness of London in November. A slight mental effort was sufficient to blot out that drab prospect and to conjure up before my mind's eye a balcony overlooking the Nile--a glimpse of dusty palms, a white wall overgrown with purple blossoms, and above all the dazzling vault of Egypt. Upon the balcony my imagination painted a figure, limning it with loving details, the figure of Kâramaneh; and I thought that her glorious eyes would be sorrowful and her lips perhaps a little tremulous, as, her arms resting upon the rail of the balcony, she looked out across the smiling river to the domes and minarets of Cairo--and beyond, into the hazy distance; seeing me in dreary, rain-swept London, as I saw her, at Gezîra beneath the cloudless sky of Egypt.

From these tender but mournful reflections I aroused myself, almost angrily, and set off through the muddy streets towards Charing Cross; for I was availing myself of the opportunity to call upon Dr. Murray, who had purchased my small suburban practice when (finally, as I thought at the time) I had left London.

This matter occupied me for the greater part of the afternoon, and I returned to the New Louvre Hotel shortly after five, and seeing no one in the lobby whom I knew, proceeded immediately to our apartment. Nayland Smith was not there, and having made some changes in my attire I descended again and inquired if he had left any message for me.

The booking-clerk informed me that Smith had not returned; therefore I resigned myself to wait. I purchased an evening paper and settled down in the lounge where I had an uninterrupted view of the entrance doors. The dinner hour approached, but still my friend failed to put in an appearance. Becoming impatient, I entered a call-box and rang up Inspector Weymouth.

Smith had not been to Scotland Yard, nor had they received any message from him. Perhaps it would appear that there was little cause for alarm in this, but I, familiar with my friend's punctual and exact habits, became strangely uneasy. I did not wish to make myself ridiculous, but growing restlessness impelled me to institute inquiries regarding the cabman who had driven my friend. The result of these was to increase rather than to allay my fears.

The man was a stranger to the hall-porter, and he was not one of the taximen who habitually stood upon the neighboring rank; no one seemed to have noticed the number of the cab.

And now my mind began to play with strange doubts and fears. The driver, I recollected, had been a small, dark man, possessing remarkably well-cut olive-hued features. Had he not worn spectacles he would indeed have been handsome, in an effeminate fashion.

I was almost certain, by this time, that he had not been an Englishman; I was almost certain that some catastrophe had befallen Smith. Our ceaseless vigilance had been momentarily relaxed--and this was the result!

At some large bank branches there is a resident messenger. Even granting that such was the case in the present instance, I doubted if the man could help me, unless, as was possible, he chanced to be familiar with my friend's appearance, and had actually seen him there that day. I determined, at any rate, to make the attempt; reentering the call-box, I asked for the bank's number.

There proved to be a resident messenger, who, after a time, replied to my call. He knew Nayland Smith very well by sight, and as he had been on duty in the public office of the bank at the time that Smith should have arrived, he assured me that my friend had not been there that day!

"Besides, sir," he said, "you say he came to deposit valuables of some kind here?"

"Yes, yes!" I cried eagerly.

"I take all such things down on the lift to the vaults at night, sir, under the supervision of the assistant manager--and I can assure you that nothing of the kind has been left with us to-day."

I stepped out of the call-box unsteadily. Indeed, I clutched at the door for support.

"What is the meaning of Si-Fan?" Detective-sergeant Fletcher had asked that morning. None of us could answer him; none of us knew. With a haze seeming to dance between my eyes and the active life in the lobby before me, I realized that the Si-Fan--that unseen, sinister power-- had reached out and plucked my friend from the very midst of this noisy life about me, into its own mysterious, deathly silence.

CHAPTER VII
CHINATOWN

"IT'S NO EASY MATTER." said Inspector Weymouth, "to patrol the vicinity of John Ki's Joy-Shop without their getting wind of it. The entrance, as you'll see, is a long, narrow rat-hole of a street running at right angles to the Thames. There's no point, so far as I know, from which the yard can be overlooked; and the back is on a narrow cutting belonging to a disused mill."

I paid little attention to his words. Disguised beyond all chance of recognition even by one intimate with my appearance, I was all impatience to set out. I had taken Smith's place in the night's program; for, every possible source of information having been tapped in vain, I now hoped against hope that some clue to the fate of my poor friend might be obtained at the Chinese den which he had designed to visit with Fletcher.

The latter, who presented a strange picture in his make-up as a sort of half-caste sailor, stared doubtfully at the Inspector; then--

"The River Police cutter," he said, "can drop down on the tide and lie off under the Surrey bank. There's a vacant wharf facing the end of the street and we can slip through and show a light there, to let you know we've arrived. You reply in the same way. If there's any trouble, I shall blaze away with this"--he showed the butt of a Service revolver protruding from his hip pocket--"and you can be ashore in no time."

The plan had one thing to commend it, viz., that no one could devise another. Therefore it was adopted, and five minutes later a taxi-cab swung out of the Yard containing Inspector Weymouth and two ruffianly looking companions--myself and Fletcher.

Any zest with which, at another time, I might have entered upon such an expedition, was absent now. I bore with me a gnawing anxiety and sorrow that precluded all conversation on my part, save monosyllabic replies, to questions that I comprehended but vaguely.

At the River Police Depot we found Inspector Ryman, an old acquaintance, awaiting us. Weymouth had telephoned from Scotland Yard.

"I've got a motor-boat at the breakwater," said Ryman, nodding to Fletcher, and staring hard at me.

Weymouth laughed shortly.

"Evidently you don't recognize Dr. Petrie!" he said.

"Eh!" cried Ryman--"Dr. Petrie! why, good heavens, Doctor, I should never have known you in a month of Bank holidays! What's afoot, then?"--

and he turned to Weymouth, eyebrows raised interrogatively.

"It's the Fu-Manchu business again, Ryman."

"Fu-Manchu! But I thought the Fu-Manchu case was off the books long ago? It was always a mystery to me; never a word in the papers; and we as much in the dark as everybody else--but didn't I hear that the Chinaman, Fu-Manchu, was dead?"

Weymouth nodded.

"Some of his friends seem to be very much alive, though" he said. "It appears that Fu-Manchu, for all his genius--and there's no denying he was a genius, Ryman--was only the agent of somebody altogether bigger."

Ryman whistled softly.

"Has the real head of affairs arrived, then?"

"We find we are up against what is known as the Si-Fan."

At that it came to the inevitable, unanswerable question.

"What is the Si-Fan?"

I laughed, but my laughter was not mirthful. Inspector Weymouth shook his head.

"Perhaps Mr. Nayland Smith could tell you that," he replied; "for the Si-Fan got him to-day!"

"Got him!" cried Ryman.

"Absolutely! He's vanished! And Fletcher here has found out that John Ki's place is in some way connected with this business."

I interrupted--impatiently, I fear.

"Then let us set out, Inspector," I said, "for it seems to me that we are wasting precious time--and you know what that may mean." I turned to Fletcher. "Where is this place situated, exactly? How do we proceed?"

"The cab can take us part of the way," he replied, "and we shall have to walk the rest. Patrons of John's don't turn up in taxis, as a rule!"

"Then let us be off," I said, and made for the door.

"Don't forget the signal!" Weymouth cried after me, "and don't venture into the place until you've received our reply...."

But I was already outside, Fletcher following; and a moment later we were both in the cab and off into a maze of tortuous streets toward John Ki's Joy-Shop.

With the coming of nightfall the rain had ceased, but the sky remained heavily overcast and the air was filled with clammy mist. It was a night to arouse longings for Southern skies; and when, discharging the cabman, we set out afoot along a muddy and ill-lighted thoroughfare bordered on either side by high brick walls, their monotony occasionally broken by gateways, I felt that the load of depression which had settled upon my shoulders must ere long bear me down.

Sounds of shunting upon some railway siding came to my ears; train whistles and fog signals hooted and boomed. River sounds there were, too, for we were close beside the Thames, that gray old stream which has borne upon its bier many a poor victim of underground London. The sky glowed sullenly red above.

"There's the Joy-Shop, along on the left," said Fletcher, breaking in upon my reflections. "You'll notice a faint light; it's shining out through the open door. Then, here is the wharf."

He began fumbling with the fastenings of a dilapidated gateway beside which we were standing; and a moment later--

"All right--slip through," he said.

I followed him through the narrow gap which the ruinous state of the gates had enabled him to force, and found myself looking under a low arch, with the Thames beyond, and a few hazy lights coming and going on the opposite bank.

"Go steady!" warned Fletcher. "It's only a few paces to the edge of the wharf."

I heard him taking a box of matches from his pocket.

"Here is my electric lamp," I said. "It will serve the purpose better."

"Good," muttered my companion. "Show a light down here, so that we can find our way."

With the aid of the lamp we found our way out on to the rotting timbers of the crazy structure. The mist hung denser over the river, but through it, as through a dirty gauze curtain, it was possible to discern some of the greater lights on the opposite shore. These, without exception, however, showed high up upon the fog curtain; along the water level lay a belt of darkness.

"Let me give them the signal," said Fletcher, shivering slightly and taking the lamp from my hand.

He flashed the light two or three times. Then we both stood watching the belt of darkness that followed the Surrey shore. The tide lapped upon the timbers supporting the wharf and little whispers and gurgling sounds stole up from beneath our feet. Once there was a faint splash from somewhere below and behind us.

"There goes a rat," said Fletcher vaguely, and without taking his gaze from the darkness under the distant shore. "It's gone into the cutting at the back of John Ki's."

He ceased speaking and flashed the lamp again several times. Then, all at once out of the murky darkness into which we were peering, looked a little eye of light--once, twice, thrice it winked at us from low down upon the oily water; then was gone.

"It's Weymouth with the cutter," said Fletcher; "they are ready ... now for Jon Ki's."

We stumbled back up the slight acclivity beneath the archway to the street, leaving the ruinous gates as we had found them. Into the uninviting little alley immediately opposite we plunged, and where the faint yellow luminance showed upon the muddy path before us, Fletcher paused a moment, whispering to me warningly.

"Don't speak if you can help it," he said; "if you do, mumble any old jargon in any language you like, and throw in plenty of cursing!"

He grasped me by the arm, and I found myself crossing the threshold of the Joy-Shop--I found myself in a meanly furnished room no more than twelve feet square and very low ceiled, smelling strongly of paraffin oil. The few items of furniture which it contained were but dimly discernible in the light of a common tin lamp which stood upon a packing-case at the head of what looked like cellar steps.

Abruptly, I pulled up; for this stuffy little den did not correspond with pre-conceived ideas of the place for which we were bound. I was about to speak when Fletcher nipped my arm--and out from the shadows behind the packing-case a little bent figure arose!

I started violently, for I had had no idea that another was in the room. The apparition proved to be a Chinaman, and judging from what I could see of him, a very old Chinaman, his bent figure attired in a blue smock. His eyes were almost invisible amidst an intricate map of wrinkles which covered his yellow face.

"Evening, John," said Fletcher--and, pulling me with him, he made for the head of the steps.

As I came abreast of the packing-case, the Chinaman lifted the lamp and directed its light fully upon my face.

Great as was the faith which I reposed in my make-up, a doubt and a tremor disturbed me now, as I found myself thus scrutinized by those cunning old eyes looking out from the mask-like, apish face. For the first time the Chinaman spoke.

"You blinger fliend, Charlie?" he squeaked in a thin, piping voice.

"Him play piecee card," replied Fletcher briefly. "Good fellow, plenty much money."

He descended the steps, still holding my arm, and I perforce followed him. Apparently John's scrutiny and Fletcher's explanation respecting me, together had proved satisfactory; for the lamp was replaced upon the lid of the packing-case, and the little bent figure dropped down again into the shadows from which it had emerged.

"Allee lightee," I heard faintly as I stumbled downward in the wake of Fletcher.

I had expected to find myself in a cellar, but instead discovered that we were in a small square court with the mist of the night about us again. On a doorstep facing us stood a duplicate of the lamp upon the box upstairs. Evidently this was designed to indicate the portals of the Joy-Shop, for Fletcher pushed open the door, whose threshold accommodated the lamp, and the light of the place beyond shone out into our faces. We entered and my companion closed the door behind us.

Before me I perceived a long low room lighted by flaming gas-burners, the jets hissing and spluttering in the draught from the door, for they were entirely innocent of shades or mantles. Wooden tables, their surfaces stained with the marks of countless wet glasses, were ranged about the place, café fashion; and many of these tables accommodated groups, of nondescript nationality for the most part. One or two there were in a distant corner who were unmistakably Chinamen; but my slight acquaintance with the races of the East did not enable me to classify the greater number of those whom I now saw about me. There were several unattractive-looking women present.

Fletcher walked up the center of the place, exchanging nods of recognition with two hang-dog poker-players, and I was pleased to note that our advent had apparently failed to attract the slightest attention. Through an opening on the right-hand side of the room, near the top, I looked into a smaller apartment, occupied exclusively by Chinese. They were playing some kind of roulette and another game which seemed wholly to absorb their interest. I ventured no more than a glance, then passed on with my companion.

"*Fan-tan!*" he whispered in my ear.

Other forms of gambling were in progress at some of the tables; and now Fletcher silently drew my attention to yet a third dimly lighted apartment--this opening out from the left-hand corner of the principal room. The atmosphere of the latter was sufficiently abominable; indeed, the stench was appalling; but a wave of choking vapor met me as I paused for a moment at the threshold of this inner sanctuary. I formed but the vaguest impression of its interior; the smell was sufficient. This annex was evidently reserved for opium-smokers.

Fletcher sat down at a small table near by, and I took a common wooden chair which he thrust forward with his foot. I was looking around at the sordid scene, filled with a bitter sense of my own impotency to aid my missing friend, when that occurred which set my heart beating wildly at once with hope and excitement. Fletcher must have seen something of this in my attitude, for--

"Don't forget what I told you," he whispered. "Be cautious!--be very cautious!..."

CHAPTER VIII

ZARMI OF THE JOY-SHOP

DOWN THE CENTER of the room came a girl carrying the only ornamental object which thus far I had seen in the Joy-Shop; a large Oriental brass tray. She was a figure which must have formed a center of interest in any place, trebly so, then, in such a place as this. Her costume consisted in a series of incongruities, whilst the entire effect was barbaric and by no means unpicturesque. She wore high-heeled red slippers, and, as her short gauzy skirt rendered amply evident, black silk stockings. A brilliantly colored Oriental scarf was wound around her waist and knotted in front, its tasseled ends swinging girdle fashion. A sort of chemise--like the *'anteree* of Egyptian women--completed her costume, if I except a number of barbaric ornaments, some of them of silver, with which her hands and arms were bedecked.

But strange as was the girl's attire, it was to her face that my gaze was drawn irresistibly. Evidently, like most of those around us, she was some kind of half-caste; but, unlike them, she was wickedly handsome. I use the adverb *wickedly* with deliberation; for the pallidly dusky, oval face, with the full red lips, between which rested a large yellow cigarette, and the half-closed almond-shaped eyes, possessed a beauty which might have appealed to an artist of one of the modern perverted schools, but which filled me less with admiration than horror. For I *knew* her--I recognized her, from a past, brief meeting; I knew her, beyond all possibility of doubt, to be one of the Si-Fan group!

This strange creature, tossing back her jet-black, frizzy hair, which was entirely innocent of any binding or ornament, advanced along the room towards us, making unhesitatingly for our table, and carrying her lithe body with the grace of a *Gházeeyeh*.

I glanced at Fletcher across the table.

"Zarmi!" he whispered.

Again I raised my eyes to the face which now was close to mine, and became aware that I was trembling with excitement....

Heavens! why did enlightenment come too late! Either I was the victim of an odd delusion, or Zarmi had been the driver of the cab in which Nayland Smith had left the New Louvre Hotel!

Zarmi place the brass tray upon the table and bent down, resting her elbows upon it, her hands upturned and her chin nestling in her palms. The smoke from the cigarette, now held in her fingers, mingled with her disheveled hair. She looked fully into my face, a long, searching look; then her lips parted in the slow, voluptuous smile of the Orient. Without moving her head she turned the wonderful eyes (rendered doubly luminous by the *kohl* with which her lashes and lids were darkened) upon Fletcher.

"What you and your strong friend drinking?" she said softly.

Her voice possessed a faint husky note which betrayed her Eastern parentage, yet it had in it the siren lure which is the ancient heritage of the Eastern woman--a heritage more ancient than the tribe of the *Ghâzeeyeh*, to one of whom I had mentally likened Zarmi.

"Same thing," replied Fletcher promptly; and raising his hand, he idly toyed with a huge gold ear-ring which she wore.

Still resting her elbows upon the table and bending down between us, Zarmi turned her slumbering, half-closed black eyes again upon me, then slowly, languishingly, upon Fletcher. She replaced the yellow cigarette between her lips. He continued to toy with the ear-ring.

Suddenly the girl sprang upright, and from its hiding-place within the silken scarf, plucked out a Malay *krîs* with a richly jeweled hilt. Her eyes now widely opened and blazing, she struck at my companion!

I half rose from my chair, stifling a cry of horror; but Fletcher, regarding her fixedly, never moved ... and Zarmi stayed her hand just as the point of the dagger had reached his throat!

"You see," she whispered softly but intensely, "how soon I can kill you."

Ere I had overcome the amazement and horror with which her action had filled me, she had suddenly clutched me by the shoulder, and, turning from Fletcher, had the point of the *krîs* at *my* throat!

"You, too!" she whispered, "you too!"

Lower and lower she bent, the needle point of the weapon pricking my skin, until her beautiful, evil face almost touched mine. Then, miraculously, the fire died out of her eyes; they half closed again and became languishing, luresome *Ghâzeeyeh* eyes. She laughed softly, wickedly, and puffed cigarette smoke into my face.

Thrusting her dagger into her waist-belt, and snatching up the brass tray, she swayed down the room, chanting some barbaric song in her husky Eastern voice.

I inhaled deeply and glanced across at my companion. Beneath the make-up with which I had stained my skin, I knew that I had grown more than a little pale.

"Fletcher!" I whispered, "we are on the eve of a great discovery--that girl ..."

I broke off, and clutching the table with both hands, sat listening intently. From the room behind me, the opium-room, whose entrance was less than two paces from where we sat, came a sound of dragging and tapping! Slowly, cautiously, I began to turn my head; when a sudden outburst of simian chattering from the *fan-tan* players drowned that other sinister sound.

"You heard it, Doctor!" hissed Fletcher.

"The man with the limp!" I said hoarsely; "he is in there! Fletcher! I am utterly confused. I believe this place to hold the key to the whole mystery, I believe ..."

Fletcher gave me a warning glance--and, turning anew, I saw Zarmi approaching with her sinuous gait, carrying two glasses and jug upon the ornate tray. These she set down upon the table; then stood spinning the salver cleverly upon the point of her index finger and watching us through half-closed eyes.

My companion took out some loose coins, but the girl thrust the proffered payment aside with her disengaged hand, the salver still whirling upon the upraised finger of the other.

"Presently you pay for drink," she said. "You do something for me--eh?"

"Yep," replied Fletcher nonchalantly, watering the rum in the tumblers. "What time?"

"Presently I tell you. You stay here. This one a strong feller?"--indicating myself.

"Sure," drawled Fletcher; "strong as a mule he is."

"All right. I give him one little kiss if he good boy!"

Tossing the tray in the air she caught it, rested its edge upon her hip, turned, and walked away down the room, puffing her cigarette.

"Listen," I said, bending across the table, "it was Zarmi who drove the cab that came for Nayland Smith to-day!"

"My God!" whispered Fletcher, "then it was nothing less than the hand of Providence that brought us here to-night. Yes! I know how you feel, Doctor!--but we must play our cards as they're dealt to us. We must wait--wait."

Out from the den of the opium-smokers came Zarmi, one hand resting upon her hip and the other uplifted, a smoldering yellow cigarette held between the first and second fingers. With a movement of her eyes she summoned us to join her, then turned and disappeared again through the low doorway.

The time for action was arrived--we were to see behind the scenes of the Joy-Shop! Our chance to revenge poor Smith even if we could not save him. I became conscious of an inward and suppressed excitement; surreptitiously I felt the hilt of the Browning pistol in my pocket. The shadow of the dead Fu-Manchu seemed to be upon me. God! how I loathed and feared that memory!

"We can make no plans," I whispered to Fletcher, as together we rose from the table; "we must be guided by circumstance."

In order to enter the little room laden with those sickly opium fumes we had to lower our heads. Two steps led down into the place, which was so dark that I hesitated, momentarily, peering about me.

Apparently some four of five persons squatted and lay in the darkness about me. Some were couched upon rough wooden shelves ranged around the walls, others sprawled upon the floor, in the center whereof, upon a small tea-chest, stood a smoky brass lamp. The room and its occupants alike were indeterminate, sketchy; its deadly atmosphere seemed to be suffocating me. A sort of choking sound came from one of the bunks; a vague, obscene murmuring filled the whole place revoltingly.

Zarmi stood at the further end, her lithe figure silhouetted against the vague light coming through an open doorway. I saw her raise her hand, beckoning to us.

Circling around the chest supporting the lamp we crossed the foul den and found ourselves in a narrow, dim passage-way, but in cleaner air.

"Come," said Zarmi, extending her long, slim hand to me.

I took it, solely for guidance in the gloom, and she immediately drew my arm about her waist, leant back against my shoulder and, raising her pouted red lips, blew a cloud of tobacco smoke fully into my eyes!

Momentarily blinded, I drew back with a muttered exclamation. Suspecting what I did of this tigerish half-caste, I could almost have found it in my heart to return her savage pleasantries with interest.

As I raised my hands to my burning eyes, Fletcher uttered a sharp cry of pain. I turned in time to see the girl touch him lightly on the neck with the burning tip of her cigarette.

"You jealous, eh, Charlie?" she said. "But I love you, too--see! Come along, you strong fellers...."

And away she went along the passage, swaying her hips lithely and glancing back over her shoulders in smiling coquetry.

Tears were still streaming from my eyes when I found myself standing in a sort of rough shed, stone-paved, and containing a variety of nondescript rubbish. A lantern stood upon the floor; and beside it ...

The place seemed to be swimming around me, the stone floor to be heaving beneath my feet....

Beside the lantern stood a wooden chest, some six feet long, and having strong rope handles at either end. Evidently the chest had but recently been nailed up. As Zarmi touched it lightly with the pointed toe of her little red slipper I clutched at Fletcher for support.

Fletcher grasped my arm in a vice-like grip. To him, too, had come the ghastly conviction--the gruesome thought that neither of us dared to name.

It was Nayland Smith's coffin that we were to carry!

"Through here," came dimly to my ears, "and then I tell you what to do...."

Coolness returned to me, suddenly, unaccountably. I doubted not for an instant that the best friend I had in the world lay dead there at the feet of the hellish girl who called herself Zarmi, and I knew since it was she, disguised, who had driven him to his doom, that she must have been actively concerned in his murder.

But, I argued, although the damp night air was pouring in through the door which Zarmi now held open, although sound of Thames-side activity came stealing to my ears, we were yet within the walls of the Joy-Shop, with a score or more Asiatic ruffians at the woman's beck and call....

With perfect truth I can state that I retain not even a shadowy recollection of aiding Fletcher to move the chest out on to the brink of the cutting--for it was upon this that the door directly opened. The mist had grown denser, and except a glimpse of slowly moving water beneath me, I could discern little of our surrounding.

So much I saw by the light of a lantern which stood in the stern of a boat. In the bows of this boat I was vaguely aware of the presence of a crouched figure enveloped in rugs--vaguely aware that two filmy eyes regarded me out of the darkness. A man who looked like a lascar stood upright in the stern.

I must have been acting like a man in a stupor; for I was aroused to the realities by the contact of a burning cigarette with the lobe of my right ear!

"Hurry, quick, strong feller!" said Zarmi softly.

At that it seemed as though some fine nerve of my brain, already strained to utmost tension, snapped. I turned, with a wild, inarticulate cry, my fists raised frenziedly above my head.

"You fiend!" I shrieked at the mocking Eurasian, "you yellow fiend of hell!"

I was beside myself, insane. Zarmi fell back a step, flashing a glance from my own contorted face to that, now pale even beneath its artificial tan, of Fletcher.

I snatched the pistol from my pocket, and for one fateful moment the lust of slaying claimed my mind.... Then I turned towards the river, and, raising the Browning, fired shot after shot in the air.

"Weymouth!" I cried. "Weymouth!"

A sharp hissing sound came from behind me; a short, muffled cry ... and something descended, crushing, upon my skull. Like a wild cat Zarmi hurled herself past me and leapt into the boat. One glimpse I had of her pallidly dusky face, of her blazing black eyes, and the boat was thrust off into the waterway ... was swallowed up in the mist.

I turned, dizzily, to see Fletcher sinking to his knees, one hand clutching his breast.

"She got me ... with the knife," he whispered. "But ... don't worry ... look to yourself, and ...*him*...."

He pointed, weakly--then collapsed at my feet. I threw myself upon the wooden chest with a fierce, sobbing cry.

"Smith, Smith!" I babbled, and knew myself no better, in my sorrow, than an hysterical woman. "Smith, dear old man! speak to me! speak to me!..."

Outraged emotion overcame me utterly, and with my arms thrown across the box, I slipped into unconsciousness.

CHAPTER IX

FU-MANCHU

MANY POIGNANT RECOLLECTIONS are mine, more of them bitter than sweet; but no one of them all can compare with the memory of that moment of my awakening.

Weymouth was supporting me, and my throat still tingled from the effects of the brandy which he had forced between my teeth from his flask. My heart was beating irregularly; my mind yet partly inert. With something compound of horror and hope I lay staring at one who was anxiously bending over the Inspector's shoulder, watching me.

It was Nayland Smith.

A whole hour of silence seemed to pass, ere speech became possible; then--

"Smith!" I whispered, "are you ..."

Smith grasped my outstretched, questing hand, grasped it firmly, warmly; and I saw his gray eyes to be dim in the light of the several lanterns around us.

"Am I alive?" he said. "Dear old Petrie! Thanks to you, I am not only alive, but free!"

My head was buzzing like a hive of bees, but I managed, aided by Weymouth, to struggle to my feet. Muffled sounds of shouting and scuffling reached me. Two men in the uniform of the Thames Police were carrying a limp body in at the low doorway communicating with the infernal Joy-Shop.

"It's Fletcher," said Weymouth, noting the anxiety expressed in my face. "His missing lady friend has given him a nasty wound, but he'll pull round all right."

"Thank God for that," I replied, clutched my aching head. "I don't know what weapon she employed in my case, but it narrowly missed achieving her purpose."

My eyes, throughout, were turned upon Smith, for his presence there, still seemed to me miraculous.

"Smith," I said, "for Heaven's sake enlighten me! I never doubted that you were ..."

"In the wooden chest!" concluded Smith grimly, "Look!"

He pointed to something that lay behind me. I turned, and saw the box which had occasioned me such anguish. The top had been wrenched off and the contents exposed to view. It was filled with a variety of gold ornaments, cups, vases, silks, and barbaric brocaded raiment; it might well have contained the loot of a cathedral. Inspector Weymouth laughed gruffly at my surprise.

"What is it?" I asked, in a voice of amazement.

"It's the treasure of the Si-Fan, I presume," rapped Smith. "Where it has come from and where it was going to, it must be my immediate business to ascertain."

"Then you ..."

"I was lying, bound and gagged, upon one of the upper shelves in the opium-den! I heard you and Fletcher arrive. I saw you pass through later with that she-devil who drove the cab to-day ..."

"Then the cab ..."

"The windows were fastened, unopenable, and some anaesthetic was injected into the interior through a tube--that speaking-tube. I know nothing further, except that our plans must have leaked out in some mysterious fashion. Petrie, my suspicions point to high quarters. The Si-Fan score thus far, for unless the search now in progress brings it to light, we must conclude that they have the brass coffer."

He was interrupted by a sudden loud crying of his name.

"Mr. Nayland Smith!" came from somewhere within the Joy-Shop. "This way, sir!"

Off he went, in his quick, impetuous manner, whilst I stood there, none too steadily, wondering what discovery this outcry portended. I had not long to wait. Out by the low doorway come Smith, a grimly triumphant smile upon his face, carrying the missing brass coffer!

He set it down upon the planking before me.

"John Ki," he said, "who was also on the missing list, had dragged the thing out of the cellar where it was hidden, and in another minute must have slipped away with it. Detective Deacon saw the light shining through a crack in the floor. I shall never forget the look John gave us when we came upon him, as, lamp in hand, he bent over the precious chest."

"Shall you open it now?"

"No." He glanced at me oddly. "I shall have it valued in the morning by Messrs. Meyerstein."

He was keeping something back; I was sure of it.

"Smith," I said suddenly, "the man with the limp! I heard him in the place where you were confined! Did you ..."

Nayland Smith clicked his teeth together sharply, looking straightly and grimly into my eyes.

"I *saw* him!" he replied slowly; "and unless the effects of the anaesthetic had not wholly worn off ..."

"Well!" I cried.

"The man with the limp is *Dr. Fu-Manchu!*"

CHAPTER X

THE TÛLUN-NÛR CHEST

"THIS BOX," said Mr. Meyerstein, bending attentively over the carven brass coffer upon the table, "is certainly of considerable value, and possibly almost unique."

Nayland Smith glanced across at me with a slight smile. Mr. Meyerstein ran one fat finger tenderly across the heavily embossed figures, which, like barnacles, encrusted the sides and lid of the weird curio which we had summoned him to appraise.

"What do you think, Lewison?" he added, glancing over his shoulder at the clerk who accompanied him.

Lewison, whose flaxen hair and light blue eyes almost served to mask his Semitic origin, shrugged his shoulders in a fashion incongruous in one of his complexion, though characteristic in one of his name.

"It is as you say, Mr. Meyerstein, an example of early Tûlun-Nûr work," he said. "It may be sixteenth century or even earlier. The Kûren treasure-chest in the Hague Collection has points of similarity, but the workmanship of this specimen is infinitely finer."

"In a word, gentlemen," snapped Nayland Smith, rising from the armchair in which he had been sitting, and beginning restlessly to pace the room, "in a word, you would be prepared to make me a substantial offer for this box?"

Mr. Meyerstein, his shrewd eyes twinkling behind the pebbles of his pince-nez, straightened himself slowly, turned in the ponderous manner of a fat man, and readjusted the pince-nez upon his nose. He cleared his throat.

"I have not yet seen the interior of the box, Mr. Smith," he said.

Smith paused in his perambulation of the carpet and stared hard at the celebrated art dealer.

"Unfortunately," he replied, "the key is missing."

"Ah!" cried the assistant, Lewison, excitedly, "you are mistaken, sir! Coffers of this description and workmanship are nearly always complicated conjuring tricks; they rarely open by any such rational means as lock and key. For instance, the Kûren treasure-chest to which I referred, opens by an intricate process involving the pressing of certain knobs in the design, and the turning of others."

"It was ultimately opened," said Mr. Meyerstein, with a faint note of professional envy in his voice, "by one of Christie's experts."

"Does my memory mislead me," I interrupted, "or was it not regarding the possession of the chest to which you refer, that the celebrated case of 'Hague versus Jacobs' arose?"

"You are quite right, Dr. Petrie," said Meyerstein, turning to me. "The original owner, a member of the Younghusband Expedition, had been unable to open the chest. When opened at Christie's it proved to contain jewels and other valuables. It was a curious case, wasn't it, Lewison?" turning to his clerk.

"Very," agreed the other absently; then--"Have you endeavored to open this box, Mr. Smith?"

Nayland Smith shook his head grimly.

"From its weight," said Meyerstein, "I am inclined to think that the contents might prove of interest. With your permission I will endeavor to open it."

Nayland Smith, tugging reflectively at the lobe of his left ear, stood looking at the expert. Then--

"I do not care to attempt it at present," he said.

Meyerstein and his clerk stared at the speaker in surprise.

"But you would be mad," cried the former, "if you accepted an offer for the box, whilst ignorant of the nature of its contents."

"But I have invited no offer," said Smith. "I do not propose to sell."

Meyerstein adjusted his pince-nez again.

"I am a business man," he said, "and I will make a business proposal: A hundred guineas for the box, cash down, and our commission to be ten per cent on the proceeds of the contents. You must remember," raising a fat forefinger to check Smith, who was about to interrupt him, "that it may be necessary to force the box in order to open it, thereby decreasing its market value and making it a bad bargain at a hundred guineas."

Nayland Smith met my gaze across the room; again a slight smile crossed the lean, tanned face.

"I can only reply, Mr. Meyerstein," he said, "in this way: if I desire to place the box on the market, you shall have first refusal, and the same applies to the contents, if any. For the moment if you will send me a note of your fee, I shall be obliged." He raised his hand with a conclusive gesture. "I am not prepared to discuss the question of sale any further at present, Mr. Meyerstein."

At that the dealer bowed, took up his hat from the table, and prepared to depart. Lewison opened the door and stood aside.

"Good morning, gentlemen," said Meyerstein.

As Lewison was about to follow him--

"Since you do not intend to open the box," he said, turning, his hand upon the door knob, "have you any idea of its contents?"

"None," replied Smith; "but with my present inadequate knowledge of its history, I do not care to open it."

Lewison smiled skeptically.

"Probably you know best," he said, bowed to us both, and retired.

When the door was closed--

"You see, Petrie," said Smith, beginning to stuff tobacco into his briar, "if we are ever short of funds, here's something"--pointing to the Tûlun-Nûr box upon the table--"which would retrieve our fallen fortunes."

He uttered one of his rare, boyish laughs, and began to pace the carpet again, his gaze always set upon our strange treasure. What did it contain?

The manner in which it had come into our possession suggested that it might contain something of the utmost value to the Yellow group. For we knew the house of John Ki to be, if not the head-quarters, certainly a meeting-place of the mysterious organization the Si-Fan; we knew that Dr. Fu-Manchu used the place--Dr. Fu-Manchu, the uncanny being whose existence seemingly proved him immune from natural laws, a deathless incarnation of evil.

My gaze set upon the box, I wondered anew what strange, dark secrets it held; I wondered how many murders and crimes greater than murder blackened its history.

"Smith," I said suddenly, "now that the mystery of the absence of a key-hole is explained, I am sorely tempted to essay the task of opening the coffer. I think it might help us to a solution of the whole mystery."

"And I think otherwise!" interrupted my friend grimly. "In a word, Petrie, I look upon this box as a sort of hostage by means of which-- who knows--we might one day buy our lives from the enemy. I have a sort of fancy, call it superstition if you will, that nothing--not even our miraculous good luck--could save us if once we ravished its secret."

I stared at him amazedly; this was a new phase in his character.

"I am conscious of something almost like a spiritual unrest," he continued. "Formerly you were endowed with a capacity for divining the presence of Fu-Manchu or his agents. Some such second-sight would appear to have visited me now, and it directs me forcibly to avoid opening the box."

His steps as he paced the floor grew more and more rapid. He relighted his pipe, which had gone out as usual, and tossed the match-end into the hearth.

"To-morrow," he said, "I shall lodge the coffer in a place of greater security. Come along, Petrie, Weymouth is expecting us at Scotland Yard."

CHAPTER XI

IN THE FOG

"BUT, SMITH," I began, as my friend hurried me along the corridor, "you are not going to leave the box unguarded?"

Nayland Smith tugged at my arm, and, glancing at him, I saw him frowningly shake his head. Utterly mystified, I nevertheless understood that for some reason he desired me to preserve silence for the present. Accordingly I said no more until the lift brought us down into the lobby and we had passed out from the New Louvre Hotel, crossed the busy thoroughfare and entered the buffet of an establishment not far distant. My friend having ordered cocktails--

"And now perhaps you will explain to me the reason for your mysterious behavior?" said I.

Smith, placing my glass before me, glanced about him to right and left, and having satisfied himself that his words could not be overheard--

"Petrie," he whispered, "I believe we are spied upon at the New Louvre."

"What!"

"There are spies of the Si-Fan--of Fu-Manchu--amongst the hotel servants! We have good reason to believe that Dr. Fu-Manchu at one time was actually in the building, and we have been compelled to draw attention to the state of the electric fitting in our apartments, which enables any one in the corridor above to spy upon us."

"Then why do you stay?"

"For a very good reason, Petrie, and the same that prompts me to retain the Tûlun-Nûr box in my own possession rather than to deposit it in the strong-room of my bank."

"I begin to understand."

"I trust you do, Petrie; it is fairly obvious. Probably the plan is a perilous one, but I hope, by laying myself open to attack, to apprehend the enemy--perhaps to make an important capture."

Setting down my glass, I stared in silence at Smith.

"I will anticipate your remark," he said, smiling dryly. "I am aware that I am not entitled to expose *you* to these dangers. It is *my* duty and I must perform it as best I can; you, as a volunteer, are perfectly entitled to withdraw."

As I continued silently to stare at him, his expression changed; the gray eyes grew less steely, and presently, clapping his hand upon my shoulder in his impulsive way--

"Petrie!" he cried, "you know I had no intention of hurting your feelings, but in the circumstances it was impossible for me to say less."

"You have said enough, Smith," I replied shortly. "I beg of you to say no more."

He gripped my shoulder hard, then plunged his hand into his pocket and pulled out the blackened pipe.

"We see it through together, then, though God knows whither it will lead us."

"In the first place," I interrupted, "since you have left the chest unguarded----"

"I locked the door."

"What is a mere lock where Fu-Manchu is concerned?"

Nayland Smith laughed almost gaily.

"Really, Petrie," he cried, "sometimes I cannot believe that you mean me to take you seriously. Inspector Weymouth has engaged the room immediately facing our door, and no one can enter or leave the suite unseen by him."

"Inspector Weymouth?"

"Oh! for once he has stooped to a disguise: spectacles, and a muffler which covers his face right up to the tip of his nose. Add to this a prodigious overcoat and an asthmatic cough, and you have a picture of Mr. Jonathan Martin, the occupant of room No. 239."

I could not repress a smile upon hearing this description.

"No. 239," continued Smith, "contains two beds, and Mr. Martin's friend will be joining him there this evening."

Meeting my friend's questioning glance, I nodded comprehendingly.

"Then what part do *I* play?"

"Ostensibly we both leave town this evening," he explained; "but I have a scheme whereby you will be enabled to remain behind. We shall thus have one watcher inside and two out."

"It seems almost absurd," I said incredulously, "to expect any member of the Yellow group to attempt anything in a huge hotel like the New Louvre, here in the heart of London!"

Nayland Smith, having lighted his pipe, stretched his arms and stared me straight in the face.

"Has Fu-Manchu never attempted outrage, murder, in the heart of London before?" he snapped.

The words were sufficient. Remembering black episodes of the past (one at least of them had occurred not a thousand yards from the very spot upon which we now stood), I knew that I had spoken folly.

Certain arrangements were made then, including a visit to Scotland Yard; and a plan--though it sounds anomalous--at once elaborate and simple, was put into execution in the dusk of the evening.

London remained in the grip of fog, and when we passed along the corridor communicating with our apartments, faint streaks of yellow vapor showed in the light of the lamp suspended at the further end. I knew that Nayland Smith suspected the presence of some spying contrivance in our rooms, although I was unable to conjecture how this could have been managed without the connivance of the management. In pursuance of his idea, however, he extinguished the lights a moment before we actually quitted the suite. Just within the door he helped me to remove the somewhat conspicuous check traveling-coat which I wore. With this upon his arm he opened the door and stepped out into the corridor.

As the door slammed upon his exit, I heard him cry: "Come along, Petrie! we have barely five minutes to catch our train."

Detective Carter of New Scotland Yard had joined him at the threshold, and muffled up in the gray traveling-coat was now hurrying with Smith along the corridor and out of the hotel. Carter, in build and features, was not unlike me, and I did not doubt that any one who might be spying upon our movements would be deceived by this device.

In the darkness of the apartment I stood listening to the retreating footsteps in the corridor. A sense of loneliness and danger assailed me. I knew that Inspector Weymouth was watching and listening from the room immediately opposite; that he held Smith's key; that I could summon him to my assistance, if necessary, in a matter of seconds.

Yet, contemplating the vigil that lay before me in silence and darkness, I cannot pretend that my frame of mind was buoyant. I could not smoke; I must make no sound.

As pre-arranged, I cautiously removed my boots, and as cautiously tiptoed across the carpet and seated myself in an arm-chair. I determined there to await the arrival of Mr. Jonathan Martin's friend, which I knew could not now be long delayed.

The clocks were striking eleven when he arrived, and in the perfect stillness of that upper corridor. I heard the bustle which heralded his approach, heard the rap upon the door opposite, followed by a muffled "Come in" from Weymouth. Then, as the door was opened, I heard the sound of a wheezy cough.

A strange cracked voice (which, nevertheless, I recognized for Smith's) cried, "Hullo, Martin!--cough no better?"

Upon that the door was closed again, and as the retreating footsteps of the servant died away, complete silence--that peculiar silence which comes with fog--descended once more upon the upper part of the New Louvre Hotel.

CHAPTER XII

THE VISITANT

THAT FIRST HOUR of watching, waiting, and listening in the lonely quietude passed drearily; and with the passage of every quarter-- signalized by London's muffled clocks--my mood became increasingly morbid. I peopled the silent rooms opening out of that wherein I sat, with stealthy, murderous figures; my imagination painted hideous yellow faces upon the draperies, twitching yellow hands protruding from this crevice and that. A score of times I started nervously, thinking I heard the pad of bare feet upon the floor behind me, the suppressed breathing of some deathly approach.

Since nothing occurred to justify these tremors, this apprehensive mood passed; I realized that I was growing cramped and stiff, that unconsciously I had been sitting with my muscles nervously tensed. The window was open a foot or so at the top and the blind was drawn; but so accustomed were my eyes now to peering through the darkness, that I could plainly discern the yellow oblong of the window, and though very vaguely, some of the appointments of the room--the Chesterfield against one wall, the lamp-shade above my head, the table with the Tûlun-Nûr box upon it.

There was fog in the room, and it was growing damply chill, for we had extinguished the electric heater some hours before. Very few sounds penetrated from outside. Twice or perhaps thrice people passed along the corridor, going to their rooms; but, as I knew, the greater number of the rooms along that corridor were unoccupied.

From the Embankment far below me, and from the river, faint noises came at long intervals it is true; the muffled hooting of motors, and yet fainter ringing of bells. Fog signals boomed distantly, and train whistles shrieked, remote and unreal. I determined to enter my bedroom, and, risking any sound which I might make, to lie down upon the bed.

I rose carefully and carried this plan into execution. I would have given much for a smoke, although my throat was parched; and almost any drink would have been nectar. But although my hopes (or my fears) of an intruder had left me, I determined to stick to the rules of the game as laid down. Therefore I neither smoked nor drank, but carefully extended my weary limbs upon the coverlet, and telling myself that I could guard our strange treasure as well from there as from elsewhere ... slipped off into a profound sleep.

Nothing approaching in acute and sustained horror to the moment when next I opened my eyes exists in all my memories of those days.

In the first place I was aroused by the shaking of the bed. It was quivering beneath me as though an earthquake disturbed the very foundations of the building. I sprang upright and into full consciousness of my lapse.... My hands clutching the coverlet on either side of me, I sat staring, staring, staring ... at *that* which peered at me over the foot of the bed.

I knew that I had slept at my post; I was convinced that I was now widely awake; yet I *dared* not admit to myself that what I saw was other than a product of my imagination. I dared not admit the physical quivering of the bed, for I could not, with sanity, believe its cause to be anything human. But what I saw, yet could not credit seeing, was this:

A ghostly white face, which seemed to glisten in some faint reflected light from the sitting-room beyond, peered over the bedrail; gibbered at me demoniacally. With quivering hands this night-mare horror, which had intruded where I believed human intrusion to be all but impossible, clutched the bed-posts so that the frame of the structure shook and faintly rattled....

My heart leapt wildly in my breast, then seemed to suspend its pulsations and to grow icily cold. My whole body became chilled horrifically. My scalp tingled: I felt that I must either cry out or become stark, raving mad!

For this clammily white face, those staring eyes, that wordless gibbering, and the shaking, shaking, shaking of the bed in the clutch of the nameless visitant--prevailed, refused to disperse like the evil dream I had hoped it all to be; manifested itself, indubitably, as something tangible--objective....

Outraged reason deprived me of coherent speech. Past the clammy white face I could see the sitting-room illuminated by a faint light; I could even see the Tûlun-Nûr box upon the table immediately opposite the door.

The thing which shook the bed was actual, existent--to be counted with!

Further and further I drew myself away from it, until I crouched close up against the head of the bed. Then, as the thing reeled aside, and--merciful Heaven!--made as if to come around and approach me yet closer, I uttered a hoarse cry and hurled myself out upon the floor and on the side remote from that pallid horror which I thought was pursuing me.

I heard a dull thud ... and the thing disappeared from my view, yet--and remembering the supreme terror of that visitation I am not ashamed to confess it--I dared not move from the spot upon which I stood, I dared not make to pass that which lay between me and the door.

"Smith!" I cried, but my voice was little more than a hoarse whisper--"Smith! Weymouth!"

The words became clearer and louder as I proceeded, so that the last-- "Weymouth!"--was uttered in a sort of falsetto scream.

A door burst open upon the other side of the corridor. A key was inserted in the lock of the door. Into the dimly lighted arch which divided the bed-room from the sitting-room, sprang the figure of Nayland Smith!

"Petrie! Petrie!" he called--and I saw him standing there looking from left to right.

Then, ere I could reply, he turned, and his gaze fell upon whatever lay upon the floor at the foot of the bed.

"My God!" he whispered--and sprang into the room.

"Smith! Smith!" I cried, "what is it? what is it?"

He turned in a flash, as Weymouth entered at his heels, saw me, and fell back a step; then looked again down at the floor.

"God's mercy!" he whispered, "I thought it was you--I thought it was you!"

Trembling violently, my mind a feverish chaos, I moved to the foot of the bed and looked down at what lay there.

"Turn up the light!" snapped Smith.

Weymouth reached for the switch, and the room became illuminated suddenly.

Prone upon the carpet, hands outstretched and nails dug deeply into the pile of the fabric, lay a dark-haired man having his head twisted sideways so that the face showed a ghastly pallid profile against the rich colorings upon which it rested. He wore no coat, but a sort of dark gray shirt and black trousers. To add to the incongruity of his attire, his feet were clad in drab-colored shoes, rubber-soled.

I stood, one hand raised to my head, looking down upon him, and gradually regaining control of myself. Weymouth, perceiving something of my condition, silently passed his flask to me; and I gladly availed myself of this.

"How in Heaven's name did he get in?" I whispered.

"How, indeed!" said Weymouth, staring about him with wondering eyes.

Both he and Smith had discarded their disguises; and, a bewildered trio, we stood looking down upon the man at our feet. Suddenly Smith dropped to his knees and turned him flat upon his back. Composure was nearly restored to me, and I knelt upon the other side of the white-faced creature whose presence there seemed so utterly outside the realm of possibility, and examined him with a consuming and fearful interest; for it was palpable that, if not already dead, he was dying rapidly.

He was a slightly built man, and the first discovery that I made was a curious one. What I had mistaken for dark hair was a wig! The short black mustache which he wore was also factitious.

"Look at this!" I cried.

"I am looking," snapped Smith.

He suddenly stood up, and entering the room beyond, turned on the light there. I saw him staring at the Tûlun-Nûr box, and I knew what had been in his mind. But the box, undisturbed, stood upon the table as we had left it. I saw Smith tugging irritably at the lobe of his ear, and staring from the box towards the man beside whom I knelt.

"For God's sake, what does it man?" said Inspector Weymouth in a voice hushed with wonder. "How did he get in? What did he come for?--and what has happened to him?"

"As to what has happened to him," I replied, "unfortunately I cannot tell you. I only know that unless something can be done his end is not far off."

"Shall we lay him on the bed?"

I nodded, and together we raised the slight figure and placed it upon the bed where so recently I had lain.

As we did so, the man suddenly opened his eyes, which were glazed with delirium. He tore himself from our grip, sat bolt upright, and holding his hands, fingers outstretched, before his face, stared at them frenziedly.

"The golden pomegranates!" he shrieked, and a slight froth appeared on his blanched lips. "The golden pomegranates!"

He laughed madly, and fell back inert.

"He's dead!" whispered Weymouth; "he's dead!"

Hard upon his words came a cry from Smith:

"Quick! Petrie!--Weymouth!"

CHAPTER XIII

THE ROOM BELOW

I RAN INTO the sitting-room, to discover Nayland Smith craning out of the now widely opened window. The blind had been drawn up, I did not know by whom; and, leaning out beside my friend, I was in time to perceive some bright object moving down the gray stone wall. Almost instantly it disappeared from sight in the yellow banks below.

Smith leapt around in a whirl of excitement.

"Come in, Petrie!" he cried, seizing my arm. "You remain here, Weymouth; don't leave these rooms whatever happens!"

We ran out into the corridor. For my own part I had not the vaguest idea what we were about. My mind was not yet fully recovered from the frightful shock which it had sustained; and the strange words of the dying man--"the golden pomegranates"--had increased my mental confusion. Smith apparently had not heard them, for he remained grimly silent, as side by side we raced down the marble stairs to the corridor immediately below our own.

Although, amid the hideous turmoil to which I had awakened, I had noted nothing of the hour, evidently the night was far advanced. Not a soul was to be seen from end to end of the vast corridor in which we stood ... until on the right-hand side and about half-way along, a door opened and a woman came out hurriedly, carrying a small hand-bag.

She wore a veil, so that her features were but vaguely distinguished, but her every movement was agitated; and this agitation perceptibly increased when, turning, she perceived the two of us bearing down upon her.

Nayland Smith, who had been audibly counting the doors along the corridor as we passed them, seized the woman's arm without ceremony, and pulled her into the apartment she had been on the point of quitting, closing the door behind us as we entered.

"Smith!" I began, "for Heaven's sake what are you about?"

"You shall see, Petrie!" he snapped.

He released the woman's arm, and pointing to an arm-chair near by--

"Be seated," he said sternly.

Speechless with amazement, I stood, with my back to the door, watching this singular scene. Our captive, who wore a smart walking costume and whose appearance was indicative of elegance and culture, so far had uttered no word of protest, no cry.

Now, whilst Smith stood rigidly pointing to the chair, she seated herself with something very like composure and placed the leather bag upon the floor beside her. The room in which I found myself was one of a suite almost identical with our own, but from what I had gathered in a hasty glance around, it bore no signs of recent tenancy. The window was widely opened, and upon the floor lay a strange-looking contrivance apparently made of aluminum. A large grip, open, stood beside it, and from this some portions of a black coat and other garments protruded.

"Now, madame," said Nayland Smith, "will you be good enough to raise your veil?"

Silently, unprotestingly, the woman obeyed him, raising her gloved hands and lifting the veil from her face.

The features revealed were handsome in a hard fashion, but heavily made-up. Our captive was younger than I had hitherto supposed; a blonde; her hair artificially reduced to the so-called Titian tint. But, despite her youth, her eyes, with the blackened lashes, were full of a world weariness. Now she smiled cynically.

"Are you satisfied," she said, speaking unemotionally, "or," holding up her wrists, "would you like to handcuff me?"

Nayland Smith, glancing from the open grip and the appliance beside it to the face of the speaker, began clicking his teeth together, whereby I knew him to be perplexed. Then he stared across at me.

"You appear bemused, Petrie," he said, with a certain irritation. "Is this what mystifies you?"

Stooping, he picked up the metal contrivance, and almost savagely jerked open the top section. It was a telescopic ladder, and more ingeniously designed than anything of the kind I had seen before. There was a sort of clamp attached to the base, and two sharply pointed hooks at the top.

"For reaching windows on an upper floor," snapped my friend, dropping the thing with a clatter upon the carpet. "An American device which forms part of the equipment of the modern hotel thief!"

He seemed to be disappointed--fiercely disappointed; and I found his attitude inexplicable. He turned to the woman--who sat regarding him with that fixed cynical smile.

"Who are you?" he demanded; "and what business have you with the Si-Fan?"

The woman's eyes opened more widely, and the smile disappeared from her face.

"The Si-Fan!" she repeated slowly. "I don't know what you mean, Inspector."

"I am not an Inspector," snapped Smith, "and you know it well enough. You have one chance--your last. To whom were you to deliver the box? when and where?"

But the blue eyes remained upraised to the grim tanned face with a look of wonder in them, which, if assumed, marked the woman a consummate actress.

"Who are you?" she asked in a low voice, "and what are you talking about?"

Inactive, I stood by the door watching my friend, and his face was a fruitful study in perplexity. He seemed upon the point of an angry outburst, then, staring intently into the questioning eyes upraised to his, he checked the words he would have uttered and began to click his teeth together again.

"You are some servant of Dr. Fu-Manchu!" he said.

The girl frowned with a bewilderment which I could have sworn was not assumed. Then--

"You said I had one chance a moment ago," she replied. "But if you referred to my answering any of your questions, it is no chance at all. We have gone under, and I know it. I am not complaining; it's all in the game. There's a clear enough case against us, and I am sorry"--suddenly, unexpectedly, her eyes became filled with tears, which coursed down her cheeks, leaving little wakes of blackness from the make-up upon her lashes. Her lips trembled, and her voice shook. "I am sorry I let him do it. He'd never done anything--not anything big like this--before, and he never would have done if he had not met me...."

The look of perplexity upon Smith's face was increasing with every word that the girl uttered.

"You don't seem to know me," she continued, her emotion growing momentarily greater, "and I don't know you; but they will know me at Bow Street. I urged him to do it, when he told me about the box to-day at lunch. He said that if it contained half as much as the Kûren treasure-chest, we could sail for America and be on the straight all the rest of our lives...."

And now something which had hitherto been puzzling me became suddenly evident. I had not removed the wig worn by the dead man, but I knew that he had fair hair, and when in his last moments he had opened his eyes, there had been in the contorted face something faintly familiar.

"Smith!" I cried excitedly, "it is Lewison, Meyerstein's clerk! Don't you understand? don't you understand?"

Smith brought his teeth together with a snap and stared me hard in the face.

"I do, Petrie. I have been following a false scent. I do!"

The girl in the chair was now sobbing convulsively.

"He was tempted by the possibility of the box containing treasure," I ran on, "and his acquaintance with this--lady--who is evidently no stranger to felonious operations, led him to make the attempt with her assistance. But"--I found myself confronted by a new problem--"what caused his death?"

"His ... *death*!"

As a wild, hysterical shriek the words smote upon my ears. I turned, to see the girl rise, tottering, from her seat. She began groping in front of her, blindly, as though a darkness had descended.

"You did not say he was dead?" she whispered, "not dead!--not ..."

The words were lost in a wild peal of laughter. Clutching at her throat she swayed and would have fallen had I not caught her in my arms. As I laid her insensible upon the settee I met Smith's glance.

"I think I know that, too, Petrie," he said gravely.

CHAPTER XIV

THE GOLDEN POMEGRANATES

"WHAT WAS IT THAT HE CRIED OUT?" demanded Nayland Smith abruptly. "I was in the sitting-room and it sounded to me like 'pomegranates'!"

We were bending over Lewison; for now, the wig removed, Lewison it proved unmistakably to be, despite the puffy and pallid face.

"He said 'the golden pomegranates,'" I replied, and laughed harshly. "They were words of delirium and cannot possibly have any bearing upon the manner of his death."

"I disagree."

He strode out into the sitting-room.

Weymouth was below, supervising the removal of the unhappy prisoner, and together Smith and I stood looking down at the brass box. Suddenly--

"I propose to attempt to open it," said my friend.

His words came as a complete surprise.

"For what reason?--and why have you so suddenly changed your mind?"

"For a reason which I hope will presently become evident," he said; "and as to my change of mind, unless I am greatly mistaken, the wily old Chinaman from whom I wrested this treasure was infinitely more clever than I gave him credit for being!"

Through the open window came faintly to my ears the chiming of Big Ben. The hour was a quarter to two. London's pulse was dimmed now, and around about us that great city slept as soundly as it ever sleeps. Other sounds came vaguely through the fog, and beside Nayland Smith I sat and watched him at work upon the Tûlun-Nûr box.

Every knob of the intricate design he pushed, pulled and twisted; but without result. The night wore on, and just before three o'clock Inspector Weymouth knocked upon the door. I admitted him, and side by side the two of us stood watching Smith patiently pursuing his task.

All conversation had ceased, when, just as the muted booming of London's clocks reached my ears again and Weymouth pulled out his watch, there came a faint click ... and I saw that Smith had raised the lid of the coffer!

Weymouth and I sprang forward with one accord, and over Smith's shoulders peered into the interior. There was a second lid of some dull, black wood, apparently of great age, and fastened to it so as to form knobs or handles was an exquisitely carved pair of _golden pomegranates!_

"They are to raise the wooden lid, Mr. Smith!" cried Weymouth eagerly.

"Look! there is a hollow in each to accommodate the fingers!"

"Aren't you going to open it?" I demanded excitedly--"aren't you going to open it?"

"Might I invite you to accompany me into the bedroom yonder for a moment?" he replied in a tome of studied reserve. "You also, Weymouth?"

Smith leading, we entered the room where the dead man lay stretched upon the bed.

"Note the appearance of his fingers," directed Nayland Smith.

I examined the peculiarity to which Smith had drawn my attention. The dead man's fingers were swollen extraordinarily, the index finger of either hand especially being oddly discolored, as though bruised from the nail upward. I looked again at the ghastly face, then, repressing a shudder, for the sight was one not good to look upon, I turned to Smith, who was watching me expectantly with his keen, steely eyes.

From his pocket the took out a knife containing a number of implements, amongst them a hook-like contrivance.

"Have you a button-hook, Petrie," he asked, "or anything of that nature?"

"How will this do?" said the Inspector, and he produced a pair of handcuffs. "They were not wanted," he added significantly.

"Better still," declared Smith.

Reclosing his knife, he took the handcuffs from Weymouth, and, returning to the sitting-room, opened them widely and inserted two steel points in the hollows of the golden pomegranates. He pulled. There was a faint sound of moving mechanism and the wooden lid lifted, revealing the interior of the coffer. It contained three long bars of lead--and nothing else!

Supporting the lid with the handcuffs--

"Just pull the light over here, Petrie," said Smith.

I did as he directed.

"Look into these two cavities where one is expected to thrust one's fingers!"

Weymouth and I craned forward so that our heads came into contact.

"My God!" whispered the Inspector, "we know now what killed him!"

Visible, in either little cavity against the edge of the steel handcuff, was the point of a needle, which evidently worked in an exquisitely made socket through which the action of raising the lid caused it to protrude. Underneath the lid, midway between the two pomegranates, as I saw by slowly moving the lamp, was a little receptacle of metal communicating with the base of the hollow needles.

The action of lifting the lid not only protruded the points but also operated the hypodermic syringe!

"Note," snapped Smith--but his voice was slightly hoarse.

He removed the points of the bracelets. The box immediately reclosed with no other sound than a faint click.

"God forgive him," said Smith, glancing toward the other room, "for he died in my stead!--and Dr. Fu-Manchu scores an undeserved failure!"

CHAPTER XV

ZARMI REAPPEARS

"COME IN!" I cried.

The door opened and a page-boy entered.

"A cable for Dr. Petrie."

I started up from my chair. A thousand possibilities--some of a sort to bring dread to my heart--instantly occurred to me. I tore open the envelope and, as one does, glanced first at the name of the sender.

It was signed "Kâramaneh!"

"Smith!" I said hoarsely, glancing over the massage, "Kâramaneh is on her way to England. She arrives by the *Nicobar* to-morrow!"

"Eh?" cried Nayland Smith, in turn leaping to his feet. "She had no right to come alone, unless----"

The boy, open-mouthed, was listening to our conversation, and I hastily thrust a coin into his hand and dismissed him. As the door closed--

"Unless what, Smith?" I said, looking my friend squarely in the eyes.

"Unless she has learnt something, or--is flying away from some one!"

My mind set in a whirl of hopes and fears, longings and dreads.

"What do you mean, Smith?" I asked. "This is the place of danger, as we know to our cost; she was safe in Egypt."

Nayland Smith commenced one of his restless perambulations, glancing at me from time to time and frequently tugging at the lobe of his ear.

"*Was* she safe in Egypt?" he rapped. "We are dealing, remember, with the Si-Fan, which, if I am not mistaken, is a sort of Eleusinian Mystery holding some kind of dominion over the eastern mind, and boasting initiates throughout the Orient. It is almost certain that there is an Egyptian branch, or group--call it what you will--of the damnable organization."

"But Dr. Fu-Manchu----"

"Dr. Fu-Manchu--for he lives, Petrie! my own eyes bear witness to the fact--Dr. Fu-Manchu is a sort of delegate from the headquarters. His prodigious genius will readily enable him to keep in touch with every branch of the movement, East and West."

He paused to knock out his pipe into an ashtray and to watch me for some moments in silence.

"He may have instructed his Cairo agents," he added significantly.

"God grant she get to England in safety," I whispered. "Smith! can we make no move to round up the devils who defy us, here in the very heart of civilized England? Listen. You will not have forgotten the wild-cat Eurasian Zarmi?"

Smith nodded. "I recall the lady perfectly!" he snapped.

"Unless my imagination has been playing me tricks, I have seen her twice within the last few days--once in the neighborhood of this hotel and once in a cab in Piccadilly."

"You mentioned the matter at the time," said Smith shortly; "but although I made inquiries, as you remember, nothing came of them."

"Nevertheless, I don't think I was mistaken. I feel in my very bones that the Yellow hand of Fu-Manchu is about to stretch out again. If only we could apprehend Zarmi."

Nayland Smith lighted his pipe with care.

"If only we could, Petrie!" he said; "but, damn it!"--he dashed his left fist into the palm of his right hand--"we are doomed to remain inactive. We can only await the arrival of Kâramaneh and see if she has anything to tell us. I must admit that there are certain theories of my own which I haven't yet had an opportunity of testing. Perhaps in the near future such an opportunity may arise."

How soon that opportunity was to arise neither of us suspected then; but Fate is a merry trickster, and even as we spoke of these matters events were brewing which were to lead us along strange paths.

With such glad anticipations as my pen cannot describe, their gladness not unmixed with fear, I retired to rest that night, scarcely expecting to sleep, so eager was I for the morrow. The musical voice of Kâramaneh seemed to ring in my ears; I seemed to feel the touch of her soft hands and to detect, as I drifted into the borderland betwixt reality and slumber, that faint, exquisite perfume which from the first moment of my meeting with the beautiful Eastern girl, had become to me inseparable from her personality.

It seemed that sleep had but just claimed me when I was awakened by some one roughly shaking my shoulder. I sprang upright, my mind alert to sudden danger. The room looked yellow and dismal, illuminated as it was by a cold light of dawn which crept through the window and with which competed the luminance of the electric lamps.

Nayland Smith stood at my bedside, partially dressed!

"Wake up, Petrie!" he cried; "you instincts serve you better than my reasoning. Hell's afoot, old man! Even as you predicted it, perhaps in that same hour, the yellow fiends were at work!"

"What, Smith, what!" I said, leaping out of bed; "you don't mean----"

"Not that, old man," he replied, clapping his hand upon my shoulder; "there is no further news of *her*, but Weymouth is waiting outside. Sir Baldwin Frazer has disappeared!"

sleep. I rubbed my eyes hard and sought to clear my mind of the vapors of

"Sir Baldwin Frazer!" I said, "of Half-Moon Street? But what----"

"God knows *what*," snapped Smith; "but our old friend Zarmi, or so it would appear, bore him off last night, and he has completely vanished, leaving practically no trace behind."

Only a few sleeping servants were about as we descended the marble stairs to the lobby of the hotel where Weymouth was awaiting us.

"I have a cab outside from the Yard," he said. "I came straight here to fetch you before going on to Half-Moon Street."

"Quite right!" snapped Smith; "but you are sure the cab is from the Yard? I have had painful experience of strange cabs recently!"

"You can trust this one," said Weymouth, smiling slightly. "It has carried me to the scene of many a crime."

"Hem!" said Smith--"a dubious recommendation."

We entered the waiting vehicle and soon were passing through the nearly deserted streets of London. Only those workers whose toils began with the dawn were afoot at that early hour, and in the misty gray light the streets had an unfamiliar look and wore an aspect of sadness in ill accord with the sentiments which now were stirring within me. For whatever might be the fate of the famous mental specialist, whatever the mystery before us--even though Dr. Fu-Manchu himself, malignantly active, threatened our safety--Kâramaneh would be with me again that day--Kâramaneh, my beautiful wife to be!

So selfishly occupied was I with these reflections that I paid little heed to the words of Weymouth, who was acquainting Nayland Smith with the facts bearing upon the mysterious disappearance of Sir Baldwin Frazer. Indeed, I was almost entirely ignorant upon the subject when the cab pulled up before the surgeon's house in Half-Moon Street.

Here, where all else spoke of a city yet sleeping or but newly awakened, was wild unrest and excitement. Several servants were hovering about the hall eager to glean any scrap of information that might be obtainable; wide-eyed and curious, if not a little fearful. In the somber dining-room with its heavy oak furniture and gleaming silver, Sir Baldwin's secretary awaited us. He was a young man, fair-haired, clean-shaven and alert; but a real and ever-present anxiety could be read in his eyes.

"I am sorry," he began, "to have been the cause of disturbing you at so early an hour, particularly since this mysterious affair may prove to have no connection with the matters which I understand are at present engaging your attention."

Nayland Smith raised his hand deprecatingly.

"We are prepared, Mr. Logan," he replied, "to travel to the uttermost ends of the earth at all times, if by doing so we can obtain even a meager clue to the enigma which baffles us."

"I should not have disturbed Mr. Smith," said Weymouth, "if I had not been pretty sure that there was Chinese devilry at work here: nor should I have told you as much as I have, Mr. Logan," he added, a humorous twinkle creeping into his blue eyes, "if I had thought you could not be of use to us in unraveling our case!"

"I quite understand that," said Logan, "and now, since you have voted for the story first and refreshments afterward, let me tell you what little I know of the matter."

"Be as brief as you can," snapped Nayland Smith, starting up from the chair in which he had been seated and beginning restlessly to pace the floor before the open fireplace--"as brief as is consistent with clarity. We have learnt in the past that an hour or less sometimes means the difference between----"

He paused, glancing at Sir Baldwin's secretary.

"Between life and death," he added.

Mr. Logan started perceptibly.

"You alarm me, Mr. Smith," he declared; "for I can conceive of no earthly manner in which this mysterious Eastern organization of which Inspector Weymouth speaks, could profit by the death of Sir Baldwin."

Nayland Smith suddenly turned and stared grimly at the speaker.

"I call it death," he said harshly, "to be carried off to the interior of China, to be made a mere slave, having no will but the great and evil man who already--already, mark you!--has actually accomplished such things."

"But Sir Baldwin----"

"Sir Baldwin Frazer," snapped Smith, "is the undisputed head of his particular branch of surgery. Dr. Fu-Manchu may have what he deems useful employment for such skill as his. But," glancing at the clock, "we are wasting time. Your story, Mr. Logan."

"It was about half-past twelve last night," began the secretary, closing his eyes as if he were concentrating his mind upon certain past events, "when a woman came here and inquired for Sir Baldwin. The butler informed her that Sir Baldwin was entertaining friends and that he could receive no professional visitors until the morning. She was so insistent, however, absolutely declining to go away, that I was sent for--I have rooms in the house--and I came down to interview her in the library."

"Be very accurate, Mr. Logan," interrupted Smith, "in your description of this visitor."

"I shall do my best," pursued Logan, closing his eyes again in concentrated thought. "She wore evening dress, of a fantastic kind, markedly Oriental in character, and had large gold rings in her ears. A green embroidered shawl, with raised figures of white birds as a design, took the place of a cloak. It was certainly of Eastern workmanship, possibly Arab; and she wore it about her shoulders with one corner thrown over her head-- again, something like a *burnous*. She was extremely dark, had jet-black, frizzy hair and very remarkable eyes, the finest of their type I have ever seen. She possessed beauty of a sort, of course, but without being exactly vulgar, it was what I may term *ostentatious;* and as I entered the library I found myself at a loss to define her exact place in society--you understand what I mean?"

We all nodded comprehendingly and awaited with intense interest the resumption of the story. Mr. Logan had vividly described the Eurasian Zarmi, the creature of Dr. Fu-Manchu.

"When the woman addressed me," he continued, "my surmise that she was some kind of half-caste, probably a Eurasian, was confirmed by her broken English. I shall not be misunderstood"--a slight embarrassment became perceptible in his manner--"if I say that the visitor quite openly tried to bewitch me; and since we are all human, you will perhaps condone my conduct when I add that she succeeded, in a measure, inasmuch as I consented to speak to Sir Baldwin, although he was actually playing bridge at the time.

"Either my eloquence, or, to put it bluntly, the extraordinary fee which the woman offered, resulted in Sir Baldwin's agreeing to abandon his friends and accompany the visitor in a cab which was waiting to see the patient."

"And who was the patient?" rapped Smith.

"According to the woman's account, the patient was her mother, who had met with a street accident a week before. She gave the name of the consultant who had been called in, and who, she stated, had advised the opinion of Sir Baldwin. She represented that the matter was urgent, and that it might be necessary to perform an operation immediately in order to save the patient's life."

"But surely," I interrupted, in surprise, "Sir Baldwin did not take his instruments?"

"He took his case with him--yes," replied Logan; "for he in turn yielded to the appeals of the visitor. The very last words that I heard him speak as he left the house were to assure her that no such operation could be undertaken at such short notice in that way."

Logan paused, looking around at us a little wearily.

"And what aroused your suspicions?" said Smith.

"My suspicions were aroused at the very moment of Sir Baldwin's departure, for as I came out onto the steps with him I noticed a singular thing."

"And that was?" snapped Smith.

"Directly Sir Baldwin had entered the cab the woman got out," replied Logan with some excitement in his manner, "and reclosing the door took her seat beside the driver of the vehicle--which immediately moved off."

Nayland Smith glanced significantly at me.

"The cab trick again, Petrie!" he said; "scarcely a doubt of it." Then, to Logan: "Anything else?"

"This," replied the secretary: "I thought, although I could not be sure, that the face of Sir Baldwin peered out of the window for a moment as the cab moved away from the house, and that there was strange expression upon it, almost a look of horror. But of course as there was no light in the cab and the only illumination was that from the open door, I could not be sure."

"And now tell Mr. Smith," said Weymouth, "how you got confirmation of your fears."

"I felt very uneasy in my mind," continued Logan, "for the whole thing was so irregular, and I could not rid my memory of the idea of Sir Baldwin's face looking out from the cab window. Therefore I rang up the consultant whose name our visitor had mentioned."

"Yes?" cried Smith eagerly.

"He knew nothing whatever of the matter," said Logan, "and had no such case upon his books! That of course put me in a dreadful state of mind, but I was naturally anxious to avoid making a fool of myself and therefore I waited for some hours before mentioning my suspicions to any one. But when the morning came and no message was received I determined to communicate with Scotland Yard. The rest of the mystery it is for you, gentlemen, to unravel."

CHAPTER XVI

I TRACK ZARMI

"WHAT DOES IT MEAN?" said Nayland Smith wearily, looking at me through the haze of tobacco smoke which lay between us. "A well-known man like Sir Baldwin Frazer is decoyed away--undoubtedly by the woman Zarmi; and up to the present moment not so much as a trace of him can be found. It is mortifying to think that with all the facilities of New Scotland Yard at our disposal we cannot trace that damnable cab! We cannot find the headquarters of the group--we cannot *move!* To sit here inactive whilst Sir Baldwin Frazer--God knows for what purpose!-- is perhaps being smuggled out of the country, is maddening--maddening!" Then, glancing quickly across to me: "To think ..."

I rose from my chair, head averted. A tragedy had befallen me which completely overshadowed all other affairs, great and small. Indeed, its poignancy was not yet come to its most acute stage; the news was too recent for that. It had numbed my mind; dulled the pulsing life within me.

The s.s. *Nicobar*, of the Oriental Navigation Line, had arrived at Tilbury at the scheduled time. My heart leaping joyously in my bosom, I had hurried on board to meet Kâramaneh....

I have sustained some cruel blows in my life; but I can state with candor that this which now befell me was by far the greatest and the most crushing I had ever been called upon to bear; a calamity dwarfing all others which I could imagine.

She had left the ship at Southampton--and had vanished completely.

"Poor old Petrie," said Smith, and clapped his hands upon my shoulders in his impulsive sympathetic way. "Don't give up hope! We are not going to be beaten!"

"Smith," I interrupted bitterly, "what chance have we? what chance have we? We know no more than a child unborn where these people have their hiding-place, and we haven't a shadow of a clue to guide us to it."

His hands resting upon my shoulders and his gray eyes looking straightly into mine.

"I can only repeat, old man," said my friend, "don't abandon hope. I must leave you for an hour or so, and, when I return, possibly I may have some news."

For long enough after Smith's departure I sat there, companioned only by wretched reflections; then, further inaction seemed impossible; to move, to be up and doing, to be seeking, questing, became an imperative necessity. Muffled in a heavy traveling coat I went out into the wet and dismal night, having no other plan in mind than that of walking on through the rain-swept streets, on and always on, in an attempt, vain enough, to escape from the deadly thoughts that pursued me.

Without having the slightest idea that I had done so, I must have walked along the Strand, crossed Trafalgar Square, proceeded up the Haymarket to Piccadilly Circus, and commenced to trudge along at the Oriental rugs displayed in Messrs. Liberty's window, when an incident aroused me from the apathy of sorrow in which I was sunken.

"Tell the cab feller to drive to the north side of Wandsworth Common," said a woman's voice--a voice speaking in broken English, a voice which electrified me, had me alert and watchful in a moment.

I turned, as the speaker, entering a taxi-cab that was drawn up by the pavement, gave these directions to the door-porter, who with open umbrella was in attendance. Just one glimpse I had of her as she stepped into the cab, but it was sufficient. Indeed, the voice had been sufficient; but that sinuous shape and that lithe swaying movement of the hips removed all doubt.

It was Zarmi!

As the cab moved off I ran out into the middle of the road, where there was a rank, and sprang into the first taxi waiting there.

"Follow the cab ahead!" I cried to the man, my voice quivering with excitement. "Look! you can see the number! There can be no mistake. But don't lose it for your life! It's worth a sovereign to you!"

The man, warming to my mood, cranked his engine rapidly and sprang to the wheel. I was wild with excitement now, and fearful lest the cab ahead should have disappeared; but fortune seemingly was with me for once, and I was not twenty yards behind when Zarmi's cab turned the first corner ahead. Through the gloomy street, which appeared to be populated solely by streaming umbrellas, we went. I could scarcely keep my seat; every nerve in my body seemed to be dancing--twitching. Eternally I was peering ahead; and when, leaving the well-lighted West End thoroughfares, we came to the comparatively gloomy streets of the suburbs, a hundred times I thought we had lost the track. But always in the pool of light cast by some friendly lamp, I would see the quarry again speeding on before us.

At a lonely spot bordering the common the vehicle which contained Zarmi stopped. I snatched up the speaking-tube.

"Drive on," I cried, "and pull up somewhere beyond! Not too far!"

The man obeyed, and presently I found myself standing in what was now become a steady downpour, looking back at the headlights of the other cab. I gave the driver his promised reward.

"Wait for ten minutes," I directed; "then if I have not returned, you need wait no longer."

I strode along the muddy, unpaved path, to the spot where the cab, now discharged, was being slowly backed away into the road. The figure of Zarmi, unmistakable by reason of the lithe carriage, was crossing in the direction of a path which seemingly led across the common. I followed at a discreet distance. Realizing the tremendous potentialities of this rencontre I seemed to rise to the occasion; my brain became alert and clear; every faculty was at its brightest. And I felt serenely confident of my ability to make the most of the situation.

Zarmi went on and on along the lonely path. Not another pedestrian was in sight, and the rain walled in the pair of us. Where comfort-loving humanity sought shelter from the inclement weather, we two moved out there in the storm, linked by a common enmity.

I have said that my every faculty was keen, and have spoken of my confidence in my own alertness. My condition, as a matter of fact, must have been otherwise, and this belief in my powers merely symptomatic of the fever which consumed me; for, as I was to learn, I had failed to take the first elementary precaution necessary in such case. I, who tracked another, had not counted upon being tracked myself! ...

A bag or sack, reeking of some sickly perfume, was dropped silently, accurately, over my head from behind; it was drawn closely about my throat. One muffled shriek, strangely compound of fear and execration, I uttered. I was stifling, choking ... I staggered--and fell....

CHAPTER XVII

I MEET DR. FU-MANCHU

MY NEXT IMPRESSION was of a splitting headache, which, as memory remounted its throne, brought up a train of recollections. I found myself to be seated upon a heavy wooden bench set flat against a wall, which was covered with a kind of straw matting. My hands were firmly tied behind me. In the first agony of that reawakening I became aware of two things.

I was in an operating-room, for the most conspicuous item of its furniture was an operating-table! Shaded lamps were suspended above it; and instruments, antiseptics, dressings, etc., were arranged upon a glass-topped table beside it. Secondly, I had a companion.

Seated upon a similar bench on the other side of the room, was a heavily built man, his dark hair splashed with gray, as were his short, neatly trimmed beard and mustache. He, too, was pinioned; and he stared across the table with a glare in which a sort of stupefied wonderment predominated, but which was not free from terror.

It was Sir Baldwin Frazer!

"Sir Baldwin!" I muttered, moistening my parched lips with my tongue-- "Sir Baldwin!--how----"

"It is Dr. Petrie, is it not?" he said, his voice husky with emotion. "Dr. Petrie!--my dear sir, in mercy tell me--what does this mean? I have been kidnaped--drugged; made the victim of an inconceivable outrage at the very door of my own house...."

I stood up unsteadily.

"Sir Baldwin," I interrupted, "you ask me what it means. It means that we are in the hands of Dr. Fu-Manchu!"

Sir Baldwin stared at me wildly; his face was white and drawn with anxiety.

"Dr. Fu-Manchu!" he said; "but my dear sir, this name conveys nothing to me--nothing!" His manner momentarily was growing more distrait. "Since my captivity began I have been given the use of a singular suite of rooms in this place, and received, I must confess, every possible attention. I have been waited upon by the she-devil who lured me here, but not one word other than a species of coarse badinage has she spoken to me. At times I have been tempted to believe that the fate which frequently befalls the specialist had befallen me? You understand?"

"I quite understand," I replied dully. "There have been times in the past when I, too, have doubted my sanity in my dealings with the group who now hold us in their power."

"But," reiterated the other, his voice rising higher and higher, "what does it mean, my dear sir? It is incredible--fantastic! Even now I find it difficult to disabuse my mind of that old, haunting idea."

"Disabuse it at once, Sir Baldwin," I said bitterly. "The facts are as you see them; the explanation, at any rate in your own case, is quite beyond me. I was tracked ..."

"Hush! some one is coming!"

We both turned and stared at an opening before which hung a sort of gaudily embroidered mat, as the sound of dragging footsteps, accompanied by a heavy tapping, announced the approach of *some one*.

The mat was pulled aside by Zarmi. She turned her head, flashing around the apartment a glance of her black eyes, then held the drapery aside to admit the entrance of another....

Supporting himself by the aid of two heavy walking sticks and painfully dragging his gaunt frame along, *Dr. Fu-Manchu entered!*

I think I have never experienced in my life a sensation identical to that which now possessed me. Although Nayland Smith had declared that Fu-Manchu was alive, yet I would have sworn upon oath before any jury summonable that he was dead; for with my own eyes I had seen the bullet enter his skull. Now, whilst I crouched against the matting-covered wall, teeth tightly clenched and my very hair quivering upon my scalp, he dragged himself laboriously across the room, the sticks going *tap--tap--tap* upon the floor, and the tall body, enveloped in a yellow robe, bent grotesquely, gruesomely, with every effort which he made. He wore a surgical bandage about his skull and its presence seemed to accentuate the height of the great domelike brow, to throw into more evil prominence the wonderful, Satanic countenance of the man. His filmed eyes turning to right and left, he dragged himself to a wooden chair that stood beside the operating-table and sank down upon it, breathing sibilantly, exhaustedly.

Zarmi dropped the curtain and stood before it. She had discarded the dripping overall which she had been wearing when I had followed her across the common, and now stood before me with her black, frizzy hair unconfined and her beautiful, wicked face uplifted in a sort of cynical triumph. The big gold rings in her ears glittered strangely in the light of the electric lamps. She wore a garment which looked like a silken shawl wrapped about her in a wildly picturesque fashion, and, her hands upon her hips, leant back against the curtain glancing defiantly from Sir Baldwin to myself.

Those moments of silence which followed the entrance of the Chinese Doctor live in my memory and must live there for ever. Only the labored breathing of Fu-Manchu disturbed the stillness of the place. Not a sound penetrated to the room, no one uttered a word; then--

"Sir Baldwin Frazer." began Fu-Manchu in that indescribable voice, alternating between the sibilant and the guttural, "you were promised a certain fee for your services by my servant who summoned you. It shall be paid and the gift of my personal gratitude be added to it."

He turned himself with difficulty to address Sir Baldwin; and it became apparent to me that he was almost completely paralyzed down one side of his body. Some little use he could make of his hand and arm, for he still clutched the heavy carven stick, but the right side of his face was completely immobile; and rarely had I seen anything more ghastly than the effect produced upon that wonderful, Satanic countenance. The mouth, from the center of the thin lips, opened only to the left, as he spoke; in a word, seen in profile from where I sat, or rather crouched, it was the face of a dead man.

Sir Baldwin Frazer uttered no word, but, crouching upon the bench even as I crouched, stared--horror written upon every lineament--at Dr. Fu-Manchu. The latter continued:--

"Your experience, Sir Baldwin, will enable you readily to diagnose my symptoms. Owing to the passage of a bullet along a portion of the third left frontal into the postero-parietal convolution--upon which, from its lodgment in the skull, it continues to press--hemiplegia of the right side has supervened. Aphasia is present also...."

The effort of speech was ghastly. Beads of perspiration dewed Fu-Manchu's brow, and I marveled at the iron will of the man, whereby alone he forced his half-numbed brain to perform its function. He seemed to select his words elaborately and by this monstrous effort of will to compel his partially paralyzed tongue to utter them. Some of the syllables were slurred; but nevertheless distinguishable. It was a demonstration of sheer *Force* unlike any I had witnessed, and it impressed me unforgettably.

"The removal of this injurious particle," he continued, "would be an operation which I myself could undertake to perform successfully upon another. It is a matter of some delicacy as you, Sir Baldwin, and"-- slowly, horribly, turning the half-dead and half-living head towards me--"you, Dr. Petrie, will appreciate. In the event of clumsy surgery, death may supervene; failing this, permanent hemiplegia--or"--the film lifted from the green eyes, and for a moment they flickered with transient horror--"idiocy! Any one of three of my pupils whom I might name could perform this operation with ease, but their services are not available. Only one English surgeon occurred to me in this connection, and you, Sir Baldwin"--again he slowly turned his head-- "were he. Dr. Petrie will act as anaesthetist, and, your duties completed, you shall return to your home richer by the amount stipulated. I have suitably prepared myself for the operation, and I can assure you of the soundness of my heart. I may advise you, Dr. Petrie"--again turning to me-- "that my constitution is inured to the use of opium. You will make due allowance for this. Mr. Li-King-Su, a graduate of Canton, will act as dresser."

He turned laboriously to Zarmi. She clapped her hands and held the curtain aside. A perfectly immobile Chinaman, whose age I was unable to guess, and who wore a white overall, entered, bowed composedly to Frazer and myself and began in a matter-of-fact way to prepare the dressings.

CHAPTER XVIII
QUEEN OF HEARTS

"SIR BALDWIN FRAZER," said Fu-Manchu, interrupting a wild outburst from the former, "your refusal is dictated by insufficient knowledge of your surroundings. You find yourself in a place strange to you, a place to which no clue can lead your friends; in the absolute power of a man--myself--who knows no law other than his own and that of those associated with him. Virtually, Sir Baldwin, you stand in China; and in China we know how to *exact* obedience. You will not refuse, for Dr. Petrie will tell you something of my *wire-jackets* and my *files*...."

I saw Sir Baldwin Frazer blanch. He could not know what I knew of the significance of those words--"my wire-jackets, my files"--but perhaps something of my own horror communicated itself to him.

"You will not *refuse*" continued Fu-Manchu softly; "my only fear for you is that the operation my prove unsuccessful! In that event not even my own great clemency could save you, for by virtue of your failure I should be powerless to intervene." He paused for some moments, staring directly at the surgeon. "There are those within sound of my voice," he added sibilantly, "who would flay you alive in the lamentable event of your failure, who would cast your flayed body"--he paused, waving one quivering fist above his head, "to the rats--to the rats!"

Sir Baldwin's forehead was bathed in perspiration now. It was an incredible and a gruesome situation, a nightmare become reality. But, whatever my own case, I could see that Sir Baldwin Frazer was convinced, I could see that his consent would no longer be withheld.

"You, my dear friend," said Fu-Manchu, turning to me and resuming his studied and painful composure of manner, "will also consent...."

Within my heart of hearts I could not doubt him; I knew that my courage was not of a quality high enough to sustain the frightful ordeals summoned up before my imagination by those words--"my files, my wire-jackets!"

"In the event, however, of any little obstinancy," he added, "another will plead with you."

A chill like that of death descended upon me--as, for the second time, Zarmi clapped her hands, pulled the curtain aside ... and Kâramaneh was thrust into the room!

There comes a blank in my recollections. Long after Kâramaneh had been plucked out again by the two muscular brown hands which clutched her shoulders from the darkness beyond the doorway, I seemed to see her standing there, in her close-fitting traveling dress. Her hair was unbound, disheveled, her lovely face pale to the lips--and her eyes, her glorious, terror-bright eyes, looked fully into mine....

Not a word did she utter, and I was stricken dumb as one who has plucked the Flower of Silence. Only those wondrous eyes seemed to look into my soul, searing, consuming me.

Fu-Manchu had been speaking for some time ere my brain began again to record his words.

"----and this magnanimity," came dully to my ears, "extends to you, Dr. Petrie, because of my esteem. I have little cause to love Kâramaneh"--his voice quivered furiously--"but she can yet be of use to me, and I would not harm a hair of her beautiful head--except in the event of your obstinacy. Shall we then determine your immediate future upon the turn of a card, as the gamester within me, within every one of my race, suggests?

"Yes, yes!" came hoarsely.

I fought mentally to restore myself to a full knowledge of what was happening, and I realized that the last words had come from the lips of Sir Baldwin Frazer.

"Dr. Petrie," Frazer said, still in the same hoarse and unnatural voice, "what else can we do? At least take the chance of recovering your freedom, for how otherwise can you hope to serve--your friend...."

"God knows!" I said dully; "do as you wish"--and cared not to what I had agreed.

Plunging his hand beneath his white overall, the Chinaman who had been referred to as Li-King-Su calmly produced a pack of cards, unemotionally shuffled them and extended the pack to me.

I shook my head grimly, for my hands were tied. Picking up a lancet from the table, the Chinaman cut the cords which bound me, and again extended the pack. I took a card and laid it on my knee without even glancing at it. Fu-Manchu, with his left hand, in turn selected a card, looked at it and then turned its face towards me.

"It would seem, Dr. Petrie," he said calmly, "that you are fated to remain here as my guest. You will have the felicity of residing beneath the same roof with Kâramaneh."

The card was the Knave of Diamonds.

Conscious of a sudden excitement, I snatched up the card from my knee. It was the Queen of Hearts! For a moment I tasted exultation, then I tossed it upon the floor. I was not fool enough to suppose that the Chinese Doctor would pay his debt of honor and release me.

"Your star above mine," said Fu-Manchu, his calm unruffled. "I place myself in your hands, Sir Baldwin."

Assisted by his unemotional compatriot, Fu-Manchu discarded the yellow robe, revealing himself in a white singlet in all his gaunt ugliness, and extended his frame upon the operating-table.

Li-King-Su ignited the large lamp over the head of the table, and from his case took out a trephine.

"Other points for your guidance from my own considerable store of experience"--Fu-Manchu was speaking--"are written out clearly in the notebook which lies upon the table...."

His voice, now, was toneless, emotionless, as though his part in the critical operation about to be performed were that of a spectator. No trace of nervousness, of fear, could I discern; his pulse was practically normal.

How I shuddered as I touched his yellow skin! how my very soul rose up in revolt! ...

"There is the bullet!--quick! ... Steady, Petrie!"

Sir Baldwin Frazer, keen, cool, deft, was metamorphosed, was the enthusiastic, brilliant surgeon whom I knew and revered, and another than the nerveless captive who, but a few minutes ago, had stared, panic-stricken, at Dr. Fu-Manchu.

Although I had met him once or twice professionally, I had never hitherto seen him operate; and his method was little short of miraculous. It was stimulating, inspiring. With unerring touch he whittled madness, death, from the very throne of reason, of life.

Now was the crucial moment of his task ... and, with its coming, every light in the room suddenly failed--went out!

"My God!" whispered Frazer, in the darkness, "quick! quick! lights! a match!--a candle!--something, anything!"

There came a faint click, and a beam of white light was directed, steadily, upon the patient's skull. Li-King-Su--unmoved--held an electric torch in his hand!

Frazer and I set to work, in a fierce battle to fend off Death, who already outstretched his pinions over the insensible man--to fend off Death from the arch-murderer, the enemy of the white races, who lay there at our mercy! ...

"It seems you want a pick-me-up!" said Zarmi. Sir Baldwin Frazer collapsed into the cane arm-chair. Only a matting curtain separated us from the room wherein he had successfully performed perhaps the most wonderful operation of his career.

"I could not have lasted out another thirty seconds, Petrie!" he whispered. "The events which led up to it had exhausted my nerves and I had no reserve to call upon. If that last ..."

He broke off, the sentence uncompleted, and eagerly seized the tumbler containing brandy and soda, which the beautiful, wicked-eyed Eurasian passed to him. She turned, and prepared a drink for me, with the insolent *insouciance* which had never deserted her.

I emptied the tumbler at a draught.

Even as I set the glass down I realized, too late, that it was the first drink I had ever permitted to pass my lips within an abode of Dr. Fu-Manchu....

I started to my feet.

"Frazer!" I muttered--"we've been drugged! we ..."

"You sit down," came Zarmi's husky voice, and I felt her hands upon my breast, pushing me back into my seat. "You very tired ... you go to sleep...."

"Petrie! Dr. Petrie!"

The words broke in through the curtain of unconsciousness. I strove to arouse myself. I felt cold and wet. I opened my eyes--and the world seemed to be swimming dizzily about me. Then a hand grasped my arm, roughly.

"Brace up! Brace up, Petrie--and thank God you are alive! ..."

I was sitting beside Sir Baldwin Frazer on a wooden bench, under a leafless tree, from the ghostly limbs whereof rain trickled down upon me! In the gray light, which, I thought, must be the light of dawn, I discerned other trees about us and an open expanse, tree-dotted, stretching into the misty grayness.

"Where are we?" I muttered--"where ..."

"Unless I am greatly mistaken," replied my bedraggled companion, "and I don't think I am, for I attended a consultation in this neighborhood less than a week ago, we somewhere on the west side of Wandsworth Common!"

He ceased speaking; then uttered a suppressed cry. There came a jangling of coins, and dimly I saw him to be staring at a canvas bag of money which he held.

"Merciful heavens!" he said, "am I mad--or did I *really* perform that operation? And can this be my fee? ..."

I laughed loudly, wildly, plunging my wet, cold hands into the pockets of my rain-soaked overcoat. In one of them, my fingers came in contact with a piece of cardboard. It had an unfamiliar feel, and I pulled it out, peering at it in the dim light.

"Well, I'm damned!" muttered Frazer--"then I'm not mad, after all!"

It was the Queen of Hearts!

CHAPTER XIX

"ZAGAZIG"

FULLY TWO WEEKS elapsed before Nayland Smith's arduous labors at last met with a slight reward. For a moment, the curtain of mystery surrounding the Si-Fan was lifted, and we had a glimpse of that organization's elaborate mechanism. I cannot better commence my relation of the episodes associated with the Zagazig's cryptogram than from the moment when I found myself bending over a prostrate form extended upon the table in the Inspector's room at the River Police Depôt. It was that of a man who looked like a Lascar, who wore an ill-fitting slop-shop suit of blue, soaked and stained and clinging hideously to his body. His dank black hair was streaked upon his low brow; and his face, although it was notable for a sort of evil leer, had assumed in death another and more dreadful expression.

Asphyxiation had accounted for his end beyond doubt, but there were marks about his throat of clutching fingers, his tongue protruded, and the look in the dead eyes was appalling.

"He was amongst the piles upholding the old wharf at the back of the Joy-Shop?" said Smith tersely, turning to the police officer in charge.

"Exactly" was the reply. "The in-coming tide had jammed him right up under a cross-beam."

"What time was that?'

"Well, at high tide last night. Hewson, returning with the ten o'clock boat, noticed the moonlight glittering upon the knife."

The knife to which the Inspector referred possessed a long curved blade of a kind with which I had become terribly familiar in the past. The dead man still clutched the hilt of the weapon in his right hand, and it now lay with the blade resting crosswise upon his breast. I stared in a fascinated way at this mysterious and tragic flotsam of old Thames.

Glancing up, I found Nayland Smith's gray eyes watching me.

"You see the mark, Petrie?" he snapped.

I nodded. The dead man upon the table was a Burmese dacoit!

"What do you make of it?" I said slowly.

"At the moment," replied Smith, "I scarcely know what to make of it. You are agreed with the divisional surgeon that the man--unquestionably a dacoit--died, not from drowning, but from strangulation. From evidence we have heard, it would appear that the encounter which resulted in the body being hurled in the river, actually took place upon the wharf-end beneath which he was found. And we know that a place formerly used by the Si-Fan group--in other words, by Dr. Fu-Manchu-- adjoins the wharf. I am tempted to believe that this"--he nodded towards the ghastly and sinister object upon the table--"was a servant of the Chinese Doctor. In other words, we see before us one whom Fu-Manchu has rebuked for some shortcoming."

I shuddered coldly. Familiar as I should have been with the methods of the dread Chinaman, with his callous disregard of human suffering, of human life, of human law, I could not reconcile my ideas--the ideas of a modern, ordinary middle-class practitioner--with these Far Eastern devilries which were taking place in London.

Even now I sometimes found myself doubting the reality of the whole thing; found myself reviewing the history of the Eastern doctor and of the horrible group of murderers surrounding him, with an incredulity almost unbelievable in one who had been actually in contact not only with the servants of the Chinaman, but with the sinister Fu-Manchu himself. Then, to restore me to grips with reality, would come the thought of Kâramaneh, of the beautiful girl whose love had brought me seemingly endless sorrow and whose love for me had brought her once again into the power of that mysterious, implacable being.

This thought was enough. With its coming, fantasy vanished; and I knew that the dead dacoit, his great curved knife yet clutched in his hand, the Yellow menace hanging over London, over England, over the civilized world, the absence, the heart-breaking absence, of Kâramaneh--all were real, all were true, all were part of my life.

Nayland Smith was standing staring vaguely before him and tugging at the lobe of his left ear.

"Come along!" he snapped suddenly. "We have no more to learn here: the clue to the mystery must be sought elsewhere."

There was that in his manner whereby I knew that his thoughts were far away, as we filed out from the River Police Depôt to the cab which awaited us. Pulling from his overcoat pocket a copy of a daily paper--

"Have you seen this, Weymouth?" he demanded.

With a long, nervous index finger he indicated a paragraph on the front page which appeared under the heading of "Personal." Weymouth bent frowningly over the paper, holding it close to his eyes, for this was a gloomy morning and the light in the cab was poor.

"Such things don't enter into my sphere, Mr. Smith," he replied, "but no doubt the proper department at the Yard have seen it."

"I *know* they have seen it!" snapped Smith; "but they have also been unable to read it!"

Weymouth looked up in surprise.

"Indeed," he said. "You are interested in this, then?"

"Very! Have you any suggestion to offer respecting it?"

Moving from my seat I, also, bent over the paper and read, in growing astonishment, the following:--

ZAGAZIG-Z,-a-g-a;-z:-*I*-g,a,-a,ag-*a,z*;- I;-g:z-a-g-A-z;i-:g;-Z,,-a;-gg-_-z-i;- G;-z-,a-g-:a-Z_*I*;-g:-z-a-g;-a-:Z-,i-g: z,a-g,-a:z,i-g.

"This is utterly incomprehensible! It can be nothing but some foolish practical joke! It consists merely of the word 'Zagazig' repeated six or seven times--which can have no possible significance!"

"Can't it!" snapped Smith.

"Well," I said, "what has Zagazig to do with Fu-Manchu, or to do with us?"

"Zagazig, my dear Petrie, is a very unsavory Arab town in Lower Egypt, as you know!"

He returned the paper to the pocket of his over-coat, and, noting my bewildered glance, burst into one of his sudden laughs.

"You think I am talking nonsense," he said; "but, as a matter of fact, that message in the paper has been puzzling me since it appeared--yesterday morning--and at last I think I see the light."

He pulled out his pipe and began rapidly to load it.

"I have been growing careless of late, Petrie," he continued; and no hint of merriment remained in his voice. His gaunt face was drawn grimly, and his eyes glittered like steel. "In future I must avoid going out alone at night as much as possible."

Inspector Weymouth was staring at Smith in a puzzled way; and certainly I was every whit as mystified as he.

"I am disposed to believe," said my friend, in his rapid, incisive way, "that the dacoit met his end at the hands of a tall man, possibly dark and almost certainly clean-shaven. If this missing personage wears, on chilly nights, a long tweed traveling coat and affects soft gray hats of the Stetson pattern, I shall not be surprised."

Weymouth stared at me in frank bewilderment.

"By the way, Inspector," added Smith, a sudden gleam of inspiration entering his keen eyes--"did I not see that the s.s. *Andaman* arrived recently?"

"The Oriental Navigation Company's boat?" inquired Weymouth in a hopeless tone. "Yes. She docked yesterday evening."

"If Jack Forsyth is still chief officer, I shall look him up," declared Smith. "You recall his brother, Petrie?"

"Naturally; since he was done to death in my presence," I replied; for the words awoke memories of one of Dr. Fu-Manchu's most ghastly crimes, always associated in my mind with the cry of a night-hawk.

"The divine afflatus should never be neglected," announced Nayland Smith didactically, "wild though its promptings may seem."

CHAPTER XX

THE NOTE ON THE DOOR

I SAW LITTLE of Nayland Smith for the remainder of that day. Presumably he was following those "promptings" to which he had referred, though I was unable to conjecture whither they were leading him. Then, towards dusk he arrived in a perfect whirl, figuratively sweeping me off my feet.

"Get your coat on, Petrie!" he cried; "you forget that we have a most urgent appointment!"

Beyond doubt I had forgotten that we had any appointment whatever that evening, and some surprise must have shown upon my face, for--

"Really you are becoming very forgetful!" my friend continued. "You know we can no longer trust the 'phone. I have to leave certain instructions for Weymouth at the rendezvous!"

There was a hidden significance in his manner, and, my memory harking back to an adventure which we had shared in the past, I suddenly glimpsed the depths of my own stupidity.

He suspected the presence of an eavesdropper! Yes! incredible though it might appear, we were spied upon in the New Louvre; agents of the Si-Fan, of Dr. Fu-Manchu, were actually within the walls of the great hotel!

We hurried out into the corridor, and descended by the lift to the lobby. M. Samarkan, long famous as *maître d'hôtel* of one of Cairo's fashionable *khans*, and now principal of the New Louvre, greeted us with true Greek courtesy. He trusted that we should be present at some charitable function or other to be held at the hotel on the following evening.

"If possible, M. Samarkan--if possible," said Smith. "We have many demands upon our time." Then, abruptly, to me: "Come, Petrie, we will walk as far as Charing Cross and take a cab from the rank there."

"The hall-porter can call you a cab," said M. Samarkan, solicitous for the comfort of his guests.

"Thanks," snapped Smith; "we prefer to walk a little way."

Passing along the Strand, he took my arm, and speaking close to my ear--

"That place is alive with spies, Petrie," he said; "or if there are only a few of them they are remarkably efficient!"

Not another word could I get from him, although I was eager enough to talk; since one dearer to me than all else in the world was in the hands of the damnable organization we knew as the Si-Fan; until, arrived at Charing Cross, he walked out to the cab rank, and--

"Jump in!" he snapped.

He opened the door of the first cab on the rank.

"Drive to J---- Street, Kennington," he directed the man.

In something of a mental stupor I entered and found myself seated beside Smith. The cab made off towards Trafalgar Square, then swung around into Whitehall.

"Look behind!" cried Smith, intense excitement expressed in his voice-- "look behind!"

I turned and peered through the little square window.

The cab which had stood second upon the rank was closely following us!

"We are tracked!" snapped my companion. "If further evidence were necessary of the fact that our every movement is watched, here it is!"

I turned to him, momentarily at a loss for words; then--

"Was this the object of our journey?" I said. "Your reference to a 'rendezvous' was presumably addressed to a hypothetical spy?"

"Partly," he replied. "I have a plan, as you will see in a moment."

I looked again from the window in the rear of the cab. We were now passing between the House of Lords and the back of Westminster Abbey ... and fifty yards behind us the pursuing cab was crossing from Whitehall! A great excitement grew up within me, and a great curiosity respecting the identity of our pursuer.

"What is the place for which we are bound, Smith?" I said rapidly.

"It is a house which I chanced to notice a few days ago, and I marked it as useful for such a purpose as our present one. You will see what I mean when we arrive."

On we went, following the course of the river, then turned over Vauxhall Bridge and on down Vauxhall Bridge Road into a very dreary neighborhood where gasometers formed the notable feature of the landscape.

"That's the Oval just beyond," said Smith suddenly, "and--here we are."

In a narrow *cul de sac* which apparently communicated with the boundary of the famous cricket ground, the cabman pulled up. Smith jumped out and paid the fare.

"Pull back to that court with the iron posts," he directed the man, "and wait there for me." Then: "Come on, Petrie!" he snapped.

Side by side we entered the wooden gate of a small detached house, or more properly cottage, and passed up the tiled path towards a sort of side entrance which apparently gave access to the tiny garden. At this moment I became aware of two things; the first, that the house was an empty one, and the second, that some one--some one who had quitted the second cab (which I had heard pull up at no great distance behind us) was approaching stealthily along the dark and uninviting street, walking upon the opposite pavement and taking advantage of the shadow of a high wooden fence which skirted it for some distance.

Smith pushed the gate open, and I found myself in a narrow passageway in almost complete darkness. But my friend walked confidently forward, turned the angle of the building and entered the miniature wilderness which once had been a garden.

"In here, Petrie!" he whispered.

He seized me by the arm, pushed open a door and thrust me forward down two stone steps into absolute darkness.

"Walk straight ahead!" he directed, still in the same intense whisper, "and you will find a locked door having a broken panel. Watch through the opening for any one who may enter the room beyond, but see that your presence is not detected. Whatever I say or do, don't stir until I actually rejoin you."

He stepped back across the floor and was gone. One glimpse I had of him, silhouetted against the faint light of the open door, then the door was gently closed, and I was left alone in the empty house.

Smith's methods frequently surprised me, but always in the past I had found that they were dictated by sound reasons. I had no doubt that an emergency unknown to me dictated his present course, but it was with my mind in a wildly confused condition, that I groped for and found the door with the broken panel and that I stood there in the complete darkness of the deserted house listening.

I can well appreciate how the blind develop an unusually keen sense of hearing; for there, in the blackness, which (at first) was entirely unrelieved by any speck of light, I became aware of the fact, by dint of tense listening, that Smith was retiring by means of some gateway at the upper end of the little garden, and I became aware of the fact that a lane or court, with which this gateway communicated, gave access to the main road.

Faintly, I heard our discharged cab backing out from the *cul de sac*; then, from some nearer place, came Smith's voice speaking loudly.

"Come along, Petrie!" he cried; "there is no occasion for us to wait. Weymouth will see the note pinned on the door."

I started--and was about to stumble back across the room, when, as my mind began to work more clearly, I realized that the words had been spoken as a ruse--a favorite device of Nayland Smith's.

Rigidly I stood there, and continued to listen.

"All right, cabman!" came more distantly now; "back to the New Louvre-- jump in, Petrie!"

The cab went rattling away ... as a faint light became perceptible in the room beyond the broken panel.

Hitherto I had been able to detect the presence of this panel only by my sense of touch and by means of a faint draught which blew through it; now it suddenly became clearly perceptible. I found myself looking into what was evidently the principal room of the house--a dreary apartment with tatters of paper hanging from the walls and litter of all sorts lying about upon the floor and in the rusty fireplace.

Some one had partly raised the front window and opened the shutters. A patch of moonlight shone down upon the floor immediately below my hiding-place and furthermore enabled me vaguely to discern the disorder of the room.

A bulky figure showed silhouetted against the dirty panes. It was that of a man who, leaning upon the window sill, was peering intently in. Silently he had approached, and silently had raised the sash and opened the shutters.

For thirty seconds or more he stood so, moving his head from right to left ... and I watched him through the broken panel, almost holding my breath with suspense. Then, fully raising the window, the man stepped into the room, and, first reclosing the shutters, suddenly flashed the light of an electric lamp all about the place. I was enabled to discern him more clearly, this mysterious spy who had tracked us from the moment that we had left the hotel.

He was a man of portly build wearing a heavy fur-lined overcoat and having a soft felt hat, the brim turned down so as to shade the upper part of his face. Moreover, he wore his fur collar turned up, which served further to disguise him, since it concealed the greater part of his chin. But the eyes which now were searching every corner of the room, the alert, dark eyes, were strangely familiar. The black mustache, the clear-cut, aquiline nose, confirmed the impression.

Our follower was M. Samarkan, manager of the New Louvre.

I suppressed a gasp of astonishment. Small wonder that our plans had leaked out. This was a momentous discovery indeed.

And as I watched the portly Greek who was not only one of the most celebrated *maîtres d'hôtel* in Europe, but also a creature of Dr. Fu-Manchu, he cast the light of his electric lamp upon a note attached by means of a drawing-pin to the inside of the room door. I immediately divined that my friend must have pinned the note in its place earlier in the day; even at that distance I recognized Smith's neat, illegible writing.

Samarkan quickly scanned the message scribbled upon the white page; then, exhibiting an agility uncommon in a man of his bulk, he threw open the shutters again, having first replaced his lamp in his pocket, climbed out into the little front garden, reclosed the window, and disappeared!

A moment I stood, lost to my surroundings, plunged in a sea of wonderment concerning the damnable organization which, its tentacles extending I knew not whither, since new and unexpected limbs were ever coming to light, sought no less a goal than Yellow dominion of the world! I reflected how one man--Nayland Smith--alone stood between this powerful group and the realization of their project ... when I was aroused by a hand grasping my arm in the darkness!

I uttered a short cry, of which I was instantly ashamed, for Nayland Smith's voice came:--

"I startled you, eh, Petrie?"

"Smith," I said, "how long have you been standing there?"

"I only returned in time to see our Fenimore Cooper friend retreating through the window," he replied; "but no doubt you had a good look at him?"

"I had!" I answered eagerly. "It was Samarkan!"

"I thought so! I have suspected as much for a long time."

"Was this the object of our visit here?"

"It was one of the objects," admitted Nayland Smith evasively.

From some place not far distant came the sound of a restarted engine.

"The other," he added, "was this: to enable M. Samarkan to read the note which I had pinned upon the door!"

CHAPTER XXI

THE SECOND MESSAGE

"HERE YOU ARE, PETRIE," said Nayland Smith--and he tossed across the table the folded copy of a morning paper. "This may assist you in your study of the first Zagazig message."

I set down my cup and turned my attention to the "Personal" column on the front page of the journal. A paragraph appeared therein conceived as follows:--

ZAGAZIG-Z-a-g-*a*;-z:-I:-*g*;z-a,g;- A-,*z;i:*G,-z:*a;g*-A,z-*i*;-gz *A*;*g*aZ-*i*;*g*-:a z i g

I stared across at my friend in extreme bewilderment.

"But, Smith!" I cried, "these messages are utterly meaningless!"

"Not at all," he rapped back. "Scotland Yard thought they were meaningless at first, and I must admit that they suggested nothing to me for a long time; but the dead dacoit was the clue to the first, Petrie, and the note pinned upon the door of the house near the Oval is the clue to the second."

Stupidly I continued to stare at him until he broke into a grim smile.

"Surely you understand?" he said. "You remember where the dead Burman was found?"

"Perfectly."

"You know the street along which, ordinarily, one would approach the wharf?"

"Three Colt Street?"

"Three Colt Street, exactly. Well, on the night that the Burman met his end I had an appointment in Three Colt Street with Weymouth. The appointment was made by 'phone, from the New Louvre! My cab broke down and I never arrived. I discovered later that Weymouth had received a telegram purporting to come from me, putting off the engagement."

"I am aware of all this!"

Nayland Smith burst into a loud laugh.

"But *still* you are fogged!" he cried. "Then I'm hanged if I'll pilot you any farther! You have all the facts before you. There lies the first Zagazig message; here is the second; and you know the context of the note pinned upon the door? It read, if you remember, 'Remove patrol from Joy-Shop neighborhood. Have a theory. Wish to visit place alone on Monday night after one o'clock.'"

"Smith," I said dully, "I have a heavy stake upon this murderous game."

His manner changed instantly; the tanned face grew grim and hard, but the steely eyes softened strangely. He bent over me, clapping his hands upon my shoulders.

"I know it, old man," he replied; "and because it may serve to keep your mind busy during hours when otherwise it would be engaged with profitless sorrows, I invite you to puzzle out this business for yourself. You have nothing else to do until late to-night, and you can work undisturbed, here, at any rate!"

His words referred to the fact that, without surrendering our suite at the New Louvre Hotel, we had gone upon a visit, of indefinite duration, to a mythical friend; and now were quartered in furnished chambers adjoining Fleet Street.

We had remained at the New Louvre long enough to secure confirmation of our belief that a creature of Fu-Manchu spied upon us there; and now we only awaited the termination of the night's affair to take such steps as Smith might consider politic in regard to the sardonic Greek who presided over London's newest and most palatial hotel.

Smith setting out for New Scotland Yard in order to make certain final arrangements in connection with the business of the night, I began closely to study the mysterious Zagazig messages, determined not to be beaten, and remembering the words of Edgar Allan Poe--the strange genius to whom we are indebted for the first workable system of deciphering cryptograms: "It may well be doubted whether human ingenuity can construct an enigma of the kind which human ingenuity may not, by proper application, resolve."

The first conclusion to which I was borne was this: that the letters comprising the word "Zagazig" were designed merely to confuse the reader, and might be neglected; since, occurring as they did in regular sequence, they could possess no significance. I became quite excited upon making the discovery that the *punctuation marks* varied in almost every case!

I immediately assumed that these constituted the cipher; and, seeking for my key-letter, *e* (that which most frequently occurs in the English language), I found the sign of a full-stop to appear more frequently than any other in the first message, namely ten times, although it only occurred thrice in the second. Nevertheless, I was hopeful ... until I discovered that in two cases it appeared three times *in succession!*

There is no word in English, nor, so far as I am aware, in any language, where this occurs, either in regard to *e* or any other letter!

That unfortunate discovery seemed so wholly to destroy the very theory upon which I relied, that I almost abandoned my investigation there and then. Indeed, I doubt if I ever should have proceeded were it not that by a piece of pure guesswork I blundered on to a clue.

I observed that certain letters, at irregularly occurring intervals, were set in capital, and I divided up the message into corresponding sections, in the hope that the capitals might indicate the commencements of words. This accomplished, I set out upon a series of guesses, basing these upon Smith's assurance that the death of the dacoit afforded a clue to the first message and the note which he (Smith) had pinned upon the door a clue to the second.

Such being my system--if I can honor my random attempts with the title--I take little credit to myself for the fortunate result. In short, I determined (although *e* twice occurred where *r* should have been!) that the first message from the thirteenth letter, onwards to the twenty-seventh (*id est:* I;g:-zagAz;i-;*g*;-Z,-a;-*g*azi;-) read:--

"*Three Colt Street.*"

Endeavoring, now, to eliminate the *e* where *r* should appear, I made another discovery. The presence of a letter in *italics* altered the value of the sign which followed it!

From that point onward the task became child's-play, and I should merely render this account tedious if I entered into further details. Both messages commenced with the name "Smith" as I early perceived, and half an hour of close study gave me the complete sentences, thus:--

1. *Smith passing Three Colt Street twelve-thirty Wednesday.*

2. *Smith going Joy-Shop after one Monday.*

The word "Zagazig" was completed, always, and did not necessarily terminate with the last letter occurring in the cryptographic message. A subsequent inspection of this curious code has enabled Nayland Smith, by a process of simple deduction, to compile the entire alphabet employed by Dr. Fu-Manchu's agent, Samarkan, in communicating with his awful superior. With a little patience, any one of my readers my achieve the same result (and I should be pleased to hear from those who succeed!).

This, then was the outcome of my labors; and although it enlightened me to some extent, I realized that I still had much to learn.

The dacoit, apparently, had met his death at the very hour when Nayland Smith should have been passing along Three Colt Street--a thoroughfare with an unsavory reputation. Who had killed him?

To-night, Samarkan advised the Chinese doctor, Smith would again be in the same dangerous neighborhood. A strange thrill of excitement swept through me. I glanced at my watch. Yes! It was time for me to repair, secretly, to my post. For I, too, had business on the borders of Chinatown to-night.

CHAPTER XXII

THE SECRET OF THE WHARF

I SAT IN the evil-smelling little room with its low, blackened ceiling, and strove to avoid making the slightest noise; but the crazy boards creaked beneath me with every movement. The moon hung low in an almost cloudless sky; for, following the spell of damp and foggy weather, a fall in temperature had taken place, and there was a frosty snap in the air to-night.

Through the open window the moonlight poured in and spilled its pure luminance upon the filthy floor; but I kept religiously within the shadows, so posted, however, that I could command an uninterrupted view of the street from the point where it crossed the creek to that where it terminated at the gates of the deserted wharf.

Above and below me the crazy building formerly known as the Joy-Shop and once the nightly resort of the Asiatic riff-raff from the docks-- was silent, save for the squealing and scuffling of the rats. The melancholy lapping of the water frequently reached my ears, and a more or less continuous din from the wharves and workshops upon the further bank of the Thames; but in the narrow, dingy streets immediately surrounding the house, quietude reigned and no solitary footstep disturbed it.

Once, looking down in the direction of the bridge, I gave a great start, for a black patch of shadow moved swiftly across the path and merged into the other shadows bordering a high wall. My heart leapt momentarily, then, in another instant, the explanation of the mystery became apparent--in the presence of a gaunt and prowling cat. Bestowing a suspicious glance upward in my direction, the animal slunk away toward the path bordering the cutting.

By a devious route amid ghostly gasometers I had crept to my post in the early dusk, before the moon was risen, and already I was heartily weary of my passive part in the affair of the night. I had never before appreciated the multitudinous sounds, all of them weird and many of them horrible, which are within the compass of those great black rats who find their way to England with cargoes from Russia and elsewhere. From the rafters above my head, from the wall recesses about me, from the floor beneath my feet, proceeded a continuous and nerve-shattering concert, an unholy symphony which seemingly accompanied the eternal dance of the rats.

Sometimes a faint splash from below would tell of one of the revelers taking the water, but save for the more distant throbbing of riverside industry, and rarer note of shipping, the mad discords of this rat saturnalia alone claimed the ear.

The hour was nigh now, when matters should begin to develop. I followed the chimes from the clock of some church nearby--I have never learnt its name; and was conscious of a thrill of excitement when they warned me that the hour was actually arrived....

A strange figure appeared noiselessly, from I knew not where, and stood fully within view upon the bridge crossing the cutting, peering to right and left, in an attitude of listening. It was the figure of a bedraggled old woman, gray-haired, and carrying a large bundle tied up in what appeared to be a red shawl. Of her face I could see little, since it was shaded by the brim of her black bonnet, but she rested her bundle upon the low wall of the bridge, and to my intense surprise, sat down upon it!

She evidently intended to remain there.

I drew back further into the darkness; for the presence of this singular old woman at such a place, and at that hour, could not well be accidental. I was convinced that the first actor in the drama had already taken the stage. Whether I was mistaken or not must shortly appear.

Crisp footsteps sounded upon the roadway; distantly, and from my left. Nearer they approached and nearer. I saw the old woman, in the shadow of the wall, glance once rapidly in the direction of the approaching pedestrian. For some occult reason, the chorus of the rats was stilled. Only that firm and regular tread broke the intimate silence of the dreary spot.

Now the pedestrian came within my range of sight. It was Nayland Smith!

He wore a long tweed overcoat with which I was familiar, and a soft felt hat, the brim pulled down all around in a fashion characteristic of him, and probably acquired during the years spent beneath the merciless sun of Burma. He carried a heavy walking-cane which I knew to be a formidable weapon that he could wield to good effect. But, despite the stillness about me, a stillness which had reigned uninterruptedly (save for the *danse macabre* of the rats) since the coming of dusk, some voice within, ignoring these physical evidences of solitude, spoke urgently of lurking assassins; of murderous Easterns armed with those curved knives which sometimes flashed before my eyes in dreams; of a deathly menace which hid in the shadows about me, in the many shadows cloaking the holes and corners of the ramshackle building, draping arches, crannies and portals to which the moonlight could not penetrate.

He was abreast of the Joy-Shop now, and in sight of the ominous old witch huddled upon the bridge. He pulled up suddenly and stood looking at her. Coincident with his doing so, she began to moan and sway her body to right and left as if in pain; then--

"Kind gentleman," she whined in a sing-song voice, "thank God you came this way to help a poor old woman."

"What is the matter?" said Smith tersely, approaching her.

I clenched my fists. I could have cried out; I was indeed hard put to it to refrain from crying out--from warning him. But his injunctions had been explicit, and I restrained myself by a great effort, preserving silence and crouching there at the window, but with every muscle tensed and a desire for action strong upon me.

"I tripped up on a rough stone, sir," whined the old creature, "and here I've been sitting waiting for a policeman or someone to help me, for more than an hour, I have."

Smith stood looking down at her, his arms behind him, and in one gloved hand swinging the cane.

"Where do you live, then?" he asked.

"Not a hundred steps from here, kind gentleman," she replied in the monotonous voice; "but I can't move my left foot. It's only just through the gates yonder."

"What!" snapped Smith, "on the wharf?"

"They let me have a room in the old building until it's let," she explained. "Be helping a poor old woman, and God bless you."

"Come along, then!"

Stooping, Smith placed his arm around her shoulders, and assisted her to her feet. She groaned as if in great pain, but gripped her red bundle, and leaning heavily upon the supporting arm, hobbled off across the bridge in the direction of the wharf gates at the end of the lane.

Now at last a little action became possible, and having seen my friend push open one of the gates and assist the old woman to enter, I crept rapidly across the crazy floor, found the doorway, and, with little noise, for I wore rubber-soled shoes, stole down the stairs into what had formerly been the reception-room of the Joy-Shop, the malodorous sanctum of the old Chinaman, John Ki.

Utter darkness prevailed there, but momentarily flicking the light of a pocket-lamp upon the floor before me, I discovered the further steps that were to be negotiated, and descended into the square yard which gave access to the path skirting the creek.

The moonlight drew a sharp line of shadow along the wall of the house above me, but the yard itself was a well of darkness. I stumbled under the rotting brick archway, and stepped gingerly upon the muddy path that I must follow. One hand pressed to the damp wall, I worked my way cautiously along, for a false step had precipitated me into the foul water of the creek. In this fashion and still enveloped by dense shadows, I reached the angle of the building. Then--at risk of being perceived, for the wharf and the river both were bathed in moonlight-- I peered along to the left....

Out onto the paved pathway communicating with the wharf came Smith, shepherding his tottering charge. I was too far away to hear any conversation that might take place between the two, but, unless Smith gave the pre-arranged signal, I must approach no closer. Thus, as one sees a drama upon the screen, I saw what now occurred--occurred with dramatic, lightning swiftness.

Releasing Smith's arm, the old woman suddenly stepped back ... at the instant that another figure, a repellent figure which approached, stooping, apish, with a sort of loping gait, crossed from some spot invisible to me, and sprang like a wild animal upon Smith's back!

It was a Chinaman, wearing a short loose garment of the smock pattern, and having his head bare, so that I could see his pigtail coiled upon his yellow crown. That he carried a cord, I perceived in the instant of his spring, and that he had whipped it about Smith's throat with unerring dexterity was evidenced by the one, short, strangled cry that came from my friend's lips.

Then Smith was down, prone upon the crazy planking, with the ape-like figure of the Chinaman perched between his shoulders--bending forward-- the wicked yellow fingers at work, tightening--tightening--tightening the strangling-cord!

Uttering a loud cry of horror, I went racing along the gangway which projected actually over the moving Thames waters, and gained the wharf. But, swift as I had been, another had been swifter!

A tall figure (despite the brilliant moon, I doubted the evidence of my sight), wearing a tweed overcoat and a soft felt hat with the brim turned down, sprang up, from nowhere as it seemed, swooped upon the horrible figure squatting, simianesque, between Smith's shoulder-blades, and grasped him by the neck.

I pulled up shortly, one foot set upon the wharf. The new-comer was the double of Nayland Smith!

Seemingly exerting no effort whatever, he lifted the strangler in that remorseless grasp, so that the Chinaman's hands, after one quick convulsive upward movement, hung limply beside him like the paws of a rat in the grip of a terrier.

"You damned murderous swine!" I heard in a repressed, savage undertone. "The knife failed, so now the cord has an innings! Go after your pal!"

Releasing one hand from the neck of the limp figure, the speaker grasped the Chinaman by his loose, smock-like garment, swung him back, once--a mighty swing--and hurled him far out into the river as one might hurl a sack of rubbish!

CHAPTER XXIII

ARREST OF SAMARKAN

"AS THE HIGH GOD'S WILLED IT," explained Nayland Smith, tenderly massaging his throat, "Mr. Forsyth, having just left the docks, chanced to pass along Three Colt Street on Wednesday night at exactly the hour that *I* was expected! The resemblance between us is rather marked and the coincidence of dress completed the illusion. That devilish Eurasian woman, Zarmi, who has escaped us again--of course you recognized her?--made a very natural mistake. Mr. Forsyth, however, made no mistake!"

I glanced at the chief officer of the *Andaman*, who sat in an armchair in our new chambers, contentedly smoking a black cheroot.

"Heaven has blessed me with a pair of useful hands!" said the seaman, grimly, extending his horny palms. "I've an old score against those yellow swine; poor George and I were twins."

He referred to his brother who had been foully done to death by one of the creatures of Dr. Fu-Manchu.

"It beats me how Mr. Smith got on the track!" he added.

"Pure inspiration!" murmured Nayland Smith, glancing aside from the siphon wherewith he now was busy. "The divine afflatus--and the same whereby Petrie solved the Zagazig cryptogram!"

"But," concluded Forsyth, "I am indebted to you for an opportunity of meeting the Chinese strangler, and sending him to join the Burmese knife expert!"

Such, then, were the episodes that led to the arrest of M. Samarkan, and my duty as narrator of these strange matters now bears me on to the morning when Nayland Smith was hastily summoned to the prison into which the villainous Greek had been cast.

We were shown immediately into the Governor's room and were invited by that much disturbed official to be seated. The news which he had to impart was sufficiently startling.

Samarkan was dead.

"I have Warder Morrison's statement here," said Colonel Warrington, "if you will be good enough to read it----"

Nayland Smith rose abruptly, and began to pace up and down the little office. Through the open window I had a glimpse of a stooping figure in convict garb, engaged in liming the flower-beds of the prison Governor's garden.

"I should like to see this Warder Morrison personally," snapped my friend.

"Very good," replied the Governor, pressing a bell-push placed close beside his table.

A man entered, to stand rigidly at attention just within the doorway.

"Send Morrison here," ordered Colonel Warrington.

The man saluted and withdrew. As the door was reclosed, the Colonel sat drumming his fingers upon the table, Nayland Smith walked restlessly about tugging at the lobe of his ear, and I absently watched the convict gardener pursuing his toils. Shortly, sounded a rap at the door, and--

"Come in," cried Colonel Warrington.

A man wearing warder's uniform appeared, saluted the Governor, and stood glancing uneasily from the Colonel to Smith. The latter had now ceased his perambulations, and, one elbow resting upon the mantelpiece, was staring at Morrison--his penetrating gray eyes as hard as steel. Colonel Warrington twisted his chair around, fixing his monocle more closely in its place. He had the wiry white mustache and fiery red face of the old-style Anglo-Indian officer.

"Morrison," he said, "Mr. Commissioner Nayland Smith has some questions to put to you."

The man's uneasiness palpably was growing by leaps and bounds. He was a tall and intelligent-looking fellow of military build, though spare for his height and of an unhealthy complexion. His eyes were curiously dull, and their pupils interested me, professionally, from the very moment of his entrance.

"You were in charge of the prisoner Samarkan?" began Smith harshly.

"Yes, sir," Morrison replied.

"Were you the first to learn of his death?"

"I was, sir. I looked through the grille in the door and saw him lying on the floor of the cell."

"What time was it?"

"Half-past four A.M."

"What did you do?"

"I went into the cell and then sent for the head warder."

"You realized at once that Samarkan was dead?"

"At once, yes."

"Were you surprised?"

Nayland Smith subtly changed the tone of his voice in asking the last question, and it was evident that the veiled significance of the words was not lost upon Morrison.

"Well, sir," he began, and cleared his throat nervously.

"Yes, or no!" snapped Smith.

Morrison still hesitated, and I saw his underlip twitch. Nayland Smith, taking two long strides, stood immediately in front of him, glaring grimly into his face.

"This is your chance," he said emphatically; "I shall not give you another. You had met Samarkan before?"

Morrison hung his head for a moment, clenching and unclenching his fists; then he looked up swiftly, and the light of a new resolution was in his eyes.

"I'll take the chance, sir," he said, speaking with some emotion, "and I hope, sir"--turning momentarily to Colonel Warrington--"that you'll be as lenient as you can; for I didn't know there was any harm in what I did."

"Don't expect any leniency from me!" cried the Colonel. "If there has been a breach of discipline there will be punishment, rely upon it!"

"I admit the breach of discipline," pursued the man doggedly; "but I want to say, here and now, that I've no more idea than anybody else how the-----"

Smith snapped his fingers irritably.

"The facts--the facts!" he demanded. "What you *don't* know cannot help us!"

"Well, sir," said Morrison, clearing his throat again, "when the prisoner, Samarkan, was admitted, and I put him safely into his cell, he told me that he suffered from heart trouble, that he'd had an attack when he was arrested and that he thought he was threatened with another, which might kill him----"

"One moment," interrupted Smith, "is this confirmed by the police officer who made the arrest?"

"It is, sir," replied Colonel Warrington, swinging his chair around and consulting some papers upon his table. "The prisoner was overcome by faintness when the officer showed him the warrant and asked to be given some cognac from the decanter which stood in his room. This was administered, and he then entered the cab which the officer had waiting. He was taken to Bow Street, remanded, and brought here in accordance with some one's instructions."

"*My instructions*" said Smith. "Go on, Morrison."

"He told me," continued Morrison more steadily, "that he suffered from something that sounded to me like apoplexy."

"Catalepsy!" I suggested, for I was beginning to see light.

"That's it, sir! He said he was afraid of being buried alive! He asked me, as a favor, if he should die in prison to go to a friend of his and get a syringe with which to inject some stuff that would do away with all chance of his coming to life again after burial."

"You had no right to talk to the prisoner!" roared Colonel Warrington.

"I know that, sir, but you'll admit that the circumstances were peculiar. Anyway, he died in the night, sure enough, and from heart failure, according to the doctor. I managed to get a couple of hours leave in the evening, and I went and fetched the syringe and a little tube of yellow stuff."

"Do you understand, Petrie?" cried Nayland Smith, his eyes blazing with excitement. "Do you understand?"

"Perfectly."

"It's more than I do, sir," continued Morrison, "but as I was explaining, I brought the little syringe back with me and I filled it from the tube. The body was lying in the mortuary, which you've seen, and the door not being locked, it was easy for me to slip in there for a moment. I didn't fancy the job, but it was soon done. I threw the syringe and the tube over the wall into the lane outside, as I'd been told to do."

"What part of the wall?" asked Smith.

"Behind the mortuary."

"That's where they were waiting!" I cried excitedly. "The building used as a mortuary is quite isolated, and it would not be a difficult matter for some one hiding in the lane outside to throw one of those ladders of silk and bamboo across the top of the wall."

"But, my good sir," interrupted the Governor irascibly, "whilst I admit the possibility to which you allude, I do not admit that a dead man, and a heavy one at that, can be carried up a ladder of silk and bamboo! Yet, on the evidence of my own eyes, the body of the prisoner, Samarkan, was removed from the mortuary last night!"

Smith signaled to me to pursue the subject no further; and indeed I realized that it would have been no easy matter to render the amazing truth evident to a man of the Colonel's type of mind. But to me the facts of the case were now clear enough.

That Fu-Manchu possessed a preparation for producing artificial catalepsy, of a sort indistinguishable from death, I was well aware. A dose of this unknown drug had doubtless been contained in the cognac (if, indeed, the decanter had held cognac) that the prisoner had drunk at the time of his arrest. The "yellow stuff" spoken of by Morrison I recognized as the antidote (another secret of the brilliant Chinese doctor), a portion of which I had once, some years before, actually had in my possession. The "dead man" had not been carried up the ladder; he had climbed up!

"Now, Morrison," snapped Nayland Smith, "you have acted wisely thus far. Make a clean breast of it. How much were you paid for the job?"

"Twenty pounds, sir" answered the man promptly, "and I'd have done it for less, because I could see no harm in it, the prisoner being dead, and this his last request."

"And who paid you?"

Now we were come to the nub of the matter, as the change in the man's face revealed. He hesitated momentarily, and Colonel Warrington brought his fist down on the table with a bang. Morrison made a sort of gesture of resignation at that, and--

"When I was in the Army, sir, stationed at Cairo," he said slowly, "I regret to confess that I formed a drug habit."

"Opium?" snapped Smith.

"No, sir, hashish."

"Good God! Go on."

"There's a place in Soho, just off Frith Street, where hashish is supplied, and I go there sometimes. Mr. Samarkan used to come, and bring people with him--from the New Louvre Hotel, I believe. That's where I met him."

"The exact address?" demanded Smith.

"Café de l'Egypte. But the hashish is only sold upstairs, and no one is allowed up that isn't known personally to Ismail."

"Who is this Ismail?"

"The proprietor of the café. He's a Greek Jew of Salonica. An old woman used to attend to the customers upstairs, but during the last few months a young one has sometimes taken her place."

"What is she like?" I asked eagerly.

"She has very fine eyes, and that's about all I can tell you, sir, because she wears a yashmak. Last night there were two women there, both veiled, though."

"Two women!"

Hope and fear entered my heart. That Kâramaneh was again in the power of the Chinese Doctor I knew to my sorrow. Could it be that the Café de l'Egypte was the place of her captivity?

CHAPTER XXIV
CAFÉ DE L'EGYPTE

I COULD SEE that Nayland Smith counted the escape of the prisoner but a trivial matter by comparison with the discovery to which it had led us. That the Soho café should prove to be, if not the headquarters at least a regular resort of Dr. Fu-Manchu, was not too much to hope. The usefulness of such a haunt was evident enough, since it might conveniently be employed as a place of rendezvous for Orientals--and furthermore enable the cunning Chinaman to establish relations with persons likely to prove of service to him.

Formerly, he had used an East End opium den for this purpose, and, later, the resort known as the Joy-Shop. Soho, hitherto, had remained outside the radius of his activity, but that he should have embraced it at last was not surprising; for Soho is the Montmartre of London and a land of many secrets.

"Why," demanded Nayland Smith, "have I never been told of the existence of this place?"

"That's simple enough," answered Inspector Weymouth. "Although we knew of this Café de l'Egypte, we have never had the slightest trouble there. It's a Bohemian resort, where members of the French Colony, some of the Chelsea art people, professional models, and others of that sort, foregather at night. I've been there myself as a matter of fact, and I've seen people well known in the artistic world come in. It has much the same clientele as, say, the Café Royal, with a rather heavier sprinkling of Hindu students, Japanese, and so forth. It's celebrated for Turkish coffee."

"What do you know of this Ismail?"

"Nothing much. He's a Levantine Jew."

"And something more!" added Smith, surveying himself in the mirror, and turning to nod his satisfaction to the well-known perruquier whose services are sometimes requisitioned by the police authorities.

We were ready for our visit to the Café de l'Egypte, and Smith having deemed it inadvisable that we should appear there openly, we had been transformed, under the adroit manipulation of Foster, into a pair of Futurists oddly unlike our actual selves. No wigs, no false mustaches had been employed; a change of costume and a few deft touches of some water-color paint had rendered us unrecognizable by our most intimate friends.

It was all very fantastic, very reminiscent of Christmas charades, but the farce had a grim, murderous undercurrent; the life of one dearer to me than life itself hung upon our success; the swamping of the White world by Yellow hordes might well be the price of our failure.

Weymouth left us at the corner of Frith Street. This was no more than a reconnaissance, but--

"I shall be within hail if I'm wanted," said the burly detective; and although we stood not in Chinatown but in the heart of Bohemian London, with popular restaurants about us, I was glad to know that we had so stanch an ally in reserve.

The shadow of the great Chinaman was upon me. That strange, subconscious voice, with which I had become familiar in the past, awoke within me to-night. Not by logic, but by prescience, I knew that the Yellow doctor was near.

Two minutes walk brought us to the door of the café. The upper half was of glass, neatly curtained, as were the windows on either side of it; and above the establishment appeared the words: "Café de l'Egypte." Between the second and third word was inserted a gilded device representing the crescent of Islâm.

We entered. On our right was a room furnished with marble-topped tables, cane-seated chairs and plush-covered lounges set against the walls. The air was heavy with tobacco smoke; evidently the café was full, although the night was young.

Smith immediately made for the upper end of the room. It was not large, and at first glance I thought that there was no vacant place. Presently, however, I espied two unoccupied chairs; and these we took, finding ourselves facing a pale, bespectacled young man, with long, fair hair and faded eyes, whose companion, a bold brunette, was smoking one of the largest cigarettes I had ever seen, in a gold and amber cigar-holder.

A very commonplace Swiss waiter took our orders for coffee, and we began discreetly to survey our surroundings. The only touch of Oriental color thus far perceptible in the café de l'Egypte was provided by a red-capped Egyptian behind a narrow counter, who presided over the coffee pots. The patrons of the establishment were in every way typical of Soho, and in the bulk differed not at all from those of the better known café restaurants.

There were several Easterns present; but Smith, having given each of them a searching glance, turned to me with a slight shrug of disappointment. Coffee being placed before us, we sat sipping the thick, sugary beverage, smoking cigarettes and vainly seeking for some clue to guide us to the inner sanctuary consecrated to hashish. It was maddening to think that Kâramaneh might be somewhere concealed in the building, whilst I sat there, inert amongst this gathering whose conversation was of abnormalities in art, music, and literature.

Then, suddenly, the pale young man seated opposite paid his bill, and with a word of farewell to his companion, went out of the café. He did not make his exit by the door through which we entered, but passed up the crowded room to the counter whereat the Egyptian presided. From some place hidden in the rear, emerged a black-haired, swarthy man, with whom the other exchanged a few words. The pale young artist raised his wide-brimmed hat, and was gone--through a curtained doorway on the left of the counter.

As he opened it, I had a glimpse of a narrow court beyond; then the door was closed again ... and I found myself thinking of the peculiar eyes of the departed visitor. Even through the thick pebbles of his spectacles, although for some reason I had thought little of the matter at the time, his oddly contracted pupils were noticeable. As the girl, in turn, rose and left the café--but by the ordinary door--I turned to Smith.

"That man ..." I began, and paused.

Smith was watching covertly, a Hindu seated at a neighboring table, who was about to settle his bill. Standing up, the Hindu made for the coffee counter, the swarthy man appeared out of the background--and the Asiatic visitor went out by the door opening into the court.

One quick glance Smith gave me, and raised his hand for the waiter. A few minutes later we were out in the street again.

"We must find our way to that court!" snapped my friend. "Let us try back, I noted a sort of alley-way which we passed just before reaching the café."

"You think the hashish den is in some adjoining building?"

"I don't know where it is, Petrie, but I know the way to it!"

Into a narrow, gloomy court we plunged, hemmed in by high walls, and followed it for ten yards or more. An even narrower and less inviting turning revealed itself on the left. We pursued our way, and presently found ourselves at the back of the Café de l'Egypte.

"There's the door," I said.

It opened into a tiny cul de sac, flanked by dilapidated hoardings, and no other door of any kind was visible in the vicinity. Nayland Smith stood tugging at the lobe of his ear almost savagely.

"Where the devil do they go?" he whispered.

Even as he spoke the words, came a gleam of light through the upper curtained part of the door, and I distinctly saw the figure of a man in silhouette.

"Stand back!" snapped Smith.

We crouched back against the dirty wall of the court, and watched a strange thing happen. The back door of the Café de l'Egypte opened outward, simultaneously a door, hitherto invisible, set at right angles in the hoarding adjoining, opened *inward!*

A man emerged from the café and entered the secret doorway. As he did so, the café door swung back ... and closed the door in the hoarding!

"Very good!" muttered Nayland Smith. "Our friend Ismail, behind the counter, moves some lever which causes the opening of one door automatically to open the other. Failing his kindly offices, the second exit from the Café de l'Egypte is innocent enough. Now--what is the next move?"

"I have an idea, Smith!" I cried. "According to Morrison, the place in which the hashish may be obtained has no windows but is lighted from above. No doubt it was built for a studio and has a glass roof. Therefore----"

"Come along!" snapped Smith, grasping my arm; "you have solved the difficulty, Petrie."

CHAPTER XXV

THE HOUSE OF HASHISH

ALONG THE LEADS from Frith Street we worked our perilous way. From the top landing of a French restaurant we had gained access, by means of a trap, to the roof of the building. Now, the busy streets of Soho were below me, and I clung dizzily to telephone standards and smoke stacks, rarely venturing to glance downward upon the cosmopolitan throng, surging, dwarfish, in the lighted depths.

Sometimes the bulky figure of Inspector Weymouth would loom up grotesquely against the star-sprinkled blue, as he paused to take breath; the next moment Nayland Smith would be leading the way again, and I would find myself contemplating some sheer well of blackness, with nausea threatening me because it had to be negotiated.

None of these gaps were more than a long stride from side to side; but the sense of depth conveyed in the muffled voices and dimmed footsteps from the pavements far below was almost overpowering. Indeed, I am convinced that for my part I should never have essayed that nightmare journey were it not that the musical voice of Kâramaneh seemed to be calling to me, her little white hands to be seeking mine, blindly, in the darkness.

That we were close to a haunt of the dreadful Chinamen I was persuaded; therefore my hatred and my love cooperated to lend me a coolness and address which otherwise I must have lacked.

"Hullo!" cried Smith, who was leading--"what now?"

We had crept along the crown of a sloping roof and were confronted by the blank wall of a building which rose a story higher than that adjoining it. It was crowned by an iron railing, showing blackly against the sky. I paused, breathing heavily, and seated astride that dizzy perch. Weymouth was immediately behind me, and--

"It's the Café de l'Egypte, Mr. Smith!" he said, "If you'll look up, you'll see the reflection of the lights shining through the glass roof."

Vaguely I discerned Nayland Smith rising to his feet.

"Be careful!" I said. "For God's sake don't slip!"

"Take my hand," he snapped energetically.

I stretched forward and grasped his hand. As I did so, he slid down the slope on the right, away from the street, and hung perilously for a moment over the very cul de sac upon which the secret door opened.

"Good!" he muttered "There is, as I had hoped, a window lighting the top of the staircase. Ssh!--ssh!"

His grip upon my hand tightened; and there aloft, above the teemful streets of Soho, I sat listening ... whilst very faint and muffled footsteps sounded upon an uncarpeted stair, a door banged, and all was silent again, save for the ceaseless turmoil far below.

"Sit tight, and catch!" rapped Smith.

Into my extended hands he swung his boots, fastened together by the laces! Then, ere I could frame any protest, he disengaged his hand from mine, and pressing his body close against the angle of the building, worked his way around to the staircase window, which was invisible from where I crouched.

"Heavens!" muttered Weymouth, close to my ear, "I can never travel that road!"

"Nor I!" was my scarcely audible answer.

In a anguish of fearful anticipation I listened for the cry and the dull thud which should proclaim the fate of my intrepid friend; but no such sounds came to me. Some thirty seconds passed in this fashion, when a subdued call from above caused me to start and look aloft.

Nayland Smith was peering down from the railing on the roof.

"Mind your head!" he warned--and over the rail swung the end of a light wooden ladder, lowering it until it rested upon the crest astride of which I sat.

"Up you come!--then Weymouth!"

Whilst Smith held the top firmly, I climbed up rung by rung, not daring to think of what lay below.

My relief when at last I grasped the railing, climbed over, and found myself upon a wooden platform, was truly inexpressible.

"Come on, Weymouth!" rapped Nayland Smith. "This ladder has to be lowered back down the trap before another visitor arrives!"

Taking short, staccato breaths at every step, Inspector Weymouth ascended, ungainly, that frail and moving stair. Arrived beside me, he wiped the perspiration from his face and forehead.

"I wouldn't do it again for a hundred pounds!" he said hoarsely.

"You don't have to!" snapped Smith.

Back he hauled the ladder, shouldered it, and stepping to a square opening in one corner of the rickety platform, lowered it cautiously down.

"Have you a knife with a corkscrew in it?" he demanded.

Weymouth had one, which he produced. Nayland Smith screwed it into the weather-worn frame, and by that means reclosed the trapdoor softly, then--

"Look," he said, "there is the house of hashish!"

CHAPTER XXVI

"THE DEMON'S SELF"

THROUGH THE GLASS panes of the skylight I looked down upon a scene so bizarre that my actual environment became blotted out, and I was mentally translated to Cairo--to that quarter of Cairo immediately surrounding the famous Square of the Fountain--to those indescribable streets, wherefrom arises the perfume of deathless evil, wherein, to the wailing, luresome music of the reed pipe, painted dancing-girls sway in the wild abandon of dances that were ancient when Thebes was the City of a Hundred Gates; I seemed to stand again in el Wasr.

The room below was rectangular, and around three of the walls were divans strewn with garish cushions, whilst highly colored Eastern rugs were spread about the floor. Four lamps swung on chains, two from either of the beams which traversed the apartment. They were fine examples of native perforated brasswork.

Upon the divans some eight or nine men were seated, fully half of whom were Orientals or half-castes. Before each stood a little inlaid table bearing a brass tray; and upon the trays were various boxes, some apparently containing sweetmeats, other cigarettes. One or two of the visitors smoked curious, long-stemmed pipes and sipped coffee.

Even as I leaned from the platform, surveying that incredible scene (incredible in a street of Soho), another devotee of hashish entered-- a tall, distinguished-looking man, wearing a light coat over his evening dress.

"Gad!" whispered Smith, beside me--"Sir Byngham Pyne of the India Office! You see, Petrie! You see! This place is a lure. My God! ..."

He broke off, as I clutched wildly at his arm.

The last arrival having taken his seat in a corner of the divan, two heavy curtains draped before an opening at one end of the room parted, and a girl came out, carrying a tray such as already reposed before each of the other men in the room.

She wore a dress of dark lilac-colored gauze, banded about with gold tissue and embroidered with gold thread and pearls; and around her shoulders floated, so ethereally that she seemed to move in a violet cloud; a scarf of Delhi muslin. A white yashmak trimmed with gold tissue concealed the lower part of her face.

My heart throbbed wildly; I seemed to be choking. By the wonderful hair alone I must have known her, by the great, brilliant eyes, by the shape of those slim white ankles, by every movement of that exquisite form. It was

Kâramaneh!

I sprang madly back from the rail ... and Smith had my arm in an iron grip.

"Where are you going?" he snapped.

"Where am I going?" I cried. "Do you think--"

"What do you propose to do?" he interrupted harshly. "Do you know so little of the resources of Dr. Fu-Manchu that you would throw yourself blindly into that den? Damn it all, man! I know what you suffer!--but wait--wait. We must not act rashly; our plans must be well considered."

He drew me back to my former post and clapped his hand on my shoulder sympathetically. Clutching the rail like a man frenzied, as indeed I was, I looked down into that infamous den again, striving hard for composure.

Kâramaneh listlessly placed the tray upon the little table before Sir Byngham Pyne and withdrew without vouchsafing him a single glance in acknowledgment of his unconcealed admiration.

A moment later, above the dim clamor of London far below, there crept to my ears a sound which completed the magical quality of the scene, rendering that sky platform on a roof of Soho a magical carpet bearing me to the golden Orient. This sound was the wailing of a reed pipe.

"The company is complete," murmured Smith. "I had expected this."

Again the curtains parted, and a *ghazeeyeh* glided out into the room. She wore a white dress, clinging closely to her figure from shoulders to hips, where it was clasped by an ornate girdle, and a skirt of sky-blue gauze which clothed her as Io was clothed of old. Her arms were covered with gold bangles, and gold bands were clasped about her ankles. Her jet-black, frizzy hair was unconfined and without ornament, and she wore a sort of highly colored scarf so arranged that it effectually concealed the greater part of her face, but served to accentuated the brightness of the great flashing eyes. She had unmistakable beauty of a sort, but how different from the sweet witchery of Kâramaneh!

With a bold, swinging grace she walked down the center of the room, swaying her arms from side to side and snapping her fingers.

"Zarmi!" exclaimed Smith.

But his exclamation was unnecessary, for already I had recognized the evil Eurasian who was so efficient a servant of the Chinese doctor.

The wailing of the pipes continued, and now faintly I could detect the throbbing of a *darabûkeh*. This was el Wasr indeed. The dance commenced, its every phase followed eagerly by the motley clientele of the hashish house. Zarmi danced with an insolent nonchalance that nevertheless displayed her barbaric beauty to greatest advantage. She was lithe as a serpent, graceful as a young panther, another Lamia come to damn the souls of men with those arts denounced in a long dead age by Apolonius of Tyana.

"She seemed, at once, some penanced lady elf, Some demon's mistress, or the demon's self...."

Entranced against my will, I watched the Eurasian until, the barbaric dance completed, she ran from the room, and the curtains concealed her from view. How my mind was torn between hope and fear that I should see Kâramaneh again! How I longed for one more glimpse of her, yet loathed the thought of her presence in that infamous house.

She was a captive; of that there could be no doubt, a captive in the hands of the giant criminal whose wiles were endless, whose resources were boundless, whose intense cunning had enabled him, for years, to weave his nefarious plots in the very heart of civilization, and remain immune. Suddenly--

"That woman is a sorceress!" muttered Nayland Smith. "There is about her something serpentine, at once repelling and fascinating. It would be of interest, Petrie, to learn what State secrets have been filched from the brains of habitues of this den, and interesting to know from what unsuspected spy-hole Fu-Manchu views his nightly catch. If ..."

His voice died away, in a most curious fashion. I have since thought that here was a case of true telepathy. For, as Smith spoke of Fu-Manchu's spy-hole, the idea leapt instantly to my mind that *this* was it--this strange platform upon which we stood!

I drew back from the rail, turned, stared at Smith. I read in his face that our suspicions were identical. Then--

"Look! Look!" whispered Weymouth.

He was gazing at the trapdoor--which was slowly rising; inch by inch ... inch by inch ... Fascinatedly, raptly, we all gazed. A head appeared in the opening--and some vague, reflected light revealed two long, narrow, slightly oblique eyes watching us. They were brilliantly green.

"By God!" came in a mighty roar from Weymouth. "It's Dr. Fu-Manchu!"

As one man we leapt for the trap. It dropped, with a resounding bang-- and I distinctly heard a bolt shot home.

A gutteral voice--the unmistakable, unforgettable voice of Fu-Manchu-- sounded dimly from below. I turned and sprang back to the rail of the platform, peering down into the hashish house. The occupants of the divans were making for the curtained doorway. Some, who seemed to be in a state of stupor, were being assisted by the others and by the man, Ismail, who had now appeared upon the scene.

Of Kâramaneh, Zarmi, or Fu-Manchu there was no sign.

Suddenly, the lights were extinguished.

"This is maddening!" cried Nayland Smith--"maddening! No doubt they have some other exit, some hiding-place--and they are slipping through our hands!"

Inspector Weymouth blew a shrill blast upon his whistle, and Smith, running to the rail of the platform, began to shatter the panes of the skylight with his foot.

"That's hopeless, sir!" cried Weymouth. "You'd be torn to pieces on the jagged glass."

Smith desisted, with a savage exclamation, and stood beating his right fist into the palm of his left hand, and glaring madly at the Scotland Yard man.

"I know I'm to blame," admitted Weymouth; "but the words were out before I knew I'd spoken. Ah!"--as an answering whistle came from somewhere in the street below. "But will they ever find us?"

He blew again shrilly. Several whistles replied ... and a wisp of smoke floated up from the shattered pane of the skylight.

"I can smell *petrol*!" muttered Weymouth.

An ever-increasing roar, not unlike that of an approaching storm at sea, came from the streets beneath. Whistles skirled, remotely and intimately, and sometimes one voice, sometimes another, would detach itself from this stormy background with weird effect. Somewhere deep in the bowels of the hashish house there went on ceaselessly a splintering and crashing as though a determined assault were being made upon a door. A light shone up through the skylight.

Back once more to the rail I sprang, looked down into the room below-- and saw a sight never to be forgotten.

Passing from divan to curtained door, from piles of cushions to stacked-up tables, and bearing a flaming torch hastily improvised out of a roll of newspaper, was Dr. Fu-Manchu. Everything inflammable in the place had been soaked with petrol, and, his gaunt, yellow face lighted by the evergrowing conflagration, so that truly it seemed not the face of a man, but that of a demon of the hells, the Chinese doctor ignited point after point....

"Smith!" I screamed, "we are trapped! that fiend means to burn us alive!"

"And the place will flare like matchwood! It's touch and go this time, Petrie! To drop to the sloping roof underneath would mean almost certain death on the pavement...."

I dragged my pistol from my pocket and began wildly to fire shot after shot into the holocaust below. But the awful Chinaman had escaped-- probably by some secret exit reserved for his own use; for certainly he must have known that escape into the court was now cut off.

Flames were beginning to hiss through the skylight. A tremendous crackling and crashing told of the glass destroyed. Smoke spurted up through the cracks of the boarding upon which we stood--and a great shout came from the crowd in the streets....

In the distance--a long, long way off, it seemed--was born a new note in the stormy human symphony. It grew in volume, it seemed to be sweeping down upon us--nearer--nearer--nearer. Now it was in the streets immediately adjoining the Café de l'Egypte ... and now, blessed sound! it culminated in a mighty surging cheer.

"The fire-engines," said Weymouth coolly--and raised himself on to the lower rail, for the platform was growing uncomfortably hot.

Tongues of fire licked out, venomously, from beneath my feet. I leapt for the railing in turn, and sat astride it ... as one end of the flooring burst into flame.

The heat from the blazing room above which we hung suspended was now all but insupportable, and the fumes threatened to stifle us. My head seemed to be bursting; my throat and lungs were consumed by internal fires.

"Merciful heavens!" whispered Smith. "Will they reach us in time?"

"Not if they don't get here within the next thirty seconds!" answered Weymouth grimly--and changed his position, in order to avoid a tongue of flame that hungrily sought to reach him.

Nayland Smith turned and looked me squarely in the eyes. Words trembled on his tongue; but those words were never spoken ... for a brass helmet appeared suddenly out of the smoke banks, followed almost immediately by a second....

"Quick, sir! this way! Jump! I'll catch you!"

Exactly what followed I never knew; but there was a mighty burst of cheering, a sense of tension released, and it became a task less agonizing to breathe.

Feeling very dazed, I found myself in the heart of a huge, excited crowd, with Weymouth beside me, and Nayland Smith holding my arm. Vaguely, I heard;--

"They have the man Ismail, but ..."

A hollow crash drowned the end of the sentence. A shower of sparks shot up into the night's darkness high above our heads.

"That's the platform gone!"

CHAPTER XXVII

ROOM WITH THE GOLDEN DOOR

ONE NIGHT EARLY in the following week I sat at work upon my notes dealing with our almost miraculous escape from the blazing hashish house when the clock of St. Paul's began to strike midnight.

I paused in my work, leaning back wearily and wondering what detained Nayland Smith so late. Some friends from Burma had carried him off to a theater, and in their good company I had thought him safe enough; yet, with the omnipresent menace of Fu-Manchu hanging over our heads, always I doubted, always I feared, if my friend should chance to be delayed abroad at night.

What a world of unreality was mine, in those days! Jostling, as I did, commonplace folk in commonplace surroundings, I yet knew myself removed from them, knew myself all but alone in my knowledge of the great and evil man, whose presence in England had diverted my life into these strange channels.

But, despite of all my knowledge, and despite the infinitely greater knowledge and wider experience of Nayland Smith, what did I know, what did he know, of the strange organization called the Si-Fan, and of its most formidable member, Dr. Fu-Manchu?

Where did the dreadful Chinaman hide, with his murderers, his poisons, and his nameless death agents? What roof in broad England sheltered Kâramaneh, the companion of my dreams, the desire of every waking hour?

I uttered a sigh of despair, when, to my unbounded astonishment, there came a loud rap upon the window pane!

Leaping up, I crossed to the window, threw it widely open and leant out, looking down into the court below. It was deserted. In no other window visible to me was any light to be seen, and no living thing moved in the shadows beneath. The clamor of Fleet Street's diminishing traffic came dimly to my ears; the last stroke from St. Paul's quivered through the night.

What was the meaning of the sound which had disturbed me? Surely I could not have imagined it? Yet, right, left, above and below, from the cloisteresque shadows on the east of the court to the blank wall of the building on the west, no living thing stirred.

Quietly, I reclosed the window, and stood by it for a moment listening. Nothing occurred, and I returned to the writing-table, puzzled but in no sense alarmed. I resumed the seemingly interminable record of the Si-

Fan mysteries, and I had just taken up my pen, when ... two loud raps sounded upon the pane behind me.

In a trice I was at the window, had thrown it open, and was craning out. Practical joking was not characteristic of Nayland Smith, and I knew of none other likely to take such a liberty. As before, the court below proved to be empty....

Some one was softly rapping at the door of the chambers!

I turned swiftly from the open window; and now, came *fear*. Momentarily, the icy finger of panic touched me, for I thought myself invested upon all sides. Who could this late caller be, this midnight visitor who rapped, ghostly, in preference to ringing the bell?

From the table drawer I took out a Browning pistol, slipped it into my pocket and crossed to the narrow hallway. It was in darkness, but I depressed the switch, lighting the lamp. Toward the closed door I looked --as the soft rapping was repeated.

I advanced; then hesitated, and, strung up to a keen pitch of fearful anticipation, stood there in doubt. The silence remained unbroken for the space, perhaps of half a minute. Then again came the ghostly rapping.

"Who's there?" I cried loudly.

Nothing stirred outside the door, and still I hesitated. To some who read, my hesitancy may brand me childishly timid; but I, who had met many of the dreadful creatures of Dr. Fu-Manchu, had good reason to fear whomsoever or whatsoever rapped at midnight upon my door. Was I likely to forget the great half-human ape, with the strength of four lusty men, which once he had loosed upon us?--had I not cause to remember his Burmese dacoits and Chinese stranglers?

No, I had just cause for dread, as I fully recognized when, snatching the pistol from my pocket, I strode forward, flung wide the door, and stood peering out into the black gulf of the stairhead.

Nothing, no one, appeared!

Conscious of a longing to cry out--if only that the sound of my own voice might reassure me--I stood listening. The silence was complete.

"Who's there?" I cried again, and loudly enough to arrest the attention of the occupant of the chambers opposite if he chanced to be at home.

None replied; and finding this phantom silence more nerve-racking than any clamor, I stepped outside the door--and my heart gave a great leap, then seemed to remain inert, in my breast....

Right and left of me, upon either side of the doorway, stood a dim figure: I had walked deliberately into a trap!

The shock of the discovery paralyzed my mind for one instant. In the next, and with the sinister pair closing swiftly upon me, I stepped back--I stepped into the arms of some third assailant, who must have entered the chambers by way of the open window and silently crept up behind me!

So much I realized, and no more. A bag, reeking of some hashish-like perfume, was clapped over my head and pressed firmly against mouth and nostrils. I felt myself to be stifling--dying--and dropping into a bottomless pit.

When I opened my eyes I failed for some time to realize that I was conscious in the true sense of the word, that I was really awake.

I sat upon a bench covered with a red carpet, in a fair-sized room, very simply furnished, in the Chinese manner, but having a two-leaved, gilded door, which was shut. At the further end of this apartment was a dais some three feet high, also carpeted with red, and upon it was placed a very large cushion covered with a tiger skin.

Seated cross-legged upon the cushion was a Chinaman of most majestic appearance. His countenance was truly noble and gracious and he was dressed in a yellow robe lined with marten-fur. His hair, which was thickly splashed with gray, was confined upon the top of his head by three golden combs, and a large diamond was suspended from his left ear. A pearl-embroidered black cap, surmounted by the red coral ball denoting the mandarin's rank, lay upon a second smaller cushion beside him.

Leaning back against the wall, I stared at his personage with a dreadful fixity, for I counted him the figment of a disarranged mind. But palpably he remained before me, fanning himself complacently, and watching me with every mark of kindly interest. Evidently perceiving that I was fully alive to my surroundings, the Chinaman addressed a remark to me in a tongue quite unfamiliar.

I shook my head dazedly.

"Ah," he commented in French, "you do not speak my language."

"I do not," I answered, also in French, "but since it seems we have one common tongue, what is the meaning of the outrage to which I have been subjected, and who are you?"

As I spoke the words I rose to my feet, but was immediately attacked by vertigo, which compelled me to resume my seat upon the bench.

"Compose yourself," said the Chinaman, taking a pinch of snuff from a silver vase which stood convenient to his hand. "I have been compelled to adopt certain measures in order to bring about this interview. In China, such measures are not unusual, but I recognize that they are out of accordance with your English ideas."

"Emphatically they are!" I replied.

The placid manner of this singularly imposing old man rendered proper resentment difficult. A sense of futility, and of unreality, claimed me; I felt that this was a dream-world, governed by dream-laws.

"You have good reason," he continued, calmly raising the pinch of snuff to his nostrils, "good reason to distrust all that is Chinese. Therefore, when I despatched my servants to your abode (knowing you to be alone) I instructed them to observe every law of courtesy, compatible with the Sure Invitation. Hence, I pray you, absolve me, for I intended no offense."

Words failed me altogether; wonder succeeded wonder! What was coming? What did it all mean?

"I have selected you, rather than Mr. Commissioner Nayland Smith," continued the mandarin, "as the recipient of those secrets which I am about to impart, for the reason that your friend might possibly be acquainted with my appearance. I will confess there was a time when I must have regarded you with animosity, as one who sought the destruction of the most ancient and potent organization in the world-- the Si-Fan."

As he uttered the words he raised his right hand and touched his forehead, his mouth, and finally his breast--a gesture reminiscent of that employed by Moslems.

"But my first task is to assure you," he resumed, "that the activities of that Order are in no way inimical to yourself, your country or your King. The extensive ramifications of the Order have recently been employed by a certain Dr. Fu-Manchu for his own ends, and, since he was (I admit it) a high official, a schism has been created in our ranks. Exactly a month ago, sentence of death was passed upon him by the Sublime Prince, and since I myself must return immediately to China, I look to Mr. Nayland Smith to carry out that sentence."

I said nothing; I remained bereft of the power of speech.

"The Si-Fan," he added, repeating the gesture with his hand, "disown Dr. Fu-Manchu and his servants; do with them what you will. In this envelope"--he held up a sealed package--"is information which should prove helpful to Mr. Smith. I have now a request to make. You were conveyed here in the garments which your wore at the time that my servants called upon you." (I was hatless and wore red leathern slippers.) "An overcoat and a hat can doubtless be found to suit you, temporarily, and my request is that you close your eyes until permission is given to open them."

Is there any one of my readers in doubt respecting my reception of this proposal? Remember my situation, remember the bizarre happening that had led up to it; remember, too, ere judging me, that whilst I could not doubt the unseen presence of Chinamen unnumbered surrounding that strange apartment with the golden door, I had not the remotest clue to guide me in determining where it was situated. Since the duration of my unconsciousness was immeasurable, the place in which I found myself might have been anywhere, within say, thirty miles of Fleet Street!

"I agree," I said.

The mandarin bowed composedly.

"Kindly close your eyes, Dr. Petrie," he requested, "and fear nothing. No danger threatens you."

I obeyed. Instantly sounded the note of a gong, and I became aware that the golden door was open. A soft voice, evidently that of a cultured Chinaman, spoke quite close to my ear--

"Keep your eyes tightly closed, please, and I will help you on with this coat. The envelope you will find in the pocket and here is a tweed cap. Now take my hand."

Wearing the borrowed garments, I was led from the room, along a passage, down a flight of thickly carpeted stairs, and so out of the house into the street. Faint evidences of remote traffic reached my ears as I was assisted into a car and placed in a cushioned corner. The car moved off, proceeded for some distance; then--

"Allow me to help you to descend," said the soft voice. "You may open your eyes in thirty seconds."

I was assisted from the step on to the pavement--and I heard the car being driven back. Having slowly counted thirty I opened my eyes, and looked about me. This, and not the fevered moment when first I had looked upon the room with the golden door, seemed to be my true awakening, for about me was comprehensible world, the homely streets of London, with deserted Portland Place stretching away on the one hand and a glimpse of midnight Regent Street obtainable on the other! The clock of the neighboring church struck one.

My mind yet dull with wonder of it all, I walked on to Oxford Circus and there obtained a taxicab, in which I drove to Fleet Street. Discharging the man, I passed quickly under the time worn archway into the court and approached our stair. Indeed, I was about to ascend when some one came racing down and almost knocked me over.

"Petrie! Petrie! Thank God you're safe!"

It was Nayland Smith, his eyes blazing with excitement, as I could see by the dim light of the lamp near the archway, and his hands, as he clapped them upon my shoulders, quivering tensely.

"Petrie!" he ran on impulsively, and speaking with extraordinary rapidly, "I was detained by a most ingenious trick and arrived only five minutes ago, to find you missing, the window wide open, and signs of hooks, evidently to support a rope ladder, having been attached to the ledge."

"But where were you going?"

"Weymouth has just rung up. We have indisputable proof that the mandarin Ki-Ming, whom I had believed to be dead, and whom I know for a high official of the Si-Fan, is actually in London! It's neck or nothing this time, Petrie! I'm going straight to Portland Place!"

"To the Chinese Legation?"

"Exactly!"

"Perhaps I can save you a journey," I said slowly. "I have just come from there!"

CHAPTER XXVIII

THE MANDARIN KI-MING

NAYLAND SMITH strode up and down the little sitting-room, tugging almost savagely at the lobe of his left ear. To-night his increasing grayness was very perceptible, and with his feverishly bright eyes staring straightly before him, he looked haggard and ill, despite the deceptive tan of his skin.

"Petrie," he began in his abrupt fashion, "I am losing confidence in myself."

"Why?" I asked in surprise.

"I hardly know; but for some occult reason I feel afraid."

"Afraid?"

"Exactly; afraid. There is some deep mystery here that I cannot fathom. In the first place, if they had really meant you to remain ignorant of the place at which the episodes described by you occurred, they would scarcely have dropped you at the end of Portland Place."

"You mean ...?"

"I mean that I don't believe you were taken to the Chinese Legation at all. Undoubtedly you saw the mandarin Ki-Ming; I recognize him from your description."

"You have met him, then?"

"No; but I know those who have. He is undoubtedly a very dangerous man, and it is just possible----"

He hesitated, glancing at me strangely.

"It is just possible," he continued musingly, "that his presence marks the beginning of the end. Fu-Manchu's health may be permanently impaired, and Ki-Ming may have superceded him."

"But, if what you suspect, Smith, be only partly true, with what object was I seized and carried to that singular interview? What was the meaning of the whole solemn farce?"

"Its meaning remains to be discovered," he answered; "but that the mandarin is amicably disposed I refuse to believe. You may dismiss the idea. In dealing with Ki-Ming we are to all intents and purposes dealing with Fu-Manchu. To me, this man's presence means one thing: we are about to be subjected to attempts along slightly different lines."

I was completely puzzled by Smith's tone.

"You evidently know more of this man, Ki-Ming, than you have yet explained to me," I said.

Nayland Smith pulled out the blackened briar and began rapidly to load it.

"He is a graduate," he replied, "of the Lama College, or monastery, of Rache-Churân."

"This does not enlighten me."

Having got his pipe going well--

"What do you know of animal magnetism?" snapped Smith.

The question seemed so wildly irrelevant that I stared at him in silence for some moments. Then--

"Certain powers sometimes grouped under that head are recognized in every hospital to-day," I answered shortly.

"Quite so. And the monastery of Rache-Churân is entirely devoted to the study of the subject."

"Do you mean that that gentle old man----"

"Petrie, a certain M. Sokoloff, a Russian gentleman whose acquaintance I made in Mandalay, related to me an episode that took place at the house of the mandarin Ki-Ming in Canton. It actually occurred in the presence of M. Sokoloff, and therefore is worthy of your close attention.

"He had had certain transactions with Ki-Ming, and at their conclusion received an invitation to dine with the mandarin. The entertainment took place in a sort of loggia or open pavilion, immediately in front of which was an ornamental lake, with numerous water lilies growing upon its surface. One of the servants, I think his name was Li, dropped a silver bowl containing orange-flower water for pouring upon the hands, and some of the contents lightly sprinkled M. Sokoloff's garments.

"Ki-Ming spoke no word of rebuke, Petrie; he merely *looked* at Li, with those deceptive, gazelle-like eyes. Li, according to my acquaintance account, began to make palpable and increasingly anxious attempts to look anywhere rather than into the mild eyes of his implacable master. M. Sokoloff, who, up to that moment, had entertained similar views to your own respecting his host, regarded this unmoving stare of Ki-Ming's as a sort of kindly, because silent, reprimand. The behavior of the unhappy Li very speedily served to disabuse his mind of that delusion.

"Petrie--the man grew livid, his whole body began to twitch and shake as though an ague had attacked him; and his eyes protruded hideously from their sockets! M. Sokoloff assured me that he *felt* himself turning pale--when Ki-Ming, very slowly, raised his right hand and pointed to the pond.

"Li began to pant as though engaged in a life and death struggle with a physically superior antagonist. He clutched at the posts of the loggia with frenzied hands and a bloody froth came to his lips. He began to move backward, step by step, step by step, all the time striving, with might and main, to *prevent* himself from doing so! His eyes were set rigidly upon Ki-Ming, like the eyes of a rabbit fascinated by a python. Ki-Ming continued to point.

"Right to the brink of the lake the man retreated, and there, for one dreadful moment, he paused and uttered a sort of groaning sob. Then, clenching his fists frenziedly, he stepped back into the water and immediately sank among the lilies. Ki-Ming continued to gaze fixedly-- at the spot where bubbles were rising; and presently up came the livid face of the drowning man, still having those glazed eyes turned, immovably, upon the mandarin. For nearly five seconds that hideous, distorted face gazed from amid the mass of blooms, then it sank again ... and rose no more."

"What!" I cried, "do you mean to tell me----"

"Ki-Ming struck a gong. Another servant appeared with a fresh bowl of water; and the mandarin calmly resumed his dinner!"

I drew a deep breath and raised my hand to my head.

"It is almost unbelievable," I said. "But what completely passes my comprehension is his allowing me to depart unscathed, having once held me in his power. Why the long harangue and the pose of friendship?

"That point is not so difficult."

"What!"

"That does not surprise me in the least. You may recollect that Dr. Fu-Manchu entertains for you an undoubted affection, distinctly Chinese in its character, but nevertheless an affection! There is no intention of assassinating *you*, Petrie; *I* am the selected victim."

I started up.

"Smith! what do you mean? What danger, other than that which has threatened us for over two years, threatens us to-night?"

"Now you come to the point which *does* puzzle me. I believe I stated awhile ago that I was afraid. You have placed your finger upon the cause of my fear. *What* threatens us to-night?"

He spoke the words in such a fashion that they seemed physically to chill me. The shadows of the room grew menacing; the very silence became horrible. I longed with a terrible longing for company, for the strength that is in numbers; I would have had the place full to overflowing--for it seemed that we two, condemned by the mysterious organization called the Si-Fan, were at that moment surrounded by the entire arsenal of horrors at the command of Dr. Fu-Manchu. I broke that morbid silence. My voice had assumed an unnatural tone.

"Why do you dread this man, Ki-Ming, so much?"

"Because he must be aware that I know he is in London."

"Well?"

"Dr. Fu-Manchu has no official status. Long ago, his Legation denied all knowledge of his existence. But the mandarin Ki-Ming is known to every diplomat in Europe, Asia and American almost. Only *I*, and now yourself, know that he is a high official of the Si-Fan; Ki-Ming is aware that I know. Why, therefore, does he risk his neck in London?"

"He relies upon his national cunning."

"Petrie, he is aware that I hold evidence to hang him, either here or in China! He relies upon one thing; upon striking first and striking surely. Why is he so confident? I do not know. Therefore I am afraid."

Again a cold shudder ran icily through me. A piece of coal dropped lower into the dying fire--and my heart leapt wildly. Then, in a flash, I remembered something.

"Smith!" I cried, "the letter! We have not looked at the letter."

Nayland Smith laid his pipe upon the mantelpiece and smiled grimly. From his pocket he took out square piece of paper, and thrust it close under my eyes.

"I remembered it as I passed your borrowed garment--which bear no maker's name--on my way to the bedroom for matches," he said.

The paper was covered with Chinese characters!

"What does it mean?" I demanded breathlessly.

Smith uttered a short, mirthless laugh.

"It states that an attempt of a particularly dangerous nature is to be made upon my life to-night, and it recommends me to guard the door, and advises that you watch the window overlooking the court, and keep your pistol ready for instant employment." He stared at me oddly. "How should you act in the circumstances, Petrie?"

"I should strongly distrust such advice. Yet--what else can we *do*?"

"There are several alternatives, but I prefer to follow the advice of Ki-Ming."

The clock of St. Paul's chimed the half-hour: half-past two.

CHAPTER XXIX
LAMA SORCERY

FROM MY POST in the chair by the window I could see two sides of the court below; that immediately opposite, with the entrance to some chambers situated there, and that on the right, with the cloisteresque arches beyond which lay a maze of old-world passages and stairs whereby one who knew the tortuous navigation might come ultimately to the Embankment.

It was this side of the court which lay in deepest shadow. By altering my position quite slightly I could command a view of the arched entrance on the left with its pale lamp in an iron bracket above, and of the high blank wall whose otherwise unbroken expanse it interrupted. All was very still; only on occasions the passing of a vehicle along Fleet Street would break the silence.

The nature of the danger that threatened I was wholly unable to surmise. Since, my pistol on the table beside me, I sat on guard at the window, and Smith, also armed, watched the outer door, it was not apparent by what agency the shadowy enemy could hope to come at us.

Something strange I had detected in Nayland Smith's manner, however, which had induced me to believe that he suspected, if he did not know, what form of menace hung over us in the darkness. One thing in particular was puzzling me extremely: if Smith doubted the good faith of the sender of the message, why had he acted upon it?

Thus my mind worked--in endless and profitless cycles--whilst my eyes were ever searching the shadows below me.

And, as I watched, wondering vaguely why Smith at his post was so silent, presently I became aware of the presence of a slim figure over by the arches on the right. This discovery did not come suddenly, nor did it surprise me; I merely observed without being conscious of any great interest in the matter, that some one was standing in the court below, looking up at me where I sat.

I cannot hope to explain my state of mind at that moment, to render understandable by contrast with the cold fear which had visited me so recently, the utter apathy of my mental attitude. To this day I cannot recapture the mood--and for a very good reason, though one that was not apparent to me at the time.

It was the Eurasian girl Zarmi, who was standing there, looking up at the window! Silently I watched her. Why was I silent?--why did I not warn Smith of the presence of one of Dr. Fu-Manchu's servants? I cannot explain, although later, the strangeness of my behavior may become in some measure understandable.

Zarmi raised her hand, beckoning to me, then stepped back, revealing the presence of a companion, hitherto masked by the dense shadows that lay under the arches. This second watcher moved slowly forward, and I perceived him to be none other than the mandarin Ki-Ming.

This I noted with interest, but with a sort of *impersonal* interest, as I might have watched the entrance of a character upon the stage of a theater. Despite the feeble light, I could see his benign countenance very clearly; but, far from being excited, a dreamy contentment possessed me; I actually found myself hoping that Smith would not intrude upon my reverie!

What a fascinating pageant it had been--the Fu-Manchu drama--from the moment that I had first set eyes upon the Yellow doctor. Again I seemed to be enacting my part in that scene, two years ago and more, when I had burst into the bare room above Shen-Yan's opium den and had stood face to face with Dr. Fu-Manchu. He wore a plain yellow robe, its hue almost identical with that of his gaunt, hairless face; his elbows rested upon the dirty table and his pointed chin upon his long, bony hands.

Into those uncanny eyes I stared, those eyes, long, narrow, and slightly oblique, their brilliant, catlike greenness sometimes horribly filmed, like the eyes of some grotesque bird....

Thus it began; and from this point I was carried on, step by step through every episode, great and small. It was such a retrospect as passes through the mind of one drowning.

With a vividness that was terrible yet exquisite, I saw Kâramaneh, my lost love; I saw her first wrapped in a hooded opera-cloak, with her flower-like face and glorious dark eyes raised to me; I saw her in the gauzy Eastern raiment of a slave-girl, and I saw her in the dress of a gipsy.

Through moments sweet and bitter I lived again, through hours of suspense and days of ceaseless watching; through the long months of that first summer when my unhappy love came to me, and on, on, interminably on. For years I lived again beneath that ghastly Yellow cloud. I searched throughout the land of Egypt for Kâramaneh and knew once more the sorrow of losing her. Time ceased to exist for me.

Then, at the end of these strenuous years, I came at last to my meeting with Ki-Ming in the room with the golden door. At this point my visionary adventures took a new turn. I sat again upon the red-covered couch and listened, half stupefied, to the placid speech of the mandarin. Again I came under the spell of his singular personality, and again, closing my eyes, I consented to be led from the room.

But, having crossed the threshold, a sudden awful doubt passed through my mind, arrow-like. The hand that held my arm was bony and clawish; I could detect the presence of incredibly long finger nails--nails long as those of some buried vampire of the black ages!

Choking down a cry of horror, I opened my eyes--heedless of the promise given but a few moments earlier--and looked into the face of my guide.

It was Dr. Fu-Manchu!...

Never, dreaming or waking, have I known a sensation identical with that which now clutched my heart; I thought that it must be death. For ages, untold ages--aeons longer than the world has known--I looked into that still, awful face, into those unnatural green eyes. I jerked my hand free from the Chinaman's clutch and sprang back.

As I did so, I became miraculously translated from the threshold of the room with the golden door to our chambers in the court adjoining Fleet Street; I came into full possession of my faculties (or believed so at the time); I realized that I had nodded at my post, that I had dreamed a strange dream ... but I realized something else. A ghoulish presence was in the room.

Snatching up my pistol from the table I turned. Like some evil jinn of Arabian lore, Dr. Fu-Manchu, surrounded by a slight mist, stood looking at me!

Instantly I raised the pistol, leveled it steadily at the high, dome-like brow--and fired! There could be no possibility of missing at such short range, no possibility whatever ... and in the very instant of pulling the trigger the mist cleared, the lineaments of Dr. Fu-Manchu melted magically. This was not the Chinese doctor who stood before me, at whose skull I still was pointing the deadly little weapon, into whose brain I had fired the bullet; _it was Nayland Smith!_

Ki-Ming, by means of the unholy arts of the Lamas of Rache-Churân, had caused my to murder my best friend!

"Smith!" I whispered huskily--"God forgive me, what have I done? What have I done?"

I stepped forward to support him ere he fell; but utter oblivion closed down upon me, and I knew no more.

"He will do quite well now." said a voice that seemed to come from a vast distance. "The effects of the drug will have entirely worn off when he wakes, except that there may be nausea, and possibly muscular pain for a time."

I opened my eyes; they were throbbing agonizingly. I lay in bed, and beside me stood Murdoch McCabe, the famous toxicological expert from Charing Cross Hospital--and Nayland Smith!

"Ah, that's better!" cried McCabe cheerily. "Here--drink this."

I drank from the glass which he raised to my lips. I was too weak for speech, too weak for wonder. Nayland Smith, his face gray and drawn in the cold light of early morning, watched me anxiously. McCabe in a matter of fact way that acted upon me like a welcome tonic, put several purely medical questions, which at first by dint of a great effort, but, with ever-increasing ease, I answered.

"Yes," he said musingly at last. "Of course it is all but impossible to speak with certainty, but I am disposed to think that you have been drugged with some preparation of hashish. The most likely is that known in Eastern countries as *maagûn* or *barsh*, composed of equal parts of *cannabis indica* and opium, with hellebore and two other constituents, which vary according to the purpose which the *maagûn* is intended to serve. This renders the subject particularly open to subjective hallucination, and a pliable instrument in the hands of a hypnotic operator, for instance."

"You see, old man?" cried Smith eagerly. "You see?"

But I shook my head weakly.

"I shot you," I said. "It is impossible that I could have missed."

"Mr. Smith has placed me in possession of the facts," interrupted McCabe, "and I can outline with reasonable certainty what took place. Of course, it's all very amazing, utterly fantastic in fact, but I have met with almost parallel cases in Egypt, in India, and elsewhere in the East: never in London, I'll confess. You see, Dr. Petrie, you were taken into the presence of a very accomplished hypnotist, having been previously prepared by a stiff administration of *maagûn*. You are doubtless familiar with the remarkable experiments in psycho-therapeutics conducted at the Salpêtrier in Paris, and you will readily understand me when I say that, prior to your recovering consciousness in the presence of the mandarin Ki-Ming, you had received your hypnotic instructions.

"These were to be put into execution either at a certain time (duly impressed upon your drugged mind) or at a given signal...."

"It was a signal," snapped Smith. "Ki-Ming stood in the court below and looked up at the window," I objected.

"In that event," snapped Smith, "he would have spoken softly, through the letter-box of the door!"

"You immediately resumed your interrupted trance," continued McCabe, "and by hypnotic suggestion impressed upon you earlier in the evening, you were ingeniously led up to a point at which, under what delusion I know not, you fired at Mr. Smith. I had the privilege of studying an almost parallel case in Simla, where an officer was fatally stabbed by his *khitmatgar* (a most faithful servant) acting under the hypnotic prompting of a certain *fakîr* whom the officer had been unwise enough to chastise. The *fakîr* paid for the crime with his life, I may add. The *khitmatgar* shot him, ten minutes later."

"I had no chance at Ki-Ming," snapped Smith. "He vanished like a shadow. But has has played his big card and lost! Henceforth he is a hunted man; and he knows it! Oh!" he cried, seeing me watching him in bewilderment, "I suspected some Lama trickery, old man, and I stuck closely to the arrangements proposed by the mandarin, but kept you under careful observation!"

"But, Smith--I shot you! It was impossible to miss!"

"I agree. But do you recall the *report?*"

"The report? I was too dazed, too horrified, by the discovery of what I had done...."

"There was no report, Petrie. I am not entirely a stranger to Indo-Chinese jugglery, and you had a very strange look in your eyes. Therefore I took the precaution of unloading your Browning!"

CHAPTER XXX

MEDUSA

LEGAL BUSINESS, connected with the estate of a distant relative, deceased, necessitated my sudden departure from London, within twenty-four hours of the events just narrated; and at a time when London was for me the center of the universe. The business being terminated--and in a manner financially satisfactory to myself--I discovered that with luck I could just catch the fast train back. Amid a perfect whirl of hotel porters and taxi-drivers worthy of Nayland Smith I departed for the station ... to arrive at the entrance to the platform at the exact moment that the guard raised his green flag!

"Too late, sir! Stand back, if you please!"

The ticket-collector at the barrier thrust out his arm to stay me. The London express was moving from the platform. But my determination to travel by that train and by no other over-rode all obstacles; If I missed it, I should be forced to wait until the following morning.

I leapt past the barrier, completely taking the man by surprise, and went racing up the platform. Many arms were outstretched to detain me, and the gray-bearded guard stood fully in my path; but I dodged them all, collided with and upset a gigantic negro who wore a chauffeur's uniform--and found myself level with a first-class compartment; the window was open.

Amid a chorus of excited voices, I tossed my bag in at the window, leapt upon the footboard and turned the handle. Although the entrance to the tunnel was perilously near now, I managed to wrench the door open and to swing myself into the carriage. Then, by means of the strap, I reclosed the door in the nick of time, and sank, panting, upon the seat. I had a vague impression that the black chauffeur, having recovered himself, had raced after me to the uttermost point of the platform, but, my end achieved, I was callously indifferent to the outrageous means thereto which I seen fit to employ. The express dashed into the tunnel. I uttered a great sigh of relief.

With Kâramaneh in the hands of the Si-Fan, this journey to the north had indeed been undertaken with the utmost reluctance. Nayland Smith had written to me once during my brief absence, and his letter had inspired a yet keener desire to be back and at grips with the Yellow group; for he had hinted broadly that a tangible clue to the whereabouts of the Si-Fan head-quarters had at last been secured.

Now I learnt that I had a traveling companion--a woman. She was seated in the further, opposite corner, wore a long, loose motor-coat, which could not altogether conceal the fine lines of her lithe figure, and a thick veil hid her face. A motive for the excited behavior of the negro chauffeur suggested itself to my mind; a label; "Engaged," was pasted to the window!

I glanced across the compartment. Through the closely woven veil the woman was watching me. An apology clearly was called for.

"Madame," I said, "I hope you will forgive this unfortunate intrusion; but it was vitally important that I should not miss the London train."

She bowed, very slightly, very coldly--and turned her head aside.

The rebuff was as unmistakable as my offense was irremediable. Nor did I feel justified in resenting it. Therefore, endeavoring to dismiss the matter from my mind, I placed my bag upon the rack, and unfolding the newspaper with which I was provided, tried to interest myself in the doings of the world at large.

My attempt proved not altogether successful; strive how I would, my thoughts persistently reverted to the Si-Fan, the evil, secret society who held in their power one dearer to me than all the rest of the world; to Dr. Fu-Manchu, the genius who darkly controlled my destiny; and to Nayland Smith, the barrier between the White races and the devouring tide of the Yellow.

Sighing again, involuntarily, I glanced up ... to meet the gaze of a pair of wonderful eyes.

Never, in my experience, had I seen their like. The dark eyes of Kâramaneh were wonderful and beautiful, the eyes of Dr. Fu-Manchu sinister and wholly unforgettable; but the eyes of this woman were incredible. Their glance was all but insupportable; the were the eyes of a Medusa!

Since I had met; in the not distant past, the soft gaze of Ki-Ming, the mandarin whose phenomenal hypnotic powers rendered him capable of transcending the achievements of the celebrated Cagliostro, I knew much of the power of the human eye. But these were unlike any human eyes I had ever known.

Long, almond-shaped, bordered by heavy jet-black lashes, arched over by finely penciled brows, their strange brilliancy, as of a fire within, was utterly uncanny. They were the eyes of some beautiful wild creature rather than those of a woman.

Their possessor had now thrown back her motor-veil, revealing a face Orientally dark and perfectly oval, with a clustering mass of dull gold hair, small, aquiline nose and full, red lips. Her weird eyes met mine for an instant, and then the long lashes drooped quickly, as she leant back against the cushions, with a graceful languor suggestive of the East rather than of the West.

Her long coat had fallen partly open, and I saw, with surprise, that it was lined with leopard-skin. One hand was ungloved, and lay on the arm-rest--a slim hand of the hue of old ivory, with a strange, ancient ring upon the index finger.

This woman obviously was not a European, and I experienced great difficulty in determining with what Asiatic nation she could claim kinship. In point of fact I had never seen another who remotely resembled her; she was a fit employer for the gigantic negro with whom I had collided on the platform.

I tried to laugh at myself, staring from the window at the moon-bathed landscape; but the strange personality of my solitary companion would not be denied, and I looked quickly in her direction--in time to detect her glancing away; in time to experience the uncanny fascination of her gaze.

The long slim hand attracted my attention again, the green stone in the ring affording a startling contrast against the dull cream of the skin.

Whether the woman's personality, or a vague perfume of which I became aware, were responsible, I found myself thinking of a flower-bedecked shrine, wherefrom arose the smoke of incense to some pagan god.

In vain I told myself that my frame of mind was contemptible, that I should be ashamed of such weakness. Station after station was left behind, as the express sped through moonlit England towards the smoky metropolis. Assured that I was being furtively watched, I became more and more uneasy.

It was with a distinct sense of effort that I withheld my gaze, forcing myself to look out of the window. When, having reasoned against the mad ideas that sought to obsess me, I glanced again across the compartment, I perceived, with inexpressible relief, that my companion had lowered her veil.

She kept it lowered throughout the remainder of the journey; yet during the hour that ensued I continued to experience sensations of which I have never since been able to think without a thrill of fear. It seemed that I had thrust myself, not into a commonplace railway compartment, but into a Cumaean cavern.

If only I could have addressed this utterly mysterious stranger, have uttered some word of commonplace, I felt that the spell might have been broken. But, for some occult reason, in no way associated with my first rebuff, I found myself tongue-tied; I sustained, for an hour (the longest I had ever known), a silent watch and ward over my reason; I seemed to be repelling, fighting against, some subtle power that sought to flood my brain, swamp my individuality, and enslave me to another's will.

In what degree this was actual, and in what due to a mind overwrought from endless conflict with the Yellow group, I know not to this day, but you who read these records of our giant struggle with Fu-Manchu and his satellites shall presently judge for yourselves.

When, at last, the brakes were applied, and the pillars and platforms of the great terminus glided into view, how welcome was the smoky glare, how welcome the muffled roar of busy London!

A huge negro--the double of the man I had overthrown--opened the door of the compartment, bestowing upon me a glance in which enmity and amazement were oddly blended, and the woman, drawing the cloak about her graceful figure, stood up composedly.

She reached for a small leather case on the rack, and her loose sleeve fell back, to reveal a bare arm--soft, perfectly molded, of the even hue of old ivory. Just below the elbow a strange-looking snake bangle clasped the warm-flesh; the eyes; dull green, seemed to hold a slumbering fire--a spark--a spark of living light.

Then--she was gone!

"Thank Heaven!" I muttered, and felt like another Dante emerging from the Hades.

As I passed out of the station, I had a fleeting glimpse of a gray figure stepping into a big car, driven by a black chauffeur.

CHAPTER XXXI

THE MARMOSET

HALF-PAST TWELVE was striking as I came out of the terminus, buttoning up my overcoat, and pulling my soft hat firmly down upon my head, started to walk to Hyde Park Corner.

I had declined the services of the several taxi-drivers who had accosted me and had determined to walk a part of the distance homeward, in order to check the fever of excitement which consumed me.

Already I was ashamed of the strange fears which had been mine during the journey, but I wanted to reflect, to conquer my mood, and the midnight solitude of the land of Squares which lay between me and Hyde Park appealed quite irresistibly.

There is a distinct pleasure to be derived from a solitary walk through London, in the small hours of an April morning, provided one is so situated as to be capable of enjoying it. To appreciate the solitude and mystery of the sleeping city, a certain sense of prosperity--a knowledge that one is immune from the necessity of being abroad at that hour--is requisite. The tramp, the night policeman and the coffee-stall keeper know more of London by night than most people--but of the romance of the dark hours they know little. Romance succumbs before necessity.

I had good reason to be keenly alive to the aroma of mystery which pervades the most commonplace thoroughfare after the hum of the traffic has subsided--when the rare pedestrian and the rarer cab alone traverse the deserted highway. With more intimate cares seeking to claim my mind, it was good to tramp along the echoing, empty streets and to indulge in imaginative speculation regarding the strange things that night must shroud in every big city. I have known the solitude of deserts, but the solitude of London is equally fascinating.

He whose business or pleasure had led him to traverse the route which was mine on this memorable night must have observed how each of the squares composing that residential chain which links the outer with the inner Society has a popular and an exclusive side. The angle used by vehicular traffic in crossing the square from corner to corner invariably is rich in a crop of black board bearing house-agent's announcements.

In the shadow of such a board I paused, taking out my case an leisurely selecting a cigar. So many of the houses in the southwest angle were unoccupied, that I found myself taking quite an interest in one a little way ahead; from the hall door and from the long conservatory over the porch light streamed out.

Excepting these illuminations, there was no light elsewhere in the square to show which houses were inhabited and which vacant. I might have stood in a street of Pompeii or Thebes--a street of the dead past. I permitted my imagination to dwell upon this idea as I fumbled for matches and gazed about me. I wondered if a day would come when some savant of a future land, in a future age, should stand where I stood and endeavor to reconstruct, from the crumbling ruins, this typical London square. A slight breeze set the hatchet-board creaking above my head, as I held my gloved hands about the pine-vesta.

At that moment some one or something whistled close beside me!

I turned, in a flash, dropping the match upon the pavement. There was no lamp near the spot whereat I stood, and the gateway and porch of the deserted residence seemed to be empty. I stood there peering in the direction from which the mysterious whistle had come.

The drone of a taxicab, approaching from the north, increased in volume, as the vehicle came spinning around the angle of the square, passed me, and went droning on its way. I watched it swing around the distant corner ... and, in the new stillness, the whistle was repeated!

This time the sound chilled me. The whistle was pitched in a curious, inhuman key, and it possessed a mocking note that was strangely uncanny.

Listening intently and peering towards the porch of the empty house, I struck a second match, pushed the iron gate open and made for the steps, sheltering the feeble flame with upraised hand. As I did so, the whistle was again repeated, but from some spot further away, to the left of the porch, and from low down upon the ground.

Just as I glimpsed something moving under the lee of the porch, the match was blown out, for I was hampered by the handbag which I carried. Thus reminded of its presence, however, I recollected that my pocket-lamp was in it. Quickly opening the bag, I took out the lamp, and, passing around the corner of the steps, directed a ray of light into the narrow passage which communicated with the rear of the building.

Half-way along the passage, looking back at me over its shoulder, and whistling angrily, was a little marmoset!

I pulled up as sharply as though the point of a sword had been held at my throat. One marmoset is sufficiently like another to deceive the ordinary observer, but unless I was permitting a not unnatural prejudice to influence my opinion, this particular specimen was the pet of Dr. Fu-Manchu!

Excitement, not untinged with fear, began to grow up within me. Hyde Park was no far cry, this was near to the heart of social London; yet, somewhere close at hand, it might be, watching me as I stood--lurked, perhaps, the great and evil being who dreamed of overthrowing the entire white race!

With a grotesque grimace and a final, chattering whistle, the little creature leapt away out of the beam of light cast by my lamp. Its sudden disappearance brought me to my senses and reminded me of my plain duty. I set off along the passage briskly, arrived at a small, square yard ... and was just in time to see the ape leap into a well-like opening before a basement window. I stepped to the brink, directing the light down into the well.

I saw a collection of rotten leaves, waste paper, and miscellaneous rubbish--but the marmoset was not visible. Then I perceived that practically all the glass in the window had been broken. A sound of shrill chattering reached me from the blackness of the underground apartment.

Again I hesitated. What did the darkness mask?

The note of a distant motor-horn rose clearly above the vague throbbing which is the only silence known to the town-dweller.

Gripping the unlighted cigar between my teeth, I placed my bag upon the ground and dropped into the well before the broken window. To raise the sash was a simple matter, and, having accomplished it, I inspected the room within.

The light showed a large kitchen, with torn wall-paper and decorator's litter strewn about the floor, a whitewash pail in one corner, and nothing else.

I climbed in, and, taking from my pocket the Browning pistol without which I had never traveled since the return of the dreadful Chinaman to England, I crossed to the door, which was ajar, and looked out into the passage beyond.

Stifling an exclamation, I fell back a step. Two gleaming eyes stared straightly into mine!

The next moment I had forced a laugh to my lips ... as the marmoset turned and went gamboling up the stairs. The house was profoundly silent. I crossed the passage and followed the creature, which now was proceeding, I thought, with more of a set purpose.

Out into a spacious and deserted hallway it led me, where my cautious footsteps echoed eerily, and ghostly faces seemed to peer down upon me from the galleries above. I should have liked to have unbarred the street door, in order to have opened a safe line of retreat in the event of its being required, but the marmoset suddenly sprang up the main stairway at a great speed, and went racing around the gallery overhead toward the front of the house.

Determined, if possible, to keep the creature in view, I started in pursuit. Up the uncarpeted stairs I went, and, from the rail of the landing, looked down into the blackness of the hallway apprehensively. Nothing stirred below. The marmoset had disappeared between the half-opened leaves of a large folding door. Casting the beam of light ahead of me I followed. I found myself in a long, lofty apartment, evidently a drawing-room.

Of the quarry I could detect no sign; but the only other door of the room was closed; therefore, since the creature had entered, it must, I argued, undoubtedly be concealed somewhere in the apartment. Flashing the light about to right and left, I presently perceived that a conservatory (no doubt facing on the square) ran parallel with one side of the room. French windows gave access to either end of it; and it was through one of these, which was slightly open, that the questioning ray had intruded.

I stepped into the conservatory. Linen blinds covered the windows, but a faint light from outside found access to the bare, tiled apartment. Ten paces on my right, from an aperture once closed by a square wooden panel that now lay upon the floor, the marmoset was grimacing at me.

Realizing that the ray of my lamp must be visible through the blinds from outside, I extinguished it ... and, a moving silhouette against a faintly luminous square, I could clearly distinguish the marmoset watching me.

There was a light in the room beyond!

The marmoset disappeared--and I became aware of a faint, incense-like perfume. Where had I met with it before? Nothing disturbed the silence of the empty house wherein I stood; yet I hesitated for several seconds to pursue the chase further. The realization came to me that the hole in the wall communicated with the conservatory of the corner house in the square, the house with the lighted windows.

Determined to see the thing through, I discarded my overcoat--and crawled through the gap. The smell of burning perfume became almost overpowering, as I stood upright, to find myself almost touching curtains of some semi-transparent golden fabric draped in the door between the conservatory and the drawing-room.

Cautiously, inch by inch, I approached my eyes to the slight gap in the draperies, as, from somewhere in the house below, sounded the clangor of a brazen gong. Seven times its ominous note boomed out. I shrank back into my sanctuary; the incense seemed to be stifling me.

CHAPTER XXXII

SHRINE OF SEVEN LAMPS

NEVER CAN I FORGET that nightmare apartment, that efreet's hall. It was identical in shape with the room of the adjoining house through which I had come, but its walls were draped in somber black and a dead black carpet covered the entire floor. A golden curtain--similar to that which concealed me--broke the somber expanse of the end wall to my right, and the door directly opposite my hiding-place was closed.

Across the gold curtain, wrought in glittering black, were seven characters, apparently Chinese; before it, supported upon seven ebony pedestals, burned seven golden lamps; whilst, dotted about the black carpet, were seven gold-lacquered stools, each having a black cushion set before it. There was no sign of the marmoset; the incredible room of black and gold was quite empty, with a sort of stark emptiness that seemed to oppress my soul.

Close upon the booming of the gong followed a sound of many footsteps and a buzz of subdued conversation. Keeping well back in the welcome shadow I watched, with bated breath, the opening of the door immediately opposite.

The outer sides of its leaves proved to be of gold, and one glimpse of the room beyond awoke a latent memory and gave it positive form. I had been in this house before; it was in that room with the golden door that I had had my memorable interview with the mandarin Ki-Ming! My excitement grew more and more intense.

Singly, and in small groups, a number of Orientals came in. All wore European, or semi-European garments, but I was enabled to identify two for Chinamen, two for Hindus and three for Burmans. Other Asiatics there were, also, whose exact place among the Eastern races I could not determine; there was at least one Egyptian and there were several Eurasians; no women were present.

Standing grouped just within the open door, the gathering of Orientals kept up a ceaseless buzz of subdued conversation; then, abruptly, stark silence fell, and through a lane of bowed heads, Ki-Ming, the famous Chinese diplomat, entered, smiling blandly, and took his seat upon one of the seven golden stools. He wore the picturesque yellow robe, trimmed with marten fur, which I had seen once before, and he placed his pearl-encircled cap, surmounted by the coral ball denoting his rank, upon the black cushion beside him.

Almost immediately afterward entered a second and even more

striking figure. It was that of a Lama monk! He was received with the same marks of deference which had been accorded the mandarin; and he seated himself upon another of the golden stools.

Silence, a moment of hushed expectancy, and ... yellow-robed, immobile, his wonderful, evil face emaciated by illness, but his long, magnetic eyes blazing greenly, as though not a soul but an elemental spirit dwelt within that gaunt, high-shouldered body, Dr. Fu-Manchu entered, slowly, leaning upon a heavy stick!

The realities seemed to be slipping from me; I could not believe that I looked upon a material world. This had been a night of wonders, having no place in the life of a sane, modern man, but belonging to the days of the jinn and the Arabian necromancers.

Fu-Manchu was greeted by a universal raising of hands, but in complete silence. He also wore a cap surmounted by a coral ball, and this he placed upon one of the black cushions set before a golden stool. Then, resting heavily upon his stick, he began to speak--in French!

As on listens to a dream-voice, I listened to that, alternately gutteral and sibilant, of the terrible Chinese doctor. He was defending himself! With what he was charged by his sinister brethren I knew not nor could I gather from his words, but that he was rendering account of his stewardship became unmistakable. Scarce crediting my senses, I heard him unfold to his listeners details of crimes successfully perpetrated, and with the results of some of these I was but too familiar; other there were in the ghastly catalogue which had been accomplished secretly. Then my blood froze with horror. My own name was mentioned--and that of Nayland Smith! We two stood in the way of the coming of one whom he called the Lady of the Si-Fan, in the way of Asiatic supremacy.

A fantastic legend once mentioned to me by Smith, of some woman cherished in a secret fastness of Hindustan who was destined one day to rule the world, now appeared, to my benumbed senses, to be the unquestioned creed of the murderous, cosmopolitan group known as the Si-Fan! At every mention of her name all heads were bowed in reverence.

Dr. Fu-Manchu spoke without the slightest trace of excitement; he assured his auditors of his fidelity to their cause and proposed to prove to them that he enjoyed the complete confidence of the Lady of the Si-Fan.

And with every moment that passed the giant intellect of the speaker became more and more apparent. Years ago Nayland Smith had asssure me that Dr. Fu-Manchu was a linguist who spoke with almost equal facility in any of th civilized languages and in most of the barbaric; now the truth of this was demonstrated. For, following some passage which might be susceptible of misconstruction, Fu-Manchu would turn slightly, and elucidate his remarks, addressing a Chinaman in Chinese, a Hindu in Hindustanee, or an Egyptian in Arabic.

His auditors were swayed by the magnetic personality of the speaker, as reeds by a breeze; and now I became aware of a curious circumstance. Either because they and I viewed the character of this great and evil man from a widely dissimilar aspect, or because, my presence being unknown to him, I remained outside the radius of his power, it seemed to me that these members of the evidently vast organization known as the Si-Fan were dupes, to a man, of the Chinese orator! It seemed to me that he used them as an instrument, playing upon their obvious fanaticism, string by string, as a player upon an Eastern harp, and all the time weaving harmonies to suit some giant, incredible scheme of his own--a scheme over and beyond any of which they had dreamed, in the fruition whereof they had no part--of the true nature and composition of which they had no comprehension.

"Not since the day of the first Yuan Emperor," said Fu-Manchu sibilantly, "has Our Lady of the Si-Fan--to look upon upon whom, unveiled, is death--crossed the sacred borders. To-day I am a man supremely happy and honored above my deserts. You shall all partake with me of that happiness, that honor...."

Again the gong sounded seven times, and a sort of magnetic thrill seemed to pass throughout the room. There followed a faint, musical sound, like the tinkle of a silver bell.

All heads were lowered, but all eyes upturned to the golden curtain. Literally holding my breath, in those moments of intense expectancy, I watched the draperies parted from the center and pulled aside by unseen agency.

A black covered dais was revealed, bearing an ebony chair. And seated in the chair, enveloped from head to feet in a shimmering white veil, was a woman. A sound like a great sigh arose from the gathering. The woman rose slowly to her feet, and raised her arms, which were exquisitely formed, and of the uniform hue of old ivory, so that the veil fell back to her shoulders, revealing the green snake bangle which she wore. She extended her long, slim hands as if in benediction; the silver bell sounded ... and the curtain dropped again, entirely obscuring the dais!

Frankly, I thought myself mad; for this "lady of the Si-Fan" was none other than my mysterious traveling companion! This was some solemn farce with which Fu-Manchu sought to impress his fanatical dupes. And he had succeeded; they were inspired, their eyes blazed. Here were men capable of any crime in the name of the Si-Fan!

Every face within my ken I had studied individually, and now slowly and cautiously I changed my position, so that a group of three members standing immediately to the right of the door came into view. One of them--a tall, spare, and closely bearded man whom I took for some kind of Hindu--had removed his gaze from the dais and was glancing furtively all about him. Once he looked in my direction, and my heart leapt high, then seemed to stop its pulsing.

An overpowering consciousness of my danger came to me; a dim envisioning of what appalling fate would be mine in the event of discovery. As those piercing eyes were turned away again, I drew back, step my step.

Dropping upon my knees, I began to feel for the gap in the conservatory wall. The desire to depart from the house of the Si-Fan was become urgent. Once safely away, I could take the necessary steps to ensure the apprehension of the entire group. What a triumph would be mine!

I found the opening without much difficulty and crept through into the empty house. The vague light which penetrated the linen blinds served to show me the length of the empty, tiled apartment. I had actually reached the French window giving access to the drawing-room, when--the skirl of a police whistle split the stillness ... and the sound came from the house which I had just quitted!

To write that I was amazed were to achieve the banal. Rigid with wonderment I stood, and clutched at the open window. So I was standing, a man of stone, when the voice, the high-pitched, imperious, unmistakable voice of *Nayland Smith,* followed sharply upon the skirl of the whistle:--

"Watch those French windows, Weymouth! I can hold the door!"

Like a lightning flash it came to me that the tall Hindu had been none other than Smith disguised. From the square outside came a sudden turmoil, a sound of racing feet, of smashing glass, of doors burst forcibly open. Palpably, the place was surrounded; this was an organized raid.

Irresolute, I stood there in the semi-gloom--inactive from amaze of it all--whilst sounds of a tremendous struggle proceeded from the square gap in the partition.

"Lights!" rose a cry, in Smith's voice again--"they have cut the wires!"

At that I came to my senses. Plunging my hand into my pocket, I snatched out the electric lamp ... and stepped back quickly into the utter gloom of the room behind me.

Some one was crawling through the aperture into the conservatory!

As I watched I saw him, in the dim light, stoop to replace the movable panel. Then, tapping upon the tiled floor as he walked, the fugitive approached me. He was but three paces from the French window when I pressed the button of my lamp and directed its ray fully upon his face.

"Hands up!" I said breathlessly. "I have you covered, Dr. Fu-Manchu!"

CHAPTER XXXIII

AN ANTI-CLIMAX

ONE HOUR LATER I stood in the entrance hall of our chambers in the court adjoining Fleet Street. Some one who had come racing up the stairs, now had inserted a key in the lock. Open swung the door--and Nayland Smith entered, in a perfect whirl of excitement.

"Petrie! Petrie!" he cried, and seized both my hands--"you have missed a night of nights! Man alive! we have the whole gang--the great Ki-Ming included!" His eyes were blazing. "Weymouth has made no fewer than twenty-five arrests, some of the prisoners being well-known Orientals. It will be the devil's own work to keep it all quiet, but Scotland Yard has already advised the Press."

"Congratulations, old man," I said, and looked him squarely in the eyes.

Something there must have been in my glance at variance with the spoken words. His expression changed; he grasped my shoulder.

"*She* was not there," he said, "but please God, we'll find her now. It's only a question of time."

But, even as he spoke, the old, haunted look was creeping back into the lean face. He gave me a rapid glance; then:--

"I might as well make a clean breast of it," he rapped. "Fu-Manchu escaped! Furthermore, when we got lights, the woman had vanished, too."

"The woman!"

"There was a woman at this strange gathering, Petrie. Heaven only knows who she really is. According to Fu-Manchu she is that woman of mystery concerning whose existence strange stories are current in the East; the future Empress of a universal empire! But of course I decline to accept the story, Petrie! if ever the Yellow races overran Europe, I am in no doubt respecting the identity of the person who would ascend the throne of the world!"

"Nor I, Smith!" I cried excitedly. "Good God! he holds them all in the palm of his hand! He has welded together the fanatics of every creed of the East into a giant weapon for his personal use! Small wonder that he is so formidable. But, Smith--*who* is that woman?"

"Petrie!" he said slowly, and I knew that I had betrayed my secret, "Petrie--where did you learn all this?"

I returned his steady gaze.

"I was present at the meeting of the Si-Fan," I replied steadily.

"What? What? *You* were present?"

"I was present! Listen, and I will explain."

Standing there in the hallway I related, as briefly as possible, the astounding events of the night. As I told of the woman in the train--

"That confirms my impression that Fu-Manchu was imposing upon the others!" he snapped. "I cannot conceive of a woman recluse from some Lamaserie, surrounded by silent attendants and trained for her exalted destiny in the way that the legendary veiled woman of Tibet is said to be trained, traveling alone in an English railway carriage! Did you observe, Petrie, if her eyes were *oblique* at all?"

"They did not strike me as being oblique. Why do you ask?"

"Because I strongly suspect that we have to do with none other than Fu-Manchu's daughter! But go on."

"By heavens, Smith! You may be right! I had no idea that a Chinese woman could possess such features."

"She may not have a Chinese mother; furthermore, there are pretty women in China as well as in other countries; also, there are hair dyes and cosmetics. But for Heaven's sake go on!"

I continued my all but incredible narrative; came to the point where I discovered the straying marmoset and entered the empty house, without provoking any comment from my listener. He stared at me with something very like surprised admiration when I related how I had become an unseen spectator of that singular meeting.

"And I though I had achieved the triumph of my life in gaining admission and smuggling Weymouth and Carter into the roof, armed with hooks and rope-ladders!" he murmured.

Now I came to the moment when, having withdrawn into the empty house, I had heard the police whistle and had heard Smith's voice; I came to the moment when I had found myself face to face with Dr. Fu-Manchu.

Nayland Smith's eyes were on fire now; he literally quivered with excitement, when--

"*Ssh!* what's that?" he whispered, and grasped my arm. "I heard something move in the sitting-room, Petrie!"

"It was a coal dropping from the grate, perhaps," I said--and rapidly continued my story, telling how, with my pistol to his head, I had forced the Chinese doctor to descend into the hallway of the empty house.

"Yes, yes," snapped Smith. "For God's sake go on, man! What have you done with him? Where is he?"

I clearly detected a movement myself immediately behind the half-open door of the sitting-room. Smith started and stared intently across my shoulder at the doorway; then his gaze shifted and became fixed upon my face.

"He bought his life from me, Smith."

Never can I forget the change that came over my friend's tanned features at those words; never can I forget the pang that I suffered to see it. The fire died out of his eyes and he seemed to grow old and weary in a moment. None too steadily I went on:--

"He offered a price that I could not resist, Smith. Try to forgive me, if you can. I know that I have done a dastardly thing, but--perhaps a day may come in your own life when you will understand. He descended with me to a cellar under the empty house, in which some one was locked. Had I arrested Fu-Manchu this poor captive must have died there of starvation; for no one would ever have suspected that the place had an occupant...."

The door of the sitting-room was thrown open, and, wearing my great-coat over the bizarre costume in which I had found her, with her bare ankles and little red slippers peeping grotesquely from below, and her wonderful cloud of hair rippling over the turned-up collar, Kâramaneh came out!

Her great dark eyes were raised to Nayland Smith's with such an appeal in them--an appeal for *me*--that emotion took me by the throat and had me speechless. I could not look at either of them; I turned aside and stared into the lighted sitting-room.

How long I stood so God knows, and I never shall; but suddenly I found my hand seized in a vice-like grip, I looked around ... and Smith, holding my fingers fast in that iron grasp, had his left arm about Kâramaneh's shoulders, and his gray eyes were strangely soft, whilst hers were hidden behind her upraised hands.

"Good old Petrie!" said Smith hoarsely. "Wake up, man; we have to get her to a hotel before they all close, remember. *I* understand, old man. That day came in my life long years ago!"

CHAPTER XXXIV

GRAYWATER PARK

"THIS IS A SINGULAR SITUATION IN WHICH WE FIND OURSELVES." I said, "and one that I'm bound to admit I don't appreciate."

Nayland Smith stretched his long legs, and lay back in his chair.

"The sudden illness of Sir Lionel is certainly very disturbing," he replied, "and had there been any possibility of returning to London to-night, I should certainly have availed myself of it, Petrie. I share your misgivings. We are intruders at a time like this."

He stared at me keenly, blowing a wreath of smoke from his lips, and then directing his attention to the cone of ash which crowned his cigar. I glanced, and not for the first time, toward the quaint old doorway which gave access to a certain corridor. Then--

"Apart from the feeling that we intrude," I continued slowly, "there is a certain sense of unrest."

"Yes," snapped Smith, sitting suddenly upright--"yes! You experience this? Good! You are happily sensitive to this type of impression, Petrie, and therefore quite as useful to me as a cat is useful to a physical investigator."

He laughed in his quick, breezy fashion.

"You will appreciate my meaning," he added; "therefore I offer no excuse for the analogy. Of course, the circumstances, as we know them, may be responsible for this consciousness of unrest. We are neither of us likely to forget the attempt upon the life of Sir Lionel Barton two years ago or more. Our attitude toward sudden illness is scarcely that of impartial observers."

"I suppose not," I admitted, glancing yet again at the still vacant doorway by the foot of the stairs, which now the twilight was draping in mysterious shadows.

Indeed, our position was a curious one. A welcome invitation from our old friend, Sir Lionel Barton, the world-famous explorer, had come at a time when a spell of repose, a glimpse of sea and awakening countryside, and a breath of fair, untainted air were very desirable. The position of Kâramaneh, who accompanied us, was sufficiently unconventional already, but the presence of Mrs. Oram, the dignified housekeeper, had rendered possible her visit to this bachelor establishment. In fact it was largely in the interests of the girl's health that we had accepted.

On our arrival at Graywater Park we had learnt that our host had been stricken down an hour earlier by sudden illness. The exact nature of his seizure I had thus far been unable to learn; but a local doctor, who had left the Park barely ten minutes before our advent, had strictly forbidden visitors to the sick-room. Sir Lionel's man, Kennedy, who had served him in many strange spots in the world, was in attendance.

So much we had gathered from Homopoulo, the Greek butler (Sir Lionel's household had ever been eccentric). Furthermore, we learned that there was no London train that night and no accommodation in the neighboring village.

"Sir Lionel urgently requests you to remain," the butler had assured us, in his flawless, monotonous English. "He trusts that you will not be dull, and hopes to be able to see you to-morrow and to make plans for your entertainment."

A ghostly, gray shape glided across the darkened hall--and was gone. I started involuntarily. Then remote, fearsome, came muted howling to echo through the ancient apartments of Graywater Park. Nayland Smith laughed.

"That was the civet cat, Petrie!" he said. "I was startled, for a moment, until the lamentations of the leopard family reminded me of the fact that Sir Lionel had transferred his menagerie to Graywater!"

Truly, this was a singular household. In turn, Graywater Park had been a fortress, a monastery, and a manor-house. Now, in the extensive crypt below the former chapel, in an atmosphere artificially raised to a suitably stuffy temperature, were housed the strange pets brought by our eccentric host from distant lands. In one cage was an African lioness, a beautiful and powerful beast, docile as a cat. Housed under other arches were two surly hyenas, goats from the White Nile, and an antelope of Kordofan. In a stable opening upon the garden were a pair of beautiful desert gazelles, and near to them, two cranes and a marabout. The leopards, whose howling now disturbed the night, were in a large, cell-like cage immediately below the spot where of old the chapel alter had stood.

And here were we an odd party in odd environment. I sought to make out the time by my watch, but the growing dusk rendered it impossible. Then, unheralded by any sound, Kâramaneh entered by the door which during the past twenty minutes had been the focus of my gaze. The gathering darkness precluded the possibility of my observing with certainty, but I think a soft blush stole to her cheeks as those glorious dark eyes rested upon me.

The beauty of Kâramaneh was not of the typed which is enhanced by artificial lighting; it was the beauty of the palm and the pomegranate blossom, the beauty which flowers beneath merciless suns, which expands, like the lotus, under the skies of the East. But there, in the dusk, as she came towards me, she looked exquisitely lovely, and graceful with the grace of the desert gazelles which I had seen earlier in the evening. I cannot describe her dress; I only know that she seemed very wonderful--so wonderful that a pang; almost of terror, smote my heart, because such sweetness should belong to me.

And then, from the shadows masking the other side of the old hall, emerged the black figure of Homopoulo, and our odd trio obediently paced into the somber dining-room.

A large lamp burned in the center of the table; a shaded candle was placed before each diner; and the subdued light made play upon the snowy napery and fine old silver without dispersing the gloom about us. Indeed, if anything, it seemed to render it more remarkable, and the table became a lighted oasis in the desert of the huge apartment. One could barely discern the suits of armor and trophies which ornamented the paneled walls; and I never failed to start nervously when the butler appeared, somber and silent, at my elbow.

Sir Lionel Barton's *penchant* for strange visitors, of which we had had experience in the past, was exemplified in the person of Homopoulo. I gathered that the butler (who, I must admit, seemed thoroughly to comprehend his duties) had entered the service of Sir Lionel during the time that the latter was pursuing his celebrated excavations upon the traditional site of the Daedalian Labyrinth in Crete. It was during this expedition that the death of a distant relative had made him master of Graywater Park; and the event seemingly had inspired the eccentric baronet to engage a suitable factotum.

His usual retinue of Malay footmen, Hindu grooms and Chinese cooks, was missing apparently, and the rest of the household, including the charming old housekeeper, had been at the Park for periods varying from five to five-and-twenty years. I must admit that I welcomed the fact; my tastes are essentially insular.

But the untimely illness of our host had cast a shadow upon the party. I found myself speaking in a church-whisper, whilst Kâramaneh was quite silent. That curious dinner party in the shadow desert of the huge apartment frequently recurs in my memories of those days because of the uncanny happening which terminated it.

Nayland Smith, who palpably had been as ill at ease as myself, and who had not escaped the contagious habit of speaking in a hushed whisper, suddenly began, in a loud and cheery manner, to tell us something of the history of Graywater Park, which in his methodical way he had looked up. It was a desperate revolt, on the part of his strenuous spirit, against the phantom of gloom which threatened to obsess us all.

Parts of the house, it appeared, were of very great age, although successive owners had added portions. There were fascinating traditions connected with the place; secret rooms walled up since the Middle Ages, a private stair whose entrance, though undiscoverable, was said to be somewhere in the orchard to the west of the ancient chapel. It had been built by an ancestor of Sir Lionel who had flourished in the reign of the eighth Henry. At this point in his reminiscences (Smith had an astonishing memory where recondite facts were concerned) there came an interruption.

The smooth voice of the butler almost made me leap from my chair, as he spoke out of the shadows immediately behind me.

"The '45 port, sir," he said--and proceeded to place a crusted bottle upon the table. "Sir Lionel desires me to say that he is with you in spirit and that he proposes the health of Dr. Petrie and his fiancée', whom he hopes to have the pleasure of meeting in the morning."

Truly it was a singular situation, and I am unlikely ever to forget the scene as the three of us solemnly rose to our feet and drank our host's toast, thus proposed by proxy, under the eye of Homopoulo, who stood a shadowy figure in the background.

The ceremony solemnly performed and the gloomy butler having departed with a suitable message to Sir Lionel--

"I was about to tell you," resumed Nayland Smith, with a gaiety palpably forced, "of the traditional ghost of Graywater Park. He is a black clad priest, said to be the Spanish chaplain of the owner of the Park in the early days of the Reformation. Owing to some little misunderstanding with His Majesty's commissioners, this unfortunate churchman met with an untimely death, and his shade is said to haunt the secret room--the site of which is unknown--and to clamor upon the door, and upon the walls of the private stair."

I thought the subject rather ill chosen, but recognized that my friend was talking more or less at random and in desperation; indeed, failing his reminiscences of Graywater Park, I think the demon of silence must have conquered us completely.

"Presumably," I said, unconsciously speaking as though I feared the sound of my own voice, "this Spanish priest was confined at some time in the famous hidden chamber?"

"He was supposed to know the secret of a hoard of church property, and tradition has it, that he was put to the question in some gloomy dungeon ..."

He ceased abruptly; in fact the effect was that which must have resulted had the speaker been suddenly stricken down. But the deadly silence which ensued was instantly interrupted. My heart seemed to be clutched as though by fingers of ice; a stark and supernatural horror held me riveted in my chair.

For as though Nayland Smith's words had been heard by the ghostly inhabitant of Graywater Park, as though the tortured priest sought once more release from his age-long sufferings--there came echoing, hollowly and remotely, as if from a subterranean cavern, the sound of *knocking*.

From whence it actually proceeded I was wholly unable to determine. At one time it seemed to surround us, as though not one but a hundred prisoners were beating upon the paneled walls of the huge, ancient apartment.

Faintly, so faintly, that I could not be sure if I heard aright, there came, too, a stifled cry. Louder grew the frantic beating and louder ... then it ceased abruptly.

"Merciful God!" I whispered--"what was it? What was it?"

CHAPTER XXXV

THE EAST TOWER

WITH A CIGARETTE between my lips I sat at the open window, looking out upon the skeleton trees of the orchard; for the buds of early spring were only just beginning to proclaim themselves.

The idea of sleep was far from my mind. The attractive modern furniture of the room could not deprive the paneled walls of the musty antiquity which was their birthright. This solitary window deeply set and overlooking the orchard upon which the secret stair was said to open, struck a note of more remote antiquity, casting back beyond the carousing days of the Stuart monarchs to the troublous time of the Middle Ages.

An air of ghostly evil had seemed to arise like a miasma within the house from the moment that we had been disturbed by the unaccountable rapping. It was at a late hour that we had separated, and none of us, I think, welcomed the breaking up of our little party. Mrs. Oram, the housekeeper, had been closely questioned by Smith--for Homopoulo, as a new-comer, could not be expected to know anything of the history of Graywater Park. The old lady admitted the existence of the tradition which Nayland Smith had in some way unearthed, but assured us that never, in her time, had the uneasy spirit declared himself. She was ignorant (or, like the excellent retainer that she was, professed to be ignorant) of the location of the historic chamber and staircase.

As for Homopoulo, hitherto so irreproachably imperturbable, I had rarely seen a man in such a state of passive panic. His dark face was blanched to the hue of dirty parchment and his forehead dewed with cold perspiration. I mentally predicted an early resignation in the household of Sir Lionel Barton. Homopoulo might be an excellent butler, but his superstitious Greek nature was clearly incapable of sustaining existence beneath the same roof with a family ghost, hoary though the specter's antiquity might be.

Where the skeleton shadows of the fruit trees lay beneath me on the fresh green turf my fancy persistently fashioned a black-clad figure flitting from tree to tree. Sleep indeed was impossible. Once I thought I detected the howling of the distant leopards.

Somewhere on the floor above me, Nayland Smith, I knew, at that moment would be restlessly pacing his room, the exact situation of which I could not identify, because of the quaint, rambling passages whereby one approached it. It was in regard to Kâramaneh, however, that my misgivings were the keenest. Already her position had been strange enough, in those unfamiliar surroundings, but what tremors must have been hers now in the still watches of the night, following the ghostly manifestations which had so dramatically interrupted Nayland Smith's story, I dared not imagine. She had been allotted an apartment somewhere upon the ground floor, and Mrs. Oram, whose motherly interest in the girl had touched me deeply, had gone with her to her room, where no doubt her presence had done much to restore the girl's courage.

Graywater Park stood upon a well-wooded slope, and, to the southwest, starting above the trees almost like a giant Spanish priest, showed a solitary tower. With a vague and indefinite interest I watched it. It was Monkswell, an uninhabited place belonging to Sir Lionel's estate and dating, in part, to the days of King John. Flicking the ash from my cigarette, I studied the ancient tower wondering idly what deeds had had their setting within its shadows, since the Angevin monarch, in whose reign it saw the light, had signed the Magna Charta.

This was a perfect night, and very still. Nothing stirred, within or without Greywater Park. Yet I was conscious of a definite disquietude which I could only suppose to be ascribable to the weird events of the evening, but which seemed rather to increase than to diminish.

I tossed the end of my cigarette out into the darkness, determined to turn in, although I had never felt more wide awake in my life. One parting glance I cast into the skeleton orchard and was on the point of standing up, when--although no breezed stirred--a shower of ivy leaves rained down upon my head!

Brushing them away irritably, I looked up--and a second shower dropped fully upon my face and filled my eyes with dust. I drew back, checking an exclamation. What with the depth of the embrasure, due to the great thickness of the wall, and the leafy tangle above the window, I could see for no great distance up the face of the building; but a faint sound of rustling and stumbling which proceeded from somewhere above me proclaimed that some one, or something, was climbing either up or down the wall of the corner tower in which I was housed!

Partially removing the dust from my smarting eyes, I returned to the embrasure, and stepping from the chair on to the deep ledge, I grasped the corner of the quaint, diamond-paned window, which I had opened to its fullest extent, and craned forth.

Now I could see the ivy-grown battlements surmounting the tower (the east wing, in which my room was situated, was the oldest part of Graywater Park). Sharply outlined against the cloudless sky they showed ... and the black silhouette of a man's head and shoulders leant over directly above me!

I drew back sharply. The climber, I thought, had not seen me, although he was evidently peering down at my window. What did it mean?

As I crouched in the embrasure, a sudden giddiness assailed me, which at first I ascribed to a sympathetic nervous action due to having seen the man poised there at that dizzy height. But it increased, I swayed forward, and clutched at the wall to save myself. A deadly nausea overcame me ... and a deadly doubt leapt to my mind.

In the past, Sir Lionel Barton had had spies in his household; what if the dark-faced Greek, Homopoulo, were another of these? I thought of the '45 port, of the ghostly rapping; and I thought of the man who crouched upon the roof of the tower above my open window.

My symptoms now were unmistakable; my head throbbed and my vision grew imperfect; there had to be an opiate in the wine!

I almost fell back into the room. Supporting myself by means of the chair, the chest of drawers, and finally, the bed-rail, I got to my grip, and with weakening fingers, extracted the little medicine-chest which was invariably my traveling companion.

Grimly pitting my will against the drug, but still trembling weakly from the result of the treatment, internal and subcutaneous, which I had adopted, I staggered to the door out into the corridor and up the narrow, winding stairs to Smith's room. I carried an electric pocket-lamp, and by its light I found my way to the triangular, paneled landing.

I tried the handle. As I had expected, the door was locked. I beat upon it with my fist.

"Smith!" I cried--"Smith!"

There was no reply.

Again I clamored; awaking ancient echoes within the rooms and all about me. But nothing moved and no answering voice rewarded my efforts; the other rooms were seemingly unoccupied, and Smith--was drugged!

My senses in disorder, and a mist dancing before my eyes, I went stumbling down into the lower corridor. At the door of my own room I paused; a new fact had suddenly been revealed to me, a fact which the mazy windings of the corridors had hitherto led me to overlook. Smith's room was also in the east tower, and must be directly above mine!

"My God!" I whispered, thinking of the climber--"he has been murdered!"

I staggered into my room and clutched at the bed-rail to support myself, for my legs threatened to collapse beneath me. How should I act? That we were victims of a cunning plot, that the deathful Si-Fan had at last wreaked its vengeance upon Nayland Smith I could not doubt.

My brain reeled, and a weakness, mental and physical, threatened to conquer me completely. Indeed, I think I must have succumbed, sapped as my strength had been by the drug administered to me, if the sound of a creaking stair had not arrested my attention and by the menace which it conveyed afforded a new stimulus.

Some one was creeping down from the landing above--coming to my room! The creatures of the Yellow doctor, having despatched Nayland Smith, were approaching stealthily, stair by stair, to deal with *me!*

From my grip I took out the Browning pistol. The Chinese doctor's servants should have a warm reception. I burned to avenge my friend, who I was persuaded, lay murdered in the room above. I partially closed the door and took up a post immediately behind it. Nearer came the stealthy footsteps--nearer.... Now the one who approached had turned the angle of the passage....

Within sight of my door he seemed to stop; a shaft of white light crept through the opening, across the floor and on to the wall beyond. A moment it remained so--then was gone. The room became plunged in darkness.

Gripping the Browning with nervous fingers I waited, listening intently; but the silence remained unbroken. My gaze set upon the spot where the head of this midnight visitant might be expected to appear, I almost held my breath during the ensuing moments of frightful suspense.

The door was opening; slowly--slowly--by almost imperceptible degrees. I held the pistol pointed rigidly before me and my gaze remained fixed intently on the dimly seen opening. I suppose I acted as ninety-nine men out of a hundred would have done in like case. Nothing appeared.

Then a voice--a voice that seemed to come from somewhere under the floor snapped:--

"Good God! it's Petrie!"

I dropped my gaze instantly ... and there, looking up at me from the floor at my feet, I vaguely discerned the outline of a human head!

"Smith!" I whispered.

Nayland Smith--for indeed it was none other--stood up and entered the room.

"Thank God you are safe, old man," he said. "But in waiting for one who is stealthily entering a room, don't, as you love me, take it for granted that he will enter *upright*. I could have shot you from the floor with ease! But, mercifully, even in the darkness, I recognized your Arab slippers!"

"Smith," I said, my heart beating wildly, "I thought you were drugged-- murdered. The port contained an opiate."

"I guessed as much!" snapped Smith. "But despite the excellent tuition of Dr. Fu-Manchu, I am still childishly trustful; and the fact that I did not partake of the crusted '45 was not due to any suspicions which I entertained at that time."

"But, Smith, I saw you drink some port."

"I regret to contradict you, Petrie, but you must be aware that the state of my liver--due to a long residence in Burma--does not permit me to indulge in the luxury of port. My share of the '45 now reposes amid the moss in the tulip-bowl, which you may remember decorated the dining table! Not desiring to appear churlish, by means of a simple feat of legerdemain I drank your health and future happiness in claret!"

"For God's sake what is going on, Smith? Some one climbed from your window."

"I climbed from my window!"

"What!" I said dazedly--"it was you! But what does it all mean? Kâramaneh----"

"It is for her I fear, Petrie, now. We have not a moment to waste!"

He made for the door.

"Sir Lionel must be warned at all cost!" I cried.

"Impossible!" snapped Smith.

"What do you mean?"

"Sir Lionel has disappeared!"

CHAPTER XXXVI

THE DUNGEON

WE WERE OUT in the corridor now, Smith showing the way with the light of his electric pocket-lamp. My mind was clear enough, but I felt as weak as a child.

"You look positively ghastly, old man," rapped Smith, "which is no matter for wonder. I have yet to learn how it happened that you are not lying insensible, or dead, as a result of the drugged wine. When I heard some one moving in your room, it never occurred to me that it was *you*."

"Smith," I said--"the house seems as still as death."

"You, Kâramaneh, and myself are the only occupants of the east wing. Homopoulo saw to that."

"Then he----"

"He is a member of the Si-Fan, a creature of Dr. Fu-Manchu--yes, beyond all doubt! Sir Lionel is unfortunate--as ever--in his choice of servants. I blame my own stupidity entirely, Petrie; and I pray that my enlightenment has not come too late."

"What does it all mean?--what have you learnt?"

"Mind these three steps," warned Smith, glancing back. "I found my mind persistently dwelling upon the matter of that weird rapping, Petrie, and I recollected the situation of Sir Lionel's room, on the southeast front. A brief inspection revealed the fact that, by means of a kindly branch of ivy, I could reach the roof of the east tower from my window."

"Well?"

"One may walk from there along the roof of the southeast front, and by lying face downwards at the point where it projects above the main entrance look into Sir Lionel's room!"

"I saw you go!"

"I feared that some one was watching me, but that it was you I had never supposed. Neither Barton nor his man are in that room, Petrie! They have been spirited away! This is Kâramaneh's door."

He grasped me by the arm, at the same time directing the light upon a closed door before which we stood. I raised my fist and beat upon the panels; then, every muscle tensed and my heart throbbing wildly, I listened for the girl's voice.

Not a sound broke that deathly stillness except the beating of my own heart, which, I thought, must surely be audible to my companion. Frantically I hurled myself against the stubborn oak, but Smith thrust me back.

"Useless, Petrie!" he said--"useless. This room is in the base of the east tower, yours is above it and mine at the top. The corridors approaching the three floors deceive one, but the fact remains. I have no positive evidence, but I would wager all I possess that there is a stair in the thickness of the wall, and hidden doors in the paneling of the three apartments. The Yellow group has somehow obtained possession of a plan of the historic secret passages and chambers of Graywater Park. Homopoulo is the spy in the household; and Sir Lionel, with his man Kennedy, was removed directly the invitation to us had been posted. The group will know by now that we have escaped them, but Kâramaneh ..."

"Smith!" I groaned, "Smith! What has we do? What has befallen her? ..."

"This way!" he snapped. "We are not beaten yet!"

"We must arouse the servants!"

"Why? It would be sheer waste of priceless time. There are only three men who actually sleep in the house (excepting Homopoulo) and these are in the northwest wing. No, Petrie; we must rely upon ourselves."

He was racing recklessly along the tortuous corridors and up the oddly placed stairways of that old-world building. My anguish had reinforced the atropine which I had employed as an antidote to the opiate in the wine, and now my blood, that had coursed sluggishly, leapt through my veins like fire and I burned with a passionate anger.

Into a large and untidy bedroom we burst. Books and papers littered about the floor; curios, ranging from mummied cats and ibises to Turkish yataghans and Zulu assegais, surrounded the place in riotous disorder. Beyond doubt this was the apartment of Sir Lionel Barton. A lamp burned upon a table near to the disordered bed, and a discolored Greek statuette of Orpheus lay overturned on the carpet close beside it.

"Homopoulo was on the point of leaving this room at the moment that I peered in at the window," said Smith, breathing heavily. "From here there is another entrance to the secret passages. Have your pistol ready."

He stepped across the disordered room to a little alcove near the foot of the bed, directing the ray of the pocket-lamp upon the small, square paneling.

"Ah!" he cried, a note of triumph in his voice--"he has left the door ajar! A visit of inspection was not anticipated to-night, Petrie! Thank God for an Indian liver and a suspicious mind."

He disappeared into a yawning cavity which now I perceived to exist in the wall. I hurried after him, and found myself upon roughly fashioned stone steps in a very low and narrow descending passage. Over his shoulder.

"Note the direction," said Smith breathlessly. "We shall presently find ourselves at the base of the east tower."

Down we went and down, the ray of the electric lamp always showing more steps ahead, until at last these terminated in a level, arched passage, curving sharply to the right. Two paces more brought us to a doorway, less, than four feet high, approached by two wide steps. A blackened door, having a most cumbersome and complicated lock, showed in the recess.

Nayland Smith bent and examined the mechanism intently.

"Freshly oiled!" he commented. "You know into whose room it opens?"

Well enough I knew, and, detecting that faint, haunting perfume which spoke of the dainty personality of Kâramaneh, my anger blazed up anew. Came a faint sound of metal grating upon metal, and Smith pulled open the door, which turned outward upon the steps, and bent further forward, sweeping the ray of light about the room beyond.

"Empty, of course!" he muttered. "Now for the base of these damned nocturnal operations."

He descended the steps and began to flash the light all about the arched passageway wherein we stood.

"The present dining-room of Graywater Park lies almost due south of this spot," he mused. "Suppose we try back."

We retraced our steps to the foot of the stair. In the wall on their left was an opening, low down against the floor and little more than three feet high; it reminded me of some of the entrances to those seemingly interminable passages whereby one approaches the sepulchral chambers of the Egyptian Pyramids.

"Now for it!" snapped Smith. "Follow me closely."

Down he dropped, and, having the lamp thrust out before him, began to crawl into the tunnel. As his heels disappeared, and only a faint light outlined the opening, I dropped upon all fours in turn, and began laboriously to drag myself along behind him. The atmosphere was damp, chilly, and evil-smelling; therefore, at the end of some ten or twelve yards of this serpentine crawling, when I saw Smith, ahead of me, to be standing erect, I uttered a stifled exclamation of relief. The thought of Kâramaneh having been dragged through this noisome hole was one I dared not dwell upon.

A long, narrow passage now opened up, its end invisible from where we stood. Smith hurried forward. For the first thirty of forty paces the roof was formed of massive stone slabs; then its character changed; the passage became lower, and one was compelled frequently to lower the head in order to avoid the oaken beams which crossed it.

"We are passing under the dining-room," said Smith. "It was from here the sound of beating first came!"

"What do you mean?"

"I have built up a theory, which remains to be proved, Petrie. In my opinion a captive of the Yellow group escaped to-night and sought to summon assistance, but was discovered and overpowered."

"Sir Lionel?"

"Sir Lionel, or Kennedy--yes, I believe so."

Enlightenment came to me, and I understood the pitiable condition into which the Greek butler had been thrown by the phenomenon of the ghostly knocking. But Smith hurried on, and suddenly I saw that the passage had entered upon a sharp declivity; and now both roof and walls were composed of crumbling brickwork. Smith pulled up, and thrust back a hand to detain me.

"*Ssh!*" he hissed, and grasped my arm.

Silent, intently still, we stood and listened. The sound of a guttural voice was clearly distinguishable from somewhere close at hand!

Smith extinguished the lamp. A faint luminance proclaimed itself directly ahead. Still grasping my arm, Smith began slowly to advance toward the light. One--two--three--four--five paces we crept onward ... and I found myself looking through an archway into a medieval torture-chamber!

Only a part of the place was visible to me, but its character was unmistakable. Leg-irons, boots and thumb-screws hung in racks upon the fungi-covered wall. A massive, iron-studded door was open at the further end of the chamber, and on the threshold stood Homopoulo, holding a lantern in his hand.

Even as I saw him, he stepped through, followed by on of those short, thick-set Burmans of whom Dr. Fu-Manchu had a number among his entourage; they were members of the villainous robber bands notorious in India as the dacoits. Over one broad shoulder, slung sackwise, the dacoit carried a girl clad in scanty white drapery....

Madness seized me, the madness of sorrow and impotent wrath. For, with Kâramaneh being borne off before my eyes, I dared not fire at her abductors lest I should strike *her*!

Nayland Smith uttered a loud cry, and together we hurled ourselves into the chamber. Heedless of what, of whom, else it might shelter, we sprang for the group in the distant doorway. A memory is mine of the dark, white face of Homopoulo, peering, wild-eyed, over the lantern, of the slim, white-clad form of the lovely captive seeming to fade into the obscurity of the passage beyond.

Then, with bleeding knuckles, with wild imprecations bubbling from my lips, I was battering upon the mighty door--which had been slammed in my face at the very instant that I had gained it.

"Brace up, man!--Brace up!" cried Smith, and in his strenuous, grimly purposeful fashion, he shouldered me away from the door. "A battering ram could not force that timber; we must seek another way!"

I staggered, weakly, back into the room. Hand raised to my head, I looked about me. A lantern stood in a niche in one wall, weirdly illuminating that place of ghastly memories; there were braziers, branding-irons, with other instruments dear to the Black Ages, about me--and gagged, chained side by side against the opposite wall, lay Sir Lionel Barton and another man unknown to me!

Already Nayland Smith was bending over the intrepid explorer, whose fierce blue eyes glared out from the sun-tanned face madly, whose gray hair and mustache literally bristled with rage long repressed. I choked down the emotions that boiled and seethed within me, and sought to release the second captive, a stockily-built, clean-shaven man. First I removed the length of toweling which was tied firmly over his mouth; and--

"Thank you, sir," he said composedly. "The keys of these irons are on the ledge there beside the lantern. I broke the first ring I was chained to, but the Yellow devils overhauled me, all manacled as I was, half-way along the passage before I could attract your attention, and fixed me up to another and stronger ring!"

Ere he had finished speaking, the keys were in my hands, and I had unlocked the gyves from both the captives. Sir Lionel Barton, his gag removed, unloosed a torrent of pent-up wrath.

"The hell-fiends drugged me!" he shouted. "That black villain Homopoulo doctored my tea! I woke in this damnable cell, the secret of which has been lost for generations!" He turned blazing blue eyes upon Kennedy. "How did *you* come to be trapped?" he demanded unreasonably. "I credited you with a modicum of brains!"

"Homopoulo came running from your room, sir, and told me you were taken suddenly ill and that a doctor must be summoned without delay."

"Well, well, you fool!"

"Dr. Hamilton was away, sir."

"A false call beyond doubt!" snapped Smith.

"Therefore I went for the new doctor, Dr. Magnus, in the village. He came at once and I showed him up to your room. He sent Mrs. Oram out, leaving only Homopoulo and myself there, except yourself."

"Well?"

"Sandbagged!" explained the man nonchalantly. "Dr. Magnus, who is some kind of dago, is evidently one of the gang."

"Sir Lionel!" cried Smith--"where does the passage lead to beyond that doorway?"

"God knows!" was the answer, which dashed my last hope to the ground. "I have no more idea than yourself. Perhaps ..."

He ceased speaking. A sound had interrupted him, which, in those grim surroundings, lighted by the solitary lantern, translated my thoughts magically to Ancient Rome, to the Rome of Tigellinus, to the dungeons of Nero's Circus. Echoing eerily along the secret passages it came-- the roaring and snarling of the lioness and the leopards.

Nayland Smith clapped his hand to his brow and stared at me almost frenziedly, then--

"God guard her!" he whispered. "Either their plans, wherever they got them, are inaccurate, or in their panic they have mistaken the way." ... Wild cries now were mingling with the snarling of the beasts.... "They have blundered into the old crypt!"

How we got out of the secret labyrinth of Graywater Park into the grounds and around the angle of the west wing to the ivy-grown, pointed door, where once the chapel had bee, I do not know. Light seemed to spring up about me, and half-clad servants to appear out of the void. Temporarily I was insane.

Sir Lionel Barton was behaving like a madman too, and like a madman he tore at the ancient bolts and precipitated himself into the stone-paved cloister barred with the moon-cast shadows of the Norman pillars. From behind the iron bars of the home of the leopards came now a fearsome growling and scuffling.

Smith held the light with a steady hand, whilst Kennedy forced the heavy bolts of the crypt door.

In leapt the fearless baronet among his savage pets, and in the ray of light from the electric lamp I saw that which turned my sick with horror. Prone beside a yawning gap in the floor lay Homopoulo, his throat torn indescribably and his white shirt-front smothered in blood. A black leopard, having its fore-paws upon the dead man's breast, turned blazing eyes upon us; a second crouched beside him.

Heaped up in a corner of the place, amongst the straw and litter of the lair, lay the Burmese dacoit, his sinewy fingers embedded in the throat of the third and largest leopard--which was dead--whilst the creature's gleaming fangs were buried in the tattered flesh of the man's shoulder.

Upon the straw beside the two, her slim, bare arms outstretched and her head pillowed upon them, so that her rippling hair completely concealed her face, lay Kâramaneh....

In a trice Barton leapt upon the great beast standing over Homopoulo, had him by the back of the neck and held him in his powerful hands whining with fear and helpless as a rat in the grip of a terrier. The second leopard fled into the inner lair.

So much I visualized in a flash; then all faded, and I knelt alone beside her whose life was my life, in a world grown suddenly empty and still.

Through long hours of agony I lived, hours contained within the span of seconds, the beloved head resting against my shoulder, whilst I searched for signs of life and dreaded to find ghastly wounds.... At first I could not credit the miracle; I could not receive the wondrous truth.

Kâramaneh was quite uninjured and deep in drugged slumber!

"The leopards thought her dead," whispered Smith brokenly, "and never touched her!"

CHAPTER XXXVII

THREE NIGHTS LATER

"LISTEN!" cried Sir Lionel Barton.

He stood upon the black rug before the massive, carven mantelpiece, a huge man in an appropriately huge setting.

I checked the words on my lips, and listened intently. Within Graywater Park all was still, for the hour was late. Outside, the rain was descending in a deluge, its continuous roar drowning any other sound that might have been discernible. Then, above it, I detected a noise that at first I found difficult to define.

"The howling of the leopards!" I suggested.

Sir Lionel shook his tawny head with impatience. Then, the sound growing louder, suddenly I knew it for what it was.

"Some one shouting!" I exclaimed--"some one who rides a galloping horse!"

"Coming here!" added Sir Lionel. "Hark! he is at the door!"

A bell rang furiously, again and again sending its brazen clangor echoing through the great apartments and passages of Graywater.

"There goes Kennedy."

Above the sibilant roaring of the rain I could hear some one releasing heavy bolts and bars. The servants had long since retired, as also had Kâramaneh; but Sir Lionel's man remained wakeful and alert.

Sir Lionel made for the door, and I, standing up, was about to follow him, when Kennedy appeared, in his wake a bedraggled groom, hatless, and pale to the lips. His frightened eyes looked from face to face.

"Dr. Petrie?" he gasped interrogatively.

"Yes!" I said, a sudden dread assailing me. "What is it?"

"Gad! it's Hamilton's man!" cried Barton.

"Mr. Nayland Smith, sir," continued the groom brokenly--and all my fears were realized. "He's been attacked, sir, on the road from the station, and Dr. Hamilton, to whose house he was carried----"

"Kennedy!" shouted Sir Lionel, "get the Rolls-Royce out! Put your horse up here, my man, and come with us!"

He turned abruptly ... as the groom, grasping at the wall, fell heavily to the floor.

"Good God!" I cried--"What's the matter with him?"

I bent over the prostrate man, making a rapid examination.

"His head! A nasty blow. Give me a hand, Sir Lionel; we must get him on to a couch."

The unconscious man was laid upon a Chesterfield, and, ably assisted by the explorer, who was used to coping with such hurts as this, I attended to him as best I could. One of the men-servants had been aroused, and, just as he appeared in the doorway, I had the satisfaction of seeing Dr. Hamilton's groom open his eyes, and look about him, dazedly.

"Quick," I said. "Tell me--what hurt you?"

The man raised his hand to his head and groaned feebly.

"Something came *whizzing*, sir," he answered. "There was no report, and I saw nothing. I don't know what it can have been----"

"Where did this attack take place?"

"Between here and the village, sir; just by the coppice at the cross-roads on top of Raddon Hill."

"You had better remain here for the present," I said, and gave a few words of instruction to the man whom we had aroused.

"This way," cried Barton, who had rushed out of the room, his huge frame reappearing in the door-way; "the car is ready."

My mind filled with dreadful apprehensions, I passed out on to the carriage sweep. Sir Lionel was already at the wheel.

"Jump in, Kennedy," he said, when I had taken a seat beside him; and the man sprang into the car.

Away we shot, up the narrow lane, lurched hard on the bend--and were off at ever growing speed toward the hills, where a long climb awaited the car.

The head-light picked out the straight road before us, and Barton increased the pace, regardless of regulations, until the growing slope made itself felt and the speed grew gradually less; above the throbbing of the motor, I could hear, now, the rain in the overhanging trees.

I peered through the darkness, up the road, wondering if we were near to the spot where the mysterious attack had been made upon Dr. Hamilton's groom. I decided that we were just passing the place, and to confirm my opinion, at that moment Sir Lionel swung the car around suddenly, and plunged headlong into the black mouth of a narrow lane.

Hitherto, the roads had been fair, but now the jolting and swaying became very pronounced.

"Beastly road!" shouted Barton--"and stiff gradient!"

I nodded.

That part of the way which was visible in front had the appearance of a muddy cataract, through which we must force a path.

Then, as abruptly as it had commenced, the rain ceased; and at almost the same moment came an angry cry from behind.

The canvas hood made it impossible to see clearly in the car, but, turning quickly, I perceived Kennedy, with his cap off, rubbing his close-cropped skull. He was cursing volubly.

"What is it, Kennedy?"

"Somebody sniping!" cried the man. "Lucky for me I had my cap on!"

"Eh, sniping?" said Barton, glancing over his shoulder. "What d'you mean? A stone, was it?"

"No, sir," answered Kennedy. "I don't know what it was--but it wasn't a stone."

"Hurt much?" I asked.

"No, sir! nothing at all." But there was a note of fear in the man's voice--fear of the unknown.

Something struck the hood with a dull drum-like thud.

"There's another, sir!" cried Kennedy. "There's some one following us!"

"Can you see any one?" came the reply. "I thought I saw something then, about twenty yards behind. It's so dark."

"Try a shot!" I said, passing my Browning to Kennedy.

The next moment, the crack of the little weapon sounded sharply, and I thought I detected a vague, answering cry.

"See anything?" came from Barton.

Neither Kennedy nor I made reply; for we were both looking back down the hill. Momentarily, the moon had peeped from the cloud-banks, and where, three hundreds yards behind, the bordering trees were few, a patch of dim light spread across the muddy road--and melted away as a new blackness gathered.

But, in the brief space, three figures had shown, only for an instant-- but long enough for us both to see that they were those of three gaunt men, seemingly clad in scanty garments. What weapons they employed I could not conjecture; but we were pursued by three of Dr. Fu-Manchu's dacoits!

Barton growled something savagely, and ran the car to the left of the road, as the gates of Dr. Hamilton's house came in sight.

A servant was there, ready to throw them open; and Sir Lionel swung around on to the drive, and drove ahead, up the elm avenue to where the light streamed through the open door on to the wet gravel. The house was a blaze of lights, every window visible being illuminated; and Mrs. Hamilton stood in the porch to greet us.

"Doctor Petrie?" she asked, nervously, as we descended.

"I am he," I said. "How is Mr. Smith?"

"Still insensible," was the reply.

Passing a knot of servants who stood at the foot of the stairs like a little flock of frightened sheep--we made our way into the room where my poor friend lay.

Dr. Hamilton, a gray-haired man of military bearing, greeted Sir Lionel, and the latter made me known to my fellow practitioner, who grasped my hand, and then went straight to the bedside, tilting the lampshade to throw the light directly upon the patient.

Nayland Smith lay with his arms outside the coverlet and his fists tightly clenched. His thin, tanned face wore a grayish hue, and a white bandage was about his head. He breathed stentoriously.

"We can only wait," said Dr. Hamilton, "and trust that there will be no complications."

I clenched my fists involuntarily, but, speaking no word, turned and passed from the room.

Downstairs in Dr. Hamilton's study was the man who had found Nayland Smith.

"We don't know when it was done, sir," he said, answering my first question. "Staples and me stumbled on him in the dusk, just by the big beech--a good quarter-mile from the village. I don't know how long he'd laid there, but it must have been for some time, as the last rain arrived an hour earlier. No, sir, he hadn't been robbed; his money and watch were on him but his pocketbook lay open beside him;-- though, funny as it seems, there were three five-pound notes in it!"

"Do you understand, Petrie?" cried Sir Lionel. "Smith evidently obtained a copy of the old plan of the secret passages of Graywater and Monkswell, sooner than he expected, and determined to return to-night. They left him for dead, having robbed him of the plans!"

"But the attack on Dr. Hamilton's man?"

"Fu-Manchu clearly tried to prevent communication with us to-night! He is playing for time. Depend on it, Petrie, the hour of his departure draws near and he is afraid of being trapped at the last moment."

He began taking huge strides up and down the room, forcibly reminding me of a caged lion.

"To think," I said bitterly, "that all our efforts have failed to discover the secret----"

"The secret of my own property!" roared Barton--"and one known to that damned, cunning Chinese devil!"

"And in all probability now known also to Smith----"

"And he cannot speak! ..."

"*Who* cannot speak?" demanded a hoarse voice.

I turned in a flash, unable to credit my senses--and there, holding weakly to the doorpost, stood Nayland Smith!

"Smith!" I cried reproachfully--"you should not have left your room!"

He sank into an arm-chair, assisted by Dr. Hamilton.

"My skull is fortunately thick!" he replied, a ghostly smile playing around the corners of his mouth--"and it was a physical impossibility for me to remain inert considering that Dr. Fu-Manchu proposes to leave England to-night!"

CHAPTER XXXVIII
THE MONK'S PLAN

"MY INQUIRIES IN THE MANUSCRIPT ROOM OF THE BRITISH MUSEUM," said Nayland Smith, his voice momentarily growing stronger and some of the old fire creeping back into his eyes, "have proved entirely successful."

Sir Lionel Barton, Dr. Hamilton, and myself hung upon every word; and often I fond myself glancing at the old-fashioned clock on the doctor's mantel-piece.

"We had very definite proof," continued Smith, "of the fact that Fu-Manchu and company were conversant with that elaborate system of secret rooms and passages which forms a veritable labyrinth, in, about, and beneath Graywater Park. Some of the passages we explored. That Sir Lionel should be ignorant of the system was not strange, considering that he had but recently inherited the property, and that the former owner, his kinsman, regarded the secret as lost. A starting-point was discovered, however, in the old work on haunted manors unearthed in the library, as you remember. There was a reference, in the chapter dealing with Graywater, so a certain monkish manuscript said to repose in the national collection and to contain a plan of these passages and stairways.

"The Keeper of the Manuscripts at the Museum very courteously assisted me in my inquiries, and the ancient parchment was placed in my hands. Sure enough, it contained a carefully executed drawing of the hidden ways of Graywater, the work of a monk in the distant days when Graywater was a priory. This monk, I may add--a certain Brother Anselm-- afterwards became Abbot of Graywater."

"Very interesting!" cried sir Lionel loudly; "very interesting indeed."

"I copied the plan," resumed Smith, "with elaborate care. That labor, unfortunately, was wasted, in part, at least. Then, in order to confirm my suspicions on the point, I endeavored to ascertain if the monk's MS. had been asked for at the Museum recently. The Keeper of the Manuscripts could not recall that any student had handled the work, prior to my own visit, during the past ten years.

"This was disappointing, and I was tempted to conclude that Fu-Manchu had blundered on to the secret in some other way, when the Assistant Keeper of Manuscripts put in an appearance. From him I obtained confirmation of my theory. Three months ago a Greek gentleman--possibly, Sir Lionel, your late butler, Homopoulo--obtained permission to consult the MS., claiming to be engaged upon a paper for some review or another.

"At any rate, the fact was sufficient. Quite evidently, a servant of Fu-Manchu had obtained a copy of the plan--and this within a day or so of the death of Mr. Brangholme Burton--whose heir, Sir Lionel, you were! I became daily impressed anew with the omniscience, the incredible genius, of Dr. Fu-Manchu.

"The scheme which we know of to compass the death, or captivity, of our three selves and Kâramaneh was put into operation, and failed. But, with its failure, the utility of the secret chambers was by no means terminated. The local legend, according to which a passage exists, linking Graywater and Monkswell, is confirmed by the monk's plan."

"What?" cried Sir Lionel, springing to his feet--"a passage between the Park and the old tower! My dear sir, it's impossible! Such a passage would have to pass under the River Starn! It's only a narrow stream, I know, but----"

"It *does*, or *did*, pass under the River Starn!" said Nayland Smith coolly. "That it is still practicable I do not assert; what interests me is the spot at which it terminates."

He plunged his hand into the pocket of the light overcoat which he wore over the borrowed suit of pyjamas in which the kindly Dr. Hamilton had clothed him. He was seeking his pipe!

"Have a cigar, Smith!" cried Sir Lionel, proffering his case--"if you *must* smoke; although I think our medical friends frowning!"

Nayland Smith took a cigar, bit off the end, and lighted up. He began to surround himself with odorous clouds, to his evident satisfaction.

"To resume," he said; "the Spanish priest who was persecuted at Graywater in early Reformation days and whose tortured spirit is said to haunt the Park, held the secret of this passage, and of the subterranean chamber in Monkswell, to which it led. His confession-- which resulted in his death at the stake!--enabled the commissioners to recover from his chamber a quantity of church ornaments. For these facts I am indebted to the author of the work on haunted manors.

"Our inquiry at this point touches upon things sinister and incomprehensible. In a word, although the passage and a part of the underground room are of unknown antiquity, it appears certain that they were improved and enlarged by one of the abbots of Monkswell--at a date much later than Brother Anselm's abbotship--and the place was converted to a secret chapel----"

"A *secret* chapel!" said Dr. Hamilton.

"Exactly. This was at a time in English history when the horrible cult of Asmodeus spread from the Rhine monasteries and gained proselytes in many religious houses of England. In this secret chapel, wretched Churchmen, seduced to the abominable views of the abbot, celebrated the Black Mass!"

"My God!" I whispered--"small wonder that the place is reputed to be haunted!"

"Small wonder," cried Nayland Smith, with all his old nervous vigor, "that Dr. Fu-Manchu selected it as an ideal retreat in times of danger!"

"What! the chapel?" roared Sir Lionel.

"Beyond doubt! Well knowing the penalty of discovery, those old devil-worshipers had chosen a temple from which they could escape in an emergency. There is a short stair from the chamber into the cave which, as you may know, exists in the cliff adjoining Monkswell."

Smith's eyes were blazing now, and he was on his feet, pacing the floor, an odd figure, with his bandaged skull and inadequate garments, biting on the already extinguished cigar as though it had been a pipe.

"Returning to our rooms, Petrie," he went on rapidly, "who should I run into but Summers! You remember Summers, the Suez Canal pilot whom you met at Ismailia two years ago? He brought the yacht through the Canal, from Suez, on which I suspect Ki-Ming came to England. She is a big boat-- used to be on the Port Said and Jaffa route before a wealthy Chinaman acquired her--through an Egyptian agent--for his personal use.

"All the crews, Summers told me, were Asiatics, and little groups of natives lined the Canal and performed obeisances as the vessel passed. Undoubtedly they had that woman on board, Petrie, the Lady of the Si-Fan, who escaped, together with Fu-Manchu, when we raided the meeting in London! Like a fool I came racing back here without advising you; and, all alone, my mind occupied with the tremendous import of these discoveries, started, long after dusk, to walk to Graywater Park."

He shrugged his shoulders whimsically, and raised one hand to his bandaged head.

"Fu-Manchu employs weapons both of the future and of the past," he said. "My movements had been watched, of course; I was mad. Some one, probably a dacoit, laid me low with a ball of clay propelled form a sling of the Ancient Persian pattern! I actually saw him ... then saw, and knew, no more!"

"Smith!" I cried--whilst Sir Lionel Barton and Dr. Hamilton stared at one another, dumbfounded--"you think *he* is on the point of flying from England----"

"The Chinese yacht, *Chanak-Kampo*, is lying two miles off the coast and in the sight of the tower of Monkswell!"

CHAPTER XXXIX

THE SHADOW ARMY

THE SCENE OF OUR RETURN to Graywater Park is destined to live in my memory for ever. The storm, of which the violet rainfall had been a prelude, gathered blackly over the hills. Ebon clouds lowered upon us as we came racing to the gates. Then the big car was spinning around the carriage sweep, amid a deathly stillness of Nature indescribably gloomy and ominous. I have said, a stillness of nature; but, as Kennedy leapt out and ran up the steps to the door, from the distant cages wherein Sire Lionel kept his collection of rare beasts proceeded the angry howling of the leopards and such a wild succession of roars from the African lioness that I stared at our eccentric host questioningly.

"It's the gathering storm," he explained. "These creatures are peculiarly susceptible to atmospheric disturbances."

Now the door was thrown open, and, standing in the lighted hall, a picture fair to look upon in her dainty kimono and little red, high-heeled slippers, stood Kâramaneh!

I was beside her in a moment; for the lovely face was pale and there was a wildness in her eyes which alarmed me.

"*He* is somewhere near!" she whispered, clinging to me. "Some great danger threatens. Where have you been?--what has happened?"

"Smith was attacked on his way back from London," I replied. "But, as you see, he is quite recovered. We are in no danger; and I insist that you go back to bed. We shall tell you all about it in the morning."

Rebellion blazed up in her wonderful eyes instantly--and as quickly was gone, leaving them exquisitely bright. Two tears, like twin pearls, hung upon the curved black lashes. It made my blood course faster to watch this lovely Eastern girl conquering the barbaric impulses that sometimes flamed up within, her, because *I* willed it; indeed this was a miracle that I never tired of witnessing.

Mrs. Oram, the white-haired housekeeper, placed her arm in motherly fashion about the girl's slim waist.

"She wants to stay in my room until the trouble is all over," she said in her refined, sweet voice.

"You are very good, Mrs. Oram," I replied. "Take care of her."

One long, reassuring glance I gave Kâramaneh, then turned and followed Smith and Sir Lionel up the winding oak stair. Kennedy came close behind me, carrying one of the acetylene head-lamps of the car. And--

"Just listen to the lioness, sir!" he whispered. "It's not the gathering storm that's making her so restless. Jungle beasts grow quiet, as a rule, when there's thunder about."

The snarling of the great creature was plainly audible, distant though we were from her cage.

"Through your room, Barton!" snapped Nayland Smith, when we gained the top corridor.

He was his old, masterful self once more, and his voice was vibrant with that suppressed excitement which I knew well. Into the disorderly sleeping apartment of the baronet we hurried, and Smith made for the recess near the bed which concealed a door in the paneling.

"Cautiously here!" cried Smith. "Follow immediately behind me, Kennedy, and throw the beam ahead. Hold the lamp well to the left."

In we filed, into that ancient passage which had figured in many a black deed but had never served the ends of a more evil plotter than the awful Chinaman who so recently had rediscovered it.

Down we marched, and down, but not to the base of the tower, as I had anticipated. At a point which I judged to be about level with the first floor of the house, Smith--who had been audibly counting the steps--paused, and began to examine the seemingly unbroken masonry of the wall.

"We have to remember," he muttered, "that this passage may be blocked up or otherwise impassable, and that Fu-Manchu may know of another entrance. Furthermore, since the plan is lost, I have to rely upon my memory for the exact position of the door."

He was feeling about in the crevices between the stone blocks of which the wall was constructed.

"Twenty-one steps," he muttered; "I feel certain."

Suddenly it seemed that his quest had proved successful.

"Ah!" he cried--"the ring!"

I saw that he had drawn out a large iron ring from some crevice in which it had been concealed.

"Stand back, Kennedy!" he warned.

Kennedy moved on to a lower step--as Smith, bringing all his weight to bear upon the ring, turned the huge stone slab upon its hidden pivot, so that it fell back upon the stair with a reverberating boom.

We all pressed forward to peer into the black cavity. Kennedy moving the light, a square well was revealed, not more than three feet across. Footholes were cut at intervals down the further side.

"H'm!" said Smith--"I was hardly prepared for this. The method of descent that occurs to me is to lean back against one side and trust one's weight entirely to the foot-holes on the other. A shaft appeared in the plan, I remember, but I had formed no theory respecting the means provided for descending it. Tilt the lamp forward, Kennedy. Good! I can see the floor of the passage below; only about fifteen feet or so down."

He stretched his foot across, placed it in the niche and began to descend.

"Kennedy next!" came his muffled voice, "with the lamp. Its light will enable you others to see the way."

Down went Kennedy without hesitation, the lamp swung from his right arm.

"I will bring up the rear," said Sir Lionel Barton.

Whereupon I descended. I had climbed down about half-way when, from below, came a loud cry, a sound of scuffling, and a savage exclamation from Smith. Then----

"We're right, Petrie! This passage was recently used by Fu-Manchu!"

I gained the bottom of the well, and found myself standing in the entrance to an arched passage. Kennedy was directing the light of the lamp down upon the floor.

"You see, the door was guarded" said Nayland Smith.

"What!"

"Puff adder!" he snapped, and indicated a small snake whose head was crushed beneath his heel.

Sir Lionel now joined us; and, a silent quartette, we stood staring from the dead reptile into the damp and evil-smelling tunnel. A distant muttering and rumbling rolled, echoing awesomely along it.

"For Heaven's sake what was that, sir?" whispered Kennedy.

"It was the thunder," answered Nayland Smith. "The storm is breaking over the hills. Steady with the lamp, my man."

We had proceeded for some three hundred yards, and, according to my calculation, were clear of the orchard of Graywater Park and close to the fringe of trees beyond; I was taking note of the curious old brickwork of the passage, when--

"Look out, sir!" cried Kennedy--and the light began dancing madly. "Just under your feet! Now it's up the wall!--mind your hand, Dr. Petrie!"

The lamp was turned, and, since it shone fully into my face, temporarily blinded me.

"On the roof over your head, Barton!"--this from Nayland Smith. "What can we kill it with?"

Now my sight was restored to me, and looking back along the passage, I saw, clinging to an irregularity in the moldy wall, the most gigantic scorpion I had ever set eyes upon! It was fully as large as my open hand.

Kennedy and Nayland Smith were stealthily retracing their steps, the former keeping the light directed upon the hideous insect, which now began running about with that horrible, febrile activity characteristic of the species.

Suddenly came a sharp, staccato report.... Sir Lionel had scored a hit with his Browning pistol.

In waves of sound, the report went booming along the passage. The lamp, as I have said, was turned in order to shine back upon us, rendering the tunnel ahead a mere black mouth--a veritable inferno, held by inhuman guards. Into that black cavern I stared, gloomily fascinated by the onward rolling sound storm; into that blackness I looked ... to feel my scalp tingle horrifically, to know the crowning horror of the horrible journey.

The blackness was spangled with watching, diamond eyes!--with tiny insect eyes that moved; upon the floor, upon the walls, upon the ceiling! A choking cry rose to my lips.

"Smith! Barton! for God's sake, look! The place is *alive* with scorpions!"

Around we all came, panic plucking at our hearts, around swept the beam of the big lamp; and there, retreating before the light, went a veritable army of venomous creatures! I counted no fewer than three of the giant red centipedes whose poisonous touch, called "the zayat kiss," is certain death; several species of scorpion were represented; and some kind of bloated, unwieldy spider, so gross of body that its short, hairy legs could scarce support it, crawled, hideous, almost at my feet.

What other monstrosities of the insect kingdom were included in that obscene host I know not; my skin tingled from head to feet; I experienced a sensation as if a million venomous things already clung to me--unclean things bred in the malarial jungles of Burma, in the corpse-tainted mud of China's rivers, in the fever spots of that darkest East from which Fu-Manchu recruited his shadow army.

I was perilously near to losing my nerve when the crisp, incisive tones of Nayland Smith's voice came to stimulate me like a cold douche.

"This wanton sacrifice of horrors speaks eloquently of a forlorn hope! Sweep the walls with light, Kennedy; all those filthy things are nocturnal and they will retreat before us as we advance."

His words proved true. Occasioning a sort of *rustling* sound--a faint sibilance indescribably loathsome--the creatures gray and black and red darted off along the passage. One by one, as we proceeded, they crept into holes and crevices of the ancient walls, sometimes singly, sometimes in pairs--the pairs locked together in deadly embrace.

"They cannot live long in this cold atmosphere," cried Smith. "Many of them will kill one another--and we can safely leave the rest to the British climate. But see that none of them drops upon you in passing."

Thus we pursued our nightmare march, on through that valley of horror. Colder grew the atmosphere and colder. Again the thunder boomed out above us, seeming to shake the roof of the tunnel fiercely, as with Titan hands. A sound of falling water, audible for some time, now grew so loud that conversation became difficult. All the insects had disappeared.

"We are approaching the River Starn!" roared Sir Lionel. "Note the dip of the passage and the wet walls!"

"Note the type of brickwork!" shouted Smith.

Largely as a sedative to the feverish excitement which consumed me, I forced myself to study the construction of the tunnel; and I became aware of an astonishing circumstance. Partly the walls were natural, a narrow cavern traversing the bed of rock which upcropped on this portion of the estate, but partly, if my scanty knowledge of archaeology did not betray me, they were *Phoenician!*

"This stretch of passage," came another roar from Sir Lionel, "dates back to Roman days or even earlier! By God! It's almost incredible!"

And now Smith and Kennedy, who lid, were up to their knees in a running tide. An icy shower-bath drenched us from above; ahead was a solid wall of falling water. Again, and louder, nearer, boomed and rattled the thunder; its mighty voice was almost lost in the roar of that subterranean cataract. Nayland Smith, using his hands as a megaphone, cried;--

"Failing the evidence that others have passed this way, I should not dare to risk it! But the river is less than forty feet wide at the point below Monkswell; a dozen paces should see us through the worst!"

I attempted no reply. I will frankly admit that the prospect appalled me. But, bracing himself up as one does preparatory to a high dive, Smith, nodding to Kennedy to proceed, plunged into the cataract ahead....

CHAPTER XL

THE BLACK CHAPEL

OF HOW WE achieved that twelve or fifteen yards below the rocky bed of the stream the Powers that lent us strength and fortitude alone hold record. Gasping for breath, drenched, almost reconciled to the end which I thought was come--I found myself standing at the foot of a steep flight of stairs roughly hewn in the living rock.

Beside me, the extinguished lamp still grasped in his hand, leant Kennedy, panting wildly and clutching at the uneven wall. Sir Lionel Barton had sunk exhausted upon the bottom step, and Nayland Smith was standing near him, looking up the stairs. From an arched doorway at their head light streamed forth!

Immediately behind me, in the dark place where the waters roared, opened a fissure in the rock, and into it poured the miniature cataract; I understood now the phenomenon of minor whirlpools for which the little river above was famous. Such were my impressions of that brief breathing-space; then--

"Have your pistols ready!" cried Smith. "Leave the lamp, Kennedy. It can serve us no further."

Mustering all the reserve that remained to us, we went, pell-mell, a wild, bedraggled company, up that ancient stair and poured into the room above....

One glance showed us that this was indeed the chapel of Asmodeus, the shrine of Satan where the Black Mass had been sung in the Middle Ages. The stone altar remained, together with certain Latin inscriptions cut in the wall. Fu-Manchu's last home in England had been within a temple of his only Master.

Save for nondescript litter, evidencing a hasty departure of the occupants, and a ship's lantern burning upon the altar, the chapel was unfurnished. Nothing menaced us, but the thunder hollowly crashed far above. To cover his retreat, Fu-Manchu had relied upon the noxious host in the passage and upon the wall of water. Silent, motionless, we four stood looking down at that which lay upon the floor of the unholy place.

In a pool of blood was stretched the Eurasian girl, Zarmi. Her picturesque finery was reft into tatters and her bare throat and arms were covered with weals and bruises occasioned by ruthless, clutching fingers. Of her face, which had been notable for a sort of devilish beauty, I cannot write; it was the awful face of one who had did from strangulation.

Beside her, with a Malay krîs in his heart--a little, jeweled weapon that I had often seen in Zarmi's hand--sprawled the obese Greek, Samarkan, a member of the Si-Fan group and sometime manager of a great London hotel!

It was ghastly, it was infinitely horrible, that tragedy of which the story can never be known, never be written; that fiendish fight to the death in the black chapel of Asmodeus.

"We are too late!" said Nayland Smith. "The stair behind the altar!"

He snatched up the lantern. Directly behind the stone altar was a narrow, pointed doorway. From the depths with which it communicated proceeded vague, awesome sounds, as of waves breaking in some vast cavern....

We were more than half-way down the stair when, above the muffled roaring of the thunder, I distinctly heard the voice of *Dr. Fu-Manchu!*

"My God!" shouted Smith, "perhaps they are trapped! The cave is only navigable at low tide and in calm weather!"

We literally fell down the remaining steps ... and were almost precipitated into the water!

The light of the lantern showed a lofty cavern tapering away to a point at its remote end, pear-fashion. The throbbing of an engine and churning of a screw became audible. There was a faint smell of petrol.

"Shoot! shoot!"--the frenzied voice was that of Sir Lionel--"Look! they can just get through! ..."

Crack! Crack! Crack!

Nayland Smith's Browning spat death across the cave. Then followed the report of Barton's pistol; then those of mine and Kennedy's.

A small motor-boat was creeping cautiously out under a low, natural archway which evidently gave access to the sea! Since the tide was incoming, a few minutes more of delay had rendered the passage of the cavern impossible....

The boat disappeared.

"We are not beaten!" snapped Nayland Smith. "The *Chanak-Kampo* will be seized in the Channel!"

"There were formerly steps, in the side of the well from which this place takes its name," declared Nayland Smith dully. "This was the means of access to the secret chapel employed by the devil-worshipers."

"The top of the well (alleged to be the deepest in England)," said Sir Lionel, "is among a tangle of weeds close by the ruined tower."

Smith, ascending three stone steps, swung the lantern out over the yawning pit below; then he stared long and fixedly upwards.

Both thunder and rain had ceased; but even in those gloomy depths we could hear the coming of the tempest which followed upon that memorable storm.

"The steps are here," reported Smith; "but without the aid of a rope from above, I doubt if they are climbable."

"It's that or the way we came, sir!" said Kennedy. "I was five years at sea in wind-jammers. Let me swarm up and go for a rope to the Park."

"Can you do it?" demanded Smith. "Come and look!"

Kennedy craned from the opening, staring upward and downward; then--

"I can do it, sir," he said quietly.

Removing his boots and socks, he swung himself out from the opening into the well and was gone.

The story of Fu-Manchu, and of the organization called the Si-Fan which he employed as a means to further his own vast projects, is almost told.

Kennedy accomplished the perilous climb to the lip of the well, and sped barefooted to Graywater Park for ropes. By means of these we all escaped from the strange chapel of the devil-worshipers. Of how we arranged for the removal of the bodies which lay in the place I need not write. My record advances twenty-four hours.

The great storm which burst over England in the never-to-be-forgotten spring when Fu-Manchu fled our shores has become historical. There were no fewer than twenty shipwrecks during the day and night that it raged.

Imprisoned by the elements in Graywater Park, we listened to the wind howling with the voice of a million demons around the ancient manor, to the creatures of Sir Lionel's collection swelling the unholy discord. Then came the news that there was a big steamer on the Pinion Rocks--that the lifeboat could not reach her.

As though it were but yesterday I can see us, Sir Lionel Barton, Nayland Smith and I, hurrying down into the little cove which sheltered the fishing-village; fighting our way against the power of the tempest....

Thrice we saw the rockets split the inky curtain of the storm; thrice saw the gallant lifeboat crew essay to put their frail craft out to sea ... thrice the mighty rollers hurled them contemptuously back....

Dawn--a gray, eerie dawn--was creeping ghostly over the iron-bound shore, when the fragments of wreckage began to drift in. Such are the currents upon those coasts that bodies are rarely recovered from wrecks on the cruel Pinion Rocks.

In the dim light I bent over a battered and torn mass of timber--that once had been the bow of a boat; and in letters of black and gold I read: "S. Y. *Chanak-Kampo.*"

www.ingramcontent.com/pod-product-compliance
Ingram Content Group UK Ltd.
Pitfield, Milton Keynes, MK11 3LW, UK
UKHW041259180426
11947UKWH00008B/561